Mehala
Lady of Sealandings

Jonathan Grant is the real name of Jonathan
Gash, author of the bestselling Lovejoy novels
which are watched by millions on television.

As well as being an author, he is a doctor
specialising in Tropical Medicine. He is
married with three daughters and four
grandchildren, and lives near Colchester in
Essex.

GW00631151

MEHALA
Lady of
Sealandings

Jonathan Grant

ARROW

First published 1993

1 3 5 7 9 10 8 6 4 2

The right of Jonathan Grant to be identified as the author
of this work has been asserted by him in accordance
with the Copyright, Designs and Patents Act, 1988

First published in Great Britain by Century in 1993

This edition published by Arrow in 1994
Random House, 20 Vauxhall Bridge Road, London SW1V 2SA

Random House Australia (Pty) Limited
20 Alfred Street, Milsons Point, Sydney,
New South Wales 2061, Australia

Random House New Zealand Limited
18 Poland Road, Glenfield
Auckland 10, New Zealand

Random House South Africa (Pty) Limited
PO Box 337, Bergvlei, South Africa

Random House UK Limited Reg. No. 954009

A CIP catalogue record for this book
is available from the British Library

ISBN 0 09 978730 X

Printed and bound in Great Britain by
Cox & Wyman Ltd, Reading, Berkshire

'PROMPTITUDE IS THE duty of servants,' Harriet Treggan said as she waited for the hanging, 'but is the *gift* of ladies.' She scanned the crowd below, impatient at being kept waiting.

The Suffolk town of Saint Edmundsbury had been thronged since before dawn. Squabbles had already broken out among people struggling for the best vantage points. A fairground could not be more boisterous than this expectant multitude, with jugglers, pedlars, beggars, whores and sellers of sweetmeats competing for attention. Musicians and acrobats had their paid stalwarts clearing space for their dances and displays. Pickpockets, the notorious subtle-mongers of every crowd, moved with seeming innocence through the mob.

'Harriet!' her husband Rodney Treggan exclaimed. 'Has promptness no place in gentlemen's society?'

Harriet smiled behind her pictorial ivory fan. 'Were I provoked, I should reply that no gentleman need ask!'

The rejoinder drew loud laughter, with especial applause from Brillianta Astell, who was seated in the window beside Harriet. 'You see, Rodney, how we ladies manage to barb our words without letting fly!'

'He comes now!' Harriet cried, forgetting the flirtatious conversation. A roar heralded the approach of the hanging cart.

She tried to lean nearer the casement light, excitedly surveying the people. Soldiers were pushing ahead of the cart to butt a way through. In spite of the boos and catcalls, some folk were cheering as William Corder moved into the square. The horrific murder at nearby Polstead had caused disturbances throughout the Eastern Hundreds.

'See how brazen he stands!' Harriet cried. 'Oh, the cruel murderer! How poor Maria's soul must rejoice in Heaven!'

'The hangman is on the scaffold, see, ladies!' Alex Waite called. 'Ready for his gold sovereign!'

'From whom, pray?' Harriet asked, incensed. 'Such a fee? For letting drop a wooden trapdoor?'

'No, Mistress Treggan. From the murderer.'

'A to-insure-promptness, a *tip*, Mr Waite?' Harriet was scandalised. 'Why, that is a most outrageous suggestion!'

'It encourages the hangman to provide a secure knot, that the hanged man's neck will be broken immediately.'

'Please, Mr Waite,' Brillianta Astell said faintly to the young visitor. 'You Scotch talk too readily of these events.'

'But we are all here to observe every thrilling detail, Brillianta, are we not?' Harriet nudged mischievously. 'Tell me, Mr Waite. What would happen otherwise?'

Alex Waite was uncomfortably aware of the glances being exchanged among the company. He could ill afford to be thought too loose of manner among such exalted gentry. His aim was to enter society. So far he had done creditably, as he wrote to his father in Montrose.

'Were that the case, Miss Brillianta, the murderer would slowly strangle, from the hangman's loosely tied rope.'

Harriet Treggan cried out in mock alarm, delighted to cause the North Briton such discomfiture. 'Be informed that I certainly do not regret *any* manner of passing for this foul fiend! William Corder murdered poor young Maria Marten in cold blood, at that red barn. Imagine the poor girl's screams!'

'Enough, Harriet!' Brillianta Astell exclaimed. 'You spoil our entertainment!'

The younger of the two Astell sisters was disinclined to allow Harriet Treggan much more licence. The wretched woman assumed too much, wearing an impossible plum-coloured redingote of scotia silk with, if you please, a silver – *silver*! – soprano, an absurd mixture of styles. And a ferroniere round the wanton lady's head, under a hat so absurd as to be indescribable except as a spray of feathers.

Brillianta thought Harriet was determined to spoil the holiday. It had promised such a marvellously joyous day, with her bossy elder sister Lorela unable to come to the celebratory jaunt of the public hanging, in the company of so many gentlemen. And dear darling Lorela happily home in Arminell nursing an ague! A double blessing, for a senior sister would have taken preference at every juncture. Now the odious Harriet Treggan, with her new wedding ring, threatened to spoil this exciting rout. Brillianta was already irritated with the woman, for putting on airs now she was married to Rodney Treggan – and therefore well past any gentleman's consideration except in the matter of general politeness. Yet the silly woman was flirting outrageously, quite trying to outdo the single ladies present in the large room overlooking the scaffold. It was high time she turned her mind to receiving from Rodney Treggan and announcing an impending birth, instead of behaving like a girl at her first gathering.

'And, Harriet,' Brillianta pursued with pretended severity, 'I shall not have Mr Waite disturbed!'

Alex Waite gratefully tried to recoup his losses. 'If my seriousness gives offence, Mistress Treggan, I beg you to attribute it to a North Briton's natural gravity. I am unused to such merriment, even on so happy an occasion.'

'Mistress Treggan is quite right, Waite,' Sir Charles Golding said, oblivious to nuance. He was already well into his bottle of Portugal, though yet showing no sign. 'The duties of the labouring folk are quite separate, and should remain so. It is just a pity that Sir Robert Peel's administration to His Majesty sees fit to abolish the death penalty for so many transgressions against law.'

'Indeed, Sir Charles,' Harriet exclaimed. 'I even heard one gentleman say that hanging should no longer be a public spectacle, but carried out within prison walls! Its salutary effects upon the labouring mob would then be totally lost!'

'See!' Brillianta cried out to distract the company, for Charles Golding was undeserving, even though rich and a bachelor. She cast about for something to catch everybody's eye, and finally pointed. 'The constables by the scaffold! Yet who is the cloaked man?'

'Surgeon,' Golding said. He looked away.

Something in his voice drew Brillianta's attention to the young man standing by the scaffold steps. Until Charles Golding's terse answer she had not really looked. Now she stared, wishing for a quizzing glass to inspect the silent figure. As she looked, the young man tried to fend away the closer members of the crowd pressing close, as if he carried something valuable. He seemed vaguely familiar, and she remembered.

'Why,' she remarked, with ill-concealed pleasure, 'is that not the doctor from Sealandings?'

'Who?' Harriet searched for the surgeon in the melee. 'You have a tradesman's acquaintanceship, Brillianta?'

'No!' Brillianta reproved with sufficient coldness. This Treggan gargoyle was becoming insufferable, implying that a mere quack, a doctor, was of sufficient social standing to claim 'acquaintance-ship' with one of her class, daughter of the august Sir Edward Astell, senior magistrate of Maidborough. 'The staff and servants at Arminell are served by Maidborough's local physician. My father fetches our own chirurgeon from London when necessary. And a physician from the Royal College will always take a bribe to extend beyond the seven-mile London limit. But that man's face . . . Sir Charles?'

Golding drained his glass. A servant leapt to pour, having swiftly learned of the noble's temper. 'He *is* the dog-leech from Sealandings, I believe.'

Harriet Treggan's gaze found the man at last. 'I see him!' She was smiling, ready to make another jibe at Brillianta Astell, when something in the man's attitude struck her.

He was young, shabby, and stood tense and watchful. Even in the jostling throng he seemed turned to stone, looking towards the uproar at the far end of the square. His attire was rough, almost crude, a poor countryman's garb. An old beaver hat on his brow, a shock of hair protruding beneath. A surtout coat, patched at the shoulder seams. *It will be too long*, Harriet thought in a shock of recognition. *The surtout will flap about his half-jack boots as he walks. He was always carelessly attired.*

'I forget his name,' Golding remarked, in a voice that announced the contrary.

'Carmichael,' Harriet heard herself say, to her horror.

'That is it!' Waite said, pleased to be joining on what he thought a safe conversation. 'I saw him once mend a fellow's shoulder in the blacksmith's there. Saved the arm without an amputation!'

'Why, Harriet!' Brillianta cooed, interrupting Alex Waite's reminiscences. 'The sawbones is *your* acquaintance rather than mine!'

4

'One of your father's former servants, I think, Mistress Treggan?' Rodney put in deftly, sensing his wife's need of a rescue. 'Moved him out of Sealandings, did you, Charles?'

'No, Rodney,' Golding answered, irritably holding out his glass for another filling, 'he is still out on the coast.' He added with an hint of malice, 'Him and his doxy.'

Brillianta observed Harriet's bloodless countenance. She looked about the crowd. 'He has no doxy with him, Sir Charles,' she complained. 'I should like to see her. Shouldn't you, Harriet dear?'

The glint in Harriet's eyes at the mention of the doctor's woman thrilled Brillianta. She purred, indicating the wedge of soldiery driving into the crowd, longarms raised to club the crowd. So Harriet knew the intent young doctor better than any lady ought to know any tradesman! Brillianta smiled, for the first time getting a good glimpse of the murderer William Corder and feeling horror that almost made her faint. The day was rescued from impending disaster after all. Such a happy coincidence.

'Now, Harriet!' she chided, deliberately misinterpreting Harriet's fret. 'You shall *not* get upset! This criminal earned his punishment. This sanction restores belief in law. Thus he serves as an example to the commonalty, the mob of servants. And gives us an entertainment!'

'Well uttered, Miss Brillianta!' Alex Waite exclaimed.

'The Empress Tsarina of the Russias, Catherine the Second, abolished the death penalty for all crimes except treason,' Golding said morosely. 'So where is punishment?'

'Punishment inflicted is duty done!' Brillianta concluded, knowing the remark would gratify. '*Is* the doxy with him, Charles?'

Rodney Treggan watched his wife from the corner of his eye. She was out of the conversation, looking about the crowd with new intensity. She paid no attention to the approaching murderer's cart and the pandemonium surrounding it.

'I do not see her, Miss Astell,' Golding said, his voice thick with anger. 'But she is here.'

'*Is*, Sir Charles?' Brillianta cooed, fluttering her eyelashes. There was mystery here, worth several coffee-tastings of gossip. 'You mean, she *may* possibly be?'

'No,' Golding said with a curtness bordering on incivility. 'Where he, there she.'

'Has she a name, this ephemeral creature whose presence is so ubiquitously certain?' Brillianta was now intrigued by the intent young doctor at the scaffold and the strange atmosphere engendered in the room by the mention of him.

'Mehala,' Golding and Waite said together, then exchanged glances before looking away.

'Mehala! What a rare name!' Brillianta kept her eyes on the doctor. 'So memorable! I must try to guess her.' She turned to Harriet sweetly. 'Perhaps you already have her acquaintance, Harriet. Would you point her out?'

Ven Carmichael resisted the shoves of a group of farm labourers trying a concerted rush to the scaffold. He had been here since dawn, seen the crowd assemble, heard over and again the jingles, tunes of the English arm-pipers, the raucous shouts of the broadsheet-mongers whose pamphlets described the terrible last moments of the man about to be hanged and the brutal murder he had perpetrated. Twice he had argued with a master of a dancing bear, who had wanted to put his animal by the scaffold steps. He had produced his warrant from the town constables as the hanging surgeon, but had only kept his place under a torrent of abuse from the bear master, pie-sellers, toy-vendors with their ingenious miniature gallows, the travelling prostitutes from the fairground, and the townsfolk who saw him as an intruder.

It was a golden opportunity, though, and he fought hard for his appointed place. He could smell the new wood of the scaffold, see the dowel pegs that would hold the structure firm when the murderer's body jerked. He prayed that it would be swift, to spare the man the distress of a prolonged suffocation. Sport to the crowd, of course, who wanted a protracted death – always the cause of much merriment – but the cause of desperate grief for sympathisers.

Wagers were being placed with an almost incoherent fury as the shouting crowd fell back before the advancing soldiery. No drumbeat, as there would be for a military execution, just the rattle of the cart as it trundled nearer in the hubbub.

A man pushed close and grabbed Ven's arm. 'Here, Doctor. You the hangman's leech this day?'

Ven Carmichael hesitated. The man was a townsman by his clothes. No farm labourer would wear a spencer jacket with a half shirt adorned by chitterlings. Already the man seemed tipsy, ale sour on his breath.

'Yes. I am appointed to pronounce death.'

'Can you stand the tip, then, Doctor?' The man leered, winking. 'Time the murderer's death at five minutes after the drop. I've a pretty penny on the outcome. Two pounds six and eightpence, doctor booy, for yourself!'

'I must go by the law,' Ven said, recovering his arm.

'Think, booy! I'll make it two pounds thirteen and fourpence! No questions asked!'

'I'm sorry, but no.'

The man turned ugly. 'You bain't local. You'm from the coast, booy. It's a long walk you got.' He grabbed Ven's arm fiercely, brown teeth bared in threat. 'I'll leave you in some ditch afore you've gone a mile beyond the tollgate stone.'

The front rank of soldiers had almost reached the scaffold platform. The crowd was baying in renewed fervour.

'I'll thank you to leave me be, sir,' Ven said desperately. 'I must be about my duty.'

A sudden screech made heads turn, as the gambler's hat was swiped off. A young woman seized the crushed beaver and climbed over the two men's shoulders onto the scaffold. She wore a small cottager, tightly latched under her chin, and a home-made pelisse-robe of coarse dun hessian with a fringed whittle shawl.

'Folk of Edmundsbury!' she shouted, waving the man's hat and skilfully evading the constables. 'Which gambler tries to cheat honest bettors of a true hangman's time? He tries to bribe the hanging surgeon! Who knows the false man?'

A roar of anger rose at her words, then silence fell. Ven watched Mehala in distress. She was taking an impossible risk, simply to deflect the man's threat. People had been killed in rioting from less serious accusations than this.

'Name him!' somebody bellowed from the crowd. Bookmakers on the outskirts of the mob began shouting for his name.

'Half-a-crown to whoever brings me that hat for identification!'

Mehala shrieked, 'I'd tell you the name, sir, but there's no label. Your betrayer cannot write an ex, even!'

Amid roars of laughter she waved the hat. Ven saw the gambler duck into the crowd.

'There he goes, townsfolk!' Mehala cried out. 'His hat'll find him!'

She skimmed the beaver. It almost hit the man. The constables on the platform hesitated, forbidden to leave the gallows until after the hanging. Below, fights were breaking out among the crowd as the man was caught, struggling. A mounted officer of the Suffolk Militia drove his mare into the crowd, will-he-nill-he slashing with his whip to separate the brawlers. Six foot-soldiers followed the lieutenant, jabbing the stocks of their flintlocks indiscriminately into paunch and face.

Mehala jumped down beside Ven and linked her arm with his, slightly breathless. 'Unscathed, Ven?'

'Thank you, Mehala,' he said awkwardly. 'It was an ugly moment. I thought I had lost my chance of a corpse dissection.'

She gave a shiver. 'If it pleases you, Ven, so it shall be.'

'He comes,' Ven said, worried now more than ever. His instrument case was safe, thank God, and if all went well – went terribly for the murderer, that was to say – then he would, for the first time in his life, view the internal organs of a human being. He would learn more true anatomy than in all his student years at the London Hospital in Whitechapel's slums. He had been too poor to afford the entrance fees to lectures at famous London anatomy schools, getting it all second-hand from student hearsay to supplement borrowed books.

'May God forgive him,' Mehala said, awed.

She was almost as nervous as Ven. Apart from the ghastly work he had to do this day, and the demented gaiety of the Edmundsbury folk, she had begun to sense an odd threat for no reason she could identify.

The hangman clambered past to a roar of applause from the crowd. His heap of chains was already on the platform.

'Chains, chains,' some chanted in the mob.

'There is a move to abolish hanging bodies in chains after a hanging,' Ven told Mehala in answer to her questioning look. 'Laws might well be enacted soon.'

'These are the supporters, then?' Mehala glanced at the yelling faction.

'Yes. They make money from the corpses, by arrangement with the hangman. Sellers of ghoulish mementoes of the corpse.'

They were almost jostled apart as the platoon of soldiers thrust forward with advanced weapons. Their flintlocks seemed huge, the uniformed soldiers sweating from exertion. Each infantryman carried forty pounds of equipment, the encumbrance quickening their tempers in the effort of controlling the mass.

The cart was dragged forward, to cheers and insults. Stones were flung at the murderer. Corder was struck. The militia officer shouted an order, and two soldiers moved into the crowd with a constable to seek out the thrower. It was becoming ugly. Never before had ten thousand people crammed into Saint Edmundsbury before the gaol.

'Two pounds for the rope, hangman!' somebody bawled.

'Guineas, hangman!'

'Four, if complete! On the nail!'

The hangman waved away the bids. He had every intention of selling the rope – his property, after all – piecemeal, and had already received bids of over four shillings and threepence an inch. By nightfall, as tavern celebrations mounted once Corder's corpse was in the hands of the prison doctor, he hoped for half-a-guinea an inch. Ten shillings and sixpence! He smiled inwardly at the knowledge of his canvas sack under the scaffold containing spare lengths of hemp. With luck he could sell both, and get away scot-free. How terrible to live in Finland, where capital punishment had lately been abolished in 1824. Or in Prussia's strict kingdom, where a sword finished the job. Or Brunswick, where a murderer such as Corder would have been axed in utter seclusion. How fortunate he was, to live in so liberal a land as Great Britain, where a hangman's job was yet safe and such side benefits came easy! He was envious of London's John Calcraft, the young hangman newly appointed this very Year of Grace, who could milk an enthusiastic Newgate crowd for a fortune at every hanging. Why, already two had been hanged in the past three months – Catherine Walsh, and William Rea the highwayman. An honest hangman deserved superb milkings, for a woman and a romantic robber hero such as Rea. But tonight he himself would have the pick of almost any woman, aye, of titled ladies and all. Nothing made a bedworthy woman lust more than a hangman fresh from his labour.

'I cannot look, Ven,' Mehala said quietly.

'You must, Mehala.' He was pale in spite of the August heat. 'You know the rule betwixt us. I ask you to observe it.'

'I am afraid to see a man die so . . .'

They held each other's eyes, oblivious to the contumely.

'You promised to learn all, when I took you as my true apprentice, just as though you were not of the weaker sex. Hold fast.'

'But why?'

People were roaring now, as Corder was led on to the platform. A parson gabbled prayers, unheeded in the din. Ven and Mehala were communicating by looking at the other's lips.

'Remember what I told you when first we decided you were to become a doctor? Observation is all. Learning cannot be done once removed.'

'Yes, Ven.' She turned her pale face up to the gallows.

Corder was on the trapdoor now, head in the noose. He was sweating heavily, white as death. The parson was reading inaudibly from the Book of Common Prayer.

'Remember the mole-catcher's daughter, Corder!' A furious, stout farmer strove to reach the steps. A soldier clubbed the man away. The crowd took up the cry for the murdered Maria Marten.

'Quartering! A quartering!'

'No rich Brentford lady to hide you now, Corder!' Youths from Polstead, Maria Marten's village, howled jubilant reminders of Corder's attempted escape by marrying an heiress he had found through a matrimonial advertisement.

'Less'n you broadsheet for another, booy!' The sally earned roars of laughter.

'Or the bastard brings in his school for young ladies!'

That proved the final joke. The crowd rocked with merriment. A piece of offal was flung at the murderer. Corder and his new-found wife had kept a profitable school, until Maria Marten's mother had prevailed upon her husband to act on her recurring dream about her missing daughter, shot and buried at Polstead's Red Barn.

'Watch, Mehala.' Ven grasped her firmly. 'We must see what we shall examine later.'

The signal was given. The hangman nodded to the constables, acknowledged the sheriff's presence, and in almost total silence

10

released the trap. Corder's body fell and jerked once with an audible crack as the neck snapped at the limit of the rope. He struggled, his legs flailing reflexly. The crowd erupted in cheers and laughter as a trickle of urine made its way down his breeches. The body swung. Farm lads sang a crude ditty in time with the swings, starting up a morris dance in mockery.

Ven was thrust towards the steps by the boisterous mob.

'Make it three minutes, Doctor!' someone yelled.

'Two and twenty seconds, leech!'

Ven stood white-faced by the trapdoor. He could hear the rope creaking, see the lopsided body in its slow pendular motion. Oddly, the uproar dwindled to nothing. He was conscious only of the loss of a human life, even that of a murderer. When *did* a life end? Perhaps, away in some magical future, might doctors know the secrets of life itself? Or, more terribly, of death, the end of all? Might a human body be suspended between life and death, for medical purposes? And then be restored marvellously to life after some healing process?

To utter such thoughts would be regarded as blasphemous. This crowd, now calling out eager suggestions, would tear him to pieces for such perfidy, for blasphemy was the most corrosive destroyer of society. All people had to conform. Differ in some, any, opinion and you were marked as treasonous, heretical, rebellious. For that there was only one remedy.

The body twitched, seemed to give a great shudder. Was *that* the end of Corder? Ven did not know. His shame returned. Medical students were taught nothing of death, its signs, how to define it. He had simply nothing to go on, except a few tricks taught him by old Doctor Arbuthnot, for whom he had worked unpaid after qualifying from the London Hospital. Stories of hanging were only folklore. Yet it was possible to survive hanging. Why, in 1447 there occurred the famous 'Gloucester Five', gentlemen attached to the Duke of Gloucester. Condemned for treason, they were hanged, swiftly cut down, their naked bodies marked for quartering, then pardoned and set free – alive. But how swift was swiftly? How long could life's transient spark stay before it was extinguished? Did it depend on air, the act of breathing? Or was it something less evidential, like the spinal cord's continuity?

'One minute!' the constable cried.

The crowd roared. Bets were paid off. Ven was subjected to a chorus of abuse from losers. A few winning gamesters applauded him as they collected.

Ven could recall a young woman lying moribund in the dark-tiled wards of the London Hospital, dead to every inspection. No breath stirred her body, no flutter of her eyelids showed as he had lifted one with a thumb to peer at her pupil by the light of a candle. She had been found in the Thames near the Wapping Stairs, brought in by a penny boatman one night. Cold, extremities blue, she had been cast onto the board flooring in the entrance of a surgical ward, but only because the boatman had claimed she had been alive when he dragged her ashore. Without much hope, Ven had wearily started to compress her chest, relaxing every few moments. He had no real understanding, had heard that it sometimes proved successful for farm animals born in traumatic birth. Two other students on a surgical 'firm', as those adhering to senior surgeons were known, stopped to laugh at his efforts.

'What goes on here, Carmichael?' a loud, dandily-dressed youth called. Septon Peveril was no friend, ostentatiously preaching that only those students who could afford the profession should be allowed to enter. 'Polishing cadavers now, are we? To gain a few pence for tomorrow's pharmacy lectures?'

'I'll show him how to handle a female any day, Peveril,' Peveril's friend George Godrell said in a stage whisper.

Ven remembered the feeling of stupidity that had enveloped him. Indeed, what was he doing? Trying useless chest compressions, almost as if the dead woman was nothing more than a mere animal.

The woman retched, arched up her recumbent form in a spasm, and vomited filthy water into Ven's face. How long had she seemed dead? An hour? Two? Which was in itself a horror, for how often had physicians, surgeons, country doctors, abandoned hope when they might still have saved a life? The students had gone off in disgust, for the woman was a vagrant and unable to pay her fee, and Ven Carmichael was again their butt. Peveril and Godrell were now affluent doctors in London, prominent in the Royal Colleges and at the Apothecaries Hall. Inevitably so, for Godrell was of Debenham's richest land-owning family, and Peveril was well connected in Mayfair society.

'Two minutes!'

'Gone to sleep, crocus?' Somebody yelled the abusive term.

'Wake the dog-leech up, for God's sake! I shall lose –'

'Time! Call time, Doctor!'

Septon Peveril had become something of an enemy during Ven's final student year. He took to needling Ven whenever they passed, joking loudly about country bumpkins and pointedly ordering the most expensive meals whenever Ven was nearby. He goaded Ven for his dour, obsessed learning, his country accent, jeered at his non-existent prospects for appointment to fashionable practices. Only a chance encounter with the ebullient eccentric Doctor Arbuthnot had enabled Ven to find lodgement and training in an established man surgery.

The murderer's body swung, slowly.

How swift *was* swift? Once, as a child, he had seen a frozen man rescued from a snowdrift, and carried into a tavern by a rejoicing crowd. The man had actually waved as he was placed by the log fire. And died within minutes before the shocked taproom crowd. So time was only one factor. There were others. Warmth? Chill? The movements a body made in its death throes?

He came to as the scaffold platform rocked. He recovered his balance. Several fights had broken out round the gallows between gamblers disputing the number of kicks the hanged murderer had made.

'Doctor!' The lieutenant nudged his mount closer. 'Harley, Suffolk Militia. Best decide soon, man, or we'll have a sorry time getting home this e'en!'

'Yes, Lieutenant Harley. Very soon now.'

'I s'll be obliged, Doctor.'

The body was still now, no jerks, no kicks. It swung more gently. The rope creaked softer.

'He be gone, booy,' the hangman said quietly, 'I swear it.'

By experience? Intuition? Astute observation? Some signs he, Doctor Carmichael, did not know? Ven looked blankly at him. 'You're sure? Why?'

The hangman shrugged. 'You can feel it, see?'

Ven thought a moment. To let down a convicted murderer's body, which then miraculously recovered in the hands of friends who stole it away for resuscitation, was the fear. Charges of connivance were cheaply made, but only expensively refuted. And a spontaneous recovery might seem proof of having taken a bribe. William Corder's family was well-to-do, rich even. The suspicion of trickery always sprouted from a gallows tree.

'Now,' he called, raising his hand to let it fall.

A roar of cheering rose. The hangman unceremoniously hauled the body up and perched it on the trapdoor edge. To let it fall by releasing the rope would mean theft of his now-so-valuable rope by the horde of scavenging children waiting beneath the gallows in hopes of stealing some trinkets from the murderer. He deftly undid the knot, wound the rope round his waist and tied it securely.

He nodded at the cadaver. 'All yours, leech.'

'Thank you.'

'A warning.' The hangman gestured to the crowd who beseeched him for a piece of the rope, coins in their hands. 'Do not cut the skin too clumsily. The prison doctor wants the skin, to bind his book of the Corder trial.'

'Thank you, hangman.'

Ven quickly performed a rudimentary examination of the body. The neck was scored by the burn marks from the rope. The head flopped limply. No breath from the nostrils on his fragment of mirror. No pulse along the carotid artery. No response of the pupils to light. It was all that he knew. He beckoned the sheriff's men, who rough-handledly threw Corder's body on to the cart. He jumped down beside it, following the soldiers. Mehala walked beside him with his case.

As they headed for the prison, Mehala caught sight of a carriage, a coat of arms clearly emblazoned on its door and the ornate hammer-cloth over the Salisbury coach box. She glanced at the coachman, but did not recognise him. Nonetheless, she knew Sir Charles Golding was among the spectators. And the tavern at the corner of the square was likeliest. From there, she had felt an emanation of hatred when waiting for the hangman. She trusted her feeling. Malice was in the air, directed at Ven and herself.

She could not resist giving a sharp glance towards the tavern. A woman's face, intent and questioning, was framed in the window. She did not know the woman, but her appraising gaze proved that the woman knew Ven. The woman quickly turned aside behind her fan, making a remark to gentlemen standing behind her.

The cart trundled through the prison gates, soldiers beating aside the noisy importuners who reached for scraps of clothing from Corder's body. Mehala walked close to Carmichael. The gates slammed shut on the milling crowds, and they were inside the prison, the tumbril wheels rattling on the flint cobbles.

2

TWO MILES DUE eastward from Saint Edmundsbury on the coast road, Saxelby Hall stood in its ancient moat. There was nothing pretentious about the Treggan country house. Recent stands of trees, established soon after the deer park, proved a success, but this showed that the Treggans were newcomers to the Eastern Hundreds, not indigenous gentry. The Treggans could not hope to pass themselves off as anything other than virtual strangers. Rodney Treggan himself was well regarded, being a scion of some West Country family with estates in Devon. The lady, Harriet Treggan, was famously from London, though little was known of her locally. Saxelby was pleased that the Corder hanging had attracted many noble guests and their entourages to the manor after the entertainment.

Brillianta Astell was pleased she had had the foresight to persuade her father Sir Edward to allow her to sojourn for the Treggans' banquet. Her lanky half-cousin Ralph Chauncey was to attend her. A sober Latin scholar with stark leanings towards a reformed Church, he was roused to passion only by the mention of religious preferment at Cambridge's Trinity College. Her Aunt Artemisia Astell of Maidborough had given sombre approval of cousin Ralph Chauncey's attendance, with strict abjurations that at no time was Brillianta to travel in any carriage unescorted, or to remain in any withdrawing-room unless *all* the company proved acceptable. The outing had been uncommonly difficult.

No greater difficulty than that of procuring a secret messenger by the good offices of her coachman, without Ralph Chauncey's eagle eye observing.

'I have mislaid my reticule, Cousin Ralph,' Brillianta had said woefully as they were about to embark. 'I shall send a footman to the innkeeper.'

'Cousin Brillianta,' Ralph interposed smoothly. 'You could never be a burden. Leave the problem in my charge.'

She had entered the carriage fuming, thwarted by that idiot relative. Her plan was a simple deception, merely the kind of, well, play which a lady could enjoy while entertaining the rest of the company. Where was the harm in summoning Doctor Carmichael on some perfectly trustworthy pretext? When he came – to attend on whatever vapours she would mimic for the purpose – why, all the guests could inspect him! That he was the hangman's surgeon was common knowledge; no other doctor in the Eastern Hundreds would assume that responsibility. And Doctor Carmichael, she had learned at the inn after the death cart had rumbled away in the guard of the Suffolk Militia, was to engage in anatomical dissection. The very thought made her feel faintish, though intrigued. And excited almost as if . . . no. The very idea was absurd. Ladies did not demean themselves for hedonistic purposes. Titillation was sophisticated, not a sordid physical indulgence.

So resolved, she was delighted when an opportunity presented itself to guide events her own way the instant the party had assembled at Saxelby.

'We have a paltry fare for your sustenance,' Harriet announced to the company. She looked quite well recovered, though a little too brittle to convince Brillianta. 'I hope a few dishes will sustain you before supper.'

Two long trestled tables were lavishly laid with cuts and hot collations. Hashed grouse was a must, of course, in such sporting company, with eighteen different meat dishes and a miscellany of sauces, filleted soles, salmon, hams, roasted fowl, stewed eels, minced veal, black game, salmi of game, and a score of puddings including Harriet's own specialities, amber pudding and noyau cream, the new and highly-favoured fruit called pine apple, and marbled jelly. It was not much to appease appetites after so engrossing an entertainment as a hanging, but the ladies naturally praised her provisions to the skies, cooing and exclaiming, while the gentlemen smiled and allowed themselves well served.

Harriet was pleased with the admiration, though of course Sylvia Newborough had to whine to Alexander Waite that, no thank you, she would forgo the Marlborough pudding as it tended to remain heavily upon her, the implication being that she was too willowy, a veritable picture of youth, to cope with that sweetmeat. The absurd girl wore a silly Gallo-Greek bodice, quite wrong, in pink, making her positively drain every ounce of colour from the ornate floral walls. Doubtless, Harriet thought, smiling brightly at the company as they distributed themselves around the piecrust occasional tables, Sylvia Newborough's delight at having her father at last receive the profits from the one merchant ship that managed to creep cargo home from the Orient was making her feel a cut above. The Newboroughs were a mercantilist family, the new sort, famous for their climbing nature in these days of ridiculously liberal opinions.

A disturbance at the far end of the dining hall caught her attention. She hurried to where an elderly lady was seated, fanning herself vigorously. Other ladies were murmuring anxiously about her. Brillianta Astell, Harriet saw with annoyance, had already taken charge.

'I shall send for an apothecary, saving your presence, Harriet.' Brillianta tapped her sombre cousin Ralph and glided swiftly down the room, beckoning to the senior footman.

'What is it, Miss Cashel?' Harriet summoned a screen and a chaise longue.

Miss Cashel was one of Rodney's elderly relatives from Blackrock in Ireland, and was notorious for her need of attention. Stout and vaporous, she gained centre stage by complaints of languor, tottering to win notice. Harriet had already succumbed, from inexperience of the lady, but quickly recognised Miss Cashel's device for what it was. Now the lady was crying wolf yet again. At her advanced age – fifty-two if a day – she had clearly to be indulged, but how ridiculous for so elderly a lady to wear an impossibly tall Medici collar, of Dresden lace! How a hostess had to suffer!

It took time to settle the company after such excitement. The lady was recovered and the music playing by the time the apothecary arrived. The two violins and a viol, with a new type of upright pianoforte as made in William Southwell's manufactory, were entertaining the gathering before evening dinner. Harriet sent to dismiss him, but Brillianta prevailed upon her to allow Miss Cashel to be waited on by the tradesman.

18

'You cannot be too careful, Harriet.' Brillianta's smile should have warned Harriet. She was too irritated by Miss Cashel's uncertainties, and naively hoped it would be done in a moment.

Maids-of-all were instructed to assist Miss Cashel's own abigail, and help her into a withdrawing-room. Harriet waited by the door as the necessary cushions were laid and aromas wafted through for Miss Cashel's approval. In the dining hall, servants hurried to lay for dinner, the butler's wine stewards moving slowly so as not to disturb the clarets and Portugals as they arrived from the cellars.

Doctor Carmichael entered and stood regarding the scene. Harriet stared, feeling herself go pale as she understood Brillianta's trick. He stood there, dishevelled as ever, in his long surtout that reached the mid-calves of his half-jacks, his beaver hat in his hand. Behind him stood a girl, momentarily caught in the shadows of the Argand lamps. She was quite still, and carried his case.

'Is this the patient?' he asked. The voice was gentle as ever, foolishly questioning. Hopeless for a physician, worse for the surgeon he represented himself to be, his very inflexion announced his poor knowledge, hope for certainty in a world of ignorance.

'Yes,' Miss Cashel said, stirring, immediately angered by the dolt's attitude. *This* indeed! 'Come, my man. I have had an attack of the vapours.'

'Doctor Carmichael?' Brillianta asked. 'Sealandings?'

'At your pleasure, madam.' He advanced into the room with a long step. 'Who will chaperone me as I make examination?'

'Why, Miss Cashel's own abigail,' Brillianta said before Harriet could speak. 'And Mistress Treggan and myself. I believe you have Mistress Treggan's acquaintance?'

Carmichael paused for a moment, then he bowed. 'Your servant, ladies. May I enquire of the patient's symptoms?'

The Doctor's cursory evasion annoyed Brillianta. It would not do. She swept forward. She had gone to considerable thought to devise this meeting and exploit Harriet's distress to the uttermost. She would not be baulked.

'Of *course*! What are we thinking of?' She pointed, and Miss Cashel's abigail hurriedly closed the doors. Mehala stepped inside carrying the instrument case. Brillianta saw her opportunity. 'I see you have brought your maid-of-all. Send her outside.'

'Your pardon, Miss Astell,' Carmichael said with candour. 'Mehala is my assistant. She remains, or I cannot.'

Harriet felt matters slipping out of her control. She had not shown herself mistress of the house.

'You *are* acquainted with Miss Astell, then, Doctor?' she put in neatly. 'Please get on, for Miss Cashel is distressed.'

Brillianta suppressed her irritation. 'Assistant? Surely you cannot mean *medical* assistant, Doctor? There is no such thing as a female apprentice, be that physician or surgeon. Unless this helper is a very remarkable creature indeed!'

'Just so, Miss Astell.'

Carmichael advanced, declining further conversation, and knelt beside the white-and-gold scroll-ended Grecian squab on which Miss Cashel reclined. She started moaning slightly and gave a restless thrash, keeping her eyes on him.

'He is the hanging surgeon, is he not?' she whispered.

'Yes.' Brillianta felt this exploit was not going quite her way, though it had reduced Harriet to a silent spectator. 'I trust, Doctor, that you finished your labours at the prison?'

'I was unfortunately called away before getting properly started, as you are aware. I should have declined your summons, had it not been addressed to me by name.'

Harriet's intake of breath made Brillianta's cheeks colour at the revelation that she had deliberately avoided summoning the town apothecary. She remained mute. Carmichael signed for oil lamps to be brought. Miss Cashel's abigail hurried to comply.

He smelt the lady's breath, observed her pupils in the feeble light. He held out his hand, and she placed hers in his, a gratified smile about her lips, her breathing quickened.

'Pains, m'lady?'

'Yes.' Miss Cashel indicated her whole body. 'Fierce, as if burning in a fever.'

'Breathless?' He saw her flabby stoutness, her thick wrist, her ability to move at will while claiming an incapacitating pain. He had once seen a man pass a stone after a horrendous fortnight of utter distress that had made the poor patient roll in agony. The relief had been instantaneous, accompanied with torrential sweats and rigors.

'I cannot breathe, Doctor. My heart throbs, my head spins.'

She was gross, Ven observed. She stank of Portugal, brandy, and unless he was much mistaken, distilled Geneva spirit also. She was delighted by his attention. He asked several terse questions. From his meagre knowledge, she had all known symptoms, each one contradicting the next.

Abruptly he released her wrist. The hand fell on the squab. 'M'lady. Do you wish me to pronounce my diagnosis, in company? Or in solitude, saving only Mehala?'

'Here, Doctor.' Miss Cashel could not avoid looking at the Doctor's hands. To think that those hands, but an hour ago, had been dissecting the cadaver of William Corder, the cruel murderer hanged this very day! She moaned, her breath driven faster by the thought. 'Before these ladies, if you please. All should know the seriousness of my ailments.'

'Very well.' He straightened and stepped away. 'M'lady, you are drunk. The imbibition of Geneva, that people now abbreviate to gin, is ferocious to the constitution, especially yours, because you are too fat. You are dressed wrongly. Your attire is too youthful, being far too tight for corpulence. Eat a deal less. Drink only mild fluids, in moderate quantity.'

Miss Cashel sat bolt upright, apoplectic with fury at his frankness. 'You hear him?' she screeched in rage. 'You hear this man? Rodney Treggan! This instant! Arrest this . . . this impostor – for defamation!'

Carmichael was standing motionless when the door burst open and Treggan entered, with Charles Golding and Alex Waite alongside. They halted, seeing nothing amiss except Miss Cashel screaming on the squab and the rest observing her. Doctor Carmichael's recognition of Treggan and Charles Golding was immediate. He stiffened, but continued remorselessly.

'The medical facts are, m'lady, that you are suffering the effects of excess assorted drink. I advise you for the sake of your health to consume less intoxicating fluid, preferably little or none. You are six stones too heavy for the capacity of your heart and lungs. Over eighty needless pounds. Frugality, m'lady, is next to godliness.'

'Hear him, Rodney!' Miss Cashel wailed. 'I demand protection!'

'The superstition, to accept food at Christmas, applies to mince pies only, m'lady,' Ven continued, his voice cold with disapproval. 'The rest of the year, it is customary to avoid gluttony.'

'Carmichael!' Treggan said sharply. 'You have said enough!'

Harriet glanced at Brillianta, and saw with dismay that she had realised Treggan knew and disliked Carmichael. Ven was oblivious to the tension. He was only concerned with the absurdity of being called from important anatomical work to minister to a fat, wheezing woman whose gluttony was ruining her health. He saw there would be no escape except by appealing to holiness by way of hypocrisy. It had served him well in the past, and he hoped it would serve him now.

'Our Lord and Saviour ate sparingly, m'lady, as you will recall from the Scriptures. His diet was frugal, his form revealing to us mortals that moderation is the path to follow.' He gazed at the gentlemen in the doorway. Golding was whispering to Rodney Treggan. 'I thank you for your courtesy in summoning me instead of a more fashionable physician, but regret that, as you suffer no medical ailments here, I must now report back to Edmundsbury to complete my task for the Governor there. Mehala.'

He bowed and retreated, Miss Cashel weeping loudly and snapping as her abigail rushed to minister to her. Brillianta was appalled yet delighted by her plan's interesting fruition. Harriet was distraught, comforting the hysterical Miss Cashel. Treggan left quickly, not following the doctor and his doxy, Brillianta observed, but going through the dining hall, from where he could quickly intercept. She slipped out after him.

'Cousin Brillianta.'

'Yes, Ralph.' The wretched gloom-monger barred her path.

He led her aside. 'Brillianta. I have to tender my sincerest apologies. That a lady should have been compelled to listen to such a revolting display of ill manners! I feel inclined to horse-whip that ignorant quack who so disgraced –'

Brillianta cut across his twaddle, trying to conceal her screaming impatience with the pompous fool. 'Ralph. Dear cousin. One thing I can always rely on, I know, is your unfailing devotion to good manners, to breeding, which only a devoted relative can provide. I am indebted. But I am so overcome by the distressing spectacle that I must rest.'

She saw consternation leap into his eyes and hastily corrected the impression she had created. The last thing she wanted was for Cousin Ralph to hoist her away to Arminell Hall, just when matters were fascinating. She glided with becoming grace down the dining hall, paused to inspect her appearance in a pier glass, leaning on the pier table to give exactly the right impression of faintness to that ever-vigilant pest. Then, gathering herself with a breath, she moved sedately out of his sight beyond the double doors. She hurried with swift quiet across the entrance hall towards the corridor which led to the tradesmen's side entrance, slowing as she heard voices and stopping beside a hanging corridor cupboard. Rodney Treggan's voice was thick with restrained anger.

'I want no reminders of your past allegiances, quack!'

'Nothing was further from my mind, sir. I was summoned by your ladies to treat a sick person.'

Treggan snorted in derision. "And seized the opportunity to intrude among your betters! Always your failing, assuming breeding and status not your own!'

Carmichael spoke only after a pause, his voice shaking. 'Your mention of past allegiances discredits your wife far more than it discommodes me. I have forgot any and all admirations, ever since I met the lady you see here as my assistant. She alone holds my admiration. She excels. All pale in comparison.'

'How dare you, you cheap crocus!' Treggan seemed to take a step, but a slap sounded and Brilliant heard him gasp. 'Of all —'

The girl's voice cried, 'That will be one sovereign, sir!'

'You have the impertinence to — ?'

The girl called loudly, 'Will any servant at Saxelby Hall pay for his master? 'Llowing this gentleman's solvency, will any gentleman loan money for this Treggan fellow to pay his debt?'

'Silence!' Treggan thundered, but the girl shouted all the louder, her voice carrying across the wide entrance hall. 'I shall have you taken in charge, Carmichael, as God is my judge! You shall not proceed a furlong!'

'Debtors!' the girl was shouting, quite calmly but with renewed intensity. 'Bad debtors, gentlemen!'

'Mehala,' Brillianta heard Doctor Carmichael say, 'let us away.'

'Away, you dog-quack?' Treggan was yelling. 'Vettars! Crombie! Bring my bailiff! By God —'

'Bad debtors!' Mehala kept shouting, ever angrier. 'Bad debtors at Saxelby Hall!'

23

Footfalls sounded in the corridor and Sir Charles Golding came past with Miss Newborough, Alex Waite, Ralph Chauncey, followed by several ladies.

'*Silence!*'

The old, quavering voice had little sound but great authority. Two thumps caused Brillianta's feet to vibrate. With so many now present, she felt it safe to move from concealment.

By the low doorway that formed the tradesmen's entrance stood Rodney Treggan. Mehala had interposed herself between Carmichael and his accuser. She seemed strangely exalted, almost happy, at finding herself in a position of danger. Her hair shone dark, tinged with streaks of gleaming russet in the oblique light from the curved porch window. Treggan's cheek showed where she had struck him. She looked up at him completely unfazed. Brillianta was astonished. *She is enjoying this*, she realised. Though it truly was serious, for a hireling's doxy to accuse one of the established gentry of a debt default was tantamount to begging for imprisonment. False accusers were once hanged out of hand and, since Henry the Eighth's time, were branded with an 'F' on the face before further punishment. Mehala was not beautiful, but so compelling that all eyes were on her. Including, Brillianta noted with a start of alarm, the glittering eyes of an old austere lady standing on the stairs.

She was dressed in an old-fashioned pelisse-robe with a shoulder-cape, the walking gown latchings not yet fastened. Her hair was arranged under a chaperone, itself covered by a pale green dormouse of French style. Black walking-out slippers indicated that she had been intending to take the air, which accounted for her informal attire. She leaned on a tall gold-mounted ash stick.

'I am waiting! What is the cause of this?'

'Lady Faith,' Treggan spoke with difficulty, glaring at Mehala, 'I apologise for the disturbance created by these intruders. I shall take them in charge –'

'Bad debtors, m'lady,' Mehala interrupted, 'are given to magistrates, not creditors.'

'So, miss.' The old lady's eyes raked the faces below her. 'You were the harridan I heard shrieking about money?'

'Yes, Lady Hunterfield, and with cause.'

24

Several servants were in the corridor now, a bailiff and stewards working their way forward. Treggan beckoned them angrily.

The old lady's gaze was on Mehala. 'You are either impertinent or courageous, girl. Mr Treggan, please allow all to leave, save this wench and her tradesman.'

'Very well.'

Reluctantly the crowd dispersed, the bailiff taking his stewards through the outer door. Brillianta was about to move off after Charles Golding and Sylvia Newborough, but Lady Hunterfield called.

'Miss Astell! Stay, if you please. It will save you having to skulk beside the hanging press, in such a skimpy Piedmont gown!'

Brillianta halted, her face flaming. 'Yes, Lady Faith.'

The old lady slowly descended the rest of the steps to stand with Treggan facing Carmichael and the girl.

'You would be tried before my nephew,' she announced. 'I wish to hear what caused this affray.'

'This leech caused trouble, and sorely insulted Miss Cashel,' Treggan said tightly. 'He accused her of drunkenness, gluttony, and pretended symptoms. I intend to punish him with utmost severity.'

'Mr Treggan,' Lady Faith's bird-like eyes were everywhere, 'would you indulge a lady, sir?'

Rodney Treggan swallowed. 'Why, of course, ma'am.'

'Then allow me to sentence this pair myself. After all,' she said gravely, 'I seem to be the one most disturbed by their noisy presence here, do I not? And handling tradesmen is no talk for a gentleman. It is so much better left to an experienced lady.'

Treggan glanced at Brillianta, at Carmichael, Mehala, then nodded. 'Very well, Lady Faith. As you will.'

'Miss Brillianta can chaperone me in your stead, Mr Treggan. She has been so *very* attentive to these proceedings.'

'With your ladyship's permission.' Treggan strode with deliberation along the corridor until his footsteps faded.

'Now, miss. How did you know my name?'

Mehala found herself almost quailing. She did not retreat before the intent gaze, but strove to hold her own steady.

'M'ladyship's likeness is at Lorne House, the fourth painting in the west wing. It is m'lady when young.'

'You do well to recognise me. That daub! You have been in Sir Henry Hunterfield's home?'

'Yes, m'lady. As has Doctor Carmichael.'

'Carmichael,' Faith Hunterfield said quietly. Her brow cleared. 'You then must be Mehala, and this the redoubtable Doctor from Shalamar.' She held up a restraining hand as he made to murmur his name in introduction. 'No silliness, Doctor. I am tired. My walk through the orangery is ruined. Brillianta?'

'Yes, Lady Faith?'

'What did Doctor Carmichael tell Miss Cashel?'

Brillianta glanced from the imperious old lady to Mehala and Carmichael. She exhaled, unable to utter a word. Lady Hunterfield gave an unexpected bark of a laugh.

'That says it all, Brillianta! So!' She rounded on Carmichael. 'You told Miss Cashel the truth! Have you no sense, Doctor? You will not get very far!' Ven stammered an approximate apology, but the old lady would have none of it. 'And Mehala. Pulled from the sea, wasn't it? Brought to Sealandings harbour without a memory?'

'Just so, m'lady.' Mehala's tone was quietly guarded.

'Hmmmph. If you say so, girl. You look remarkably self-possessed to me. Who's this bad debtor?'

'Doctor Carmichael was being abused, m'lady. I demanded payment for his services.'

'A sovereign is a high fee for a country quack, miss!'

'Doctor Carmichael's advice would save Miss Cashel's life, were she to heed it. Does Treggan deem his relation's life to be worth less?'

The old lady appraised her candidly. 'You argue well, for a sea-fetched waif. Perhaps too smartly for your own good!'

'Forgive me, m'lady,' Carmichael put in, starting to stammer. 'I ask no payment.'

'Doctor Carmichael was summoned here by name,' Mehala said. 'A fee is due. If it is not forthcoming –'

Lady Hunterfield's face wrinkled in a sudden disarming smile. 'I remember being like you, Mehala,' she said reminiscently. 'It is a lovely and beautiful time. So young, you would rather have the hatred than the solution! As would any woman worth her salt. True, Miss Astell?'

'Oh, very true, m'lady!' Brillianta exclaimed, hardly caring what she answered as long as she escaped unscathed from this old dragon. It was just her ill luck that it was time for the old lady's evening walk. It had spoiled everything.

'Your ladyship,' Ven interposed, desperate to be away. 'I am commanded by the Governor of Edmundsbury gaol to be back at the soonest, and am already mortal tardy.'

'You will anatomise the hanged man?'

'Yes, m'lady. I do it without fee, to learn the structure of *Homo sapiens*. There is a move afoot in Parliament to forbid the dissection of hanged corpses, as now is allowed. There might soon be no means of studying human anatomy at all!' He was almost beside himself with anxiety lest the opportunity be wrested away.

Very well. She thought, then smiled. 'I must provide a punishment to fit the crime, must I not? Your host Rodney Treggan insists! You are the doctor who saved Sealandings from the cattle plague, the murrain; and who combats the croup in dying children?'

He flushed, and stammered. 'N-n-none of my learning, m'lady. Only of my application. So many theories in medicine suffer indirect speculation, when more direct methods might –'

'Mmm, well,' she said. 'Be that as it may, Doctor, you are hereby appointed to help the workhouse at Sealandings, for a full year, when time permits. Your salary shall be half of a London physician's equivalent.'

'But, m'lady,' Ven countered, frowning, 'I fear you err –'

'Thank you, your ladyship.' Mehala curtseyed quickly. She held Ven's arm, trying to propel him out. 'Doctor Carmichael wishes to thank you for your kind intervention and promises to do everything possible to perform satisfactorily.'

The old lady hid a smile as Mehala edged Carmichael away, still explaining in his nervous stutter.

'Vettars!' she called. 'See this pair of . . . of medical folk travel back to the prison by the speediest means!'

'Yes, your ladyship,' a man's voice answered.

Brillianta realised the astute old lady had guessed that Treggan had stationed his men outside. The formidable old trout stared at Brillianta until she began to shift uneasily.

'And Brillianta Astell. How is your father, Sir Edward?'

27

'Very well, thank you, m'm.'

'You shall accompany me on my evening promenade through the orangery,' Lady Hunterfield announced as though awarding a prize. 'Tell me of his doings lately.'

'Thank you, m'm,' Brillianta said desperately, 'but I must speak with Harriet on matters of intimacy –'

'Which', Lady Faith boomed in an unexpected louring voice, 'you will sacrifice to give me the pleasure of your company.'

'Yes, Lady Hunterfield,' Brillianta said miserably. 'Thank you, Lady Hunterfield.'

Together they left for the orangery, the old lady leaning on Brillianta at least as heavily as on her gold-mounted cane.

3

THE JOURNEY TO the prison took less than half an hour. Even considering the dry condition of the rutted roads, it was a remarkable achievement. Ven thanked the coachman, and together he and Mehala were admitted to the prison yard. Three torches burned smokily, reflecting on the slimed, dripping walls. A warder led them down into the damp cellar set aside for anatomy.

The cadaver was on the rough-hewn table, a sheet over it, exactly as when they had been called by the gentry's summons. Mehala lit her two candles from the warder's lanthorn. He harrumphed at her parsimony.

'Taking your candles!' he complained as she placed the first candle for Ven's work. 'Shows meanness, that do, gal.'

'So you can swap mine for your inferior hog tallows?' Mehala flared, instantly roused. 'I've seen how your candles gutter and spit.' Cruelly she mimicked. 'Shows thievery, that do, booy!'

Ven paused, hanging up his Cambridge and spencer jacket on a protruding nail. 'Please to remember the presence of a person's mortal remains.'

'Yes, Doctor,' she said quietly. She followed the disgruntled warder and held the door, to call after him, 'My candles are half sheep and half bullock tallow with none of your pressed greaves left in, to defraud the buyer, and steal from prisoners!'

'Mehala!' Ven called, sharper. 'Please attend to your duty.'

'Yes, Doctor.' She came meekly enough, glancing to see how far she had overstepped her mark. 'The greaves, pressed cake left after the tallow is properly boiled and extracted, is scavenged by dogs, Doctor. That is all it is good for –'

'Thank you, Mehala.' He was worried, holding out his arms. 'Do I not hold the cotton threads while you judge the right amount of twist for the best candle?'

She fetched a thick white apron out of a jute bag. 'I had a clean one in reserve,' she explained when he expressed surprise. 'Nettles grow well at Shalamar, so I made several nettlelinen aprons. It lasts better than flax, though needs soaking a good five months longer before it can be beaten. Lovely nettle cloth!' She tied his apron's back latchings.

'I wondered where my discarded bloodstained apron had got to.'

'Shhh!' She looked towards the steps to make sure the warder was not eavesdropping. 'I slipped it through the bars for a prisoner to use, or sell.'

'Was that proper, Mehala?' He was constantly startled by the things she did, her knowledge and skills. 'Justice rules prisoners and judges alike. A gift, even a nettle linen apron, might be seen as perfidious encouragement of leniency.'

'Oh, indeed, Doctor,' she agreed innocently. 'Though were some physician to drop, quite accidentally, the last of his coins by the grating where the poorest prisoners are kept, that would be permissible?'

He reddened, caught out. 'A true accident, Mehala! My pocket flap, ah, happened to catch my arm. The coins spilled.'

'Do not fear, Doctor,' she said disarmingly. 'I shall say nothing to the authorities.'

'Enough talk, Mehala,' he said gruffly, annoyed. The poorest prisoners were kept in the most piteous circumstances, in rat-infested recesses of cellars that ran wet from the sewage and ordure of richer prisoners on the floor above. They succumbed quickest to gaol fever, the terrible typhus that was the most grim of all the Ancient World's legacies. With a few coppers, the chained sufferers could buy a little food or even new straw from the gaolers. 'Let us get on with our work.'

They removed the sheet, Mehala blanching and turning away at the sight of the partly dissected corpse. Ven reached for his lancet. He took a pair of leather retractors from the instrument case and fitted the wooden spatulas into them to hold them firmer.

'We had reached the point, Mehala,' he instructed, peering in the dim candlelight, 'where I showed you the ligaments of the liver, how the diaphragm is attached to the body's walls. See, I hold aside the stomach and lift the intestines superiorly towards the head.'

'Yes, Doctor.' She looked, holding herself stiff.

'No, Mehala,' he said quietly. 'Remember the Latin tag: *Humani nihil a me alienum puto*. We must accept all that is human. Take a retractor, and reflect the intestines so. Inspect the organ lying in the crook of the stomach.'

She breathed deeply. The stench almost made her retch but she managed to comply.

The glistening tubes were astonishingly like the lights of an animal, she saw, fascinated in spite of herself. Remarkable! Was a human nothing more than an extension of a mere animal? The heretical thought was almost blasphemy. It crossed her mind that perhaps the similarities Ven often referred to, and occasionally depended on as a means of learning, were greater than even he supposed.

'The sweetbread, Ven?' she asked.

'The pancreas, yes. Retract inferiorly – towards the feet – to see one of the kidneys. There!'

He traced the ureter towards the bladder, then cut through the fat omentum that tethered the intestines.

'The kidney lies behind and out of the belly cavity!' he exclaimed, pleased at the observation. 'Imagine if the renal organ were a great abscess, Mehala. It would track down, and present somewhere far below . . .' He cut, following the plane of fascia with his fingers.

'It is a sheet, Ven! A transparent covering.'

Wondering, he paused to look. 'Can this be the peritoneum, Mehala, of which I heard so much? It is a sac, yet is not a sac. Do you see? It explains why purulent fluids seem to originate in one organ, yet present elsewhere!' He stood back, wiping his hands on the coarse cloth she provided. 'I feel so useless, love. So hopeless. Do you know what I envisaged, never having seen this structure before?' He gave a dejected smile. 'I saw the peritoneum covering as a kind of, well, towel. Can you believe my ignorance?'

She wanted to touch him, give him comfort. 'Blame your poverty, Ven. Ignorance is blameless.'

'It wasn't just that, Mehala. Not even wealthy students at the London Hospital ever *saw* a cadaver. They too had to rely on books, freehand drawings in lecture theatres, by doctors who had never seen a corpse dissected in their whole lives. Shameful. We know so little, and I the least of all.'

'You learn as best you may, Ven. And teach me!'

He smiled. 'Our contract is binding, Mehala. One day, after the requisite and proper time, you will know all I can teach. Then you too will be a doctor. And then . . .' He stared blankly at the candle's shifting shadows, blank with surprise and dismay. 'And then,' he resumed hesitantly, his stammer returning, 'I will provide you with your letters, and you will be free . . .'

'It is a dream, Ven,' she said, her heart sinking at the thought of leaving. 'I shall learn, and you teach. Beyond that, we can not see.'

'Yes. That is sensible.' Relieved, he resumed the dissection. 'I now turn to the neck, Mehala. I want to see what we call glands actually are. They are palpable in certain diseases. There are theories, one being that they only appear when sickness causes them to do so. Another is that they are there all the time in some quiescent form, like an inert pea beneath the skin, only to become larger when disease spreads inflammation into them.'

'How will we recognise them?'

He cut along the skin of the dead man's neck, shrugging helplessly. 'I simply do not know. I asked surgeons at the London during my years, and listened to student arguments in taverns. It was all guesswork, for none knew. So I will search where they usually appear, along the line of arteries and veins. In inflammation they feel like lead shot chained along a child's neck . . .'

Dissecting down the great blood vessels of the neck took over an hour, as every so often he had to pause and inspect the area in the candleglim, mopping away the blood caused by the hangman's rope, the force of which had ruptured veins and arteries alike.

'Here! Mehala! I see them!'

Small greyish beads were there, in a recess of fascia, showing dully in the light. Mehala brought a candle nearer and together they peered at the small nodules. He turned to her, eyes glowing.

'We have made a discovery, Mehala! They exist even in the normal person! Simply waiting in these grooves, perhaps all over the body, for inflammation!'

'Why, Ven?'

His enthusiasm waned. 'I do not know. Who does? Perhaps to combat the infection? To delay it? Reasons yet unknown?'

Footfalls sounded on the steps and a lanthorn swung shadows eerily. The warder came with a chink of keys.

'Time ahead, Doctor,' he growled. 'You've had long enough.'

'If you will permit only another hour or two, sir –'

'Doctor, finish! The prison surgeon is concerned lest you damage the skin. He wants it whole.'

'Very well.' Disconsolately Ven complied, covering the cadaver with the sheet. 'Do please extend my gratitude, for my appointment as hanging doctor and the opportunity of dissection.'

'Half a guinea is payable, warder,' Mehala said. 'To whom does my master apply for it?'

'To me, as head gaoler.' The man grinning. 'And in vain! The pair of you have cost me more than the whole prison together, so be off.'

Mehala started towards the man, but Ven interposed and gestured her to gather their belongings. 'I shall have the Governor on your back, booy!' she cried, hauling an eshet of water for Ven to wash his hands free of fat and congealed blood.

'The Governor and me are mortal friends, gal!' the gaoler laughed, and went off, shaking his head at her credulity.

'Mehala,' Ven said quietly, 'no more contumely. Respect the deceased. He has served us, made some reparation for his crime.'

'Yes, well,' she said, angry at being defrauded, 'money might have served us better this night, Ven. Imagine staying at some tavern, travelling home to Sealandings tomorrow on the post-chaise!'

He was smiling as he took the soap paste she offered in its leaf wrapping. 'Mehala, you hide even more dreams than I!'

'Careful. That is all the soap I have, not having enough chalk to bring it in a pot. I had to use sea salt at the boiling stage, while making it from old tallow. That makes it go less far.'

He washed his hands, silenced by her range of skills, always able to produce something marvellous when they were destitute. 'I feel ashamed, Mehala.'

'Why, sir?' she chided, offering him her own discarded nettle apron. Its upper part was unstained.

He flapped his hands before drying them. 'Look around.' She obeyed, seeing the stone walls dripping excrement, the flickering shadows, rats skulking along runnels. 'A sight for the despairing. Filth, cold, dank, as foul a prison as could be. You hear only the cries of the inmates, the suffering who are imprisoned. Men, women, babes.' He turned haggard features towards her. 'You see? This is all I have brought you to. After . . . how many months we have been together at Sealandings?'

'Many, Ven. And many more to come!' She spoke with spirit, knowing that Ven's sadnesses took hold; ever a man's way but never a woman's. 'These terrible conditions have to be fought, Ven. We are here to conquer. You dwell on the sorrows, live inside your soul too much. A woman cannot, nor should she. It is my duty to lift you, that you gain strength to carry on. That way, we do better, bring life when hope is failing.'

They faced each other, the candlelight throwing silhouettes on the walls.

'But the world ought not to be so terrible, Mehala. In one day we have witnessed dreadful events: a hanging, fraud, gambling, bullying, riots of mobs making merry over a human being's death, not to mention that gluttonous lady pretending she was ill.'

Mehala smiled. 'It *is* terrible, Ven. And we cannot remake it, nor mend all its ills. We simply must live and do the best we can. You utter the man's fervent wish, while I make the woman's clear observation: it is always so, and ever shall be.'

His shoulders sagged wearily. 'I understand nothing, Mehala.' He looked at two bowls she had set by the cadaver. 'Why did you place those, and fill them with water?'

She laughed. 'A little milked water, Ven, with hoarhound plant crushed in as a powder. I brought it from Shalamar.'

He looked blankly at her. She coloured. ''Tis an old folk remedy against flies. You observe that there is none now, nor was there on our return from Saxelby Hall? Hoarhound steeped in milk is said to speedily kill flies, however many there be. The problem was preventing the warder from stealing my clay bowls!'

'How did you?'

'I lied,' she said candidly. 'A little superstition goes a long way. I whispered to him, when we were interrupted by the Lady Brillianta's summons, that the bowls were borrowed from Saint Edmund's tomb, that they once caught the Saint's blood when the Norsemen so cruelly slew him.'

'A lie, Mehala!' Ven was shocked.

Mehala was unconcerned, but argued against his reprimand. 'Our Saint would rather have his name used for good than evil,

Ven. Did I not prevent the sin of theft by the chief gaoler whose soul, we already know, needs every bit of assistance?'

He started to speak, then cleared his throat and paused, nonplussed. She smiled. He was always so concerned to do right that he sometimes exasperated her.

'Come, dearest,' she said gently. 'We have far to go to lay our head at Shalamar. I was very pleased with you.'

'Pleased?' he asked, puzzled, as they regained their coats and belongings. 'For why?'

'For telling that Miss Cashel a home truth,' she said lightly. And for looking straight at your former love Harriet Ferlane, now Mistress Treggan, to whom you once proposed long before I met you, and never showing the slightest emotion, so proving she is nothing. She thought this, but did not say.

He frowned as they made their way up from the cellar and into the evening air. It was coming on to rain.

'That was my duty, Mehala,' he said seriously. 'When making a diagnosis, you must pronounce it in a way the patient understands.'

'Yes, Doctor,' she said formally, taking his instrument case from him as they set out down the yard.

Cries for alms rose from the gratings, taken up by the rest of the prisoners as it was realised they were no longer accompanied by the gaoler.

'For God's pity, sir, a coin. My babe here is mortal famished . . .'

'Lady, lady! A farthing, for food on the morrow!'

'Sir! An y'please, I did nothing, save protect my father from scoundrels –'

Ven walked on as Mehala paused to shove the bloodstained aprons between the bars. Hands reached through to claim the garments amid scuffling. She placed her two bowls on gratings further along. They were swiftly scrabbled out of sight, to cries of gratification. She hurried to catch Ven up. His eyes were streaming. He looked at the ground as they were discharged from the prison gate by the night gaoler.

Mehala touched his arm. 'Do not take on so.'

He shook her hand off angrily. 'I thank you not to jump to conclusions,' he corrected coldly. 'I am not weeping. It is simply the effect of the chill night air.'

'Of course, Doctor,' she said. 'I am deceived by the poor torchlight from the gates.'

'That and the smoke from the candles,' he added sternly.

'Just so.'

'A brisk pace, then.' He was mollified. 'We have far to go.'

'Doctor,' Mehala called after. 'That way leads inland. Here lies the direction coastward.'

Sheepishly he retraced his steps. 'You should have reminded me, Mehala.'

She was smiling in the darkness as they set off through the town. It was still noisy, with singers and entertainers clustered outside the alehouses, and whores plying their trade along the streets and in church doorways. She held on to the sleeve of his surtout so that, should one stumble in some sludge trickling from the houses they passed, the other could prevent a fall of both into the mire.

They reached the corner. She gave a glance back at the louring mass of the prison as it passed from sight. She inhaled the sour stench of the congested town with pleasure, for they were now facing the coast. She imagined she inhaled the breeze of her lovely North Sea shores at Sealandings, which was home.

4

A LEX WAITE WAS addressing a rapt audience of ladies at
Saxelby when the newcomer arrived and stood listening
unnoticed by Lady Hunterfield's chair.

'No, Miss Newborough,' Waite was saying. 'I saw it with my
own eyes. No second-hand news, this.'

'And that leech's carry-all actually handled a weapon?' Sylvia
Newborough was outraged.

'Not merely handled. She held it as a sailor does when boarding
an enemy ship, that is rotated, firing pan uppermost.'

'It cannot be done!' Miss Newborough exclaimed, scandalised.

'I assure you. Then she fired, holding it rock steady, and hit a
single stave stuck in the ground!'

'Unwholesome, sir!' Brillianta cried, having heard rumours of
this when visiting Sealandings, but never talked of it with a
witness. 'Unnatural! For one of the female gender to execute
things so mannishly, why!'

'As I stand here, Miss Astell. In a horse fair, before many score
witnesses. Furthermore, Mehala actually prepared to fight a duel
against another girl, over a matter of selling ale in Sealandings
cattle and horsebreeders' market.'

'Duel?' The ladies were faint with horror.

Alex Waite was enjoying the attention. 'Duel, ladies! The other
girl fled, losing all her impudence. She was routed.'

The newcomer spoke quietly to his Aunt Faith, shaking his head
to prevent the head servant making the customary announcement.
'She was here?'

'Indeed, Henry,' Faith Hunterfield said, as quietly. She made her
way to sit on a window, her nephew beside her. 'Unfazed by the
company, causing disturbances at least as disturbing as those
occasioned by her beau!'

Hunterfield did not reply. His elderly aunt was remarkable for the gossip she could cull from the most innocent conversation. He listened to the North Briton's account of Mehala's prowess.

Faith Hunterfield's only nephew was too shrewd by half, she thought with some irritation. She had used the word beau to goad him, suspecting his unspoken longing for the girl. Sealandings was an outlandish harbour on the North Sea coast, in the rural remoteness of the Eastern Hundreds. Her own Gloucester was a mighty city in the west country, virtually at the crossroads of all the commercial activities in England. But the families of the established gentry extended into every county in the Kingdom. Events at Sealandings were not as remote as he might suppose.

'She is remarkable, Henry,' Faith Hunterfield told him mischievously. 'I admire her. After all, to sacrifice the position of housekeeper to that drunken sot Charles Golding, and take up residence with an impecunious quack, is a considerable act of faith, optimism, hope. I wish you had been here. Do you not?'

'I was delayed, Aunt Faith. A report of some disease imported in the north. It seems rumour.' Hunterfield smiled in wry apology as Waite held the company enthralled.

'. . . team of oxen! Mehala drove it to the floods, and helped to save the sea dykes!'

'All these peasants' skills, yet she cannot remember her past, sir?' Brillianta asked Waite sweetly.

'Indeed. She was taken from the sea a-drowning, and recalls nothing!'

As the ladies exclaimed, Aunt Faith nudged her nephew. 'You know differently by now, Henry. As I.'

Hunterfield glanced at the old lady. 'You have seen her before, Aunt Faith?'

'Once. In Colchester. She had been married only three days to that madman at Red Hall, Elijah Rebow. He drowned with his new wife Mehala, I heard afterwards.' She looked at him. 'It is time you settled, Henry. Brillianta Astell sets her cap at you, as does her sister Lorela. Among others in the Eastern Hundreds as elsewhere.'

He could not expect Aunt Faith to be ignorant of his affair with Thalia De Foe. She was warning him that many knew of his troublesome passion. That that restless vixen was exiled by her husband Fellows De Foe to St Albans, as preventive punishment, was not enough in Aunt Faith's opinion, Hunterfield guessed. A great deal of what Aunt Faith said was of course his sister Lydia's opinion circling in the gyre of family rumour.

'Is this a command to wed, Aunt?' he asked mildly.

'Were I your sainted mother, I should answer affirmatively, Henry Hunterfield,' she said tartly. 'You see twenty ladies in this company! I advocate Brillianta Astell. She does not come up to Mehala's qualities, but who does?'

It was strange to hear Mehala's name spoken so frankly. He had gone to much trouble to confirm Mehala's man's drowning, and his burial at St Edmund's church on the Isle of Southwold, facing the sea that had taken his life. In Sealandings she was merely Mehala, though many blamed her for living in sin with Doctor Carmichael. The hint that he himself had leanings towards the girl was another nudge from his absent sister Lydia.

'Mercy Carmady soon returns to the coast, I believe, Henry,' Aunt Faith quietly speculated. 'Her brother, lately a lieutenant of His Majesty's marine, seeks residence in the Eastern Hundreds. Natural for a naval man to want sight of the ocean, but I hear that his wish is blown along by his sister's eagerness for your Lorne House. Let me see her.'

'Gloucester is a city of rumours, Aunt Faith,' Henry said in dry reprimand. 'Percy Carmady leans to my sister Tabitha. I charged Lydia with getting Tabby settled in life, and soon.'

Aunt Faith pondered this. Tabitha Hunterfield had been too wayward for the family's good since her nonage. She was worry, which, coupled with the fact that Henry had not yet risen to the bait, was infuriating.

'I saw Mistress Rebow', she said pointedly, 'calm a terrified horse near St Peter's church in Colchester. It would have plunged down that steep hill had she not stepped from her carriage and taken charge of the maddened beast.'

'I saw her whip – *whip*, Aunt Faith – a captain's hat from his head, when she considered herself insulted.'

She observed his reflective smile. Alex Waite was now telling the story of the girl saving somebody's life from the muddy estuary in Sealandings Bay.

'Which raises the question, Henry, of the breeding she hides by forgetting, does it not?'

39

'She has no family, Aunt,' he said, watching two ladies rise to welcome a group of gentlemen. 'No children. Her mother died, and lies in Mersea Island. She serves simply as Doctor Carmichael's housekeeper by all accounts, nothing more.'

Clever girl, Faith Hunterfield thought grimly. Remarkable of talent, the right age, but a widow. The landage of Red Hall must be extensive, so Mehala could become wealthy by simply reclaiming her rightful possessions. Yet she still pretends to be mind-lost, in order to remain with an impoverished leech? It did not add up.

'. . . outbreak of cattle plague in the Eastern Hundreds!' Waite was concluding. 'Carmichael predicted the disease's end, once he had devised the plan of burning and restrictions. Mehala served as his principal factotum, I heard!'

'That I know to be true, sir!' Brillianta Astell said in a determined interruption. Things had gone too far. This was becoming a paean of praise for the wretched girl. 'Which only goes to show how splendidly the gentry with large estates *do* manage to instruct their underlings, does it not?'

'A farm girl, one might suppose?' from Sylvia Newborough.

Brillianta cooed. 'Or some fisherman's woman cast adrift.'

'Hunterfield,' Golding called, seeing the Lord of Sealandings standing by the lady dowager. He was more than slightly intoxicated, Hunterfield saw. 'You missed the hanging! A splendid entertainment! What delayed you, man?'

Rodney Treggan, uncomfortable at Golding's boisterousness, gestured for the chief servant to announce the new guest. Hunterfield made his excuses to Aunt Faith.

'Sir Henry Hunterfield, Lord of Sealandings,' the man intoned. Hunterfield rose and bowed to the company, raised his aunt, and joined the others, who were agog to tell them of the good-humoured affrays that had attended the hanging. For the while, Mehala and her penniless leech were forgotten.

5

THEY SPENT THE night in a barn on the outskirts of Woolpit, a small place almost midway between Saint Edmundsbury and Stowmarket. It was wise to follow the turnpike, because footpads and roaming vagabonds were fewer than on the side roads. A reluctant farmer allowed them to sleep by one of his shippons, but only after a converse with his wife and Mehala's claim to be staunchly of the Established Church persuasion. He had heard of Polstead, yes, and the hanging. Mehala said nothing of the part Ven had played. She managed somehow to convince the farmer that Ven was a young newly-qualified doctor heading for Ipswich, she his wife. They slept on stooks, and rose at five to the whooping noises of the stockboys. The farmer's wife gave them a torn loaf of yeoman's bread, and kindly allowed them to drink from the yard pump. Eight of the farmer's twelve children came to watch them eat in the yard among the chickens. Mehala played Queen Anne with the youngest, chanting,

> 'Queen Anne sits in the sun,
> Fair as a lily, brown as a bun.
> We've brought you three letters, so pray read one!'

Ven tried to join in, but his chanting of the old guessing game was so different that the children fell to laughing. He pretended indignation.

'You forgot the black gypsies!' he cried in mock outrage. 'And the kittens within!' He struggled to guess which of the three girls had the hidden ball, awry every time.

'That's wrong, isn't it, Lil?' Mehala's swift facility with children's names was enviable. 'This London gentleman does not know the true words!'

The game broke up as the farmwife called the older ones to work, as the day had long since begun, it being now six o'clock. Ven and Mehala thanked her generosity, and crossed the yard towards the gate. Two of the farmer's men had hung back, delaying while strangers remained in the place. Mehala was envious; the farmhouse seemed the height of affluence.

'One day, Ven, you shall have only the finest white manchet wheaten bread for your break-of-fast, I promise. We shall manage well enough today from plants I shall find along the roadside, but –' Mehala's words were uttered with such ferocity that Ven had to laugh. She rounded on him angrily, but was forced to relent when she saw his chagrin.

He hitched his instrument case on his shoulder and opened the farmyard gate. Mehala waved a salutation towards the bright Suffolk-pink farmhouse. The wife was watching them go, a flock of the smallest children at her skirts.

'Shame makes me laugh, Mehala.' They set off along the track between the hedges. 'I depend on you for so much. For directions – do we take the Stowmarket turnpike? For sustenance – what food, until we reach Shalamar? For finding shelter – without you, I should have been beaten from their door!'

She smiled, proud. 'No, Ven. Without me, you would not even have asked! You would have blundered on in silence, foolish man! That is the difference. As a pair, we must differ but as one.'

'Thirty miles, Mehala? Thirty-five?'

'As the crow might fly.' She gauged the sky with a rueful look. 'As we must go, forty.' She tied up her skirt latchings for a freer walk. 'Add a third to the crow's distance, and there's our journey. Rain before noon, and wet all day.'

He exclaimed. 'Why a third? Why not a tenth? You see what I mean, Mehala? *How* do you know rain is coming? If only I knew more, not merely of the medical art, but of all things.'

'A journey is always a third longer than a straight line because it is so,' she said. 'There are no explanations.'

'Never! There *must* be explanation, Mehala!' he argued. 'We have to believe that! Then we can discover reasons! In medicine, in life. It is the first step towards being able to control all things; Man's destiny!'

'Just listen to you, Ven!' she chided. 'All things are obvious.

When you worry about reasons, they become troublesome. The scarlet pimpernel tells us rain is coming by closing early — hence we call it the poor man's weather glass. Simple!'

Their familiar argument was serious. 'Why *is* manchet bread pure ground flour? What does manchet mean? We do not know.'

His gravity over such obvious trivia brought her frankest smile. 'It means what it means, for heaven's sakes! Hot tansies are called so from their look — see those by the roadside?' She pointed to the golden flower heads. 'What more could resemble the fried yellow tansies I make for you of a morning, while providing a principal ingredient?'

Ven stopped in astonishment. The plants stood two feet tall, with flattened gold blossoms heaped on each stalk.

'It looks exactly like!' His interest was kindled.

'Amazing, Mehala! I had never noticed! How many common plants signify their uses in their very form?' He drooped in resignation.

'An amazement, doctor?' Mehala saw his mood was no more than a despond at their poverty and only natural. She must jolt him out of it. 'Every child!' She grimaced. 'Forgive me, I meant *almost* every child!'

He smiled apology as they skirted enormous water-filled pot-holes in the roadway. 'How will we be greeted in Sealandings, Mehala, after word spreads? Me, the hangman's quack?'

So that was it. 'They will think even the worse of us, Ven, when we cadge onto a dung cart for part of the journey.'

The stinking dung carts would soon be out on the roads from the villages and townships, taking night soil to the fields. With their great four-and-a-half-inch tyres the familiar vehicles did enormous damage to East Anglia's hideously bad roads. Their groaning approach could be heard a mile away, for like most country carts they were still made with whole axle-trees of wood. The complete iron axle-trees forged in modern industrial towns like Wolverhampton and smoky Lambeth were far too expensive, though Mehala had pointed out several inland farm carts wearing new iron axle-ends, bought ready-made as so-called 'boxes', fitted by iron bolts to the wooden axle trees.

She had him laughingly arguing the best direction before they had gone a furlong beyond the scent of the farmhouse's wood-smoke. His encounter with the grand gentry the night before was in his mind, she knew. When it returned to trouble him she would be ready to dispel his worries over the future. That was her role, her purpose. So far she had done her duty well among the coastal folk of Sealandings.

'You will never regret your return, Euterpe,' Reverend Baring announced as they boarded the coach. 'But I must warn you, there have been many changes in Sealandings since you made your ill-advised retreat. Be prepared!'

The carriage's interior smelled musty. She had said little since they had disembarked at Saint Edmundsbury to change from the Royal Mail to the cross-Suffolk coach. Festivities attending from some dreadful punishment being meted out had caused delay. Euterpe could not bring herself to think of the event, much less join the boisterous crowds. She had remained in her inn room, reading, wondering why she had finally succumbed to her brother's relentless importuning to return as housekeeper to his rectory at Sealandings. Josiah, of course, held strong opinions on punishment, and tried to persuade her to enjoy the spectacle of duty necessarily done.

Her brother leant from the coach window. He was incensed – when was he not? – arguing vehemently with the coachman about the half-fare passengers accepted in the tavern yard. Josiah, always pompous, always furious, saw decadence and moral shirking in anything that eased life. The two extra outsiders, only children after all, would in any case be made to ride in the conveniency, the huge iron basket attached to the coach between the high rear wheels. Where was the harm in that, as long as they suffered no danger and did no harm?

'Please, Josiah,' she asked, already tired and the next stage of the journey not yet begun. 'These children will have to suffer the weather's inclemency, as well as having to disembark and trudge up every incline to ease the horses.'

Reverend Baring swivelled to glare into the interior of the coach. 'So they ought, sister! Is it not blunt thievery, to defraud the coaching company of half the legitimate fare, that they may ride? God gave children legs, Euterpe! They should use them!'

The two miserable half-fares were ten and eleven years of age, cloaked ready for a return to school and put on by a coachman from the Royal Mail at the same inn.

'Already we inside passengers pay twice the outsider rate, Euterpe! Five pence a mile! It should be only fourpence-halfpenny, but for the horses' provisions being so costly.'

He came back to his seat, grumbling. 'Penny a mile tax duty, so long as only four folk travel! You see my point? Now, with two half-fares, two outsider passengers on top, and we two, the coachers pay *more* duty! Which makes for dearer fares! Improvidence!'

'But think of the benefit to the children, Josiah!'

'You are governed by emotion, Euterpe,' he said sternly, as the coach pulled at last from the inn yard to shouts of 'Beware before! Beware before!' 'You are indisciplined! Think of the twenty-five shillings annual duty on each coachman! Of horsing this four-horse stage coach per double mile, at three pounds each double mile per calendar month!' She listened resignedly as he preached on. 'Of course, *were* a coach to go slow, it would be less. But these fantastic speeds of nine – even *ten* – miles per hour have to be maintained, such is the rush to progress!'

Such is the rush to wordage, Euterpe thought drily. Her brother knew so much, yet so little. A knock sounded on the carriage door. It opened to admit a young gentleman. He doffed his beaver hat, and clambered into the moving coach with an easy economy that had him seated in a single movement.

'Good morning, sir, madam.'

Reverend Baring greeted him sourly, doubtless thinking of the extra passenger's weight. Euterpe inclined her head. To her surprise she recognised the gentleman, but gave no sign.

'Do I have the honour of greeting the Rector of Sealandings?' the newcomer asked. 'And Miss Baring? Forgive my forwardness, but may I present myself? Mr Carmady.'

Reverend Baring unbent a little. 'Late of His Majesty's naval service, the lieutenant?'

'The same. Plain esquire now, since I left the King's employ.' Percy Carmady saw the lady's tiredness. 'I hope our journey to the east coast does not prove too wearisome, Miss Baring. Suffolk's roads are less negotiable than the rivers!'

Euterpe rewarded his rough attempt at levity with a smile.

'Indeed,' her brother said pompously. 'I was informing my sister of the deplorable condition of Suffolk's roads. Ten thousand miles of roads, governed by incompetent turnpikers!'

'Forgive me, Reverend,' Carmady said. 'Barely eleven per cent of Suffolk's roads are turnpiked or paved, as in towns. Some two thousand nine hundred miles are not paved or turnpiked.'

'Hmmmh,' Baring said, drawing breath to put the upstart right, but the insolent young man was clearly trying to ingratiate himself. Outside, the coach was having difficulty manoeuvring through crowds struggling out of town, the press pushing folk off pavements everywhere.

'I avoided the hanging,' Carmady said conversationally, 'and the wassailing. I slept the sounder for it.'

'Duty must be seen to be done, sir,' Reverend Baring said sternly. 'Hanging is a moral duty.'

Percy Carmady acquiesced without interest. He tried to avoid staring too obviously at the lady before him, but her face drew his gaze. He saw a quiet-looking, dark-haired woman in her early twenties, slight of form, with pale oval features. Her manner showed an intelligent awareness of his attitude. He knew instantly that she understood his exasperation with her brother, and that she was wryly amused. Yet her expression revealed nothing. He guessed that she had felt the same emotion times without number, and looked away as her gaze met his in sardonic appraisal.

'I am to Lorne House, Reverend,' Carmady mentioned amiably. 'Squire Hunterfield expects me two days from now, but I could not wait among the Edmundsburians in case of delays on the road.' He smiled to show no ill intent after their brief difference. 'I was pleased to see how well the militia controlled the mobs.'

'Insufficient force was used, sir,' Reverend Baring countered. 'As a naval gentleman, you surely understand the implications of excessive leniency?'

'In some circumstances, Reverend,' Carmady began carefully, but was interrupted.

'In my frank view, Mr Carmady, the magistracy inclines to a gentleness that even the present Government condones! I deplore it, sir! Why, in Sealandings —' The cleric paused as Euterpe stirred, uncomfortably aware that he risked a dangerous transgression.

46

He improvised quickly, 'Even in Sealandings, we are blessed with a magnanimous chief Justice, Sir Henry Hunterfield, your friend. Other Hundreds are not so fortunate.'

'I note your kind remark, Reverend,' Carmady said evenly. 'The Lord of Sealandings would be gratified by your support.'

'Speak as one finds.' Reverend Baring was pleased at the younger man's reply.

Carmady's irony was not lost on Euterpe. Carmady was a personable gentleman, seeming even-tempered and with a ready smile. She knew of his popularity at Lorne House with the Hunterfield ladies, and that he was a particular friend of Hunterfield himself. It was rumoured Hunterfield favoured Carmady's purchase of an estate in Sealandings with a view to settling there. His sister Mercy was notoriously difficult to please, though Euterpe guessed that the presence of Henry Hunterfield would lessen any impediment. She wanted to know more, and assayed a gentle politeness.

'May I inquire after Mr Carmady's sister? She is well?'

'Very well indeed, thank you, Miss Euterpe.' He laughed. 'Notice how I try to avoid mentioning my sister's name when answering? Mercy Carmady and Percy? We were named after various ancestors of my mother's. As children we so hated our Christian givens that we pretended different ones, to no avail!'

'Mercy is a proud appellation, sir,' Josiah Baring intoned sombrely. 'I shall sermonise on the link between names and the prime virtues. I trust Miss Carmady will attend, if she visits Sealandings?'

'I promise to inform her of the opportunity, Rector,' Percy Carmady said, seriousness hiding his amusement. He tried to change the subject. 'When last I had the pleasure of staying on the coast, Miss Euterpe was earning high commendation for her support of the children's school. Your charity thrives, I trust?'

Josiah Baring cleared his throat. 'My sister gave needless assistance. Is anything worse than throwing good money to waste?' He indicated the thinning crowd as the coach bullied past the town boundary. 'These people should be at their labours, and their children busy in gainful employment. Why teach them to be above their station?'

'Charity, sir?'

Reverend Baring gave a bleak smile and adjusted his posture.

Euterpe's heart sank. She recognised the signs of an improvised sermon. There would be no stopping her brother now, with an audience trapped for hours to hear his entrenched beliefs.

'How much charity is true Christian charity, Mr Carmady?' he began. 'Look from the coach window – what do you see?'

Percy Carmady obligingly looked out. 'Hedgerows, distant farms, a hamlet, clusters of people withdrawing to the verges to make way for our coach. Have I missed something?'

'Yes, sir!' Euterpe heard Josiah begin. Why *was* he so galling? She could hardly remember him wearing a sincere smile. If only he would marry, she could leave him, her conscience clear. Surely there was some decent Sealandings woman willing to restore his common sense? 'Yes, sir, you have indeed missed something! A clear division of the people into two groups! One group is law-abiding, labouring in their proper station at farm and forge! The other group are the improvident and irresponsible! The first group are the ones who stayed loyally labouring for their masters!'

Euterpe thought cryptically, all work is easy at a distance.

'And the others, Rector?' Carmady asked.

'Are those who throw aside their tools, tempted to a sinful vagabondage by any passing whim!' Euterpe saw the usual red blotches mark her brother's cheeks as the vehemence of his convictions took hold. 'Too many shirk their duty! It is a modern disease, sir! Furthermore . . .'

Carmady caught Euterpe's eye. His attempt to draw her out of her reticence was disastrous. Now there seemed no chance of any conversation with the lady. There was apology and regret in his glance. She felt herself colour slightly, and let her gaze move slowly towards the window.

As the four horses gathered impetus and the coach crashed and jingled forward, Carmady listened dully to a monologue from Reverend Baring, when he would have preferred to learn more about Euterpe Baring.

They had been travelling less than an hour when he saw Mehala.

'Just think, Mehala,' Ven Carmichael was saying, 'of the diseases women suffer in childbirth.'

'Careful, Ven!'

She drew him to a prominence on the bank by the road where a

48

stile started a footpath across fields, and they perched on the wooden crosspiece. She gave him a leather bottle she had filled at the farmer's well before leaving the Woolpit farm.

She watched with real pleasure as he undid the thong, extracted the wooden plug and tilted his head to drink. 'We risk constant trouble at Sealandings because people claim you blaspheme against religion, when treating the sick.'

'Who is to hear us, Mehala?' He gestured at the countryside. 'You promised me a cadge on a dung cart, and so far not a yard!'

There was only a distant cowman moving a herd of cows.

Mehala bridled at his reminder, and accepted the leather flask. 'The dung man hadn't washed his cart wheels, sirrah, so begging a ride would have filthed us. Mud is cleaner, so we walk!'

'And I thought you countryfolk so wise, Mehala!'

She drank, replaced the stopper and tutted to find it off its string. 'Not all, Ven. Yonder cowman wouldn't earn bread on any farm of mine!'

Ven pushed himself to sit up and peer. 'Why not?'

'He drives his herd too fast to their shippon milking. That always means less milk in Suffolks – you can tell them from their squarish udder, hollow chine, snakey head and ridged backbone. They come from the Galloway breed, and can't be bullied.' She eyed the herd with annoyance. 'And I'd sack his cowmaster. See, there are even some small-horned cows among them, the wretched man!'

'So?' He was mystified.

'Polled cows, that have no horns, are the most valuable milkers. But Galloway stock cast up throwbacks with small horns. A cowmaster who breeds wrong beasts deserves the workhouse.'

Ven shook his head. It was all beyond him. There were so many tantalising yet elusive medical clues in the countryside's ancient lore, yet none seemed logical.

'Do cows suffer from a kind of childbed fever, Mehala? Or is the human disease reserved solely for mankind?'

'Yes. Mares hardly at all, but cows and ewes quite often.'

He stared at her as she stood and held out her hand for his instrument case. She never failed to astonish. He gave it and rose. 'Is that true? But you hardly hear of it in Sealandings –'

'Silly innocent!' She actually laughed. 'You think farmers would broadcast such a disease? They hide it, Ven!'

He did not laugh with her. 'They bleed a cow thoroughly, I've heard. Is that true?'

'Much they know,' she scathed. 'They're all as ignorant as . . .' She coloured, adjusted her cottage bonnet and stepped round a pothole.

'As ignorant as we doctors, Mehala?'

She rounded on him almost angrily. 'Yes, if you will, Ven! As ignorant as all who insist on bleeding a poor beast nigh to death when it already struggles for life!'

He sighed. There were times when his ignorance weighed so heavily upon him that he wanted to hide, and emerge after hibernation as a simple rustic with no responsibility to anyone.

'Do you know, Ven,' she coursed on in anger, 'there are cowmen who actually drive a poor cow about *at a fast run* when her time approaches? Can you believe such cruelty? Thinking in their ignorance that will prevent the dropping fever?'

'I've seen that, once.'

'A cow instinctively seeks a quiet hedgerow where she may drop her calf in peace, far from the herd and untroubled by us cruel creatures! *That* is her best chance of survival!'

'Indeed.' He was too unhappy to argue further. How long they would have walked together in silence he never knew, for there was a growing rattle on the road behind. 'Coach, Mehala!'

'I hear, Ven.' She came beside him, backing beneath the safety of the roadside hedge's overhang to let the coach pass. 'It will be the Edmundsbury cross flier to Stowmarket.'

The coach approached, its noise increasing as it breasted a rise and the lathered horses pounded closer. A grand spectacle, Ven thought, cheered by the excitement of such speed. The tremendous majesty of the large coach horses, the irresistible impetus of the vehicle as it slithered down the narrow road was so modern and wondrous to him that he could not imagine anything that could surpass such grandeur.

He smiled with pleasure as the coach hurtled up and for a moment passed close. He looked up, saw the face of Euterpe Baring at the window, saw her brother Reverend Baring in the interior shadow with the indistinct figure of another gentleman. Then it was gone, with two children, heavily cloaked, clinging miserably inside the huge iron conveniency fastened to the rear, jolting and swaying every yard.

They stood watching the coach recede. It was only after they resumed walking that Mehala spoke.

'Miss Baring and Reverend,' she said quietly. 'Lieutenant Carmady.'

Ven said nothing, just answered with a curt nod.

'So she returns to Sealandings.' She slipped her arm through his. 'We have seen more coastal gentry inland in two days than we do in a three-month in Sealandings, Ven.'

'It is as if they haunt us, Mehala.'

'No, Ven, dearest.' She pulled him close and put her mouth to his quickly, moving breathlessly apart. 'No. Always remember that haunting is something we permit! If we deny a spirit the strength to haunt, it can do nothing. And I refuse every spirit that power! *Always* remember that you are safe with me.'

He gave a shrug of exasperation. 'I should protect you, Mehala. Instead, you defend me. If only I wasn't so hopeless.'

'One day, Ven, I shall shelter you with one of those Hanway implements that I've heard of, an ingenious portable penthouse to keep you dry even as you walk!'

'An umbrella!' His humour lightened. 'I saw one in London, though the poor merchant was abused by sedan chairmen and hire-coach drivers. Street children threw dung at him and mocked him for a Frenchman, even as Jonas Hanway was when he introduced it to London before Tyrant Napoleon's wars . . .'

'A coach, a sedan chair, servants, and the protection of a silk umbrella, Ven!' She laughed, though serious still. She sang him songs as the rain started and the road ran wet.

6

ENDERCOTTE ROSE TO address the meeting.
He was conscious of the effect he created. Sombre of mien,
bearded, clothed entirely in black except for his white wide
Geneva collar of the Puritans, he affected a threatening stance
in his old-fashioned knee-buttoned breeches. His attitude
announced that he alone spoke with God and everyone should
beware. With his hooked nose and thin figure, he invoked fear.

'It's the Wandsworthian,' somebody whispered, to Endercotte's
gratification.

He cleared his throat and let the buzz die. Fewer than sixty
people were crammed into the school's meeting hall, mostly
fisherfolk from the harbour cottages, with a scattering of awed
children, and some farm people. The sexes were equally
represented, Endercotte observed. Women were necessary for the
spirit to be moved; they responded with greater swings of mood
than their taciturn menfolk. And it was a woman who had
summoned him to Sealandings, to extirpate evil. Her insistence on
the secrecy of her payments to him was entirely praiseworthy, for
not all of Heaven's supporters needed be visible to the people.

Two silent figures were less than seriously in awe of him,
however. He knew them only slightly. The two gentlemen sat well
apart, signifying their doctrinal differences. The one to be
reckoned with was the rich Quaker, Bettany, who owned the only
windmill in Sealandings. Strict and unyielding, he lived by the
Good Book and his miller's accounts. Endercotte's gaze shifted
scornfully to Robert Parker, a milder man who owned the public
stables on the Norwich road. Leader of the Methodists, he had a
thinner disciplinarian streak than a true believer needed. In short,
a weakling. The Wesleyans were diminished by such an elder.
Weakness was disgusting.

He began the meeting.

'Brothers and sisters in the Lord, I welcome you in the name of the Almighty. First, we pray – each according to conscience,' he added quickly, as Bettany the miller stirred in offence. 'Many here are of the Society of Friends, who do not indulge in what they call *vain repetition*. In silence, then, let us pray . . .'

Heads bowed. Endercotte waited, eyes alert to judge the moment, then into the silence his voice thundered out.

'God hates, brothers!'

'Amen!' his wife croaked as the meeting came to with startled gasps. She also was adorned in plain black, and remained standing to await her cues.

'God *hates* the sins we perpetrate!'

'Amen, amen!'

Endercotte held the moment, then resumed in a whisper, 'Yet we speak of God's inestimable love. Do we not?'

'Yes!' Heads nodded. Emanuel Bettany made no move. He remained silent.

'Very well!' Endercotte's voice was cleverly modulated, rising and falling as he warmed to his pitch. 'Let us make amends, brothers and sisters! Let us think *why* we must fear God's hatred.' He paced across the front of the crowd, staring threateningly down. 'Is it something we have done in Sealandings? Or is it – perhaps worse! – what we merely condone?'

His sudden stillness gripped them. He waited until they began to stir uncomfortably, then thundered, 'Speak!'

The front rows cowered back before his glare. He drew himself up and intoned, hand outstretched, 'Sealandings has committed a terrible sin of omission! We failed to speak out against ungodliness!'

'In what regard, Mister Endercotte?' Bettany demanded, his voice calm. He knew these enthusiasts and their techniques. He tried to maintain a detached air, as if merely approaching somebody in the flint-cobbled lanes by the main square.

'Is there, or is there not, Master Bettany, a couple here in Sealandings living in sin? Yes or no?'

Bettany made no reply, but murmurs arose.

Endercotte gave a wintry smile. 'I ask again, yes or no? Shall I answer for you? Yes! *Yes!* Those sinners are Doctor Carmichael and his evil woman Mehala! Are they married? Yes or no?'

'No,' somebody muttered. The answer was taken up, by women's voices answering, 'No! No!'

'Shall I continue, then?' Endercotte demanded, now almost purring. Elderly folk cupped their ears to hear. 'Has Sealandings done anything – *anything!* – to stop the cheap quackery that he practises on the orphanage children and workhouse idlers?' He stood akimbo, glaring round. 'Answer me! Yes or no?'

'No, no.'

'Why not?'

No answers came now, though many were exchanging glances and speaking in undertones. Endercotte saw several heads nodding. The women were on his side. He felt a familiar excitement.

'Then let me answer for the true godly people of this fair town! The answer . . .' He clasped his hands together in fervent prayer, and forced himself on. 'The answer is *no!* And why? Because, friends, we shirked our godly duty! Cut off the hand that betrays us! What does the Good Book say, brothers and sisters?' He held his book aloft for all to see. 'It reveals our holy task! We must drive these sinners from our midst, and save the very soul of Sealandings!'

'Amen!' his wife croaked from the back of the hall.

'Amen! Amen!'

Endercotte raised his face and babbled a torrent of meaningless sounds. People prayed in alarm. A trio of older women began exclaiming of the Holy Spirit.

Bettany listened in dismay to the growing clamour. The tactics of the wretched rabble rouser were all too plain to a man such as himself, familiar with the frenzies of the modern enthusiasts who drove folk to believe they were touched by God and given the gift of Tongues. The deception, for such he believed it was, implied that the furious speaker was in direct communion with the Almighty, with the right – he drew a sharp breath – to be obeyed.

He glanced along the row at Robert Parker, the Methodist elder. The man was sitting as if mesmerised, mouth open and eyes on Preacher Endercotte. Bettany found himself on his feet, turning to face the mass of the audience.

'Good people of Sealandings,' he called, sweating at his plight. 'Let us, in our various ways, ask guidance of the Lord.'

Remaining standing, he bowed his head, seeing under his

lowered brows hands clasp and hearing several fisherfolk begin to mumble the Lord's Prayer. A slow relief spread through him. The babble gradually calmed as more joined in. At the end, he spoke quickly before Endercotte could resume his tirade.

'Now, fellow Sealanders,' he said pointedly excluding the vehement visitor, 'let us leave this meeting with our thoughts on the trust we have in God and each other! Amen!'

'Amen!' several echoed mechanically, and Bettany smiled as if dismissing one of his own religious meetings, deliberately shuffling his feet and moving his Suffolk rush chair.

'Now, Endercotte!' Bettany reached across and gripped his arm. 'We shall walk together to wherever you might be lodging, and exchange ideas about the ancient Euchites. Have they relevance for these modern times?'

Endercotte's eyes stared redly at the Quaker. Bettany realised he had made an enemy, but almost forcibly propelled the man along with him, calling out to Parker to join them in discussion. The Puritan freed his arm. He could hardly speak from rage as the people began to leave, the tension relaxed.

'Bettany, my mission is divine. I shall not be deterred.'

Bettany kept his smile with difficulty. 'Who deters the Lord's work? Not I, for sure! Nor these godly people.'

They moved slowly out into the evening cool. The rain had stopped. Beyond the main square where the weekly markets were held, the lights of the harbour were visible. The roof of the Corn Mart glistened from wetness in a gibbous moon that sat among scudding clouds. A few lanterns showed among the cottages. Nearby the dark mass of the Church of St Edmund stood among the ancient yews that shushed in the night breeze.

Endercotte faced Bettany. 'Those who condone sin, Bettany, serve Satan! I shall stay hereabouts. Those who are not for me are against me. I do Heaven's work. Remember that.'

'May Heaven triumph over all its enemies.'

'How say you, Parker?' Endercotte demanded harshly.

'I . . . I . . . It will be necessary for me to speak with the other elders of my persuasion, Preacher Endercotte.' Robert Parker unhappily wanted the approval of everybody. His public stables were vulnerable to any tide of opinion, for his livelihood depended upon the patronising gentry of the east coast. He wanted to explain this dilemma but knew there was no victory here, only defeat. He wished he had not come.

'For or against, Parker! Remember that! For or against!'

Endercotte strode furiously away. His wife flitted quickly after him like a slender bat.

'Disaster was narrowly averted, Bettany,' Parker said, wiping the inside of his beaver hat with a neckerchief. 'You did it most ably.'

Bettany had no time for the stable owner, whom he regarded as an utter ingrate. 'I wished I had not been the only one moved to lessen the meeting's fervour, Parker. I lacked support.'

'How could I know how to help?' Parker asked plaintively, mentally comparing Bettany's virtual monopoly with his own uncertain status. A windmill master was invariably the richest merchant, since almost every farmer used Emanuel Bettany's grinding stones to obtain sellable flour from his wheat. Only the sea mill at Watermillock offered any competition. 'I was not even sure of the main issue.'

'The issue is, Parker,' Bettany said as they walked the slope towards the Norwich road, 'that Preacher Endercotte has decided to use Reverend Baring's absence as opportunity to rouse the passions of the people.'

'You have no fondness for Carmichael, yet you defended him. And', the stableman added innocently, 'Mehala.'

'I condemn their unsanctified relationship.' Bettany stopped, to emphasise his point. 'And the girl – woman – Mehala has proved a disturbing influence ever since she was saved from the North Sea. But she and her doctor consort *would* attend St Edmund's services, were he not banned by Reverend Baring. And they live at Shalamar under the protection of Lord Hunterfield, having saved the entire Sealandings Hundred from the cattle plague.'

They resumed walking. Parker wanted the miller's approval. 'I see that, Bettany. I was simply concerned lest there was any truth in Endercotte's view.'

'Some, Parker,' Bettany said grimly. 'There is always *some*. But that is for the Almighty to judge, not us.'

'What do you think he will do?' Parker asked nervously. 'He has done wonders in God's name. Miracles, even!'

'*Do*, Parker?' Bettany said. 'That does not concern me, so much as where he will do it. I pray he leaves Sealandings on the first available coach down the South Toll road.'

'Amen,' Parker said miserably. A plain honest owner of public stables could only lose, when troubles of this magnitude threatened. And this tiresomely rich Quaker striding beside him was right; all troubles seemed to stem somehow from Mehala. He sometimes wished *The Jaunty* had never rescued the girl – no, no, he didn't mean that. But perhaps she would recover her memory, and be claimed by some family far away from these coast lands. Then the Eastern Hundreds could return to peace.

They walked in silence, each with his own thoughts, passing the gate lantern of the notorious Two Cotts brothel in frigid disapproval. Soon after, the driveway of Bettany's Mill split the dark line of the hedgerows. The miller turned off with a pious 'Goodnight and God save,' leaving the stabler to plod on alone. Enviously he heard young Richard Bettany the miller's son call out with the boisterousness of his fifteen years, and heard too the grave reproof Bettany made at the boy's levity.

Parker sighed. Maybe his feckless brother Thomas was right, that there was too much gloom in God. Did it all come down to God versus Mehala, in some strange way? He suppressed the blasphemous thought, and prayed guiltily as he made it home.

7

CARRADINE KICKED THE whore and reached for the Portugal. Barely the lees remained; the liquid was undrinkable.

'What's this?' he demanded, thumping her.

The girl gasped at the blow. 'I s'll bring another, sir.'

He swore as the girl scurried from the room, and leaned back on the selour. He felt disgusted. The entire expedition to Edmundsbury was a waste of time. For a start, he had lost his heavy wager on the hanged man's death. Surely to God the murderer William Corder's own weight would strangulate in two minutes, even if the hangman failed to get a clean jerk-and-break. He had sent a man to bribe the executioner's doctor, and failed even in that.

Then Mehala had been there, and the hangman's quack none other than that odious, incompetent Sealandings leech. Carradine had instantly known the affair would be a disaster. Every time his path crossed Mehala's he suffered. She was a witch, working satanic forces against him. And that fool doctor, treasonably liberal, did more harm than he mended.

Carradine looked about the grim little bedroom. Thirty-three whole shillings the night, for Christ's sweet sake, and disappointment! The first girl they'd sent was frightened and incompetent, the second insolent and sluttish. This last one satisfied him, but by then he'd been past caring, so angry was he at Carmichael's declaration of the murderer's death breath that had lost him four hundred guineas. Jesus, but life was hard, lately well-nigh impossible.

The bed's selour wobbled when he leaned back. He looked up at the cracked ceiling – of course, no tester, decorated or otherwise, so no seeing-glass suspended there, for a working whore's reflection to entertain a gentleman at natural pleasure. Edmundsbury was supposed to be a major centre in East Anglia's interior

Hundreds! Not a patch on Newmarket, now so rapidly growing with its horse races rivalling the Duke of Richmond's park races at Goodwood, famous since the turn of the century. But at least the Jockey Club's accumulated rules of racing, amassed this Year of Grace into one code, still left room for bending by a cunning gambler, thank God.

The girl returned with the new bottle of wine, trying to hold her night shift at her throat. She poured, but in her anxiety spilled some over the clap table. Carradine swore, sickened by the attempts to make the room, indeed the whole brothel, gentrified instead of allowing what it really was, a spilling shed.

'Bring me breakfast in a while.' He gestured her back into bed. 'And make sure it's better than last night's fare. A man can not live on crumbs.'

'Please, sir, I told downstairs you were displeased by the Cromwell's Favourite, saying the veal shoulder was less seasoned –'

'Less meal!' Carradine grumbled, holding his glass out to be refilled. 'Fewer than ten courses insults a gentleman's money!'

He inspected her. He had made her shed her night mob cap, a stupid women's invention. Ridiculous to sacrifice attractiveness for warmth, but they were brainless. Latterly he had used a titled merchant's wife who had had the insolence to welcome him abed wearing the ridiculous biggin, that enormous loose mob cap without latchings. She had earned her punishment.

'What gentlemen have you served here this week, girl?'

'Please sir, we are instructed not to tell that.'

He clouted her, cursing her truculence when the refilled glass spilled out over his hand, making her squeal. 'Tell.'

'Nobody of title, but Sir Treggan used Jenny, as usual.'

Rodney Treggan of Saxelby Hall, the girl meant.

'As usual?'

'He comes every third eve, sir.' Relieved at his interest, she decided to be wiser than obedient and prattled all she knew. 'From Saxelby Hall on the Thetford turnpike that leads nor'ard. A fine gentleman, very good to Jenny. He come early, sir, because of visitors to enjoy the hanging. He willn't use her these next few evenings. Jenny's mortal out of countenance. The whoremistress is famous kind, sir. Jenny gets to keep eighteen pence of his gold half-guinea!'

So a crowd was gathered at the Treggans. He felt a surge of anger, but kept it in rein. He did not want this little bitch telling every detail she learned about Carradine of Carradine Manor, Sealandings, to any Tom, Dick or Harry. But it was a prime insult for an upstart new-penny swine like Rodney Treggan to exclude Carradine yet invite every social climber in East Anglia. Carradine had duelled men to death for less. East Anglia was vast, but a whisper of disgrace passed swifter about the estuaries and fens than a heron in flight. Yet these same people were those who had once grovelled to catch his eye. And their daughters would jump at the chance to exchange more than glances with him, given half a chance.

Perhaps he should ride back to Sealandings by way of Saxelby? And remind Treggan of his discourtesy. A little social chastising of the man would do no harm.

'That is kind,' he concurred. Many a nuggin-shop's whore-mistress kept her nightgowners on starvation victuals, and allowed no pay. It was generosity gone mad, the sort of lunatic largesse that would be the ruination of England.

He looked at the watch stand where his fob timepiece hung. Three hours was ample. He put down his glass and pulled her over him, sliding down the bed. 'Get to work, girl. I s'll breakfast in an hour, and you must bath me before then.'

She quickly knelt up and astride him, smiling as his eyelids flickered and her power took possession of him. It amazed her, this extraordinary authority her slut's form had over such highborns. She started to croon and rock, grunting as his fingers dug into her thighs and the force moved them both as one.

Carradine rode unannounced into Saxelby just as the Astell coach was preparing to leave. The coachman had mounted his Salisbury and positioned his feet on the decorated foot rest when Treggan called him to stay. Rodney only recognised Carradine when the man was reining up, but greeted him warmly, hiding his hope that this was only a passing call.

Brillianta Astell, already seated in the coach and her goodbyes said, felt a wash of relief as Carradine hauled his mount unceremoniously to a halt. She knew him well as a transitory neighbour, after a series of gambling-incurred debts had caused him to leave Sealandings for Maidborough, where her father was principal magistrate. She was newly dismayed by the presence of Ralph Chauncey. The lanky nuisance insisted on travelling back to Maidborough with her, even though this was her father's own emblazoned coach, and Ryde, her own groom since she was six years old, was her coachman with fat Billie Toddy the first postillion. Burdened with Ralph Chauncey, the gloomiest man on earth, all on the orders of Aunt Artemisia. Please God that old dragon doesn't settle at Arminell, Brillianta prayed, for I have had enough interfering old battleaxes with Lady Faith Hunterfield's meddling. In fact enough of women, what with the odious Harriet Treggan affecting a headache (well she might!) after yesterday, and that repellent Sylvia Newborough and her ugly dresses successfully slighted at break-of-fast.

'Afraid I cannot stop, Treggan,' Carradine said before the man could begin digging for motives. 'I was nearby for the hanging jaunt, and will leave my card.'

'Very civil of you, Carradine. Are you sure you would not care for a St Giles's cup before you continue on?'

Everybody smiled except for Chauncey, who frowned at the allusion. A cup of spiritous liquid was traditionally given to the condemned on their way to execution as the tumbril paused at St Giles's Church near the Charing Cross road.

Carradine laughed aloud, controlling his mount. 'I see you are lucky enough to have welcomed the Astell ladies, Treggan!'

Brillianta showed herself at the window, to Ralph's displeasure.

'Only the one, sir,' she answered. 'I regret to say that my dear sister Lorela is unavoidably detained in London City.' Thanks to Heaven's mercy, she added inwardly.

Carradine smiled. Brillianta's aversion towards her sister was as marked as her unvaried title for Lorela, 'dear sister'.

'A disappointment,' Carradine said with ponderous gravity. 'I trust you are well chaperoned for your journey home?'

'Thank you, sir,' Chauncey said, appearing at the window, touching his Wellington but not lifting it from his head. Carradine avoided noticing the slight. 'I escort Miss Brillianta.'

'How pleased I am to see you there, Chauncey!' Carradine exclaimed. 'You will not mind if I ride on?'

'Thank you, Carradine, not in the slightest.'

'I hope, Miss Brillianta, that I shall have the pleasure of meeting you anon. I saw you overlooking the celebrations, but was otherwise engaged.'

'Pity you could not join us, Carradine,' Treggan exclaimed.

'Is Mistress Treggan well?' Carradine's inquiry was perfunctory, no more than a routine politeness, but he caught Treggan's slight frown and Brillianta's ill-concealed smile.

Treggan started to speak, but he was interrupted by Brillianta.

'Poor Harriet had something of a shock, Carradine,' she said with charmed innocence. 'She encountered a young doctor who was summoned. She used to know him quite well.'

'Is that so!' Carradine kicked his horse to cease its fidgeting.

'And his doxy Mehala, from your coast, I believe?'

'Indeed.' He looked sour, which pleased Brillianta further.

'Are you sure you need no sustenance?' Treggan asked, wanting this ferreting talk ended and the lot of them gone.

'Thank you, Treggan, but I must decline.'

'You will be anxious to see your friend Henry Hunterfield, no doubt.' Brillianta was delighted to see Carradine's face cloud over at his enemy's name.

'As eager as ever, Miss Astell,' he said coldly. 'Do please give my compliments to your pretty sister.' Which was tit for tat, since Lorela was the lovelier, and Brillianta the plain. 'Best wishes to Mistress Treggan, Rodney, and Sir Edward!'

They called their goodbyes and watched him ride at a canter down the long drive and out onto the cross-country Stowmarket road. He cut a handsome figure. Brillianta was oddly disturbed by the encounter rather than gratified.

Ryde clicked the four horses to a slow walk. Brillianta fumed at the funereal pace. Ryde was too careful a coachman to whip up the beasts until they were on a clear stretch. Until then it would be a snail's trundle. The one time you want a coach to rattle the teeth in your head with its speed, it travelled like a bavin-tug filled with bavins of timber, slower even than a market woman. Life was a mess, simply a horrid mess.

She sulked, out of countenance, and would not answer Ralph when he started on his most interesting subject, the Established Church's influence on country habits and dress in the previous century. Carradine was on her mind, and the chances of seeing

Henry Hunterfield. There was no doubt in her mind, the Lord of Sealandings was the ideal man for her. Presentable, and with a certain charm in spite of his three utterly offensive sisters — two safely married, though — he was virtual ruler of the Sealandings Hundred and its entire coast. Yet Carradine, that uncontrollable rogue, had streaks of cruelty that belied his lineage, and were weirdly compelling to a woman. Why? She could not answer.

If she had power over both, which would she choose, Carradine or Sir Henry Hunterfield? The bad or the good? Or did she mean the desirable versus the merely acceptable?

It was urgent that she reach home as soon as possible, and give Father a sound reason to send her to Sealandings.

8

VEN INSPECTED THE man. He lay on a cot bed, white as death and sweating profusely. 'I shall need to see his shoulder, Mistress,' he told the cottage wife.

'I can not strip him, for he screams like a child when I touch him.' Womanlike, she turned to Mehala to explain more. 'It is the size of a bladder. Three days agone he fell on the master's machine.'

'What machine?'

'Ar, a mortal frightening monster of iron and wheels. My man Taw is a ploughman labourer, so drives the horses for the reaping. They mislike the engine.'

'Which sort?' Mehala asked, but Ven interrupted.

They had reached the outskirts of Debenham, famous grain country. Begging some sweet water from an isolated cottage, they were allowed to slake their thirst at the handpump. The distressed woman regaled them with the plight of her man, unpaid by reason of an injured arm and worsening hourly. She had asked the head ploughman for help, but received nothing.

Mehala wanted instinctively to withdraw and talk about the wisdom, or unwisdom, of interfering, but unhappily saw the light of interest glow in Ven's eyes.

With some reluctance she told the woman, 'My husband is a doctor, but –'

'A doctor?' The woman's grasp almost pulled him off his feet. 'Would you see him, sir? I beg. What if he dies, sir? I should be put out with the littles . . .'

'I may not be able to help,' Ven said carefully. 'But I –'

'My husband is reluctant,' Mehala put in firmly. 'What arrangements does your master make for his men's ailments?'

'None, Mistress,' the woman said, desperately seizing the

chance. 'There are doctors in Debenham Town, but mortal costly, and they won't see us 'bout our master's approval.'

'We waste time,' Ven said. 'I shall see him.'

'Go and prepare your man,' Mehala told the woman. 'The doctor wants to get his instruments ready.'

'No, Mehala, there is no need –' Ven began, but the woman had already fled. Mehala restrained him. 'What is it?'

'Ven. Take care.' She stood between him and the cottage. 'This is a charitable thing, but you do not know country ways. What if this man dies?'

'I must treat him, Mehala.'

'Treated or left untreated, Ven, word will spread. A mob will come after us.' She was pale. 'We faced them in Sealandings, yes. But we had the protection of Hunterfield and so were spared – by his help and your successes.'

'The man is sick, Mehala.' He put her gently aside.

'Hunterfield's writ does not run this far inland, Ven!'

He smiled sadly. 'My writ has no boundaries, Mehala. Now,' he straightened, 'you will observe what I do. Inspection of the man – age, state, breathing rate, pulse, eyes, tongue, all I have taught you. I shall explain to you my treatment, what I do and the prognosis.'

'Yes, Ven.'

With misgiving, she followed him into the cottage where the woman was eagerly waiting with her children. He asked for the children to be sent out during his examination. Frightened by their father's sickness, they stood outside staring at the cottage.

The labourer was no more than twenty-two. He was hot and dry, in pain from his arm and shoulder, yet he was able to answer.

'You were well before the ploughing accident, Taw?'

Even in such distress the man gave a feeble grin. 'You be no farmer, Doctor. Reaping, not ploughing. The master has a reaping engine. It cost thirty whole pounds!'

Mehala inhaled sharply. Such an enormous sum, for a mere machine to scythe grain.

'What happened? You bumped against it and cut the skin?'

'No, Doctor. I drive the horses, see. Two good Suffolks they be. But they must push the reaper, not give an honest pull. Unnatural. They drove on the kilter. I tried to align them. My shoulder twisted. I was bagged from employ there and then.'

Ven asked the woman to strip her husband to his waist, by cutting the clothes if need be, and drew Mehala aside. His relief as the torso appeared surprised Mehala. Taw's left shoulder was hugely swollen. The arm seemed to project down at an odd angle. Ven asked the woman to turn her man over so he lay prone.

'Prone, Doctor?'

Mehala explained. 'Lay him grublins, face down.'

But it was impossible, the man groaning with pain, so Ven let him remain supine, and asked, 'You could eat, but for the pain?'

'Ar, Doctor. I do drink still. I can move my fingers.'

'The feeling remains, in your hand and arm?'

'Yes.'

He responded well when Ven tested him with cold and hot irons. The skin was hardly discoloured even where it ballooned into a massive swelling at the point of his shoulder. The shoulder's natural round contour had gone, and the shoulder tip projected outwards, making an unnatural hollow beneath. Apart from that recess the shoulder was one tight mass. The ache seemed in the man's neck, causing him to lie with his head aslant.

'There is not enough light,' Ven told the woman. 'I shall ask Taw to come outside into open air, and there I shall see what can be done.'

'Walk, Doctor?' The woman was appalled.

'His legs are sound. It is his shoulder that is awry.'

Ven went to wait in the cottage garden with Mehala while the woman helped Taw outside. He was strong, but ashen with the pain. The children helped Mehala to bring a blanket and lay it over straw they spread on the ground at Ven's direction.

'It seems a shoulder dislocation, Mehala,' Ven said quietly as Taw lay down. The man groaned and once cried out with pain at his change of position. In broad daylight the deformity seemed horrendous. 'It is best dealt with straight away after injury, for delay spoils the ease of reduction to its normal position. It is as if the whole joint tissues settle into one mass of hard yet moist turgidity, we do not know how. If my diagnosis is correct –'

'Can it be wrong, Ven?'

He eyed her resignedly. 'Yes. Blood vessels may be damaged. I may damage them when I reduce the dislocation. That is grave, and internal bleeding serious.'

'Dear God, Ven —'

He stepped away with a curt instruction for her to watch, and went to stand beside the man.

'Listen, Taw. Your shoulder is out of its position. I shall try to restore it. I want you to relax as much as possible in a particular way. Do not pull against me. You understand?'

'Yes. Will I be better after?'

'Please God. First, drink what spirits your wife has, slowly, until you are a little merry.'

'I have none!' The woman wrung her hands. 'My man bought seed, pledging wages against it.' She indicated the neat, wide vegetable garden in front of the cottage. 'Hoping to provide, should we have more children, see.'

'Then laudanum, surely? Or opium?'

'Not even that. We never had need to dose the children while we labour, not like those with larger families in factories.'

Ven looked at Mehala. She took a shilling from her reticule. 'Send the children for whatever spirits this will bring most of,' she said. 'Is there an inn nearby?'

During the children's absence, the cottager provided them with a gofer cake, good but stale round its crimped margins. Mehala gave Ven a look, but merely thanked the woman for the cake and the bread and cheese that followed. They sat apart and drank a little water while Ven went over the anatomy of the shoulder, regretting the little time they had been allowed with the corpse of William Corder.

'You see how essential anatomy is, Mehala? By dissection I could have seen with my own eyes how a joint dislocates! But all I know comes mostly from watching that wretch Eldridge.' Eldridge was the Sealandings butcher, a rich townsman less than honest with the customers, and like as not to sell dead meat, that of beasts found dead of disease in the pasture.

The children returned with their leather flask half filled with spirits. Mehala unstoppered it and tasted it cautiously.

'It is the dregs!' she exclaimed with distaste. 'Half metheglin, with half green noyau.'

'It will do, Mehala.'

Ven went to Taw and persuaded him to let him take his injured arm. Gently, as the man cried out, Ven slowly tried to move it away from the body into a reaching position.

'Stretch it out if you can, Taw, scarecrow position. Do what you like with the good arm. Your wife can sit by.'

Ven told Taw to drink. They waited. Ven wistfully told Mehala of the wondrous effects that doctors of the Ancient World had achieved by their soporific herbal infusions. She sat by him in the herb garden, listening. This was the time she loved best, hearing his hopes for the future, when he too would have a great stock of medicinals, unguents and lotions, and bring off the most startling medical cures.

'A fellow student, Ward, with whom I correspond, had a translation of Galen,' Ven remembered dreamily. 'And the works of Ibn Sinna, the great Arab physician of olden days, whom we call Avicenna. The learning in them, Mehala!' he exclaimed, his eyes shining. 'Drugs compounded from plants that could dull pain! Can you imagine? Potions to calm the most grievous madness! It is miraculous, Mehala!'

She encouraged him by asking what plants from the hot eastern lands might have cousin kin in English hedgerows, but his knowledge of Avicenna's botany was meagre.

'I used to hire the book, for sixpence a day,' Ven remembered blissfully. 'A terrible sum I could hardly ever afford. But when I could, oh, what days they were, Mehala! I would beg used candle stumps – hog fat, any sort of tallow – and cheaper rush lights when I could hire a book and be sore grieved if I could not stay awake the full twenty-four hours!'

One day, Mehala promised silently, you shall have any book you desire, however expensive, and a sedan chair for town journeys, with a pony-and-whisky for calls further afield. And she would be by his side, the first woman doctor in the kingdom.

And there would come a time too when they would marry, in church, before an altar, instead of this marriage she herself had conducted. She turned the iron ring on her finger, remembering the day she and Ven had been banished by Reverend Baring. She had declared herself Ven's wife outwith religion or laws. It was still done often enough, men taking women irrespective of clergy. But one day, only months from now, she would be free to marry him legally, and nothing would stand in her way.

Ven was in the middle of a discourse about the possibilities of inducing tranquillity in insanity cases by means of plant infusions, when she nudged him and pointed. Taw was snoring gently, his wife sitting beside him on the blanket looking their way.

Ven rose quietly. The children were playing 'Farmer, Farmer', so could be forgotten for the moment.

'Get a ribbon from the cottage,' he said. 'I want you to tie it round Taw's arm above the elbow, and pull when I say.'

That was arranged without disturbing Taw. He had drunk a third of the spirits, and came drowsily awake as they tied the ribbon and arranged themselves about him.

'Taw, your hand.' Ven sat on the blanket and took off his left half-jack boot. It was Taw's left shoulder that was dislocated.

'Done, Doctor.' Mehala showed Ven the knotted ribbon on Taw's upper arm. He gestured for her to sit beside him and to take up the ribbon ends.

'Taw, I s'll want your wife to hold your good hand away.'

Taw nodded, less drowsy than before but befuddled, as his wife, seeing the point, grasped his right hand and knelt close.

Ven extended Taw's left arm slowly until it was straight. The man shifted uneasily, his eyes moving in enquiry.

'Now, Taw, you will feel some pain for a little time. Try not to resist.' Ven said quietly to Mehala, 'When I say, pull gently but steadily towards you. Our purpose is to let the muscles be overcome with a gradual stretching. I shall do the rest.'

He slowly shoved his unshod heel into the armpit, nodded to Mehala and started to lean away, pulling on Taw's arm. The man whimpered as Ven dug his heel deep into the armpit.

They pulled steadily, Ven once jerking his head for Mehala to increase the traction on her ribbons and, using his own weight, drawing Taw's arm down and away from the shoulder as if trying to stretch the arm to a greater length.

In an astonishingly short time he felt the opposing tension gradually relax as the muscle spasm was bested. Taw screeched in agony as the tissues shifted. His body bucked. He tried to reach with his good hand, but his wife held on.

Ven now drove his heel in with all his strength, feeling it come hard against the shoulder blade. 'Keep up the pull!' he gasped, straining. 'Keep it steady.'

The crack when it came was like a gunshot. The shoulder gave. 'Stop pulling!' Ven called, letting the injured arm give and the dislocation reduce into position.

Taw's groaning was interrupted as he vomited to one side, leaning on his good elbow and heaving. Ven kept hold of the wrist, checked the shoulder to see the sinister recession and angularity quite gone. He bent the arm across the man's chest and told the wife to bring a towel. With it, as Taw sank back gasping and blinking away sweat, Ven bound the arm across Taw's body.

'Done!' He knelt up smiling at Taw and the woman. 'Let it be thus for two days, without work.'

'It is healed, Doctor?' the woman asked.

'As good as new! It will not take heavy labour, but will be in use after a week. Now, Taw, go and do the same to the other shoulder!'

The man smiled at the feeble quip. 'Doctor, I can not pay.'

'No matter,' Ven said, while Mehala looked. 'We have had an excellent repast, Taw, so are well repaid.'

They said their goodbyes, but the children walked them to the wooded crest where the path rejoined the road.

It was as Mehala and Ven waved a last farewell to the cottage below that she noticed, only fifty yards away, a lady in a ponied whisky watching their departure. Beside her was a tall mounted gentleman sitting his gelding with casual ease. Both seemed to have been there some time, and observed the scene unabashed by discovery.

Ven would have spoken, but Mehala felt it was not their place to greet gentry.

'A good part of the day is left,' she said quietly. 'Let us use it to best advantage. It is too much to hope that we make south of Beccles by nightfall, but a good foot under and tomorrow we'll be home at Shalamar, please the Almighty.'

He was amused. 'Very well, Mehala. Though bidding somebody a good day, however highborn or low, costs nothing!'

'Usually, Ven,' she said tartly, 'but only usually.'

She wanted to look back at the elegant pair, feeling she had seen one of them before, but that would have shown weakness or doubt, and she was unwilling to. It had not been in Sealandings, she was sure.

In a hundred yards they were out of sight, and she relaxed as they began to cover the ground towards the coast.

'*She*, George!' Sylvia Newborough said. 'That lady Mehala!'

The mounted man nodded. 'And I recognise Carmichael.'

'You do?' The lady was astonished, then thought. 'But of course, George! I forgot! You yourself were a famous surgeon!'

'Hardly, Sylvia,' George Godrell said. 'Never soiled my hands. I left all that to serfs like yon Carmichael. He was always grubbing about wards for coppers. Hardly a penny to his name.'

'He seemed most proficient, George.'

Down in the cottage garden, the sick man was already experimenting with his mended shoulder, flexing his hand and smiling with relief.

Godrell snorted. 'Any leech needs only seconds! Carmichael was born to serve. Once a peasant, always so!'

Sylvia Newborough was more than a little interested. She had only agreed to drive this way home because George Godrell, the escort she was having to endure today, suddenly urged her. It was when passing an inn that they heard folk laughing at some travelling leech actually paying his own money to buy spiritous liquors for an ailing man. Godrell wanted to see the cause of such hilarity. Sylvia was especially intrigued, for the change in George was instantaneous. She heard him question the two children. Then, there was no dissuading him from changing her planned route to spy on the doctor and his doxy.

'Are we done, George?' she asked, provoking. There seemed more to the young couple than met the eye. 'Or must we stay here all day looking at your labourer's cottage?'

George Godrell was deep in thought, but came to at her needling. 'My apologies, Sylvia. On our way, you must tell of your encounter with that pair at Saxelby.'

The lady casually shook the reins of her whisky. 'If you wish. But why so interested?'

'Scarcely interested, Sylvia.' He rode at a slow walk.

'I should hope not! After all, a country quack can hardly trouble Suffolk's most extensive landowner!'

'I came into lands by the sad demise of relatives,' Godrell reminded her. 'It was a sorrowful occasion.'

'Indeed, George.' But transient sorrow. Sylvia thought of the lavish ball thrown to celebrate his fortune.

'One thing.' Godrell came back to the subject. It seemed to fascinate him, which was itself curious. 'You refer to Carmichael's doxy as "that lady". And seemed to infer that she also caught Brillianta Astell's interest in an uncommon way.'

'Lady?' Sylvia thought a moment. 'Because she is so, George. Why she stays so low sunk, I cannot imagine. She has known wealth and position. I wonder what made it so intolerable to her?'

'I wonder,' Godrell said. It was worth a separate ride, to Taw's cottage, later and alone.

Judith ordered Carradine to escort her. He obeyed, subduing his anger. The woman he had, he now hated. The one he was denied, he craved. This shapely dark-haired woman trapped him. The other was unattainable, with hair that appeared lit from within by half-glimpsed russet fires. Judith was his captress, his possessor. Mehala had chosen a penniless quack.

'You never write letters, Judith.'

She smiled. It was her pleasure to perambulate each morning with Carradine; so gentry on the Norfolk road must see them on the terrace, and know she ruled Carradine Manor.

'I have no need.'

No, he thought, reminded of her many relatives among the artisans on the Carradine estates, but I have exactly such a need. 'I must go to London. The estate funds in –'

'No, Rad.' She spoke the command gently. 'I send your messages. I allowed you to go to the Corder hanging. Stay.'

'You make me a prisoner.'

She faced him, full of her power over this handsome rake, with hates as absolute as her own. Almost. 'No, Rad. You made yourself prisoner. Without me you would be an eighty-shilling man, a pedlar touting his ped afoot round East Anglia's hamlets. I saved your estates, your family name. I could sell all on a whim.'

His silence proved her victory. She heard a distant coach, a grand four-horse landau by its sound. She raised her face in a pretty little-girl movement, standing on tiptoe.

'Kiss me, darling.'

Stiffly he obeyed, conscious of the fond scene exhibited to the coach's passengers.

'Now an embrace, I think . . .'

He embraced her without passion, unable to avoid glancing up. He glimpsed the great landau among the roadside trees. It was definitely that of Hunterfield, Lord of Sealandings.

'Now call me darling, Rad.'

He paused, gathered himself. 'Darling,' he said, with hate. His escape must be soon, perfect and complete.

'Again,' she commanded, conscious of servants' eyes on them from the mansion windows. 'Louder.'

9

HUNTERFIELD TOOK HIS place at the table aware that it was going to be a disturbing day, beyond his control. Tabitha seemed particularly keyed up this morning. Already she had criticised the preparation of the breakfast dishes, though her feud with Mrs Kitchiner, cook at Lorne House, was unrelenting and likely to remain so. The chief maid Rebecca greeted him pleasantly, but her face showed high spots of colour indicating that Tabitha had waged war earlier. He caught the glances between two breakfast maids.

'Good morning, Tabitha.'

'Good morning, Henry. I trust you slept well after last night's intrusion?'

'Intrusion? A deranged woman is nothing unusual.'

'You ordered her confined?'

'Indeed. That will be our first duty today, sister.'

Tabitha's face clouded. '*Our*, Henry? Must I come to see every vagrant passing through Sealandings?'

'This one, yes.' Henry spoke with finality. Tabitha knew her morning was doomed.

It was as she feared. Late last evening, a constable had called at Lorne House asking for a ruling on a vagrant woman found rambling, evidently quite mad, at the open Corn Mart building and taken in custody. It was for Henry, senior magistrate of the whole Sealandings Hundred and hereditary Lord of the manorial district as far as neighbouring Whitehanger, to dispose of vagrants.

'See, Henry!' she gushed, to weaken his resolve. 'I have some of Walton's minnow tansies, yellow and succulent, perfect!'

He always started with collared meats, broiled kidneys and several potted meats. Rump chops he had given little attention the past two mornings. She provided some nine or ten such meat dishes on the expansive horseshoe tables of the breakfast room, but she felt he was only perfunctory in his choice. Her six kinds of bread and eleven different toasts were probably enough to tempt his appetite, and the four variants of breakfast cakes always pleased him. Summer was generous in East Anglia, thank heaven, so the fruits, preserves and marmalades made a pretty display to offset the bacons and sliced muttons.

He began on muffins, with poached eggs and broiled mackerels, and kindly accepted six of Isaac Walton's cowslip-flavoured and primrosed minnow tansies. Tabitha's hopes rose.

'How did you manage this wonder, Tabby? A spring dish in the height of summer?'

'The ice house, Henry!' The building of the deep dome-covered structure, with its steep steps to underground, had been last year's major enterprise. It had been built at her elder sister Lydia's instigation, like the expansive orangery, but the less Lydia was remembered the better. She, Tabitha, now wore the chatelaine at Lorne House, and her two sisters both married off, thank God. She smiled. 'My suggestions are now literally bearing fruit! I had Mrs Kitchiner lay down many surprises in the ice house for later in the year! Last winter's hoar frosts were marvellous helpful. I arranged many an ice moon, for gathering sawn ice!' She laughed at her claim.

Henry smiled. 'Very wise to make the weather obey, Tabby!'

'Amn't I just?'

He watched her indulgently. He had always allowed Tabitha more licence. And he could honestly say that, with Lydia now inland with her husband Captain James Vallance back from India, and the quiet Letitia successfully married – beneath her – to that exotic artist William Maderley of nearby Watermillock sea mill, Tabitha behaved prettily as mistress of Lorne. Young, yes, vivacious and captivating. Before long all and sundry would be card-calling. And that would be that.

And then?

Then, he would be alone at Lorne House, Lord of Sealandings without an heir except those provided by his sisters. They would be bountiful, God willing. A period of freedom, without sisters inveigling with every breath, was not altogether unpleasant. He had no illusions about Tabitha. Since the domineering Lydia had gone to meet her husband and Letitia settled at Watermillock, Tabitha had been the semblance rather than substance of lady of the manor. He had to rely on the elderly butler Crane for details of the household, and was seriously thinking of broaching the idea of taking on a lady housekeeper. But Tabitha would see it as a mortal slight.

There were no American breakfast cakes, which the extraordinary New Englanders fed themselves hot under butter. He suppressed his irritation. The fashion to copy the Bostonites had come quickly to East Anglia but was on the wane. So he would have to go without. He let the matter go, and made do with Swaffham potted herring, though even here the parsley was ill chopped, occasional stalks left unminced. This fault testified to kitchen distress. Like the hot Norfolk spoon dumplings that Lydia always insisted should be 'as light as love', after their mother's saying. Here, they lay stodgy as lead under their melted butter and sprinkled sugar. He had difficulty finishing his eighth. Such a loss of appetite would never have happened under Lydia.

'Henry, I have one more surprise! Guess who is coming to my tea morning!' Tabitha exaggerated her enthusiasm, a ploy she used often with great success. 'Brillianta Astell, with her cousin Ralph Chauncey! I am sure you wish news of the entertainment at Edmundsbury when that terrible brute Corder was hanged –'

Hunterfield winced. 'Tabby, my duties lie in the Hundred. Your company', he added pointedly, 'makes sordid tasks pleasant.'

'My company, Henry?' she almost shrieked. 'But Brillianta –'

'Thank you for thinking of me, Tabitha.' His tone was not unkind. 'Kindly concede! I must see the lunatic woman –'

Tabitha wailed, 'But Henry –'

He said firmly: 'Since your tea tastings are at eleven, we must make a reasonable start. Kindly be ready.'

'Yes, Henry,' she said miserably, feeling her temper rise. She signalled one of the breakfast maids to summon Crane.

'The conveyance, thirty minutes,' Henry told her, well aware that something more important was on her mind than a visit from Miss Astell and her grim cousin. Could Tabitha be using Brillianta as a distraction for some scheme she was hatching?

'That is impossible!' Tabitha blurted out, then tried to cover her

76

bluntness with a disarming smile. 'I shall need at least two hours, if you please. I want to see my new pelisse robe, which I designed in pink with a pelisse shoulder mantle –'

'I am sure it will be charming, Tabitha.' He saw old Crane enter. 'We leave Lorne for duty in half an hour. The light pilentum, I think. Have Mosston drive.' He smiled benignly at his sister. 'Miss Hunterfield will accompany me as chaperone while I inspect the captured lunatic woman.'

'Very well, Sir Henry.'

Tabitha begged to be excused and left the table glowering, the two maids shrinking as she passed. Hunterfield sighed and settled down to finish breakfast in peace. There was so little quietude at Lorne House these days. To be away when Brillianta arrived would be a bonus, for he much preferred her older sister Lorela, though did not admit to an affection for either.

He had a few slices of collared meat, four sorts of breakfast breads, and a Lowestoft fish pie – though here again he found a small bone, an unspeakable crime to Lydia. The Norfolk bread dumplings he left in pointed reprimand, but managed the Ipswich almond pudding.

'Are you well, Sir Henry?' old Crane asked.

'Thank you, Crane, yes.' Hunterfield washed his fingers in the rosewater bowl and held out a hand for the linen cloth.

'Will you resume breakfast on your return, sir?'

'No, Crane. I shall try to manage on what I have had. The day's duties preoccupy me now. Miss Hunterfield will leave instructions for her visitors' reception. Oh, Crane,' Hunterfield hesitated, 'Doctor Carmichael. Have you his whereabouts?'

Crane spoke a moment with the breakfast maids. 'It seems he is gone afoot to Saint Edmundsbury, Sir Henry, on, ah, medical duties. He will return afoot today.'

'And his . . . housekeeper?'

'Miss Mehala is with him, sir.' The old man's disapproval showed. That man and woman should live together as so-say married was an outrageous affront to morality. It was intolerable. Some were so weak as to call Mehala 'Mistress Carmichael', but not the servants at Lorne House in Crane's hearing.

'Then I shall have the overseer as witness.' Hunterfield rose, thanked the servants with a nod, and went to prepare for the ride.

He had not seen the vagrant woman yet, but she represented the country's greatest problem. Since the recent war, when Tyrant Napoleon bestrode Europe and had the world in turmoil, no country had restored itself to its former peace. East Anglia was in worse upheaval now than before. In the past, and still by statute laws, every one of the King's subjects was 'settled', deemed to have a parish of origin, where he or she was entitled to reside. There he could work, obtain Poor Law relief if destitute – harsh indeed, but something rather than nothing. There too children got shelter, however abysmal. In theory, nobody starved. But now?

His manservant Grindon had his frock coat laid out ready. Hunterfield decided against the strap pantaloons, which were too dressy for the task in hand. It would be a good day when foppery was done away with and simpler styles of dress allowed for country gentlemen. The frock coat was acceptable, with seamed waist, lapels and collars, and the narrow flaps over the hip pockets were an ingenious advantage.

Within minutes they were being driven towards the petty constable's dwelling, Tabitha in one of her memorable sulks. That meant, Hunterfield realised with foreboding, that her scheme was far more important than he had realised. He would have to watch out. Lydia's schemes were always meticulously planned and carefully introduced. Letitia's were gentle, oblique, harmless. But Tabitha's? They were as tactful as a thunderclap, to be avoided at all costs. It would probably concern her likely expectations, or his own eligibility, one or the other.

The pilentum turned out of the Lorne House drive onto the Whitehanger coast road and headed sedately towards Sealandings. He quelled his impulse to speak. Tabitha for once was silent.

Pleasence met the carriage, doffing his beaver and jumping forward to hold the door in ingratiating display. He was a stout man, pompous and eager. Tabitha followed her brother down the uneven paving, trying to avoid the man. His soiled spencer, pretentiously made of Manchester velvet cotton, his muddied jackboots, his soiled half-shirt masquerading as a gentleman's chitterlings over unthinkable grime beneath, all testified to Pleasence's slovenliness. His wife, hovering in the background, was as repellent, with a leather apron under her calico, a blouse over a man's cut-down shirt, and a mob cap under a stained cottage bonnet frayed at every margin. Pleasence had cast aside his leather apron on the path.

'Good morning, Sir Henry!' he exclaimed, bowing. 'It gives me great pleasure to welcome you to our properly-licensed abode!'

'Good day, Pleasence. The vagrant woman?'

'With the others, sir! Can I invite you and Miss Hunterfield to partake of a little refreshment before I show you the sad article brought me last night?'

'Thank you, no. Is she well?'

'As well as any in her state, Sir Henry.' The man ran ahead, fussily waving away his wife as she curtseyed.

The building stood apart from Pleasence's house. Whereas the cottage was of traditional wattle-and-daub construction, bright Suffolk-pink plaster beneath its patterned reed thatch, the workhouse was of flint and mortar with a red treble-tile roof. It was not unpleasing to the casual gaze, for its build was in form similar to the new chapels that had sprung up across the fens and throughout the rest of East Anglia as methodists gained ground. An orderly vegetable garden seemed well tended. Several small children were hoeing and stacking. Others were deepening the bed of a muddy stream nearby. Older children were hauling a crude two-wheel cart along to the fields where nettles grew tall and thick.

'Hah, sir!' Pleasence pointed with pride. 'You see how carefully I manage the economy here? The night soil and effluvium produced by the inmates themselves is conveyed to yonder fields!' He smirked, delighted to prove his worth. 'And what makes nettles grow best? Why, that selfsame night soil! The gain is immense, Sir Henry! For, you see, the inmates cull the nettles, and from it is made all manner of things – a nourishing nettle soup, nettle linen for shirts better than any fustian or cambrics!'

'Your thrift must save the Poors' Rate much.'

'Thank you, Sir Henry! I but try!'

'I hope the moneys saved go recorded for the Justices?'

'Indeed, Sir Henry!' Pleasence's jocularity lessened. 'But m'lord will recall the inordinate expenses of these people. Dreadful drains on the purse, they. But I take pride in performing a commendable parish duty! Even if my onerous tasks are such that nobody else would have the Christian devotion to perform!'

Hunterfield paused to watch one mite struggling to lift a hoe. He could not have been more than two years old, and wore only a filthed smock. 'Why does the child limp?'

'His leg's awry, sir. Always was, since born.'

The child was heaving the hoe along. A girl, almost as small as he was, took it for him, placed it between rows of lettuces. Both were frightened, trying to avoid looking at the august visitors hoping to go unnoticed. The tiny boy stood lopsided.

'Pity.' Hunterfield made a quick count of the children. 'Seventeen, Pleasence?'

'Correct, sir. Fifteen adults, all usefully employed!' Pleasence fawned his way ahead of the Hunterfields. 'Plus one or two hard at outside work! This way, sir, lady.'

Tabitha held her skirts, trying desperately not to let anything touch her hem. She should have worn a guard-hem, of coarse linsey that could afterwards be removed and given to some deserving servant. What was the use of having one's shoe strings properly ironed so the ribbon showed gracefully, in this offensive den?

Pleasence entered the workhouse, Hunterfield stooping to avoid the lintel. The light inside was poor, except for one long grimy window that ran the length of the main room. On one side were stalls containing pallets, raised against the bare wall. Ranged down the other, women sorted rags, raising a thick choking dust that dimmed the light. The windows wore rims of accumulated dust. Four men carried in bundles of rags for a preliminary sorting. The women nearest the entrance sloshed the pieces into a trough and beat them with ash sticks. A constant coughing was the only background noise, all racking with every breath.

'Today is rags day, Sir Henry, for paper manufacture. Processed rags are sold – but', Pleasence added hastily, 'for very little, all duly accounted for! And the expense is high!'

Hunterfield turned away, trying not to cough as he breathed the scarifying dust. 'The woman, Pleasence.'

'Why, here, sir!'

'Where?'

Pleasence pointed behind the door, a small space enclosed by a blackened iron basket. Hunterfield looked inquiringly at the overseer. 'There is no one.'

Pleasence kicked the ironwork. It was no more than a cage measuring a yard across, almost spherical, with manacles and shackles hanging inside on a bundle of rags. 'There, sir!'

Tabitha gagged as the rags stirred. A flickering haze of fleas rose at the overseer's kick. Hunterfield stepped back. The bundle moaned.

'Put her in there last night. The petty constable brought her, quite off her head, fighting anybody. But I bested her!'

'How is she now?'

'Mad, sir. In my estimate, for the lunatic asylum.'

Hunterfield nodded as the figure's face appeared. The eyes were matted, the hair a mess of congealed filth. The woman keened, hurled herself at the ironwork, which rolled a foot or two then was stopped by the wall chain.

'More costs on the Poors' Rate, but less in the long run.'

'Indeed, Sir Henry. I s'll arrange –'

The light reduced even further. Carmichael was standing in the doorway. He was breathing hard, as if he had run.

'Good morning, Sir Henry. Who signed the woman, Pleasence?'

'I speak with the Lord of Sealandings, Carmichael,' Pleasence answered. 'Without permission to enter this workhouse, you trespass!'

'What doctor saw the woman?' Carmichael asked. He was angry but holding it within. 'Sir Henry, a doctor needs to certify a subject as insane, a troublesome idiot or a lunatic pauper –'

'Sir Henry!' Pleasence complained angrily, shoving himself forward. 'You yourself gave orders for this creature! Now comes this interfering dog-leech to whine about her! I know his sort, sir! This woman is a dangerous lunatic! How can a crocus who wasn't even here come trespassing to create a disturbance on property that I – *I*, sir! – have paid licence fee of ten whole pounds, that I may keep ten lunatics –'

'In the most degrading –'

'That will do.' Hunterfield's command silenced the overseer and aborted Carmichael's retort. His voice was quiet. 'Outside, if you please. I'll not have contumely before the inmates.'

They moved out, Tabitha almost retching. The children were working feverishly in the garden, sensing trouble.

'Pleasence has a point, Carmichael.' Hunterfield glanced about and failed to see Mehala. 'How came you here?'

'Ran from the Norwich turnpike on seeing your pilentum, sir, believing I might help the woman newly imprisoned.'

'How did you know there was a new lunatic?' Hunterfield asked, curious.

Carmichael reddened. 'You only come then, Sir Henry.'

Hunterfield gave a curt nod. The man had the knack of fuelling his anger whenever they met, with his air of apology and anguish combining to give offence with every word he uttered. That he was correct was irritation enough for one morning.

'Examine the woman, then.'

'I shall need a chaperone.' Carmichael looked directly at Tabitha Hunterfield.

'Not I.' Tabitha withdrew. She had not even a nosegay to counteract the stench of the place, and her smelling salts were unaccountably elsewhere.

'Mehala will . . . cope.' Carmichael let the barb fall where it would. Tabitha coloured in anger at such insolence, furious at a brother so weak as to let a country quack demean his sister before labouring urchins and a filthy overseer.

She looked along the path and saw the woman Mehala approaching. She was attired as any country woman on a long walking journey, but carried herself with assurance. Her cottage was latched loosely, chinstays flapping beneath her chin in a way that was improper, even wanton.

Tabitha swept away. Mehala moved aside into the vegetable patch, skirts lifted to avoid damaging the plants and let the lady pass. Mehala gave a curtsey, but so perfunctorily that it was almost insulting. Tabitha was further enraged to see the slut smile in an unconcealed aside at some filthy little brat. Such were the manners of the insolent lower orders these days, in districts where the lord of the manor was too condescending to enforce strict discipline. Carradine was right, she fumed, stalking back to the carriage.

'Good morning, sirs.'

'Mehala,' Carmichael cut in, 'there is a poor woman enchained inside. I need to examine her. If you please, Pleasence?' Carmichael held out his hand.

'What now, leech?'

'The key. Or will you take her from the cage yourself?'

'Sir Henry!'

'Get on, man,' Hunterfield snapped.

Pleasence took a bunch of keys from his spencer and handed it over. Carmichael gestured to Mehala, and they entered the workhouse.

The iron cage was simple to unlock, but extracting the woman was more difficult. She clawed and scratched even before the padlocks were undone, and kept up a high keening, gibbering in fear and trying to use the chains to flail at them. It took Mehala a full quarter of an hour's quiet talking to reduce the woman to a semblance of control. Mehala passed her a piece of bread through the bars and the leather water flask.

'Look, Ven!' Mehala indicated the woman's actions.

Ven Carmichael saw then that the creature was probably no more than sixteen. He felt his eyes lose their vision for a moment, and rose from his kneeling position. He became aware that the long workhouse room behind him was silent. He looked, to see the paupers, old and young, staring through the dust-filled murk at him, Mehala, and at the girl in rags in the iron cage.

'Bring her out, Mehala. Leave the keys.'

'Yes, Ven.'

He saw Mehala weeping, and blinked his own eyes clear before stepping out to where Hunterfield and Pleasence waited.

'Well?' Pleasence demanded truculently. 'Go on, quack! Tell the Squire here that she be mad as a hatter! Then if I be pleased you can certify her mad and –'

'When was she fed?' Ven heard his voice as if from a distance. Hunterfield was observing him.

'Fed?' Pleasence shrugged. 'She was given gruel earlier.'

'And drink, Pleasence?'

'For sure.' The overseer glanced from Carmichael to Hunterfield, losing assurance. 'Inmates are fed and watered better than they have a right, seeing they're nothing, but taxpayers' burdens.'

'You tended her yourself, Pleasence?' Ven asked. He felt giddy.

'Indeed I did, with my wife. We put her in the iron cage ourselves, fighting like a mad beast she was all the time.'

'Why was she apprehended?'

Pleasence looked at Sir Henry in outrage. The Lord of

Sealandings had said nothing. 'She was stealing from the bakery. It took two strong men to apprehend her.'

'Ven.' Mehala led the girl out by her ragged shawl.

'Could you gentlemen withdraw, please? I will show you.' The girl was filthed down her legs, unbelievably dirty and stinking. Lice were evident, and fleas flickered their silent dance about her tattered form. 'Please look, Sir Henry.'

Ven gently reached out and lifted one corner of the rags over the girl's arms, which seemed crossed about her breast. The girl whimpered, but Ven patted her and tried to smile.

'You shall come home with me and Mehala, miss,' he whispered.'Just let me see, then we can all go home and get something to eat, hot and sweet. Will that be all right?'

Hunterfield saw the rag lift, already knowing before he caught sight of the dead baby's face what he would see. The babe was not even a few days old. It was shrivelled, its eyes partly open, the glaze dulled by the death skin over the corneas. Its mouth was filled with shreds of grass, showing the girl had desperately tried to feed it with pluckings from hedgerows.

'She delivered herself, I think,' Ven said, finding it hard to speak. 'Tried to feed it as best she knew how.' He let the cloth fall back over the dead child's face, and spoke to Hunterfield. 'Probably trying to steal bread, she fought with a parent's instinct for a child.'

'That still does not allow . . .' Pleasence began, but quailed to silence before Hunterfield's gaze.

'You did not report that she was delivered of a child.'

Pleasence's voice dropped to a whine. 'Sir Henry, I could not see that she carried a babe, her screaming and fighting like a mad thing. The constable will tell you, sir.'

'May I take her in Mehala's charge to Shalamar, Sir Henry?'

'Yes, Doctor. Make report to the churchwardens tomorrow of her condition. Charge recompense for upkeep on the Poors' Rate.'

Carmichael returned Hunterfield's look levelly. 'I am banned by the church, Sir Henry. She will be welcome to share what Shalamar has. One more thing, with permission: Lady Hunterfield of Gloucester sentenced me to a particular duty at this workhouse for a disturbance that arose at Saxelby Hall.'

Hunterfield could not admit having learned of the event by his aunt's tattle. 'You have lost me, Doctor.'

'I was accused of slander in Treggan's mansion, Sir Henry. Lady Hunterfield sentenced me for transgression.'

Mehala angrily interrupted: 'Answering false charges!'

Hunterfield wearily waved for silence. 'Sentence, Carmichael?'

'To be supervisory doctor for paupers in the Sealandings workhouse.' Ven heard the overseer start to bluster.

Mehala added, 'At a certain rate of pay, sir!'

'You were given anything in writing, Doctor?'

'No, sir.'

Never mind, Hunterfield thought drily, there will soon be letters flying about the Eastern Hundreds enough to satisfy any jury of cynical parsimonious churchwardens.

'I trust on trust, Doctor. Commence duty with this girl.'

Pleasence reached for Hunterfield's hand. 'Please, Squire! Overseers are appointed at Easter, and it is nigh Michaelmas. This is without precedent! Who knows where this madwoman has settlement? This dog-leech battens her on our good Sealandings people's Poors' Rate! There will be an outcry –'

'*Silence!*'

Pleasence almost stifled on the command. He watched Mehala lead the girl down the path.

'May I influence the care here also, Sir Henry?'

'Yes, Doctor. Good day.' Hunterfield strode away, overtaking Mehala and the girl but not glancing their way.

'Pleasence,' Ven said. 'I shall not make inspection. Nor shall I make adverse report about you.'

Pleasence brightened. 'So we can . . .' He checked that the Squire was out of earshot. 'So we can reach an understanding?'

Ven said candidly, 'I want to see all the paupers, young or old, so we can make a better show.'

Pleasence smiled openly. 'Very commendable, if I may say. And my small mistake, not noticing she carried a breast-babe, well, everybody makes oversights, true?'

He accompanied Carmichael to the road. The Hunterfield pilentum had already left. Pleasence stood at the edge of his garden as they turned left down the incline towards Market Square. He waved amiably, sure now that all would be as before.

'Come any time, Doctor!'

'Thank you, Pleasence,' Ven called back. 'I shall!'

10

THE MOP FAIR was a bedraggled mob of men standing disconsolately in the livestock field. Once it had been a grand affair, but now was an assembly of the poverty stricken who sought employment.

Carradine's stallion stood a hand taller than the mare ridden by his estate steward, Rossar, a tiny man neat as a pin with black hair sleeked down with oil of lavender, stinking like a whore, as Carradine registered with disgust. Judith Blaker had appointed Rossar while the master was away at Saint Edmundsbury, and presented him to the returned Carradine as a *fait accompli*.

'A fine day for a Mop Fair, master,' Rossar chirruped, beady eyes everywhere. He seemed to stick to his saddle like glue, his tiny feet turned in, following the beast's contour.

Another of Judith's relatives, Carradine noted in fury. This man was a piker, a road wanderer. He had been saluted as they rode from the Carradine grounds, several gardeners raising hats to Rossar. No doffed beavers to the master.

'Fine? It pours rain,' Carradine growled.

'All the better. They hire cheaper in wet than sun!'

And a damned sight too familiar. The situation was intolerable, and Carradine at the end of his tether. 'I do not believe it.'

Rossar refused to be put down by a master's surliness. 'Hire wet, discharge dry. My personal saying, sir, always bears me out.'

They rode on to the field. The steward dismounted to lead his mare. Carradine watched him approach the line of men.

They stood, drenched in their smocks, displaying the tools of their trade. Shepherds had an uncombed lock of sheep's wool in their hats. Carters and drivers had whipcord on sticks tied in bands on their soaked beavers. Unemployed grooms hoping for hire held up sponges or small brushes as the steward walked perkily along the line. Farm labourers shouldered billhooks, coopers sported a piece of ash chimer hoop to signify their expertise in barrel-making. Hardly a man looked directly at the steward. Hardly one had a hope.

Rossar returned to discuss the selection with Carradine. This angered Carradine further. A master was above hiring and such trivialities. That was for hirelings, merchants, and money-grubbers like Rossar himself.

'You see their expressions, sir?'

'Sullen, miserable, worthless.' Carradine did not mind who heard. A man wearing a wrap-round entered by the field gate and paused, seeing Carradine. 'Come, man!' Carradine called irritably.

'Thank you, sir.'

John Weaver, taverner of the Donkey and Buskin, went slowly down the line. They numbered some forty-five or fifty, and had come to Sealandings from surrounding hamlets. Most seemed dishevelled from hedgerow sleeping. Weaver was a pleasant, open-featured man, slow-moving and capable. He greeted each man with a word, giving each a moment, explaining his requirement, causing some to look towards others further along.

'Their expressions', Rossar said, unabashed, 'indicate how low I can pay. A cheerful group'd cost more than this sorry lot. I can have any of these labourers for tenpence a day, five shillings and tenpence a week. 'Tis cheaper than ploughing, to hire a dozen men to dig a field of four acres at ninepence, tenpence a day, life is beautiful.' The Steward beamed with pleasure at the thought. 'Men! Cheaper than horses! Life comes full circle!'

Carradine eyed the man. 'How so? The country is beset with discontent. Labourers burn their masters' barns. Look at the notorious outbreaks of pillaging! Worse than anything Tyrant Napoleon could do! Traitors, the lot! I have even heard them call for "another good war", when times were best!'

The countryside was impoverished, as farm prices slumped from the early part of the decade. Discontent was rising, folk being dispossessed by enclosures. Villages decayed across the whole Hundreds. The traditional ancient open-field system had been replaced by larger enclosed estates, small farms failing every-where. Poor parishes were mocked by the splendid medieval churches that dominated their villages. Deserted cottages were commonplace, and prosperity barely a memory.

'Ah, sir, that is only part of the tale,' Rossar said with a rueful expression. 'Some of these be dissidents, men to be shunned. I looks them in the eye, and sees they are but malcontents itching for a fight. They would argue with your servants in your own house, that parsons slip glebe rents and tithes into their own fat purses while folk go hungry.'

Carradine suspected Rossar was merely voicing his own opinion under the pretext of condemning it in others.

'They would say, sir,' the steward went on, 'all of these things and worse, accusing rich of getting richer and the poor getting poorer, blaming the gentry as tax-eaters who drive folk into the city wens. But I counter that argument, sir.'

'How?' Carradine saw John Weaver speaking with the cooper. The man eagerly showed the taverner by gestures of his competence, answering questions about his former service.

'By action, sir!' Rossar shook in a fit of self-congratulation. 'Bitter or recalcitrant men, I ignore. Any that is properly servile, him I match in my mind's eye against the rest. That way, the haters and levellers succumb to poverty, which is after all self-induced. The obedient will survive, and so will the nation.'

'We shall always have malcontents, Rossar. Look throughout the land: Carlisle, Sunderland, Sussex, Anglesey.'

Rossar grinned, his face seeming to crumple. 'Frankly, sir, I enjoy challenge, always have! As their demands grow more preposterous, so must we reply the firmer! Thirty pence for a married man's daily labour? Ridiculous! Two shillings for a single man? No, sir. The greater their demands, the less they get!'

'Where did you work previously, Rossar?' Carradine asked.

'Oh, inland quite a way. Near St Alban's. A new gentleman bought the estates. I misliked the terms of employment, sir, so came to where a fond relative is already serving. I was fortunate enough to be hired by your kind grace.'

Carradine guessed the 'relative' was Judith Blaker, and this slime Rossar yet another 'cousin'. She already had half the Carradine estates staffed by vague relatives, and had the rest in her gift, with himself powerless to do anything about it. Since Judith Blaker came to his rescue, he had to ask permission to come, go, a servant to the mistress of Carradine Manor.

He reined himself in. It would not do, before these ragtaggle destitutes, to show anger. St Albans, though? There, Thalia De Foe had gone from Sealandings less than a twelvemonth since, driven from her own Milton Hall by the machinations of that bitch Mehala and her idiot dog-leech. Her husband Fellows, friend of Hunterfield, had finally turned, as all worms must, forcing Thalia to the austere grandeur of St Albans. That had lost Carradine his staunchest ally. There were other women, true, like the loyal and docilely obedient Barbara Tyll, his former housekeeper, useful in more ways than many, compliant to the point of total subjection. But Thalia De Foe had been an abettor, not merely a bedwarmer like Mistress Tyll. She had political influence, and despite her craving for him had furthered his private ambitions, until she had overreached herself and found herself victim.

If only he could get a letter to her secretly. But that was impossible. Even in the journey to Edmundsbury, he had been shadowed by a private groom — and of course that groom was a sallow-skinned silent man, recently employed by Judith Blaker, 'to make your journey the more secure, darling . . .' Letters would be intercepted or magically lost. It was impossible to use a go-between in established society. He had crossed too many people to risk offending the rich and influential Fellows De Foe.

But one day, Carradine vowed, he would reclaim Thalia De Foe. She would fall on him like the vixen she was, begging him for more rough usage of her body, to his brief relief and her gasping ecstasy. And help his ambitions, chief being the riddance of Judith Blaker.

'The taverner has decided on that rascally-looking cooper,' Carradine observed, leaning nonchalantly in the saddle. 'See? He gives the man his earnest shilling.'

John Weaver handed over a coin as proof of contract. The cooper touched his soaked hat, received his instructions, and followed the taverner without a glance at the disappointed men still waiting, who all looked enviously after him.

'He paid too much,' Rossar said with disapproval. 'He offered him nine shillings a week, all found. He could have got him for three shillings less, with an agreed 'bating for slowth.'

'As you will, Rossar?'

'Yes, sir. Overpay, and all are masters and no men.'

Carradine had heard Judith say those very words, when seated at his hearth. He wondered uneasily how close the woman really was to these men she seemed to know instantly by name, trade, aptitude, and speech. He was suddenly disgruntled, being here to lend credibility to this charade of fools. 'Hire as you will, Rossar,' he said abruptly, and kicked his mount to ride through the gate. It was high time he took a hand in at Carradine, and became his own master. Too long he had been docile and under the bitch's spell. It had to change, whoever had to suffer in the transformation.

'You notice something strange, Mehala?' Ven Carmichael asked.

They approached Shalamar, Mehala tutting at the weeds that had already taken hold in their few days' absence. She talked quietly to the deranged girl, who was stumbling and hardly fit to walk another yard, but it would have been wrong to let her rest alone while they went to prepare for her. Mehala had been softly telling her about their place, that would also become her home.

'What, Ven?'

'Look at Shalamar.' He sounded pleased to be home.

The huge expanse of mansion stood tall and wide. Once it had been a great house of splendour and beauty. Now, its leaded windows were covered in creepers. The roof was partly tumbled. Windows were tied with straw-ropes to prevent their fall from rusted hinges. The steps were wide ornamental stone, but the balustrades were covered in twining greenery. It was a picture of dereliction. A french-style double window was crudely boarded against draughts, with daub to infill where the wet wind might intrude. Several windows were broken. A start at repairs had been made near the kitchen vestibule, but two seasons of neglect had run the plaster down the walls; horsehair stiffening had frayed as if the wall had become unstuffed. Birds competed in the vines. The verandah was only partly cleared. That was Mehala's work, as was the Flora Dial she was growing again in the garden after it had been removed by an old enemy – a woman, of course; no man would have seen the potential for cruelty in removing Mehala's circle of flowers, the most ancient emblem of love.

'I see it, Ven, thank God,' she answered. 'I s'll see if Mrs Trenchard has cooked something to welcome us home! And see if old Trenchard and his dog are awake and at their duties of idle roaming!'

91

Ven was smiling. 'No, Mehala. *How* do we enter?'

'Why, through the vestibule that leads to . . .' She paused. They had moved off the drive and started round the front of Shalamar, avoiding the steps and the main door. 'I see.'

'We never enter through the front! Always the kitchen or the old footman's door at the rear. Why, I wonder?'

Mehala laughed. He was so amazed by simple things; even astonished at this habit. He would refer to it two or three times before the day was out. She was ecstatic to be back at Shalamar. The journey to Edmundsbury had promised so full of adventure and worth for Ven, and so was pleasing to her, but now all she could think was to reach home, virtual ruin though it was, settle herself in at the home she had made, for herself and Ven. And now for the poor simple girl.

'Maybe because we both know that Shalamar is not ours, Ven. We are here because Willoughby, De Foe family agent, was somehow prevailed upon to let us stay.'

'Hunterfield's instigation.' Ven lost his humour.

'Because you saved Sealandings from the cattle disease, Ven.'

'And you helped to save the flooded sealands, Mehala.' Ven could have added more but kept silent.

'That is all past.' Mehala felt the girl start to withdraw as they reached the vestibule. She was still clutching her bundle of rags about the dead baby. Mehala coaxed her forward, having difficulty turning the kitchen door handle. The key was on the lintel. She opened it, rust squealing, and pushed inside.

'Mrs Trenchard?' Mehala called.

'The grate is cold, Mehala.'

There was no sign of life. The sparse furniture was there, the crudely fashioned stools old Trenchard had joined, and the table they had dragged from the great hall to save it from the incoming rain and mould there. But provisions were lacking. Mehala felt the grate. It had not been lit for days.

'Ven?' Mehala said. He had gone, puzzled, up the steps from the kitchen into the hallway. She could hear his boots clumping on the bare wooden floor as he entered his study, one of the rooms that Thalia De Foe had ordered refurbished when she had evicted them, and reclaimed Shalamar for her lover Carradine. But that was before the terrible events that had led to Ven's return.

'Yes? All is here, still.'

All, Mehala thought ruefully. He had a few pages, goose quills she herself had made, inks she had brewed for him to write his precious medical notes with, and a ledger to record details of diseases in Sealandings. His surgery was what he carried in his leather case, and even those few instruments were the gift of Hunterfield. She went to the steps and called along the corridor. 'The fire was let out as soon as we embarked, Ven.'

The girl was rocking and crooning to the shrouded babe. Mehala went to the kitchen door and looked across the herb garden to the cottage that stood at the end of the copse path. That too showed no signs of life. Mehala waited until Ven returned, then went down to knock. Here old Mrs Trenchard and her man had lived since their young days, having served as caretakers as the great house, left destitute, had begun to crumble to ruin. Mehala peered through the windows, tried the door to find it swinging ajar at a touch, and inspected the interior. It already smelled dank and empty.

She returned to Shalamar, disturbed to see so many signs of neglect, though she did find a bunch of angelica outside the vestibule door where old Trenchard had left his worn ash stick. Some memory nudged her, but she hurried to take over from Ven, who was trying to start a fire. A small fireside press held straw and firewood. Ven carried in some damp, sawn logs.

'Trenchard did not stock firewood, Mehala,' he said ruefully. 'I shall set to in the dawn, cull wood from the copse.'

'Have you the tinderbox, Ven?'

Ven struck the spark for her, keeping himself between the steel and flint and the girl in case the sparks flew too far. The wisp of cotton caught the third spark, and he sat to blow steadily, but was too eager and the spark wore itself to a charred shred. He was surprised to feel fingers plucking his sleeve. The girl took the steel and flint, and expertly struck a spark first time onto the cotton. She was matter-of-fact, quite at ease as she blew steadily and got flame rising. The candle stub, made by Mehala of good fat tallow, caught the flame. Ven smiled thanks, leading Mehala in a show of applause. The girl almost smiled, then returned to rocking.

Mehala lit the straw twists she had placed in the grate beneath rafts of old apple twigs. All three watched the fire draw and the crackling sounds begin. Mehala knelt by the grate, smiling at the girl, at Ven. This was the centre of life in a house, the fire burning giving warmth for the acceptance of strangers and family alike.

Mehala told the girl, 'Welcome home, to Shalamar.'

The girl said nothing. Mehala's eyes signalled to Ven, who awkwardly cleared his throat. 'You can stay until you are well,' he said, checking that Mehala approved. 'We are poor, but manage.'

'So!' Mehala said briskly. 'Now we must see to victuals, scrape something together! A vegetable porridge? A meatless stew? There will be milk at a neighbouring farm, perhaps.'

She moved about the kitchen, making almost a child's show of surprising herself when finding some treasure, a few potatoes here, a clutch of old yeast-cakes in the bread bin.

Mehala took one to show the girl. 'See how stale they are? That's what comes from using baker's dough! Nutmeg saves them an extra day. But always bake them in baking tins, and slice as you wish.' Mehala halted. She was going to repeat the age-old wisdom, that only for children were kitchen cakes made small, as buns.

'Only for us today, eh, Mehala?' Ven quickly put in.

The girl's stench was more noticeable in the kitchen. She was beginning to look about, at Mehala, at Ven.

'Ven,' Mehala said, matter-of-fact, 'may I suggest you go to make your notes? It will be an hour before we two have something worth offering.'

'Yes.' He paused, passing the window. 'Your friend, Mehala.'

Mehala went to see. Little Jane was scurrying towards the house, strangely from the direction of the Trenchards' cottage instead of the South Toll road. Mehala was pleased, but worried by Little Jane's furtive air. She wore her coarse woollen rateen shawl gathered tight, her hair covered only by an informal soft chaperone, proving that she'd hurried. Mehala touched the vagrant girl's shoulder.

'Our friend comes to visit!' She went to kiss Little Jane at the kitchen door and draw her inside, trying to signal by her manner the need for care. 'See? This is Little Jane, my first friend when I was fetched from the North Sea!'

'Mehala! I am thrilled to see you home, because I have . . .' Jane drew away, seeing the state of the girl.

'But now Little Jane is a grand housekeeper, over at Bures House, to Sir Charles Golding!'

'*Under*-housekeeper, Mehala! And I would not have that post were it not for you.' She beckoned Mehala to one side, but Mehala held her ground so the girl would overhear. 'Shall I speak? It is not good, Mehala, for you and Doctor Carmichael.'

'We already guess there is something amiss.'

'An incomer is here, Mehala. A holy man, very Puritan, very accusing. He has already called prayer meetings.'

'I have heard of him. From Wenham, is he not?' Mehala spoke drily. 'Very zealous in the Lord's work, I believe.'

In her anxiety Little Jane missed the irony. 'Endercotte rails dreadful. Nobody knows how to respond. The Quakers meet today, and the Methody folk gathered yester night.'

'He speaks against me and Ven, Jane?' Mehala went on in Little Jane's silence, 'I could tell. The Trenchards are too old to traipse the land, yet their cottage is vacant and Shalamar untended.' It was almost too sad to say. 'They lived here most of their lives. Why should they leave, unless driven out by bigotry?'

'Shhh, Mehala!' Little Jane cautioned feverishly. 'Endercotte sees everything as witchcraft! I beg –'

'It is the same story, Jane.' Mehala sank to the bench. 'Ven and I are easy prey. We married in our hearts. We do for the sick what others shirk, so incur the guilt of better folk.'

'The Trenchards lodged in the fisherfolk cottages, a cousin. Endercotte drove them out, Mehala. I came to warn.'

'I did wonder.' Mehala hesitated. The vagrant girl was still now. Twice she had looked fearfully at Little Jane, but the women's voices were having an effect. She was slowly coming to. Mehala was reluctant to risk upsetting her. The significance of old Trenchard's ash stick, driven upright outside the vestibule, and the spray of angelica she had found beside it, now struck her. No other wood was so powerful against witchcraft, for witches shunned the ash tree. It was not simply for its strength and elasticity that ash wood was so favoured by country people. Why, she herself had ordered the planting of an ash grove nearby an important dwelling she herself once ruled. And sprays of angelica, like bundles of ash seeds, were also a powerful guard. The Trenchards had left signs to warn. Or to test her innocence?

'Well, Little Jane,' Mehala said with a calm she did not feel, 'accusers only aim at the rich, so they can seize the wealth of those accused. There are few pickings at Shalamar!' She could not resist asking: 'Where is this Endercotte?'

'Beyond the Goat and Compass, the last North Mole cottage.'

Mehala knew the harbour well, and the tavern. She had good reason. The memories of Ven imprisoned there were too recent, and the animosity of the publican Fowler would never leave.

'Has Endercotte a patron in Sealandings, Jane?'

Even before Little Jane answered, Mehala had guessed. 'Yes, Mehala. Endercotte lodges by permission of Carradine Manor.'

It could only be so. Mehala had known ever since she was a little girl that hatreds combined. They never stayed separate, to be coped with piecemeal. They clustered in horrid packs, like the mob she and Ven had witnessed at the hanging. Hatreds were without soul, and the more evil because of it.

'Carradine. It could only be.'

And, Mehala added to herself, Rad Carradine's sinister house-keeper – so she was called, with many reservations. Yes, Judith Blaker would have a hand in it, however recently this repellent Endercotte had come to Sealandings.

'Thank you for coming, Jane.' She smiled with assumed brightness at the girl. 'When we are settled, Little Jane shall visit for Bohea tea and Yarmouth biscuits.'

The girl gave a shy nod, avoiding looking at either. Mehala felt her spirits rise. The poor thing was coming round. She accompanied Little Jane to the vestibule and walked her out.

'Little Jane. Is it so serious?'

'Oh, Mehala, I am so frightened! People are saying this man is God-driven, to heed him. Others are afeared, though they might say different if they had courage to utter a word.'

'He mentioned Doctor Carmichael by name?'

'Yes. But where he got knowledge of him I do not know.'

'That is it, then.' Mehala was quite calm. 'It is a prearranged scheme. So be it. I shall prepare as best I can. And Ven's actions always speak for themselves, plain and truthful.'

They said their goodbyes. Mehala watched the diminutive figure hurry down and vanish beyond the Trenchards' thatched cottage. She sighed and moved back into the kitchen. Well, in God's time the old gamekeeper and his lady might return. The cottage might do for the girl, if she recovered her sanity.

11

THE SHOOTING PARTY'S guns erupted in smoke with the characteristic flash, pause, crack of the flintlock smoothbore. Birds tumbled as if willing their own descent to earth. Carradine laughed as one managed to fly helter-skelter and plummet to earth nearby for the dogs to hunt. Carradine was first to move towards the victuals. He had outscored his guests.

'Such shooting, Rad!' Alex Waite said. 'Who taught you?'

'My father, grandfathers.' Carradine tapped his gun. 'Start young, Waite. And stick to your last, as they say. Start with a double-barrelled Manton, stay with it all your life.'

'The same gun?'

'The very same.' Carradine held it obliquely for the other to see. 'Damascus twist barrel – none of this British rubbish; I want the Spanish-made Toledo. It is the Mediterranean air quality, you see. And none of your follderols, like Purdy's percussion system. That is a woman's toy.'

The young Scotsman smiled. 'I notice you permit no Forsyth weaponry on your estates.' He risked a slight taunt. 'Even though James Purdy was Joseph Manton's most brilliant pupil?'

Carradine acknowledged the jibe. 'Plenty of people realise to their cost the improvidence of swapping fashion for practical achievement. Many shooting parties carry home more than the sport they sought.'

Waite nodded sombrely. 'True, Rad.'

Castor Deeping, a principal guest, noticed the restraint in the North Briton's manner. It almost approached deference, but then Fifers were noted for their desperate social climbing.

'Except, Alex,' Deeping countered, 'your fulminate percussion lock can shoot all weathers.' He called to the gunsmith Bartholomew Hast, who was busy appraising the stock of weapons nearby. He looked up and took a step nearer in inquiry. 'Is it not so, Hast, that percussions fire even in wind and rain?'

'Indeed, sir,' the gunsmith answered. 'The Aberdeenshire vicar made experiments some years since, proving that his rotary magazine could hold enough powder for twenty-five shots, reliably firing in sleet and hail 999 times in a thousand tries! *And* more powerfully than any flintlock!'

Carradine appraised the young gunsmith. Tradesmen seemed to wear a new-found truculence these days. It was disturbing, especially so in one of this gunmaker's stripe, who saw remedy for all social ills in the development of craftsmanship. The incompetent but traitorous radical quack Carmichael – significantly English born, but with evidence of the sinister Gael revealed in his name – similarly strove for equality. Lunatic.

'Is this not leveller talk, Hast?' Carradine asked. 'Too many these disturbing days want all to be equal, without the background or family to provide justification.'

Hast gave a great cheerful grin. 'Whatever you say, sir,' he assented, indicating his low cart filled with long arms and powder flasks. 'I know nothing of such matters, nor is it my place to speculate. Firearms are my trade, and that is it. My family were gunsmiths since ever guns came into being. It is not for me to question my betters. All I know is that percussion shoots faster and with greater force than flintlock, though I love the old flinter more than the new fulminate.'

Well answered, Carradine thought sardonically, but a deal too predictable. He suspected Hast of thinking too freely behind his facade of docile obedience, but gave a nod of dismissal. The trio strolled towards where the lady was seated on a knoll among screens erected to protect from the onshore breeze.

Castor Deeping was another, Carradine registered as the merchant began to discuss the terrible shooting accidents that sometimes occurred. Of a long-established Maidborough family, true, and sufficiently formal to be accepted by county families, Deeping was still only a mercantilist, one whose mind tended to commerce, product prices, and Excise duties levied on imports and exports. A gentleman's blood should do a gentleman's thinking, and lineage be his sole guide.

But there was no doubt that the Maidborough man was well

connected. It was not his wealth that made him a friend and neighbour of the Astells. He was particularly well thought of by old Sir Edward Astell of Arminell, father of Brillianta and Lorela. Carradine had had this connection in mind for some time. Lorela was possible, yes, but Brillianta was accessible. Definitely, Brillianta might be the way out that he was seeking. And Castor Deeping, a neighbour at Arminell, might provide the circuitous route to her.

'Why, only ten years ago, Mr Cocking of Broadholme in Lincoln shot his friend dead by a hanging fire from a flintlock!' Deeping's heart was not in rural pursuits, though he was flattered enough to pretend enthusiasm when invited over for a weekend's sport.

'I reflect this seditionistic talk against the flintlock, Castor,' Carradine said, smiling at Judith Blaker as they approached. 'Nobody in his right mind trusts a hanging fire. Remember the famed caution from Markland's *Pteryplegia*? It remarks that "lurking seeds of death may hiss" in any flintlock that flashes in the pan without discharging its shot.'

'Improper storage of loaded weapons,' Alex Waite conceded. 'I see how meticulous you are, Rad, bringing your gunmaster to check every weapon.'

Judith Blaker welcomed them with a smile, motioning her travelling maids away now the gentlemen had come.

'Not my gunmaster, Waite, merely the Sealandings gunmaker. I would not risk my own gunhandlers!'

The others laughed at the sally. Carradine was amused to hear them respond to what was no joke but a simple statement of practicality. People who assumed the best were fools.

'We are discussing the improvements in guns, Mistress Blaker,' Carradine told her. 'I hope we have agreed that it is a disaster for sportsmanship.'

'And nations,' Waite added. 'Were the military given percussion, war would be too terrible, and civilisation collapse.'

'Yet,' Castor Deeping said, laying aside his Wellington shooting hat upturned on the blankets, 'traditional flints are now displaced everywhere on the sports fields, are they not? And duelling pistols are all percussion.' He caught himself in apology. 'I mean *target* pistols!'

All laughed at his mistake. Duels still occurred, but were everywhere being checked by public opinion. 'Hast still sells fine duellers of both kinds,' Carradine said. 'I believe the duel to be an essential regulator of behaviour. It is a proper entry to society. I was the first to order the Code in the Sealandings Hundred!' The famous book, *The British Code of Duel*, had been published only four years before, and was approved by the Duke of Wellington himself.

Judith Blaker saw Alex Waite and the merchant becoming slightly discomfited at the conversation. Carradine's past, and his notorious temper, were too incendiary for chats about duels at a casual gathering.

'Please, gentlemen. I shall *not* allow such talk at my pick nick! Instead, I demand to know the stories you have of Saint Edmundsbury, Maidborough, and North Britain.'

'My fault, mistress,' Waite said. 'I grumbled, scoring only a third of Rad's successes.'

Deeping made a face, accepting the glass of red Portugal. 'I was hardly better, Alex.'

She saw that Carradine was gratified, and busied herself with the silver picknick plates.

'Then you should stay longer, and make practice,' she said easily, wanting to know their intentions. 'I am sure Rad would be only too pleased to have your company a little longer.'

'Alas, family affairs call me back to Maidborough,' Deeping said, with a show of regret.

'And I must discover a residence,' Waite said. 'I intend to scour Sealandings, and hope that a year's lease will be easily found on some appropriate house.'

'Wonderful news!' Judith exclaimed. 'Please do start on this rather rough fare, gentlemen. I have only a dozen hot dishes, but I hope some may please. The cold meats and fish should balance the hot game and fowl before we move on to the sweet courses.'

'I hoped for a viaticum, and am overwhelmed with viands,' Deeping praised elegantly, toasting the lady.

He was not altogether at ease. His attendance at Carradine's estate was more difficult for him than for Waite. The North Briton could be excused, but his own presence might cause problems. He had accepted Carradine's invitation on Brillianta Astell's account.

She had urged him to come, but he had no illusions. Her unstated motive could only be for him to act the spy on the relationship between Judith Blaker and Carradine.

The woman, nominally Carradine's housekeeper, seemed to exert an influence far beyond her position. Local gossip awarded her an authority rightly belonging to a wife. There were times when Carradine deferred with startling meekness. What was infinitely more intriguing, the Astell sisters openly admitted, was the woman's background, for she had come from nowhere, though reputedly had vague London connections. And no noble family scion would stoop to marry a housekeeper, though that was known among traders and other lower levels of society. A new-found wariness about Rad Carradine disturbed Castor Deeping. Not that he was a close acquaintance of Carradine, but he had visited the large estate when a boy, though mostly on commercial matters his father had executed for Sealandings families. It was odd. The cavalier rake Carradine had gone. In his place there was this brooding man, far more dangerous and unpredictable. That was it, Deeping noted to himself; it was Carradine's uncertainty that was so unsettling, as if he struggled to subdue himself. And the tension could only come from this woman, the one new entity at Carradine Manor. Worryingly, it was impossible for a gentleman to report such a conclusion to an unmarried lady like Brillianta, for what words could describe such indelicate matters?

As the conversation veered to the difficulties of obtaining supplies of French wines, Deeping was pleased to hear Alex Waite express definite opinions on the cost of licences to distillers of strong waters in North Britain, though the merchant forbore correcting the Fifer's wrong estimate. The fee was a mere two pounds, for ordinary dwellings distilling their own aqua vitae, and only one pound in the Highlands. He was tempted to expound on the difference between distillers who worked on ratable property and those who did not, when he caught the expression on Mistress Blaker's face, and he thought *Judith Blaker knows*.

'French wines are favoured,' Waite was saying, 'when the Exchequer ought to help our own.'

Deeping was curious. He helped himself to potted mackerel, spreading it on a roll of Coltishall bread that he tapped to approve its hollow sound, to Judith's obvious pleasure.

'The Customs levy a duty of seven shillings and sixpence per gallon, Alex,' he said casually. 'That is costly enough.'

The lady drew breath to speak, but merely asked if the potted fish was to his liking. Deeping sensed that she wanted to correct his deliberate error.

'Or is it seven and threepence?' he amended. 'It is anyway returned when the wine is re-exported.'

'Enough, gentlemen,' Judith begged, serving the Souchong. 'I am eager to assist Mr Waite to find a dwelling. Might I ask what purpose it would serve, sir?'

'Oh, a rural retreat, Mistress Blaker, nothing more than perhaps two seasons a year. The rest I shall spend in London.'

'There is an excellent gentleman's house locally,' she suggested. 'On the South Toll. Presently it is occupied by itinerants, and is dilapidated, but beautifully placed.'

'I'm indebted for the information. Its name?'

'Shalamar.' She smiled. 'I can see you in it now, restoring it to its former splendour. It deserves better than it has!'

'When was it inhabited, mistress?' Deeping asked innocently.

She looked directly at him in a way he found disturbing: with no malice, but such a stark intensity that he was shocked.

Carradine stirred as if about to interpose. He alone remained standing, drinking his Portugal and declining food, and so was able to deflect attention from the talk quickly.

'What is going on over there?'

A skeletal man in black attire was speaking to the men by the gunhandlers' dogcart phaeton. The gunsmith was trying to get the handlers back to work, but they were hesitant, even though Bartholomew Hast derided them by doing most of the dogloading himself.

'Please, Rad,' Judith remonstrated, pleased to show her authority, 'let me send a maid. Prettiance!'

A maid of singular plainness scurried over. 'Yes, mistress?'

'Go to the shooting gig and ask what disturbs us.' Judith urged the gentlemen to resume their meal.

'Looks like a wandering preacher,' Deeping offered.

Waite stirred. 'North Britain has suffered from zealots. I mislike them in Sealandings.'

'All religious are parasitic, Waite,' Carradine said bluntly. 'But the authentic ones must be borne for the good of the illiterate lower orders.'

Judith Blaker pretended to be deep in thought. 'Could I suggest another dwelling, Mr Waite? The residence Stanton Lodge, by Lorne. In the gift of Squire Hunterfield.'

'That is impossible,' Carradine rebuked, coming to. 'Alex is a friend of the Hunterfields. He could not ask.'

'Of course!' Judith said sweetly. 'Do forgive me. Yes, Prettiance?'

'Please, mistress, the preacher is a Puritan, wanting the men to desist working, for it be Saturday eve.'

'So?' Judith Blaker looked her surprise.

'Saturday is part of Sunday, for abstinence's sake.'

Carradine swung towards the gun phaeton in sudden fury, but the lady soothed the situation. 'Prettiance. Go instantly, and tell the man to call at Carradine Manor the day after tomorrow to discuss this matter. Instruct him to leave the estate forthwith.' She smiled demurely at Carradine. 'Sir, you have not had a *single* mouthful! Have I nothing to please?'

'It is splendid fare, Rad,' Deeping complimented. 'I shall beat you to the pigeon pie, though.'

Carradine relented, but was still glowering after the black scarecrow even after he took the track to the Norwich road.

Judith Blaker was especially charming after the episode, delighted by the way things had turned out. Endercotte had made his appearance exactly as she had instructed, and done all that she required of him. Now, she could legitimately receive him at Carradine Manor as a religious devotee with nothing more malevolent than God on his mind. The coming affray excited her. Endercotte would provide the voice, she the malice.

Hatred was beautiful. Mehala was doomed, the instant Judith had planned an innocent day's sport shooting on the sealands.

The swelling distended the man's middle finger to the size of a small cobble stone. The labourer was in agony. Mehala had admitted him.

'I crushed it, Doctor, cutting rushes.'

'On a bank?' Ven knew the injury. 'It does not seem broken, but I need to lessen its thickness. Look away.'

He made the man lower his injured finger into the dish of

leeches. The creatures fastened onto the skin. Ven waited. Their bodies slowly distended with the man's blood. Mehala watched, fascinated.

'The *Hirudinidae* are valuable for this, Mehala. In medicine, we use mostly Bohemian or Hungarian leech. Nigh on a hundred body rings. You see the six yellowish lines along the back?' He smiled, reassuring the man. 'Of course, it does not merely suck. It has jaws, with semicircular toothed edges like a curved saw. Wholly admirable! Up to seven inches long!'

'Will East Anglian leeches not do?'

'Indeed! The *medicinalis* species is the same, the belly spotted. But drainage of fens, ponds and bogs has made them rare. I caught these two years ago, by the old method, standing naked in a marsh in spring and letting them leech onto me! They must be a year or two old to perform, fickle things.'

The leeches were sucking vigorously, swelling perceptibly as they gorged, their olive-green bodies glistening. Ven saw the peristaltic motion of their feeding slow. He lifted the man's hand out, leeches dangling bulbously, dripping water.

'Now the wick, Mehala.'

Grimacing, Mehala touched a wick to the candle, blew it to smouldering redness, and moved it slowly towards each of the creatures. They released themselves at the heat, and plopped fatly into their dish like huge distended prunes.

'That is it!' Ven exclaimed. 'See? The swelling is already reduced! Bandage it tightly, and it should be well in two days.' He examined the leeches. 'I wish I had more than four, Mehala. They are so costly. Better make them sick their blood and fluids up, instantly, so they will be hungry for more work!'

Mehala brought the salt. The man left, paying her his sixpenny fee. She sprinkled salt into the dish, and watched each creature spew its ingested blood. She fished them out as they became slender, and replaced them in their own jar.

'Done!' Ven said, delighted. 'Was that not a splendid example of God's provision for mankind?'

12

THEY BURIED THE baby in unconsecrated ground, without benefit of a service. Ven carried the little coffin on his shoulder all the way. Mehala had washed and dressed the minute form, making a tiny burial alb from Ven's one spare linen shirt, mentally promising him a replacement when the battered nettle cloth bleached sufficiently white on the grass.

The girl still had not spoken, but wept copiously as they started out on the long walk down the South Toll road. Mehala had suggested a time before five o'clock, when few if any sealands folk would be about except for harbour fishermen. The wharf was too far east for anybody on the hard to catch sight of the trio heading for the churchyard. Ven worried that the girl might be mute, like Simple Tom who was groom to Squire Hunterfield, but guessed from her keening that she had full voice.

'Have you the paper, Mehala?' Ven asked as they approached Market Square. 'I do not want to cross Reverend Baring further.'

'Here, Ven.' She carried it in a reticule, wrapped in an oiled cloth against the wet morning. The rector's reply barely acknowledged Ven's written request to bury the baby, and contained a bill for the four-shilling fee payable to the churchwardens.

'See it is to hand, Mehala.' He was sweating from the exertion after a few hundred yards. The church tower was visible through the trees, and already they could see the first cottages.

'I shall.' She walked hand-in-hand with the girl. 'It will be a proper ceremony, miss. We shall see to it.'

Mehala had dressed the girl in her only other full garment, a smocked shirt-dress over a garment cut down from a once-elegant redingote, and found her one of old Mrs Trenchard's straw bonnets to cover the mob cap. She herself had settled for her usual patched dress with a plunket shawl and cottage bonnet. She found some freesias growing near the stream that flowed through Shalamar's wildly uncontrolled gardens, and tied them into a wreath with a kissing string ribbon from her own working cap.

Mercifully Market Square was still empty except for one small goosegirl minding a flock of geese near the corner. The stolid open building, the Corn Mart, was public. Mehala could see an older goosegirl sitting there in deep conversation with a young fisherman called Hal Baines. She had cause to remember him, being one of the crew of *The Jaunty* that had rescued her from the sea. She repressed a shudder at the memory, and hurried ahead to open the lych-gate.

'Not this way!'

Reverend Baring stood on the path between the tall yews. Heavily cloaked against the early mist, he looked startlingly threatening in the dawn light.

'Good morning, Reverend. I have your written permission.'

'Not this way.' Baring pointed. 'This is consecrated earth.'

Ven fell in with Mehala and the girl as they retraced their steps and walked the hedged footpath towards the three-barred gate that opened at the rear of the churchyard. There he halted, looking at Mehala for guidance. The fossor had left his spade, but was missing. Mehala tried to raise their spirits at the deliberate slight.

'Now we can make the resting place exactly as we wish!'

Ven caught the intention and looked about for a place to lay the coffin. 'Find a pleasant spot while I prepare.'

'A few more flowers, I think, while you start, Ven.'

He looked at her blankly, glancing round. 'Where?'

'With Bella! She would love the company!' Mehala smiled at the girl. 'Bella was lovely. She will welcome the babe, mind it for you until the proper time. Will that be all right?'

The girl said nothing, stared dully at Mehala.

Ven coughed apologetically. 'I'll make a start.'

Mehala was conscious of the cloaked figure of Reverend Baring glaring their way as she and the girl garnered wild flowers and tied them into bundles. Ven marked out an area in the tall grass near Bella's overgrown grave, and began to dig. In a few moments he had cast off his surtout and worked steadily.

He tried to remember how long it was since he and Mehala had stood here, praying over the drowned prostitute. Those had been

106

troubled times, with the whole populace outraged, only Mehala standing between him, certain gaol and possible deportation. She had saved him when he had been at his most ineffectual. Now, his medical art had brought him to this, the mundane job of sexton, grave digger for a mite he ought to have saved instead of plodding the Eastern Hundreds to dissect corpses feebly attempting to teach himself anatomy.

It was done, he saw finally. The grave was five feet down, the soil roughly heaped nearby and the grass trodden down. He had had to widen it more than he had intended, in order to stand in and wield the spade. Digging the heavy clay was hard. He really needed boards to shore the sides, but solved the problem by sloping the grave.

'Here!' Mehala exclaimed in pretended pleasure when Ven called her to see. 'We need some of our blossoms, quite a carpet!'

She gave Ven several bunches. With Mehala's assistance he lowered the small coffin and placed the flowers on it. Mehala took the last of the freesias, and they stood beside the girl looking down after they had cast them, neither knowing quite what to say.

'Thank you.'

The girl spoke the words so softly that for a moment Ven wondered if he had heard anything at all.

Mehala indicated with a look that it was time to return to Shalamar. He nodded, and watched them slowly leave. The ominous figure of the rector had vanished. He stretched and grasped the spade. Sealandings was awakening, people moving in Market Square. He could hear the goosegirls coming to the flocks they had left in the charge of their little sisters. They would feed the noisy flocks before driving them on the last stage of their journey towards the new public livestock fields Hunterfield had set aside for northern drovers. A cart jolted and thumped into Market Square, doubtless some early farm or estate vehicle heading for the wharf for provender. Somebody called a good morning to someone too surly to reply. The sky was breaking into cracks of bright grey light. It would soon be day. He must get on. Though most of Sealandings knew of the girl by now, it would hardly be thought proper for him to be seen at a burying.

As he worked at infilling, he said aloud what he could remember of the burial service, several times pausing for breath. He fashioned a small cross from twigs and pushed it into the ground, donned his surtout and stood looking at the earth.

'Ven.' The woman's voice was familiar. 'Ven?'

'Good morning, Euterpe,' he managed at last, still not looking her way.

'I was just taking the air,' she said lamely in explanation. 'Ven. I apologise for Josiah.' Euterpe Baring came to stand facing him across the earth. 'It is unforgivable.'

His voice was dull with defeat. 'What is unforgivable, Euterpe? That your brother denies a babe the burial service? So the Book of Common Prayer rules. He only obeys. That he charges a fee, then excludes the fossor from preparing the grave?' He shrugged. 'Spite harms none, save him who harbours that emotion.'

'His hatred of you.'

'Oh, I forgive him! See how easy life is, Euterpe!' He still avoided looking at her.

She paused. 'You threw rosemary in, Ven.'

'Just a sprig. Habit, I suppose.'

'And scattered rowan berries, I think? And ash keys.'

'Old habits die hard.' He liked Euterpe Baring. But for Mehala, his fondness might have strengthened, becoming more. 'My father did that, I remember, heaven knows why.'

'The basil that you brought from your pocket, guarantees eternal life. Dill protects from evil. So it is said among sea coast folk.'

'Only by the foolish.' He was so tired. 'Please conceal my customs, or the rector will condemn me.'

'You planted a birch seedling. The cross is elder.'

He shrugged, trying to seem offhand. 'They were what I found.' His eyes raised to hers at last. She was cloaked, the hood raised. 'So you came home to Sealandings.'

She almost stepped back upon meeting his gaze. His eyes seemed sunken, his face gaunter than she remembered. Before, he had appeared always buoyed up, striving to maintain the image of competence. Now he was thinner, a man grieving when the mask with which he faced the world was cracking.

'Yes, Ven. I came home. Are you well?'

'Thank you, yes.'

'I saw Mehala. And the girl.' Euterpe said carefully, 'You care for her. A charge laid on the parish –'

'Hunterfield's order!' he interrupted. 'Not my asking!'

'I heard my maid-of-all Bridget's gossip last evening. And I hear more, Ven. There is a preacher here who will see ominous threats to religion in your care for the girl, performing this service, using the old charms as you have. Endercotte spoke against you once before, at your trial.'

'I remember the trial.'

'Hunterfield's intervention saved you then. Please take care. You may get no more strokes of fortune.'

'You are kind to warn me, Euterpe.'

She coloured slightly. 'It is my duty, nothing more. There is another precaution I should speak of. Letters have come from the churchwardens of the Isle of Southwold.' The significance did not strike him immediately. It slowly came to him as she continued. 'The man they found washed ashore there. The Isle Church demands its fee from Squire Hunterfield. As Lord of the Manor who made enquiry on Mehala's behalf . . .' She petered out.

Ven nodded. 'Thank you, Euterpe.'

'Sir Henry will have received his copied letter by now. As the man was Mehala's spouse, Ven . . .' She caught herself and quickly amended, 'Former spouse, I mean. Mehala will be charged through his place of residence.'

He felt trapped. He had always known the news had to come, this way or some other made no difference. 'You are well informed, Euterpe.'

'Surely I am the last in Sealandings to know, Ven.' She wanted to soothe him, so clearly in pain. 'I will be the rectory friend that you deserve but have never had.'

'I wish all were as kind, Euterpe.'

'I am only concerned for Sealandings,' she said to her own horror, sensing a serious mistake, and concluded lamely, 'I mean that Sealandings can ill afford to lose a dedicated doctor. The newspapers say there is sickness in the north. We might need you all the more, Ven.'

'I could not wish for a kinder sentiment, Euterpe.'

He wanted to pursue her news but felt the conversation might cause scandal now that the jingle of waggons and shouts of drivers had become a steady background noise in the growing day. It was imperative he take Euterpe's ominous news to Mehala immediately. She would have reached Shalamar by now, and might already be off to some farm for provisions.

'Will you stay in Sealandings, Euterpe?'

She met his eyes. 'Yes, Ven. While I can do some good.'

He tried to smile. 'Then you are a permanence, as I. Thank you, Miss Baring. I bid you a good day. The fee will be paid before noon, as required.'

He almost dithered, wanting to stay, but finally left, donning his beaver hat at the hedge gate.

She gathered her cloak about her, suddenly cold. The familiar folklore was customary at a burial. Nobody could criticise him for having planted a birch seedling. The mountain ash, the cross of elder for permanent after life, rosemary for remembrance, basil, dill, all were primitive but reassuring tokens of eternity coupled with hope and life. The hazel nuts he had dropped near the tiny grave were less usual in these parts, as the rowan, but still could be regarded as nothing more than plain custom.

She drew some long grass over the birch seedling Ven had planted, the better to conceal it from the few passers by that came into the churchyard, and made her way to the rectory where her brother would be preparing to leave for morning service.

When Ven reached Shalamar, Mehala had already gone with the girl. She had left him a breakfast of bread and cheese, and her old black kettle steamed on the hob. A note was propped on the table; she would be home in a trice with victuals.

His instrument case was ready, should need arise. There was enough Bohea leaf tea in the teapot on the kitchen range. He sat looking out of the window. Without Mehala he felt lost, only half there even within his own self. He thought of Euterpe, but found the news of Mehala's spouse occupying his mind.

He was half through his breakfast when a footman brought a message from Lorne House. Sir Henry Hunterfield, Squire of Sealandings, wanted to see Mehala instantly.

13

THE WHORE WAS not worth the sovereign, but fairly comely and trustworthy. So she said.

Carradine was dissatisfied. The quality of nightgowners in Two Cotts, the only brothel in Sealandings, was deplorable, hardly worth a gentleman's time. Lucy, his favourite, had been swept off to a humdrum life with a cattleman from far-off Lincolnshire. He was disgusted. The trollop he had to make do with was docile to the point of bovinity, not a brain in her head, incapable of an inventive sexual act. She rutted like a sack. He had actually had to instruct the bitch how to grunt, how to use her mouth on him. And as for ministering to a gentleman's wants, she was useless.

She was promised by the whoremistress, Wren, to bed superbly. He had yet to receive any evidence in performance. Lucky for her that he was here for other things.

'Did Mistress Wren give you instructions?'

'Please sir, yes.'

She answered like a child, though she was all of fourteen. Swelling breasts unmarked and her bodily hair all in place. That was the first thing, for he had never yet been palmed off with a prostitute who wore the merkin, the telltale pubic wig that betokened as well as concealed the balding areas of old smallpox.

'What did she tell you?'

'That you are the most important of our gentlemen.'

'And?' Carradine wanted bathing, but to order hot water now would mean more delay. Like blood from a stone, but it was his most reliable source of information about Sealandings, especially now he was subordinate to Judith Blaker. Whorehouse news had served well in the past.

'And I am to do your every bidding, sir. I am to answer your questions truthfully.'

And Mistress Wren was as sly as ever, Carradine thought wrily, sure to have supplied him with a girl who knew little of what passed at the whorehouse. She should never have let Lucy abscond, losing him an invaluable spy on moral and immoral people alike.

'Tell me who comes here.' Carradine drank the Geneva spirit.

Without permission she sat on the edge of the bed so naturally that Carradine was almost amused. 'There is Eldridge the butcher. I hate him, says nothing and gives less, the girls say. There is the great gentleman, but I don't know his name yet –'

'Describe him, what he wears.' Carradine was all attention.

'Tallish, not local, rich, talks Londonish.'

'He uses you?'

'No, sir.' The girl sounded wistful. 'He uses the two girls together, sisters from Lowestoft, great slammakens they are. Sisters have unfair advantage on us lone girls.'

A stranger? 'When did he start coming here?'

'Three times so far, sir, leaves a to-insure-promptness separate for each, one sister no more than the other.'

'He comes in a carriage?'

'Yes, master. Drawn from a common stablers in Maidborough. Though he did come once from stables in Whitehanger.'

'Are you sure?'

'The coachman was recognised from the window. He worked one of the girls less than a month since.' The girl smiled, showing remarkably even white teeth. Mistress Wren deprived all her girls of sugar and sweetmeats, to lessen the blackening.

'What makes you laugh?'

'The girl said the driver was so addled he was fooky.' Carradine looked his enquiry. She was pleased to explain. 'So drunk his member was all soft, boggy, like marsh ground.'

'Ah. Did he reveal anything of his master?'

'No, sir. I could ask for you.'

Her willingness was gratifying. She might yet yield well.

'I want you to be diligent. You understand?' He spoke directly into her wide eyes. 'I shall reward you, and will see you are better treated.'

'Am I to be your special girl, sir?'

'No,' he said, restraining his impatience. 'There would be no way for you to discover news about other gentlemen.'

She was disappointed. 'I wish . . .'

'There will be money for you above your usual pay. I shall give part of it direct, without Mistress Wren knowing.'

She gasped in alarm. 'Oh, she is like to kill me –'

'She will not. It will be a secret between us. You will tell her only what I say. You understand?'

'I s'll be your creature secretwise, then?'

'Yes. I will tell Mistress Wren I am well satisfied, and will want you next time.'

'You will ask for me by name, sir?'

'Yes. Tell it, and whence you came.'

'I'm Corrie, sir, sold from Ipswich a month since, supposed for a maid-of-all. It was that or on the parish.'

Which was good. A local girl would have gossiped more – and certainly spread more about him, to others. He wanted his visits to Two Cotts to be utterly clandestine, hence his attendance at this outlandish hour.

'Corrie, stick to the bargain, or I shall be cross.'

'Yes, sir. And thank you.'

'You can serve me before I go. No,' he corrected wearily as she jumped over him with alacrity, 'take your time. I s'll use you kneeling this time, I think. Remember what I told you about the noises you must make, and when.'

'Yes, sir,' she said meekly, moving onto all fours. Carradine sighed. The bitch had already forgotten. It was ridiculous. A gentleman's life was one long battle against incompetence. There were usually enough titled whores to satisfy him most of the time, though the problem was to find one with wealth and estates – and a doting father, who would accept Carradine as a son-in-law. He might then free himself of that intolerable gypsy woman Judith, who now queened over Carradine Manor.

He buffeted the girl so she spread herself and accommodated him easily. Judith Blaker's horde of relatives throttled his estates, serving as wheelwrights and groundsmen and God-knows-what, and maids like that ugly Prettiance with the incongruous name. He moved absently in the kneeling girl, thinking.

But with fresher news than most, he might achieve a self-rescue. Judith served sex well enough, but what woman with motive did not? And she saw to it that the mansion was perfectly run. But the hold she had over him was a burden he could not endure. It made him a serf in his own domain, the ultimate shame for a Carradine.

The girl began to cry out her 'Shuuf, shuuf.' Silly bitch. He clouted her savagely across her shoulders.

'Not yet, you ignorant mare.' He resignedly worked on through her babbled apologies.

It was coming so that a gentleman had to do everything while the whole world lay idle. This whore was shapely, though. He liked the dropping curve of her loins and the way her waist moved under his thrusts. He felt peace descend. Sweat began to trickle down his spine. She moaned with pleasure, which made him warm to her a little. He felt the sweet ache start inside his chest, his hands moving roughly over her. Within moments, he would be in that precious oblivion that sometimes seemed to him the purest state of being.

He fisted her to move her faster, and reached round for her breasts as she obeyed. She was learning. Perhaps she was going to be some use to him after all.

Mehala named Rosie, seeing the girl look at a pink budding dogrose. She decided to take the girl with her to Lorne House, perhaps in self-defence, and they set out to obey Hunterfield's summons. She described Sealandings to Rosie as they walked.

'If you are tired, say and we shall rest. It is not far. These shops are all that Sealandings has, in the open square.'

'The cottages are pretty,' Rosie said. She looked across to St Edmund's tower. Mehala had said nothing.

'Treble tiling is the style hereabouts, against the onshore gales, though they serve no better than northern slate.'

Rosie paused as the hedges began, with the sea's vast grey expanse beyond. Mehala did not urge her, just halted and waited. It was mid-morning now and the township was abustle. The cottages by the harbour all showed opened doors, older folk sitting on stools watching the activity, whittling or knitting. Between dwellings they could see the shipping, and out to sea a Revenue cutter slowly patrolled the horizon.

'There is a small wooden bridge over the River Affon by the town limit.' Mehala pointed, holding Rosie's hand. 'Beyond lies Whitehanger, a harbour some miles distant. Nice folk, if they like you. If not, then it is another story.'

'Where do we go, Mehala?'

It was the first time Rosie had uttered Mehala's name. She was absurdly pleased.

'To Sir Henry Hunterfield. What for, I shall soon find. It is something legal, I shouldn't wonder, to do with my coming. I was rescued from the North Sea by yonder fisher folk.' She indicated the harbour. 'Doctor Carmichael took me, and now . . . He had need of a housekeeper.'

Rosie looked with disturbing directness. 'You love him, Mehala.'

'Good heavens!' Mehala coloured at the frankness. 'Is that for you to ask, miss?' There was barely a handful of years between them, but Mehala felt ages Rosie's senior.

'And he loves you, Mehala.'

'Enough, Rosie! We shall be rebuked for lateness.'

'He was the nobleman at the . . . at the place?'

'The workhouse,' Mehala said. 'Yes. He has kind instincts. Some gentry – not in his presence – deplore his liking for the coast people. He takes his duties seriously.'

'He knows our speech,' Rosie said, to Mehala's astonishment. 'He smiled when a child called that her hands were slabbied.'

Rosie was mending fast, remembering so.

'I want to be home when Ven returns from his call. We must make reasonable noonings, or we s'll all be famished for the rest of the day! What shall we have?'

They were still debating when they reached the great ironwork gates of Lorne House, and were directed towards the servant entrance. Rosie revealed a surprising expertise about cookery, though Mehala was reluctant to ask how she came by it.

Hunterfield kept her waiting barely twenty minutes before Simple Tom conducted them to the counting house beyond the second herb garden.

He came almost on her heels, expressing no surprise at seeing Rosie, clean now in her cast-offs. He greeted them both.

'You wish the girl to remain, Mehala?' he asked without preliminary. 'Some news hears best in confidence.'

'Please allow her to stay, Sir Henry.'

'Very well.' He took a letter from a rent table, and sat at a tablet chair to check the contents before handing it to Mehala.

'The churchwardens of the Isle of Southwold request the moneys for the services they performed in respect of one Elijah Rebow, found washed ashore some time since.' He was reluctant to go on, seeing Mehala's ashen look, but could find no easier way. 'The military who discovered the drowning were paid the five shillings discovery reward, as King George the Third's statute law forty-eight demands. The churchwardens estimate the fee at seven pounds and eleven shillings.'

Rosie gasped at the huge sum, but Mehala read steadily on until she came to the end of the letter. She returned it.

'I shall find the sum, Sir Henry, and thank you.'

He cleared his throat. There were times when, her guard down, she spoke like a lady accustomed to the exercise of authority.

'This brings me to another matter. You married without benefit of clergy, and see yourself the wife of Doctor Carmichael. Reverend Baring condemns the act as blasphemous, an affront to established religion.'

'Our marriage is godly. The Church's laws say that nobody needs sibberidge. The betrothed who do the marrying.'

'Even so, Mehala, custom and rules must be observed.'

'I wear no gold ring, that folk will not take offence.' She remained stubbornly sure of her ground.

'You gave him a ring, Mehala. Iron.'

'One for the both, made by Temple the blacksmith.'

Hunterfield made a brief note using the chair's writing surface. Women had a greater ferocity, he sometimes thought. His sisters, like Mehala, were no exception in their different ways.

'Be as it may, Mehala, Reverend brings a legal action.'

Mehala felt her blood drain, her cheeks prickling. 'Wherefore sir?'

'Under the Public Worship rules. Reverend Baring seems to have taken legal advice, Mehala,' Hunterfield added drily. 'He cites under First William, cap eighteen: *Entry into church or chapel and maliciously or contemptuously disquiet* . . . et cetera.' He looked up. 'I have profound misgivings, Mehala, but Reverend Baring has some legal grounds for it.'

'Does he need witnesses?'

Hunterfield recognised her astuteness. 'Two.'

'And he has them, sir?'

'He says yes.'

'We married alone, in the churchyard.'

'The churchyard represents church grounds, Mehala. You have no way out of this. You were not "married" – you simply declared yourself married to the man. There is a difference.'

'When will it be, my trial for observing God's rule rather than the Church's?'

Hunterfield looked uncomfortable. 'I shall call a hearing. If it goes against you, as I fear it might, you will need to find two sureties in the sum of fifty pounds.'

Mehala blanched. 'And if I cannot?'

'Trial at the next quarter sessions. That said, it might . . .' He faltered. 'It might count somewhat in your favour if you were to find replacements for the Trenchards at Shalamar. I hear they are gone?'

'They left while we were at Edmundsbury, sir.'

'They are old respectable folk, Mehala. Not', he added in haste, 'that you or Carmichael lack respectability. But two unmarried people living alone might seem scandalous. You understand my meaning? And with only a girl vagrant –'

'Allocated to our care by the senior magistrate of Sealandings, Sir Henry.'

'I recall, Mehala,' he answered drily, pleased at her attempt at humour under the circumstances. 'But take care.'

'I shall, Sir Henry, and thank you for your patience.'

'I will allow you a month, Mehala. Please inform Carmichael of this conversation.'

'You are generous, Sir Henry.'

Mehala inclined her head to Simple Tom, and caught Rosie by the hand. They left the counting house.

Hunterfield slowly replaced the Southwold churchwardens' letter in the rent table drawer.

The grounds at Lorne were among the most extensive in all Sealandings Hundred, and were remarkable even among other Eastern Hundreds. Leaving the counting house, Hunterfield felt it was almost sinfully proud to feel gratified at the lawns, the flower beds, the orangery, the new ice house, the lines of trees demarcating sympathetic walks through the home estate.

'Good morning, Henry,' Sylvia Newborough called from the slope where the haha began. 'You change your mind again, sir?'

'Good morning, Miss Newborough,' he called back, his pleasure fading. Some women did nothing but interrupt, however graciously they joined a gentleman's company. Others were the opposite – however much you wanted them to interrupt, they kept away. Like Mehala. 'Who changes his mind?'

He watched her approach, stepping lightly through the line of harebells that flecked blue on the grass. They were his favourites, those and wallflowers. He loved them for having been England's national flower, long before the rose assumed prominence. Now, only common folk affections preserved the nodding slate-blue brilliance down the generations. Many estate keepers saw it as a weed, even though Shakespeare himself cited it so dearly as the blue-bell, and people miscalled it now for a woodland flower.

Sylvia Newborough was attractive, no doubt about it. Tabitha's idea of tact was to invite this lady. And she dressed well, her pink pelisse-robe full skirted with dusty pink bows fastening the front down to the hem, and a decorative 'zone', as it used to be called in his parents' day, of the same darker hue moulding above her breast. It was of changeable silk, that folk now called 'shot', a term his sister Lydia forbade as vulgar. Her yeoman hat was rather extreme, its crown gathered in a broad band, but matching the dyed front feather. Yes, an agreeable and vivacious picture.

So why his irritation at meeting her?

'I can see thoughts flitting through your brain, Henry!' Sylvia fell in beside him so he was obliged to walk with her. To stand speaking with a lady, even openly in his own sculpted gardens, would suggest a certain intimacy, and he did not want anyone to make assumptions. 'The lake you will create has new boundaries today, has it not?'

His brow cleared with relief. He had forgotten last night's supper talk about a proposal for an extra ornamental lake in Lorne's grounds. He was engaging people from the sea millers at Watermillock to discuss possibilities. The men had proved so staunch in combating recent floods on the sealands that he wished to reward them. With his sister Letitia married to that odd artist Maderley who owned the sea mill – well, it would be reason to see her more often.

'How perceptive you are, Miss Newborough!' he said lightly. 'Lorne has so many possibilities that I want to lose none!'

Sylvia smiled. 'Promise you will take me boating when it is completed, Henry! I must be the first lady to enjoy the pleasure.'

'How kind!' he said with easy evasion. He had three sisters, and experience. 'What if Tabitha commands me?'

'She would not dare!'

'How little you know Tabitha, Miss Newborough!' He kept his tone casual, but his manner formal. Her determination was all very well, but her company was proving too relentless.

'Now, Henry,' she said playfully,' I know you for a very astute man! Were you not at your duties *very* early this morning? I saw you in conference in the counting house. No other gentleman is half so devoted to his servants!'

'Not servants, Miss Newborough. Merely two Sealandingers.'

'Really?' Sylvia swung the conversation neatly. 'Have I seen the older woman somewhere before? I happened to glance her way.'

It was an unkind description of Mehala, who was younger than Sylvia. 'She lives in Sealandings,' was all he would say.

'I think I recall her now!' she answered, as if realising.

'Indeed,' Hunterfield said, offhand. 'My stewards want the new lake brought this far. You see where the cotton easters stand?'

'In fact, it was at Harriet Treggan's place in Saxelby. Your aunt Lady Faith interviewed her after some misdemeanour.'

'Oh? The lake's acreage –'

Sylvia Newborough would not let go. 'She seems to have acquired a new familiar in that younger female. She accompanied some leech busily disgracing his calling – making quite a fool of himself, in fact – and earning the opprobrium of the gentry present. *And* being as insolent as his woman to his betters.'

'I do not know –'

'Curiously,' she persisted, 'I was escorted later by George Godrell. You know the Godrells, Henry? An old titled family, and George now at the height of opulence. She sauntered the county, bold as brass, while her leech touted for custom and did his worst on anyone with an aching arm! Disgusting!'

'Really,' Hunterfield affected boredom, heartily sick of the woman and her malicious prattle.

'The woman is called Mehala, I think. The one in patched

Philip-and-Cheney camlet stuff she has cobbled together.' Sylvia smiled, venom in her voice. 'What a pity that she tries to put on airs! A decent subservience ages a woman so much less!'

Hunterfield judged Mehala hardly twenty, possibly three years younger than Miss Newborough. The conversation had taken a disagreeable turn. 'The question is,' he said casually, 'should I lose those bushes if my stewards have their way?'

She was put out by his unwillingness to enjoy a jibe at Mehala's expense, but thought well, if his preoccupation with a patch of muddy grass is to be the subject, then so be it – for the moment. She talked brightly of his wretched pond all the way back to Lorne House.

14

'I WANT TO see every inmate, Pleasence.' Ven stood his ground. The workhouse master's attitude had changed. 'Where is your written order?'

'What written order?' Ven was unsure of the procedure, but was not going to give way. Lady Faith Hunterfield's instruction, admittedly as a sentence for misbehaviour, had not been overruled by Hunterfield himself on this very spot, so it must count.

Pleasence grinned. 'Tell me, leech. What order do *you* mean? From the overseers, the churchwardens?'

Ven hesitated, now out of his depth. The slightest slip now would encourage Pleasence to eject him and bar entry for good. The law on the Poors' Rate was notoriously difficult.

'I intend to ask . . .' He faltered.

'Or from the guardians themselves, perhaps?' Pleasence leered, enjoying this impudent quack's dilemma. 'I s'll have you know that I am not merely the master of this poor house, but its governor! Appointed by written letter of law!'

'You agreed in Lord Hunterfield's presence that I attend the sick in need, Pleasence, and my duties –'

Pleasence guffawed. The children working in the long fields kept busy with almost frenetic haste. Ven felt his old helplessness stealing over him. He had no weapons against laws. Truth to tell, he had precious few weapons against disease.

'*Need*, pill-poisoner? *Necessity*, the law says.' Pleasence tapped Ven's surtout lapel, increasing the force to push Ven back along the workhouse path.

'The order –'

'Baffled, are you, crocus?' Pleasence stood apart as if in deep thought. 'Let me quote from memory. The *Magistrate's Manual* states that an apothecary or surgeon be provided by the governor "when there shall appear necessity for it". Your necessity, leech?'

'The children,' Ven said lamely. 'Some I saw last time, and see now here, are clearly unwell.'

'Unwell? I see only laziness, Carmichael. My duty is to work them. Can you imagine what the parish would say if I failed to work them enough to pay at least part of their keep? The parish Poors' Rate is already a shilling in the pound on every rateable property, for Christ's sake! Twelve whole pence in every two hundred and forty! For parasites!'

He advanced aggressively on Ven, who fell back before the abuse. 'Coming here with your traitor's leveller talk! You want the world to heed you – but not at your expense, oh no! You will spend from everybody else's pocket, never your own!'

Ven felt a hand on his arm. Mehala stood beside him.

'Mr Pleasence, no less!' she said gaily. 'Good afternoon.'

'It is not yet noon. Have you taken leave of your senses?'

'Not I, sir. But you have, I think.'

The workhouse master eyed her. She needed putting in her place, with her offensive truculence. If this feeble quack was not man enough, she had come to the right one for correction.

'I s'll cite you for trespass. You have one minute.'

Mehala examined Ven's expression, and quickly reached a decision. 'Very well, Mr Pleasence. We are leaving. Come, Doctor.' She drew him slowly away, calling over her shoulder, 'Good fortune with the indictments, Mr Pleasence!'

It took several paces for the workhouse master to reply. He called after her, 'What indictments?'

'*Do* tell Sir Charles Golding that we shall visit him in the House of Correction! Good day!'

'What?' Ven was asking blankly as Pleasence caught them up. 'Wait! What about Sir Charles Golding?'

Mehala held Ven's arm so they turned together. 'Doctor Carmichael was too kind to bring it to your notice, Mr Pleasence. But failing to provide a medical inspection is a neglect of duty. The Act of Queen Elizabeth rules that neglect is punishable by indictment. Sir Charles will never pay the five pound fine – can you imagine the slur on his family honour? So it will be the House of Correction for him. We admire your principles, Mr Pleasence.'

Pleasence caught her. 'Sir Charles Golding's name is not on any overseer instruction I have ever seen.'

'His family helped to codify the old act, and were made parish officers in perpetuity.' She smiled pleasantly. 'Your principles have saved us time. We must get on with other calls.'

'A moment.' Pleasence's mind worked. To cross Golding would mean the end of all he had built up in Sealandings. It was a sinecure, money, power, all right on his own doorstep. To lose all because of some legal nicety would be disastrous. Give an inch today, recover a yard tomorrow.

'No more moments, Mr Pleasence,' Mehala said. 'It was our observation, when meeting Reverend Baring this morning before five o'clock, that brought us here in the first place, so please do not trouble yourself. We shall report of this visit.'

'Observation?' Pleasence felt things were slipping away. He had been enjoying himself until this bitch arrived.

'Yes. We saw field lights burning well before five o'clock, and saw children working in the fields. I well remember the old trick, a lantern at the end of each hoeing row!'

'So? It is my duty to make them work.'

'From six of the morning to four of the afternoon.' Mehala's voice hardened. Her manner lost its blitheness. 'Lady Day to Michaelmas, sir, you shall call the inmates to labour by the ring of a bell. Your evil trick of ringing the bell at six o'clock shall not protect you. You slave these children from four-thirty! Doctor Carmichael is too lenient, sir, but I am not!'

'Please, mistress.' Pleasence darted round to delay their departure, assaying a feeble grin. 'Please. I would not impede your bounden duty, Doctor Carmichael. I did not understand.'

'Very well.' Ven glanced at Mehala, not quite understanding how victory had suddenly come, saw her almost imperceptible nod, and started back to the building.

'Seven children with rickets, Mr Pleasence,' he said an hour later.

'I know, Doctor,' Pleasence sighed theatrically. 'I get bad breeders. Stands to reason. They should be gainfully employed. As it is, sour blood makes sorry beasts.'

'Is that so?' Mehala looked at Ven, who said nothing.

'Of course it is so!' Pleasence expanded on the theme. 'Who gets

123

rickets? The last children of large families! And the poorest of the poor! Miserable infants born to feeble parents who ought to work harder and earn more!'

Ven was examining the last child, a little girl of four. She had a pigeon chest, outwardly bowed legs, the typical protruding forehead and large head. He wanted to explain to Mehala the signs of the crushed pelvis, where the innominate bones had failed to expand properly. This was ominous in the case of female children, for the pelvis retained its narrowed form and led to difficult labour in childbirth, and even death for both mother and child from arrested labour. He kept silent for the child's sake. The spine was already badly curved from side to side: the feared scoliosis, with the vertebrae unable to bear the little girl's increasing weight.

The child's ankles and knee joints were disproportionately large, the legs seeming spindly by comparison. He smiled at the child, turning her round to look into her face. Pale as death, she stood anxiously before him, stunted and frail.

'There!' he exclaimed. 'Off you go!'

The child tried to trot away, but managed only a few steps before slowing to a weary walk. The other children watched apprehensively.

Ven had told Pleasence to halt all work while the medical examinations were performed. The rag picking was stilled and the workers brought out to rest.

'You see how useless these are as labour?' Pleasence said bluntly. 'I am expected to maintain these inmates, work them profitably, and what thanks do I get? The ungrateful louts –'

'Mr Pleasence, it is grave news, I am afraid.'

Pleasence affected sadness. 'You can not disappoint me, Doctor. These poor-bred waifs. Hardly a one has an ounce of power. The older ones get feebler every passing day –'

'Three are consumptives, Mr Pleasence.'

Pleasence beamed at the chance of showing his diligence. 'I wager I could name the very ones! I know the idlest in my flock, if nought else!'

'I measured the children, Mr Pleasence.' Ven suppressed his rage. Why be angry? And anger at what? At disease, always with mankind from the dawn of time itself? He even felt a blind rage at the children themselves for looking at him with large frightened eyes; for their fear, when he wanted so badly to help, to cure, to prevent further illnesses in their tiny frames.

'Hardly a one with any breeding at all! Am I right?'

'Children ought to grow from two to three inches a year. These children are stunted.'

'Simple bad blood, Doctor!' Pleasence rubbed his hands. 'Now back to work, eh? We've lost over two hours. Very pleased you could come, Doctor, and thank you for all your –'

'Not yet, Mr Pleasence.' Mehala was writing down the last of the children's names. She had made a portable quill pen, and pointed it at him. 'There is another quarter of an hour, from the striking of the church clock.'

'To go?' Pleasence demanded, lost.

'The inmates were worked two hours early. Count quarter of an hour for rising, they are owed the remainder.' Into Pleasence's bluster she continued, 'And there is the interior.'

'The interior? Why, that is empty!' He laughed, trying to hurry them away. 'Where is the value in examining an empty building, eh, Doctor? With you so busy!'

'I heard someone crying in there a few moments ago, Mr Pleasence.' Mehala put away the pen. 'Shall we see?'

Pleasence glowered. 'I tell you there is no one left!'

'The accommodation must be reported on,' Mehala said calmly.

'Waste of time.' Pleasence was glaring and furious.

'Nonetheless.' Ven rose and entered the workhouse with Mehala.

The rag-dust clouds had not settled. The long bins, filled with caustic, choked him as he went forward through the haze, coughing in the rasping air. His old trick of breathing through a balled handkerchief in the noisesome and spreading slums of Whitechapel came in useful, except he was unprepared for the stench where a narrow corridor led to several small cell-like cubicles.

Mehala halted. He bumped into her in the gloaming. 'Here.'

'Listen to me!' Pleasence stormed.

'Stand to one side, Pleasence,' Ven said harshly.

The cubicle was no wider than three feet, with a flagged floor and a bare grille, letting in filtered daylight. A half-door was bolted on the outside, with a single plank fixed to the flintstone walling. A small figure occupied the cell.

'Can you come out?' Ven asked.

The figure began to whimper.

Pleasence pushed forward. 'Look, Doctor. This child doesn't count. He is lodged here temporarily, nothing to do with the workhouse.'

'Mehala, please. Bring the child out.'

Ven walked away. Pleasence followed, wheedling explanations. 'You see, there is obligation – a very serious obligation – foistered on me. Not that I am disloyal when I say that. Nobody more loyal than Pleasence of Sealandings, sir! But I must make a small amount on the side – no more than a coin or two. This is a case in point, Doctor!'

'A case of what?'

'Of improvidence, sir, that's what!' Pleasence exclaimed portentously, scurrying after Ven. They reached the door to the open air where Ven waited for Mehala and the child. 'His parents fail to pay some school fees, so the boy is made an out-boarder!'

'School? You mean Miss Gould's school, in Sealandings?'

Pleasence guffawed. 'No! The one in Rustonhall, not far off. A fine boarding institution. Modelled on the very best of the Yorkshire schools, so famed for their teaching of children . . .'

Mehala appeared in the doorway with a boy, leading him by the hand. He was quite blind. His attire was good quality, but badly filthed. He lacked shoes, but otherwise he would have been described as well clothed, were it not for the excrement soiling his trousers and half shirt. Lice dotted his hair. Fleas flickered about him. His eyelids were matted and adherent with dried pus. Fresh yellow purulence showed in streaks like lemon-tinted tears running down his cheeks. His face was flecked with red flea-bites, and his dirty hands showed excoriations where he had scratched.

'Who are you?' Ven asked.

'Clement Wellins, sir.' The boy's head turned, questing.

'See the state of him; what I must put up with?' Pleasence sighed. 'Too blind even to find the privy! Parents gone on the lam,' Pleasence explained casually. 'What can I do but lodge him, see if his sight recovers or his parents return? A damned nuisance –'

'This is a highly dangerous instance of contagious blindness, Mr Pleasence,' Ven said weightily. He stroked his chin with all the gravity he could assume.

'Contagious? Does that mean – ?'

'You are at risk, from contact with this boy.'

'I have never touched him!' Pleasence bleated.

'Good! Consign him to solitude.' Ven frowned at the work-house master. 'Where is your separate quarantine place?'

'A. . . ?' Pleasence gasped. 'I do not know what that is!'

'There is nothing else for it, then.' Ven heaved a heavy sigh. 'Mehala. I know it will be difficult, but you must take this boy to Shalamar, lest this blindness strikes more deserving folk!'

'Very well, Doctor.' Mehala quickly caught his intent. 'Shall I summon a conveyance from the public stables?'

'Certainly not, woman!' Ven growled in simulated anger. 'And spread the disease everywhere? No! Walk him there this instant!' Ven looked seriously at Pleasence. 'You did well to summon me, Mr Pleasence. I shall take your assiduity into account when making my report.'

They left with the boy, Pleasence calling fulsome gratitude. Out of earshot, Ven thanked Mehala for coming to his rescue.

'I should have been there from the start, Ven.'

'Where is the girl?'

'Rosie waits at St Edmund's. She wanted to sit in the church-yard. I said she may, but not to stray.'

The boy stumbled with weariness and faltered from blindness. He kept tight hold of their hands, several times pausing when a rut jolted unexpectedly. They walked slowly.

'Ven,' Mehala said, 'one thing. You would not explain the deformities while the children were within hearing.'

He coloured. 'Think of the effect on the child, Mehala, if I had.'

She looked at him curiously. 'What effect, Ven?'

'When I was small, I was one day called in front of the whole school. The teacher inspected my head, watched by all. I was upbraided, having lice on my head and body. I have never forgot the shame.'

'How cruel!'

He smiled. 'Every doctor on earth carries home lice and fleas at some time, Mehala. If you are to progress in medicine, it will also be your lot.'

'Indeed.'

'I am explaining about fleas and lice to Mehala, Clement,' Ven told the boy. 'Thereafter, I hated every school hour.'

'Doctor?' the boy said. 'May I speak? Am I . . . am I rescued?'

Ven looked away a moment. 'Yes, Clement, you are rescued. You now live with us – Mehala and me – at a house called Shalamar. We are poor.'

Mehala put her arm round the child. 'Shall I tell you what lies all around us as we walk? This road is called the Norwich road. It is a downward slope, for the most part between hedgerows, and leading into Market Square. A furlong distant is the livestock field where drovers and goosegirls gather for our market . . .'

15

THEY HAD PORRIDGE for breakfast, no salt or milk. Mehala found some pears in the garden that the wasps had not yet attacked. They showed Clement round the kitchen by feel, and agreed that he be allowed to sleep on a straw pallet by the hearth. Mehala gave him the gill of honey drink she found in the nook at the bend of the cellar stairs, joking to ease him.

'We shall soon have the cellars well stocked, so his lordship can partake of all he wishes!'

'Are the stairs steep, Mehala?'

She glanced sharply toward Ven at the boy's fear. 'We rarely use them, Clement.' She drew him close on the bench. 'Do not form a wrong impression, Clement, for if Doctor manages to cure your sight you will be shocked at our poverty.'

'Poverty? It echoes like a mansion, a truly great house.'

'It was once.' She smiled at Ven and grimaced. 'There must have been two score servants here. We have heard there were great balls, jousting and mock tournaments, with even the King's court on the grand lawns. Now . . .'

'Now?'

'Now all is overgrown, Clement. Truly a Sleeping Beauty's castle, with nought but rotting plaster and fallen tapestries, mouldy woodwork, broken windows. We used to have an old couple, the Trenchards, but they seem not to be here any more.'

'Were you long away?'

'No. Just enough . . .' She glanced at Ven, whose spoon had paused in warning. 'Just long enough for Doctor Ven to accomplish a task inland, through Suffolk. Now we are home in Shalamar, safe and sound! And as for the housework, a score of derelict bedrooms is too much to manage, what with harvesting food, making clothes, cooking, culling plants for my weaving, spinning, making simples and unguents from my herb garden.'

'She does little enough, Clement,' Ven interrupted, seeing apprehension forming on the boy's features.

'Sir?' Mehala cried, pretending shock.

'Do not interrupt her, please. It is hard enough to start her!'

'Wait until Clement has his day sleep, Ven! I shall –'

'Shush, woman!'

He confided to Clement in a stage whisper, 'Always control a woman, or she assumes all power! Was it so at your home?'

Clement was silent a moment. 'We had . . . some servants,' he said with difficulty. 'Father went to the new Indian Empire, and Mother sailed soon after. My uncle passed away two months since. I was not paid for at the school, so was farmed . . .'

'Then we must all manage here as best we can!'

'As best *I* can,' Mehala corrected with pretended sternness. 'You two idle scapegraces are nothing but a pair of connivers who mar my days . . .'

She paused. A shadow had fallen against the glass of the vestibule door. Ven rose and went to see. A man stood there, with a small deformed boy slightly behind him.

He was soot black, head to foot, and so was the crippled boy. His beaver was crumpled, his clothes in tatters. He wore a blackened leather apron, with half-jack boots patched with bits of kid crudely sewn. His face, hands, neck, were so soot-ingrained that his eyes showed white and red-rimmed, and his mouth was a pink slit that seemed startlingly raw.

The boy wore no hat, and stood barefoot. His clothes were rags. Early moisture from grass had washed his feet clean, making him seem even more frail. His hair was matted, his face streaked white in rivulets so he seemed extraordinarily mottled, almost like a child from a harlequinade.

'You the leech?' the man said.

'Yes.' Even standing there, Ven could hear the man's wheezing, his rattling inspirations.

'See to this boy. He does badly at work.'

'Very well. Wait a moment.' Ven turned to smile at Mehala, consternation in his eyes. 'Mehala, make Clement familiar with the house. I must examine this boy.'

'Yes, Doctor.' She drew Clement off, looking doubtfully back.

Sweeps were said to be notorious thieves. She consoled herself that Shalamar's poverty would disappoint any burglar.

'What is the illness?' Ven asked.

The sweep growled up his phlegm and spat into the hearth. 'Little bastard goes slothful on me.'

'Why so?'

'You tell me that, leech! Good money I paid for him, described as healthy and willing! Now look at the laggard!'

'Tell me, little friend.' Ven seated himself, drawing the boy with both hands to stand before him, trying to seem reassuring. His heart was heavy with dread at the probable cause of the boy's seeming lameness. "Do you hurt?'

'Please sir, yes.' It was a whisper. The child was even frailer than he thought.

'Where?' The boy's frightened glance at the master sweep was sufficient. Ven made his hold on the boy's hands firmer. 'You tell me. I shall try to help you. Please?'

'It be here.'

'In your groin? Let me see.'

'Always complaining,' the sweep muttered. 'This wart was not willing to clear a flue for a pissing-candle!' The pissing-candle was the smallest, a makeweight candle thrown in to make up the pound by which tallows were sold. 'I am hard pressed to support a climbing boy who only wants the life of a palliard!'

'A moment, and I shall be able to tell you.'

The palliard was the deliberate beggar, complete with self-inflicted sores, often with borrowed infants and cleverly-taught children desperate from sham hunger, who went about mimicking lameness. It was a cruel accusation, for climbing boys worked harder in their short lives than people knew.

Ven managed to strip the reluctant boy. He shivered, kept hold of his half-shirt as if fearing it would be stolen, and clung to his breeches when Ven insisted.

The lesion was extensive, already too far gone. The boy's scrotum was a tumescent, fungating growth with raised, everted edges, forming a corrugated mass the size of Ven's palm.

'I must feel . . .' *to see how far it has already killed you.* He felt close to tears at the boy's looming death.

He touched the edge, feeling along the skin surface. Underneath the black encrusted soot, the tumour would be a savage dark scarlet with areas glistening with exudates that the boy's body would be secreting. Why? To minimise the effects of infection, destruction, of the cancer itself? Ven did not know.

No wonder the child was having to walk stooped and bent like an elderly man with a stroke. His trailed leg and breeches had excoriated the penis and scrotal sac, so the child's genitalia were not only tumorous but leathery under the encrusted soot.

Ven could palpate large nodules along the groin. Were these the pink nodes he had discovered when dissecting the hanged man's body? He did not know. He could do nothing to help the boy's dying days. How long? Perhaps a month; less. That also, he told himself bitterly, I do not know.

'Very well,' he said with cheer. 'Dress up! I shall give you some medicine to take away with you!'

'Please. Will it make me better?'

'It will surely try,' Ven said, smiling to conceal his despair.

'"I have no money to waste on draughts for this sluggard,' the sweep grumbled, hawking sputum up and noisily projecting a single squirt to splatter on the hearth.

'That is included,' Ven said. He wanted to strike the man, but what good would anything but a feeble smile and pretence do? The sweep would starve if he did not carry out his trade, though he too had but a few narrow years to live, judging by the sound of his soot-kippered lungs. The boy would last another week climbing inside the chimneys of great houses, scraping with his little hands inside the flues of mansions.

Twice Ven had seen London climbing boys brought out dead from inside chimneys, a calamity regarded as self-inflicted by a boy's own carelessness. He had once helped to carry the limp body of such a child to the pauper burial grounds, the whole journey made to the accompaniment of the master sweep's complaints about the dead boy's stubborn disobedience.

'Where did you get the boy?' Ven asked.

'Bought him as apprentice,' the sweep said. 'Much good it did. And him supposed to be a fit eight years old!'

Employ was a sentence of death from disease, in these times. Ven shivered.

'Here,' he said, as if making a discovery, 'it must be about time for your dockey!' The dockey was the country meal taken about ten o'clock in the morning by field labourers. 'Some porridge left over for you both.'

To give to the boy alone would incur the sweep's wrath. To feed both would lead the sweep to believe the boy's plight had encouraged charity, and make him less savage on the lad. He set them both devouring the remnants of the meal, serving the sweep the cooking bowl and the boy his own half-finished plate.

The only medicine he had that might apply was one small phial of a powder of hops, and another, not yet ground, of the soft, dried tops of motherwort. If he combined the two . . .

He made excuses, and withdrew to compound the two powders in a stone mortar. It took only a few minutes, and he returned to offer them water before they went on.

'Keep this powder. Take a pinch, enough to fill a . . .' the boy had probably never seen a thimble, 'enough to fill an acorn cup. Swallow it. It will ease the pain of . . . that you feel.'

'Thank you, sir.'

'How much?' the sweep demanded. 'I am a poor man, and get paid little enough.'

'There is no fee. Let the boy eat as well as he may with what you earn, that is all I ask.'

'He eats like a horse as it is!'

'Wait.' Ven hesitated, decided it could do no harm to speak out. 'Go outside, boy, and sit by the well.'

The boy went slowly into the garden, looking about. Ven spoke low. 'Sweep, the boy is dying. You know that?'

The man spat. 'Little bastard. Nothing but a lobcock, bad cess to him. Kept him like my own, now he does this.'

'It is a disease called a cancer, that commonly eats away the scrotum of climbing children. It is incurable, as far as we know.' Ven swallowed. That plural was a doctor's pompous rejection of a responsibility. He corrected grimly, 'As far as I know.'

'How long?'

'He will fail in days.'

'Just my luck!' The sweep cursed in fury. 'The brat brings it on himself, from devilment. I met a sweep in Essex whose climbers last but a month apiece, so obstinate are they!'

There should be laws against evil, but there was none. There should be help for the dying, but there was none.

Ven swallowed. 'Please show the child kindness.'

'Kindness?' the man laughed, shaking his head in disbelief. ''Tis well for you, leech, with a grand house, a girl to rut, and money from selling your dog-Latin to anyone stupid enough to buy. But me? Black chimneys, and ill pay! At times they want to pay nothing but a cold meal and a kicked arse.'

'What will you do with him?'

The sweep shrugged. 'Get some work out of the little bastard while I may. What else?'

'And then?'

'Pass him to some charity lunatic enough to take him.'

Ven all but winced. Charity was an evil sentence in these times, even if it could be found.

He went to the door to watch them leave. With feigned heartiness he gave them some fruit. It was piteous, seeing the boy limping, swivelling his body with each step to lessen the scraping of his soot-stiffened breeches against the cancerous growth that would soon be his death. He remained standing there, unseeing and lone, when a child from the fisher folk came at a run with two other smaller children squealing behind her.

'Please, Doctor! Come quickly! There is a great King's ship in the harbour, and all is lost!'

He grabbed his case and ran.

'I am taking you to the buttery,' Mehala explained, holding Clement by the hand and moving slowly.

'I loved the buttery.'

His eyes were still matted, though Ven had irrigated them twice with water. Clement's wistful remark told her much.

'And I wager you were a mortal nuisance when there was butter-making to be done!'

'Yes!' he answered unexpectedly, making them both laugh so that he stumbled on one of the raised bricks. 'They said so, but I was spared beatings. Dairy maids never tell!'

'Here at Shalamar, the buttery is apart from the main house.' She described as she went. 'There is a moat, but it lies on two sides only now. It was filled to make part of the garden.'

'The orangery? Ice house?'

'Alas, none yet!' Mehala was impressed. Few dwellings were as grand as the one Clement had known. Hunterfield, of course, had all any man could ever want in appurtenances, commodities and grandeur. Why, her own Red Hall, with its many servants and expansive lands, had made do without an orangery, though her ice house was well constructed and . . .

'What is it, Mehala?' Clement stopped.

'Nothing, Clement. I thought of something horrid.'

'Was it something I said?'

'Of course not. My silly imaginings, that is all. Now here on the left is the buttery continuance. Moss overgrowing thatch as ever in this rain-soaked county!'

'Sewing rooms for the maids above?'

'Yes,' she answered, surprised. 'Dairy, cheese room, herb rooms – two, linked by an arch – and at the end the stores.'

Clement followed gingerly, sniffing. 'Your still room?'

'Very astute, sir,' she said admiringly, 'to detect the scent of brewing yeast! I use it well enough. Porter, enough small beer to keep us. Doctor Ven insists on our using small beer as a staple. He believes that our well waters and streams carry effluvia dangerous to health. You will soon notice that we boil every drop of water we drink in Shalamar. All food is heated or scrubbed to vanishing!'

'Is your bakery separate?'

'Indeed it is! Bakery fires burn down to the flagstones.'

'Always the bakery burns, never the forge!'

So Clement's home had once a forge, doubtless smiths too, with bakery, still rooms for brewing potables, all a grand estate could desire. But so had she, once, at Red Hall. Did it now stand as derelict as Shalamar? She linked her arm to Clement's, and walked out underneath the huge cedars.

'Do not cry, Mehala.'

'I do not, sir.' She squeezed his hand.

They sat on the flintstone wall overlooking the moat. She had no love for Red Hall, or the man she married. Indeed, she felt such hatred that the emotion lingered even beyond his death. She wondered how long hate lasted, if it was as enduring as its opposite passion, if the one outlived the other.

Shalamar was different. She would have loved it even had she come as a buttery girl or seamstress sewing in the rooms over the herbal. Its dereliction was grievous, of course, yet it felt a home, friendly, all-embracing, warm even in the coldest winter months.

'Will you stay here, Mehala?' Clement asked.

For all his youth, he was a perceiving child. Mehala smiled, brought them both upright and said they should walk on. 'Yes, Clement, and so shall you, as long as we may.'

'Thank you.'

They heard a child's shrill calling, the squeal of other children and excited shouts about a ship that was utterly lost in the harbour. The vestibule door slammed, and Ven's footfalls pounded on the drive. Mehala instinctively made as if to start after him, then realised Clement would be left blind and alone.

'Doctor has been called away,' she said lightly. 'It often happens. Thank goodness it is only to the harbour!'

And thank God, she prayed fervently, that the day is calm; at least I know that he will be safe.

The Sealandings harbour was not a picture of catastrophe at all, when Ven arrived.

A brig-sloop was peacefully moored against the south mole, its sails already stowed. Ven slowed, sweating heavily from the long run through Market Square and down among the fisher cottages. His surtout and instrument case were impediments to speed. He felt the lack of a dog cart.

'On the mole, Doctor,' a young fisherboy called. 'That Baltic brig-sloop, in on the first tide.'

'Thank you, Hal.'

Hal Baines, of *The Jaunty*, once Mehala's rescuer, started to walk with him. 'She brung some man who is sore a-fallen, Doctor.'

'Badly injured?'

'In faith, Doctor,' Hal swore politely. 'The second mate says he will be blessed to sail Baltic again!'

'Baltic?' Ven eyed the vessel. 'She seems too big.'

'Not a Baltic sloop, Doctor, for they be small, one-masted and square of hull with but one small cross top sail. They never do goow anywhere, 'cept blown off course. I means she comes from the Baltic Sea.'

136

'Does she indeed?'

He noticed Carradine, mounted, his stallion at a stand, watching from rising ground near the hill between Sealandings and the rival Whitehanger.

'Are you the leech?' someone aboard called down.

'Yes. Doctor Carmichael of Sealandings. Late of Whitechapel.'

'Come aboard. We shall be glad of your help.'

Ven walked up the gangplank, holding to the rope for balance, and stepped from the gunwale. A seaman was lying unattended by a hatch. The man who greeted him was a plethoric, stout man with weathered features.

'See to him, but first what be your fee?'

'Whatever you pay.'

'Hmph. I want him to work, not waste. Get on.'

'What happened?'

The injured man was still wearing his leather shoes, but the latchings of one were undone. It was his right foot.

'I was at the gaff, and fell.'

'You landed on your right foot?'

'Aye. Straight down, jarred the teeth from my head and sent me daft for a whole hour.'

'You heard a crack?'

'Aye, that I did.'

Ven bent and managed to remove the man's footwear. He made comparison of the injured and uninjured ankles. The right foot was badly misshapen, everted so that the line of the limb was angled outward. Ven felt along the bones. It seemed astonishingly swollen, and suspicion grew.

'When was this done?'

'Three days since, Doctor.'

'Three *days*? Could you not ask for a surgeon earlier?' He looked round, addressing the question to the mate.

The man grinned, unabashed. 'You darst not ask our captain idiot's questions, leech. He stops for nothing, God nor man, but gets the cargo home fast as may be.'

Ven was angered by the man's nonchalance. He took the ship's scent. 'What cargo that will not wait? Wood of some sort?'

'Wood, aye, but much as ballast and voyages free, you might say. The rest is silver wares, ambers and specie.'

'Precious metals and decoratives can tolerate delay!'

The mate grinned. 'Not on board our captain's ship, leech!'

'Where is he, if I may?'

'Called to talk with one of your gentry. See there?'

Ven raised his head to see. Carradine was in conversation with a man in a short but embroidered seaman's spencer.

The mate crouched down, waving two seamen away who had come to watch, fascinated by the mystique of a healer's art.

'Betwixt you and me, Doctor,' the mate said quietly, 'this vessel will suffer no rest until she docks in the port of Lunnon, and that be God's truth.'

'But you put in here at Sealandings, for heaven's sake!'

'Aye, by request, not by Christian charity. Not even the Baltic's diseases will stop her. Our captain be a driving man, that is for sure.'

'Diseases? Of what nature?'

The mate looked uncomfortable. 'Nothing you could tell, to another. But tales abound where tales never did afore.'

Ven wanted to question further but the injured man groaned, and he bent to explain. 'You have suffered a fracture. It is of the fibula, the ankle's clasp-bone. It is got by falling directly down, with your foot turned aside.'

'Will it heal?' The seaman waited with resignation.

'It will heal,' Ven said heavily, wishing he could make it an outright accusation. 'It would have healed a deal better had you been treated early. As you have suffered a double fracture – with the tibia, the strength bone – it is serious.'

'What does that mean?'

Ven gathered himself. It had been a grim day, what with the sweep's doomed climbing boy and now this stricken seaman.

'I can splint it for you, to start healing and lessen the pain. You have what is known as a Pott's fracture –'

'Pott's?' The name alarmed the man.

'Nothing to do with how the bone breaks, not like a pot. Called for a London doctor, Percivall Pott. It is always a problem. You need it made straight. I must put your great toe in line with the inner edge of the knee-pan. It will take only a moment, and prevent lasting deformity. Have you a ship's carpenter?'

'Aye.'

Ven pulled off his surtout and laid it on the deck, reassuring the seaman. 'No, friend,' he said. 'No amputation. I shall lay your leg straight on a splint of wood, supported by a folded sheet with wadding, bandaged to be firm. Then, crutches. And . . .'

'Then?' the seaman asked. He was resigned, accepting the ruined life that lay before him.

'It is up to God,' Ven said. God had proved little use today. 'Perhaps the owners will be benevolent.'

He greeted the carpenter who came up from below, and explained what was needed, a splint to extend below the ankle by three inches, with a notch cut to facilitate bandaging.

He wished Mehala was with him, for she learned as quickly as any male apprentice, and retained details with admirable clarity. He would take her through the method of forcing bone fragments into position, with diagrams, when he got home.

'Keep your knee moved at least twice daily, to prevent stiffening,' he said, trying to distance himself from the man's plight. 'In four or five weeks the splints can be removed, after which a bandage will do.'

It was the best he could do. He sat on the deck by the man, asking him about his voyage, but wondering throughout why Carradine could want to see a sea captain from a Baltic ship.

16

ROSIE RECOVERED WITH every passing hour, or so Mehala thought. She invited her help, explaining patiently.

'Clement will help,' she said, leading the boy to the table. 'You will manage famously!'

Rosie was still reluctant to say much, but seemed glad to have somebody in her charge. She held Clement's hand as they sat. The stink of sulphur ointment about him was almost as noticeable as that emanating from Rosie. Mehala had them smiling about it.

'You two are like bonnets – sulphur-bleached! But the noisome aroma will not last long.'

'Will Doctor let us be rid of the ointment, Mehala?' Clement wanted to know. His eyes were red, but he could occasionally open them with a determined wrinkling of his forehead.

'One more day for Rosie, two more for you, Clement!' Ven smiled at the scene. 'I only hope my unguents do not carry into the pudding!'

Mehala tutted disparagingly. 'Just listen to the man! Pudding, indeed! It is a marasquin that we are making, so many gooseberries and no pastry. Away with you, while we get on!'

Her eyes let him know she would come to him as soon as she had the young pair distracted by work. Rosie giggled in horror at Mehala's mock anger.

'And shall I see again soon?' Clement asked.

'I do not know.' She tried to sound assured. 'Doctor can tell us in two days. Rosie, the cherry leaves and gooseberries are not to be touched until you have washed your hands scrupulously – otherwise the *pudding* will be most offensive!'

'Tell me in order, please, Mehala.'

'As you like.' Mehala smiled a mute instruction to Rosie to assume responsibility. 'Marasquin is simple. Weigh out eight pounds of ripe gooseberries – see that Clement uses the Surrey scales, Rosie, so he can feel their balance. Only ripe ones, please, no red ones! One pound of black cherry leaves, from our old tree. Bruise them, add water, and yeast to ferment.'

'Can I do that?'

'Share the labour, or I s'll put salt on your tails!' Mehala scolded. 'We distil it in a few days, when the fermentation is done. I will show you how.'

'Mehala.' Clement's face clouded. His eyes were closed. Some encrustations still showed in the corners. He was embarrassed by the mob cap he was made to wear. 'Shall we still be here then?'

'We shall be here for ever! For heaven's sake get on! I must see if Doctor needs notes taking.'

She left them, hearing with delight Rosie speak quietly to the boy almost before she had closed the door.

Ven was standing in the hall. He beckoned her along the empty hallway into the room that was partially restored. It held a plain table, a wheatsheaf-back upright chair and a stool that old Trenchard had joined. Scrim hung over the walls near the windows, and more scrim was plastered to strengthen the decayed patches, showing where the repair work had been abandoned. Mehala had wanted to lay a fire, but Ven had said to keep the logs for the kitchen. He wore his old spencer against draughts, as always when reading or making up medicaments.

'Luxuries like fires will come in due time, Mehala.'

'Please God, Ven.' She drew up the stool and hugged her worn Norwich around her shoulders as he sat. As with all cloths of silk warp and woollen weft in fill-over pattern, the wool wore faster, leaving the silk showing in elegant if barer patches. She caught his glance and coloured. 'Forgive my appearance, Ven. I will finish a Scotch cloth shawl soon, with a winsey lining.'

'Yet more nettle?'

Mehala was annoyed. 'There is nothing wrong with nettle cloth!' she exclaimed. 'It has clothed more folk than –'

'I am sorry, Mehala.' He put his hand on her shoulder. On her low stool, she had to crane to see his drawings.

'Hush, Ven. We say sorry too often. We are together, and do what we can. There is an end to it. What am I to learn today?'

'Fleas, lice, the scabies itch. Are they occupied?'

'As you asked.' She concealed a laugh in her shawl. 'I expended all my ripe gooseberries to find them a task that will not carry their odour! The poor things stink so!'

'My fault, Mehala, but no apology!' He gave the first paper to her. 'We all know the remedy for head lice – comb out, cut hair, wash, comb with burrs continuously. The dreadful excoriations and scabs that come from other infestations are not so easily treated. What did we do?'

She knew he would ask her this, and had the response ready. She counted on her fingers, frowning in concentration.

'We made up an ointment of six ounces each of sulphur and my best soft soap. White hellebore two ounces, half a drachm of bergamot essence, the whole porridged into lard.'

'Good!' He was suddenly wistful. 'Nitre is said to strengthen the ointment, but it is so expensive. Continue.'

'Clothes into the boiler. When dry, iron with the hottest possible smoothing iron from the range. Then air them a whole day. Other clothes, burn immediately.'

'Very good.' He corrected the list, and gave it to her. 'Here are the other treatment possibilities. Those that work instantly, I put a tick.'

She read. 'So many, Ven!'

He tried to smile. 'I had no books of my own. My friend Ward – I mentioned him – was kindly to me on occasion. But the lecture fees were financially crippling, every day another door ticket, another fee! The wards were free, so working there was the cheapest activity of all!'

She shared his wistfulness, but was eager to alleviate it. 'You are giving me that gift, Ven.'

'I wish I were able to, properly. Buy you books, unlearned though they are even now in these modern days.' He found his hand on her shoulder, and tapped the table. 'The young people must be checked for fleas and lice again. You will scrutinise Rosie, I Clement. New scarifications, new red spots, bites. Tell me where especially.'

'The collar ring, folds of skin, nape, groin.'

'Good.' He hesitated. 'That is about all, Mehala. I should warn you against the blue ointment of mercury. It causes as much trouble as it cures – if indeed it cures any!'

'Thank you, Doctor.' She did not rise and leave immediately, but looked at him closely. 'What is it, Ven?'

'Nothing.' He was unable to form the question.

She had only briefly told him of Hunterfield's interview. It was time to speak out. 'Ven. I think I have an answer for our position. It may not be to your liking, and will be hateful to me. It *is* a solution, though. Will you walk with me in the garden?'

He came easily. They went through the great hall, footfalls echoing as they moved to the balustraded walk that extended across the front of gaunt and broken windows.

Mehala gave a half-laugh of reproof. 'See where I swept away the broken glass, Ven? Trenchard carried it to market. Guess who bought it? Hast, the gunsmith!' She was so pleased that he too smiled. 'Seven sacks of rubbish!'

'He will make new glass from it, of course. The pure metal is so easily melted, and his furnace is always on the go. A skilled gunmaker has all the abilities to spin a hollow hand-mandrel and blow it. That is why gunsmiths often have cheap unmarked glasses for sale, by the back door!'

In spite of the anxieties hanging over them, she felt an extraordinary happiness, walking among the weeds that were now everywhere in the drive. She had worked to create patches of order, only to see her rescue attempts devastated by Thalia De Foe. It was a natural duty to protect Ven. If it was his intention to make her the first-ever female doctor, then that vanity had to be nurtured. His dreams deserved care.

'See, Ven?' She pointed, clapping her hands in joy as butterflies skipped across her view. 'Oh, I love them!'

He listened with unconcealed pleasure to her sudden gush of words, the names of the butterflies she had known as a girl.

'I know that your sainted father loved nature, Ven! As I. See how blessed we are? Why, on the sea marshes I would see them all!' She waited, breathless as a child, pointing them out. 'Gatekeepers! See? And the Essex Skipper: my favourites, always such impudence, like naughty infants! Peacock butterflies, the small Tortoiseshells, and Meadow Browns!' She laughed as memories came flooding back, pulling him quickly through the garden to even wilder areas.

'I only ever remember large Cabbage Whites!'

'I do not believe it for an instant!' she shot back. 'I know from Mistress Prothero's remarks that you used to come as a boy with your father on expeditions, drawing and observing along the coast near Whitehanger and beyond the Sealandings marshes. You *must* have seen the green-veined Whites delving and diving; they love the purple sea lavender blooms!'

'I do not have your love of the sea saltings, Mehala.'

'What nonsense!' She would have none of his modesty. 'The weeds we called fat-hen weeds collect butterflies like a net. We played counting games, who could get the most alighting on one chosen fat-hen!'

'I knew the Clouded Yellows, I think.'

'That is not truly East Anglian. It blows in on summer air, it is said, from lands over the sea.'

'Does it?' His easy manner left him.

'Why, so they say.' She tried to recapture the gaiety of moments before. 'See? A White Admiral! It is not common, not like the Painted Lady or the Speckled Wood or the Large Blue . . .'

He paused. They were in a part of the garden he rarely entered, except when helping Mehala to find medicinal plants. 'Is this where. . . ?'

'My Flora Dial? Yes, Ven.' She glanced back at the house. 'You can see it from . . . from there.'

'I know.' The circle still showed, where Mehala had dug the ground and planted the rich soil with her sequence of plants. 'It signifies eternity in love, I hear.'

She felt her face colour. 'So people say. But it is also pretty, Ven. To have the hours forever marked by a silent blossoming of flowers, hour upon hour, through the day and through the night, telling all nature that love never sleeps.'

'Pretty indeed.'

'Ven. This action Reverend Baring brings against me –'

'Us, Mehala.'

'Us.' She held his arm tighter. 'We have a way out, Ven. The sums are vast, two sureties of fifty pounds in coin. And fees.'

'There is no question of our affording a lawyer.'

She looked away. 'We can survive independently of Sea-landings.'

'You mean leave?'

'No, Ven.' She faced him. 'We have not spoken of my past, before I was rescued. But you realise I was married, and that . . . the person is drowned. I am in fact a widow in law.'

He was uncomfortable. 'Mehala —'

'Please, darling. Let me. My home was at Red Hall, in seamarshes by the Colne and the Blackwater, beyond Suffolk's south border. It was extensive, its herds prolific, the land productive.'

'No, Mehala. Not for me.'

'Please hear me out. I could claim the estates, appoint a good steward. Hunterfield could advise us —'

'No.' He had a streak of stubbornness, remembering Hunterfield's attitude towards her.

'Or I could seek one from Maningtree or elsewhere. We could afford our defence, our surety. I could buy Shalamar, if you desired. Then what could anybody say?'

'Even more than they do now.' He could not help his bitterness. 'A grand lady and a penniless leech? You can hear them say it!'

'They would not say it for long!' Mehala said angrily.

'We can think about it, Mehala.'

She stared at him. Did he mean no? He seemed odd. The White Admiral had gone somewhere. She tried to remember if it was early in the year for them, or was time already too far gone for that loveliest of butterflies, causing it to hurry away in sudden understanding of the lateness of its hour? She shivered slightly.

'What is it, Ven?'

'Oh, the hanging, what has happened since.'

'It must be Hunterfield's warning.' She craned to see his eyes. He was hiding something. 'Or that man Pleasence?'

'Not directly, Mehala.' He gathered himself. 'Did you hear the rumours while we were in Saint Edmundsbury?'

She looked blank. 'Rumours? There are always rumours, about the King, government, coming storms, society scandals . . .'

He resolved on frankness. 'There is rumour of a disease, Mehala. What kind, I do not know, but it seems alarming.'

'Rumour, Ven? How many have we heard since we found each other? Two epidemics a day, and all figments!'

'Except the one, Mehala.'

'Which only proves how rarely truth follows after tattle, Ven!'

She wanted no more upsets. 'And you managed it superbly, earning the gratitude of Hunterfield and Sealandings!'

'This may be different; far worse.' He gestured at a yellowish butterfly that fluttered on a plant nearby. 'You spoke of butterflies blown over the sea by summer winds. It seems some sort of disease might be heading our way.'

Her hand gathered her shawl. 'How did you hear?'

'The talk of the crowd at the hanging was similar to what I overheard at two of the taverns we called at for small beer. I resorted to cunning, Mehala. I wrote to a friend.'

'You wrote? I saw no letter.'

'I wrote it late, the night we returned. And Doctor Ward answered. He practises on the Humber.' Ven apologised, 'I kept back ninepence from our funds, that being the cost of a letter between eighty and a hundred-and-twenty miles.'

'And?'

'It seems there is substance to the stories.'

'Is the sickness already here?'

'Not yet, but it might come, unless something checks it.'

'Can we do anything?'

'I am racking my brains to make some sort of plan.' He smiled, taking her hand with resolution, as Rosie called from the house. 'Keep up a brave face, a physician's first duty.'

'I already know.' They started back. 'It is my nature.'

'Is the ink ready, Mehala?'

'Yes. Not yet strained, so dip from the top of the well. You may then write without sediment coming down the quill.'

She carried the standish to him carefully. The well was whittled by old Trenchard from an oak bowl, and smoothed by coarse sand. 'I lacked enough scrapings from green rust of iron, but added enough gum senegal. I swapped my recipe for sauce of hen lobster for it – Little Jane at Bures House was preparing a brill dish. Your ink has our own nutgalls, pound to a gallon.'

Ven peered into the ink. 'I hate the thought of bullock blood being added.'

Mehala cuffed him playfully. 'Only by the careless housekeeper, Ven Carmichael, not at Shalamar! It worsens the ink but looks better! Just as well you do not run this household!'

He took up a quill to inspect the point. She fired her parting shot. 'And you will find no fancy turmeric staining of *my* quills, thank you!'

'Sorry, sorry.'

Mehala's quills were an emblem of their life, in a way, for her ingenuity was marvellous. French women prepared their quills in a bed of hot sand; Dutch housewives used swift immersion in hot water; the Austrians bested the famed Hamburg women by steaming their goose quills in the vapour from boiling kettles for four hours. Mehala outdid them all by adapting the old English method of quickly plunging her quills into dying embers for less than a heartbeat, and immediately scraping it between the grate's top bar and a knife. In the dark quiet of evening, he had watched her, making her laugh at his ineptitude when copying her skill. She did all the actions in a trice. He split the quill every time. She would cry that all her lovely feathers were being ruined, and forbid him. Her hands were beautiful, scouring each stripped quill with rough dogfish skin, then tying one score per bundle. This quill was perfect, as everything touched by Mehala. He brought himself to, for postponing a hard duty.

He dipped the quill in the ink, and wrote to the Lord of Sealandings.

Sir,

It has come to my notice that disease afflicts the Baltic ports, though of its nature I am yet ignorant. I shall make endeavour to ascertain its true character from medical correspondents, and report when I have sure news.

Until then, Sir, I urge that you impose an order on the harbour imposing quarantine on any ship arriving at any landfall within your jurisdiction, expressing my willingness to assist the execution of such in any manner.

I remain, Sir,

Your humble servant,

He read the letter several times. Further steps were impossible, lacking evidence. He could only warn. Would there ever come a day when health was protected throughout the Kingdom, based on sure foreknowledge? London doctors seemed to aim at such a hope, but with such vagueness that he felt no optimism.

'Mehala,' he called, rising to show her his letter. She was always wiser than he. He was halfway along the corridor in search of her when he halted, stricken with guilt. He had forgotten to wash the quill's tip in the steam-water she laid to hand for the purpose, but sighed and went on. Perhaps she would not notice. A forlorn hope, for she always did.

17

UGLINESS, JUDITH BLAKER thought with satisfaction as she watched Prettiance approach, is that, whatever her youth, her features will deny her a favourable first impression. This negates a shapely girl's advantage. Youth is far more treacherous than age. Barely sixteen, Prettiance looked attractive from a distance, but once her features came clearly into view she was finished.

Yet a spy, especially one in Carradine Manor, needs less beauty than slyness, and Prettiance had that in plenty. She had an even greater worth, for she was related – thank God, not closely! – and blood counted more than money or friendship among the Romany.

'Yes?' She knew who had come even before Prettiance spoke.

'The *piro-mengro*, Judith,' the maid said with casual insolence. 'The one that thinks himself a *rashi*.'

'Not in Romany,' Judith said, furious her instruction was ignored. The travelling man, that thinks himself a priest. Not too wild a description of Endercotte, however. 'And keep your voice down. Remember you are a servant, and I mistress.'

'*Tugnis amande!*' Prettiance cried, but with the same sluttish indifference that had Judith fuming. 'Woe is me! I forget you are a grand *gorgio* lady. Shall I admit him?'

Judith retained her composure. She would punish the girl in her own time. 'Not here. In the great hall.'

'He's from *Match-Eneskey Gav*, m'lady.' Prettiance went to the door, deliberately switching her skirts to taunt. 'Yarmouth, the Town of Fish. Be on your guard for slipperiness.'

'Get out!'

Judith watched the trollop pause before the door mirror to adjust the puffed caul of her mob cap before sauntering out. Prettiance deliberately allowed the double door to slam. For an instant Judith sat in rage, eyes closed.

She herself – *she*, unaided – had come to Sealandings off the road, literally without prospect or post. True to her tenets, she had schemed to find a rich place, a situation among the *gorgios*, and was now one of the most influential ladies in the Eastern Hundreds. An eligible landowner, of a highly esteemed local family of lineage, was her lover, and she had manipulated him into being a virtual puppet.

She glared at the blue and gold patterns on the doors through which that young bitch had just swept – barely seen her sixteenth birthday and flouting the mistress of the house!

Had she been too loyal to her kin? The Carradine estates were peopled with her tribe. The *yag-engroes*, the gamekeepers, were cousins, and the *wardo-mescroes*, the carters and coopers, were also of her clan. On the northern aspect of Sealandings, where Carradine lands lay in a great crescent from the sea saltings inland, her own relatives worked in peace, unhindered by the subtle conflict of competing *gorgios* and Romany. Here they were in Paradise, did they but know it – thanks to her, Judith, alone. Yet she was taunted and even rebuked by that chit Prettiance, ugly as sin and ignorant as a mare. She would be starving on some heathland but for the charity of Judith Blaker.

She had clearly been too soft, on staff, on Carradine. It was time she forced the man to marry her, instead of this.

Rising, she removed her muffetees from her wrists, rang the bell-pull for a maid to open the door, then glided out.

Endercotte was standing beside the great door, for all the world as if he had just been admitted from that direction instead of through the servant entrance beside the great kitchens. A sense of theatricality, Judith observed, making a surprisingly favourable impression. A woman always approved the right display, in flesh, fish, or fowl. Or even in a puritanical rabble-rouser.

The man's skeletal frame accorded well with his narrow visage, his cheeks indrawn as if he sucked some astringent berries. His beard was less stubble than a sparse mat of feeble threads, and he wore black. His white Geneva collar, striking the white of his eyes, created a sense of unrelenting aggression, yet he bowed with a meekness that would have been laughable if Judith did not know what kind of man he was.

'Kemp Endercotte, your servant – after the Lord's.'

'Endercotte.' She took in his manner. Not servile but taut, quivering with barely controlled passion. Interesting but uncertain, and uncertainty to a woman meant trouble. 'Yes?'

'Mistress,' the man intoned on cue, 'I come to make abject apology for the intrusion I caused upon your pique nique gaiety.'

She acknowledged this. He had learned his words well enough, but the thought of folk actually enjoying themselves he found a bitter pill. How curious some men are, she thought, intrigued. What had that Prettiance said, about his coming from Yarmouth? She supposed it would be the greater Yarmouth, a port thriving enough for bawds and sin, but not to rear a holy roarer like this.

'Come, Endercotte. We shall perambulate.'

They left the house by the rear, and slowly moved to the paved walk above the ornamental gardens. She smiled. In the distance she counted no fewer than six of her own people working diligently. In the estate, almost forty. An army! And here was another recruit, come for other reasons than money, ties of blood, or ambition. As if there were anything else! Clearly a deranged fool, but one that would be useful.

'You know the girl Mehala?'

'I do.'

Judith smiled. His sepulchral timbre moderated at Mehala's name. It was an effect the bitch had. Even over a preacher, the mare extended her malign influence. Well, not for long.

'What do you know exactly?'

'I know her sins, mistress.' He seemed to choke, but went on. 'She cohabits with one Carmichael, a so-say apothecary-cum-surgeon of Sealandings, a leech of ill fame.'

'Why do you say so?'

'Not only is he a sinner against the Lord, he is a leveller, intent on the destruction of society! He treats without fee. He opposes sicknesses, God's punishment. His avowed intent is to alleviate pain, and relieve poverty!'

She concurred with a sad smile. 'I feel exactly as you do, Endercotte. There is a viper in our midst –'

'Who,' the preacher cut in harshly, 'by her foul example leads the mad quack astray. She erodes the structures by which our world is sustained! And what is done?'

She was fascinated in spite of herself. The man seemed to grow taller. A fleck of spittle whitened to foam, his thin lips trembling, his eyes becoming red as fire.

'We can do so little, Master Endercotte.' She almost whispered the words. The man had a certain grim power. She could imagine the effects he had on an illiterate crowd.

'So little?' he thundered, raising his arm. 'Those who do not do their uttermost in the name of the Lord condone sin! They are as mortally evil as the sinners who perpetrate sacrilege to the limits of swinishness!'

'What can be done against?' she prompted.

'Mehala can be extirpated!' he cried. She found herself actually shrinking. 'She and her satanic familiar can be driven out! She can be brought before the watchers of God, who are unafraid to rise up and condemn for the Lord!'

'How?' she whispered.

'By allowing it!' He quietened, regained his former demeanour. 'Simply by allowing it, Mistress Blaker.'

'But allowing what?'

'Allowing her to be seen for what she is,' he said. 'Mehala cannot have come from the sea, and in a single year captivate all on whom she turns her face! It is not humanly possible.'

'Humanly?'

'Only by powers above life, mistress.'

She thought quickly, seeing Carradine dismounting by the stables at the end of the great east lawns. He must have ridden from the sea coast, or he would have arrived at the western stables, where she had expected him. She stored the thought. 'You shall have your wish, Endercotte,' she promised swiftly. 'But say nothing as yet. A time will come, and soon. Tell me what you will need.'

He smiled, like a sleet storm in midwinter. 'The word of God, mistress, and the permission of the Lord of Sealandings.'

'And then?'

'Then,' he said, losing his smile, exaltation in his unseeing eyes, 'then the sinners shall be delivered unto me.' He paused. 'You will be able to find me –'

It was her turn to smile. 'I shall know where you are every second, Master Endercotte. When I want you, I shall send.'

For an instant he seemed taken aback, then he nodded and went striding round the side of the house. She adjusted her black satin Venetian cloak, and tripped down the terrace steps to meet Carradine. He had seen the preacher leave, but she had ready the explanation for his visit. Endercotte was a superb find, whose worth would soon be proved in the flame and the rope.

'Spirits of nitre?'

The gunsmith was pleased to see Carmichael. Sealandings being a small coastal town, with every inhabitant busy, there was little time for social intercourse except with neighbours. With Eldridge the unpleasant butcher on one side, and Tizzard the elderly haberdasher on the other, Bartholomew Hast had lately felt an undue restlessness shadowing his usually sunny disposition.

'Yes. Only a small quantity, for a trial.'

Hast was beating metal wire on a heated mandrel, sweating profusely. Young Jed Baines, barely ten years, was feeding the wire. He a Baines, the only one to shun the sea for a land trade. It was his older brother Hal who, on the slow Yorkshire lugger *The Jaunty*, had found Mehala in the waters.

The gunmaker's furnace was in a workshop at the rear of the premises that faced onto Market Square. Hast had the building freehold, by a bequest of moneys from the famous Colchester gunsmithing family of Hasts, to which he was cousin. He had served his apprenticeship there, and was enviable for his sure expertise, his open friendliness.

'Will you have tea, Doctor?' Hast beat with his hammer, ignoring the sparks flying. Ven shook his head and stepped away a pace. 'Old Mistress Gomme there can hurry to your service.'

'No thank you.' Ven joined in the laughter. Mistress Gomme wagged a finger at the gunmaker. Her husband was an elderly balding man whose work lay in planing walnut stock blanks from bare wood, in an alcove. 'I am in haste.'

'Haste? For a drop of aqua fortis?'

Hast stopped work, appraising Ven. This was the first real call he had made. Mehala had come once, asking for help, but in a more turbulent time. Hast could not quite make Ven out. Shoddy in spite of the patches and sprucing that Mehala seemed to spend her time on, he was so diffident that he irritated rather than reassured. Yet there had been times – the cattle plague that had almost extinguished Sealandings, an amputation in a sinking ship in autumnal storms, the resolve with which he had faced mob hatred – that gave the lie to his stuttering.

'I s'll get the flask, Master!' Jed sprang up eagerly.

'You s'll do no such thing!' Hast grinned at Carmichael. 'He be my Blue Monday apprentice, jack-o'sleep and master of nod! I pay good money to hire idleness!'

Hast's perennial joke, that he alone worked here, gave his three helpers continual amusement. Blue Monday, that preceded Lent, was a traditional holiday countrywide. The gunsmith saw Ven start to fumble for coins. He put aside his two-pound hammer and cast his leather apron. Naked to the waist, his trunk shone with sweat, speckles of light in the furnace glow.

'Come through, Doctor.'

Ven followed to the shop, by contrast a cool airy place but dour with chains that held the weapons along one wall.

Hast caught Ven's glance. 'You would be astonished at how many visiting folk take more notice of my precautions – locks, chains, door grilles – than look at my wares, Doctor!'

'You mean they come to see if they might steal?'

Hast laughed. 'Never lose your innocence, Doctor! It pleases me that Sealandings has at least one honest soul!' He sobered. 'Yes, robbers in abundance, especially when Market Square is filled with pedlars, licensed or no!'

The country had suffered a great deal since the ending of the wars against Tyrant Napoleon. The countryside was plagued with footpads and robbers, and vagrants however innocent were looked upon with mistrust everywhere. It was said that even in the outskirts of London ladies now walked with minute muff pistols for protection.

'Spirits of nitre, Doctor. How much a quantity?'

Ven hesitated, and brought out a silver sixpence. 'Enough to render this fluid. Is that possible?'

Hast examined the coin, puzzled. 'An ordinary sixpence.'

'Yes. I have heard that a compound may be formed of its silver by spiritous activity in the nitre.'

Hast was doubtful. 'It is true that spiritous fluids corrode metals. Why would you want the compound?'

'I shall test it on my eye.' Ven explained, becoming animated. 'I expect gossip has already reached you, of the sick boy sent to the Poor House from some school?'

'Rustonhall.' Hast nodded. 'I heard. An infamous place.'

'The boy is Clement Wellins. His fees went unpaid, so he was sent to be lodged in the workhouse. The boy's eyes were quite blind from purulent disease. I have cleaned him with salt lotions several times a day, but the purulence continues. I remember something from my student days after leaving the London. I worked for an elderly physician, Doctor Arbuthnot, who used nitrate of silver on the eyes of foreign seamen at London Docks. Many had a strange granularity of the eye, and were so blind that they walked with the head turned – their corneas were quite opaque from some fermentation along diseased –'

'Please, Doctor.' Hast was agitated. It was extraordinary how swiftly this medical ditherer became an enthusiast explaining his gruesome work. 'I would rather not hear details. Your compound is to make a treatment?'

'Yes.' Ven was disappointed, as well as rather curious. Bartholomew Hast was strangely pale, and now sitting on the serving stool behind the counter. How odd. Such a strong man, in the fullness of his muscular youth, yet wilting at the simplest description of treating an ailment. Or was it perhaps some ague that Hast had acquired out in the countryside? Or the change from the heat to the chill of the shop? 'Arbuthnot's treatment might eradicate the pus, by washing the eye fornices –'

'I shall give you the nitrous spirit, Doctor.'

'Give? But I can pay, Mr Hast.'

The gunmaker looked up from the stool. 'There is no charge, Doctor.' His hands were trembling and his pallor now extreme.

Ven reached for his hand, found it clammy and cold. 'Mr Hast,' he said solemnly. 'You should go and lie down. The cold air does not suit, after leaving the hot workshop –'

'Ven,' the gunmaker said wearily, 'please go and make your trial with your sixpence and the spirit, and let me get on.'

'Very well. Thank you.' Ven took the small flask, and went towards the door. 'You are so busy, and generous. Perhaps we can resume our conversation another time? I am sure you would find my account of eye purulence –'

'Excuse me, Doctor.' Hast left hurriedly. Ven called an anxious goodbye, and young Jed came to unlock and let him leave.

'Shall I not go through the workshop, and say my farewells to the Gommes, Jed?'

'I shall say them for you, Doctor.' Jed was grinning. 'You must leave by a different door than you arrive.'

'Ah. I had forgot the custom.'

He left, not hearing Bartholomew Hast throwing up in the privy beyond the furnace room.

18

BACK AT SHALAMAR that evening, the excitement in the kitchen was intense. Clement was desperate to see but had to accept the commentary. Mehala was rather frightened, remembering how she once assisted Ven to brew some dangerous fluids and catch the evolving chlorinaceous gas. Anxiously she sought his reassurance that this experiment would not be so dangerous.

Ven was almost as worried. 'I do not know the outcome, Mehala. We did have lectures on chemical philosophy, but I afforded to go only to one, they being among the most expensive. It was incomprehensible, I am ashamed to say. I learned what little I know from overhearing earnest students talking in the Black Bull tavern in Whitechapel.'

Mehala gazed at the small container with its oily fluid, and held Rosie and the boy away. She had procured a small porcelain dish. Its margin was cracked but its base was intact.

'The principle, as far as I remember, is that spirits of nitre can be decomposed somehow by silver. In the absence of pure silver, we can offer it sixpences or threepenny pieces.'

'Will we get our money back, Ven?'

'I should be afeared to use them,' Rosie said quietly. She was improving with every moment. Mehala had given her almost complete responsibility for the boy, and had even given her a gentle but unfounded scolding for tardiness, so making Clement and the girl complicitors against tyranny.

'Alas, Rosie. If my experiment works, they will be gone.'

'Gone where, Ven?' Mehala asked. A custom was growing for apothecaries and druggists to display imposing coloured bottles openly in their windows, to imply wisdom and knowledge. Some said it was nothing more than trumpery, as in fairgrounds, but the suggestion of magic still clung to the unknown.

'Into the aqua fortis. That is the acid's proper name.' Ven ran his fingers through his disordered thatch. 'We must see what happens. I shall place some drops of the aqua fortis in the dish, and carefully drop in our smallest silver coin.'

'It will not explode?'

'I have heard not, Mahala. It should accept its own decomposition, and give us the substance.' Ven sat on the bench facing them, and pulled Clement close to sit beside him. 'Look at Clement's eyes.'

They still ran yellowish, and had to be bathed each morning to part the lids. Pus, solidifying each night, formed hard mats of the lashes. Already one eyelid was showing an ugly twist along its margin where scar tissue deformed the edge.

'You can see a little, Clement? Tell me truthfully.'

'Not really, Doctor. A faint shining, as if under water.'

'This is the purpose of our experiment.' Ven did not quite know how to begin. Truth was often horrid in medicine. For a moment he remembered old Doctor Arbuthnot and almost smiled at the memory of the old man, sitting there uncoiling his catheter from inside his hat before his study fire.

'See these books, m'boy?' he would bark, breathless on account of his corpulence, foot on his gout stool. His study was lined with tomes. 'Hopeless, the lot of them! Not a medical one worth reading – except those we cannot even translate!'

'You mean Galen, Sir?' Ven would ask, hoping to keep the old cynic garrulous, then he learned gems of honesty about medicine.

'Galen?' Arbuthnot had pondered. 'The slavishness with which hospitals tout his name is ridiculous. Everything hospitals do, however cruel and larded with ignorance, is justified by saying that Galen said *this* and Galen said *that*. Balderdash. Teaching is a collection of fables, m'boy.'

'I would give a great deal to be able to study Galen's works,' Ven remembered saying with passion, and was hurt to hear the old doctor emit a bark of laughter.

'Did you say *study*? There on the shelf is Doctor Hooper's famous *Lexicon Medicum*. Take it down. Read what that inestimable physician of St Mary-Le-Bone Infirmary says about Galen – and Hooper as ignorant as the rest of us! Son, Galen was a vicious competitor, whose sole aim was to do down his fellow doctors, m'boy! Made such a mystery of our pathetic inept craft that he hoodwinked us for fifteen hundred years! A nasty ambitionist.' Arbuthnot's eyes had twinkled as he flung back a glass of red Portugal. 'Like us!'

Ven had gazed in wonder at the bookshelves, admiring their leather bindings in the firelight. 'Is there none worth reading?'

'Indeed there is! But he is beyond us, unless you know the eastern tongues. His name is Avicenna, a man from Chorasan. He studied at a city of Persia called Bagdat. A doctor at eighteen! Wrote that thing up there, enormous *Canon of Medicine*.' Arbuthnot grunted as Ven hesitated, daring to take the remarks as an invitation to examine the volumes. 'No good, m'boy. It is in their heathen script, unreadable to us . . .' his eyes showed a disturbing cynical shrewdness, '. . . *civilised* people!'

'Is it so marvellous?'

'I had a traveller once from the eastern ships, a polyglot who could hardly read but could talk any damned tongue on earth. He fumbled a few passages out for me, until I cured the pagan swine and he left. Cataract.' The old man sighed. 'Can you believe it? Avicenna was performing cataract operations – actually cutting out the thickened, opaque lens from blind eyes – before William The Bastard came from Normandy!'

Ven was nonplussed. 'There is no treatment for cataract!'

'It seems logical, does it not?' The old doctor was almost talking to himself by now. 'The lens goes opaque, so simply cut it out, and the eye sees once more!'

'Is that in Doctor Avicenna's book, sir?'

'It seems so.' Ven could not tell if the old man was weeping, or if his rheumy old eyes were just watering. 'The terrible question comes to me some nights, what else is in Avicenna's writings, that we have not yet even begun to learn? So I trust nothing but what I see myself, m'boy.'

The next day Doctor Arbuthnot had showed him how to treat serious eye infections with a silver salt. The case had been a prostitute from Aldgate, who plied her trade near the Minories, serving the evening carriage trade by Aldgate Pump. It had been successful, and Ven had carried out the same treatment on several other cases. It seemed epochs away from the kitchen at Shalamar, where the three awaited his explanation.

'This is our experiment,' he resumed, coming to. 'I shall tell it how I learned from the old doctor. Take silver into aqua fortis. It evaporates and deposits crystals. London doctors may actually buy that deposit under the name of *causticum lunare* – lunar caustic – in sticks fashioned inside small iron tubes, for air blackens the crystals and makes them insoluble. That old name *luna* means silver. We doctors always hide our ignorance!'

He smiled to make a joke, but recognised his words as the old physician's cynicism. Mehala was watching closely. Sometimes Ven's bitterness was barely concealed. She spoke up.

'Should we not use the coins to buy the caustic?'

'From where, Mehala? Sealandings has no apothecary. In any case, who can tell if some scoundrel druggist cheats, if we send on the mailcoach for the substance? I do not know how to test physics for honesty. Many medicaments are simply fradulent. The lunar caustic I shall make – if we succeed – will at least be the true material. And it will take less time. We shall soon have the substance.' He had heard of a newly invented instrument called an eriometer, used for optical measurement of cotton fibres, that might serve to view the crystals in detail, but that too was wishful thinking.

'It is to put in my eyes, Doctor?' Clement asked.

'Yes. But first I shall test it in my own, lest it harm.'

He ignored Mehala's sharp breath, and unstoppered Hast's container, pouring some aqua fortis into the dish. Fumes rose. He pushed the dish to the table centre. He slid a coin down the side of the dish so it entered the liquid without a splash.

The coin seemed to agitate the fluid. 'Bubbles, and a slight fuming, accompany the process,' he guessed, trying to recall the words of the richer fellow students on the subject. 'Aqua fortis is dangerous to the skin.'

Rosie quietly began to describe to Clement what Ven was doing as the second coin was added, then more fluid was poured into the dish, then a third coin.

The experiment was finished after two hours, during which they sat watching the dish. It had grown hot. Rosie made some camomile infusion, and as they drank Ven wistfully told how he longed for the means to test if acid remained on the crystals.

'Lacmus is a marvellous substance, I hear. It comes from the Auvergne, a place in France with mountains where a moss plant grows in rock cavities. A yellow dye-stuff it is. The smallest drop turns bright yellow if acid remains. It goes blue with caustics, that philosophers call alkaline. It is imported from Holland.' He smiled with a confidence he did not feel. 'I shall evaporate this mess in your dish, Mehala, giving the crystals time to form, then repeat the same with water, as if washing them free of the aqua fortis. Dissolved in ordinary water, the crystals should be safe to run under my eyelids, and later under Clement's!'

'Are you sure, Ven?' Mehala asked, knowing the answer.

'No.' Carefully he carried the dish across to the kitchen range where the fire was now fading to a glow. He placed the dish by the black iron roasting jack. 'So far, our experiment seems successful, for the silver coins have vanished and the liquid does not seem to fume anything like as much.'

The crystals formed before midnight. Ven remembered the word rhombic, but did not know what it meant. He added boiled water from Mehala's kettle and they successfully dissolved. Rosie took Clement off to put him to bed, and soon after she too said her goodnights, leaving Mehala with Ven to watch the dish.

Two evaporations were complete by four in the morning. Ven made a solution with the crystals' weight of water. Its taste was metallic and bitter. Was that too strong? He added twice that volume, counting drops. Before Mehala could protest he dipped his finger in and touched it to his eyelid.

It stung, and made his eye run with tears. He looked in the piece of cheval reflecting glass. Mehala held a guttering flame of a hog-fat rush lit from the embers, and saw that his eye looked untroubled. His vision was unimpaired.

Mehala washed Bartholomew's container out, testing it for traces of the aqua fortis by touching her tongue to the rim before giving it a final rinse. She poured the final colourless solution into the vial, and with relief inserted the stopper.

At seven o'clock next morning, Mehala made a small pouring vessel, an undine, from clay under Ven's direction, and fashioned a tiny spout from a hollowed reed.

Clement's eyes were washed clean and ungummed of their sticky yellow pus by Mehala's latherwort-plant soap in warm water, then given their first treatment. He complained of no real pain, and Ven showed Mehala how to perform the treatment. Clement made fun of her by calling her Doctor and Surgeon, but he went too far and called her Quack Mehala, receiving a laughing rebuke for his levity.

19

BEYOND ONE SIDE of the workhouse stood a mixed orchard of pear and apple trees, Ven saw with pleasure. That meant a regular supply of fruit for the inmates.

'You can store hard fruits, Mehala,' he enthused as they approached. 'The folk can have a goodly supply.'

'There seems to be fewer,' Mehala observed.

'Fewer?' Ven was excited at the prospect of starting his regular visits. 'They will probably be at their ablutions round the rear.'

'Children, and men.' Mehala indicated the vegetable fields to the left and down towards the shallow vale where woods began. 'How many did Pleasence say?'

'You see, Mehala,' Ven said, serious, 'most doctors, fashionable surgeons and physicians alike, would accuse me of meddling in the Almighty's plans. But I reject their opinions.'

'You had that argument when you were a student?' Mehala asked, still scanning the fields and the workhouse building.

'Indeed! Many claimed that prevention was a sin, worse than neglecting the diseases themselves! I think it proper to care for the healthy as well as the sick. Think of the benefits to children!'

'Ven,' Mehala said quietly, 'the looms are silent.'

'Looms?'

'Handlooms, beyond the main long room.'

Ven smiled, confident nothing would be found amiss. 'Do not worry, Mehala. We have put paid to Pleasence's subterfuges!'

'Possibly. I hope so, Ven.'

He thought her misgivings too mistrustful, and said so. 'We have shown the man just how serious we are!'

'Perhaps, Ven.'

He laughed outright. 'What *is* this, Mehala? Possibly? Perhaps? No, Mehala, we are certain!'

She smiled at his exuberance and stood aside as he entered, reverting to their roles of servant and master.

The rag picking was proceeding at only half the pace, with scarcely a dozen women and children at the benches. The mounds of discarded materials were even larger, though, and the air as foul and reeking of night soil as before. Mehala hurried to open windows.

'Mistress,' Ven asked a woman, 'where are the other inmates?'

'They are gone to work, sir.'

'It is only seven o'clock. Where to?'

'They were taken by the master, Mr Pleasence.'

Mehala moved ahead, speaking quietly to the women, fondling the children. One women was carrying, Ven observed, some six months. She had a racking cough. He bade her sit by a window.

'Ven,' Mehala came to whisper. 'The windows are sealed.'

Gnats and mosquitoes whined in the air. Several of the younger children had blotched faces, almost as if sickening with pox. Their exposed arms and legs were excoriated, showing where they had scratched at the fleas and lice during their night hours.

'Nothing has been done!' Ven was aghast.

'You wanted to inspect the beds, Doctor.'

'Yes.' He went through to the sleeping areas. There, handlooms had been set up, the pallets raised against the walls.

Ven stood back in the doorway, extending a hand to bar Mehala. He stamped suddenly on the plank flooring, and stood away, stooping to look at knee height.

'Mehala? See that flickering?'

Mehala stooped with him, puzzled, then her brow cleared. 'There is a faint shimmering, Ven, as if . . .'

'. . . the floor was covered with fleas. They are always roused by stamping on floorboards.' He straightened. 'There will not be one inmate free of them. And lice also.'

He left while Mehala spoke with the rag pickers. Outside, he drew in the fresh air and walked round the buildings.

He knocked on the house's side door. Pleasence himself opened it. He wore a wrap-rascal, as if he had just returned home.

'Ah, our good leech!' He was effusive, and stepped out quickly. 'You have come to make your visit, then?'

'Mr Pleasence. What improvements have you made since I called?'

'Well, I have sent several of the inmates out harvesting, for the fresh sea breezes! You will understand, a country man like us all!'

'The windows are sealed. The rag pickers get no air.'

'Ah, well, that is good modern practice, Doctor!' Pleasence led the way. 'Can you imagine if there was a wild wind swirling around the place, how thick the air would be with dust? Very light stuff, cottons and wools! Those idlers would make no progress at all.'

'Are you sure?'

'Sure?' Pleasence guided Ven by the arm. 'Have I not tried it a score of times, a hundred? Everything these modern days must be efficiency, Doctor. I am sure you will agree!'

'Have you discussed this with the parish churchwardens?'

'A thousand times! They are in full agreement!' Pleasence's heartiness dropped and he became serious. 'I am very like you, Doctor Carmichael, in more ways than one! The milk of human kindness is in our souls. But the churchwardens, the payers of the Poors' Rate in Sealandings, those who own property, why, they maintain places such as this, the charity school, heaven knows what else. They rule us, and insist on economy.' He resumed walking, shaking his head dolefully. 'Nothing would please me more than to let the inmates lie about the live-long day, breathing God's good clean air, sitting smoking their tobaccos, sporting themselves in games. But the churchwardens? The overseers? What would *they* say?'

'I am concerned, Mr Pleasence, by the number in there who have serious coughing ailments.'

'Their rising time, as your young lady reminded us recently, is six o'clock, to work until six or four of the afternoon, depending on the season.' Pleasence wagged his head, sighing, showing Ven the progress made in the orchard. Six men and two small children were working, picking the fruit into wicker baskets. 'See? Labour is progress!'

'The children look cachectic – debilitated, underfed.'

Pleasence was friendly and affable. 'Doctor, they cannot be provided with separate accommodation. It is the rule. They cannot be given special treatment. That too is the rule. Feeding?' He was the picture of compassion. Ven watched him. 'Children under nine years are to be fed *at discretion*. I quote the law. Where do you think that puts me, Doctor? Having to find for their little mouths, yet there is no proper column in which to write their demands – and they incessantly clamour for food.' He smiled fondly. 'Yet we are one great wholesome family.'

'How constrained are you by the churchwardens?'

Pleasence shrugged. 'Totally, sir, totally!' He plucked Ven's sleeve, drawing him closer for a confidentiality. 'Hear this, Doctor: if there was, say, a fit and able-bodied child, as they term it, of nine, who refused to work for perhaps a single hour – picking fruit, such as you have just seen. Now, what would you say to such a recalcitrant?'

'Urge him to go with the others?'

'Ah, Doctor!' Pleasence gave a sad, knowing laugh. 'That is what *you* might say, in your kindness! And I! But the church-wardens? They invoke the law. And you know what the law says on this point?'

'No?'

'The law *insists* that youth must be committed to gaol, or to the House of Correction for hard labour. And for how long? Twenty-one days!' He blew his nose on a puce handkerchief.

'It does?'

'As God is our judge, Doctor. You see what I do here? My policy is to encourage compliance with the churchwardens' interpreta-tion of the law! By encouraging obedience, I save these poor folk from worse! By *making* a youngster work for that one hour, I rescue him from hard labour in the worst conditions in the world!'

Ven was indecisive. 'Even so, Mr Pleasence, I do urge you to provide them with cleaner conditions.'

'They are spotless, Doctor!' Pleasence was shocked. 'Show me one who is not! I shall punish him myself!'

'No, you misunderstand. I want the lice and fleas eradicated.'

'Fleas? Lice?' The man was honestly puzzled. 'Everybody has them! They are everywhere, on every living thing! All God's creatures, from birds to the lowest crawling thing!'

Ven smiled. 'That seems to be true, but need not. I shall have those creatures eliminated, Mr Pleasence. At my expense. It will become a tribute to you and your management of this work-house.'

'It can never be done, Doctor! Kings, queens, even perhaps

Christ himself, had them. They are a vehicle for health, and prompt us to greater activity!'

'Yes, that is said.'

'They are even called "Nature's Friends" !'

'That *is* one theory,' Ven said pleasantly. 'But think how marvellous it will look, Mr Pleasence! Any visitor would be proud to say they visited your workhouse, a model of cleanliness! And at a time when workhouses are being amalgamated.'

'You mean, as in Nacton?' The man was suddenly uneasy.

It was Ven's turn to sigh. 'Gilbert's Act of 1782 has encouraged incorporation, Mr Pleasence. It puts workhouse masters out of employment!'

'I have heard so.' Pleasence wondered where this led.

'Can you imagine it?' Ven gestured at the workhouse complex. 'All these buildings, the poor hard at work, your house there with all its comforts, and your wages, all gone?'

'Gone?' Pleasence croaked.

'That is incorporation. Separate Hundreds combine to set up a House of Industry. Now *there* is efficiency!'

'But –'

'But indeed!' Ven said regretfully, working out his argument. 'They will never allow you to take charge of a House of Industry if Maidborough and Sealandings incorporate.'

'No.' He was outraged, but trying to keep calm.

Ven said, as if in sorrow, 'Such a highly paid appointment will go to some official with connections, as in Samford to the south, Blything, Lothingland, Wangford. In this life, Mr Pleasence, it is always the decent individual who suffers! You do see we must prevent such a move?'

Pleasence's complaint was almost strangled. 'Have you heard incorporation is likely?'

'Efficiency, Pleasence! Fight them with their own weapons!'

'But how?'

Ven looked about as if for eavesdroppers. 'Supposing that officials came to inspect your workhouse. What would impress them?'

'Efficiency? Cheapness?'

'And cleanliness, Mr Pleasence! Cleanliness *is* next to godliness, is it not? And might it prove your diligence in the welfare of these inmates, however idle and stupid they are? The august visitors would be sure to leave highly impressed!'

'True, Doctor!' The man was beside himself with eagerness. 'How do we go about it?'

'I shall do it for you, Mr Pleasence.' Ven reached out and shook Pleasence's hand fervently. 'Never fear. We shall succeed.'

'Thank you, Doctor!' He turned with Ven, and almost bumped into Mehala who was standing listening. 'I shall expect another visit from you soon, then?'

'Indeed you must.'

'Thank you for your visit, Doctor.'

Ven paused as if in afterthought. 'Oh, Mr Pleasence, one thing. Have you the list of all your inmates? Then I could estimate the materials, physic, unguents, that might be needed.'

Pleasence's ingratiating smile faded. 'I *think* I could have a copy prepared soon, Doctor.'

'And I might receive it, say, by four o'clock today, then?'

'Very well.' The concession was forced from him.

'And it will be accurate in all respects?'

'Of course, Doctor.'

'Thank you, Mr Pleasence.' Ven smiled at the workhouse master. 'We must save the inmates as best we can!'

The man watched them go, staring doubtfully after Ven and wondering if there had been any double meaning in his words.

Out of earshot, Mehala heaved a sigh of relief. 'Ven Carmichael, I have misjudged you!'

'Me? How so?' He was quiet.

'I heard almost every word. At first I was astonished you were hoodwinked so easily by that reptile. Then I realised.'

'Mmmh?'

'Do not play the innocent, sir!' Mehala cried softly, hugging his arm. 'You deceived that deceiver, bent him to your will by a mixture of half-truths and evasions!'

'You misheard, Mehala.' He gazed at her with equanimity. 'But now we have a serious task ahead – to cleanse that poor place, make all pristine and free of body lice and such kin.'

'Is there such urgency, Ven?'

'Yes.' He took in the movements of the trees, the bright weather, the reflection of the North Sea. 'I am becoming disturbed, Mehala.

That ship, remember, the brig-sloop from the Baltic? I heard tales of diseases across the Baltic Sea from the crew.'

'Could such sickness come to Sealandings?'

He tried to allay her alarm. 'Nobody knows how to predict illness, or prevent them. Do you remember the prisoners?'

'At Edmundsbury? Yes, poor things.'

'They will suffer from gaol fever, the epidemic typhus we all know. It is fearsome, but we who are not prisoners, or inmates in lunatic hospitals like Bedlam, or in workhouses, rejoice because it mostly kills *in* such establishments.'

'Ven?' She slowed, looking into his face. 'You are afraid.'

'I have no real reasons, so can take none to the authorities. But yes, Mehala. I am frightened for what might come.'

20

THE RACE MEETING was Carradine's notion. On account of his former debtor's status, however, he had obtained Sir Charles Golding's agreement to champion the cause. It was run on the heath beyond Calling Farm. Prothero's lands were among the most extensive, spreading round the public livestock field, lately donated by Hunterfield for the use of drovers and local horse fairs, to the borders of Carradine's estates.

'Who knows?' Sir Charles asked Percy Carmady as they rode to the meeting. 'This might be our answer to, what, the Duke of Richmond's races at Goodwood!'

'Has Sealandings enough society, Charles?' Carmady asked. 'His Grace of Richmond's famous park was ideal country even back in 1802 when they began, nigh thirty years since.'

He rode uncomfortably. It was true what they said – horses were hideous at both ends and damned awkward in the middle – but as a seafaring man he naturally thought ill of anything caballine.

'Carradine's land has space, good runs.' Golding was only slightly tipsy, and not above enjoying a jibe or two at another's expense. 'Is not this diverting, Carmady?' He indicated the scene on the heath. 'Over sixty people here, the ladies at their prettiest, the gentlemen on their best behaviour?'

'Splendid indeed,' Percy Carmady conceded. Nearer three hundred, by his count, excluding the children. But fashionable gentry only mentioned – in fact, only *saw* – those of high degree, and not the commonalty. A fine judge Golding would make at sea, where skill, not breeding, mattered.

'We have a grand tented structure for our victuals, Percy.' Golding was pleased, hoping to create a good impression on the visitor, who was Hunterfield's guest. 'The ladies have argued about the decorations for a fortnight.' Such as would speak with Judith Blaker, he thought with more candour.

'As long as I am spared taking part,' Percy Carmady cautioned. 'I saw Newmarket's races only last year, and was dismayed by the ferocity of the riders, with royalty looking on!'

'Do not compare Sealandings with that Cambridgeshire sprawl, Carmady,' Golding answered as they breasted a rise and viewed the course marked out with bunting. 'When King Charles the Second established a stand-house for horse races there in 1667, it was immediately sanctified by a burnt sacrifice! Sealandings cannot hope for such a stroke of luck!'

The King's stand had been accidentally burnt down in the March races of 1683, necessitating his early return to London. The timely accident had saved him from the infamous Rye House Plot.

'Sealandings has more favourable aspects,' Percy praised kindly. 'The sea air, the harbour, a healthy, loyal town.' He would rather have reined in to watch jugglers spinning their coloured cudgels for the amusement of the crowds, but Golding was anxious to get to the victuals and urged him to canter.

'Carradine wants a word with you particularly, Carmady!' Golding called. 'He will already be at the wine! We must get apace lest he drinks every drop before we arrive!'

Aye, Carmady thought wryly, and there will never be enough wine for your likes, Golding. He had seen much addiction to Mistress Drink at sea, and recognised that vicious servitude only too well. It was life slavery, without remission.

'A word? What about?'

A large gathering of coaches clustered about the coloured tents adorned with brilliant gonfalons near the long seaward slope, and it was there that Golding set his mount. Carmady clumsily followed, jolting breathlessly on his mare.

'About your wish to settle in this happy Hundred. Look at the Astell barouche, Carmady! Surely that's a Hooper? Did you ever see such greys? Splendid!'

So? Another dull carriage, Carmady thought, even if made by London's most fashionable carriage maker. The countryside passions for horseflesh and vehicles was quite beyond him. Shots were being fired in fusilade beyond the tinkers' waggons and decorated carriages, causing Carmady to exclaim as his mount pricked nervously. Golding laughed while the visitor regained control. He had no such problem, of course, the mark of the bred gentleman.

'It is nothing, only the gun competition.'

Carmady cursed, hauling on the reins until the mare was quietened. 'Shooting competition? At a race meeting?'

'One before the other, Percy.' Golding was amused by the other's worry. 'So both can proceed in tranquillity!'

'With proper haviour in each!' the other grumbled, only partly in jest. 'Gramineous pastimes ill suit a seaman.'

They made their way slowly through the crowd, Golding still laughing at Carmady's remark. A fair was set up, with jugglers and pedlars crying for attention. A mangy bear with a ring through its nose was rocking side to side, doing its slow agitated stamp while folk mocked, threw clods of earth and taunted it with handfuls of grass. Its dancing master was laughing his forced bellow, tugging the chain to get the animal on its hind legs. Whores were out in pairs, and gypsies paraded their horses in single file past the gentry in hopes that one at least might be tipsy enough to admire a beast and buy it before their grooms could be called to examine it for defects. Fiddlers capered, and the ubiquitous ullan pipers made their plaintive thready sound on all sides.

The folk of Sealandings had their favours out, some families sporting lucky flowers. Others wore ribbons on their best bonnets, and were spreading shawls on the grass for meals. The men were exchanging tobacco and talk of work, comparing sea and farm.

As Percy guessed, Golding immediately headed for a group of gentry between two of the grandest carriages where drinks were laid.

'Hulloo, ladies!' Golding called, sliding from the saddle and throwing the reins to a groom.

'See who I bring!'

Carmady thankfully pulled the mare in and painstakingly dismounted. He doffed his Wellington, relieved he had been well fitted out. His Wellington frock coat might be thought dated by many country gentry, with its Prussian collar that lacked any lapel, but it buttoned to the waist and was more like the compact attire he was used to at sea. No cut-in at the front, of course, but with side pleats and hip buttons it felt oddly ostentatious. The fish dart at his waist made it fit tight about his midriff, which was all to the good as it carried into the seam there. The flapped pockets were a godsend, for on land he never seemed to have anywhere to carry money or other small items.

'Allow me to introduce you to everyone, Mr Carmady!'

Brillianta Astell was hostess over this particular encampment, courageously managing with only eight maids-of-all.

'I have already had the honour of meeting most.' Percy felt even more out of his depth. Judith Blaker, housekeeper at Carradine Manor, was as elegantly dressed as the other ladies, all of whom sported varied riding coat dresses with ornamental brandenbergs. One lady had even adapted a redingote style to her riding wear in bright shock pink. 'Miss Newborough!'

'Lieutenant Percy Carmady!' the pink lady responded, offering him her hand. 'Last year's ball, in the company of Thalia De Foe, when last we met, was it not?'

All eyes turned on Carradine, who was talking with Golding. He made no sign that he had overheard, to everyone's relief. It was then that his bankruptcy had become known.

'A happy occasion, Miss Newborough.'

She forged on, sensing she had somehow trespassed. 'I am escorted by one who is eager to become better acquainted with Sealandings. You know George Godrell, I think?'

'I shall be pleased to meet him, Miss Newborough.'

He greeted Alex Waite, wagged a casual hand at Carradine, and was appropriately obsequious to each of the ladies. It was unfortunate that he had to apologise for missing the party thrown at Saxelby by Harriet Treggan, who was more flamboyantly dressed even than Sylvia Newborough in a bottle green riding dress coat cut with imbecile sleeves and sporting a large folding calash over her hair. Rodney Treggan accepted the apology graciously.

'You missed the hanging, Percy,' he sympathised. 'It was one of our best for many a day. At least as amusing as those in London, even with that new hangman.'

'I heard something of it.' Carmady had been present when a seaman had been hanged for maiming a sleeping gunner over some dispute. The memory of the execution was worse than any sea action.

'And where is your lovely sister, Percy?' Brillianta asked,

quickly cutting Harriet Treggan out of the conversation. 'I gathered she will be with us today?'

'She will be along presently, Miss Brillianta.' Judith Blaker, always surprising, finished the explanation for him.

'With Squire Hunterfield,' the housekeeper said with a smile. 'Sir Henry will arrive by the first pursuit.'

Brillianta's manner stiffened. The lady from Arminell was outraged but kept her smile, thinking the Blaker woman had become insufferable. It was not for a common housekeeper to make remarks uninvited, even if everybody here was paying lip service to her presence by pretending she had a right to be among her betters. Clearly she was nothing but a social climber striving to mimic a breeding she did not possess. Percy Carmady suspected Brillianta's attitude, but it was all beyond him.

'Thank God Hunterfield will be risen betimes!' Carradine strolled over to join them, leaving Charles Golding toping at the wine benches and arguing with the steward about the disputative practice of 'qualifying' Spanish wines by coopering them with brandy. 'Morning, Carmady! I have a notion for you!'

Carmady was taken aback. This was becoming as unknowable as horse riding. He had agreed to ride out early only to stop Golding getting drunker as the morning wore on – a tactic that had evidently failed – and in hopes of seeing his friend Hunterfield. Barely a day or two in Sealandings, and already he was regretting having accepted Golding's invitation to stay at Bures House. He ought to have stayed at Lorne, but instinct had nudged him from that perch for his sister Mercy was frankly enamoured of Henry Hunterfield. She could become better acquainted with the man unhindered by a brother.

'Notion, Rad?'

'Financially, nautically, take your pick.' Carradine was impeccably dressed in Hussar boots, with a high hunting necktie, its requisite three creases perfect on each side and converging with the ends secured by diamond fastenings that people now called tie-pins. His short-skirted red riding coat was tailored, the pockets in the pleats ignoring the recent fashion, popularised in London, to have flapped pockets on the hips. His shirt was a froth of chitterlings, his hat the fashionable russet Wellington beaver, its crown the exact eight inches and wider than the brim.

'See, gentlemen!' Sylvia cried. 'The races are about to begin!' She was annoyed at being left out of the conversation, and pointed to where the people were assembling as a dozen mounts were brought into a line.

'It is the parade, Miss Sylvia,' Alex Waite explained. 'The rules newly put about by the Jockey Club want the horses first showed to the public.'

'Why so, Mr Waite?'

'The people can then see the races are honestly run, Miss Sylvia.' Waite looked uncomfortable. 'The Strand jews made fortunes, when horses were swapped or treated before races.'

'How terrible!'

Brillianta was undeceived by Sylvia's show of horror and added, 'More terrible, Sylvia, is the interference of some committee in London into our local practices! I recall attending the Horseheath races, when there was no such ostentation. Gentlemen simply brought their beasts and raced them. Life is altogether too complicated these modern days!'

'Here is Hunterfield now.'

The company fell silent. A compact landau was approaching, driven by a coachman with two liveried outriders. Two ladies sat with the Lord of Sealandings. Carradine snorted quietly, but received a sharp correcting glance from Judith.

'Bloody man,' Carradine muttered, unheard by all except his housekeeper. 'Lord of Sealandings, and just look! His carriage looks more like a Vidler! Ought to be painted maroon –'

'Silence, sir.' Judith's low correction was caught by one of the group. Carmady turned in astonishment, then was suddenly red-faced as the lady hastily smiled to correct the impression of ordering her employer to behave better. 'I think the landau looks superb, do you not agree, Mr Carmady?'

'Splendid!'

Carradine forced a smile to cover his anger. 'It is an old joke, Mr Carmady. As a boy I once, ah, painted my father's private brougham maroon, covering up his coat-of-arms on the doors, and received a thorough belting!'

Carmady pretended to believe the impromptu tale, but knew Carradine had intended the insult. John Vidler, the London coachbuilder, had taken over Besant's and supplied the nation's

Royal Mail coaches since 1791, with side panels painted maroon to contrast with the stark black of the rear boot and four upper-quarter panels.

'How charming Miss Tabitha looks!' Sylvia gushed, lifting her skirts to advance and meet the newcomers. 'And Miss Carmady also!'

But her eyes were for Hunterfield alone, Alex Waite noted with chagrin. Since the meeting at Saint Edmundsbury she had occupied more of his thoughts than had pleased him.

Local people were doffing hats and bobbing curtseys as the landau passed. Carradine too doffed his hat and went forward to greet Hunterfield, thinking that at least the man, ruler of the Sealandings Hundred, had had the sense not to drive himself this time. As the others went to the victuals chatting about the coming horse pursuits he managed to deflect Hunterfield aside, trying for informality.

'Squire Henry. It is fortunate that all the ingredients are here.' He beckoned Percy, who came to join them with relief. 'I propose a new venture for Sealandings, and want your approval.'

'Morning, Percy.' Hunterfield was amused at his friend. 'Are you somewhat frayed by the foiling and fencing of our coast gentry?'

Carmady grinned shamefacedly. 'I always feel it is Kissing Friday but nobody will tell me the date!'

'You will get used to Sealandings.' Hunterfield turned to Carradine. 'Venture? That sounds uncommonly commercial.'

'The harbour, Squire Henry.' Carradine pointed seawards. Below the greensward, the north mole could just be seen, with several small fishing vessels in the harbour. An Excise vessel, *Hunter*, lay against the longer south mole. 'This will be the last time *Hunter* will chandler and victual here. She will be displaced soon. We shall be lucky to see government vessels ever again.'

'So I hear, Carradine,' Hunter answered drily. 'If your scheme is to approach Parliament on the matter —'

'No, Squire. My scheme will increase the shipping in our harbour so that Customs vessels will be superfluous!'

Hunterfield eyed the man. Rad Carradine was always the restless one. Of all the gentry of Sealandings, he alone had fought duels, and killed. And brought himself to the brink of ruin by heavy gambling. Of all the scandal-bringers, Carradine was the leader. His exploits with the beauties of the London salons were widely known. Not only that, but he was unpredictable, vicious, and harboured grudges. Hunterfield suddenly felt a strong inclination to look at Mistress Blaker. Since that woman had taken the housekeeper's chatelaine at Carradine Manor, Carradine had been quiet. Tabitha had begun to speak of the reformed Carradine in tones of admiration. It was clear that Carradine had become a focus for the Sealandings ladies now he seemed more settled. But Hunterfield wanted to know how the arrival of a housekeeper, however skilled she might be in domestic matters, could effect such a transformation. Not long since, Carradine had lost every penny and acre on a prizefight. It was Hunterfield's experience that the most complex changes needed but one reason. That reason could only be Judith Blaker.

'A scheme, for all Sealandings?'

'For the harbour, the town.' Carradine drew breath and took a pace encouraging them to obtain a more seaward view. 'We lose, Squire,' he said bluntly. 'We are a harbour town, a port; but it is Felixstowe, the greater Yarmouth, Harwich, the ports of northern Norfolk, Colchester and Maldon, that gain.'

'At our expense?' Hunterfield's manner was mild, though Percy shifted uncomfortably. Carradine's was direct criticism.

'In a way of speaking, yes. I will redress the balance.'

Hunterfield chuckled suddenly as two little boys in smock-frocks and quarter caps scampered past, a harassed sister in a smock and tattered, old-fashioned whittle shawl chasing. 'I s'll give thee! Spilling the bottle, and the family kisky!'

'Here,' he called, and a groom instantly caught the girl and brought her over. She was afraid and panting, but his smile eased her. 'Kisky, are you? How many go thirsty, then?'

'Please, Squire, six and father. They spilled the beer.'

Hunterfield nodded to his mute personal groom who had brought the girl. 'Tom. See they get enough for the day.' The groom raised his hand in acquiescence and took the girl off, her awed brothers following in silence. Hunterfield laughed to cloak his embarrassment. 'Their old speechways amuse me. Percy, you shall have to learn a word or two!'

'I shall avoid cant at every opportunity, Henry,' Carmady

vowed. 'I have not forgiven you for making me listen to caterwauling elbow pipes the other day. That is the reason I went to stay with Golding!'

'I have funds,' Carradine interposed impatiently. 'With permission, I shall start trade with the Baltic.'

Taken aback by the intention – stranger still from Carradine – Hunterfield looked at Carmady, who was immediately all interest.

'What sort of ship, sir?'

'A sufficient ship, Carmady.' Carradine glowed. The man was hooked. All that was needed was to reel him in. Hunterfield himself might come swimming in. 'That is the problem.'

Carmady smiled. 'Ships are no problem, Carradine. It is land that is the difficulty!'

'What ship should one buy, for maximum cargo between here and the Baltics?' Carradine frowned as if he had given the matter serious thought. He could not care less, as long as the vessel did what was required. 'They all look alike, except some are painted different colours and have eccentric sails –'

'Trade what?' Hunterfield put in quietly. 'I want nothing amiss in this harbour, Carradine.'

Carradine swallowed at the blunt warning but gathered himself before replying so his words emerged with calm. Judith would know every single sentence spoken, and would take him to task if he spoke out of turn to the powerful Hunterfield.

'Nor shall there be, Squire.' Carradine almost choked, making his submission. Since his past confrontation with Hunterfield, all caused by that Mehala bitch, he had been obliged to address Hunterfield with utter formality, when his own lineage was as august as that of Hunterfield's. 'All I need is expert advice on purchase, and seamanship enough to sail her.'

'Seamen are abundant in every hedgerow,' Carmady said sombrely. 'Since the overthrow of Tyrant Napoleon, half the blackguards in country lanes are seamen or discharged militiamen. Things have not changed in fifteen years.'

'And authority on board.' Carradine knew he was too ponderous, but Carmady only nodded as if considering the possibility. 'I would be greatly obliged for advice, Carmady.'

'To my best ability!'

'Trade what, Carradine?' asked Hunterfield a second time.

'Merchants will answer that, Sir Henry. They have lists of commodities as long as my arm. Precious amber, found between Königsberg and Memel in Prussia; Baltic timbers, that are now in fashion; raw ores and silverwares. Exports would be cloths –'

'It is a fact', Carmady intruded, prompted by Hunterfield's raised eyebrow, 'that the Baltic Sea is the most frequented, with the exception of the China Seas. Over thirteen thousand vessels passed through the Sound in 1829. But it is frozen for three or four months. Its sandbanks are as dangerous as ours.'

'What is danger to a brave seafarer?' Carradine demanded.

'How dangerous, Percy?' Hunterfield asked.

Carmady grimaced. 'Of those thirteen thousand four hundred ships, Henry, two out of every hundred were lost, and hardly a man rescued. Yet on the Atlantic trade with America's New England, only one per cent of ships founders each year.'

'Think, though, Carmady!' Carradine urged. 'Think of Sweden, Prussia, the Russias, all Scandinavia! The wines –'

'Wines!' Golding was with them, nodding perfunctorily to Hunterfield. 'That is what is needed! German wines fetched through the Baltics, and no perfidious practices of the French vintners! Did you know that they colour their wines openly with log-wood chips, sweeten them with sugar of lead and alum?'

A series of shots sounded, and several voices cried out simultaneously in a distant roar.

'What the devil – ?' Hunterfield exclaimed.

There were shouts from the edge of the copse where the shooting contest was being held. Somebody came running.

'Something amiss.' Hunterfield shouted for Simple Tom, and gestured for his mount. 'Please God nobody is seriously hurt. Tom?' he called as his personal groom came at a run. 'Find Doctor Carmichael, and bid him yonder.'

Carradine saw a figure running in the distance, her skirts held before her and her bonnet flying back from her head. It was Mehala. He should have known. Always, when one of his schemes needed an untroubled passage, that bitch baulked him. Rudely he shoved Golding aside, grabbed the reins of Carmady's mare, flung himself on her back and kicked into a swift canter in the direction of the shouting.

21

MEHALA HAD SEEN Ven off an hour before the horse racing was due to start, going as far as the Norwich road to watch him from sight. She allowed him to go with misgiving. When they were separated, something evil always seemed to happen. He had insisted that his journey would be brief, and that much of the road was turnpiked beyond Tyll's tollgate at the boundary of Sealandings, and likely to be well frequented. He could walk the few miles to Rustonhall, offer his treatment to the headmaster, and cite the dramatic improvement in Clement Wellins' eyesight after only a few administrations of the marvellous lunar caustic solution. There was happily enough left for a dozen children with similar infections. According to Pleasence, the school was a very fine institution. He could treat the children, and be home before 'foorzes', as local labourers called the afternoon tea rest. Mehala watched him leave, reckoning in her mind that she had given him enough food to manage: cheese, bread, two apples, two pints of small beer in an earthenware flask stoppered by a waxed plug, a cold boiled egg, and strips of mackerel.

Ven only just remembered to pause and wave back. She waved, ostentatiously blowing him a kiss which made him quickly lower his head and resume his uphill walk in embarrassment. That made her smile all the more. She went along the footpath opposite the great mass of Bettany's windmill to join the trickle of people heading for the heath.

'The gypsies are your particular concern today, Mehala,' Ven had instructed her. 'They will bring scores of herbs. I want you to see if they have any of those on my list.'

Frowning, he had gone over the names, indicating the overseas rarities that gypsies liked to tout at horse fairs and markets. She knew of most, but was particularly fascinated by the

Dalmatian daisy flower that Ven described in somewhat clumsy detail.

'Its seeds are available, they say, though I am confused by the types. I think of it as the Persian Pellitory, or the Dalmatian, though my old student friend says it has a Latin name now, *cineraraefolium*. It came into East Anglia two years ago in 1826, via interested gentlemen, and adapts well.'

'For what?'

'It is like common feverfews,' Ven had told her haltingly, but when pressed had grinned like a child caught out, and conceded, 'It seems to kill insects.' He would say no more.

The rest of the listed plants numbered some two dozen, but many of them she could find herself, so wisely put them out of her mind and concentrated on those unfamiliar to her.

Today she put on her red cloak with its hood, feeling quite full of herself. Ven could come to little harm on a relatively safe road with so many titled families driving to the horse racing. Practically everybody in the Home Counties wore red cloaks at one time, and no lady in Hertfordshire's rich countryside would be seen without one, high born or low. But during the early part of the 1820's they had begun to decline, for no known reason, and now they represented adherence to custom rather than a response to fashion. She had been given the red cloak by Miss Gould from the charity school, with whom she was in favour, thank heavens, in spite of Reverend Baring's antagonism.

The heathland was crowding well when she arrived. Already the tumblers and jugglers were attracting crowds, and the cutpurses were doubtless as active as ever. In the distance she saw a cluster of tents, the gentry assembling nearby. Carradine's figure was unmistakable, while Sir Charles Golding was predictably assaulting the wine tables. A slighter figure was not immediately familiar, one who was uncomfortably stiff in his walk when dismounting. Then she knew him for Lieutenant Carmady, lately retired from the King's Navy and come to seek a house in Sealandings, a close friend of Hunterfield.

She saw the Hunterfield landau arrive, and Miss Newborough prance out to meet it. Tabitha Hunterfield, eyes roaming the crowds, descended gracefully in her tight plum-coloured riding coat dress of redingote pattern. Mehala wished she were close enough to inspect the serpent 'dragons' of hair Miss Hunterfield affected, such a risk in view of the predilection of actresses and other loose elements for that persistent early Regency style. Mercy Carmady alighted and stood self-effacingly until introduced, then she mingled discreetly, keeping herself among the ladies. She alone made no demur when Carmady and Hunterfield were drawn to one side by Carradine in deep conversation, whereupon she began to converse with Mr Waite when the North Briton engaged her.

Mehala saw the racers emerge, and the gentry who would ride begin to put down their glasses of Madeira wine and stroll down to the mounts. Wagers were being made on all sides. Mehala saw gypsies pass their sale horses to tethering stakes guarded by gypsy children. They seemed rough men, coming lighting clay pipes, talking volubly in their slithery tongue.

Mehala's nose wrinkled. They smoked the pungent tabak of the Syrias and Levant, yet it was mildly scented. She grew interested, for it must be admixed during drying with a sufficiency of Croatia tobacco, or that from Dalmatia. Her heartbeat quickened at the realisation. She took careful note of the men's garb so as to be able to recognise them later. Where the tobacco came from, so would the seeds Ven wanted for his mysterious insect-killing properties. Gypsies had supplies denied to others.

By the shooting staves, a scatter of people was watching the competition. Two of Carradine's men acted as stewards, and had marked out the targets and shooting positions with a long bilbouquet consisting of two sticks connected by measured twine. Most of the weapons were old flintlock and black powder smoothbores, the kind she herself had often fired on Ray Island far to the south. She decided to ignore the gentry on the crest of the incline, and to enjoy the firing tests for a while, at least until the horse racing. By then the pedlars would be easy to haggle with. This was a difficulty in such a holiday as this, for most wandering hawkers had a licence costing four whole pounds. Those who 'travelled with a beast of burden', as the law put it, must pay another four pounds in coin, and were in the majority. Mehala smiled to herself. Hardly a one would admit to being a pedlar or hawker unless they carried a licence. Even at this early stage she saw one, who carried the statutory sign of *Licensed Hawker* painted on his ped sack, swiftly slip a folded paper to another at the petty constable's approach, playing the twindle – one licence, two pedlars.

There was something reassuring about familiar practices, she thought, spreading her shawl on the grass and sinking down on it to watch the guns. Even when custom was damaging, it was enough to enjoy, being a spur to memory.

On the Ray Island sea marshes she liked to watch wading birds, and had startled them away when sporting gentlemen had been about to shoot them dead. The times she had risen from the samphire and the sea grass, laughing in the face of their anger! As a small girl, she had played that dangerous game successfully only by escaping through runnels across the low mud flats of the Blackwater and the Colne estuaries. Despoiling sport was a fearsome risk. Later, as Mistress of Red Hall and wife of the evil Rebow, she had been suddenly the lady, able to indulge her spoiling to her heart's content. Once, she had saved the life of a red-necked stint, a rare visitor from Siberia, it was said, in the Empire of the Russias, though how could anyone ever know that? At a grand lady's playfulness, the astounded gentlemen in the shooting parties had been obliged to pretend amusement while seething inwardly. They had gone their ways, their lethal sport spoiled.

'Good morning, Mistress Mehala.'

'Good morning, Mr Hast.'

The gunsmith was smiling as he doffed his low beaver and indicated the low cart he had hired.

'May I offer you a weapon from my stock?'

'Me, sir?'

'You are more fitted to handle these long arms and pistols than most of the competitors here! I wish I had been there the day you shot the stake at, how far was it, three miles?'

She laughed. 'The distance grows in the telling, Mr Hast! I was standing next to the marker post when the pistol accidentally discharged.' His kindness was evident in his mode of address; to call her Miss Mehala would deny her marital status.

'Just look!' Bartholomew grumbled. 'Seven gentlemen, each with his own weapon, plus three with my new guns, firing at tree stumps big as houses, missing every time!'

'They forget to hold firm once the sear spring gives,' Mehala said. 'A child's mistake.'

'True.' He smiled at the scene. There was quite a panorama from their vantage point; the harbour, the luggers of Yorkshire and Mousehole styles, an occasional skaffie fishing boat from far North Britain, the smaller smacks and hoys, the distant sweep of the Bay of Sealandings and the hills curving down to the sealands, the faint smudge of Whitehanger's rival harbourside. 'Does this remind you, Mehala?'

'Remind?' Her heart squeezed in warning: Bartholomew Hast, relative of the Colchester Hasts, gunmakers. It was to Colchester that she had ridden in her four-horse landau, to St Peter's Church on North Hill for evensong, or to St James' on East Hill to listen to the solid pedantic sermons of John Dakins, still rector though his ministry began in 1799 . . . 'No. I glimpse fragments from the past, but nothing more.' She ignored his quizzical look. 'Though I feel a strong affinity for these shores.'

Did he remember her, from some chance encounter when visiting his gunsmith cousins? For they too had contributed charitable donations to the new Essex and Colchester General Infirmary, on one occasion donating brewings for the patients' and infirmary servants' beer at the large sum of eight pounds and four shillings. Nostalgia seduced her attention, and her mind worked out the sum again. *To brewing in the seven-hundred-weight copper by Mr Fincham; malt for 3 butts (i.e. 6 hogsheads) 18 bushels = 6.15.0d.; with hops, 18 lbs is in total 8.4s.2d.* Mehala found herself smiling at the argument she had had with Mr Fincham, whose labour had been raised in 1827 to ten whole shillings per brew. 'A pocket of hops at ten pounds two shillings, Mr Fincham, that is 168lbs weight of hops . . .'

'You spoke, Mehala?'

She caught herself. 'No, Bartholomew. I wandered a moment.'

He knew, she felt immediately. Was this why he seemed drawn to her for closer friendship? Surely it could not be anything more, for he was friendly with Bridget, the maid-of-all at the rectory, among others. She gave him a smile and rose. Inattention was dangerous. She must look to her duty and find Ven's herbs.

'I seek the pedlars. Thank you for your company.'

'And you for yours, Mehala.'

The first race was almost about to begin. The new fashion of perambulating the mounts, that folk were now calling a 'parade', was already under way, impromptu betting still going on. Mehala saw Miss Gould with children chattering about her, and went to speak. The teacher had always been kind to Ven and herself.

'Good morning, Matilda. You have charges even on holiday!'

'Good morning, Mehala. Yes, I am always troubled by these scoundrels. They can never be controlled!'

The children laughed at her mock scolding and moved away to see the start of the first race.

'You see I am wearing my red cloak, Matilda?'

'It suits you better than it ever did me! I only wish it was in sounder condition, not so worn.' The schoolteacher coloured at the implication of Mehala's poverty. 'I hope I give no offence.'

'You never could, Matilda.' Mehala hesitated. 'There may be some change in our circumstances, fairly soon. I mean, it seems that charges are being brought against us. It may go badly.'

Matilda paled. 'Charges? For what reason?'

'Reverend Baring brings them. You can guess their substance. I just want to say that it would be wiser if you were to avoid my company. No taint endures like the faintest. Your standing in Sealandings might possibly be damaged.'

A shout rose, joined by several other voices. Two shots had sounded together, then three others . . . or more?

'Down! A man down!'

'Assist here, sirs!'

'Please God, no loss,' Matilda gasped, straining to see.

The shooters were milling about a figure on the ground. Mehala stared, then started to run. She was almost sure it was Bartholomew Hast. She flew across the greensward, arrived in moments, and struggled to push her way through.

Hast lay sprawled on the grass, pale as death, blood spreading from his thigh and over his waist. Red blood, already congealing, blotched his shirt and hands.

'It was not my fault!' The man who spoke was Codgie, a longshoreman. 'I shot, but the gun hung fire –'

'You should have disbelieved it, you damned fool!' somebody swore inelegantly among the crowd.

'It was no fault of mine! The long arm failed on me.'

The injured gunsmith seemed unconscious. Mehala could not see the wound, but fresh blood was pooling beneath him.

'What happened?' she cried into the babble.

'I tell thee, gul,' Codgie resumed hoarsely, ' 'twere no blame on me –'

'He pulled the trigger, the cock sprung onto the steel.' The voice was that of Jason Prothero of Calling Farm.

'A flash in the pan, then?' Mehala said directly into his eyes, hating the man even now. 'So whence the injury?'

'The man did not wait,' Prothero told her. The crowd quietened, listening. 'He slacked his arm, turned to Hast.'

'The spark smouldered through and the gun fired?'

'Seems so.' Prothero raised his voice so all could hear. 'Let no one bring charge against me as owner of part of this land. I never gave written approval for this shooting contest; nor did I authorise Hast's weapons!'

'Where did the bullet enter?' Mehala demanded. 'And what was the bore? Show me the weapon.'

'Here, Mistress,' Codgie cried, shoving the gun at her.

She inspected it. It was an old smoothbore Twigg and Bass long arm, one barrel only, and that worn to almost incredible thinness. The Piccadilly gunmakers' partnership had ended when John Fox Twigg had died in 1790, testifying to the gun's age. No wonder that it was rusted near the lock. The barrel's browning showed naked metal down its length. She felt rage, for Bartholomew would tolerate no weapon like this.

'Twelve bore?' She tested the barrel with a thumb, feeling the heat.

'Yes, Mistress.'

Twelve bore, and unrifled. So the bullet was a spherical lead ball weighing one twelfth of a pound, thus measuring a fraction less than three-quarters of an inch in diameter. Old Abby Abraham, who had taught her sailing, had shown her how a flintlock worked, and insisted she learn by heart the dimensions of the three common flintlocks. She had written them in the dark gritty beach sand of Ray Island. So, 0.747: twelve bore.

'Where did it wound him?'

There was silence and a shuffling as Bartholomew Hast's life ebbed into the grass.

'The bullet!' she shouted angrily at the faces. 'Where did it enter the man? For Christ's sweet sake, will you *answer?*'

'Into his waist,' Prothero said. 'I saw it. No blame can be cast onto the landowner.'

'What is it here?'

The crowd parted for a gentleman in a bright blue riding coat. Mehala looked into the face of the rider whom she had last seen staring after her and Ven as they left the cottager Taw, on the long journey from Edmundsbury.

'Please can you help, sir?' she begged. 'This man is shot.'

The newcomer inspected the moribund figure on the grass. 'A waist entry, hey? No hope, then. Get him the rector for the rites. There will be one fewer within two hours.' He spoke with offensive affability over his shoulder. 'Nobody survives that, Squire Hunterfield. Sorry to spoil your occasion.'

'Are you sure, Godrell? The man is my gunmaker.'

'Sure as God gives breath.'

'Only, you being a famed surgeon –'

'Only a pastime, Hunterfield,' Godrell drawled. 'To while away crude youth!' He chuckled and drifted away.

Mehala called out, 'Squire, sir, if you please!'

'Who calls?'

'Mehala, Squire.' She was cradling Hast's head.

Hunterfield came, people making way. 'Is it so, then?' he asked, taking in Hast's deathly pallor.

'It seems so, Squire. But Doctor Carmichael is walking north to Rustonhall, taking physics to the school from where the boy Wellins came. He is gone but an hour. Can he be fetched, please?'

Hunterfield nodded. 'Very well. Can you help Hast? Godrell said most emphatically . . .'

'I shall try, Squire.'

He turned on his heel, calling instructions to Simple Tom.

Desperately she looked up. 'Please, somebody find Harold Temple the blacksmith. Ask for his farrier's knife. And somebody beg washed linen, two yards, from the haberdashers . . .'

To her fury the crowd began to drift away, muttering.

'Please, ladies! Gentlemen! Please, of your charity –'

'Let the man die in peace,' Prothero's gruff voice said, and the stout farmer was gone, shunning responsibility.

Mehala looked about in despair. A few children stood awe-stricken nearby, but the adults were dispersing. There was not even shade or shelter, and she could not leave Bartholomew even to bring his hired cart, nor could she lift him. She almost wept. She ought to have brought Rosie instead of leaving her with light duties at Shalamar with Clement. Even that young boy would have been of assistance.

'Mehala? Can I help?'

'Mistress Prothero!'

Mary Prothero stood there, her slender form accented by dun and black formal attire. She was wife of the aggressive Prothero, and had once been the heiress at Calling Farm.

Relief flooded into Mehala. 'Thank you. I need some sort of help to cut this poor man's clothing. They said the wound was in his waist. I need to see where the lead entered. I might be able to staunch the flow of blood until Ven is brought.'

'What do you wish me to do?'

'One of your men, with a keen knife to cut his clothing.'

'Perrigo! Mr Perrigo, if you will!' Mary Prothero lifted her skirts and rushed away.

Mehala observed Bartholomew's features. It was now that she needed to remember everything that Ven had taught her during the long nights of winter in Shalamar. The lines of the muscles and their insertions, the tendons and the sheaths, the course of nerves . . . The haemorrhage was now profuse. An artery? The descriptions Ven gave, and the few times she had seen new bleeding in patient injuries, were suddenly somehow less clear now. With Ven there pointing out the characteristic brightness of spurting arterial blood, and the slightly darker venous flow, it had seemed self-evident. Alone in a field with the populace shunning her and Hast seeming like to die, the responsibility was suddenly too great. The young gunsmith wore a shirt with a high neck stock bound once round, and a spencer with heavily filled pockets, moleskin breeches and half-jacks. The ground beneath was blood soaked. Blood was welling from below his belt.

'Here, Miss Mehala.'

Perrigo, Prothero's chief stockman at Calling Farm, dropped to his knees beside her, bringing out his long fletchers' cutting knife. He and his wife had worked for Mary Calling's parents, and for Mary Calling herself after she was bereaved of them.

'Thank heavens! Would you please cut away the clothing where I point? Only, here in full view . . .'

Perrigo nodded quickly. He had brought two of his men with him, standing uncertainly by. 'You two. Get some staves. Drape sacking about the man and look sharp.'

'Please. No delay, Mr Perrigo.'

'Show me where I am to cut his clothes.'

'Remove his trouser from the upper part of his legs. I want to see his belly about the hips.'

'Mistress Prothero?' Perrigo was doubtful, glancing about.

'Do as Mistress Mehala says, please.' Mary Prothero stood away as the men arrived with staves from the shooting markers. With canvas from Hast's gun cart, they formed a crude screen as the herdsman cut clumsily at the moleskins.

'They said the bullet entered the low stomach.' Mehala tutted in sudden anger at herself. She ought to have asked how far away the oaf Codgie was standing when the gun fired. There were no scorch marks on the clothes . . . yet what if the bloodstains obscured them? Ven taught that powder burns in gunshot wounding was serious, the chances of survival being much reduced for some reason, perhaps owing to damage of the skin and tissues beneath.

The blood-blotched skin showed, and the pubic hair of the gunmaker's belly. Mehala took away the knife from the herdsman with a murmur of thanks, and cut the clothes, blade upwards between her fingers to guard against damaging Hast's skin. She tugged at the moleskins, giving Perrigo a mute glance of appeal for help. He lifted Hast's hips. The injured man groaned, still unconscious, but raising Mehala's spirits at this evidence of flickering life. Perrigo grunted in dismay as his hands came away heavily smeared with blood.

Mehala peeled away the cut breeches, revealing the man's thigh where a deep hole spurted blood openly. She exclaimed in relief. Plenty of blood had been lost, but the way the gunsmith fell must have tautened his moleskin about his thigh, constricting the vessels.

The wound was charred near its gaping mouth, some two inches in diameter as far as she could judge. The exposed leg lay at an odd angle, the sign of dislocation or fracture.

'Linen. Anything. And a tie of cord, rope, a stick . . .'

Mehala thought desperately. Since she had cut away the breeches from the thigh, the freed blood flow was now gushing. Where did the artery run? And which artery was it?

Hast had been shot from slightly one side and from the front. He must have been inclined towards Codgie, perhaps reaching for the weapon to take it from the old salt. She balled her fist. The blood flowed, according to Doctor William Harvey, from the heart outwards along the arteries. What was that drawing Ven had made for her, about a month ago? The line of the femoral artery, along the inner aspect of the thigh, almost exactly where this gaping hole bled so copiously . . .

Midpoint of the inguinal fold to the hard bony prominence, the adductor tubercle, on the femur above the knee, down where the blood-soaked breeches still covered the limb. That was it! She felt savagely along the thigh, down and down until she reached the hard prominence. The femoral artery must be the one bleeding. Or was it? What internal ruin was hidden beneath?

The blood was running faster now, the spurts forcible. *The middle third of that line, Mehala*, Ven's voice reached her. *Remember that the seat of election for ligature of the femoral artery is at the apex of the femoral triangle . . .*

The femoral triangle? Yes, she had marked it on the crude clay model Ven had made, using a sharpened twig, but here?

Compress the femoral artery, Mehala, backwards against the ilio-pubic eminence, never against the head of the femur . . .

The wound was in the midshaft of the great femur bone.

So press back against the ilio-pubic eminence.

She knuckled her fist, and rammed it into place, feeling the hard pelvic bone beneath.

The blood kept spurting, but its flow lessened. She must be on the right place, but her pressure was insufficient.

She rose to her knees, grunting, and leant her whole weight on the place where the great arterial vessel ran.

The blood flow lessened still further, but kept coming.

'Mr Perrigo,' she gasped, breathless. 'Please tilt the poor man so he lies at an angle. Yes, lift.' Bartholomew groaned, but was now completely ashen, his lips a pale mauve. 'Hurry. It is a matter of seconds now.'

She saw the blood spurt anew, pushed the herdsman aside, and kicked off her shoe.

'Hold me please, so I do not overbalance.'

Perrigo steadied her. Mehala drove her heel into the gunsmith's thigh, forcing down with all her weight, compressing the skin and soft tissues against the solid bone of the ilio-public eminence.

The bleeding ceased.

She felt almost giddy, her head swimming with relief. Hast's face was shiny with a slight sweat. Now what? she thought foolishly, knowing fully for the first time the despair that Ven continually suffered. The blood flow had stopped, but what was the next stage? The artery had to be tied permanently to prevent further haemorrhage. But how did one do that? She had seen Ven perform such an operation only on three or four occasions, and none had been on an adult's thigh. If she moved, the bleeding would begin again, and the gunmaker would die.

'Cover the poor man, please,' Mary Prothero's quiet voice instructed. The men moved to obey. 'How can I assist, Mehala?'

'Thank you, Mistress Prothero.' She felt obliged to make the admission. 'I do not know, and must await Ven's return. Please God he comes soon.'

'Poor Hast,' Perrigo said. 'That Doctor Godrell was right. Nivver a galver in the poor booy no more.'

Not a throb in the poor man, Mehala translated, feeling despair well within. Then she thought of the times Ven had pressed on, even to the point of evident stupidity, when she herself suggested that all was lost.

'No!' She spoke more sharply that she should. 'Not until Doctor Carmichael himself comes will I move. Stay with me.'

The aroma of gun oil from the sacking confines almost made her gag. Oil, mildewed sacking, combined with the fright of her decisions, almost proved too much. But she stayed.

Nearly half an hour later, Ven made a breathless return. He took in the scene at a glance, listened to Mehala's halting story, nodded, and set to work. Hast was still alive. A few moments later, it began to rain.

Endercotte felt the coming rain with savage delight. He stood at the intersection of the old drovers' route across the heathland, relishing the deluge as it fell on the fair.

This was righteous pleasure that he need not suppress, the glee of observing God's wrath on the sinful. So would their riotous entertainments end, when Good triumphed over Evil! But not merely in squeakings and hurrying for shelter under the trees in their garish dresses. No, when God ruled this forsaken country by a government of Puritans, then debauchery would be outlawed, and frivolity, carnality, and cavorting. The righteous would decree punishments for sinners. Colours, furbelows, personal ornamentation serving only to draw the godly to their evil kind, would be proscribed, and transgressors would be condemned.

He had watched the fair dissolve. God-fearing righteous folk like himself would on no account ever go near such a coven of evil. Gambling, semi-nakedness, breasts of fashionable ladies almost on open display, the men as bad in their plumage and sumptuary clothing. It was blatant sinfulness.

And the common folk were as bad, dressed in their best clothes, ribbons and garlands on their bonnets, their smock frocks touched with coloured threads in a wanton parade of lustful pride. Several groups were still dancing to elbow pipers, laughing with excitement, their gaiety testifying to the sordid maliciousness brewing in their evil hearts.

And the Lord of Sealandings, Sir Henry Hunterfield, so admired by this wicked district, condoned the whole wicked gathering! Endercotte vowed to find a way. Sure as God ruled Heaven, he would find a way. God the avenger commissioned him to root out evil in Sealandings. The Almighty had sent him a servant to help in the extirpation of wrongdoers, in the meek form of Mistress Blaker. A weak creature to be sure, being only a woman and therefore unreliable because of her innate sinful soul, but one who was fortunately ensconced in a privileged position at Carradine Manor. She would prove a worthy instrument.

He, Kemp Endercotte, encharged by God to destroy evil, had Judith Blaker's promise to do her uttermost to aid him. A frail unthinking vessel she, true, but a helper who would provide the means to smite the sinners in this vineyard of the Lord. With God's good grace they would burn in the fire that alone would purify their sinners' souls for Heaven.

She would provide the means, yes, he repeated to himself, a grim smile reaching his mouth as the last races were called off because of the worsening downpour. But additional means would be provided by others. The main enemy was that sinner Mehala, one who challenged God Himself by flaunting her unmarried state before all decent people. She was clearly a witch, who encouraged an equal evil in that dog-doctor Carmichael, a man who hoped – how often had he said it, and openly? – that Death itself would one day be conquered. Could there be franker blasphemy?

And was there any further need of witnesses? In a place like Sealandings, where the canker of sin usurped all decency, yes indeed! The challenge was all the greater. It was a test set for him, Kemp Endercotte, by the Almighty. He would come through it, purified in the conflict's fire. Then would his heavenly reward be all the greater.

Thunder broke and rolled overhead. Lightning flashed three miles away, approaching swiftly from Whitehanger.

Endercotte, drenched in the rain, smiled. God had given him a sign, in the doubtless fatal wounding of Bartholomew Hast. Oh, a seeming accident, yes, but there was a more lucid explanation to a man of righteousness. God had struck Hast down in his prime by his own weapon, for which there was ample Biblical reference. So would all fall before the wrath of Heaven! It was an omen, a compelling command from God, to seek out the righteous and bend them to the work of the Lord. That work required expunging the arch sinners, smiting them and casting them out, from life itself if need be. Punishment was holy, when used for God. Mehala and Carmichael: already he had enough evidence to condemn them, but he must gather support. For so it was the will of God, that by doing well you may put to silence the ignorance of foolish men: St Peter's Epistle.

Judith Blaker would be his main instrument. The ladies of Sealandings must be his witnesses. He himself would be the destroyer on this dark and brooding coast.

'Come!' he snapped to the plain woman who waited behind him, and strode off towards the Corn Mart.

'Coming,' she answered, gathering her black shawl.

They made their way downhill, the preacher saying a psalm aloud in time with his footsteps. At the end of the day he would dismiss his wife, and walk in the dark as if in pilgrimage to Two Cotts, there to perform penance with a chosen whore. His penance for all mankind.

'We shall have to lance her eye with my scalpel, Mehala.' Ven drew a diagram. 'Her cataracts blind her. She will go on parish charity if we fail.'

'Charity!' Mehala shivered at the terrible prospect. 'Can it be done, Ven?'

They were in the cottage kitchen. 'We must try. A cataract, I explained, is the eyeball's lens becoming opaque. It blinds vision. Alice Ingall has a double cataract, though only forty years, and so is destitute, though a skilled handloom weaver.'

'I came yesterday, Ven,' Mehala said, conscious of the woman waiting alone in the other room. 'Gave her the aperient. She knows not to eat for three days, and sip only bland tea.'

'Good. You remember I dissected Corder's eye to show the lens in a capsule suspended behind the gap we call the pupil?'

'Yes.'

Ven had sharpened his scalpel until it cut an unsupported hair, had honed his hooked needle until it was all but worn away.

'So, Mehala. You have the lint and linen bandage?'

'Yes, Ven.' She came with him. The woman was propped semi-recumbent on pillows in a low bed. 'Your grandchildren are with neighbours, Alice? And your daughter will attend you for three days?'

'Yes, Mehala. I promise to stay still until you say.'

Ven asked Mehala to open the curtains as wide as possible. 'We have chosen today well, Alice. The sun shines a little! The looking-glass, Mehala.'

Mehala lodged two pieces of broken mirror to reflect light on the patient's eye, and stood behind, holding Alice's head against her breast. Ven had made her practise pinching the upper eyelid to hold it up away from the eyeball. She caught Ven's nod, and lifted Alice's eyelid.

'Now, Alice. Keep your eyes fixed ahead, as if staring. Mehala will keep your right eye covered. You will feel me pushing and pulling, and a little pain. Bear it, if you please.'

He took his small scalpel, and drove it steadily into the cornea, the eyeball indenting slightly as he kept up the pressure. The scalpel passed in front of the blue ring of the iris. He saw the scalpel point traverse inside the eye, and come out through the cornea. Halting the slow thrust when a third of the blade showed, he moved the scalpel to cut through half of the cornea, only breathing relief when the whole blade emerged.

Alice groaned. Mehala too was holding her breath.

'Not long now, Alice Ingall! Soon be done! Think how marvellous it will be, to see again!'

Ven laid the scalpel aside. He inserted the needle into the eyeball, and with minute movements lacerated the lens capsule with the sharpened, hooked tip.

'Gently now, Mehala.'

He pressed gently on the uncut half of the eyeball. Mehala almost exclaimed as the opaque lens slid out like an emerging moon to lie on the eyeball. Ven took it up on the needle tip, and breathed at last.

'Let the eyelid back, Mehala.'

Unbearably anxious, she obeyed.

'Stay as if sleeping, Alice. Three days mind! No rising, walking, no touching. Rest as you are. No peeping!'

'Yes, Doctor. Will it be well?'

'If you do as I say, please God. Mehala will dress the eye with a lint patch, but no tight bandage. I shall visit daily.'

He left an hour later. Mehala could not bring herself to touch the lens. Ven carried it in his pocket, determined to dissect it if he could borrow a magnifying glass.

'The odds for an untroubled seeing eye, Mehala, are three hundred to one.' He smiled in hope. 'Let us pray that fortune favours us this time!'

'I have much to learn, Ven.'

'I know that feeling, Mehala.' His smile disappeared. 'I would have tried the easier French method of "couching" the lens, but it needs belladonna, Deadly Nightshade.'

'I can make some, Ven! We have it in the hedgerows!'

'No. Some older patients suffer terrible pain when belladonna extract is dropped into the eye. We do not know why. If I operate, then any fault is mine, and not to be blamed on a wayside flower that cannot answer back.'

22

HARRIET TREGGAN WAS discomfited. Saxelby Hall was splendid, and certainly for the past few weeks it had held its share of society visitors. Now, though, the world had palled.

The trouble was the disposition of Saxelby. No criticism could be made of its splendid grounds; its status among the other Suffolk seats. And of its upkeep not a word could be said, for she had been raised to know that a lady's esteem lay entirely in her management of her home. Saxelby Hall was ruled with a rod of iron. Indeed her neighbours, many of them previously unknown to her, were full of praise for her control, even though she had to struggle by on a mere sixteen in-house servants, with a few occasional helpers fetched from tenant estates when required for special events like the hanging parties.

But *was* the trouble only Saxelby Hall's position in the Suffolk countryside? It lay between charming rivers and pleasant undulating valleys, amid acres of lovely grounds and well-maintained orchards.

Not if she faced herself, no. There was more to it. She felt chained, as surely as she was chained to her chatelaine, emblem and instrument of her office as Mistress of Saxelby. Rodney was preoccupied with the estates, difficult enough in a well-established pile. For newcomers it was all the harder, for one had to establish one's methods, understanding the local customs. Why, even the weights and measures of farm produce differed in these remote areas, quite seventy miles from London's cosmopolitan centre of standards and ideals! Nothing like the desperately uncouth north, of course, where every single thing was different – the Lancashire acre well over 10,000 square yards, instead of the more normal 4,840, and as for a bushel of anything . . .

She wanted a child.

She wanted company, exciting company.

Seeing Ven Carmichael it had all come flooding back. The instant his dishevelled figure had appeared in the crowd round that scaffold. Him, actually proposing marriage to her, when she was so clearly above his station! It had been unbelievable, a matter for hilarity and scorn among her relatives. Her letter had, she believed, been kindness itself, and could not possibly have been couched in more condescending terms. He had had the sense not to approach her again.

That was, in fact, a disappointment. A rejected gentleman ought to sustain his admiration for a lady, whatever the circumstances of her declining his proposal. But of course he was not a gentleman, merely a frowning, rather lost creature doing eternal studies at that terrible building in Whitechapel's slums. Her mistake had been too much kindness. She could see that now, smiling occasionally at the young man who had come to live as a quarter-share lodger in some servant's room at an indulgent neighbouring doctor's house. That old fool – was he called Arbuthnot? – proved more indulgent still as time went on, even letting him learn without fee! That only showed how different tradesmen were, compared with gentry.

For the truth was that artisans such as leeches, teachers, merchants, herded together by reason of their calling, while gentry knew distinction by their breeding. Some ladies received proposals of marriage from commercial brutes by reason of failing family fortunes, but very few succumbed to that temptation.

For a young man of breeding, of course, it was a wholly different matter. A man had to make his way in the world, and a woman alone was in need of protection. So it was more acceptable for a young gentleman of quality to propose to a wealthy merchant's daughter than it was for a marriage between a noblewoman and a merchant.

The alcove window where she sat looked out onto the stable yard. It was here this morning that the unsettled feeling had begun. A stableman's children had been playing in the yard below while watching their father, a common groom, water the horses, bringing each mount and letting the children hold the beasts to drink.

Between horses, the children had been singing nursery rhymes. One had gone,

> *Nose, nose, jolly red nose,*
> *And what gave thee that jolly red nose?*
> *Nutmeg and ginger, cinnamon and cloves,*
> *That's what gave me this jolly red nose!*

A passing maid-of-all had heard the children's rhyme, and had shushed them with anxious glances towards the main kitchen, as if afraid the children's song might give offence.

Harriet had at first been amused, and had been about to make inquiries among her maids about the little mystery, when the uses of the named spices came slowly back to her. She blushed, actually blushed openly in her own bay window. The herbs were used as aphrodisiacs, as was well known, and that scandalous rhyme mentioned them. No need to ask what symbol underlay that red nose. Nor, once she had thought of the maid-of-all's surreptitious frantic glances to make sure the children had not been heard by the chief cook, was the unspoken accusation any longer a mystery. For a woman married some months ought to be showing by now, pregnant some weeks, proudly inviting the admiration of the county ladies.

They were accusing *her*, Mistress of Saxelby Hall. The thought almost fetched her to a faint. She sat trembling, at first stunned then later becoming furious. It was an outrage. That they – serfs, underlings, who lived by the permission of the great manors – that *they* should make sly fun at her expense was the uttermost in malice.

Rodney should be told at once, she decided, but she stayed where she was as the morning slipped and the sun became almost unbearably hot. Punishment? That would only lend substance to the children's accusation.

She thought of that rather tiresome but wealthy George Godrell. A neighbour, certainly within reach as a potential visitor and one who, moreover, had been trained as a doctor, also at the London Hospital. Was it reasonable to ask his advice? Rodney was adequate in his sexual attention, and she herself was surely capable of childbearing. There had never been any hint of difficulty on either side of her family. She had three married sisters, all breeding, and one brother Clive married to Chloe, an incompetent bitch without a thought in her head or skill to her hand, who had also delivered a child. No, fecundity was certainly beyond doubt . . . except that now she felt the question had to be asked.

Ven Carmichael?

She thought of his intensity, compared with George Godrell's mannered inanity. In London, a cabriolet had run over a child, breaking its arm. A little crossing sweeper of seven or eight, the stupid boy had somehow allowed himself to be trapped between the bollard at the pavement and the great wheel of the carriage, so causing his own damage. It had happened as Doctor Arbuthnot had been descending from his whisky, returning from his Wimpole Street surgery. George Godrell had been with Arbuthnot, and they were accosted by some foolishly distraught gentleman who had come to ask help for the boy.

She had been at her own window, in the house adjacent to Arbuthnot's, and had seen Godrell's expression when the gouty old doctor had suggested that Godrell see to the lad. It had been doubt, almost total loss. The boy screamed terribly, most irritating in a decent neighbourhood, until a figure had come from the direction of the old Oxford Street and reached the injured boy. It had taken but a moment – a borrowed stick, a strip of his own surtout lining, and it seemed to be done.

Ven had helped the boy to his feet. The urchin was sickly pale under his grime. Ven had spoken to the gentleman, and seen that coins were paid to the boy who returned to do his sweeping one-handed and weeping. Ven's distress had been obvious, but his struggle to offer help immediate and total. Godrell's contribution was but fleeting bafflement, and unconcern. The boy was a worthless crossing sweeper, keeping the intersection free of slippery noisome horse dung for a penny or two, so Godrell had no real obligation. Yet he was, she felt sure from slight acquaintance-ship, a person who, had he known what to do, been only too willing to exhibit his artistry to goggling London, especially as the gentleman from the cabriolet had been a titled stranger.

No, Ven Carmichael was the one she could trust to remain silent, and to have a notion as to what might be wrong. Born low he might be, but his endeavour was beyond doubt.

For the rest of that day she racked her brains, planning how to inveigle Rodney into establishing contact with Sealandings.

Fortune played into her hands at supper that same evening. Rodney mentioned that he had had an invitation from Carradine.

'It seems to be some sort of commercial venture in which he is engaged. Carradine and commerce do not seem the right admix, but I might accept. What do you think, my dear?'

'Carradine, Rodney? What is the Sealandings weather like? I should not want to suffer even more chill.'

'Oh, similar to here. What is it, forty miles?'

'And where on earth should we stay, Rodney?' she asked cleverly. 'We know hardly anyone!'

'Oh, come, Harriet. We know a dozen good families. If Carradine's domestic circumstances bother you, why, I am sure we can communicate your concern to Charles Golding. He will jump at the chance of extending an invitation. I could then write to Carradine saying that Golding must take precedence, on some pretext.'

'If you are sure, Rodney,' Harriet said doubtfully.

'Thank you, my dear. Unless', he added, hard at the eggs à la tripe, 'you are really in serious doubt about the journey?'

'Knowing how much you enjoy the speculations of your friends in Lloyd's, I must not demur. No, Rodney, I will make myself available. How soon will we leave Saxelby? I could be ready in two days.'

He was surprised. 'I thought next week would be soon enough, Harriet. I have events on the estate.'

'No, dearest,' she countered firmly. 'I must bend my will to yours. Now, I have for the game course ortalans roasted small, stewed partidges, and spatchcocked pigeons with the Prince Regent's sauce, though as you know I add rather more shallot than His Highness permits. Which will you start with?'

Rodney was surprised and pleased at his wife's willingness. She was not always so accommodating, for reasons he did not know. And Carradine's suggested purchase of a ship for the Baltic trade was intriguing, especially as he had a sea captain ready to hand, and others already interested in contributing to the scheme. The Baltic trade was the busiest in the western world. Was there any reason that it should not contribute to the funds required for the upkeep of Saxelby Hall?

'It is time, Rad.'

Carradine did not stir. It was not for a woman to *tell* him.

Inform, support, perhaps amuse even; yes, all those, but to be rudely awakened, even with a gentle hand shaking his shoulder and words of endearment, Judith Blaker was an affront.

He said nothing, just lay on the bed.

That chance meeting with her in the lane was the most terrible day of his life – that jack-a'horse Jason Prothero and his crushed wife Mary having just taken possession of every stick and stone of his Manor. He had been seduced by Judith's eyes, her vehemence and promised help. And she had delivered, kept her word. Sexual fulfilment, yes, if a trifle predictable of late. Possession of the Manor, yes, she had somehow duped Jason Prothero out of the deeds. Carradine still did not quite understand why Prothero never sued or raised Cain over it, but the jumped-up serf had retired sullen and defeated, and left Carradine with all his former possessions and status in Sealandings. Hunterfield, that stodgy bastard, no longer laid down rules for Carradine's behaviour, accepting his new-found docility at face value. It was, or should be, enough. Peace had come to Carradine.

That was the rub.

Peace was hateful. A cow was at peace, grazing its grass. But in the distance the church clocks ticked and chimed the hours to the poor beast's doom.

That is what he, Carradine of Carradine, had become: a beast grazing life away towards demise.

He had startled Judith by mention of the Baltic scheme, over one of her coffee-tastings, now so fashionable at the hour of eleven o'clock. It had been done delicately, for him, with guile, letting her gradually into the conversation to make a suggestion here and there. He had expressed doubt quite cleverly: was it the right sort of endeavour for a gentleman? Or the sort of venture that only tradesfolk should take up? Would it demean his reputation?

It was she who had talked of Percy Carmady, young lieutenant late of His Majesty's Navy, enamoured of the east coast and coming to reside in Sealandings. Carradine had been doubtful – was the man able to sail a merchant ship? Could he be relied upon? Were there not better people obtainable on application to London's Admiralty, whose list of retired officers of greater experience. . .? All those uncertainties he had prepared in advance. She countered them, woman-like, urging that, now he had thought of the enterprise, meekness of spirit could lose it. And for the first time in their passionate relationship he saw a flash of doubt in her eyes, that told him she was wondering if she had not daunted his spirit too much.

For her machinations were profound and complex, and planned with a cunning far beyond the average woman's competence. Or man's, for that matter.

She had made the estate her own. Every man, groom, maid-of-all, were her kin or clan, or were tolerated because, local Sealandings folk as the rest were, they could be easily spied upon and controlled. Puppets to the last, and himself the most foolish puppet of all; Carradine's estates were her domain. All obeyed the silent dark-haired mistress who lay in his bed and judged pence, person, and peer in this ancient manor.

But there was one activity Judith could not control, even here on the unpredictable coast. That was the sea. The North Sea, bland and resting today, providing seafoods and occupations and trade routes, could tomorrow prove violent beyond belief, taking lives by the shipload and drowning hopes and dreams. Then perhaps by next dawn the killer sea would be bland again, but with the tranquillity of incipient madness.

Was that why Judith's clans shunned the sea? On land they were paramount, deceptively humble while ruling all. But at sea? It had come to him in a flash of inspiration. He had been staring out across the sealands, wondering about some of his past encounters in London (what *had* become of Mrs Isabella Worthington, so rich yet so jealous?). He had seen two men rowing across the bay, reminding him of the pair who had despoiled the mole's sea light the night he had pleasured Judith and learned he could recover Carradine Manor by agreeing to her terms.

Yes, the wild sea lay outside Judith's empire. No vassals out there, no allegiances beyond the sea sand. Embark, and you were beyond her reach; only for the whilst, of course, for every ship must dock, every seaman come finally to land. But freedom was worth any risk.

The sea would be his avenue to slavery's end. Many men – he thought of the despicable soak Charles Golding, Rodney Treggan and his interesting but haunted wife Harriet, Reverend Baring, Percy Carmady too perhaps – would be pleased to live in such thrall, but not Carradine. He had no illusions about Judith. She must know how many times he slipped away to the Two Cotts whores, but kept her counsel. If truth be known, she probably had spies there also.

He had lately spent time at the Goat and Compass, listening idly, and been amazed at the subjects the fisherfolk and farm labourers talked of. Naturally the North Sea recurred, the Baltic trade being spoken of with envy and admiration. He heard names like Königsberg, Riga, Oslo, Copenhagen, Hamburg, and strange names of rivers he could not even recall from his schooling days when he plagued countless tutors into tantrums.

Yes, a ship to the Baltic ports. Concealment from Judith of the profit, the cargoes, even somehow pretend a total loss – Carmady had spoken of the inordinate risks of the Baltic Sea. There was ample scope to become financially independent of this succubus. How he could achieve it he had no real idea yet, but it would bring the chance. He was certain.

The girl Mehala should have been the one, of course. No temptation would make him evade *her* wakening touch! Instead, she was probably lying beside that ignorant dog-doctor at Shalamar. Last year she simply walked away when he had propositioned the bitch. Her, a slut without a penny price, to ignore him! And finally to create the trouble that had led to this.

'Rad? Time to rouse.'

He said nothing, suddenly interested in a new train of thought. That crocus, Carmichael. Every ship needed a doctor, some crude surgeon who would hack at whatever needed hacking, some drunken sawbones. Most of those on merchantmen were running from trouble at home, or incompetents unable to make a living on land. What if Carmichael somehow got into a little bother that he could not avoid except by going to sea? Or perhaps got into debt? Then the soft-centred quack might accept a large bribe of earnest money for a voyage . . .?

It would need only one sea journey to prise Mehala free of her mad illusions. And he would be simultaneously free of Judith.

Trouble for Carmichael; entrap Mehala once she found herself alone; and rid himself of his gaoler. Those would be his profits from the Baltic. A start was now more urgent than ever.

'What do you think of Alex Waite?' he asked.

Judith laughed, her arm reaching round his belly to cup him. 'I knew you were awake, Rad. Thinking of your scheme?'

'Thinking of how the thunderstorm washed away my chance of making a good wager on the races.'

'You want to make Sealandings like . . .' Judith hesitated, trying to think of the correct name: *Boronashemeskrutan*, in her own Romany, but in English . . . 'Like Epsom race course?'

Not long since, he had wondered vaguely about her frequent hesitations in speech, but no longer. He recognised them as hitch-steps in translation from Romany. In the heat of sexual passion, her orgasm was the prompt for uttered cries in a language wholly beyond him. Revelation had come slowly – a word, an overheard conversation between Judith and some new maid – but now he was certain her tribe was everywhere.

'Alex Waite the North Briton?'

'Yes.' Carradine rolled onto his back, seeing her propped on one elbow, her long dark hair falling in waves across her naked shoulders and onto her breasts. It was always a wonder, that a woman as alluring as Judith could one minute be all that he could possibly wish for, and another, as now, seem far less desirable than the whore Corrie he had lately engaged at Two Cotts. 'Waite is eager to enter London society. I could effect that entry for him.'

'At a price?'

Carradine suppressed his anger. A gentleman never acted for money alone. He had killed a man for a lesser insult.

'No. As a favour, one gentleman for another.'

'And expecting in return . . .?'

'Nothing.' Carradine was maddened by her laughter, but this was no time for anger. For that, there was a better time coming, and it would give him greater satisfaction. That was the way of hate, as it was the way of love: storing up, keeping pent back passion until a final release gave giddy delight. 'He is a gentleman I should like to see more of.'

'We have the Treggans arriving today.'

'What more natural than to invite Waite also? A small party, for some of the pleasure we lost at the races.'

'He is wealthy, is he not? From his father in . . .' *Juvlo-Mengresky Tem, Lousy-Fellows' Country* '. . . Scotland?'

'Is he?' Carradine was offhand, yet aware of her cynical

amusement at his pose of disinterest in the young North Briton's wealth. Waite was malleable, as all lower orders seeking to climb the social scale. It would be simple to manipulate Waite into suggesting that the ship, once bought and manned, would need a surgeon, and ask if there was not a local doctor who might fill the list. The suggestion would be Waite's, and Judith would not suspect that it had originated in Carradine. She hated Mehala, as did he, but in a different way. A woman's hates were unrelenting, whereas a man's vehemence played itself out in time and was forgotten as other events came along. 'That hardly matters. But he is better informed than many. Perhaps he has advisors in Newcastle or Leith. That is all I mean.'

Judith said softly, lifting her stroking hand and inspecting him with a knowing smile, 'You speak of pleasure, Rad?'

'With Golding, Carmady, Treggan possibly, and a few others, the venture would be a certainty. It is time I thought of Sealandings. It is my duty.'

She listened warily. This was new and untrustworthy from a man like Carradine. She knew of his attendances at Two Cotts, but he was a man driven by his appetites, as every man worth his salt. That was forgivable. But to speculate on improving the lot of the harbour . . .? That was the sign of a man settling down, coming to terms with life. Thinking of Carradine the manor, and less of Carradine the man?

She hardly dared hope as her breath quickened and her hand began its slow familiar stirring. Was it finally coming to Carradine that he should now continue his lineage? That had been her one aim, since she had come to Sealandings, to become his wife, true possessor of all here, established in society as the rightful owner of the man, looked up to instead of enduring the insufferable slights of those carriaged bitches.

There was no question about his changed behaviour lately. Preoccupied, withdrawn, examining the portraits of his ancestors in unguarded moments, strolling the grounds, looking at the ornamental lakes and out to sea, as if realising that he had almost lost his inheritance. Surely a man coming to terms with the stark truth must think with fondness – at least fondness! – of the woman who had restored it all to him.

'We have very little time, Rad.'

'Make time, bitch.' His voice had thickened, his breathing becoming deeper and his body turgid. 'Come over.'

'You want me to, Rad?'

He cuffed her. 'I tell you to, bitch.'

'Ask.' She was smiling mischievously, playing the teasing game that she had played when first they came together.

He cuffed her a second time, but she only laughed and would not obey until he asked. Only then did she stop her stirring, kneel over his supine form, and start the sweet rocking that was a woman's most perfect response.

In the moment before the detumescence, the explosion of images in his mind showed him a joyous expanse of sea, limitless in its extent and freedom. He slept afterwards for the first time in weeks, and was late coming down to welcome the Treggans as their six-horse landau rolled grandly up the drive.

Clement and Rosie found the door along one of the corridors radiating from the great hall. Dust lay everywhere, and the begrimed windows were darkened by cobwebs. The double door was warped from damp, the stained glass insets in the upper halves badly buckled. Clement managed to prise the doors apart, though one brass handle tore away part of the rotten wood.

'Rosie, look!' Clement coughed at the dust. They entered cautiously. 'A church!'

That was an exaggeration. It was merely a room. An altar stood at the far end, under an arched window letting in a wash of grey. Chairs, almost crumbled from decay, showed only the occasional glint of metal among tapestry covering.

'It was a chapel. Papist, do you think?'

Rosie shook her head, indicating the area above the altar. No red votive glass showed, nor any on the walls.

Clement said in relief, 'Shalamar must have been a mansion of some great ancient family, with their own parson and everything. It is long disused.'

'That is true, Clement,' Mehala said, coming into the chapel behind them. 'I found the place by accident, seeing in from outside as I cleared the undergrowth. The window lets onto the herb garden by the old fishery pools. Mansions often had their own chapel. This is small; many held a hundred or so. Labourers and artisans from the estate and farms would come to evensong on feast days and sometimes Sundays too.'

'And in the house?' Clement asked, awed. 'The servants?'

'All as one, anciently.' She was unwilling to stay.

'And parsons could still come here for services?'

'Why, yes.'

'Then why do they not?' he asked directly.

'Reverend Baring is unwilling, and mistrusts us.'

'Why, Mehala?'

Rosie was looking, and both awaited her answer. 'Because Reverend Baring frowns on my living here with Doctor Ven. We incurred his displeasure by not marrying in his church.'

'Did you marry here, Mehala?'

'No,' she said shortly. 'I suppose this chapel will have to be cleaned up one day. It takes least priority to the rest of Shalamar! Come, both of you.'

They left the chapel, Mehala pausing to look around the walls. No figures, no plaques, just simple unadorned plainness with only the carved wood dados and the skirting intact here and there. Rats had gnawed holes in the corners, then vanished to scavenge elsewhere. She shivered. It was symbolic of the ruin that was poor Shalamar. Perhaps one day it might change.

23

A WOMAN'S PRIDE lay in her appreciation of external actions. Men, poor things, were forced in on themselves and so unable to appreciate the subtle shifts of balance when a meeting had been arranged.

Tabitha Hunterfield felt full of herself. Not, of course, in a prideful way. No, in a lady's way, from her position among the upper echelons. And today, as rightful representative of her brother Sir Henry Hunterfield, she was about to exercise her fullest authority. There was no more respected authority in the Eastern Hundreds, and no higher district authority in Sealandings, than the hereditary Lord. And it was he who had deputed her today to meet the Sealandings ladies – gentry only, of course, plus those close to – to ascertain their opinions on the charges laid against the pair at Shalamar.

This was her first commission from Henry. She would enact Henry's wishes so perfectly that he would be dazzled.

She stepped down from the small barouche slowly and with becoming gravity. She was the lady of the great Lorne House, today having summoned certain ladies to hear her opinions on the state of local morality. They must listen, while she expounded views that they would recognise as clever and worthy. They would learn.

It had been wise to seek the guidance of a senior estate steward, Mr Tayspill, to be armed against mere facts. She had certain items of history written small on card in her reticule, to consult should some lady make a protest. This proved her astuteness. Guidance? Could any suppose that she had sought *guidance* from Tayspill? Hardly that, for it made her sound deficient in some way, seeking instruction from some more expert individual. That could not be correct, for Tayspill was a mere artisan.

208

No, she had merely checked a few details with him.

Wise, though, to have prepared herself. She raised her redingote skirts to make her way along the grass path that led to the new church meeting hall. And there came Miss Euterpe Baring, a scholarly miss if ever there was one, learned in everything biblical, music and the classics. Fortunately, Miss Euterpe knew her place, as she better had, because Reverend Josiah Baring her overbearing brother lived at St Edmund the Martyr's on sufferance of Henry.

'Ladies!' Tabitha cried, overwhelmed. 'How kind of you to come!'

'Miss Hunterfield,' Euterpe Baring said, curtseying.

The other two ladies repeated the salutation, Matilda Gould the schoolmistress and Mary Prothero hurrying ahead to usher Hunterfield's sister into the small assembly room.

Its scent was of new wood, low rafters and plain wooden walls. It admitted only forty, but that it had been built at all was a miracle. Rather, Tabitha thought sweetly, it was an instance of her brother's charity, donated to the church as a gift in thanks for the delivery of Sealandings from the terrible cattle murrain. A plaque said as much; the erection of the commemorative brass had been against Henry's wishes.

Brown, the local joiner, had made the plain Suffolk chairs, rush seating, simple beechwood with two stretchers. The church had been parsimonious with Henry's largesse, an instance of Reverend Baring detaining part of the donation for his church. Quite legal, of course, but less than honest.

Tabitha smiled at the dozen or so ladies as they rose and bobbed. She made her way to the front, sitting down facing them.

She looked around the hall, enjoying herself. For far too long she had lived in the shadow of Lydia, now mercifully inland and unable to exert the slightest authority over her. And Letitia was her quiet, poetic, wistful self, and – another merciful release – likely to produce her first baby fairly soon. Now, she was Mistress of Lorne House, empowered by the weight of her brother's authority.

'Good day to you all, ladies,' she said, conscious of her charm and condescension.

They smiled and returned the greeting, heads nodding and smiles coming her way. She paused to allow Euterpe, Mary

Prothero and Miss Gould to reach their seats. The chairs had been arranged in crescents, which was somewhat unfortunate for she wanted to give admonitions. But she would direct the meeting as she wished, whoever it was had made that mistake.

The audience was highly significant. Helen Bettany, Quaker, always giving the impression of somehow straining against the confines of her Society of Friends, sat next to Bessie Parker, wife of the public stables owner and so-say reforming Methodist, weak as her facile husband. Frances Temple the blacksmith's wife, Barbara Tyll the wife of the tollgate 'farmer' on the Norwich road, and Mistress Eldridge from the butcher's place near Hast's in Market Square, with that strange-looking Mistress Endercotte. Add to those Jane, the fat aggressive wife of Leonard Sadler the corn merchant, one of the two churchwardens, and finally the brooding Gertrude Digges, always seeming on the brink of a decline from worry. This last lady was wife of the second churchwarden Finch Digges, a man much given to sudden blurting of half-digested thoughts and a great breeder of little children – seven in nine years so far.

'My purpose in accepting your kind invitation today', Tabitha began, taking in the faces, 'is to point out a few difficulties . . .' she carolled a light laugh '. . . that beset Sealandings. It is nothing that we cannot cope with. I fear the consequences, you see,' she added brightly, showing that her wish was imperative.

A lady stirred as if wanting to speak. Tabitha directed her gaze towards Miss Baring and allowed a deliberately over-long pause. The woman had the common sense to control her insolence and subside without a word.

'Charges are laid against Doctor Carmichael, resident at Shalamar, and Mehala, with whom he cohabits. The charges are under the Public Worship rules, in that this Mehala and Carmichael did cause affront in our churchyard.'

She had so far consulted no note. Her card was held in reserve. For the moment she simply frowned, she thought quite prettily, though her looks were wasted on this crowd.

'Miss Hunterfield?'

'Yes?' Tabitha was startled. Euterpe Baring had risen after all, and stood composed in her plain russet dress.

'The ladies present here know that it was my brother Reverend

Baring who laid these charges before Sir Henry. I think it beholden upon us to have the details set out before we can properly discuss them, subject to your pleasure, Miss Hunterfield.'

'Set out, you say? *Discuss?*' It was something to do with First William, she recalled quickly, but did that mean William the First? Surely not, such a distance in time. Or the first year of the latest William? She wanted to reach for her card with its now essential details, but would only make a fool of herself by doing so. She suddenly hated this pale anxious woman for her impertinence, standing there afraid at her own scandalous effrontery yet daring herself to go on.

'Yes, if you please, Miss Hunterfield. Thank you.'

The insolent bitch sat down. Tabitha had the bright idea to turn the tables.

'Very well, Miss Baring,' she cooed pleasantly. 'Let us do that, shall we, ladies? As Miss Baring's brother brought the accusation, she herself make the summary.'

There was silence. Tabitha smoothed her lace berlins over her hands and waited. 'Miss Baring?' she said, smiling, eyebrows raised. 'Please begin.'

Euterpe Baring rose slowly and stepped to one side to stand against the wall, facing the room at large.

'If it please you, Miss Hunterfield, ladies,' she began quietly. 'The custom of this realm once held that any man and woman who repeated "I do take thee for my wife", or "husband", before witnesses, established a legal and binding marriage, providing that the man kissed the lady in salutation and gave her a present of, usually, a ring, and that afterwards . . .' Euterpe's face coloured as she strove to find words delicate enough, '. . . they established marital union.'

A woman gasped, and two women bridled angrily. Mistress Bettany made as if to speak, but her lips remained shut.

Euterpe went on, 'Church law in 1604 laid down that church weddings ought to take place after eight o'clock in the morning, in the parish of bride or groom, after the reading of banns weekly for three weeks. The requirements still extant for parental approval were enforced, and the usual rules of consanguinity.'

'Thank you, Miss Baring!' Tabitha exclaimed, for the insolent cow was stealing her thunder, but the usurper had not done.

'I beg to finish, Miss Hunterfield.' Euterpe drew breath. 'There were, as many will remember from tales told by older folk, ways of avoiding these ordinations. In St James's in Duke Place, and at St Pancras, no questions were asked. Fast weddings were commonplace. Wandering clergymen married couples without licence in the Fleet Prison chapel, at taverns and coffee houses, and even in houses of ill repute, advertising their trade with painted signboards of the hands of a woman and man clasped, for between four shillings and two guineas a marriage.'

'No, no!' some lady exclaimed. 'This is indelicate!'

Mistress Temple cried out. 'Must we be so unseemly?'

'And she unmarried!' came from the grim Mistress Endercotte.

'I beg of you, Miss Hunterfield,' Euterpe said quietly. 'We are here, in the interests of Sealandings, to speak openly, guided by conscience. To evade this duty is to deny ourselves, not to support wrongdoing.'

'Very well,' Tabitha said faintly, lost. Things were getting out of hand. She had come to see that these idiot women listened to her own views, not to bray their own opinions. She lowered her head as if meekly allowing Miss Baring's point, but fervently wished the bitch would vanish into Hell, the quicker the better.

Euterpe was now white, her lips almost blue, but she stood with composure, obviously giving details she had made sure of, delivering a planned message.

'If any lady here be injured by my words, please be assured that I am merely stating the laws and customs of the land, as they have been sanctioned by King and Church.' She continued slowly. 'I was reminding us all about the swift marriages, sometimes with certificates false as to ages, names, and date of the nuptuals for purposes of legitimising a child conceived earlier.'

'Please, Miss Hunterfield!' Helen Bettany cried, but Tabitha was struck dumb by this outrageous woman's frankness, the same woman she had thought so docile.

'Lord Hardwicke it was whose Marriage Act took force in 1754, and the rule made that church weddings alone were binding. Parish registers then became the mode of recording that a proper wedding had taken place, between named couples. Marriages were taxed in 1784, and recently in 1823 a new Marriage Act was passed but partly repealed, so the former laws as yet stand. That is the current state, Miss Hunterfield. I thank you for your patience and wisdom.'

'Not at all, Miss Baring,' Tabitha said feebly, her mind a blank. There was silence.

'Miss Hunterfield, if you please?'

'Yes, Mistress Tyll?' Tabitha was thankful that someone, anyone, had risen to fill the awkward gap, but was nonetheless intrigued to see Barbara Tyll here. A devout churchgoer in the established religion, regularly attending St Edmund's. It was often remarked that she seemed to observe not only the Church's holydays, but also the more ancient holy days, which started whispers of latent Papist affections.

Until the arrival of the dark woman Judith Blaker, Barbara Tyll had held the position of Carradine's housekeeper. There had been the usual gossip, of course, that he took bluntest advantage of the woman's position, though it was not unknown for an unmarried – or even a married – gentleman to use his authority for such purposes. And there were young maids aplenty at Carradine Manor, and Carradine himself was known for his bestial reputation . . .

'I hope I do not speak out of turn, Miss Hunterfield, when I say that we here are all of one mind, that scandal should not be allowed to give bad example to the lower orders who might be influenced by the . . . the relationship established at Shalamar.'

'Amen!' Mistress Endercotte barked.

'But that does not mean we ought to exchange a poor example for a worse,' Barbara Tyll argued patiently. 'And I suggest that those who, with the best will in the world, have brought the charges, be urged to reconsider.'

'Why?' Bessie Parker demanded, almost rising in vehemence. Tabitha wondered just how afraid the woman would be, to return home to her reforming Methodist husband and account for a result he disfavoured. 'Remember the woman taken in adultery!'

'Adultery was punishable by death under the law of Moses,' Mistress Endercotte intoned harshly. 'Leviticus, chapter twenty, verse ten: *Let them both be put to death, both the adulterer and the adulteress*. It is written!'

'If I may, Mistress Endercotte,' Euterpe Baring interrupted, 'the whole verse reads differently. You give only the last half. The whole verse speaks only of adultery with *married* people. Doctor Carmichael and Mehala were unmarried.'

Tabitha drew breath to interject, but kept silent. She had overheard something being said, when Mehala and the girl Rosie attended an interview with Henry. She had only heard snatches, but then she had been put out on account of the presence of the odious Sylvia Newborough setting her cap at Henry with utter shamelessness . . .

'The Sainted Parliament established the law in 1650.' Mistress Endercotte would not surrender, though several of the ladies present looked in apprehension at the mention of the Republican Parliament of Cromwell. Even the vaguest reference to that unrelenting band of Puritans could be construed as disloyalty. 'In May the Fourteenth of that year, Parliament ordained that adultery was a capital crime, whether among the married or unmarried!'

'It was never yet enforced,' Euterepe Baring said quietly.

'Why, Mistress Tyll?' Tabitha asked. 'You want the charges rethought, without saying why.'

She waited, quite pleased at this response. She sounded like Henry! He would be so pleased with her splendid control of this meeting.

'Thank you, Miss Hunterfield.' Barbara Tyll stood, taking her time. Tabitha was not the only lady who looked at the tollkeeper's wife with renewed interest, surreptitiously scrutinising her form. 'There are two reasons. One I touched on, that we might direct the attention of susceptible folk and the young from a circumstance better left unnoticed.'

'Shame!'

Barbara Tyll ignored the preacher's wife and continued. 'The second reason is more pertinent. How often do we see people in Suffolk consorting without benefit of clergy? Here is a young couple who betrothed themselves in a manner exactly like that of our forefathers and mothers of ancient days. That is what is rumoured – I have not read the written charge. Does that mean that we must defame the memories of our forebears, who married in that manner without sibrit? I mean, by that, before the three weekly banns and church weddings were obligatory. Does it mean that kings and queens, even, who did the same, are also now damned in our eyes?'

By now the ladies were calling out in protest, and two were already leaving in anger, but Barbara Tyll went on. 'Miss Hunterfield. You summoned us here to offer our views. I believe in all honesty that the charge should be withdrawn. Let us ignore consequences – that we shall be without a doctor if Mehala and Doctor Carmichael are driven away. They have merely done what many have done before them, and that we have no way of ascertaining if they be less holy, or more holy, thereby.'

The meeting was a babble of complaints and accusations, until Tabitha rose. It was Lydia's dictum that a lady ought to retire the instant more than one voice was raised. Utterly at a loss, she remained standing until the hall fell silent.

'Ladies, I shall now take my leave,' she announced, and slowly walked to the door.

A pale and silent Euterpe Baring accompanied her to the path, and walked a pace behind her all the way to the barouche.

'Thank you, Miss Hunterfield,' she said as the coach moved slowly away.

Tabitha Hunterfield did not reply.

24

'THE IDEAL, MEHALA,' Ven was teaching in the bare with-drawing-room at Shalamar, 'is that you catch the artery in some compression. The oldest forceps, as we call the instruments, are the fingers, but Doctor Clowes, who was surgeon to Good Queen Bess, scorned them during amputation –'

'You will amputate?' Bartholomew Hast cried in fear. He was seated in a window corner, with his uncovered leg supported on two forked branches forming a crude trestle.

'If you do not stay silènt,' Ven said with mock severity. Mehala raised a hand for silence. 'Clowes said he only needed a sharp saw, a double-edged knife, and one scalpel for any amputation. Surgeons still boast as Clowes did.'

'Forceps?' Mehala inspected the instruments on the table.

'Robert Liston in London's Gower Street is our fastest surgeon, a giant of a man with brute strength and a fascination for speed. The medical students there place bets on the time he takes to cut off an arm, or leg, or hand. Twenty-five seconds is his record. Liston holds the knife in his teeth while he ties the arteries.' Ven sighed. 'But then he has many assistants. Hence the lone doctor's need for forceps.'

'Have we any?'

Ven reluctantly looked towards Hast. The gunmaker was staring out of the window now, seemingly taking little notice. He had asked to be moved from the kitchen, the only other habitable room on Shalamar's ground floor where he had been nursed since the accident.

'This case of instruments', Ven evaded lamely, 'was generously given by Squire Hunterfield, a stroke of good fortune. You remember?'

Mehala smiled. 'I remember.'

'From John Gill of Salisbury Square in London, but without advice.' He reddened and added, 'I intend no criticism. Only, had I the chance, I should have gone to Mr Grice's establishment in Whitechapel Road, London, to make my selection.'

'Are instruments bought so, at a tradesman's?'

'Indeed, yes.' He laughed, half ashamed. 'Nothing is new, Mehala. An archeologist showed me instruments from Roman times which were clearly forceps. The French forceps of Perret are excellent, I have heard, with crossed arms held closed by a spring.'

'Have you used them, Ven?' Mehala asked, then was instantly angry at her thoughtlessness as he coloured. 'No I have only heard of them from a doctor who saw them used.'

'Are they so valuable?'

'Indeed! Clamped on an artery, they stem the blood flow until the doctor can ligature the artery —'

'Ven.' Hast was ashen. 'Might I return to the kitchen?'

'Of course!' Ven was a little disappointed. 'I thought you might be interested in the surgical instruments for wounds —'

Mehala quickly intervened. 'It *is* a little chilly, Bartholomew. Let me call all hands to shift your great hulk!'

Clement and Rosie were summoned and with Ven they shuffled him slowly across the great hall and down the kitchen corridor to his old place. He settled there with relief. Ven returned with Mehala to the withdrawing-room, Mehala cautioning Clement and Rosie against letting the patient run about. Hast pretended to look about for something to throw, and she left laughing.

Ven glanced at her as they bent again over the drawings of different types of forceps.

'You are admirable, Mehala, with the boy, Hast, Rosie. How would I have managed?'

'Perhaps better?' She tried to make light of his remark. Today was the time for decision.

He stayed serious. 'You have a pleasing compassion. I lack it. You complement me.'

'Oh, Ven.' She moved the gunmaker's homemade trestle aside to stand by the window. 'My famous Floral Dial was looking the worse for wear. I have given it so little attention.'

'We had other duties.'

'Too many.' She turned to face him. 'And I heard in Market

Square that the Sealandings ladies met at the church's hall. Miss Tabitha convened the assembly.'

He stood in the attitude she knew so well, lips pursed, a hand on the table, head tilted. 'Concerning us?'

'There was antagonism, Ven. Our being here, living as . . . at Shalamar, considering ourselves married.' She shook her hair angrily, as if she could throw off her high colour. 'I was warned by Hunterfield.'

Ven seemed lost. 'Why does feeling run so strongly against us, Mehala?'

'We are different. You are barred from church only because Reverend Baring believed his sister Euterpe was enamoured of you.'

'That is beyond credulity!' Ven said, distressed.

'It is true.' Mehala put her suspicion into words. 'Euterpe spoke in our defence, from what I heard. And Mistress Tyll. The rest were against us.'

'Tyll?'

'Barbara Tyll, formerly housekeeper at Carradine before Judith Blaker took post there. She has returned to her husband's tollhouse on the Norwich road.'

'I remember. A pleasant, quiet lady.' He pretended optimism with a hopeful smile. 'Influential supporters, Mehala!'

'Not really, Ven. They will be overwhelmed. Miss Matilda *would* support us, but her position as mistress of the charity school is unenviable.' He examined her face. 'Can we not continue as we are?'

'And hope the hatred will go away?' Her love almost stopped her from going on. He was so like a child, wanting all the evil things in life to vanish and leave the world untroubled. Yet the storm clouds were gathering. Perhaps that was the woman's place in life, to be practical when her man, the ineffable dreamer, was unable to. 'No, Ven. It breaks my heart to say so, but we – I – must do something, and soon.'

He looked his dismay. 'You will not leave, Mehala?'

'No.' She suppressed the endearment that tried to come. 'But we need funds if we must respond to the charge.'

'Sir Henry Hunterfield.' It was suddenly difficult to speak. The Squire seemed too disposed to favour Mehala for Ven's liking. 'He is fair. If our trial comes before him . . .'

'It will not help, Ven. Law ties his hands. And senior justices' trials are always reviewed by higher authority.' She came to him and took his hands. They were cold. 'When Hunterfield summoned me to interview, he advised me to go south and claim my possessions.'

Ven took a moment replying. All along, Mehala had been reluctant to admit her past. She resolutely refused to remember, claiming that her near-drowning had obliterated everything. But to him she had admitted that she had once been married against her will. The few details he had discovered proved her to have been wealthy, mistress of estates somewhere on East Anglia's southern estuaries. A kind dark-haired maid-of-all, a slight girl called Praisewell at Bettany's mill, had told him that she had seen Mehala being driven through a market town in her own carriage, a lady of some standing. And there was Mehala's piecemeal account, when she broke down in tears and owned that, a widow, she was forced to mourn for two years after Rebow's drowning.

'We survive. The fees Bartholomew insists on paying –'

'No, dearest. That buys food, no more. We are five now in Shalamar. I bought some old clothing for Rosie, and I make our linen. But anything else – shoes, a coat, hats – we cannot provide. The garden vegetables last well, though meat is rarely come by, and the cost of fish on the wharf –'

'What will you do?'

There was no easy way to announce her decision. 'I will go to Red Hall, Ven, the estate I own . . .'

'Can you claim an estate so simply, after such a time?'

'I shall find a steward, Ven.'

'We know none.'

'Tayspill, of Lorne House. He is a good man, and honest.'

'Tayspill.' The man was not from Sealandings Hundred. He had proved invaluable when Ven and Mehala fought the cattle plague, though at first reluctant to accept Ven's decisions.

'I shall have to ask Hunterfield's permission to approach Tayspill,' Mehala said, wanting Ven to acknowledge that her hand was forced. 'I want you to know that if you forbid me, I shall obey you.'

'Have I the right?' His bitterness was almost too hard to bear.

'Yes. I shall stay with you lifelong, Ven. You know that.'

'Life conspires against happiness, Mehala.'

She placed her lips gently on his but stepped quickly away as a knocking sounded on the door. A man's voice was raised outside. 'Happiness must be fought for, dearest. I am simply about the business of warring for it, on our behalf.'

'It should be the man's responsibility, this fighting.'

'The man's fighting is different. This combat is a woman's career.' She left him, moving briskly out, calling for the messenger to go round to find the kitchen vestibule.

Ven stood, staring unseeing at the anatomical drawing he had made for Mehala.

There could be no doubt, not any longer, about his longing. She was all he would ever want in a woman, everything he could imagine for a wife. From the first, she had seemed his missing spirit, without which he had lumbered through existence with only half of his mind and heart. The admission was a blow to a man's self-esteem, whereas to a woman it seemed an unquestioned acceptance. But a man always ought to be complete, whole of himself, independent and free of encumbrances that seemed hostages to fortune. It was almost shaming to admit that he loved Mehala. She was essential.

What did he really know of her, though? That she had been born of a poor family living on a muddy island in East Anglia's seamarshes. That her old mother had inveigled her into marriage with a powerful but crazed landowner. That Rebow, his name, had in a fit of madness rowed her out to sea, that the boat overturned. That Mehala was rescued by a Sealandings fishing lugger. That Rebow's body lay buried on the Isle of Southwold.

Relatives? He knew nothing. Children? Also nothing.

The extent of her memory? Likewise, nothing.

Yet an almost-stranger was she, on whom he depended for happiness. He had promised to educate her as a doctor, against all common sense, in a world where no woman doctor yet existed. Where, some said, such a creature was a clear impossibility and against God's design.

He looked up to see Mehala standing in the doorway with a letter in her hand.

'The clerk to the Justices of the Peace, Ven. The charge is laid, to be heard within twenty days.' She was pale but resolute.

'Are the terms as they threatened?'

'Yes.' She passed him the note and came to stand by him. 'I shall go, Ven.'

'When?' He felt sickened.

'The sooner I leave, the sooner my return.'

'But the danger on the roads, Mehala.' He struggled to find reasons to dissuade her. 'I have yet to hear from my friend Ward in the north country about the spread of this disease –'

'Shhh.' She placed a finger on his lips. 'I shall be with you for ever, here or afar, Ven. Just remember that. And soon I shall be back, with whatever I can bring.'

'You promise?'

Mehala put her arms round him, embracing him arms and all, so he was trapped within her compass. Once before she had left him, and the result had been disastrous for them both. This was a second time, but there was not the vaguest threat. She would make sure of that.

'I promise,' she said. It was a declaration of war against all opposition.

25

HUNTERFIELD COULD NOT remember a greater anger.
Tabitha was the scatterbrain among his three sisters, a complete contrast with the other two. How strange that three sisters – same parents, with the same upbringing, identical teaching, governesses, home – should be so utterly different. It was almost as if the Almighty played perverse jokes at Man's expense. Could the quiet, poetic Letitia, contentedly domiciled at Watermillock with her artist, really be from the same stock as this moody, wholly tactless young woman? Tabitha was eager to assume responsibility, yet showed no tact. Lydia, his eldest sister, was determined but capable, minutely conscious of reefs in the uncharted oceans of ladies arguing morality, and would have returned with a guarded consensus.

Tabitha? She comes back baffled, appalled by the things said, desperate to prove that she had been unfairly treated and insulted wholesale because no lady wanted to be told what to think. He heard her with anger and disbelief.

'It is an outrage, Henry!' Tabitha blazed in the green withdrawing-room. 'They opposed me at every turn! A conspiracy! I demand that they receive the sternest correction!'

'For what, my dear?'

Tabitha was shocked at his seeming taciturnity. She stood before the fire, furious.

'For *what*, Henry? For insult, sir! For abuse! For being regarded as nothing more than . . .' She flung her hand to point to the two tea-maids standing in attendance. 'Than those!'

She saw her brother's face close, and knew she had gone too far. Aunt Faith sat on her squabbed cane day bed listening to Tabitha's harangue. The stupid girl had done for herself, of course, had she but wit to see it, for Henry Hunterfield's fondness for Sealandings would not stand this.

'I mean no presumption, sir,' Tabitha said.

Aunt Faith watched Tabitha alter her tactics with pure scorn. No Hunterfield woman in history was ever half so clumsy as Tabitha. For all her spectacular beauty, the girl was clearly impossible. Very soon she would be a total disappointment, one that would give Henry greater problems than both his other sisters together.

Hunterfield glanced at Aunt Faith. Without further ado she gestured the two maids away. They bobbed a curtsey and left, the senior pausing to see if the old lady required the Congou tea infusing further, but was dismissed. Hunterfield waited until the doors closed.

'You mean no presumption, Tabitha,' he said evenly, 'yet you presume.'

Tabitha tried, but her rage was too near the surface at the memory of that dreadful meeting.

'Henry! I obeyed you to the very best of my ability! I went to those odious peasants – they are no more! – and was deluged by contrary opinion! Can you imagine? The effrontery of that Miss Baring! And another outrageous commoner, a toll-gleaner's wife, stood to upbraid me – *me*! She said I failed to recognise the issues involved! It is treason, Henry! You must act forthwith! Suppress this disloyalty! Disloyalty to our class is disloyalty to the Crown itself! To an ordered society!'

'That will do.'

'What?' She halted, appalled at the finality of his tone.

He drew a slow breath while she stood there. The girl seemed unable to understand the mistakes she had made. His voice was cold. 'I encharged you to meet the ladies for no other purpose but to hear their opinions on the immorality charges.'

She glared at him. Aunt Faith thought, *Oh, no*. Surely not even Tabitha was so foolish as to protest once Henry reached his decision. He was slow to anger, but once it came . . .

'I did *exactly* that, Henry!' Tabitha retorted. 'Remember, sir, it was I who confronted those harridans –'

'*Silence!*' Hunterfield thundered.

Tabitha jumped and froze. Even Aunt Faith exclaimed aloud in alarm. That Hunterfield had not changed his expression was all the more disconcerting. The room fell silent.

After a moment, Hunterfield resumed in his normal voice. 'You failed abysmally, Miss Hunterfield. Not through the circumstances of the meeting, but through your own utter incompetence. You disregarded my instructions. You acted to suit your own self-esteem, which far exceeds your aptitude.'

Tabitha stood as if transfixed. Her brother paused in thought. Tabitha's desperate glance of appeal to Aunt Faith was answered by a warning frown to stay silent. Hunterfield resumed.

'Your disobedience is unacceptable. I shall not seek your assistance in any other similar matter. Of course I shall not act against the ladies at the meeting. My one regret is that you have effectively disqualified yourself from the assistance I find essential. No other sister of mine has been anything other than helpful, to the limits of their respective abilities.'

'Sir, I —'

'That will do. You may go while I speak with Aunt Faith.'

Tabitha stared, appalled. Sent from the withdrawing-room like a child? She almost appealed to Aunt Faith, but the old lady ignored her. Tabitha swallowed the correction, curtseyed, and left in silence.

Aunt Faith sighed, and poured tea. 'The trouble with this Congou, Henry, is that its infusion is too strong. Not everyone likes its high colour. I shall see that you receive Souglo or Haisven teas, if your esteemed sister has purchased some. Do your servants steal it? They do everywhere else.'

Hunterfield said nothing. The old lady passed him a cup. He placed it on the teapoy, ignoring her hiss of alarm at the risk to the mahogany. Cumbersome and awkward, she rose and placed an oak coaster beneath his saucer.

She had always hated the silences of menfolk. Henry's father, her brother, had been of a similar disposition. His quiet periods were to be enjoyed, and his mild good humour a joy. But his abstract brown studies were horrid. She had no illusions. Men were violent creatures deep down. As long as they could be kept in the emotional shallows, so to speak, they were safe. A woman could manage them without interference. It was in times like these, when a man was driven into his own depths, that he became unreachable. From such profundity a man might erupt and do untold damage. Stupid, stupid Tabitha!

But did the young women of today listen? Not to a single word.

However kindly disposed one was, they paid no heed. Yet it seemed hardly a week since she had changed this grand lord's soiled baby linen and fed him through a pap spoon.

'Aunt Faith?'

'Oh, so you speak at last, Henry!'

He ignored this. 'I want Tabitha replaced.'

'Replaced? Or displaced?'

'Both.'

She smiled to herself. He was always the quick one. But always a mite too guarded, watching himself even more closely than he watched others.

'By whom?'

'I need womanly assistance, Aunt Faith. I miss Letitia and Lydia. When we were all here I could assign duty, and not be disappointed. Now?'

'Now you are in disarray because it concerns this Mehala.'

Hunterfield was astonished. 'Mehala?'

'I rather think so, Henry.' She tasted the Congou and made a slight grimace. It had been kept too long uncovered, a clue to incompetence somewhere. She would have to explore.

'The girl is already —'

'I know, I know.' Aunt Faith overrode him. 'She invents a marriage for herself, and calls herself wedded to this bemused young doctor. That precisely means she is *not* married. The Marriage Act says so.'

'But anciently —'

'The ancients did as the ancients did. In these modern times, we are required to abide by laws. The King's writ rules. That Mehala has you and Sealandings by the ears.'

'Why do you speak of her?'

'Because you think only of her,' Aunt Faith said with asperity. 'It is clear as day. Choose now which road to drive.'

'What roads?' He was uncomfortable at the conversation, but he had wanted womanly guidance and had better listen.

'Take her, or forget her completely. And while we are speaking seriously, I shall look into this Congou's management, so costly and so far travelled.'

'Which course would you recommend?'

'That you forget her, Henry! If she had wanted you it would

have happened long since. You could have enjoyed her in secrecy – as you used to enjoy that horrid bitch Thalia De Foe over at Milton Hall. I never did like *her* evil ways. You are well shut. Anyway, she always preferred Carradine.'

Hunterfield listened while the old lady expounded on Thalia De Foe. It was all true, Fellows De Foe probably condoning his own cuckolding because of Thalia's forcefulness.

'Mehala is the stone thrown in the pond, Henry. A disturbed pond is never still thereafter. Some women have that propensity. Whether it is some quality of their nature, or whether accident, God knows but does not tell! This Mehala is one such. You have given me your answer.'

'I have?'

'Indeed, Henry. You have decided not to take Mehala. How do I know, sir? Because you would have had her months ago. You know in your heart that she would reject you and stay with her leech. She has decided, Henry. Face up to it, admit it openly to yourself. You already have in your mind. Unless there is some unforeseeable upset. She is never for you.'

Hunterfield nodded once. The old lady was right. 'I made enquiries, discreet ones, about her background. Red Hall lies in Tendring Hundred. Her husband was drowned.'

'Indeed,' Aunt Faith said with sarcasm. 'No memory is as sound as that which a woman mislays.'

'You are over-critical.'

'You are over-kind, Henry. She will remember quick enough when the occasion arises.'

'Which leaves me where I was, when Tabby proved her worth.'

'No self-pity, Henry. It never was a fault of yours, so do not make it one now. You have an immediate choice of wives, excluding the less obvious ones from lower orders. Sylvia Newborough, now. Marriageable, pretty, not too bright, but no family history of madness and not a hint of the tubercle in her lineage –'

'Aunt, please. You speak as of livestock.'

'It falls to us women to be practical, since men will not be so,' the old lady said bluntly. 'You are clever choosing horseflesh and dogs. Be at least as sensible choosing a bride. Do you like her?'

He hesitated. 'Sylvia . . . comes too close, without enough acquaintanceship.'

'A clinger. Yes, her mother Amicia was a clinger. Too eager, that's her trouble. My choice is Brillianta Astell. No phthisis of the chest, that Astell lot, though they run to croup in their boy children and groin hernias in their elderly male line. No rickets to speak of, which is always a good sign. Sir Edward would approve if you were to give him half a nod. A planner like his father, is Edward Astell. Thank God, not given to the squint. The young women, though, are too lean in the tit for my liking —'

'Aunt Faith! Please! I am not at a pig show.'

'You would say the same about beasts at a country fair, Henry.' She sniffed. 'It counts, I tell you, when your firstborn is plucking at his mother's dugs wanting more and she is distracted and her frantic chambermaids combing the villages looking for a woman with dripping udders —'

'Thank you for your advice, Aunt Faith.' Henry rose, putting his cup aside.

'Lorela Astell,' the old lady coursed on, unperturbed. 'Those two sisters hate each other. Lorela Astell has no hope of escaping a commercial marriage, the company she keeps —'

It was then that Crane interrupted by a knock, with the news that Tayspill, the estate's senior steward, requested an audience. Questioned, Crane answered that it concerned one Mehala at Shalamar.

Hunterfield avoided Aunt Faith's look of triumph, and went to the accounting room to receive the man, saying nothing.

Tayspill had proved his worth in the previous year, when Hunterfield brought him in as a second estate steward to help in the cattle epidemic. He was reliable, in spite of his air of doubt and his slow rejoinders.

'Mehala, Tayspill?'

'She came to the steward lodge, Squire. She asks permission to beg advice about an estate on the Colne river. She says she has become entitled.' Tayspill had his beaver in his hands and wore his wrap-rascal loosely about him, so Mehala had presumably come upon him when he was driving the Suffolk waggon about the estates. 'It seems a queer story to me, Squire. She is usually truthful.'

'She wants my permission?'

'Yes, Squire.'

Hunterfield pretended to give the matter some thought, as if the issue was new to him. 'I had better agree, Tayspill. But make sure that, if anything seems untoward, you let me know immediately. Give her general advice, but send her to see me about things doubtful or particular.'

The man was relieved. 'Thank you, Squire. Directly.'

Hunterfield would have preferred to interview Mehala himself, but it would have been unwise in view of what Aunt Faith had said. The old lady's presence was a two-edged sword.

26

'SEALANDINGS IS BEAUTIFUL, is it not, Mr Waite?'
Alex Waite was startled, not having heard her approach
though the path was gravelled. The North Sea was calm today.

'Mistress Blaker.' He had already seen her twice today about
Carradine Manor. 'Indeed. I was just admiring the view.'

'Is it as splendid as your north country?'

'At least as splendid,' he replied warily. Regional love he knew
well. He was advancing well in society, and did not want to
prejudice his progress by careless comment.

'The colours hereabouts must be more garish than those of your
county, I think?' she persisted, to his discomfort.

'The hues in North Britain are noted for their gentleness,' he
answered. 'Here there is a marvellous profusion.'

'Heathers are not grown enough for their beauty.'

He was unable to continue, having had very little of women's
company. At home everything was land, local rivalries, clans,
arguments about kinship. Here were subtler pathways, though he
himself had been well if brutally learned by two dour old scholasts.

She started to walk slowly along the rise, occasionally looking
down at the sea. Carradine property ran for several furlongs along
the land's edge.

'The estate's pasture falls sharply to the water along the path,'
she warned gently. 'Take care, Mr Waite.'

'Thank you, mistress.'

'Of course, you must be well used to treading warily.' Before he
could register the double meaning she went on. 'And our steep
precipices must seem trifling.'

'My countryside is bleak, and quite hilly.'

'Do you long for it?'

'I . . . I admire your lovely Suffolk, Mistress Blaker.'

She smiled, gentle reflection itself. 'That is answer enough. You miss your home. Why did you come to South Britain?'

'To see society.' He was a little embarrassed by the blunt invitation to confide. 'My father wants me to experience a greater society than Fife and Edinburgh. We have centres of manufacturing, but nothing like Birmingham, Manchester, and Leeds. And the machines in South Britain . . . But I bore you.'

'Please continue. I find it exciting, and your company . . .' She broke off, as if preventing an indiscretion. 'I share your sense of remoteness from my origins, Mr Waite.'

'Me, Mistress Blaker?'

'Judith, please, when we are able to speak, away from –'

'Thank you, ah, Judith.'

'To be denied access to one's own people is always extremely painful. Do you not agree, Alex?'

'Indeed I do.' The melancholy in his voice was revealing. 'You also are separated from your own kin, Judith?'

She watched harbourmen towing a small hopper lighter. Since the previous year's great storm Hunterfield had ordered that the harbour mouth be dredged continually. The hopper lighter boat was used to carry the dredgings out to three miles offshore, at the deepest point, opposite the River Affon that ran into the bay. The hopper had no means of propulsion, so once clear of the harbour had to be towed behind a ketch.

'Yes.' She wore her walking shawl, and pulled it close as if suddenly chilled. 'You see I try to please you. I wear my Edinburgh Kashmir, of the new Australian wool that you North Britons so admire.'

'I am honoured.' He seemed about to say more.

'Some are distanced by their birth. I am distanced . . .' She gazed frankly at him. 'Might I give you a confidence?'

'Of course.'

'I am distanced by the high rank of my father.' She had wondered if her invented tale would be going a little too far. But her impression was that he would be only too anxious to be taken into her confidence, with all the implications that might suggest.

'Your father, Judith? But that circumstance only arises when . . .' He did not gasp, but came close.

She bowed her head as if in sorrow. 'When the father is of such exalted rank that he cannot acknowledge his parenthood? Yes. I learned of it on my twelfth birthday. So I was bound to the occupation I presently hold.' She gave him a brave smile. 'I want you to know that I harbour no bitterness. That would be . . . disloyal.'

'Who knows of this?' He could hardly get the words out, thinking of the consequences of her astonishing revelation.

'You and I,' she said candidly. 'And one other, of course, in London. And an elderly guardian, but he passed away. Which necessitated my coming to Sealandings. No,' she answered his unspoken question, 'Rad does not know. He has too many responsibilities. And . . .' She made a pretty hesitation. 'And rumour tells of Carradine's lack of proper haviour with certain ladies. I should not want my natural father's indiscretion to be exposed.'

'I am honoured, Judith.'

'Oh, Alex,' she said with sudden weakening, 'it is such a relief. To speak with a gentleman who is a friend rather than a mere guest. Thank you.' She put her hand on his arm, lightly kneading with her fingers.

'I . . . Judith, I . . .'

'It would be a pleasure to talk longer.'

'The pleasure would be mine.'

'I hope for another chance meeting, Alex. This conversation means a great deal to me.'

'No more than to me.' He was awkward.

'Allow me to return to the manor alone, Alex. People assume scandal.'

The hint of complicity was not lost on Alex. He continued to walk along the low rise overlooking the shore. Only when she was among the trees bordering the pasture did he turn away from the sea.

Indoors, a few minutes later, Judith entered Carradine's library. He was sitting in his reading chair looking out to where Carmady was taking the air with Rodney and Harriet Treggan.

'We only lack that toper Golding, and we are almost complete,' he said without giving her a glance.

'I met Waite as you told me.'

'And?'

'He will fall in with the notion,' she said confidently.

'You are certain?'

'As I am of anything.'

He did not like her double meanings. She used far too many. 'Answer me plain, you bitch.'

She smiled. 'Waite will fall in, I promise, and keener than most.'

'One thing, Judith,' he rose and examined himself in the half cheval, 'Harriet has asked for a carriage to drive into Sealandings. I should like to know where she goes, without asking the coachman. Find out.'

'Every inch and word, Rad,' she promised, interested.

'I shall write to Ralph Chauncey also about the Baltic scheme, if today's meeting goes well. A few pious words about carrying the word to the Baltics and he should come to heel. And if he joins us, Castor Deeping might also be inveigled. I thought he was very susceptible at the shooting party, but have heard nothing.'

'Mr Deeping is too enamoured of Brillianta Astell to read even his own merchant's accounts these days,' Judith reported blithely, coming to adjust his white single-wrap stock.

Carradine swivelled to take her in. 'He is?'

'Of course.'

'How do you know?'

'Any woman would, Rad. Only men are blind.'

Carradine stilled while her fingers laid the stock round his neck and tightened the fit.

'Then perhaps Sir Edward Astell himself would join my venture?'

'Do not approach him, Rad. A rejection for *any* reason would be the scheme's downfall. It would never resurrect.'

'That might be true.' Judith's financial instincts often astonished him. She was so astute. But maybe this time she was too certain for her own good. The success of the Baltic enterprise would be the end of her.

She paused. He wanted more. 'Your other question, Rad?'

'Hunterfield,' he said finally, irritated that she could read his doubts. 'That man is too damned close, never lets anything out. I need to know his attitude. That blasted accident to the gunmaker at the horse meet interrupted my sounding him out. I want nothing to go wrong. It will raise us higher than we ever dreamed of.'

232

She thrilled to hear him speak of them as one. He had lately begun to talk this way, as if they were bonded for always. It had made her put aside her own unspoken plans. Only two days ago he had mentioned an estate in Hertfordshire, with purchase in mind! How wondrous to make a new start away from this Suffolk that was *Dinelo Tem*; 'Fool's County', to the Romany. And with Rad Carradine as her husband! What a triumphant return she would make to Sealandings, where the highest gentry would be honoured to give her the recognition she deserved!

'I will try to discover his mind, Rad.'

'Try?' He gave a wintry smile she did not recognise or like, and bussed her roughly on the mouth. 'Trying is not good enough. Succeed, dearest, you must succeed.'

Carradine surveyed the visitors with pleasure. He was determined to be as affable as summer. Everyone here must be nursed like babes.

'We are quite the Privy Council,' he joked, 'which stands at its meetings.'

Percy Carmady was amused at the comparison. 'Standing is my natural habit on shipboard.'

'You miss the sea, sir?' Alex Waite asked.

Carradine slyly inspected the North Briton for signs of his new-found conversion to the Baltic proposal, but was disappointed. But caution was the hallmark of these rich merchants.

'Very much, in one mood. Without war, the sea is very like the land.'

'You cannot want war, Percy?' Rodney Treggan asked.

They were on the terrace that extended across the rear of the Manor. Wide stone steps led down to a paved walk with an ornamental pool, and herbaceous borders along the red walling that bordered the lawn. Beyond, a decorative copse of deciduous trees was the principal feature, with lawns spreading down to the lake and boathouse.

Roundabout cane chairs from the East, re-exported from Amsterdam in Dutch Holland, were disposed about the tables to indicate the casual nature of the gathering. Cleverly, Judith had used range tables, for they were identical and could be quickly assembled to form one single large table should need arise. Six maids waited formally along the walls. He recognised Judith's touch in the fashionable canework back-screens waiting on the ornate trolley, to be slotted onto the roundabout chairs if a cool breeze sprang up.

Drinks were set on four matching sideboard tables, brought out as Carradine tradition demanded. The profusion of glasses and silver sparkled in the fitful sun. Hobbes the chief house steward attended, with Beckie, Joan and Dee his serving maids.

Carradine was pleased Golding was late, for he would have attacked the spirits before the visitors could have even glanced at the victuals. And they made a pretty sight, the glasses at the sideboard tables' edges on silver platters, as Swift facetiously advocated, so that their lustre would catch the light. There was a splendid array of drinks, from indigenous brews like the colourful green noyau made from gin and beech-mast, the brandy-based cherry bounce, the shining purple sloe wines and damson gins, the sweet bird-cherry brandies and wines, and the unbearably scented metheglins made from the estates' own honey. True wines, all imported nowadays since the last of the English vineyards had faded from memory, stood on the sideboard table. Carradine himself had gone over their selection. The 1825 vintage, a disastrous year for Portugal, was represented only by claret, for the same year's Rhenish and Tokay tastings had also been calamitous. He had authorised Hobbes to bring up from the cellars the rarer 1820 Portugal bottles, acknowledged by connoisseurs to be superb, and that same country's recent 1827 choice. This year's Portugal's, as last, were mediocre or frankly bad. Carradine had told Hobbes to issue that to the servants, following the Tokays and Rhenish wines. Indeed, 1829 promised a wholly evil vintage. Carradine had made Hobbes tutor him the previous evening so he could turn Golding's garrulous conversation from wine to seawater.

The visitors were discussing wars at sea. Rodney Treggan fortuitously directed attention to the issue in hand.

'Yes, Hobbes, a little Geneva, with lime. Percy, we must not forget that the Low Countries are also on the Baltic routes. So far wars have spared that sea.'

'True,' Carmady agreed. 'Since Lord Cathcart and Admiral Gambier forced the surrender of Denmark's fleet in 1807, including eighteen sail of their line, there has been no trouble.'

Carradine was gratified that naval statistics were working in his favour. This was the way the conversation should go, giving reassurance to wealth.

'And Norway's abolition of its nobility eight years ago is forgotten, while the May Treaty of Navigation the year before last between Great Britain and Sweden favours us.'

'The political constitution of Finland has been generously re-confirmed by the Tsar of the Russias,' Rodney Treggan added. 'The peace in Prussia has become a by-word since the death of Marshal Blucher, what, ten years ago.'

'But Russia is a problem,' Carmady said.

'*Can* so vast a nation be such?' Carradine angrily beckoned Hobbes to replenish all glasses as a distraction.

'Indeed she may, Rad. With Tsar Nicholas's coronation two years ago, everybody looked to the peaceful resumption of trade. Less than four weeks later he goes to war with Persia!'

'Settled in less than eighteen months, however, was it not?' Carradine put in, a little too quickly.

'Yes, in the February of this year.'

'It is disturbing,' Treggan conceded. 'And now the Tsar declares war on the Ottoman Porte, when was it, this April?'

'Two great battles; Brahilow, and one last month at Akhalzikh.' Carmady warmed to his grim tidings with relish. 'London rumours that the Russian fleet will blockade the Dardanelles soon.'

Carradine himself had to ask the question. 'What effect will that have on the Baltic? I have become quite interested.'

'Oh, a huge increase in shipping is predicted,' Carmady said, to Carradine's enormous relief. 'Especially since the Polish problem is resolved. Cracow declared as a free republic –'

Carradine laughed as if with reluctance. 'You make the scene so rosy, Percy. My family anciently had connections with St Petersburg, after it became the capital of all the Russias a century ago. I would like to re-establish links, for emotional reasons, you understand.'

'Of course,' all present murmured. Established gentry did not have commercial reasons, nor could such suspicions be voiced without mortal offence.

'But favourable political factors do not nullify the problems of the sea itself, Percy.'

Carmady had begun to suspect the drift. Conversation was being engineered by their host, with well-planned offhandedness. He found himself answering the prompt with enthusiasm.

'Think, though, Rad! The sea provides these islands with protection, an avenue of commerce, beauty. It is a gift, not our foe.'

'You speak as converted, Percy,' Carradine said amiably.

'Look back, gentlemen.' Carmady was serious now. 'You need to cast back to 1802 and the *Invincible*, when Captain Rennie and his crew perished near Yarmouth, only 126 being saved – and that a ship of the line, 74 guns! For the rest, what major ship has been lost?'

'The frigate *Circe*, 32 guns, also off Yarmouth the following year,' Treggan offered unexpectedly. 'But I do concede. The eastern shipping in these latitudes is safe.'

Carradine had forgotten Treggan's excursions into capital ventures begun in London's coffee houses.

'That seems very sound,' he said, exaggerating his caution. 'Yet, however beneficial a Baltic project would be to Sealandings generally, I confess I am baffled by the ship itself. Several shipping concerns in London have caught my attention. I frankly confess myself bewildered. I have asked my one expert to sift through them and give opinion.'

Waite, listening to the discussion, was becoming interested. His father was eager to invest capital. He stood idly facing the house, and saw a movement at an upper window. A woman had slowly passed behind the panes. He tried to direct his attention to the rest, but she moved a second time, and this time paused to look down. It was Judith. Her hair was uncovered and she had cast her shawl.

What could be more natural, for a lady to glance at guests partaking of her victuals? Yet her look was for him, he felt, rather than the quiet scene on the terrace. She awarded him a smile, then glided into the shadows. Did she raise a hand in part salutation, he wondered, or was it a finger about to touch her lips?

They had not noticed his loss of attention. He alone had no news to offer.

'I scanned the suggestions, Rad,' Carmady was saying calmly. 'There is no difficulty. There is only one vessel that will match the Baltic's need for seaworthiness.'

'Of all thirty?' Carradine asked, no longer having to dissemble. His surprise was genuine.

'Rad, consider. The Baltic Sea is less than 160,000 square miles. We here on the North Sea have the greatest shift in tides. Why, at Copenhagen the average tide is a mere twelve inches! In the famed Kattegat it is not much more. That, and the distances involved, are deciding factors. The Gulf of Bothnia, some 400 miles long, is nowhere wider than one hundred miles. Between the Danish islands and Mecklenburg is only thirty! You see how that imposes limits on the type of ship needed?'

'Well, no,' Treggan admitted.

'Nor I,' Waite added, trying to avoid looking up at Judith.

'There is but one vessel among those offered,' Carmady said. 'A Baltimore ship.'

The silence was broken by Treggan. 'A Yankee?'

Carmady's sureness was compelling. 'The Baltimore schooner is speedy – remember that prices of cargo are judged per ton. The fastest ships are priced highest.' He grimaced in retraction. 'Apologies, Rad, for this financial note, but commerce is important to the King's ships, wherein I was trained.'

'Accepted, Percy,' Carradine said. 'The ship?'

'There are two immediately on offer. I have selected one. She lies at Greenwich, finishing discharging her cargo yesterday, if she has arrived.'

Now it had come, Carradine almost lost his nerve. But the risk beckoned, as always. The craving to gamble was exhilarating.

'What is she?' Treggan asked.

'If she answers aright to her description, she is fast indeed. Two masts, both set so rakishly she will fly. Her holds capacious. This results from the hull's shape, stern deep and shallower at the fore.'

'Is that not strange?'

'For a certain ship, no. The Baltimore schooners are fast because of this, yet hold more cargo than if their kneels were level fore to aft.'

'Where is she registered?'

'Built in Liverpool, she was bought after a voyage to London and has since been registered in Greenwich.'

'What trades has she engaged in?'

Carmady paused. This was the unpleasant part. 'She was built to specifications making her swift, and able to avoid the blockades established by the Royal Navy in the American War, though she is too young to have taken part in those.' He cleared his throat and looked at Carradine. 'She was a slaver.'

'Slaves?' Even Treggan was startled out of his taciturnity.

'Yes.'

'But slavery was abolished over twenty years ago, Percy, in 1807, following the line set by Austria in 1782!'

'Many continued trading long after, Rodney.' Carradine with a nod made Hobbes start to uncover the food dishes. At the mention of slaves, even Waite was brought back from his star-gazing. 'The Americas still trade vigorously in captives from Africa. Latin states of the South New World are also adamant about their need for blackamoors. Remember, it was the Portuguese who founded that commerce, and the Spanish. The United States — as our colonies styled themselves fifty years ago — seem even less inclined to suspend the trade.'

Hobbes had the maids unveil the profusion of sweet dishes. The prospect was tempting: dozens of puddings, trifles, flummeries, fools, kickshaws, burnt creams, bloomanges, cold dumplings, mousse shapes, meringues, hedgehogs, tipsy cakes, russes and preserved fruits. The gentlemen hardly spared the inviting array a look.

'Whatever the rights and wrongs,' Carradine said, losing patience, 'the object is the purchase of the vessel.'

'As found,' Percy admitted. 'She has crew, said to be reliable, is sound of hull and hatch, sails as fast as ever, and is well reported. She could sail here for inspection, if required.'

'How soon could she be free to accept our cargoes?'

'A matter of days.'

Carradine felt the gambler's heady compulsion. It was as enticing as sex, as enthralling as a mystery, as mesmerising as a wager on the bear-baiting when the last-but-one dog was crawling wounded in the spine and the bear maddened and blinded with every sovereign hung on the beast's survival. . .

'And the cargoes?'

'Brokered, as always.' Treggan cleared his throat. 'There can be no doubt about a slave-ship's record of success. They have run blockades for years. Why not give her the benefit of inspection?'

Carradine said, still seeming casual, 'What do you think, Alex?'

'I agree, Rad.'

Carradine hid a smile. 'How is inspection arranged, Percy?'

'By letter to an agent. Or commission an independent report from London inspectors, directly at Greenwich.'

'Who would ensure that would be done correctly?'

Carmady offered eagerly, 'I would be happy to act for you, gentlemen.'

'And travel to Greenwich? Bringing details of cost and the soundness report?'

'Or the account of her hopeless condition!' Percy Carmady laughed at the image of a ramshackle schooner. The rest did not.

'I propose that we take that course,' Carradine said.

'Agreed,' Rodney Treggan said, to Carradine's relief.

'Agreed,' Waite said. 'Does this mean equal shares? I mean,' he stammered, retreating, 'I would have to seek my father's approval for a capital venture, so would need firm details.'

'Understood,' Carradine said easily. 'Of course equal shares. Though I propose that Percy here, who may want a more active part by going on the first voyage, should be allowed a third share. In view of his services as a sailing officer.'

'That is too kind, Rad,' Percy said, trying to demur, but Carradine would hear none of it and insisted.

'Agreed,' Alex Waite said.

'Agreed!' Golding came through the house, shedding his riding cloak. He was already the worse for drink. His eyes lit up at the drinks. He took the decanter of noyau from Hobbes and seized a glass. 'I agree, Rad.' He poured and gulped the glass empty, gurning to show distaste and demanding the flask of Geneva. 'That green noyau is too mild, Hobbes! Tell your brewing maids to stir themselves! They have made it a dowager's drink. What have we agreed, gentlemen?'

He flopped down, grinning blearily at them all.

27

THE DONKEY AND Buskin yard was crowded and in a ferment. The arrival of the Royal Mail coach, splendid but bespattered with mud from East Anglia's poor roads, always created excitement. In spite of the rain the fisher children played near the great coach, pestering the grooms and imitating the horses' actions. Disembarking passengers waited for their packages on benches after their long ordeal. Two pale, soaked children were being lifted down from the outside front seat behind the coachman's position. Their clothes were stained with vomit. Mehala steadied them and sat them on the nearest bench. Wet and bedraggled as they were, the turmoil inside John Weaver's tavern would be too much in their shocked state.

'Where are your parents? Guardians?'

'Please, mistress, we are named Milland, brothers travelling from London to Mr Pride's Rustonhall school,' they answered.

'Are you to be met?' There seemed to be nobody waiting. The last passengers had tottered thankfully into the taprooms.

'Please, mistress, we are to wait until fetched.'

Mehala moved them further along the bench. Piped water came into the tavern's stable yard, sealed by an enormous wooden plug when not in use. The clean water, a valuable commodity, was bought on monthly payment from the brook that ran tributary to the River Affon in the lower estate of Sir Charles Golding's Bures House. The tavern horse trough was jealously watched by Mistress Nelson the tavern cook and Nellie the chief maid, as was any risk to the huge chained alderwood plug.

She stayed with them as the horses were changed, four excited fresh beasts being brought out for harness.

Leaving Shalamar had been painful. Nothing can be as terrible as separation from a loved one. No, she corrected herself, loved ones in the plural, for there was not only Ven, but also Rosie, Clement, and her fondness for Bartholomew Hast. Infuriatingly, a woman sick with a breast abscess had come asking for help just as Mehala and Ven had been about to start down the South Toll to meet the Royal Mail coach. The woman was Mistress Dolley, wife of one of the labourers at Mary and Jason Prothero's Calling Farm. She was in agony. Ven was compelled to remain behind, and bid Mehala a shy public farewell standing before everyone at Shalamar.

The rain had been a torrent since daybreak, which made the prospect of the long journey even more disheartening.

'Mehala?'

She rose. In the yard's bustle she had not noticed the horsemen who had halted between the yard gates.

'Squire,' she greeted with a curtsey.

Hunterfield was accompanied by his dumb groom Tom. 'You go to Red Hall, then?'

'Yes, Squire, and thank you for the assistance.'

Hunterfield was silent. He wore a plain dark-red riding cloak of oiled silk delaine, and a green riding beaver with the brim tilted so the rain ran away from the collar.

'I have written to the rector of East Mersea,' he told her. 'Tay spill I have sent ahead by horse, with letters of authority about the stewardship of Red Hall. He will act for you.'

'I am ever grateful, Squire.'

'Those two. Are they travelling on, or alighting?'

Incomers were the responsibility of the parish. The Lord of Sealandings was concerned. If they were entitled to settlement, they could claim on the Poors' Rates.

She explained that Mr Pride of Rustonhall was to meet the children. Hunterfield was satisfied.

'Safe travel, then.' He seemed about to say more, but kneed Betsy away from the gate.

Mehala called her thanks. John Weaver, out to see the change of horses, came to her smiling.

'Mehala! I hear you are leaving! Why not sit inside?'

'I bide with these two,' she said.

He took her hands. 'Your memory has returned, then?'

'In part, John. Enough to become a source of trouble!'

'We hope you will remain in Sealandings, Mehala.' He was

reluctant to speak so. 'It seems a lifetime since Jervin's men laid you like death on my taproom table!'

'Sealandings is home, John. I have no life elsewhere.'

'Little Jane sends her godspeeds. I saw her this dawn when I went to pay for the month's water.'

'Thank her, John.'

The yard became busier still as the time for the coach's departure came closer. The Mail, constructed by Vidler in London on a perch undercarriage with two sets of platform springs, was truly splendid. Mehala could not imagine any progress speedier than the 'express', as people were starting to call the racing Royal Mail coaches.

Today's passengers were emerging. There was a full complement of outside passengers. The coachman on his box would have one passenger beside him. On the seat behind the coachman three other outside passengers would be seated, likewise facing forwards. The guard, his tool box strapped before him on the roof, would climb up last of all to his high circular seat, his feet on the lid covering the hind boot where passengers' bags were kept.

He would carry a brace of travelling pistols. And a blunderbuss, favoured by coach guards because of the weapon's wide mouth, a vital consideration when reloading the muzzle-loader with black gunpowder on a swaying coach.

The maroon paint gleamed wetly. The G.R. letters of the King were painted on the black sides of the front storage boot. The four stars of the Orders of Knighthood were painted on the upper-quarter panels, the Garter and Thistle stars on the nearside, the Bath and Saint Patrick on the off. Mehala was thrilled despite her sadness. The imposing words 'Royal Mail' were on the door panels, with the names of the towns limiting the coach's run. The gold paint of the Royal Arms shone brightest of all on the doors. With the scarlet wheels and undercarriage, it was beautiful.

'Good day, Mehala. You admire engineering as much as I.'

'Sir, good day.'

'Percy Carmady,' service. We are the only two inside passengers. Allow me to renew acquaintanceship.'

The naval man hauled his small seafarer's trunk up to the guard. He had a small travelling leather case, and was matter-of-fact about the journey. Her own few belongings she carried in a calfskin bag which she passed up on the guard's demand. A homemade reticule of sewn calfskin was her only other possession.

'A route is a problem,' Carmady said conversationally. 'I go to Greenwich. Easy from London, but difficult in the Eastern Hundreds.'

'Sir?'

'To cross on the latitude to Scole, meet the Norwich-to-London Royal Mail express? Or stick to this damned – forgive me, lady – slow coach crawling betwixt Greater Yarmouth and London through Saxmundham and Ipswich? Or the Scole to Ipswich?'

'I am ignorant, Mr Carmady. I am advised that this route is my most direct.'

Carmady sighed as the horses were backed into the shafts by the three grooms. 'It seems organised, Mehala, but hopelessly in-efficient. I would do anything to escape the roads. Hours of discomfort, every tooth shaken from our heads.'

'There is no alternative, sir, except horseback or foot.'

'There is the sea, Mehala!' His face lit at the thought. 'No highwaymen, no noise, no jolting, no having to trudge in the mud when the coach is enmired! A sea journey is all ease!'

He raised a hand in acknowledgement as the guard called his summons and, turning to allow Mehala to enter first, was struck by her expression.

She was facing the sea, visible between the cottages. Her face was bright with love. Her emotion astonished him.

'Yes, Mr Carmady,' she said softly. 'You are so right. The sea gives all to those who love her.'

She came to quickly. Nellie came at a rush, carrying a 'bird', as the traveller's hot food was called.

'My gift, Mehala! Got from Nelson's own hands! Excuse me, sir! Godspeed home soon!'

'Thank you, Nellie. I shall, please God.'

The 'birds' were as individual as the taverns that made them. They were eggs, potato, and meat, cooked in a parcel of pastry. Once they cooled, they were eaten. They were cheaper than the containers of hot charcoal that outside passengers could hire from the taproom.

Mehala's eyes filled at the kindness, remembering her terrible fight with Nellie. She had been a scullery maid, and managed by a ruse to save Nellie from discipline. From then on the rough girl was her declared friend.

She bade a good day to the Milland children, calling to Nellie to find them some place to wait indoors, and climbed into the coach.

The vehicle rocked as the passengers clambered aboard. The guard sounded his coach horn, warning away pedestrians or local carts, for the Royal Mail coaches took precedence over all other vehicles. The southbound express rolled majestically out onto the cobbles.

Four minutes later, still at a walk, it climbed onto the South Toll road, and passed Shalamar. The gateway was overgrown, the old gate-porter's lodge house tumbled into ruin. Shalamar moved across her view like a great derelict ship among trees. Nobody was visible, but she knew Ven would be at the window watching as the coach rolled away.

For an instant she imagined that she saw a carriage somewhere among the trees. Surely not? She thought of him and leaned back in the padded seat, but found Carmady's eyes on her. She looked away, for she and Ven were one, of themselves, and not for the intrusive quizzing of others.

The horses began to pick up speed as the coach breasted the South Toll, the guard sounding two long horn blasts to warn the toll gate ahead to open and allow the Royal Mail free passage of the bar. She was on her way to Red Hall, but would have given almost anything to be home at Shalamar.

The woman was in agony. Ven's compassion was worsened by his regret that Mehala was gone. Mistress Dolley's condition represented a missed opportunity.

She was typical example of the condition. It would be difficult to treat her with success.

'Tell me what happened, Mistress Dolley.'

'It does not seem right, Doctor, you being a child visitor at Calling Farm.'

Ven smiled. 'It is years since I came botanising with Father!'

'Happier days, Doctor,' the woman sighed, carrying her breast to lessen her pain. 'Not as we are now, at Calling Farm.'

'I must see your affliction, Mistress Dolley. Rosie here will be our assistant and chaperone.'

Rosie helped her to discard her smocked dress. 'Six years since my last was born. I should not have gathereds, should I, Doctor?'

The bare left breast was distended and reddened. Its nipple was so fissured and cracked near the areola that a split extended radially from the nipple's eye. He looked at her features. Hot and flustered, but it was not mere embarrassment. She was in fever. Ven deplored his lack of a temperature device, such as Galileo's thermoscope. Better still would have been the oil thermometer of William Cockburn, though the design had long been lost, as that excellent doctor had failed to describe, in his 1697 book on the distempers of seafarers, the instrument's actual design.

Ven felt his heart sink. Too often these days he longed for devices that were utterly beyond reach. He might never even see such instruments in his lifetime. How many patients would lose limbs, senses, even their lives, for want of equipment? Sealandings needed a hospital for suffering children. He thought of the hopelessness with which he fumbled, and guessed, or simply hoped. And how often did his ignorance of plant medicines delay the patient's recovery?

What he would give for one of the instruments now truly called thermometer, after Doctor Gabriel Fahrenheit's miraculous invention of 1720! Or, hoping wilder still, for one of the implements of Liverpool's clever James Currie, with its twin curved ends. Or even the costly new device that was used widely by wealthy London doctors after Doctor Hunter's ingenuity improved the instrument.

Tobacco dreams! Here he was with no means of judging the effect of the poor woman's ailment.

He felt the breast. It should have been flaccid like the right breast. Instead it was turgid, the skin showing an ugly dark red flush. The nipple was flaking, powdered by fine greyish-white scales. The substance was dimpled yet gross where the abscess had formed. The breast was pendulous. She had bound a piece of linen tightly round herself to cup the inflamed breast, hoping to allay the pain.

The swelling was fluctuant, showing the presence of pus deep within. He uttered a silent prayer of gratitude. If there had been no pus, he would have had to resort to cold compresses. And if those fifteen-minute applications failed, then hot ones. Nothing was yet known to diminish inflammation, so there was only surgery. The breast's floccules became 'gathered', as country people said, when some ferment within filled the breast. He had seen women driven to madness by the agony of this condition.

'I shall have to press,' he warned her. 'I need to feel the extent of the gathering.'

'Do what you must, Doctor.'

Despite her courage, she almost fainted as his fingers gently moved over the red distension. It seemed about the size of a hen's egg, with smaller bulbous extensions in the breast's lower left quadrant.

'An abscess, mistress. It needs to be allowed out. There is matter inside. It will spread otherwise.'

'Now, Doctor?'

'Soon. I want you to sit by the fire with Rosie, have a brew of tea with some honey. Then when I am ready . . .'

She caught his hand. 'Will I be well? I have children –'

'The risk is serious, mistress. If it is successful, recovery will take several days.'

He left to prepare his instruments, and met Bartholomew Hast hobbling along the corridor. Ven drew him away.

'I should not join the others in the kitchen, Bartholomew,' he warned. Mehala had finally explained the gunsmith's astonishing aversion to bodily ailments. 'I will be operating on a lady's gathered breast –'

'Thank you, Ven!' Hast hastily spun on his crutches. 'Please tell me when I am safe!'

'Wait, Bartholomew,' Ven caught him. 'I have not been able to express my gratitude,' he said awkwardly. 'It was generous of you to pay the fare for Mehala on the Royal Mail. Please accept my promissory note.'

'No, Ven. You incur no obligation.'

'I do. I must.' Ven was adamant. 'You understand why.'

'Mehala does me valuable service, Ven. I instructed my gunstock man, old Gomme, to send a quantity of Wollaston wire by Royal Mail to my Colchester cousins' gunsmithy.'

'Platina?' Wollaston's method of creating drawn wire of precious platina, the rarest and densest of all known metals, was famed among gunsmiths, since touch-holes were made of the metal, so increasing the longevity of weapons.

'Yes, Ven. I had an excess, being unable to manufacture while I lie up here. My cousins will buy my Wollaston.'

'The fare is hardly equal to that small service.'

'There is also your fee, Ven.'

Ven coloured, money being his bane. 'That is irrelevant.'

'No, Ven.' The gunmaker smiled. 'Mehala threatened me. I must keep account, and pay what I owe. Tomorrow I return home to Market Square. The Gommes can care for me. You have enough to do.' He gave a wry grin. 'And I will hear less about carnage.'

'If you say, Bartholomew. But fourpence-three farthings a mile, from the coast to the Red Lion in Colchester High Street, is an immense sum.'

'My life would cost me more, Ven. If I were poor, I could not pay. As I am not poor, I must.' He was amused by Ven's embarrassment. 'And we dare not cross Mehala!'

'Very well. Mehala shall settle on her return.'

Ven went to prepare his instruments. The current fashion among doctors – of being splashed with gore, and using only instruments crusted with fat and dried blood – had never appealed to him. London surgeons' frock coats, which they wore in wards and operating theatres, were better fitted for butchers' abattoirs than hospitals. The patients must surely be frightened by such sights. He felt instinctively that a reassured rather than a disturbed mind could only be beneficial. So he strove to keep his instruments clean by boiling them in sea water, from the old belief that water boiled became free of its fermentative capacity. Mehala kept a store of boiled cloths made of her own nettle linen.

He deliberately delayed his return. Women talked to ease their minds, whereas men usually remained silent.

The instruments cooled. He checked the few that he would need: the scalpel, a probe, a grooved needle, several wicks that Mehala made for her candles, and finally a small dish that Mehala had also made from local clay the previous winter.

He wondered if he heard a carriage and went to the window that old Trenchard had boarded over with driftwood.

Through a crack he saw the Royal Mail coach hauling slowly up the South Toll incline. Just for an instant, he imagined with a leap of his heart that he saw Mehala framed in the window of the great vehicle. But wish had fathered the thought, for the coach was gone. He listened, and heard the guard's horn signal the approach at the distant toll gate.

247

She lay on the hall floor. Rosie held both her hands. She was covered by a sheet of nettle linen, and pledgets made of linen strips were heaped on an iron salver nearby.

'I shall operate now, Mistress Dolley. It will hurt.'

'I am ready, Doctor.'

He took the breast firmly, compressing the turgid tissue between his fingers. He knelt on the woman's right side, according to the invariable rule.

Quickly he drew the scalpel across the taut skin, cutting deep. He had honed the blade on stone and stropped it on hanging leather until it was sharpened to perfection. Immediately pus oozed out, to his relief. He laid the scalpel on a linen square and pressed down on each side of the incision.

He believed that quickness was vital. It was said of amputations that the less notice the patient was given, the easier they accepted the operation. Might it be so for all surgery? It seemed wise. Intuitively he moved briskly, closing his ears to the woman's shrill squeal and her eventual continuous moan.

He drove the probe's blunt end into the locules of pus, drawing a fresh spurt from each cavity, until he was convinced all were drained of most of the yellow matter. Then the first wick, still damp from its boiling, was inserted along the probe's groove. A second, then a third, and eventually a ninth. They would serve as drains down which residual pus would flow. Only when the flow ceased would he remove them by simple pulling. The breast could then granulate along the line of the incision. All might be well.

He placed a single suture into the skin in the mid-point of his incision. That device held the wicks. Skin closure would be dangerous to the point of foolhardiness. Perhaps there might come a day when some chemical or physic unguent might act to prevent infection? But maybe God would forbid that development. Perhaps God, as religionists taught, agreed that curing disease was a sin.

He straightened and sat back on his heels.

'There. All is done.'

Her brow glistened with sweat. He nodded to Rosie to release her hands. 'Is it, Doctor?'

'Yes.' He gave his most convincing smile. 'Rosie will give you several of these linen pledgets. I shall bind the breast loosely with a linen. You will use the pledgets to clean pus that trickles down the wicks. Do not be afraid of the colour, nor the stench.'

'What else must I do?'

'Rest if you can. Get a relative to help. Do no work for three days. Give the breast a chance to heal.'

'I have a girl of eight. She be a wondrous worker. I shall ask if I can keep her back from the fields.'

'Perrigo is your herdsman. He might approve.'

'But Prothero is not condescending to us under tied thatch.'

Part-payment for labour was rent, in tied cottages. It was an iniquitous favour, proving more a crippling obligation than benefit. The abuse caused many outbreaks of violence against property in rural areas.

'Ask Perrigo in my name, Mistress Dolley. It might help. I shall call on you each morning. Rest here until you have had a piece of bread and something to drink. Rosie and Clement will walk you home. Rise slowly, go inchwise.'

'Doctor.' She groped as he wiped her forehead. 'The fee.'

He pretended to purse his lips in anger, and wafted her face with the cloth. 'There is another grave rule I forgot to lay for your observance. Silence about money. Understand?' He rose with a grunt. 'Rosie, accompany her. Take Clement. Send him running for me should anything untoward happen.'

'Yes, Doctor.'

He was almost out of the hall when Rosie's gasp brought him to a halt. The figure of a lady stood by the door leading down to the kitchen corridor. He stepped forward with an eager smile, thinking somehow it was Mehala, then saw the fine garments and the splendid bonnet, the exquisite pompadour dress and the green and gold satin esmeralda cloak.

'Miss Ferlane?' He felt dismay.

'Mistress Treggan. Good day, Ven.'

He came to, motioning to Rosie to remain. This visit was not to be secret. 'My apologies. I have just . . . Would you care to come to . . . ?' The words were ridiculous in the circumstances. He ushered the lady into the study, leaving the door ajar.

Harriet followed, ignoring the two others. She paused on the threshold then slowly entered, looking at the walls with their faded covering, the seepage water, the broken windows partly blocked, the crumbling plaster.

Two walls were completely restored, paint on the dado shining, and the picture rails and skirting boards showing new. An old table stood in the centre, with a stool. Papers and an instrument case were the only other items. A deliberate attempt had been made to make it usable.

'That girl is not your Mehala, Ven.'

For a moment he did not understand. 'Ah. She is Rosie, a girl we took in from the workhouse.'

'There is a kitchen boy with streaked eyes. Another waif?'

'Do not poke fun, mistress. He was blind until a few days ago. Now he can see.'

She stood while he rinsed his hands in a bowl and smeared his fingers with fatty paste. 'Have you no soaps?'

'This is ash-and-fat soap. Mehala makes it.' He coloured at his admission. 'Usually she stores blocks, made hard by drying through the winter. She had to sell them, for victuals. We suffered a misfortune.'

'She is not here, then?'

'No. She has been obliged to leave. She will return.'

There was defiance in his voice. She wondered if all was well between them. She would find out from servants at Carradine Manor.

'Must you remain so formal, Ven? I only call on the spur of the moment. Lieutenant Carmady is seeking a residence in Sea-landings. Shalamar might prove apt.'

'I remember being directed to observe all the formalities that lack of acquaintanceship imposes.' He dried his hands. 'Feel free to inspect the manor. I urge that you take your servant with you, for parts are unsafe, and the walls and windows unreliable.'

'Have you servants?'

'No, none.'

'Then how do you manage?'

'I do not, Mistress Treggan. Mehala manages. If you would give me leave . . .' He made to go.

'Wait!'

'I have to see to my patient.'

'A moment, Ven.' She tried to unbend, but the sight of the man maddened her beyond comprehension. He could have had everything, starting with old Doctor Arbuthnot's lucrative practice. Instead, he comes to Sealandings among these mistrustful folk with their primitive beliefs and unknowable customs. Driven, he was a poor man doomed to stay poor. She had not seen him for two, three years before that day at the hanging, yet he enraged her still. But she needed his guidance.

'I cannot help, Mistress Treggan,' he said bluntly. 'You will need the agent. Willoughby, agent for Sir Fellows De Foe.'

'It is not the house that I want to ask about.'

He looked at her. She was beautiful, the gloss of wealth upon her. He realised now he had been deranged, to believe that she would have smiled on him in anything more than an idle flirtation or a passing kindness. He felt mortified. Back then, it was a gross impertinence even to dream.

He had felt the same about Mehala at first, even though she was nothing more than a rescued pauper. It was Mehala's loving courage that had removed his absurd rectitude. Mehala had established her right to him, and he loved her freely as a result. There was nobody for him, not after loving Mehala.

She stepped to look at the overgrown gardens and the drive. It had once been a great residence, she could tell. Now, a penniless doctor and a stray woman lived in its dusty dereliction, with two waifs, so hopeless that they had to sell essential provisions for meat scraps from the market.

'I never dreamt you would fall to this, Ven.' She swung on him. He stayed by the table, his face impassive. 'You had such promise. I used to see you from my window with Doctor Arbuthnot, asking, listening, so . . . passionate.'

'My choice, Mistress Treggan.'

He would not unbend, the stupid man. Very well. Use him, then leave. Let him stew in Shalamar among the bats, draughts, falling plaster and tottering walls.

'I have a question, Doctor. Will you answer it?'

'Yes, as far as I am able. You are well?'

She gave a light disclaiming laugh. 'When I say *me*, I do not ask for myself. No, it is for a friend, a lady, who has been married approximately the same length of time as I. She is so far without issue. I want a physician's opinion as to the cause. She lives several miles inland from me. I, ah, wonder how she should conduct herself to conceive.'

'Why does the lady not consult an eminent London physician?' He was puzzled. 'I find this an unusual approach, Mistress Treggan.'

She controlled her annoyance. He was making this difficult. 'It is just that I am here, and heard you were the local doctor.'

'Has your lady any infirmity, family illnesses?'

'None.' She would have been insulted, had she been speaking of herself, to be questioned as if her breeding was somehow deficient.

'And has she the normal woman's menses?'

She answered through tight lips, 'I assume so.'

'No serious monthly loss beyond the normal amount?'

'No.' She could have struck him, with his serious frown and air of gravity.

'Has she ever conceived and lost the pregnancy early?'

'Never.'

'Then her husband and she must continue to try, Mistress Treggan. Often, unhappiness about a family event or ambition, or emotional upset, predisposes to failure.'

'It is not *failure*,' Harriet ground out, her anger showing.

'Mistress Treggan, I imply no fault on the lady's part.'

'Is that all?'

'Why, yes.' He thought a moment. 'What else is there? Stories of physics and magical potions that will produce conception after a single draught are so many old wives' tales.'

'How would *you* know?' She would have said more, but was too distressed and flung away.

'I don't, Mistress Treggan,' he said with quiet misery as she stormed out across the echoing hall.

He had dreamed for over two years, and now was relieved the interview had come to pass. The memory and emotion were laid to rest for good. Whistling, he started to wash the instruments ready for boiling.

The letter from Ward arrived an hour later, delivered by a passing labourer who had been at the Donkey and Buskin when the Royal Mail coach arrived.

28

'NEWS,' CARRADINE SAID. 'I need news.'

That other whore, Lucy. *There* was as useful a whore as ever served in any Paphian shop. She always had something to tell him. The cow had flitted away to respectability.

'I was afeared, sir.'

Corrie looked it, he thought. She needed the help of two other girls to carry enough hot water from the downstairs coppers, and had taken her time bathing him, too. Sluttishness was only to be expected in a provincial brothel, with only Wren the brothel mistress to teach them. And the towels were cold; no thought of using hot boxes for a man's comfort. No brains. But this one had no malice, which was unusual to the point of rarity.

'Afraid of what? Of whom?'

Corrie looked askance. To imply that a gentleman's protection was too weak would earn her another beating, and she already bore the marks of his anger; she had failed to move against him in his spend. Her wail had only roused him to greater passion and he had taken his belt to her.

'God, sir.'

'God?' Carradine roared with laughter, his naked body almost convulsed on the bed. 'Is God a patron?'

'No, sir. But I am mortal afraid. So is Mellie.'

'Who is Mellie?'

'She serves porters and drovers, sir, of a market day. She is cheaper than me, being older, but takes well at the Mop Fair.'

A poorer class of whore, then, this Mellie, who served only artisans or drovers reaching market after prodigious journeys from Wales or the north. These men drove their animals halfway across or down the country on two or three shillings a day plus expenses. They were rougher than most. If they were North

Britons, the whores would earn their pay, for the Scotch drovers lived wild and unsheltered on the long roads south with their cattle, and knew little of niceties.

'Mellie makes you fear God? Explain, girl.'

'She has the preacher. He do rant and rave.'

Carradine's laugh faded. He bade her stop clearing up the bath water – she had already taken an age, repeatedly emptying the small ash bucket out of the window with the shrill customary cry, 'Gardy- loo!'

'Preacher? Reverend Baring?'

'Oh, no, sir! The rector never sets foot! The new one, as has no church, sir.'

Carradine knew instantly. 'Has he a name?'

Corrie's eyes filled. 'I dare not, sir, lest –'

'Here.' Carradine took her hands, gentling her onto the bed. 'No harm will come. I already know everything about the man.'

'You promise? We will go straight to Hell –'

'You have my word, Corrie.'

The gates were opened, and she responded eagerly. 'He be the Reverend Endercotte, sir. He is most important, with a special God power! I heard him say so! He is going to rent Sealandings apart with wrath, and kill sinners and fornicators. He has the Almighty's sword of vengeance, sir.'

'Has he indeed?' Carradine said sardonically. 'He visits?'

'Late of a night, sir. He was here early once. I saw him using Mellie.'

'Using?' Carradine was even more intrigued. 'He came not to pray and condemn?'

'Him, sir?' Corrie was instantly scornful. 'He condemns nought in this vaulting-house! He weeps, froths at the mouth mortal tempestuous. Frightens Mellie to screaming.'

He was fascinated. 'Endercotte shags Mellie, then goes mad?'

'Worse than any Bedlam loon! He made a fine sight!'

Carradine shook off her comparison. Londoners went to the mad hospital of Bethlehem, now corrupted to Bedlam, where they paid a copper to goad the lunatics for an afternoon, to their amusement and the hospital's profit. 'That extreme?'

'But no vaulting, sir, not once. He makes Mellie frig him until she is quite faint! All she milks from him is a little snake-spit, like on roadside grass in a warm spring!'

'He does not mount her?' Carradine found it incredible.

'Then it is prayers and him beating his own face until blood came. Mellie screamed that she would be hanged, if folk said she had struck a minister of the cloth.'

'Quite a scene!'

'I ran in, sir, and found him lying all overcome, his fists all bloody from hitting the wall and Mellie in a swoon.'

'Did he bribe you to remain silent and say nothing?'

'No, sir. He made us kneel and swear on God that we would forget all that had passed. We should gain Heaven by it. He said he deserved punishment for his own sins, sir.'

'He was unable to fornicate, but beat Mellie?'

'Mortal bad.' Corrie shivered. 'It was not your kindly beating, that a gentleman justly gives a girl who gives offence, for which I give my sorry to you. It was chubby, nigh to kill her. That is not a gentleman's haviour, sir, though some men – women too, truth be told – do nothing else.'

The story mystified Carradine. He reached for her breast. 'He will never visit her again, I suppose?'

Corrie was gratified. She had pleased him. 'He will be back if Satan himself was in the way. You know what I think, sir? He so hates, that he can see nothing save that hate.'

'And he hates whores?'

She lay close to him, curling like a child. 'Only as he hates everybody, sir. I asked Mellie was he anguished because he could not make summerlands like other men.' The euphemism meant the ploughing of fallow ground, the heaviest operation in farming. 'Mistress Wren took us in after the minister had gone. She scolded us and 'bated us eleven whole pence, for having upset him.'

'I shall repay it, to the pair.'

'You will, sir?' Her gratitude for once did not match the gift. 'What now?'

'I am frighted that he will ask for me and Mellie together.'

'I will speak to the cat-houser and forbid it.'

'You will, sir?' She moved her face so her lips came on his. He buffeted her for impertinence. 'Thank you for your condescension, seeing as Mistress Blaker befriends him.'

Carradine froze. It was a few moments before he could speak.

'Mistress Blaker knows the preacher?'

'Did you not know, sir?' She brightened. 'He ranted that Mistress Blaker was God-sent to help in burning sinners.'

He listened to her tell his words. As with most unlettered country folk, Corrie could repeat a conversation verbatim. Endercotte had babbled Gospel, raved incoherent threats.

'Did he say anything to praise anyone, Corrie?'

The use of her name flattered her. 'No, sir. Mistress Blaker seemed his favourite. She brought him here. She alone will be saved. He would start with the Doctor and that Mehala.'

Corrie went on, but Carradine was satisfied. Judith was playing her double games. But this time he had discovered everything before the game was played. Before, he was a bewildered onlooker. Now, he was in control.

So Judith would use Endercotte to eliminate Mehala. Carradine had seen enough mobs, and knew that once roused they spared nobody in their blind fury.

But was Mehala reason enough? What other motive did Judith have? Endercotte was her instrument even though the crazed preacher believed Judith was his own weapon. Carradine had no illusions; Judith could outdo Endercotte in cunning.

No woman, or man for that matter, was as ambitious as Judith. She was already queen of her tribe at Carradine Manor. How far *did* her desire reach? Dear God, he thought. He had assumed the woman was satisfied with control over the manor, estates and himself. He now realised she had only just begun her climb. She would never stop, and people in Sealandings, Mehala and her dog-leech especially, were in the way. And himself?

It was enough to make a man's flesh crawl. But now he was forewarned, thanks to his little nightgowner.

'Corrie?'

'Yes, sir?'

'You please me. I shall take you on your side this time, and pay you well.'

'Thank you, sir.'

'Corrie. In future, I shall not ask for you by name when I come –' She started to wail, but he told her to listen. 'But that does not signify. I shall have no other girl but you. Each time I come, even without notice, you must make certain that you are next in line. Do you follow?'

'To make it seem that you get me by chance?'

'Yes. I do not want anybody – even your whore friends – to know that you are my special one.'

She was silent. He knew the girls boasted to each other of their special gentlemen.

'They may notice, Corrie,' he persisted. 'But if I hear you make it known, I shall change to Mellie, and you will not be my choice again.'

'But in time I shall become so, sir?'

'You are now, Corrie. We exchange promise for promise.'

'Yes, sir. On my life, I shall keep it secret.'

Indeed it is on your little life, Carradine thought drily, but only told her to get to work. 'Against me this time, cow, whatever the pain.'

'I shall, I shall.'

Judith's features came to him as he began to rut. He had done the right thing by hinting to Judith that he saw them both as one for life. It had cost nothing, and kept her in favour of the Baltic scheme. He found himself shoving the girl's nape so her shoulders came against his face. The curve was white and clean, the flesh lavender scented. He bared his teeth and bit savagely down, eliciting a groan. He would pay her well. Pence and punishment, they were the curbs which women understood. He would have to use both if he was to succeed against Judith Blaker, hitherto his greatest ally, now his greatest foe.

29

OLD GOMME CAME for Bartholomew, leading the same cart hired for the horse fair on Sealandings heath. Ven helped him on, with Rosie fetching and carrying. They walked out of Shalamar to Market Square where the gunsmithy stood next to Eldridge the butcher's.

Baines and Mistress Gomme were waiting, eager with pleasure.

'Am I to get the furnace up, Master?' the young apprentice cried even before the cart had come to a halt.

'A day or two yet, I think,' Ven replied.

He let them take charge now his work was done. The wound was healing well, granulating up in a thick yet flaccid mass of new tissue from deep inside the wound. The bone set well. The skin could meet as and when it would. Hast was sound. He ate what was offered him, and had had no fever for days.

They followed him in, the old lady wanting to bring out small beer to signal the gunsmith's return, but Ven demurred.

'I have a journey to make, but thank you.'

Bartholomew eyed him, settling himself carefully into a low curricle chair and hauling his crutches near. 'You go to Rustonhall after all, then?'

'Yes. It is my duty.' Ven indicated Clement, who was ardently interested in the gunshop tools which the young apprentice was showing him with all the aloofness of the expert. 'Our youngest patient recovers well. His eyes no longer run pus like sick wells. I have much lunar fluid left, and could leave it at Rustonhall, though I suppose such a wealthy school must have cured its children by now.'

Hast pursed his lips. 'Mehala charged me to see you were safe, Ven.'

Ven reddened. 'A walk to Rustonhall will not harm me. I shall be there and back within the day. I am more worried about Mehala than she should be about me.'

The other was not appeased. 'Shall I send Baines with you? He is very willing. Two travel as fast as one.'

'I am not the invalid, Bartholomew. You are the one needing help.' He tried for levity. 'You grumbled about your neglected work, so get on!'

Mistress Gomme pressed some slices of ham on him, with cheese, bread and a leather of small beer.

He made his farewells to them, particularly to Rosie. She was sad at his departure, but brightened the instant he suggested that she spend the day at the gunmaker's, to change the dressings on Hast's wound. Ven supposed she was missing Mehala and was pleased to help, though old Mistress Gomme often coped with injuries. It was natural to leave Clement there also. To Ven's surprise the boy was frankly relieved to remain at Mr Hast's. Ven had thought Clement might be eager to see his old school again.

It was Clement who came with Ven to the door as they all saw him away. 'You will come back, Doctor?'

Ven patted his head. 'For absolute certain, Clement.'

After a hesitation, Clement spoke slowly. 'Doctor. Mr Pride is a most fearsome gentleman. Please do not offend him.'

'Offend?' Ven laughed at the boy's unreasonable fears. 'I offer assistance, Clement! Free! How on earth could that give offence?'

He was still amused when he waved a goodbye and marched off through Market Square, turned right at St Edmund the Martyr's past Miss Matilda's charity school, and started up the Norwich road. The boy watched him from sight, Ven noticed, which proved what kind instincts lay in everybody, even children of very short acquaintance.

The man's body was astonishingly scarred. She was astonished; so taken aback at the silvery, puckered tissue across his midriff and chest that she almost withdrew. But by then she was too far into rut to scrutinise.

The upper room was unbearably hot. It caught the best sun on the south aspect of Carradine Manor, and besides that side of the building was where the kitchen flues passed close on the exterior wall. She had chosen this room because it was used for additional laundresses, three sharing a single truckle bed as was usual. Only that morning she had ordered it vacated, with fresh linen sheets and pillows laid ready.

She had timed it to perfection. Carradine was off on estate business, saying he would call on Sir Henry at Lorne. She was not deceived, but decided that Carradine should suffer her deception, as she his.

Alex Waite had been breathless with expectation when he had climbed the narrow winding staircase. She was amused by his apprehension. He had needed a deal of reassurance.

'Do not worry, Alex,' she said demurely, drawing him into the laundress's room and closing the door. 'I guard your reputation. All housework today is concentrated on the far wing. You are sleeping late today.'

His expression cleared as he understood. 'My reputation is nothing compared to a lady's, Judith.'

Indeed, she thought, how true. A lady found in compromising circumstances was doomed. A gentleman was merely seen as a rake, admired by men and women alike. Carradine's fury would be unimaginable were he to discover this tryst. A challenge, a duel, and Waite would join the ghostly procession of those who had crossed Rad Carradine.

'Alex,' she said softly. She started to help him off with his spencer, gently pushing it off his shoulders. 'I am glad you came. I was afraid you would think it forward of me, to put the note under your door . . .'

'I was over the moon to read it, Judith.'

'Sit with me.' There was nowhere else but the truckle bed. 'We shall be alone to make conversation.'

The double meaning almost stifled him, conversation being the euphemism for bodily pleasure. 'You do me so much honour, m'lady.'

Judith heard him with delight. It would not be long before she had that appellation by right, if all went according to plan. Whether it was with Carradine or with somebody else would hardly matter, for she controlled her own destiny. No other woman in Sealandings could make that claim.

Except Mehala?

She thrust the distasteful image from her and let Alex take her hand. She looked modestly away. They sat like children.

'Alex, I wanted you to come. I feel drawn to you.' She attempted to rise, as if overcome by a natural modesty. She was annoyed he did not pull her down, instead of merely waiting with such passivity. She could see that it was up to her to force the pace.

'You are very kind, m'lady.'

'No, Alex.' She smiled at him sadly. 'I have no other companion in whom I might confide. Oh, I know that Carradine has a stream of visitors. You can tell how invidious my position is.'

He hesitated, made himself speak. 'Being of such august origin . . .'

'And a mere housekeeper?' She smiled, sorrow catching her voice. 'There are many throughout the country, if rumour speaks truth, of highest parentage. It is a heavy cross to bear.'

'No, no!' Alex stared at Judith with fascination, completely believing that she was the daughter of such an exalted father that his very title could not be spoken without disloyalty. Other royal offspring were so well known in London that crude rhymes were sold on chapman's pamphlets at hangings and other joyous occasions.

'I need a guardian, Alex.' She smiled sadly at him, lowering her eyes. 'I am not making a plea. I would not be so forward. But you have little idea how much it would mean to me, having a friend. I feel that you are compassionate, Alex. Might I . . .?'

'I should be honoured, Judith. But . . . guardian?' That word, with all its implications, gave him doubt.

'Not in the legal sense.' She masked her irritation in a quiet sorrow. 'I have never known a father's kindness, nor even the open acknowledgement of my mother. I long for a kindred spirit to share an intimate sympathy.'

'I must leave as soon as the ship is arranged –'

She could have screamed at his tardiness, but patiently led the way through the thickets of etiquette. 'If you are a partner, then attendance at Carradine Manor is legitimate. We could . . .' She smiled shyly.

For once he took the bait. 'That would delight me more than anything.'

'You are sure, Alex? I would not wish to –'

His face was close to hers. Suddenly she raised her mouth to his, and it was done.

It was then, in compelling urgency, that she discovered the extraordinary mat of scars across his trunk, and had to check her astonishment. Even as he entered her, her hands were caressing the strange undulations. The skin was oddly smooth to the touch. She had accepted many men before, some sound, some bearing injuries from battle or wayside fights. But never before had she had one who was her own age, yet who bore such evidence of combat. He was sound of limb, and his thrusts lacked nothing for vigour. In fact she was drawn into the coupling with something approaching abandon. She felt herself grunting and heeling him with sensuous pleasure, and had to rein herself to seem more passive and let him take dominance.

Later, spent and breathless under his weight, with rivulets of his sweat pouring from him onto her, she felt a strange affection swelling in her. It was as if his innocence made him different. Yet he was sprawled on her in the oldest of positions, in the brief demise that all males had to endure after fornication. Surely he could not mean anything to her?

She found herself holding him in, though his weight was crushing. She had to get her mouth clear of his shoulder. Once, she had a similar possessive fondness for Carradine, but that was merely the natural instinct of a woman wanting security. This was weird, a curious feeling at odds with anything she had experienced.

He stirred and would have raised himself to see her face, but in sudden apprehension she clasped him and averted her own face. The strange sensation made her vulnerable. She, Judith Blaker, was invulnerable to all her lovers. She had to stay isolated, until the opportunity of seizing a truly great chance came. Only then would she commit herself totally, and not until.

The door opened slowly. She could see, in the mirror, Prettiance's mob cap, then the girl's face taking in the lovers on the bed. She silently mouthed a few words as Judith, furious that the ugly maid-of-all was staring in at her lover's scarred body, covered him with the sheet.

'*Lubbenipen*,' Prettiance mouthed, then made a throat-cutting gesture with her finger. The harlotry was finished. The insolent slut meaning, of course, that Carradine must be back sooner than expected. '*Drab-engro*,' with a finger drawn near to her scrawny breast; the poison-monger had come, meaning Doctor Carmichael. But here? For what purpose? And finally, '*Mattomengro*,' the gesture repeated with rolling eyes. The drunkard. Who else but Sir Charles Golding?

Judith gave a slow blink of dismissal. The crude bitch insolently appraised their positions, raised eyebrows inquiring about the copulation's success. Judith narrowed her gaze in threat, and Prettiance slowly withdrew.

She was shocked when Alex spoke. He had shown no sign of awareness.

'Who?' he said quietly.

'A trusted servant,' she whispered, pressing her lips to his face and holding him close. 'Visitors come, darling. You must be gone. Be reading or resting. I shall go to receive them.'

'Very well.'

It was too quick for her. She groaned aloud as he withdrew from her body and rose to find his clothes.

'Darling,' Judith said softly, 'when shall I see you?'

'Soon.' She could not take her eyes off him. 'I will openly announce my departure, and say where I shall be.'

'Thank you, darling,' she heard herself say, in a docile voice she did not recognise. She pressed his hand to her mouth.

Ridiculous, she told herself in astonishment. She was deeply disturbed, watching him dress and leave. That he did so without a glance was hurtful, especially after how they had been. He had not aroused her to the degree that, say, Carradine did. Nor had his lovemaking been inventive. He had seemed driven but distant, yet she now felt angrily possessive.

She rose and dressed quickly. She had given Prettiance instructions to steal her note back from Alex Waite's room.

Five minutes later she was sewing in the withdrawing-room overlooking the garden terrace. It was there that Carradine came on her to say he had changed his mind about calling on Hunterfield, for he had seen Hunterfield's landau carrying the Squire, old Lady Faith Hunterfield, and Miss Carmady to the harbour. He had decided to await a better opportunity.

He had not shed his riding frock coat when a servant appeared to say that Sir Charles Golding was in the drive, and that Doctor Carmichael sought an audience.

*

Ven stood with his old worn beaver in his hands, waiting.

Hobbes, the chief servant, sent a mere maid-of-all, a young girl of unprepossessing features, to summon him when the master condescended to see him.

Ven was ushered in to the hall from the servants' entrance. Carradine strode in.

'Good day, sir. Thank you for –'

'What?' Carradine jerked his head to the maid, who left.

'If you please, sir, I have important information. I am in correspondence with a physician. He lives in a port in regular trade with Baltic nations.'

'So?' Carradine heard a rider on the front drive, and stepped to the window to wave idly at some newcomer.

'I recently received a letter, sir. There have been instances of sick seamen arriving from those parts. The illness is a distemper which –'

Carradine transfixed him with a stare. 'Let me understand your stupidity, leech,' he said at last. 'You interrupt my day to tell me of some ague hundreds of miles away?'

'I heard of your intention to establish trade –'

'I do not *establish trade*, sir!' Carradine thundered, advancing on Ven, who retreated stammering.

'I acknowledge that. Only I thought you would want –'

'Where is it?'

'Sir?' Ven was stunned by the rage he had unwittingly created.

'The letter, idiot, the letter!'

'I have destroyed it, sir, by burning.'

Carradine heaved a slow breath. 'You mean there *is* no account of this famous disease? Yet you come here with –'

'Sir. I beg.' Ven's stammer was so constant that he had to speak slowly to continue. 'There is illness in the Baltic states. Ships coming into the northern ports carry it. Several have been quarantined.'

'Why have I heard nothing of this? Why do eastern harbours receive no warning?'

'I do not know, sir.'

'Then you are an idiot.' Carradine watched the man. Pale,

gaunt, standing in a worn threadbare surtout, thin half-jack boots on the kilter showing they lacked proper soles. 'Get out.'

'Please be aware, sir –'

'*Out!*'

Carradine saw him bow awkwardly and leave by the servants' entrance, thinking over what the quacksalver had said. But then Golding was announced in the green withdrawing-room. He advanced smiling on the visitor, extending his hand.

'Welcome, Charles. Is it too early to offer you a drink?'

'Never has been, Rad,' Golding said with satisfaction.

'The prospects for the venture seem to be improving, Charles,' Carradine said with all affability. 'I have heard today from an old friend, wishing to join us . . .'

In the servants' corridor Ven could hardly see. There was a singular absence of candles. He bumped into a female and recoiled with an anxious apology. He could just see that it was the maid-of-all with the unfortunate visage.

'My apologies, miss. I can hardly see an inch.'

'This way, Doctor. Mind the step, and the turn right.'

'Thank you.' He reached out for her hand with a murmur of gratitude. She led him slowly down the corridor past two store-rooms and the bakery, and out into the light by the kitchen's herb garden. 'You are very kind, miss. I am obliged.' He glanced at the splendid array of plants and the neat paths. 'You must be very happy here, miss.'

'Happy?' Her sharpness startled him.

'Such a great estate, with Carradine Manor at its centre. All friends together, as if in a busy town of its own!' He sighed wistfully. 'Friendship is such a pleasure for those who share it.'

She stared at him with disbelief. He supposed it was simply a look he did not understand.

'For some, Doctor. Not for such as I.'

Her bitterness made him uncomfortable. 'But why not? There are so many servants, of your own age.'

'Have you not seen my face?' She adopted a pose of comeliness, fingers linked beneath her chin, as a child showing off pretty features. 'I am mocked by the housekeeper down, Doctor. Features hardly matter a jot to a man. But ugliness ruins the *fair* sex.' Her distress was grievous, self-mockery only adding to the pain.

'Shhh,' he consoled. 'Miss, you led me from the darkness of the corridor and brought me into the sunlight. I was lost!' He smiled. 'How beautiful your face, your eyes, your appearance must therefore seem to me, were I wholly blind and seeing another human being for the very first time!' He took her hand again. 'No, miss. Every woman has her own beauty. Only her own disbelief betrays it, not the eyes of men. You have met only those who enjoy cruelty. They deride only their own lack of vision.'

'My name is Prettiance. The cruellest joke of all!'

'No, Prettiance. Every woman *is* her own beauty. Something in her nature outshines all. *Every* woman, Prettiance. That is not merely my truth, it is life's. Believe it. In fact, you are obliged to. When you do, it reveals of that loveliness.'

She was staring. 'I have never heard a man talk so.'

He smiled. 'Then you have met only the soul-blind, or the cruel.' He bussed her in the old custom, and pretended to be cross with himself for delaying. 'I have a walking journey to go, and here I am flirting with ladies! How will I earn my pence?'

'Goodbye, Doctor,' she called after him.

'Goodbye, Prettiance,' he called back. 'Remember!'

She was some time leaving the garden. She stood to see him head for the fence that would take him to the Norwich road, his old surtout flapping and his beaver at an angle, holding his leather bag and gradually getting into a stride. His figure dwindled, then vanished up the incline.

30

'ARE YOU GLAD to return, Mehala?'
'There is no such thing, sir,' Mehala told Carmady.

You can never go back, Ven had once told Mehala when she
asked if he longed for Whitechapel. And no, the memories of old
Arbuthnot and his grand London practice were not causes of
jealousy but mere wistfulness from a kind memory.

Never? she had asked, appalled.

He was emphatic: never. There is no such thing as return. The
very word was odious. Then she had put aside the problem in the
press of events at Shalamar – the early rising, the breakfast, the
reading of the notes of the previous day's patients, followed by the
lesson on anatomy. Then the visits to patients, the noonings, the
afternoon lesson on diseases, while trying to fit in the washing,
ironing, making candles, weaving on the old handloom, spinning
on spindle-tree bobbins, gathering food . . .

There is no such thing as return, she thought.

But she was here, back at Red Hall.

'Are you glad to return, Mehala?'
'There is no such thing, sir,' Mehala told Percy Carmady.
'No such . . .?' He glanced at her face a moment, then nodded,
taking the conversation no further.

The coach had arrived at the Red Lion in Colchester's High
Street within ten minutes of its predicted time, to everybody's
relief. The naval gentleman had been courtesy itself on the
journey, accompanying her when the Royal Mail had changed
horses and the inns were particularly rowdy. The coach had made
a brisk show, averaging a clear six miles an hour. The guard and
driver had exchanged annoyed words at the irresponsibility of
grander coaches near Ipswich. Several had been disinclined to

surrender the right of the road to the Mail even when warned by the guard's horn. Two landaus, particularly obstructive near Wickham Market and Woodbridge, were to be reported to the constabulary for delaying the Royal Mail.

Mehala had delivered the precious platina wire to Bartholomew Hast's cousins, who arrived at the Red Lion within minutes of the Mail coach. She took a written receipt signed for Philip Hast, gunmaker of 118, High Street, and witnessed by Carmady and the taverner, and saw them off with relief.

Sir Henry's steward Tayspill had left his compliments with the innkeeper. He had already paid a visit on Red Hall. He was lodged nearby in the parish of St James the Great with Reverend John Dakins. Tayspill was cousin to Elizabeth, wife of the rector. He would call on Mehala within an hour of the coach's expected arrival. Mehala left a message saying he would not be required, and retired for the night.

Percy Carmady decided to interrupt his journey and accompany her to Red Hall. He explained that, as Colchester was a famous old port with a harbour that he had never before examined, he might need to know of it should the widely-discussed Baltic venture actually come to pass. His journey through the town was a good opportunity.

'In fact, Mehala,' he told her, 'it would please me greatly were I to escort you, who are so expert in these shallow shores and strange estuaries.'

There had been a time in Sealandings when she had actually been afraid of Lieutenant Carmady. On the road outside Lorne House, Carmady had been in the Squire's company. She had known instantly that Carmady had recognised her – and it could only have been from a fleeting glimpse in Colchester. But now she was at ease with him. He was a friend of Hunterfield, whom she trusted. Their shared journey had been no place for exchanging confidences, for a succession of inside passengers had boarded, so noisy, or drunk and snoring, that Mehala's senses had been almost numbed.

That night she slept deeply in the strange bed, and awoke with a start at six from the sound of St Nicholas's church bells.

She was close to what had been home, she realised, telling herself this would be only a fleeting visit. Her duty was at home with Ven. Without her he was vulnerable, with his unworldly assumption that everyone was good at heart.

She travelled from Colchester to Red Hall in a small hired four-wheel hackney, laboriously drawn by a broken-winded Norfolk roadster with a sad shuffling gait. Mehala felt oddly ashamed. She made apologies to Percy Carmady on its behalf. He was unconcerned, being more interested in the terrain as they approached the sea.

'We should have gone by water instead of land, Mehala.'

'Indeed we should, Mr Carmady.' Her heart was pounding as familiar landmarks came into view once they were past the cross at Layer de la Haye. 'It is easier, as long as one is careful.'

'Was this the route you followed, when first you went to Red Hall?' he could not help asking. He was still surprised that she had accepted his offer to accompany her with such alacrity.

'No. My mother and I sailed our poor boat, spritsail and jib, before a north-east wind. We went down the Mersea Channel, doubled Sunken Island, and took Salcot Fleet. That channel is formed eventually from the creek separating the villages of Salcot and Virley. There I grounded. A lovely day, but preluding disaster.'

He smiled diffidently. 'This visit may prelude all manner of success! Think on that!'

She did not respond to his optimism, but stared out of the hackney window as the Norfolk hauled the carriage slowly along the trackway through Wigborough Fields.

'It was a sparkling day,' she said dreamily. 'I had never seen such multitudes of birds! The water glittering, shining as if lit! And the great gaunt windmill's black arms rotating slowly, its pump creaking and the arms groaning . . .'

She suddenly pointed. 'There is Tolleshunt Knights to the right. We go straight on here at the crossroads, skirting Salcot and Virley, to reach the Salcot side from seaward.'

'Are you well, Mehala?'

Unaccountably she had begun to shiver. 'I am well, thank you. Just a memory of my first glimpse of Red Hall.'

He was beginning to think it would have been wiser to leave her to Tayspill. He could have made good headway to London, and by now been inspecting the *Sealands* at Greenwich. But curiosity had got the better of him. Tayspill had been instructed to go ahead to Salcot and wait at Red Hall.

The wind was freshening from the east, he noted with pleasure, and brought with it the tang of the North Sea. Pity to waste the approach by trundling up in some broken carriage, instead of making a glorious landfall among these sealands. The track ran in an arc round the inlets. As the vehicle turned away from Tolleshunt D'Arcy, Carmady could see that the seamarshes extended as a low peninsula into the sea near Mersea Island.

High sea dykes seemed everywhere. The land was barren of trees. He saw the black arms of the windmill Mehala had mentioned, turning slowly, only the undulations of the ground obstructing the view across the terrain.

'Red Hall Marsh,' Mehala said quietly. 'I . . . There is a long duck decoy water established beyond that cross dyke. Look to the left, Mr Carmady.'

He peered with interest. A small wharf stood at the head of the creek, presumably the inlet near where Mehala had landed. Two boats were moored there. Others sprawled on the mudflats, waiting the tide. He leaned further, and saw Red Hall.

The roof was tiled with red pantiles, almost leached to orange by time. The building was remarkably tall to Carmady's eyes, almost tower-like above the rich pastures. The basement was formed of cellars raised at ground level, a construction he had never seen before. The low-lying nature of the land and the nearness of the tall sea dykes made him understand the purpose. Twin arches provided entrance to the cellars, which gained daylight by rounded windows at shoulder level.

'A smuggler's paradise!' he exclaimed thoughtlessly. 'Those arches and the cellar pillars are quite like cloisters!'

The main door of the grand mansion was reached by wide stone steps leading from a raised platform. Carmady looked about. What with the creeks, the marsh channels, and the navigable inlets everywhere the eye could see, it would be possible to row a small craft within a hundred yards of Red Hall on any night from almost any direction except due west. His careless exclamation had proved Red Hall's purpose and its affluence. The great dwelling was entirely brick built, brick mouldings supporting every window with brick mullions and drip stone. There was a wide moat filled with rushes and weed.

They instructed the hackney driver to wait, then walked up the steps and round the side of the house. Several walled yards were entirely brick paved. The outhouses seemed well maintained, with the bakery, stables, shippons and coach house clean, but empty.

Carmady was about to make an observation when he caught sight of Mehala's face. It was almost bloodless. He held her arm.

'Mr Tayspill!' he called, and was relieved to see the man appear from an outhouse at a brisk walk.

'Not a soul!' Tayspill called, 'but I have effected entry with the aid of the petty constable. May we go inside, Mistress?'

Carmady entered last from the terrace door, and stood a moment. At ground level, every horizon had seemed bounded by a sea wall. From the terrace, however, he was able to see the sea itself, the creeks, the friendly woods on Mersea Island, and the cultivated fields of the mainland.

'Nobody here, mistress,' Tayspill said, disgust in his voice. 'No steward or servant. The cattle have been taken by herdsmen from Gorwell Hall, your neighbour. They kept tally – they say! The rector will call on you this afternoon.'

'The estate? The pasture lands?'

'All are in good heart.' His tone expressed disgust.

'The decoy?'

'Nearly two acres lake, dug from clay, mistress, in a low willow wood. Maintained: the willows cut to fronding withies recently.'

'It is in use, then?'

'Yes. The rushes fringing it are cleared at the horns of the lake, as is proper. A few elms suffer, though.'

'The herds?'

'I have been allowed to see a small number.' Tayspill's terse reply made Mehala look at him the harder.

'Where do they stand?'

'At the Salcot Fresh Marshes, and your own Red Hall Marsh.'

'A mile square, almost, then,' Mehala said, in quiet thought. 'They are mingled?'

'They tell me not, Mistress.'

'They, Mr Tayspill?'

'Two herdsmen from Gorwell Hall. The lady and gentleman

from there sent word they will presently call.' Tayspill consulted his watch with ponderous anger.

Carmady accompanied Mehala through the ground floor. The house was spacious, all the furniture covered and neat, the curtains mostly drawn on the south side but others left undrawn.

'Mr Tayspill. Did you inspect the rest of the mansion?'

'Not yet, m'lady. I was more concerned with the estate.'

'Of course.'

A voice called from outside, and a man's cane sounded, tapping as he approached.

'Hulloo!' He came into the withdrawing-room where they were standing, and stopped as if stricken. 'By God! It really is!' he exclaimed to the lady with him, 'Mehala! Back from the dead!'

Carmady greeted the lady, was introduced to both by Mehala. Tayspill stood apart in disapproval, recognising the residents of Gorwell who had combined Red Hall's herds with their own.

'Bram Yale, Esquire, of Tolleshunt, 'service,' the gentleman said, striving a little too desperately to seem pleased. 'Melissa was only saying, Mistress Rebow, how worried all of Salcot and Virley still were at your absence!'

Mehala winced at the old name. Carmady was immediately attracted to Melissa Yale, who was extravagantly attired in a deep green merino saxony, with a light silk and wool barege cloak that showed an attractive semi-transparency about her shoulders.

'How kind,' Mehala said evenly. 'I believe your anxiety moved you to take care of my cattle, Mr Yale.'

He maintained his enthusiasm with difficulty. 'Indeed! And I protected your estate by adding your best servants to my own staff. Not altogether without cost, of course. They have proved a considerable drain on Gorwell Hall's estates.'

'Mr Tayspill,' Mehala interrupted. 'For how long might I count upon your services, during your leave from Lorne House?'

'A fortnight, Mistress Mehala, with Sir Henry's permission.'

'Very well.' She had not so far spoken to Melissa Yale. 'Mr Yale, I appoint Mr Tayspill of Sealandings my steward and agent here, to recover my beasts, horses, and –'

'And vehicles,' Tayspill added brusquely. 'I understand there are at least three?'

'Five,' Mehala said. 'Servants will be hired at Mr Tayspill's discretion. I appoint him to be steward in residence at Red Hall. He may have the senior steward's lodge.'

'Mistress Rebow,' Yale said, offended by her peremptory manner, 'I have taken every step legally –'

'And I thank you,' Mehala said coldly. 'The need for your support is ended. Mr Tayspill will take possession of all – *all*, Mr Yale – my belongings: beasts, farming implements, horses and land, forthwith.' She showed no desire to continue the conversation.

Melissa Yale's face froze at the implication. She turned on her heel. Carmady was sorry to see her leave, but pleased at Yale's chagrin. It was all but a dismissal. To mitigate the injury, he accompanied them to the terrace.

'On behalf of Mehala,' he said, as friendly as possible, 'I thank you for your kindness. I am merely an acquaintance, but I am sure Mehala would wish me to express gratitude.'

'It is gracious of you to express such sentiments, sir.' Yale was now an enemy, from his stiff reply. His wife lingered, pleased by the admiration in Carmady's eyes.

'We did only what any gentry would, sir.' Her gaze flicked towards her husband. 'I regret that we are not to have more of your company, sir. Or will you stay at Red Hall?'

'Alas no, Mistress Yale. I have lately left the King's Navy. I hope to put in to Colchester, if I take a ship to the Baltic ports.'

'If that comes to pass, perhaps you will reside in these parts? I am sure that Mistress Carmady would find our prosperous Hundred most conducive to her health and satisfaction.'

'Alas, I am a bachelor, Mistress Yale. Nonetheless, I have so far not seen an area as delightful as this.'

She lowered her eyes. 'You are kind, sir. Until then.'

'Until then. And goodbye, Mr Yale.'

The Yales left. Carmady saw they had an imposing phaeton, unusual for country living, and a driver in livery. He admired Melissa Yale. He might pay a visit to Gorwell Hall.

He found Mehala waiting. Tayspill's footsteps sounded as he climbed the small servant staircase from the ante-room. She smiled at Percy.

'Mistress Yale has made a conquest, Mr Carmady?'

He coloured a little, but shrugged. 'I tried to lessen the antagonism, Mehala.'

'I cannot abide the woman. And as for Mr Yale's protestations of neighbourliness, I know that my return is the worst news he has ever had!'

'Tayspill will serve as your steward, then?'

'Yes. He is willing. He will stay with the rector of St James the Great in Colchester, his relatives.'

'And you, Mehala? You will return here to Red Hall?'

'Hardly, Percy.' She touched his arm, seeking his complicity. 'I shall make out papers of authority for Mr Tayspill to restore the estate and take on a housekeeper and servants enough to care for Red Hall itself.'

'Then?'

'Return to Sealandings.' She felt a load lift from her. 'With joy. I shall start back at my earliest on the express Royal.' It was essential to repossess the funds available in the banks of Colchester and Maldon. Then, and only then, she would be able to resume life with Ven.

She started a desultory inspection of Red Hall, hating every minute, and the place more than ever. She had no intention of living here. It would not suit Ven, so was out of the question.

For one moment she did pause, as the inscription, cut deep into the oak lintel of the great fireplace, caught her eye: WHEN I HOLD (1636) I HOLD FAST. She felt giddy with hate. The motto's sentiment was nothing less than madness. She called out to Tayspill. 'Sir? Assemble all Red Hall estate's possessions to a state of completeness, with all expediency.'

'Very well, mistress. Then?'

'Then sell it.'

31

VEN WAS MORE tired than he had expected as Rustonhall church came into view. He had fallen in with a bulky pedlar carrying his ped with his name, Bellin, crudely painted on, the statutory words 'Licensed Hawker', and his licence number daubed in red beneath. At first, Ven was pleased to have company, but something about the man's manner was furtive; that, his uneven teeth, and his grumbling.

They had talked of the problems of obtaining money in these turbulent days. The pedlar had shown a displeasing lewdness of talk. Ven found himself replying by noncommittal remarks, wishing the hawker would branch off to some side village. But the man obstinately stayed with him, until Ven entered the hamlet of Rustonhall and the odious man continued on.

The school was an old mansion that had seen better times. Its grounds were not too badly maintained – more organised than Shalamar's – but the building itself was in disrepair. It wore an air of somnolence and poverty.

He knocked, noting rust on the door furnishings, the grimed windows. But the notice at the gate was legible; this was Rustonhall school. He felt vague misgivings.

The door opened. A soiled old woman looked out.

'Good day,' Ven said with feigned heartiness. 'Might I see the headmaster, Mr Pride?'

She stood back to allow him in. Pride came bounding out of a side room, hand extended and face ruddy with pleasure. He was a corpulent man in a tan waistcoat and moleskin breeches.

'Good day to you, sir!' He almost dragged Ven into a study where he seemed to be finishing a meal of chicken, sausage and bread and an assortment of cheeses on a trencher. 'Can I invite you to partake?'

'No, thank you.' Ven saw the other's face change as he took in his visitor's old surtout and worn half-jacks. 'I hope I was not taken for a different visitor, Mr Pride?'

'Are you a parent of a prospective pupil, sir?'

'No, Mr Pride. I am a doctor, and have walked from Sea-landings today to offer you my assistance. Doctor Carmichael.'

'Assistance in what?'

'In the problem of your boys' eyes, Mr Pride.'

The man looked quite blank. 'My pupils' *eyes*?'

'Yes. Let me explain.' Ven told how he and Mehala had visited the Sealandings workhouse, and taken charge of a boy from Rustonhall.

'Clement Wellins?'

'Why, yes, Mr Pride!' Ven was relieved to find common ground. 'That is he. I took him to Shalamar, my home. There his eyesight recovered, thank God.'

'Wellins!' Pride spoke the name with venom.

'You remember him? It was not that long ago.'

'And he urged you to come here?'

'No. I came of my own accord. Where you have one such eye infection – pus, matter, adhesions of the lids, encroaching blindness – you are sure to have several.'

'What did he tell you?'

'That you had seven or eight small boys with blind matted eyes, all confined in one room.' Ven brought out his vial. 'I have here a quantity of physic that I made, for instilling into the blind boys' eyes. They will mend within a few days. It is my pleasure to make a gift –'

'Out!' Pride rose, and swung a fist at Ven, casting about for a weapon as Ven rose in horror at the sudden transformation. '*Out!* Blackguard!'

'But I have brought your children some –'

'Out before I call the parish constable! Out! Gromond! Come quickly! Come and beat this charlatan from our door –'

Ven fled, grabbing his bag and fumbling with the door to make his escape. Luckily the school stood two or more furlongs from the centre of the hamlet, and he was able to put a safe mile or two between himself and Rustonhall without hindrance or any sign of constables following. He slowed only when out of breath, but kept walking as fast as possible. There was no accounting for people.

He realised that Clement had been trying to warn him, that the schoolteacher was either mad or wholly corrupt, a man crazed by criticism and furious at any intruder.

He maintained the pace until he had passed through two other hamlets. Only then did he slow to his usual walking speed. He was still trembling after some miles, and it was with great thankfulness that, hours later, he finally passed Mr Tyll's tollgate on the Norwich road, feeling safe from further calamity.

In the distance he saw the public livestock field just before he passed Parker's common stables. He saw a figure by the hedge, and realised it was the same Barbara Tyll who had once been housekeeper at Carradine. He paused by her.

'Are you well, Mistress Tyll?'

'Yes, Doctor, thank you.'

'Can I accompany you?' He offered his arm. 'I have just passed your husband's toll bar. As long as I am not charged!'

'Thank you, Doctor.' She leaned heavily on him. 'There is no fee for those afoot.'

'I was making pleasantry.' He judged her with a sidelong glance. 'You are seven-and-a-half, eight months?'

'Eight, Doctor.'

'In health during the carrying?'

Her wan look was enough answer. 'I ail all the time, Doctor. My head pounds, my brain spins as if I was fevered.'

'May I call? There would be no cost to yourself,' he added quickly, knowing that her finances must have tumbled since her sacking by Carradine. 'Only, I could offer guidance.'

'Please do not call, Doctor. Every pace sets me reeling. I can hardly go a perch without feeling faint. I am afraid for the babe.'

So why did she walk all the way to Carradine Manor?

'Ah. You are coming *from* Carradine, then?'

'Yes.' She allowed Ven to conduct her to the grass verge as a Norfolk carter's long-bedded waggon with its massive iron-rimmed tyres hauled past. She leaned heavily on him, breathless. 'I must tell you, Doctor. I went to appeal to Carradine. I am with child, and . . .'

'Will Mr Tyll prove condign?' It was as far as he dared go in asking outright.

Barbara Tyll looked ashen-faced. 'It is not his fault, Doctor. He must have known. The child is Carradine's, not his. He refuses to speak, and would sell me off as husbands sometimes do.'

'What did Carradine say?'

'He will not see me. I tried to leave a note for him, but was refused.'

'His very self? Or was refusal given for him?'

'I am unsure, Doctor. Mistress Blaker sent refusal.'

Ven was apalled. All around seemed to difficulties. It was as if mankind conspired to create them. Here was the most loyal of housekeepers, a woman who – very well, acknowledged that she was partner to seduction – who had stood by her master when he was condemned by all for profligacy and cruelty. Here she was now, at the most dangerous pass of all, and rejected.

The thought of blame made his anger rise. *Why* blame, when intercourse was a most natural act? What had the infant in her womb ever done to earn the stigma of blame?

'Will Tyll allow you in?'

'Yes. I prepare his meals. He eats them without a word. I fear that he will turn me out.' She was tearful, holding on to the remnants of dignity. 'He sees his livelihood at risk once word gets about.'

'Then where will you go?'

'Nowhere will have me, Doctor.'

'Have you relatives?'

She looked steadfastly away. 'Yes. But I would rather die than appeal to their clemency.'

'Has Tyll said anything openly?'

'He is close to condemning me outright, now my condition becomes apparent.'

It was a well-kept secret then, for no hint of Mistress Tyll's predicament had reached Shalamar. And though rumours had often spread about Barbara Tyll's position at Carradine Manor before the advent of Judith Blaker, the babe's parentage had never been called into question. He needed Mehala. She might be home soon.

'Mistress Tyll. I shall walk back with you to the toll house. Stay there. If you are in need, send a boy with a message, and I shall come. Do you understand?'

'Yes, Doctor.' She searched his face, wondering. 'Tyll is a good man, but I know him. As my time approaches he will burst. I know it. He has a terrible rage, if there is cause. And', she added in self-accusation, 'there is cause enough, God knows.'

'I shall find some remedy, Mistress Tyll.'

'You, Doctor? But how?'

'Rely on me to help,' he said lamely.

She caught at him. 'You will tell no one, Doctor?'

'Not a soul.'

'When I was turned from Carradine I thought of perhaps going to the churchwardens, then Squire Hunterfield, then the Poor House.'

'No, no,' Ven said, aghast at the memory of Rosie's sojourn there. No living person should suffer such atrocity. It was barbarism at its worst. 'I shall do my damnedest to see that it does not come to that.'

'Thank you.' She stayed still a moment as they faced the incline towards her home. 'Doctor. If anything happens to me . . . will you care for the babe?'

'Of course I shall.' He was worried; another promise.

'Other men I might ask to swear, Doctor.' She smiled, weary. 'Not you. From the bottom of my heart –'

'Mistress Tyll,' he exclaimed in mock severity. 'Let us get you home. It will be dark before you finish your prattle.'

Retreating to the verges as the occasional waggons passed down the incline, he took her slowly up to the tollgate, dismayed by the turn of events. Mehala only gone a brief while, and already he seemed surrounded by difficulties.

An hour after midnight, Judith Blaker descended the servants' back staircase, following Prettiance down the bakery corridor. Prettiance held a pottery Norfolk lantern with a short tallow candle to light Judith's way, and paused at the casement. She stood away.

'The *moskey*,' she whispered. 'Your spy.'

Judith ignored the ugly girl's sarcasm. She could punish her any time. For now, she needed Bellin's report. The man was standing by the shrubs near the window. She did not lean out.

'Yes, brother? *Ava pal*?'

Bellin stepped close. '*Sar shin, meeri rawnie?*'

'Well, thank you. What news?'

'I walked to Rustonhall with the *drav-engro*, your Doctor Carmichael. He must have been ill-received at the school, for he came out as if fleeing Hell itself. I trailed him back to Sealandings. He met the wife of the *stiggur-engro*, the turnpike keeper Tyll. She is *buri*, big with child.'

'Barbara Tyll?' Judith was outraged. 'She is *shuvvali?*'

'Pregnant, yes. She will need a midwife, the *mormusti*, any week now, but has the *naflipen*, sickness. She fears her husband will drive her out. You wish to know why, *rawnie?*' Prettiance heard Bellin's voice change. He was smiling, relishing his news. 'Because Carradine is the father.'

Judith stood mute, remembering. Some servant had brought a message during the afternoon, some impertinent former employee seeking an audience with Carradine. She had declined permission and ordered her sent away. It must have been Barbara Tyll, pleading paternity rights for her bastard-to-be. Hate filled her. If she hated Mehala for catching Carradine's eye, she now hated this Tyll bitch as mortally.

'And?'

'The *drav-engro* promised to care for her. He helped her home. They went *kettaney*, together.' That pleased Bellin most of all.

Judith stared past him into the darkness. If that Tyll cow had a carrying sickness, might she deliver a dead child? That would be satisfactory, especially if she was driven from hearth and home. But with that poison-monger Carmichael caring for her, the bastard might be born alive and well. She seethed with impotent hate.

'Where is Mehala? Still in the south begging?'

'*Ava, rawnie.* Evidently a great lady, your Mehala.'

'*Meklis!*' Judith spat. 'Hold your tongue! A great lady? A great witch, a *chovahani!*' But it might be all to the good. A dazzling girl had the compelling fascination of mystery, whereas a woman defined by circumstance lost all that and became tiresomely ordinary.

She would have to move against Mehala faster than she had planned. Complacency was a crime.

'Send me Endercotte early tomorrow. And keep silence about the baby being Carradine's. It is *hokkano*, a lie.'

'*Ava, rawnie*. And the Doctor at Shalamar?'

'Let it be, *mukkalis becunye*,' Judith whispered after a pause. 'Go with God. *Ja Develehi*.'

'*Az Develehi*, stay with God.'

And the man was gone.

Prettiance closed the window. Judith remained still when Prettiance made to pass and light the way along the stone-flagged corridor. The maid halted, worried at Judith's stare.

She asked nervously, '*Ava, rawnie*?'

'You brought a request today. Was it from Barbara Tyll?'

'Why, yes.'

'Why did you not tell me she was *buri* with child?'

'I did not think it mattered.'

Judith's hand lashed across the maid's cheek so savagely that the girl barely managed to avoid shattering the Norfolk lantern on the stonework. '*Lubbeny*! Harlot! Are you so stupid that you cannot see the obvious?'

'Please, *rawnie*, I –'

'Silence! As punishment, I forbid you to go to the square on market day, or to speak with anyone outside the Manor!'

'But Mistress –' Prettiance wailed. It was her only recreation. Her ugliness made her the butt of drovers' and market stall-holders' jibes, yet those outings were a serving-maid's only relief from drudgery. It was the cruellest punishment.

Judith snatched the lantern from Prettiance's fingers and swept off down the corridor, leaving the girl in darkness. For a full minute the weeping maid remained against the window until she was able to distinguish the grey rectangle of light from outside, then she slowly felt her way along the dark corridor wall.

32

TWO LETTERS ARRIVED simultaneously from the Donkey and Buskin, fetched by Rosie. She had been to see Bartholomew.
Mehala's was the first letter he had ever received from her, though he knew her handwriting from her transcriptions of his lessons. It was brief, but made him soar with pleasure.

Red Hall
Salcot

My Dearest Love,

The assistance of Mister Tayspill has been invaluable. I have now paid a visit to this accursed place of evil memory. Mister Tayspill has accepted stewardship, and will remain here with a servant loaned of Revd John Dakins, rector of St James the Great of Colchester, to whose wife Elizabeth Mister Tayspill is happily related. He will draw servants and appoint bailiffs. My herds will be reclaimed from a neighbour, Bram Yale, Esq., likewise carriages and other possessions including farm implements. I fear the place was nigh stripped, but all will be redressed.

Mister P. Carmady accompanied me the whole journey on the Royal Mail. I believe he will invite Yale to join the Baltic venture. He is welcome to the Yales's company and patronage for as long as he may care for it.

There are funds to be assigned, then I shall come home on the Royal Mail express. I believe I have laid ghosts by this journey, my dearest, so will soon justly sign myself to you with all respect.

Your loving wife,

Mehala.

He read it several times, uplifted by Mehala's evident relief at having faced the past. Percy Carmady's companionship displeased him, though he was sure the ex-lieutenant had behaved with courtesy. But did the man need to have accompanied Mehala all the way to Red Hall, when he was urgently on his way to Greenwich to examine the Baltic ship? That was the tale that Clement and Rosie brought back, suitably embellished. Why did Carmady break his journey at all? Ven smouldered for some time, cheering himself by re-reading Mehala's letter twice more and feeling reassured, before glowering again at the mental image of Carmady's journey to Red Hall.

The second letter's contents struck him like a blow. It was all the more grievous for its terse dispassion.

> Sir,
>   I regret to inform you of the demise of Doctor Ward J. St J. Ward, physician of this parish, of a sudden fever on Monday last. Your name, address and your recent letter were discovered among his effects.
>   Yours faithfully,
>   for Crame, Ashall, Wellerson, Solicitors.

The signature was illegible. Ven sat staring. He rose, stood a moment to look about, as if redress could be obtained if he could only lay his hand on it.

Ward had been one of his few medical student friends. Average height, average intellect, average expectations. In fact, Ward used to laugh, 'average everything!'

And average health, with an average man's life expectancy.

An ominous thought took hold. Ward's warnings of the disease, a mysterious malady that might be something so perilous that Ward had been unable to write his fears. But Ven had thought of an infectious fever, transmitted from man to man by fomites – things touched, bodily excrescences, fluids – or by close association.

He searched through his notes. A letter, half-completed, was still unaddressed, but it was to Ward. Ven read his own words. He had written four questions, almost peremptory in their demanding tone:

> . . . and the consequences thereof. Have you, old friend, any further notions of the transmissibility? I recall the long arguments

we entertained at the London when encountering fevers in the first-floor wards. Have you numbers of cases? Are there proposed remedies? And are you sure it is but one malady? I well recall the deceptions we met with in certain indispositions, and how we were unable to distinguish between one mild disease and another, seemingly as mild but resulting in terrible complications and death. Do not delay, Ward! Send me at your earliest a description of the outbreak you have actually witnessed! No tardiness on your part . . .

And the letter was unfinished, its urgent requests repeating some earlier correspondence. He was now sickened by his jocularity. Had Ward, poor 'average' Ward, taken some undue risk, wanting to satisfy his friend's demands, provide clues that Ward himself was unable to decipher?

He watched Rosie admonish Clement in the garden. They were trying to restore a semblance of order to the herbaceous border near the lawns, but Clement was playful now that he had his sight back.

Ven had told him nothing of the visit to Rustonhall. Clement had asked nothing, just looked hard at Ven and then gone about his task of making shoe-blacking according to Mehala's prescription. It was as if they had an unspoken agreement to avoid any mention of it. Ven felt that he was shirking his duty, by not taking the Rustonhall matter further. Clement's accounts of the sickness at the school were too stark. The children there must be in a grievous state, as tragic as the plight of the workhouse inmates.

Everything was time. He had begun to neglect that oldest imperative of all, so concerned was he with his own difficulties, Mehala, and Reverend Baring's accusations. He was losing heart, as always, without Mehala's support. She was the crux, everything to him.

He called to Rosie and Clement that he was on his way to Mr Pleasence's workhouse for an inspection, and set off without a further word. There was something on his mind, something so terrible that he could not wait. Mehala would approve.

Rosie ran to walk with him as far as the Trenchards' vacant cottage, chattering of her duties.

'We have the herbs now, Doctor. All the ones that Mehala listed. Are we to keep on collecting them?'

'Yes, Rosie. Prepare them as Mehala instructed.'

'Hey, girl!' Clement yelled from the garden. 'Come to your task or I shall unsettle you!'

Ven halted. 'No jokes about disease or settlement!'

'My apologies, sir!'

'No matter, Clement. It is only that settlement is the most valued of rights in this country, entitling people to a place called "home" whatever the vicissitudes of fortune. Without it, folk must wander and starve for ever!'

'I understand, Doctor.' The boy looked chastened, and Ven remembered that Clement soon might be in that grim plight, for nothing had been heard of his parents since his arrival at Shalamar.

'Just keep this girl in order while I am out, will you?'

'Yes, Doctor!' Clement's mischievousness returned instantly. 'Though how I can, when we visit Mistress Dolley today, I do not know!'

'Dolley? I myself will call to inspect the wound . . .' He glanced at Rosie, whose sudden high colour told him nothing.

'Don't you see, Doctor?' Clement cried, while Rosie angrily shushed him. 'Visiting the Dolleys, we must pass Market Square.'

'Yes?' Ven said, mystified. 'I know. The cottage –'

'Pay him no heed, Doctor!' Rosie scolded in fury, casting about for a stick. 'He is a naughty urchin –'

'Where stands the emporium of one Bartholomew Hast, Esquire, gunmaker of this parish!'

'I shall see him,' Ven told them, mystified. 'He is –'

But Rosie chased off after Clement with a squeal of rage. The boy fled, shouting taunts at her.

The scene was so innocent, so pretty, that Ven had to laugh. He set off without leaving further instructions. Some children's game or other, he supposed. Or had Bartholomew some entertainment for them? He put his best foot under him, and smiled absently, hearing Clement laughingly sing-shouting the old nursery rhyme,

> *Where are you going to, my pretty maid?*
> *I'm going a milking, sir, she said,*
> *Sir, she said, sir, she said . . .*

but his song was cut off, evidently stifled by the outraged Rosie.

It reminded him of the milkmaids on Calling Farm where he visited as a child. They taunted each other by that same ancient rhyme, for in many country areas to ask if you could go milking with a milkmaid was virtually a proposal. He found he had stopped, but shook his head and walked on. The gunsmith was a bachelor, a sound tradesman of reliable morals, yes. And Rosie was comely, younger than Bartholomew, trustworthy. Many might say they were matchable. But it was most unlikely because . . . why? He could think of no reason. Except that surely he would have seen signs of growing affection between the two? His one sin was that he prided himself on his clinical observation. Yet, if it were true, that if Rosie did secretly harbour affection for the gunsmith, and if Bartholomew secretly returned it, why then the nagging irritation caused by Hast's transparent admiration for Mehala would be bypassed! For a moment he brightened, then scored it as impossible.

It must simply be one of Clement's increasing mischiefs, some private niggling that he did not know about. He put it from his mind, and turned firmly to the frightening possibilities that loomed as he thought over his dead friend's warnings.

33

CORRUPTION SEEMED TO attend any nautical transaction. Percy Carmady resisted the temptation to respond to the agent's friendliness as they scanned the River Thames.

'Yes, Lieutenant,' Paisley said with a self-satisfied sigh, 'this great artery is the wonder of the nautical world. Nary a mariner expresses praise of our efficiency, from great sea-captains such as yourself, sir, down to the humblest midshipman!'

'Indeed,' Percy said drily. 'I have found London wanting.'

The agent's smile faded. 'Not nowadays, Lieutenant Carmady, sir! Everything is shipshape and Bristol! Or', he simpered ingratiatingly, 'all above board, another naval expression.'

'The question is the snow or the schooner, Mr Paisley?'

'There can be no question, sir!' the agent cried, beside himself at the thought of losing a commission. 'The schooner is the fastest —'

'Yes. Liverpool built, from the papers?'

'True English, Lieutenant! But on the lines of the Yankees, and registered in our great maritime nation !'

Carmady heard the man out with growing impatience. Everything an agent said was either famously implausible, obvious to all, or a downright lie. That had been told him by the first captain he had ever sailed under as a midshipman, and experience had confirmed every word. He had no intention of recommending any but a properly registered ship.

A registered ship had numerous benefits, including security, and the Royal Navy's protection in international waters and foreign ports. But a ship had either to be built in these islands, the colonies or dependencies. Or registered after having been taken as a battle prize at sea. Or, ominously, forfeited for breach of the slave-trade laws. Attempts to evade proper registration procedures usually failed at the outset, for any seaman alive could tell any ship's origin at a glance.

Here in the widening estuary with, a mile westward, Henry the Eighth's naval dockyard of Deptford where the King's ships were formerly built, it was possible to believe that London was becoming the most important port in the world. The number and tonnage of ships increased daily. Even Liverpool, which constructed the first wet-dock well over a century ago in 1708, was being challenged by the capital's maritime growth. Lean on the Greenwich Hospital's walls for a day, you would see every type and shape of vessel pass within a stone's throw, from the ancient and ponderous Dutch Dogger struggling in on its two jibsails, to the double-ended peter boats that were a feature of the lower Thames.

The largest vessel on the Greenwich reach was a Navy snow, gliding in with elegance. Perhaps forty or even more years old now, she could look down on any traditional brig. Carmady loved the old snows, true vessels of the northern seas. They had the oddity of an extra mast, the 'snow mast', abaft the mainmast, for a huge gaff sail.

'Beauteous snow,' he told the agent.

Mr Paisley hopefully sang its praises, though it was clear he would have extolled a passing coracle for a sale. 'Such a pity they are now combined as the man-o'war brig! I see you are a real seafarer, sir!'

'My syndicate has considered a Blackwaller, Paisley.'

'A Blackwall frigate, sir!' Paisley was clearly impressed, for the Blackwall was a trading ship made especially for the India merchants. They seemed at first sight a traditional design, but were slenderer and faster than most ships-of-the-line, even than the sumptuous, giant East Indiamen. 'A real trading vessel, sir! Who can better the Blackwall Shipbuilders?'

Percy was only testing the man. A Blackwaller would be far beyond Carradine's syndicate's means, lacking Hunterfield or new backers. And a swift three-master like the frigate-built ship would possibly outstrip Carradine's intentions.

'Sir,' Paisley said, lowering his voice as if in confidence, 'there is a splendid bark available, lying at Chatham —'

'Three-master,' Percy mused. 'No top-sail to the mizen-mast, no t'gallant sail?'

The agent tried again. 'She is most capacious, sir, and sound as a bell —'

'The same vessel refused by the Inman School examiner?' Percy jerked his chin impatiently. 'I know many such vessels, Mr Paisley, for sale after a cursory careening, unfit for navigation.'

Since the Naval College had been established by Dr Inman at Portsmouth in 1811, it had become important for merchant ships to receive favourable pre-sale recommendation from some College member.

Paisley was taken aback. 'Perhaps you mean a different vessel, sir?'

'I think not.' Percy watched two watermen race for a passenger signalling for a boat from the Greenwich steps. Each year the Thames claimed lives from such desperate contests, of passengers and boatmen alike. Watermen were as combative and foul-mouthed as the hackney cab-coaches of London's filthy streets. 'I have a gentleman from the Society for the Improvement of Naval Architecture coming to join me.'

'You have, sir?' Paisley's eagerness vanished.

'To examine the Baltimore-line schooner.' He watched the gentleman in the long new green surtout descend quickly into the boat, and seat himself in the stern without a glance. 'Unless I am mistaken, Mr Paisley, he comes now.'

The schooner *Sealands* was a delight. Percy Carmady had to admit that he was smitten.

She lay at a mooring a few cables' lengths from the shore, clean and ready. Four crewmen were swabbing and bawling some song, competing for the most raucous verse. All were good signs. Activity in port promised capability at sea. But what took his heart was her line. Rakish, the masts leaning as if wanting to race, but here with small topsails, when many schooners were designed without. The level hull belied her tonnage.

'Three jibs, four topsails,' the Society man Gilliard said approvingly as they took the boat to board.

'Splendid for speed!' Paisley exclaimed.

'If speed was all I wanted,' Percy said, knowing he was losing patience, 'I would take a Yarmouth yawl, a three-masted double-ender, that now fish from the Eastern Hundreds!'

'Of course, of course!'

Gilliard eyed Carmady. 'You have sailed, Mr Carmady?'

'Some, Mr Gilliard.'

'I have, on East Indiamen. Now', he said with a sigh, 'I live Greenwich's narrow streets, assessing vessels.'

'Your reputation is of the highest, Mr Gilliard.'

'I hope that this place will become a borough. It is only known for the Observatory and Hospital.'

Percy ignored the local politics. As the boatman rowed them against the ebb tide he spoke frankly. 'I shall be the ship's husband, Mr Gilliard, but am unsure whether to tackle from Greenwich.'

The ship's husband was the part-owner responsible for effecting repairs on behalf of all the other part-owners of a trading vessel. It was a powerful position. Ship chandlers and shipwrights sold to him, and he ordered for maintenance. Ownership was traditionally divided into sixty-fourths, so a ship's husband needed to own only one sixty-fourth to hold most of the authority. He need not even go to sea. An ex-Navy officer, the eventual captain or sailing owner who became a ship's husband was a lucrative friend.

'Sir,' the agent said, after glancing at Gilliard to judge the moment, 'might I enquire if the Lieutenant foresees the vessel as a general ship, or charter-party?'

Percy managed not to smile. He affected interest in a ketch that was having difficulty coming up to its moorings, with a ship's boy yelling insults from the bows and two crewmen bawling admonitions at the lad. The 'charter-party' was a corruption of 'charta partita', the written contract by which a ship was let wholly or in parts to merchants for conveyance of goods, with a fee per ton agreed before the voyage. The 'general' ship was one requiring a bill of lading, with several merchants using the vessel for different cargoes. A wealthy syndicate would adopt the charter-party style. Less wealthy owners would offer their ship for general use. He was unwilling to reveal more than he needed, and allowed his silence to be a stern reproof. The agent blanched. He was almost fawning by the time they clambered aboard the *Sealands*.

Percy took in the ship at a glance, and was pleased by almost everything he saw. The captain was a Warwickshire man called Hopestone, taciturn but alert. His hands were roughened by work, and his old-fashioned doublet and bishop sleeves showed he was a man of trading tradition. He shook Percy's hand warmly, ignored the agent, and gave Mr Gilliard a wary greeting.

Percy stepped back once the introductions were made. 'I have asked Mr Gilliard, from the Society for Improvement, to make examination, Captain Hopestone.'

Hopestone was pleased at the courtesy. 'My pleasure, sir.'

Percy deferred to the captain and Mr Gilliard throughout, not saying a word as they made their way through the vessel. The size of the holds astonished him. He had seen a slaver-built ship only once before, when she was taken as a prize.

Six guns a side, he saw, with additional armaments fore and aft. The crew quarters were cramped, but no worse than on a King's ship. She was clean, scented by a previous cargo of grain, and dry as a bone. Very few rat droppings. The ship was in good heart. His glimpses of the cordage, stowed sails, even the ship's boats, were all in her favour.

There was no docking problem in these modern times of the availability of wet docks. Liverpool had led the way, but times were changed since the 1770s, when Fuseli the artist complained that he could 'everywhere smell the blood of slaves'. Almost 11,000 ships sailed from London annually, a mighty commercial shipping activity almost unmatched.

'A schooner of this burthen is a formidable vessel, Captain Hopestone,' Gilliard commented when they paused during his examination of the superstructure. 'Have you had success?'

'In trade, yes indeed! The purchase comes about because owners are obliged to pass all the 'fourths of a gentlemen merchant who has lately died. His daughter benefits in a trust. *Sealands* – I captained her two years – has sailed the Baltic and to New England.'

'Mind you, gentlemen,' Paisley interrupted ingratiatingly, 'the great navigator William Adams of Gillingham, who became almost emperor of the Japans, sailed the Far East centuries ago in a ship of one hundred and sixty tons.'

Gilliard was unimpressed by the agent's remark. 'Great indeed, Mr Paisley. But times are new. Rotherhithe's wet docks began the modern port of London, but only by reason of London's need to accommodate its whaling ships and boil blubber! Difficult yet regular unloading requires a wet dock, where the levels of water are always steady, rather than a provincial small harbour where the tides dictate a ship's business.'

Percy Carmady noted with wry admiration the Society man's

astuteness. He must already have guessed that the purchasing syndicate was hoping for Baltic trade, and from a small east coast harbour. Gilliard gave Percy his frank opinion.

'London suffered the penalty for too many centuries of having to unload all her ships into lighters, with the exception of the Rotherhithe vessels. Hence the massive growth. Rotherhithe's Commercial Dock now copes admirably with the European timber and corn trade, since its forty-nine acres – four-fifths water, remember – were let to that trade as the whaling ceased.'

Percy listened in silence. It was as eloquent a recommendation to keep the *Sealands* trading from London as any man could make.

'Tyrant Napoleon's wars began the change,' Gilliard went on. 'I hate to recollect those days, with East Indiamen throughout the post-war decade struggling to unload into lighters.'

'They proved the worth of the admirable convoy system!' Paisley cried with a glance at Percy.

'True,' Gilliard said. 'But they congested London's river. It was only in 1799 that Parliament approved the building of the West India docks, at the Isle of Dogs. Their success improved Blackwall and Limehouse, the docks entrances, which though small in acreage – five and two acres respectively – can take 500 large merchant vessels at any one moment!' Gilliard's casual gaze flicked at Percy, then returned to the ship's rigging. 'They cope without effort during every political and nautical difficulty.'

'And the East India Docks are almost as capable,' Captain Hopestone added gravely. 'Not to mention the London Docks at Wapping, over seventy-one acres, water and warehouse combined! Can you imagine, sirs, a single tobacco warehouse of five whole acres? And one vault of one warehouse arched over seven acres?'

'St Katherine's Dock will be ready next month,' Gilliard said, now warning Percy directly. 'The advantage of a commercial dock between London Docks at Wapping and the Tower of London is incalculable. The two wet docks there can accept vessels of up to 800 tons.'

So far Gilliard had not made a single note, Percy observed.

'The east coast ports have wet docks.' He paused as if inviting a comment from Percy, but none came. 'Hull can take 300 ships, and Goole near the Ouse-Humber junction has now two new wet docks, one for small vessels and one for ocean-going.' He nodded his satisfaction to Captain Hopestone. 'Were I to consider a North Europe trading venture, I would be guided by these considerations.'

The inspection resumed below decks, with Percy glad he had remained silent. Carradine seemed to have assumed all along that the *Sealands* would trade directly from Sealandings. Indeed, that seemed his sole reason for embarking on this. But if Sealandings was already eclipsed by circumstances, as Gilliard implied, then there would be no purpose in the venture at all.

He followed, heeding every word and nuance. There was a clear need for far more capital than Carradine believed. His spirits were lowered even further as the inspection progressed. Commercial ventures were different from the King's Navy. He resolved to call at Bram Yale's residence on his return journey, possibly taking up the invitation hinted so clandestinely by Melissa Yale.

He wondered who the lady was, whose bequest included the lovely *Sealands* schooner with its familiar name. He might find out later, and make her acquaintance.

34

THE COMMON DROVERS' field for once was dry underfoot, the rain having ceased the previous day. Strong night breezes had dried the grass and solidified the muddy ruts. A few Sealandings cottage women used the far corners for bleaching their home-loomed cloth, for those areas were avoided by the flocks of geese and the horses. The pale material, laid on the grass in daylight, was at once an emblem and an omen to Kemp Endercotte as he inspected the assembling crowd. God provides all manner of marvels, for mankind only to destroy. But Endercotte did not need themes. He had enough. What he needed now was success. Today would prove that he could achieve it.

He could have chosen to speak in the Corn Mart, but the Lord's grace had spoken to him in the night hours. It was as if an angel had come down to warn him against speaking in the centre of Sealandings, though tradition allowed any dissenter to pray there should he wish. And the new church hall of St Edmund was consecrated ground.

So this common ground, among the last in the Sealandings Hundred since the enclosures, was the saintly choice. God's open air. He stood stock-still, as befitted one in solemn prayer before facing the legions of sin. Bareheaded, the sea breeze not stirring a hair of his black head. His wife stood behind him, head bowed and hands clasped.

A few carts and even a carriage or two were by the gate, showing the landowners' curiosity. Or perhaps wariness lest any treasonable sentiments be uttered.

But his was the mass of people standing in silence. They had come to listen to the preacher's condemnations. It was truly heartwarming. They were moved by the spirit of God. He was within reach of success, as the Lord commanded.

He stepped on to the mounting stone to speak.

'Brothers and sisters in the Lord!'

He had no intention of welcoming these people. They were here to receive his instructions. Every word must be a command.

'I am moved to speak the words of God, without fear or favour! It is your duty to hear the Almighty's commands.'

They shuffled in expectation, half-eager yet apprehensive. He felt a stir of disgust. They were cattle. How striking were God's own words, invoking comparisons between men and plain brute beasts! Cattle, sheep, flocks, herds – the Gospels scorned mankind. Rightly so.

'You have obligations!' He glared from face to face. 'It is Heaven's command that compels me to stand before you. You follow the sinner's ways. You turn against my words!' His voice deepened and rose in volume, a street speaker's trick of oratory he had learned in the stews of Mayfair listening to the Methody preachers visiting from Moorgate. 'Or you follow righteousness. Follow God in condemning sinners! Become saints on earth before due time in Paradise!'

They listened in rapt attention. Elation rose in him. He had obeyed the angel, shunning the confines of the Corn Mart, the comfort of the church hall. He was speaking as Christ spoke His Sermon on the Mount. He was truly guided this day.

'One path is the way of death. It is the way of the leveller, the sinner who says that men are born equal, and possess equal rights to bread, wealth, pay. That path I condemn!'

He saw heads nod approvingly among the folk sitting in their carts and carriages. His confidence swelled further. He let his voice rise in pitch.

'Is there a path of beauty? Is there a path of right? Is there a path of holiness, by taking which we *know* we follow God?' He paused, set his jaw, finally let the word explode. 'Yes! I cry yea verily! There *is* such a path – for those who hope in salvation! Fight the fight of Heaven! Turn against sinners! And, when God's command is heard, obey and cry amen!'

'Amen!' his wife said, head still bowed.

'Amen!' someone else spoke up. Eyes shone with excitement, and heads were raised. The preacher felt pride take hold.

'Let sinners condemn enthusiasm, brothers and sisters! But let us servants of the Lord use enthusiasm for power! Let it guide our strong right hand as it smites evil! Let the word of God subdue the foes of righteousness!'

'Amen! Amen!'

The exclamations were louder now, more spontaneous, and multiplied through the crowd. He raised his arms for silence. That the crowd was still peaceful and listening closely made no difference. He gestured as if they were crying out too loudly for him to be heard. The trick was useful, but only at the right time. He had timed it with precision.

'I have a question for the saints among you! I shall demand it of you, all and each, in words spoken plain as if from the mouth of God!'

He stood, arms akimbo, glaring at a labourer's woman whose exclamations were too prolonged. She quietened, quivering with excitement.

'But first, I am moved by the Holy Spirit to speak of poverty. The poor are always with us. They are, friends in Christ, they are! As ever, God speaks truth! Is there a reason for the poverty here in our land?'

Behind him, his wife was nodding on cue, suggesting to the crowd what the response should be.

'There surely *is*! Poverty is to be deplored. Those suffering its effects are sometimes to be pitied, and in rare cases to be helped. Yet can a world exist without poverty? It surely cannot! It drives society. It is the beast of burden that carried society. It enables our nation to progress on its great journey to holiness!'

'Amen!'

'Is not God's truth confirmed by logick? If all be rich, none would submit to the demands of another. No one would submit to drudgery! Bishop Hickes of Thetford of the Established Church solemnly declared that the poor are a necessity! Without poverty, one man could not rule over another!'

'Amen, amen!'

'There *must* be poor. God said. Thus are the poor created, to be the hands and feet of the body politick. They cleanse streets, hew wood and draw water! And do so righteously. For it is God's own appointment!'

He found himself nodding. He slowed his speech, intoning words.

'The occasional deprivations are the provision of an all-wise Providence. He graciously bestows on the poor their immediate dependence upon the rich. So it was, and so it shall be. Render to Caesar the things that are Caesar's!'

'Amen!'

'Those who are poor *must be so*! Otherwise they would never be industrious! And we need employment, with all our ability and industry! Therefore,' he pronounced with all the power he could manage, '*therefore* we must obey the God-decreed order to work. Thus we must oppose vice, gambling, drinking, and sexual licence. Those sins are the hallmarks of evil, and destroy society itself!'

Hunterfield was listening from the road in his estate manager's one-horse brougham. This gave any speaker the liberty to speak as he wished without being encumbered by the highest Sealandings authority. The carriage was readily identifiable, so familiar were local vehicles, so no deception was being perpetrated. He was only annoyed at having to resort to such a move because of Tabitha's clumsy handling of the women's meeting. So far, Endercotte had steered a clever course, skirting the usual combustible topics while giving the status quo outspoken approval.

'It is an established fact,' Preacher Endercotte went on, 'from the mouths of learned gentlemen whose loyalty is unquestionable. Excessive wages to the poor creates a dishonest poor! It encourages them to idleness! Yet every man here is willing to work his hardest in his God-given station!'

'Yes!' cried Mrs Endercotte.

The crowd joined in, 'Yes! Yes'

'And are we here not all God-fearing people? We do not swill our hard-earned money in drunken idleness!'

'True!'

'We are reasonable men,' the preacher proclaimed as if giving serious judgement, head nodding approbation. 'The destitute should be allowed to hold on to life. That too is God's command. But should we encourage idleness by encouraging profligacy? That encourages the poor to gloat in idleness, at the expense of you industrious people!'

'No, no!'

He had them now. He smiled grimly, letting them subside. 'You will remember I had a question. I promised it to you a moment ago. I keep my promise, in the Lord's name. I will pronounce it. Are you ready?'

'Yes!' his wife called out, for the first time raising her head, looking up at him almost in pious adoration.

'Will you answer it aloud, in God's holy name?'

'Yes, yes!'

'Then hear me!' He held them spellbound. Even those in the carts and carriages were craning to catch his words. 'Is there one here, in Sealandings, who is clearly the most evil sinner of all? One whose wickedness is blatantly unconcealed? Who each day grows in evil power? Who perpetrates on living and dead alike such evil that his occult powers turn the whole Hundred against God the Almighty?'

He had not yet reached his most savage. In preparation he deliberately let his voice quieten.

'I see you are chastened by responsibility, of having to speak his name! You are perhaps too timid to seize the Lord's standard! To march forward proclaiming yourself for Christ and against sin! Then let me list his transgressions!'

'Praise the Lord!' his wife cried.

'Let me speak!' Endercotte closed his eyes as if in pain. 'Is there one in Sealandings who experiments with the dead?'

The shocked gasps were as sudden as a squall.

'Is there', the preacher intoned louder, 'one here who mocks holy matrimony? Who has been seen grave-robbing in St Edmund the Martyr's churchyard? Whose witchcraft is openly practised at the graveside with his evil woman?'

They were muttering now, turning to speak names softly and nodding recognition. Endercotte's voice strengthened.

'I see some of you, those aspiring to sainthood, are willing to speak out for God against evil! I ask further: is there one in Sealandings who has abducted a girl? Who keeps her in abysmal slavery in his derelict grange for whatever wickedness he and his evil familiar perpetrate on her poor body?'

The crowd's agitation was increasing, their words louder now. He gestured angrily, letting rage show.

'Did that evil spawn abduct a boy child? Steal him from the Poor House under the eyes of your own appointed gentleman? Does he even now enslave him in unspeakable labour?'

'The leech,' his wife said softly, starting the word running round the crowd.

'And his woman!' somebody cried out. The crowd chorused the names of Mehala and Carmichael.

'And', thundered Endercotte, 'is that wickedness proved by his making . . . *this*?'

To shrieks of horror and alarm he pulled from inside his coat a small clay figure.

'Witchcraft!' his wife prompted, reeling away.

'Witchcraft!' people echoed.

'See the marks upon it! Designs of Satan! See clearly, anyone who wishes to inspect this evidence, the occult signs! Twigs pierce its limbs, its very heart! Be certain that evil will fail before the strong right hand of God! Righteousness will prevail!'

'Amen!'

The crowd was in frank disarray, people moaning in distress, many shielding their eyes from the clay anatomical figure Ven had made.

'See it destroyed!' Endercotte screeched, shattering it on the mounting stone's lower step. 'So let evil perish before God!'

In his carriage Hunterfield felt a wry admiration for the preacher's performance, for performance it was. It was at least as skilled as any of the travelling mummers, bagpipers and players.

Witchcraft and the wizard's arts had never quite vanished from the Eastern Hundreds. There was not a man, woman, or child who did not understand the language of flowers, of symbols imagined or perceived in the skies or forests, in the way the River 'Affon flowed this morning, or the ripples caused by a jackpike in the bridge pool. Every child knew and sang the old songs, the meaning clouded by time.

The country festivals themselves were shrouded in mystery. Old customs were as silly as they were baffling. Yet, were they not all innocent, by acceptance? No woman would speak to a chance-met stranger or accept money from him. Yet on Gooding Day any woman would laugh with any stranger and beg of him alms, bestowing a kiss on him in return? And did not the reverse take place on Tutty Day soon after Easter? Tutty men collected a token penny from every housewife for a kiss, as long as they called bearing their 'tutty', a nosegay of spring flowers in coloured ribbon.

For God's sweet sakes, Hunterfield thought, he had played a million games himself as a child. He still liked to see Sealandings children at their play. God knows, such merriment is short lived, all too soon exchanged for woe.

He tapped for his driver to move off. Entering Market Square, he felt the brougham slow. He heard the driver call.

He put his head from the window. Simple Tom was riding at a walk from Lorne House.

'Tom. Where is Doctor Carmichael? You went to Shalamar?'

Tom gestured with the patience of the dumb. He gave a stern frown, and moved his right hand as if flourishing a whip, looking down as if at people stooping at work in some field. Then he scratched, shifting in the saddle.

'The workhouse, Tom? He is at the workhouse?' Simple Tom nodded. 'And Mehala?'

Tom shook his head, made his gloved hand open and shut, as if a bird in flight.

'Not yet returned,' Hunterfield translated. Simple Tom held his mount at a stand. He opened his hand, palm upwards, asking for instructions. 'Look, Tom. Pass by the livestock field. There is a crowd listening to Preacher Endercotte. Gauge the mood. Discover where Endercotte goes.'

Simple Tom nodded and rode on. Hunterfield settled back, tapped his stick on the cabin for the brougham to proceed.

The preacher's facts had been correct, in a way. Ominous, if quoted in open trial. They could be presented even more vociferously in court.

He had assumed that most, if not all, of the problems at Shalamar would be resolved by Mehala's journey to the south and her repossessions. It now seemed they multiplied anew.

He wanted her back, and soon. For the sake of public order, of course, no other reason.

35

THALIA DE FOE was not dressed to her fullest advantage. She admitted this to herself as her hackney battled its way through the stews of Whitechapel's growing slums. It was by design of course, and difficult design too, for she was blindingly attractive.

Since her virtual banishment to St. Albans with her husband Fellows, life had been hell. Not the hell of physical pain, nor subjection to the bestiality of another. She could have borne that better. Carradine – her Carradine, no one else's – had given her that for year after clandestine year. She had loved him for it. Every savagery wreaked upon her she had welcomed. For brutishness was confirmation of his love. He brutalised no other woman.

There were times when she was amazed at the nature of her passion. It was incurable; she knew that. For Carradine she would kill, aye, and suffer the ultimate penalty. His own nature was feral, utterly untamed. Such a man was every woman's ultimate challenge. Lately, from misery, she had ignored her obligation to him.

The fear of being shamed in society – Fellows might feel inclined to reveal her repeated fornication with Carradine – had made her miss the whole point. Her one purpose was to possess Carradine and make him possess her. What other aim could there possibly be? She wanted Carradine. She had shirked her single duty, which was to take risks, any risks, and achieve that goal.

So she had played the base-born coward, allowed Fellows to dictate his terrible sentence: banishment from Sealandings. She had accompanied him from her lovely house of Milton Hall in Sealandings, and settled down to loneliness at the ineffably moribund Kennishton House, near St Albans. Worse, Fellows was busy reconstructing unfashionable estates in the north country. Even now he was away, thanks be to God, discussing with other lunatics inland navigation by means of carts with engines some-how moved upon iron rails, without horses. He had even made philosophical experiments, not by resorting to the writings of ancient doctors of the Church, as such researches should be, but actually having the filthy engines made by blacksmiths and similar artisans. Clear evidence of idiocy; perhaps she could persuade a doctor to condemn him as quite mad. Then, oh what a marvellous world! Back like an arrow to the arms of Carradine, rescue him from that obscenity called Judith Blaker.

The thought so nauseated her that she gagged violently. Her maid leant forward solicitously.

'Are you unwell, m'lady? Should I –?'

'No!' Thalia snarled, recovering. 'And I said for you to keep silent throughout this journey, bitch!'

The maid quailed. 'Yes, m'lady.'

Thalia eyed the cow. She had already given her two beatings this week. Such castigations seemed to have little effect upon the low classes. It was a wonder to Thalia that they repeated the same provocations, invoking the same punishment time after time. It could not be that the mistress was in the wrong – that would contradict Divine Law, since God had imposed the social orders, one upon the other in order, to carry out His divine will. No. Far more likely that God had instilled in such creatures as this sow Molly an actual desire to be beaten. So they disobeyed, to provoke a mistress into inflicting a good thrashing. That spread the word among other servants, and so reinforced society. It was education of the lower classes.

She had sworn the idiot girl to secrecy on oath, on the pain of losing her immortal soul to hellfire, if she divulged a single word about this journey. The girl had sworn on the Prayer Book. There would be no question of word getting out.

The hackney, hired from the Strand, struggled with the concourse of vehicles along the eastern route through Aldgate. Thalia heard with horror the coachman's abuse of the carters battling in the opposite direction. The traffic through Ludgate was worst of all. The slackening near St Paul's Cathedral was but a peaceful memory when Leadenhall Street was past and the nightmare tumult of Aldgate and Whitechapel came into view.

Then it was the even noisier passage of the Commercial Road, leading to the great docks, until the coachman knocked insolently on the roof, hauling up the flap that gave sight of his passengers, and called gruffly that they were at The Prospect of Whitby. The lout had not the decency to clamber down. She seethed with fury at his betrayal, and vowed to revenge herself on him when she returned to the Strand.

'Go inside,' Thalia De Foe commanded quietly to her maid. 'Ask the taverner for one Gilliard.'

'Inside, m'lady?'

'Do as you are told!'

Molly alighted, adjusting her kissing strings nervously at the sight of dock labourers drinking outside the tavern. She was saved embarrassment. A man in a sombre brown beaver hat and walking-surtout stepped from the doorway.

'M'lady?' he said, raising his hat, 'I am Gilliard.'

Thalia was relieved, but thought it important not to show it. 'Please enter, Gilliard.'

' 'Service, m'lady.' He climbed in, leaving the door ajar for the maid to follow. Thalia impatiently waved her out to stand in the rain, to the jibes of the docklands men.

'Are they always so uncouth, Gilliard?' Thalia demanded.

His chagrin was evident. 'I apologise for London, m'lady. Indeed they are. They are a special breed. I have seen many fights to the death among them. Yet on their day they are the best men on earth, loyal to a fault, capable of working until they die in their boots. Of course, m'lady,' he said to console her, 'your maid need fear nothing.'

'Indeed?'

'No, m'lady.' He was diffident, reluctant to explain. 'I was almost one of them. I worked at shipbuilding, a lowly man in the old Blackwall docks. Then I was at Wapping –'

'Were you now?' Thalia said coldly, wondering if it was wise to entrust a delicate matter to an oaf who had risen by the labour of his hands.

Gilliard drew breath. 'Is it safe to report?'

'Go on, man.'

'The inspection was satisfactory.' He kept his voice down. 'Your *Sealands* is a fine vessel: seaworthy, able founded and maintained. Captain Hopestone is reliable. She can sail soon as may be.'

'Who came?' she asked, heart in her mouth.

'One Carmady, ex-lieutenant of the King's Navy. A visitor at Sealandings, where he hopes to settle.'

'No other gentleman?' Carradine might after all be in London, had he accompanied Carmady.

'No, m'lady.'

'He has the syndicate?'

'He would not divulge the names of the gentlemen. The lady who travelled with him on the Royal –'

'Lady?' Thalia asked sharply. She wanted no new rivals for Carradine, now that she had invented this route back to him.

'One he referred to as Mistress Mehala, who came –'

'*Mehala?* Are you sure?'

'Indeed, m'lady,' Gilliard said, taken aback by her vehemence. 'I could hardly be mistaken. Her name is new to me.'

True. She herself had never known another. In fact, she wanted not even the one. But Mehala, coming south?

'Did he say more about my . . .' She forced herself to say it. '. . . friend? I am pleased to hear she is recovered enough to travel. Do you know her residence in the south?'

'No, m'lady. Mr Carmady was reticent. Except', the thought struck him, 'he did say that he wanted my report with all expedition. He hoped to disembark again at Colchester. He had to call on her near Salcot.'

'Salcot? As if he had alighted there on the way south?'

'Surely, m'lady.' Gilliard unfolded a leather case. 'The report, m'lady. Now, this particular Baltimore schooner is capable of –'

'Thank you,' Thalia De Foe cut in. 'Give it in a sealed cover to the maid.'

Gilliard was nonplussed. 'But the sale of *Sealands*. Am I to let it go ahead? Shall I argue for a higher sum? Your father after all bequeathed her to you in trust –'

'Your fee will be paid, Gilliard,' she said contemptuously. 'Tell the coachman I am ready to leave.'

'And the bill of sale, m'lady?'

She thought about that. 'My father's estate steward can receive that. Send it by my private messenger, hand-to-hand.'

'Yes, m'lady.'

'And,' she added as he alighted, 'no word of this leaves you, Gilliard. Do you understand?'

Molly embarked while the grinning dockmen called invitations to stay. Gilliard signalled the coachman, and watched the hackney trundle away towards the mayhem of Aldgate's crossings. He heaved a sigh of relief. It was the strangest transaction he had ever taken part in. To sell, but not disclose to her husband who was buying her ladyship's vessel, bequeathed by her own father? Indeed, to keep secret from her husband, it seemed, her very ownership of the *Sealands*, bequeathed in the poor old man's estates.

He entered the tavern in sore need of something to resuscitate him. His duty would soon be done, and he could return to his peaceful life in Greenwich undisturbed by such clandestine goings-on. The gentry lived in another world. Did they not see that the world was changing, that nothing – *nothing!* – would remain? That the whole world would be one of empires and communication, with the old feudal values gone for good?

36

Ven's last visit had confirmed that Pleasence knew of the charges against him. Ven's authority had virtually vanished.

'I must see them all, Mr Pleasence.' Ven tried to sound spirited.

'Why?' The man today was truculent, sensing Ven's weak position.

'It is my duty.'

'Duty, Carmichael?'

'Yes. I am here to examine the inmates.'

The man grinned, assuming the moral imperative. His post was enshrined in law.

'We have had this out, leech,' Pleasence said coolly. 'I am here to guard these poor unfortunates. Your function seems to whine!'

Ven struggled for words. His stupid stammer was fatal in an argument such as this, with a glib talker like Pleasence making destructive rejoinders.

Were Mehala here, it would be different. She had the extraordinary knack of making arguments resonate to her advantage, which meant to Ven's benefit. She was single-minded in her determination to see that things turned out best. Thus every battle – and battle it was, with this man – was worth risking, for in the end it would yield good.

'I came two days ago, Mr Pleasence,' Ven persisted haltingly.

'So, leech?'

'And you said it was not convenient for me to inspect the inmates on that occasion. I proposed this very hour.'

'Look, quack,' Pleasence said airily, 'you can see the inmates, working by the law of 1601, as parish overseers direct.'

'Why are they so few?' Ven asked.

'Some are here, some are there.' Pleasence was if anything less pleasing. He had been roused from sleep to answer this dog-crocus's knock, and was in a foul mood.

'I must see all the inmates, or I shall not leave.'

'Then stay. I shall summon you for trespass.'

'Trespass?' Ven was wearied by the man. Arguing with him was like chasing riverbed elvers, a sure failure. 'I am allowed here by my commission to inspect and advise.'

'You *have* inspected and advised. Now away with you.'

Ven had once been in the hands of the petty constable. This felt the same hideous experience. He had dragged Mehala down with him into gaol. Without her wit he would be languishing there yet.

'May I not have a list of their present duties?'

Pleasence grinned. 'No, leech.'

'Why not? I must . . .' Ven petered out, then tried a sally at random. 'I must make a report of this.'

'Report to whom?'

'Report to the Squire, and to Lady Faith.'

Pleasence sighed, as if explaining to an idiot. 'Quack. I happen to know what the rest of the parish knows. You and that bitch Mehala are to be arraigned in court for offences against religion. The charge is laid by Reverend Baring.'

Ven's mouth dried. Put thus, it sounded almost a death sentence. 'That does not alter the justice in my request.'

Pleasence spat expertly on to the toe of Ven's half-jack. 'I say it does.'

'But Squire Hunterfield expressly –'

'Squire Hunterfield will try you, leech. As the senior justice in this Hundred, he can hardly take sides in anything that concerns you. Also, there is the matter of his tenants.'

'Whose tenants?'

Pleasence was all smiles. 'The gentry have tenant farmers. Where do many hire labour from?'

'Here?' Ven had already counted. Only nine women and one infirm man worked the fields, with a smaller group of men busy stacking corn beyond. There were no children, except two or three mites among the women.

'Here indeed. Four of Squire Hunterfield's tenant farms have my labour.'

'For which they pay?'

Pleasence seemed about to enlarge boastfully, then caught himself and made a more careful admission. 'For which they pay a pittance, wages being what they are these days. Penny here, twopence there. It is very little.'

'You account to the churchwardens? To the overseers?'

'Of course!' Pleasence shouted, but curbed his anger. 'What are you suggesting, Carmichael?'

'I accuse you of hiring out children. You know that since 1819, nigh ten whole years since, it has been illegal to work a child under nine years of age! And children of ten years or more are not to be worked more than twelve hours a day!'

'You fool! That is for children in mills!'

'It is a guidance for all!'

'Let the law decide that, leech!' Pleasence shouted. 'You are on trial, not I!'

'I accuse you, Pleasence! You defraud the parish!'

'That is a criminal charge!' Pleasence started towards Ven, fists clenched.

Ven felt his blood drain from his face, but this was the best he could think of in the circumstances. 'I make it, though! I allege that you hire children out for longer than the permitted hours!'

'You are a madman!' Pleasence bawled. The inmates worked on, cringing as if expecting blows. 'You need trial witnesses, crocus? I shall be there to speak bad character, as God is my judge!'

'You cannot perjure yourself –'

'Perjure? Who speaks of perjury here but the madman who accuses a decent God-fearing workhouse master? Off, or I shall call the inmates to club you away!'

Ven retreated disconsolately. For a moment he remained at the gate while Pleasence yelled imprecations, then turned on his heel, holding his surtout against the rising wind.

Retreating from the field. He had turned tail, fled ineptly before the victor. He despised himself. Not only a coward, but one of base ineptitude. He needed anger. All Sealandings would laugh at him, at news of his ridicule. Pleasence would spread his version. Soon, every child in Sealandings would be encouraged to catcall his own words after him. Already he heard the old insults, the abusive terms for a doctor: leech, crocus, dog-poisoner, dog-leech, pill-pusher, poison-monger, breech-wiper . . .

He *knew* he had the truth of it. Pleasence had twice now refused to admit him. Hardly a child now to be seen among the fields. They must be somewhere. So they were hired out, as were many of the adults. But where, and to whom? The workhouse master admitted that he sent some to Hunterfield's tenant farms. The Poor House held a formidable number of hands. Every farmer in these penurious times would be relieved to obtain cheap labour. Frightened inmates, desperate to earn a good report for fear of more abuse. All desperate to work until they literally dropped. It was repellent.

He was powerless without Mehala. Then he paused in the centre of the track where it joined the road. Was that quite right? Could *he* not gather some evidence? The afternoon was fading. In the rain, now falling in fine blustery wafts, work would soon cease, with the harvests at the state he supposed.

They would be coming back soon! All the labourers hired to the farms, the women, the children. And they would not tarry. They would not want to return late and risk offending their tyrant, waiting with his knout at the workhouse door. They would return like ghosts, as soon as the light left the sky, so as not to offend the God-fearing folk of Sealandings.

He smiled with relief. He could do something! Mehala would be pleased, if he moved against evil.

In the fading light he went as far as the summit of the Norwich road incline. From there he would be able to hear the footfalls of anyone approaching from the tracks crossing to the upper farms. He sat under the hedge, gathering his surtout flaps. It was not dry, but he might not have to wait long. Then he would simply ask the inmates where they worked, and for how much a day. He too would have evidence! It would work to his advantage, and that of the inmates.

He came to with a start, conscious that he heard something important. A voice was raised, not too far away.

The night was quite dark. The rain had stopped, and stars were about in the heavens. He tried to rise, but his muscles screamed in silent agony. As self-chastisement he forced himself upright, ashamed of his dereliction of duty.

'Could I not watch one hour?' he moaned to himself in reproach, rubbing his limbs.

The inmates must have shuffled home – not *home*, he corrected himself angrily. Who could call that place of torment by so loving a word? He moved, and saw a glim, the night lantern at the Poor House door. They were in, and the door sealed.

He remembered what had wakened him. One stern unyielding voice expressing anger. The other spoke quietly, pleading but being shouted down. Something was thrown, something crashed, broke.

Could it be the tollhouse? He went towards the lanterns which were left burning night and day by the toll barrier. As if in a dream, he stumbled for lack of a light, into ruts, slipping so he had to extend a hand to stop himself going full length.

'I s'll not have thee back!' a man was shouting.

'The babe –'

'I s'll know thee no more, God save the babe and thee!'

'At least let me stay until the morning!'

'Leave now! It is my livelihood! You knew it then! You know it now! Carry the brat away. I s'll have none of it!'

There was a dull thud and a yelp, and the sound of some living thing falling with a splash, probably into a water-filled rut. A broad slice of bright light was slashed to darkness, as a door echoed its small thunder.

Pausing about ten yards from the tollhouse, he listened a moment. Then called out quietly, 'Mistress Tyll?'

'Here. Is that Doctor Carmichael?'

'It is.'

'Thank God,' she groaned. 'Doctor. I think my time is come.'

'Now?' He tried to locate her by swinging his face left then right, listening for the voice's direction, country fashion.

'I fear so. Can you help me?'

'I can, Mistress Tyll. Where are you?'

'By the toll. I am on the ground.'

'Keep calling. I am here.' With nothing as usual, he thought. Without my instruments, and with little knowledge. And no Mehala.

She maintained a shush-shush sound as if calling a cat until he came upon her. He reached for her hands, tried to raise her, but she only groaned.

'Wait a moment. I will speak with Tyll. Your husband will let me bring you indoors –'

The woman almost laughed at his innocence. 'Don't you see? It is my labour that provokes him! He could accept me, carrying as I was, until the pains began. Then he realised the shame.'

Ven looked about, wanting to see into the cottages, the distant farms. Below was the faint sea-glow, the riding lights of ships in the harbour. Nearer, the lanterns of the toll house, Bettany's windmill, and that on the whorehouse, Two Cotts.

Tyll the husband had banished the woman. Bettany had no liking for Mehala, and had once expelled Ven from there. Further along were the Parker stables, but he too had sided with Preacher Endercotte. Gossip had aligned all the religious folk. Reverend Baring's rectory was closed to him, as was the church itself. Miss Gould at the school was at risk of her own livelihood. Seeking her help would be an uncommon cruelty, and end her sojourn in Sealandings.

The lights by the huge wrought-iron gates of Carradine Manor were a possibility. But what if he had to ask that Judith Blaker? Once or twice he had seen her glances at Mehala, and the memory of those left no doubt. He feared for the babe's life, if it were delivered in Carradine Manor, especially if his guess about the reason for Barbara Tyll's dismissal were correct.

No. Though he had been banned from providing medical help for the prostitutes at Two Cotts, it would have to be there. Mistress Wren the whoremistress might be moved by the sight of a woman in distress.

'I shall carry you, Mistress Tyll,' he said.

'No, Doctor. I can –'

'Be quiet. I shall need all my breath for the task. Rise as best you may. Walk a step or two, then I shall porte you a few yards, then we shall take another step or two. So we shall win the race. How long are the pains?'

'I do not know.'

'You shall tell me, and I shall count between. The intervals are more important than the cramps for the whilst.' He tried to instil a smile into his voice, the way Mehala sometimes did. 'It will become different very soon, I think!'

She struggled to let him lift her to her feet. He swung her up into his arms, and with small paces on the uneven muddy trackway began the long journey of two furlongs to the brothel at Two Cotts.

37

AUNT FAITH'S ARGUMENTS made Hunterfield wish ardently that she would return to Gloucester. Not that he disliked the old lady's testy company, or found her sharp asides unamusing. But her persistence about the question of marriage was annoying.

His duties seemed to multiply daily. They concerned the charity school's money, Miss Gould's curriculum, the leaning yew tree by the lych-gate at St Edmund the Martyr, the question of the toll gate on the Norwich road, and who should be given the lucrative franchise of the tollgate 'farmer' on the South Toll. These were what folk spoke about, with the economy and the depressed condition of agriculture.

But for the Lord of Sealandings? Those concerns were trivial. The charity school? For him, it was Miss Matilda's sympathy for Mehala and Carmichael. The leaning yew at St Edmund's? For Hunterfield, it was the rector's formal charges against Mehala and Carmichael. The tollgates? It was Barbara Tyll's pregnancy, in the Norwich road tollhouse. The stern moralists of Sealandings had the hearing of bats when it came to gossip. They whispered Tyll's babe might be Carradine's by-blow.

'It is indeed,' Aunt Faith interrupted his reverie. She had to be assisted these days, fast becoming frail. She had to be lowered onto the chaise longue by maids, and supported by her two favourite damask squabs before she could settle to pour the evening coffee.

'It?' Hunterfield asked, caught out.

'Do not prevaricate, Henry. I could always see through your opacities, even when you were small.' She sighed. 'I have had an unfortunate evening. That troumadam table is a nuisance, hardly worth my playing a single game! You should replace it. Those ivory balls are far too large for me, the way my hands are. If

Tabitha had the sense she was born with, she would have bought a new troumadam the instant Lydia departed.'

'It?' Hunterfield persisted.

Aunt Faith looked critically. 'I hate that smoking chair, Henry. I trust your moving it into your blue withdrawing-room does not mean you will resort to that detestable habit?'

Hunterfield recognised this as her strategem to rid the room of maids, and waited for the obfuscation to end. He was trapped, and in for her reproaches. Marriage, he foresaw.

'I never have so far, Aunt. But if I wish –'

'All that dreadful spitting, Henry! Why would those clever London chairmakers *want* to design such a chair? The nasty little drawer that pulls from between the gentleman's legs. Quite like a commode's compartment! Nothing less than obscene.'

'It is a spittoon drawer, Aunt Faith. London clubs use them all the time.'

'Then they are wrong to do so! What gentleman needs to expectorate in company?' She glared at the maids. 'You may go. On your way, inform the housekeeper that this arabica coffee should have been tested for pallor and proper greyness *before* roasting! Some vendors much abuse the latest act.'

The senior maid hesitated, received a stare, and bobbed before leading the withdrawal.

Aunt Faith called after her, 'I will not *have* so-called British coffee. That ridiculous act licensed vendors to sell utter rubbish. Nothing but dried parsnip or roasted horse-beans!'

'Yes, m'lady.'

Henry was mildly amused at her tactics. If she knew him well enough, perhaps he knew her too well. She waited until the door closed, then darted him a look. She too was smiling.

'Do the servants see through us, Henry, as we through each other? I should hate to think that pretty maid knows our strategems.'

'No, Aunt Faith. At least, I doubt it.'

'Because', she said, tasting the coffee with suspicion, continuing only when her mistrust was unfounded, 'I should not welcome that girl's perceiving what entered my mind.'

'Something evil, Aunt Faith?'

'Yes,' she replied unexpectedly. 'Why, Henry, have you not used any of these females in Lorne?'

'Used?' Even he was taken aback by such bluntness, and he had half a lifetime of her sudden assaults. 'You cannot –'

'I do indeed *mean*, Henry.' She laid aside her cup. 'You are the most eligible gentleman in East Anglia. I am not alone in saying so. Your single state is the topic of withdrawing-rooms. Speculation is rife!'

'About what?'

'About who she is, Henry. Mercy Carmady I find pleasing, and she would give her arms to be wife to you. About Sylvia Newborough and Brillianta Astell you already have my opinion. Castor Deeping has two cousins I have lately subjected to enquiry. Both seem promising, though I have yet to hear my friend Mistress Clavering's expeditions into their character.'

Hunterfield felt uncomfortable. 'Aunt Faith, let me –'

'No, Henry. Let *me*.' She wagged a finger to stay him. 'Ever since that trollop Thalia De Foe left Sealandings – and good shuttance, I am first to say – you have been on edge. We have spoken of this. But you are not aware of your manner, Henry. You are frayed. Something is lacking in your life. It will not do.'

'And what is this lack?' He spoke gently. An old lady had to be allowed her little exercises in authority.

'A woman. You well know that.' She was letting her anger grow unplanned. 'You should take one or two of these maids-of-all, Henry. Use them regularly. A woman can manage without. God knows we often did. We would have preferred not to be abstemious while our husbands roamed the seas.'

Henry was appalled by her frankness. She had lost her usual frivolity. 'I shall –'

'Take my remarks into consideration, Henry?' She mocked his words. 'Your customary evasion! To "take into consideration" is a way of begging my silence. Another of your evasions, "I hear you, Aunt Faith," will avail you nothing. I tell you, in your father's name, that you spoil your life by procrastination.'

'I give the problem much thought, Aunt.'

'But I bring the matter out into the open!'

' "Out into the open" is a woman's phrase,' he said directly back, as open as she. 'It only means your patience is sorely tried, and you want answers. Has it not occurred to you that there might simply be no answers worth considering?'

'That Mehala,' the old lady said after a pause. She took her coffee. 'Resolve the problem, Henry. As long as she stays in Sealandings in her semi-married state, you will slide into a ruinous bachelorhood. Oh,' she stayed him with a raised hand, 'I know that you fulfil your duties perfectly. But time is running out. Not,' she added with a trace of bitterness, 'that it runs out in quite the same way for a man as it does for a woman, but that is an accident of life.'

'Mehala,' he said slowly. 'She is always there. Not only for me, but for us all, every last fisherman, cottager, farmer, the gentry.'

'This Doctor Carmichael,' Aunt Faith said. 'Let us get down to it, Henry. He will marry her?'

'Yes. When her period of mourning ends – a few months from now. I believe he cannot manage without her.'

'They are lovers?' she demanded bluntly.

'I do not know. Who could answer?'

'That means yes,' Aunt Faith said candidly. 'No woman would permit her man to let her lie, without making him tread Nature's thoroughfare. *Making*, Henry,' she said as his eyebrows raised. 'I must speak. Let us assume the worst.'

'You have already proved the worst,' he said quietly.

'You get no sympathy from me, Henry Hunterfield.' She went suddenly brisk. 'You should have taken that Brillianta months ago, and let yourself be drawn into a seemingly reluctant marriage by the talk your affair would generate. She would kill to be your wife. Sylvia Newborough would extinguish twice as many, for the same end.'

'But?'

'Buy Mehala.'

'*Buy?*'

'As in purchase; offer money for transfer of ownership.'

'Are you serious?'

'Never more in my life, Henry.' She let him digest the proposition. 'It is common enough among the lower classes. Wife sales are seen still in fairs, are they not? You yourself have adjudged on several. I have heard you speak of some.'

'With disapproval.'

'So? Let disapproval do its worst, then ignore it. I cannot see the problem, Henry!' She banged the side of the chaise longue in exasperation. 'Most gentry marriages were arranged without recourse to the principals! I myself was wed at the age of fifteen, taken in a carriage and it was done! He was eighteen. Were we any the worse? It was usual in my day! It is so still, were truth told! Only the peasantry wed for love! Women are bought, Henry – for wealth, a rich husband, a title. Join in, and bid!'

Hunterfield never ceased to be amazed at the remarkable minds of women. There was young Tabitha, of the selfsame stock as the rest of the family, yet incompetent to a fault when given the simplest of tasks: household, domestic, or otherwise. And here was this gentle old soul, wanting the head of the family to offer money for a woman he frankly could not get out of his mind.

'You approve of Mehala?'

'Of course I do, Henry!' She almost barked the words. 'She is worth ten of these docile ladies with their pretty little smiles! And she is a landed lady with considerable estates! How she came by them is a matter best not considered in detail. Before that she was a commoner, but so? Retrace our family's lineage, and before many generations we too would emerge the same!'

'Buy?' The thought still startled him. 'For what?'

'For money, advancement, a hospital, whatever.'

'He would not accept,' Hunterfield was suddenly sure.

'Of course he would not,' she said unexpectedly. 'Meaning that *he* would not. He is besotted, and loves the woman. But *she* might!'

The notion was offensive. Yes, wives were still sold by common custom. But such sales were now becoming so unusual that they were talked of with open amusement. They had even been the subject of the written word in newspapers. Mehala was not fully wedded to Carmichael, though many of the fisherfolk and farm people would be willing to let matters ride – subject to the intolerance of religion.

'Might she?'

'She loves the man, Henry. She would give up anything for him. She would even surrender him, for his good.'

'That is beyond belief.'

'Henry. Think as a woman. *If* he faced disaster by staying with her . . . You see?'

317

'Threaten Carmichael with disaster, and buy Mehala's willingness, by offering to protect the man from ruin?'

She smiled. 'You have it. You can ruin or prevent ruin.'

'It is not my way, Aunt Faith. It might ruin their lives.'

She almost exploded. 'Dear God! *Men!* You cannot see the nose in front of your face, Hunterfield!' She controlled herself with obvious effort, until her arthritic hand was steady enough to take more coffee. Henry shook his head at her mute invitation. 'A woman loves differently, Henry. Mehala will come to love you. Already she almost does.' She silenced him with a frown. 'I saw her expression when you were mentioned at Saxelby. If Carmichael were elsewhere, she would be Lady Hunterfield by now, sitting here and correcting me if I as much as blinked at her.'

'But they met. He has her, and she him.'

'Listen,' she chided more patiently. 'A woman loves differently because she is *made* to, sometimes. If she knew that you transgressed society, all tenets of your upbringing, just to possess her, at enormous cost, how do you think that would seem in her eyes? It would make her proud. The Lord of Sealandings, throwing over convention, for her! It proves love in a way that kiss-my-hand graciousness can never!'

'And she would forget him?'

'Of course not! Every so often she will think wistfully of him, wonder about him in an idle hour. She will think romantically of seeing him, by a pre-arranged chance accident. But those instances would lessen with time. They always do.'

'And if she did see him?'

Aunt Faith exclaimed in derision. 'Pshaw, Hunterfield! Can you not foretell that for yourself? She would arrange to glimpse him – accidentally of course! And what would she see? A tired man, made stout by the passage of years. His features lined, his eyes bagged, his hair thinned, his eyes rheumy with drink, snotty children wailing at his heels!'

'You paint a picture of despair, Aunt Faith.'

'Of truth, Henry,' she said, not a little saddened herself by the image. 'All prospects have but one horizon.'

'Do I have a choice?' He was amazed at himself.

'Nobody has a choice, my dear. Mehala will look from her grand incognito carriage, and see some frump that he finally married. She will be outraged that, instead of staying dedicatedly loyal to her fragrant memory, he had wed some nagging, stout, waddling woman with bad feet. Her mind will scream indignation. Cannot you hear her, Henry? *He abandoned my memory for that ugly cow!* It is', she concluded sadly, 'called "Time the Healer".'

Hunterfield felt a strange mixture of sorrow and lightness, listening to the plain speech. 'And that would cure her?'

'Of him? Not for ever, no. She will dwell on possibles from the past. We all do. Women,' she said with a smile, 'of course more than men, for we are the practical ones!'

She seemed to have proved the opposite, but he was past arguing.

'How much time do I have?'

'Very little, Henry. This Baltic venture of Carradine's. It seems the whole of Sealandings will be affected, if it comes to pass.'

'What has it to do with Mehala?'

'It will resolve all. Anticipate, rather than expect, Henry. Ask Doctor Carmichael for her purchase price, but only after you have asked Mehala what she herself will ask. It does not matter to whom you pay the fee, him or her. But ask immediately.'

'So quickly? Why?'

'Because the price will be less, the sooner you offer to buy the woman. Just be careful how you express the terms. Carmichael will not see through to the purchase, but she will.'

He was fascinated, drawn in. 'The price?'

'To Carmichael, anything. It will not matter, since he will not understand. The price you will offer Mehala is different, Henry. That must be firm as stone.'

'What will it be?'

She did not smile. 'You, Henry. Her price will be you.'

38

W<small>ARM WETNESS WAS</small> running down Ven's left arm, squishing as he moved in his soaked clothes. Breathlessly he lowered the woman to the ground at the gate of Two Cotts. He was soaked in her waters and his sweat, though it had only been yards. He breathed hard, to recover strength. She groaned anew. He held her fingers.

'Almost there, Mistress Tyll. We have time. I am not strong, but we shall get to shelter.'

The night weather was worsening as the storm moved slowly inland. The trees were roaring overhead. Leaves and twigs rained down, thickening the falling rain. He stood over the woman to give shelter, but that was foolish. They were both drenched.

The Two Cotts gate was open. The drive led straight to the front of the house. Once, the building had been two cottages, but they had been made one by building across the gap. From the road in daylight the edifice was quite imposing, almost enough for a gentleman's family. Ven had often been inside, as the physician. Then he was banned for trying to care for a girl, Bella, who had drowned. He still accused himself, blaming his inability to support the poor girl enough.

Well, tonight he would have to brave Mistress Wren a second time. This time there could be no withdrawal. He had to find shelter. Barbara Tyll was too spent to go on, and he himself could carry her no farther.

He managed to pick the woman up, through almost dropping her. She was unable to help by tightening her arm about his neck, as she had before. Only the strength of his arms held her. He leant back to keep balance. Slithering and stumbling, he splashed down the drive, thankful it was in a slight hollow, and blundered against the oak door with a thump.

The bell was a new brass handle. He pulled it twice, hearing the familiar jangle.

Almost immediately the door was opened. A maid-of-all stepped aside with a smile that instantly died. Her greeting faltered. 'Good evening, sir! Welcome to . . .'

'I am so sorry to ask your help,' Ven began, wondering where his hat had got to, 'but I have a –'

The maid fled. Ven heard her exclaiming, 'There is a wild man at the door, without a hat!'

'I shall see him!' a woman ground out.

Ven's heart sank as he recognised the coarse voice of Mistress Wren the whoremadam. Life was either famine or feast, pleasure or pall. The woman appeared in the elegant Argand light and stood glaring out at his bedraggled figure.

'Good God alive!' She actually laughed. 'The quack from Shalamar! The one with morality! I recognise you from that conscience dangling from your pocket!'

'Mistress Wren. I need your help. In all charity –'

'Carmichael. You ascribed a horrible character to me. I give you it back, sir! Be off this instant, or my men will kick you all the way into Sealandings!'

'I have a lady here, Mistress Wren. Curse me all you like, but give her shelter. She is near her time.'

The whoremistress stepped into the vestibule, folding her arms against the chill wind. 'Who is she? It looks for all the world like –'

'Mistress Tyll, the tollgate keeper's wife.'

He stepped aside to show Barbara Tyll huddled in a sodden heap, her dress and shawl awry.

'Why is she not at home? Why do you bring her here?'

'She is driven out. If you will not admit me, to deliver her, you take her inside. Surely some girl in your establishment has helped at a birth before?'

'This is a bastard, more ways than one!' the woman swore.

'I ask only for her, in the name of charity –'

'You always did plead badly, crocus!' The woman's scorn for him had not diminished.

'She has little time. Her condition worsens by the minute.' He saw several girls appear behind their whoremistress and start whispering among themselves. He raised his voice. 'I am sure any one of you would lend assistance to this poor lady!'

'My establishment cannot afford scandal,' Wren said, as if Ven was to blame for the whole affair. 'It is mortal inconvenient. Three gentlemen arrive any minute.'

'Have you perhaps a side room?' Ven begged. 'The small room I used as a medical surgery, when I treated your girls for their illnesses, Mistress?'

'Occupied,' she answered flatly. 'And here is me catching my death of cold, arguing at my own door!'

'I beg you, Mistress,' Ven wheedled, grovelling, hating himself; 'all will admire your Christian benevolence.'

Barbara Tyll gasped and doubled.

'I cannot admit her,' the woman said.

'Then have you a barn? With a lantern, a rushlight even? Anywhere out of the weather? You have two stables. Several places to the rear are converted, for I have examined gentlemen there on occasion . . .' He paused, catching sight of her expression. It had become guarded and shifty, almost apprehensive. Was it something he had said?

Desperately, he expanded on the theme. 'I examined a gentleman from Newmarket for the pox, you recall, Mistress. And was it not here that I set a gentleman's broken ribs, and attended to his wounds after a duel from beyond Whitehanger crossroads? That gentleman's friends carried him here incognito, in a friend's conveyance. You summoned me with a written note of supplication . . .'

She nodded, her lips set in an angry line. 'You bastard,' she said quietly, so the girls behind could not hear. Her fingers drummed. 'You learn fast, leech, since I threw you out and damned your name.'

He was mystified. 'Everyone does, soon or late,' he said with unfelt confidence.

'Mehala has a lot to answer for; your instructress.'

'She and you together, perhaps.' He still did not understand how the argument was turning in his favour. Rain ran down his neck. 'If you will, hurry. If not, then I must go elsewhere. And remember more details . . .' He paused suggestively.

She surrendered with ill grace. 'Very well, quack. I shall find somewhere.' She called over her shoulder for somebody to bring a carrying lantern. 'The second barn, but not up to the croft. Keep her on the straw below.'

'Thank you, Mistress Wren.'

She looked evenly at him. 'And get her off the premises as soon as possible. Make sure she makes nary a moan.'

'Yes, Mistress Wren.'

For some reason his quiet complaisance infuriated her. 'And leave no trace of her. And no word to anyone, in or out of Sealandings.'

'Yes, Mistress Wren.'

'And do not be seen leaving by anyone. D'you follow?'

'Yes, Mistress. My gratitude.'

'I want *nothing* to show she has been here. Which means the babe, should you pull it live or dead. Do you hear me?'

'Yes, Mistress Wren. And thank you.'

She glared at him, marvelling in mute rage, and slammed the door. A girl hurried out with a lantern lit from the wall Argand, pulling on her mob cap and shawl.

The whoremistress felt breathless. The man was weak as water. Any other man would have slapped her down, perhaps used her, then moved on with hardly another thought except of her arrogance.

Then again, she thought as she retired to her plush chamber, his weakness was oddly durable. Abject politeness; gaunt and bare-headed in the teeming rain; sallow features running in the downpour. Maybe it was not weakness after all . . .

She poured a glass of Geneva spirit laced with juniper. She rested on her ancient rush-seated rocking chair, the one with shallow bends on which she could sway back and forth as she had in her grandfather's house as a child. A rocking chair was considered a wild transatlantic habit, sinful and self-indulgent.

Carmichael's weakness had a strange pliability. Perhaps it was even a hidden strength? Impossible to imagine the man giving up, once he had set his mind. No, he clambered upright after each felling blow, meekly repeating his request, smiling that doubtful smile, apologising, persisting . . .

She shivered and returned to her list of gentlemen. A lady was due in this night, from inland. Her 'walker', the effete gentleman

323

who would accompany her, would wait downstairs in the blue music room while his lady took pleasures with the girl of her choice. Wren sighed, worried lest the girl the Sapphite lady selected was already booked. Carradine seemed engaged tonight, so it had been wise to send Corrie with the leech. Being a whoremistress was the most tangled occupation in the whole world, yet who gave her a moment's sympathy?

The three gentlemen should be here soon. Thank God, they would be straightforward, requiring each a whore, dinner, two bottles of Portugal, some smuggled French white wine, a little brandy. The girls would be used in the orthodox manner, and survive without too many marks, bruises or scars. That was as life should be, Mistress Wren thought primly. It was the oddities who plagued her.

She understood simple, uncomplicated people, as men in her experience ought to be. Not somebody like that Ven Carmichael, with his hesitant smile and humble gratitude for being treated like dirt. She shuddered, concentrated on her lists, basing all on normalcy.

'What is your name, miss?'

Ven was almost done for. Barbara Tyll's weight was too much now. He had tottered only ten or so paces before he had to stand Barbara down and wait until his swimming brain came to. The rain was torrential.

'Corrie, Doctor.'

'Corrie. Can you help? I can take her no more, on my own.'

The girl complied, holding Barbara Tyll's feet while he struggled along, his hands under the woman's shoulders.

'Where is this barn?' he gasped. He could see nothing but the glistening blackness and the lantern at the brothel's back door.

'Wait, sir.'

Corrie gathered her skirts and took the lantern, placing it on the ground a few yards ahead. There stood the side of a great, dark barn. She opened a door and hung the lantern on a hook within before trotting back.

'Thank you, Corrie.'

'Oh, I be strong, Doctor! I have carried many a gentleman!'

They made the barn and almost fell inside, collapsing with Barbara on straw bales. Ven was close to retching from exertion. He felt spent with exhaustion, but struggled out of his soaked surtout and cast about for something to cover the labouring woman. There was nothing save some sacking in a corner. He eyed it mistrustfully. Too many rats lurked in such places.

The dry building looked homely, to his surprise. Baled straw was stacked at one end of the lofty Suffolk barn. A gallery ran almost half-way round. A well-used ladder was placed opposite the bales. It was all meticulously cleaned.

The girl Corrie was young, perhaps four years Mehala's junior, and comely. She saw Ven's surprise and smiled with pride.

'This is a place for certain gentlemen, Doctor,' she said. 'Up that ladder is a lovely bed, wondrous liquors, all a gentleman could require for his rest, if you understand me.'

'Why here?'

'So nobody will see!' She tossed her head importantly. 'One high-born gentleman prefers me here. Two Cotts has a pair of these barns. Both are always in use.'

That explained the pristine condition. Ven regretted being deprived the use of the gallery. Mistress Tyll was now ashen. She was soaked, with rain and her own waters.

'Corrie. Have you ever helped at a delivery?'

'Why, yes, Doctor, more than a few!'

'Then you will know. Please make Mistress Tyll a straw bed. Can you bring a sheet, a blanket perhaps, from above?'

Corrie shrank at the suggestion. He did not persist, but started to drag loose straw from the nearest bale. With Corrie's assistance he formed up a thick, loose pallet.

'This can be burned afterwards,' he explained.

He closed the door. In the lantern light they carried Tyll to the bed, Ven trying to reassure her. 'We are home safe, and not sorry! And there are precedents for delivering your child in a stable barn!'

Barbara gripped his hand, her visage wan. 'Will you stay?'

'Would I miss the glad event? Of course I shall stay – if you will agree not to leave without me!'

She tried to smile her thanks, but the next pain came and she grimaced, clutching his hand tighter.

'It is quickening, Doctor.'

'So I see. Hold Corrie's hand. We must rid you of these clothes, and see where you are.'

He had no watch, so had to guess at the frequency of her contractions. They were coming at reduced intervals now. One day he would have a marvellous timepiece, he hoped wistfully. To time a patient's pulse, the rate of contractions in labour, a hundred marvellous things that might help.

His eyes met Corrie's. 'Please, Corrie?'

She nodded and went towards the ladder.

'How long is it, Doctor?'

'I do not know, Barbara,' he said, angrily vowing to answer patients truthfully from now on. He would never again hide behind mystique and black magic, sham assumed knowledge that was nothing more than a cloak for ignorance. 'I have little enough experience in medical matters, but I think all will be well, from what I have seen.'

'Thank you.' She smiled, reassured. He realised with a sinking heart that she thought he was still pretending humour to give her encouragement. Her teeth chattered lightly in the cold.

'Corrie?' he called. 'Quickly, sacking if nought else.'

'I am looking, Doctor!'

He hurried across to the sacking, and went through it. It seemed clean, but he could not use it to cover the woman. He believed the ancient Englishman of the fourteenth century, Doctor John of Aderne, who insisted on a leech's having 'clean hands and well-shapen nails, cleansed from all blackness and filth . . .' But few other doctors held to those tenets. Instead they believed that there was merit in dirt, as gardeners believed in the value of soot for soil. He was tempted, but the sacking might hold humours he knew nothing about. At least a clean sheet, well laundered and pressed by a hot smoothing iron, might have fewer noxious humours, whatever they were. He would have given anything to know the truths of such secrets.

'Doctor?' Corrie's face peered down at him from the gallery.

'Yes, Corrie? Have you found something I could use?'

'There be four lovely clean sheets and two blankets. The bed is not yet made up.'

'Bring one sheet, and a blanket. Make sure they are taken from the middle of the pile.'

'Our sheets are always fresh laundered, Doctor!' she rebuked.

In other circumstances he would have smiled at Corrie's tart rejoinder, defending the sparkling cleanliness of her whorehouse's domestic arrangements. But not now. The consequences would be serious, for theft was one of the gravest charges in the land. Punishments were severe. In the north, young girls had been hanged for the theft of small pieces of factory cloth, and not many years since, either. The repeal of laws demanding death by hanging for simple theft were still being abolished by Home Secretary Robert Peel's acts in Parliament between 1823 and last year. But theft – and a forbidden sheet counted as such – was still a crime. There were numerous instances: the nine-year-old Chelmsford boy lately hanged; a child executed for tuppenny theft; a . . .

He hesitated. Mehala would know what to do. She could always protect him from these weird rules when he proved too inept to guess how people would behave . . . Only a few years ago, in 1811, Lord Chief Justice Ellenborough had opposed revoking of the law that demanded the death penalty for shoplifters who stole less than ten shillings. What chance would a country doctor have, stealing a blanket and sheet? The counter-arguments of the praiseworthy Romilly, that cruel punishments only begat cruelty, would avail him little. The whole country believed that hanging an Essex child was reasonable, an essential deterrent.

'Corrie?' He rose, winking at Barbara Tyll's sudden anxiety. 'Corrie, show me.'

He strode to the ladder and climbed it. Even in the low glim he could see how luxurious the area was. Elegant furnishings, a handsome four-poster bed, washbasins and ewers, pedestal side tables with open wine coolers, cheval mirrors, cupboards and wardrobes, with a small glass chandelier and whole expanses of wall covered in seeing glasses that showed himself a hundred times, a scarecrow of a figure, haggard and sallow, bedraggled, hunted.

Corrie was pale with anxiety. 'Here, sir.'

Ven moved to the linen chest and took out a folded sheet. He collected a blanket. In for a penny, in for a pound, he thought. Hang for a sheep as a lamb.

'I took them, Corrie. You did not. You understand?'

'Yes, sir. Thank you, sir.'

'Come,' he said, 'let us to work.'

Ridding Barbara Tyll of her sodden clothing took an age, but she was finally bedded on dry straw, with a clean pile ready beside her and the blanket over her for cover. He had Corrie fetch the lantern close. The ornate wall lanterns in the plush gallery tempted him, but he finally discounted them. They must have cost a fortune. That these persisted at all was a wonder, as wall sconces had begun to replace the traditional lanthorns in country houses for outside use, and testified to Mistress Wren's strong affinity to elegance.

Critically he examined the woman's abdomen and pelvis. She seemed to have the female lines well enough, he saw with a wash of relief. Women whose pelvis tended to a narrower male pattern had difficulties in labour. He had no instruments, no forceps that were so talked of in London's medical schools, and nothing to aid an extraction should the babe arrest in descent.

'The blanket is welcome, Doctor,' Barbara said. She was drawing up her knees, had been for some time, and tended to raise her head as if wanting to stare at her chest.

'Your back?'

'Mortal sore, Doctor. It aches.'

'Corrie can rub it, when you wish. You do not yet need to push vigorously. Breathe regularly, if you can.'

The girl was pleased to be given the task. Ven sat to one side. The woman was advancing rapidly, or she was further on than he had supposed. But distress had serious effects on a person. None was so vulnerable as a woman at term.

It was strange, he thought, sitting counting as the contractions quickened more, how life tended to change of its own volition in spite of our plans. Astrology, the new palmistry, phrenology's measuring of bumps on the head to guess one's innermost character, the zodiacal influences, superstitions about eventual spouses, the prediction games of virgin girls on the eve of poor, martyred, twelve-year-old St Agnes to learn of their probable husbands-to-be; all was deception. Chance ruled. Chance had brought Mehala ashore in *The Jaunty*. Chance had fetched his father to Sealandings as a visitor, and so made Ven reside here.

'Your dates, Mistress Tyll?' He tried to be informal, but it was difficult. Perhaps his knowing that the child was Carradine's made him so stiff. For Carradine disliked him, and he was resolutely opposed to Carradine.

'Barbara, please, Doctor.'

'Ven, if you would.' And chance made women detect nuances; made them see instantly through a man's hesitations to the cause.

She smiled. 'Ven afterwards, Doctor.'

The pains came again, and she started to push. Sweat started on her forehead. He raised the blanket, for it was time.

The average labour for a first child, it was usually taught, took some twelve hours, but sometimes was as short as six. He had seen longer and shorter. A too-brief labour for a first child worried him, though he did not know if it was a drawback for the child. How marvellous it would be to have a great body of information on problems in obstetrics . . . He collected himself, abandoning such wistful silliness. That benefit would probably never come about. He carefully felt the abdomen, as she contracted anew and gathered herself to push.

Had her first stage been two-thirds of the whole labour, as was commonly taught? He did not know. Could he detect her progress by mere palpation? He did not know. Was *any* rule about the stages of labour correct? He did not know.

Stimulants, enemas, aperients, indeed any medicaments, were useless, he had come to believe. Perhaps one day doctors would know how to help a woman in childbirth. But for now nothing could assist. The few instruments that might help were so jealously guarded, for money, that few doctors still had access to the precious metal devices.

She was pushing now, wanting to bear down and grunting with effort. He drew the covering sheet to inspect the distending lips of her vulva. It was close. He went to the barn door, and ran into the rain. The rain barrel was overpouring. He washed his hands quickly. A gentleman was dismounting near the opposite barn, where newly-lit lanthorns shone. It was Carradine. He glimpsed Ven, and turned to look.

'Who the devil is that?' he said.

'Carmichael,' Ven called.

'What do you here?'

'I am here with permission, sir.'

'I shall inquire if you lie, leech.'

Ven had no time. As soaked as when he had first come, he fled back to the dry barn. If John of Aderne was wrong about cleanliness all those centuries ago, he too would be wrong.

The head was presenting when he knelt beside her. Corrie excitedly cried the news to Barbara, but Ven put a stop to that in case of possible disaster. He sent her to wash her hands as he had done, then to kneel opposite on her return. The head came in a quick movement that he barely had time to control. He felt around the babe's neck with a forefinger. The umbilical cord was round the babe's neck, tightly constricting its throat. He inserted his finger under the cord and pull-lifted it, freeing it over the babe's shoulder.

He sighed, and saw that the woman had caught his relief. She questioned him mutely with her eyes. He cursed himself. Letting his feelings show always did damage, whoever the patient, whatever the complaint.

'Try to resist pushing for a moment or two.'

But it proved too hard. The child's head turned slightly, heralding the main delivery. She started to bear down stronger. He always refrained from helping the pushing action, so the child was expelled gradually. Ven restrained its progress gently so the woman's fourchette was not torn with too sudden an egress. The child slipped free from his mother with a facile glide that always amazed Ven with its smoothness. He felt sweat trickle down his face. The mother gave a great groan of relief at the delivery. Ven laid the baby boy over her leg as was taught, gently shoving her left leg to form a smooth place for the babe, and watched the umbilical cord.

She was losing blood. Indeed, the straw was blood-soaked beneath her, but nothing too excessive. Ven marvelled at the resilience of womankind. They bore this trauma, yet managed to face their fate with resolve.

'The babe is free, mother. Some moments more.'

He had nothing with which to tie or cut the umbilical cord. Cursing himself for lack of foresight, he sent Corrie rushing up the ladder for the candle docker. He passed it several times through the flame of the lanthorn. He had been taught about the use of string, or a new candle wick, for tying off the umbilical cord, but mistrusted the information. He had seen several newly-born babes die soon after their first week from lockjaw, whose cords had been tied thus. Also, many old women in London's stews used ashes from any cold firepit to smear on the babe's cord, all swearing that it prevented disease. But he mistrusted that, too, and always tied the cord in a knot to stop the blood flow.

It seemed only common sense. A woman lost enough in the process. It seemed to him that patients survived often in spite of doctors, rather than with their help.

Severing the cord with a bite of the teeth was no longer fashionable. It seemed to be too far from nature. He cut the cord, and tied the babe's end quickly only tight enough to hold. He lifted the babe upside down, its ankles between his fingers, and tapped its buttocks to start respiration. The mouth was clear of fluid. Its awkward cry was a blessed relief, sounding hearty. He passed the babe to Corrie's sheet. The mother's end of the umbilical cord, still trailing from her, he grasped and held between forefinger and thumb.

'The babe, Corrie,' he instructed. She beamed, folding the sheet for the babe, passing him to lie against the mother's shoulder. 'He should be warm enough.'

'A boy child? And well?'

'As ever is, mother,' Ven said lamely. 'I shall see him over time, to judge progress. He looks a fine child.'

'Praise God!' Corrie exclaimed, as proud as if he was hers.

'Amen,' Barbara Tyll said, craning to see the child and lying back exhausted.

'You will feel cramps, mother. They will not be important for anyone except me, who will remove the afterbirth.'

'Yes, Doctor. Am I to push?'

Her third stage began on her words. She had to relinquish the babe to Corrie as the placenta slowly moved down. It rested for quite some time, until Ven gradually eased it out and laid it on the bloody straw between her legs. He returned the babe to the fatigued mother. Corrie adroitly bound up the afterbirth in twists of straw tied with plaited straw lengths. Ven watched in admiration. He had not half her skill. The girls's fingers moved with enviable alacrity. She laid the afterbirth aside, and Ven covered the mother in her blanket.

'That is all, mother,' he said wearily, feeling his tiredness for the first time. Then he reminded himself that he had done nothing; the woman had done it all.

'Thank you, Doctor.' She tried to speak.

'What is it?'

She hesitated. 'Did I hear someone, during my labour?'

'No. Just drovers, waggoners from the north.'

She accepted that. Corrie was looking strangely at him, perhaps because she had recognised Carradine's voice. The barn door had stood ajar when Ven had gone to the water butt.

Barbara drowsily opened her eyes, almost asleep. 'Doctor. What becomes of me and my babe now?'

'We rest, mother.' He tried to sound confident. Sleep was almost on him too.

He settled back. The rain was loud as ever. The gurgling and the gentle spattering sound from the channels beat with a comforting regularity. He began to feel warm. He heard Corrie rise and slip away, and glanced at mother and babe. Both were sleeping, looking a wondrous picture in the golden glow from the lanthorn.

Drowsiness took him. He wondered if Corrie had gone to her whore's duties. He no longer had care of the prostitutes . . .

He did not know how long it was before a kick woke him. He heard Barbara Tyll cry in alarm.

The whoremistress stood over him, glaring.

'So, leech, you could not accept my Christian charity without stealing my possessions? It is the petty constable for you, and the quarter session thereafter, as God is my judge!'

'Mistress Wren!' He struggled to his feet, trying to smile ingratiatingly. 'I thank you for –'

'Thanks, leech?' The woman was apoplectic with rage. 'I have had enough thanks from you! Blanket stealer. Thief!'

'They are not stolen, Mistress Wren –'

'Stolen, sir!' she screeched, pointing at the door, quivering with rage. 'One of my esteemed gentlemen clients complained of goings-on, and I find you –'

'Find what, Wren?' Mehala's voice said.

The whoremistress swung round, spitting fury. 'Find this dog-leech a-stealing of my goods! Who knows but what this has been a regular event behind my back! I shall charge . . .'

Her words petered out slowly as Mehala stepped into the

lanthorn light. Her cloak was a costly popinjay velvet edged at the throat with red roskyn, a picture of wealth. Wren stifled, scoring Mehala's costly apparel. Also, Mehala was dry. Low voices of men outside testified to her having arrived accompanied.

'Taken in charge, Wren? For what?'

'Well, for theft.' The whoremistress was nonplussed.

Mehala took in the scene, slowly coming to stand by Ven. 'Theft, Wren?'

Ven stared in astonishment at Mehala's glorious apparel. She looked majestic, quite dazzling. But her voice was hard.

'Why, yes, for I find him here —'

'You find Doctor Carmichael where I suggested we meet, woman!'

'*You* . . . ?'

'And where I find him, gentleman that he is, awaiting my coach's arrival exactly as we arranged! So? What have you to say?'

The woman's mouth gaped. She floundered, trying to stammer explanations. 'Mistress, I had no intention —'

Mehala confronted the woman, but now so savagely that the woman retreated.

'You had no sense, Wren! That is the error of your kind, not your calling! You will be paid by one of my stewards. *Out!*'

Wren fled, leaving Mehala in command. She relaxed, smiling, coming to take Ven's hands. He demurred, for they were covered in dried bloodstains, but she only held on all the harder.

'I am home, dearest.'

He reddened, indicating the apprehensive mother resting on the straw, awake. Mehala raised her eyebrows at the babe in silent praise to the new arrival and the mother's achievement.

'I leave my gentleman alone for a minute, and find him in trouble with another woman!'

'I am sorry, Mehala,' Ven said earnestly. 'I honestly did ask Mistress Wren beforehand —'

'Shhh!' Mehala put a finger over his lips. 'I am delighted you were in trouble, Ven, darling, for then I might rescue you. It gladdens me.' She looked about, brisk of a sudden. 'Now, what must we do here for the best?'

'Well, I must stay with Mistress Tyll, Mehala,' Ven explained. 'It will be a full day before she can move.'

'To where?'

'Actually, she has no place. You see –'

'Shalamar?' Mehala guessed, keeping the rue from her voice.

'Exactly what I thought, Mehala!' He was pleased.

'We shall all rest here for a moment, and have a cup of sweet Congou, or perhaps Bohea. We have all had an ordeal. Four cups, I think.'

Ven was puzzled. 'The girl Corrie who helped seems to have returned to her duties, Mehala.'

Mehala went to the door. 'Mallen! Send for Bohea tea for four, with milk and sugar, instantly.'

'Yes, Mistress!'

'Four?' Ven asked. 'That gentleman will join us?'

Mehala returned smiling. 'Just us.' She waited a moment, admiring the babe, and sank on a bale. Then, eyes still on the child, she called softly, 'You can come down now, little sweep.'

Nothing happened. Ven looked about, making to go and search, but Mehala restrained him.

'Come down,' she called. 'We have a warm drink for you. We are all in sore need of one, I think.'

There was the sound of rustling straw from the far end of the barn. The climbing boy slowly slithered into the lanthorn light down the stacked bales. He could hardly stand, but he responded to Mehala's beckoning and came to sit beside Ven.

'Shalamar?' she asked Ven.

He raised his hands in apology. 'Well, for the best . .'

Mehala counted on her fingers. 'And now we are Rosie, Clement, Mistress Tyll, the babe, you, our new friend, me. Seven!'

Ven patted the boy's hand, ignoring the terrible cachectic condition he was in. He stank and looked dire, his features sunken.

'You are among friends. Have you a name?'

'Yes, Doctor. I am Nath.'

'Welcome, Nath.' His eyes warned Mehala it will be soon.

He put his arm round the child, and drew him close. How much longer they would remain seven, he could not tell. The boy leant against him, utterly spent.

39

THE NEWS OF the *Sealands* purchase spread across the Hundred like sunshine. From Maidborough to the Fentons, from neighbouring Whitehanger to the wide forests of Thatchleys and along the coast to Kings Omney, all envied the good fortune of Sealandings. It eclipsed all talk of the inland riots, where ricks burned and agriculture was halted by the unrest among labourers and the numbers moving into towns. It seemed the end of worry.

The ship grew vaster in the telling, somehow becoming a decommissioned naval man-of-war, holding sixty-four guns, let go by the King after Tyrant Napoleon's fall and peace in Europe. Others praised it as a newly-launched commercial vessel bought at the last minute by Carradine, that would otherwise have gone to serve the new Indian Empire as an Indiaman, racing round the Cape.

In Sealandings, folk stopped to doff hats and bob curtseys to any vehicle bearing the Carradine coat-of-arms. There was knowing talk of the Carradine character as the soundest expression of breeding. The crude excesses of that gentleman were natural, for excellence of judgement descended from quality.

Cargo loading was mostly done in London, Sealandings folk heard at first with dismay. They were mollified on hearing that *Sealands* was to call at Sealandings for local goods before she struck for the ports of Scandinavia, Prussia, and the Russias.

Excitement rose when Percy Carmady returned, with strangers called Bram and Melissa Yale, clearly gentry with their own armorials. A ball was proclaimed at Carradine Manor, and the Hundred society invited. News of the *Sealands* eclipsed the minor surprise of Mehala. She had visited to the south and returned affluent, though most folk had suspected something for quite some time. Bram Yale and his beautiful wife were to stay at Milton Hall,

335

which was to be reopened by agreement with Sir Fellows De Foe, lately resident there, but who had been gone many months to live in far-off St Albans.

Squire Hunterfield, Lord of Sealandings, had become somewhat reclusive since the news, though his friendship with Mr Carmady endured as ever. Mercy Carmady the ex-lieutenant's sister arrived at Lorne House as guest of Lady Faith.

Interest grew even more when word came that a great engine, almost miraculous in its capabilities, had been manufactured in the Midlands by a Mr Boulton and his partner. It was made entirely of iron, worked somehow without horses by means of coal and a great boiler. It would be carried by the great ship *Sealands* to a Baltic port, where it would command an unbelievable price. It was a coinage machine, that stamped out solid money without any assistance from men with hammers, water-driven milling wheels, or beasts of any kind. Truly, the *Sealands* was both omen and substance. Prosperity would return to Sealandings, the Hundred, and even all East Anglia, for look at the variety and quantity of cargo! The list of goods entering the ship in London was reported each afternoon by written letter from the ship's factors. Details were learned and recited in both taverns. The tally was huge, and grew by the hour. It gave endless wonderment.

The strangest assortment of goods ever assembled on earth, everybody in the Donkey and Buskin agreed, would sail in the ship. That much of the cargo would consist of iron goods was only to be expected, knives and cutlery being especially favoured.

That hats formed a considerable and expensive proportion caused astonishment. Some disbelieved, but others knew the extraordinary truth that the country's hat trade was one of the most profitable exports in the Kingdom, rivalling manufactured iron, steel, brass objects, copper, and even weaponry. As any who had sailed abroad could testify, France's hat trade had been overtaken in quality and quantity years before, when castors or beaver hats came into demand. It was the proper mixture of coney wool, hare's wool or beaver mixed with an exact proportion of floss silk that did it, that and the Midland workfolk's excellence.

Glass was another astonishment. It was such a commonplace these modern days that hardly any thought it a thing of especial value. But it was widely agreed that foreigners could hardly be expected to have achieved the Kingdom's excellence. Woollen goods and cloth formed export staples, of course. But people were surprised by the carriages, mostly curricles and chaises, and by one particularly grand landau that had been especially sought. Surely the nobles of the Russias and Prussia had their own vehicles?

More understandable were optical instruments, including those for navigation, a special group of almost magical accuracy. Sealandings predicted a great demand overseas for those curious devices. London, being filled with weird and esoteric inventors, was the centre for such baffling contrivances.

In the Hundred itself, merchants combined for part cargoes of woollens, serges, baizes, perpetuanas, swansdowns, kerseys, and, strangely, stockings. These last invoked much amazement, for stockings seemed so usual a commodity. How strange that the North Americas seemed to lack stocking manufactories, and likewise depended on hats. Much of the Baltic trade was concerned with re-export to the New World. Goods unloaded in North Europe and even Königsberg were simply never unpacked for local use, but were shipped elsewhere without more ado.

Pewter and tin goods, that Europe seemed to use almost exclusively, were especially in demand. Cottons were another staple, dimities, calicoes, and counterpanes being the principals on this voyage. Sealandings was elated by a new-found importance. Remarks were passed that there would be nothing left in the whole country once the great *Sealands* put to sea.

On her return, she would bring not profit, but ambers, silverware, and great weights of valuable timber. Then she would sail to London for more exports, and repeat the process. Farmers, the mainstay of the Hundred, would provide malt and grain for the London market when the *Sealands* went on to London. It was the greatest achievement in all history. Carradine was the one to be thanked for it. Sealandings would equal Ipswich, outdo Kings Lynn and Maldon, and leave Colchester guttering, if not wholly extinguished. Yarmouth and Lowestoft would be nothing.

Heavy waggons began to rumble to the wharves night and day. The few artisans with factories producing expensive goods laboured ceaselessly. Horatio Veriker, clockmaker off the Norwich road, used his famous temper and bellicosity to drive his apprentice Richard Bettany, and even took on a clocksmith friend in Maidborough to help in the purchase of timepieces from the Midlands. Bartholomew Hast bought fancy weapons, percussion target pistols, on commission from his cousins in Colchester and Ipswich. Hast acknowledged that no output could compete with that of the greater manufactories in London or Birmingham, but his weapons were more embellished and cheaper, so he had confidence.

Pottery came in quantity from merchants who, hearing of the new Baltic venture, rode in ahead of their great six-horse waggons. The country's potteries outmatched any, so their goods would be virtual ballast, and profitable revenue.

Carmady and Carradine were feted several times in a fortnight. Bram and Melissa Yale, joining the syndicate and bringing additional investors, were other heroes. Two ship chandlers from Ipswich purchased cottages in Market Square and set up trade. Two ketches and a new wherry from Norfolk became their coastal vessels bringing cordage and fittings.

Hunterfield declined invitations to join the celebrations. Folk understood; it was proper for the Lord of Sealandings to take a back seat when such a massive venture was on hand. The dispute between Hunterfield and Carradine of the previous year, that had ended with Carradine's subjection, was easily forgotten, except by old fisherwomen on the wharves who remembered everything, for use when their long recollections would be of most value.

Ven and Mehala received notice that Reverend Baring's accusation was reinforced by charges notified by Preacher Endercotte and Mr Pleasence, those being lodged at Lorne with Hunterfield's clerk. Endercotte's was signed by thirty-eight people, all rate-payers and therefore people of consequence.

'I am under no misapprehensions,' Jason Prothero told Mary. 'The gentry's invitations mean gate money.'

Mary Prothero said nothing. Over her few years of marriage she had learned the wisdom of listening, as if in agreement, and waiting to see what was to come. The carriage chosen for the visit was a simple chaise. Jason was to drive, rather than have one of Calling Farm's labourers to the honours. Strange that she only remembered the younger Jason, before their marriage, as forever smiling and deferential. Once Father and Mother left her alone in a state of baffled authority, smiling Jason the herdsman was the one to turn to. His bluff firmness was a godsend.

Once wedded, he changed. He was wedded now to Calling Farm's vast acreage, and ambition. She was superfluous. Conversation, companionship, amusement, interest, love — all went for nothing. She was virtually ignored. The more personal associations between a husband and wife she forbade herself to think about under any circumstances. That way led to nightmare and madness. She knew some ladies among the gentry who'd travelled the harlot's road and seemed ecstatic, but that was not for her. One consolation, though mixed with regret, lay in allowing herself the sin of wondering how her life would now be had she married Ven Carmichael. He had stayed at Calling Farm when she was a girl. She remembered him always running, hair wild, laughing with his father on the shelving foreshore . . .

'I should have brought out the best carriage,' her husband was grumbling. 'But will not give them the satisfaction.'

'Yes, dear.'

A year ago he had been close to owning Carradine Manor. He had anticipated aggrandisement by taking armorial bearings and a splendid four-horse landau, liveried servants, and postillions. His setback, in losing the Carradine property, was something she still did not understand. It somehow involved the woman Judith Blaker, but Mary knew better than enquire.

He had dressed up for the drive to Bures House. She too had made every effort. He lacked social graces, but she had been taught that such a flaw in a husband was the fault of the wife, whose plain duty it was to lead from within a marriage, and achieve perfect domestic balance. Any failure was the wife's, not her husband's. God's unwritten laws of gender dictated so.

'Your prosperity, Jason, has persuaded Sir Charles Golding to extend the invitation.'

'They need more investors,' Prothero said bluntly, signalling the Bures House gatekeeper that he would not slow to the customary walk.

'Perhaps the Sealandings mood, Jason, invites a new community of spirit?'

'They excluded me before,' Prothero carped. She had heard his grievances many times. 'Carradine is the prime mover. He has no love for me. Why does he want me in his syndicate?'

'Your resourcefulness, Jason?'

'Hmmph! My resourcefulness almost beggared the man! I will not join without cast-iron sureness. As your idiot leech might sail in the *Sealands*, it endears me less!'

She slipped her thoughts, and watched the great mansion.

Bures House was a monstrous pile for a bachelor. Golding's drunkenness and his neglect of the estate would deter any woman from showing affectionate interest. It was a waste of eligibility, in Mary Prothero's opinion, when a man who would be improved by a good woman failed to acquire a wife. He thus condemned not women but himself. The sentence was dire, unless some radical event rescued the lone drunkard.

The girl Mehala had been housekeeper here for a brief time. It had almost been the saving of Golding, but she had gone to Ven, so throwing away the chance of a brilliant marriage. Mary was in no doubt that would have been the outcome. Tonight, the Protheros and other Sealandings guests would have been curtseying to Sir Charles and Lady Mehala. All the Hundred would envy Mehala her advancement, had she stayed at Bures. Golding would have fallen for her.

Mary Prothero alone – alone? – envied Mehala now.

Mary did not call it jealousy. She suspected that Euterpe Baring had an inkling of her sentiment. Ven was unaware, probably. Mehala? Mehala knew, deep down and sure, for a woman who loved a man was aware of every rivalry. Mary surprised herself by acknowledging that Mehala would not hate her. She shivered, drawing her cristygrey shawl round to take advantage of the fur. She wondered if it had been altogether wise to wear a satin pompadour dress this cooling evening. She always felt autumn early, but she had to look the part of Mistress Prothero of Calling Farm. Father's gentle pride and Mother's absent presence ruled so. She ought to have worn her best casaweck, the short quilted mantle, for more warmth, with its sleeves and a close-fitting collar with fur trimming.

The chaise drew up at the main steps, Jason bringing the gelding to a neat stand. Footmen came to lower the steps and hand her down.

It was early evening, the light fading quite fast from the broad skies. Swallows overhead were flitting, touching then wheeling apart. The swifts were leaving, seeming to stretch the blue expanse as they glanced at southern lands. In another week they would be gone, leaving only the swallows. They would tarry until Michaelmas Eve, when they would suddenly leave the morning skies empty. Autumn would command the whole countryside in its long vigil for the coming of winter.

'Come, woman,' Prothero growled, giving her a shove.

They ascended the steps towards the sound of music and chatter. Carradine stood with Charles Golding to one side of the great stone balustrade watching them.

'He is not essential, Charles,' Carradine reminded Golding quietly.

'Where Prothero goes, so do many others, though he is an upstart, a jack-a'back.'

Carradine felt nothing but contempt for his host, who was already in his cups and finding it hard to stay vertical. But he needed Golding to acquire Prothero for the syndicate. He disliked Prothero, but gave him grudging respect. The farmer was a grasper, a risk-taker if not an out-and-out gambler, in a sordid grubbing way. Such a man Carradine understood. He could not help comparing Prothero with Golding.

The latter was an incompetent sot who hungered to stand for Parliament, and never would. Nobody could give out enough bribes for such a toper. Golding knew that, but hoped they would move heaven and earth for a gentleman of quality who had restored commerce in the Eastern Hundreds. Carradine had encouraged Golding's delusion. It would be Carradine himself, not Golding, who would gain. He would be liberated. His rise to Parliament would remove Judith Blaker. She had allowed him a strange leeway lately, almost as if she wanted him to resume his old ways. She never demurred now when he wanted to ride out. But he was not deceived. She must only be testing him somehow, by having some sly groom flit along unseen to report back. His plan was: *Sealands*, triumph, Parliament, and freedom.

Less than two months since, the uncouth lout O'Connell had been returned for Clare County in Ireland to the Mother of Parliaments, a Roman Catholic no less, overturning the 1678 exclusion of those repetitious babblers. It was rumoured that next year the Duke of Norfolk, another idolatrist, would be seated in the Lords, when his brain, like all papists', was bottled in Rome. Was the lineage of the Carradines to be slighted by being barred? Parliament could do not wrong, nor could its elected members – though Yorkshire had gained two additional county members in 1821, transferred from the Cornish borough of Grampound, which was sharply disenfranchised for excessively flagrant bribery.

He needed a few months' grace, that was all, even a few weeks, for his Baltic scheme. The representation law of Queen Anne's ninth year ruled that every knight of the shire should possess freehold or copyhold estate of a clear six hundred pounds value. It was then that the Queen Anne Act had gone mad, insanely adding that every citizen, burgess, or Cinque Port baron up for election should possess three hundred pounds' worth of landed qualification. This was madness. Letting in any money-grubbing merchant or filthy labourer who had a few groats put aside in an ell of grass. But the gentry still held sway, even if these Reform burners wanted the voting right for every man in the Kingdom. Two knights of the shire for Suffolk, though, were electable still, and he, Rad Carradine, must be one.

Then would come the reckoning for Judith Blaker and her tribe. Bottle-tippers like Golding would grovel. The Lord of Sealandings would have to whistle for Carradine's company.

He nudged Golding, seeing Mary Prothero's pale face as she reached the front terrace, and stepped forward with a smile. Golding lurched out with a grin to greet Prothero.

'Mr Prothero, and Mistress Prothero! Welcome. May I accompany you inside? The music began only a little while since. There are many ladies who will enjoy your vivacious company!'

'Thank you,' Mary said quietly, detecting Golding's sarcasm. His taste ran to gaudy women. She hardly qualified.

Prothero however was gratified, to Carradine's disgust. The man should have knocked Golding over the balustrade for such ill-concealed derision, but was too stupid to notice he had been mocked through his woman. A retiring mouse Mary Prothero now was, but the Mary Calling he remembered from before her marriage was gently amusing and merry enough for most.

'Thank you, Sir Charles! We are delighted to come.' Prothero turned to Carradine. ' 'Servant, sir.'

' 'Service, Mr Prothero,' Carradine said evenly. 'Mistress Prothero. A pleasure to see you both.'

'I shall go inside, gentlemen,' Mary said.

Fortunately for Golding the Treggans were talking by the entrance to the music room, so Golding was able to leave Mary Prothero with them after a garbled introduction. He set out to return to Carradine and Prothero by way of the wine table. It was all informal. His under-housekeeper Little Jane was in attendance there. A tiny garrulous young woman, he was tempted to use her, but was nowadays overtaken by drink. He emptied two glasses of new madeira, scowled at the slightness of the drink, and accepted a glass of punch to last the journey back to the terrace.

'You are very fortunate, Mistress Prothero', Harriet Treggan welcomed Mary, 'to live in such a beautiful county! And to live where one was born!'

Mary Prothero acknowledged the remark, though it was more barbed than kind. She was being told she was the country yokel, the Treggans the much-travelled elite.

'I thank heaven for my good fortune, Mistress Treggan. Our seasons have unrivalled beauty and a wild sublimity of Nature at her most savage.'

Harriet Treggan was annoyed the wretched woman had not recognised the slight. She smiled brightly. 'Rodney is so pleased to rescue Sealandings! With his extensive city connections he has enormous influence over local . . . *trades*. I am delighted that he is able to further your gentry's designs.'

Mary still refused to take offence. 'He is so kind.'

'You took in guests, did you not?' Harriet needled viciously, using the phrase applied to common lodgings. 'I recall a surgical apprentice, whom you lodged as a child.'

Mary knew then that this was the same Harriet that Ven had once encountered in his London days. She let her expression show nothing.

'Guests? Yes, Mistress Treggan. My great-grandfather "took in", as you choose to express it, guests. One was His Majesty the King, of happy memory, when he progressed these Hundreds. He stayed twice at Calling.'

Rodney Treggan paled, and Harriet almost swooned. The slight on the Monarch was tantamount to treason.

'Mistress Prothero!' Lady Hunterfield laid a heavy hand unasked on Mary's arm. 'It is high time you were properly welcomed to Bures House. I am hauled from retirement into service as hostess, for silly Golding's lack of a spouse.'

Mary felt immediate relief. 'I am honoured, Lady Faith.'

The old lady cackled. 'That dark voice, Mary Calling! It was your grandmother's! Are there *so many* of whom you disapprove?'

Mary felt her face colour. 'I am content to listen to the music, Lady Faith.'

'Put me in my place, hey?' Lady Faith failed to lower her voice. 'I am thankful that gypsy was not asked to take Golding's arm. But she is satisfied parading that Scotchman.'

'Mr Waite? I have met him.' Mary was embarrassed by Lady Faith's frankness, for she too had noticed the smiling Judith Blaker wafting past in rich scarlet scotia silk, the sleeves slit and the excessively deep cleft above her tight bodice emphasised by her lace cardinal pelerine.

Lady Faith tapped her arm with her fan. 'The privilege of age, Mary, is to enjoy embarrassment without shame! Where would you choose to be seated? I cannot put you beside one of your admirers, that sloth-love Henry of my own family. He abhors salon music. Any caterwauling from wandering pipers' English bagpipes and fifes, he will hear. Otherwise . . .' She darted Mary a mischievous glance. 'Otherwise I would have fetched him, even though you are married!'

'Lady Faith!'

'I shall seat you, I think, beside that pretty Miss Euterpe, and so sustain your morals!' The old lady laughed, talking in a stage whisper as the musicians played a Handel string piece. 'I adore weaknesses, Mary, as all of my vintage – as devoutly as you young people adore strength! You are wrong, of course.'

'Shall you be seated, Lady Faith?' Safety lay in stillness.

'In a moment.' The old dowager surveyed the music room. 'Look at us! Gentlemen eye the ladies, who pretend to be so busy prattling that they cannot possibly notice the gentlemen!' Irritably she waved away a waiting-maid who was eager to serve glasses of hot punch.

Mary thought the music delightful and would have been glad to listen. 'Company is pleasing spectacle.'

The new brightness of the room almost dazzled. Mary had seen Carcel lamps before, of course. She herself favoured the Proust modification of the Argand lamp, for it did not give the annoying tick of the Carcel's clockwork mechanism. Yet it produced the steady white light so necessary for domestic life. The Geneva Argand lamp's light faded as its oil dwindled, but the Proust version was better. It operated on the principle of a bird fountain. Ladies often disliked the Proust wall lamps in parlours, for the oil reservoirs stood above the wick and so partially blocked the flame's radiance on one side. Mary firmly believed that a careful wife should so regulate her house that —

'M'lady?' She came to, startled.

'You see Margaret Swale? She, whose cramoisy-coloured redingote is impossibly trying to match her terrible platoff evening cape in pink satin? Seated by the stout lady in that hopelessly tight-bodiced dress in palmyrene?'

Mary tried not to look, but her eyes were drawn. 'Yes?'

'She hopes tonight to make her failed affianced gentleman — next to her, with the horrid roll collar — buy a sixty-fourth share of the *Sealands* catastrophe! They have lived in sin for months, and are rivals to purchase Shalamar. Though I had hoped that Castor Deeping would buy the place. He wants to bring Brillianta Astell as his bride, but what can a lady do? Old Sir Edward has always wanted that odious Chauncey to wed one of his daughters —'

'Shalamar?' Mary asked as quietly as she could above the music. Almost everybody Lady Faith mentioned was here. She was terrified lest someone overhear. 'Catastrophe, Lady Faith?'

The old lady smiled, liking Mary's response. Shalamar first, then wholesale economic disaster second?

'It will fail. Heaven knows why. Königsberg alone has half its trade with our country. But it will.' For the first time she lowered her voice to a respectable quiet. 'I wanted you for Henry, Mary. Events overtook you, poor thing. Had it come about, you would be familiar with my nephew. He can somehow perceive what these muddy virgates of Sealandings allow. Notice: he distances himself from the Treggans, Golding, Deeping, your loutish Prothero, in this matter. Not because he wants to; because instinct decrees that it will fail.'

'Why? How?'

'He cannot explain,' Lady Faith said simply. She looked troubled. 'I have seen him like this several times since he was a child. So he saves his finances, perhaps to rescue Sealandings when the venture collapses.' She indicated the groups of laughing gentry. 'Your childhood friend at Shalamar also has some sort of instinct. Enough! Let us listen to the fat German's screeching.'

She allowed a footman to place chairs, and sat ready to regale Mary with tittle-tattle of others, her eyes everywhere.

'The pity is', she confided loudly at a pause in the violins so that the company overheard, 'that lovely Mehala was not invited! She *always* enlivens proceedings . . .'

Carradine was delighted that Prothero came into line so quickly. In fact, the man's eagerness was an embarrassment.

'Three sixty-fourths is rather greedy, Prothero,' Carradine said, but kept in good humour. 'We shall be accused of favouring friends!'

Prothero felt gratified. 'Those are my terms, sir.'

'Oh, everybody will agree, when they know that it is yourself making the demand.' Carradine indicated the gathering. 'Here alone there must be forty or fifty gentlemen, all eager for a share.'

'Then they must share each other's share, sir.'

Carradine tilted his glass in surrender. 'If you insist, Prothero.' He grimaced at Golding, who was now befuddled. 'I should have known you were a man of determination.'

'Money turnover is vanity, but profit is sanity!' Prothero said weightily. 'I shall instruct my bank in the morning.'

'I am honoured to welcome you, Prothero, on your terms.'

'Honoured!' Golding cried. 'A drink to success!'

Prothero let the two high-born gentlemen bring him a cup of their expensive swill. He harboured no illusions. He was here on sufferance, because his acceptance would bring in more land-owners. When they heard he was in for a major stake, they would come begging for a fraction of his coming good fortune. It was ever the way, with those who owned land. Nothing could block this venture, except lack of capital funds. That is where the gentry needed him. Very well, but it would cost them dear.

'I shall require an equal number of extra shares.' Prothero tasted the wine – foreign muck, not half as good as his own.

Carradine stilled. Even Golding focused. '*Extra?*'

'I can pay,' Prothero said with a heavy attempt at humour. The expressions on their faces were worth every penny.

'There are only sixty-four shares in the entire venture, Prothero. You agreed three.'

Prothero was unmoved. 'Must I remind you two that I will pay a fortune for each share? You do not give them away!'

'But a *further* three shares? Six sixty-fourths?'

'Yes.' Prothero tapped his foot to the music, to show his indifference. They needed him. He needed them hardly at all. 'I might farm them out to friends. I might not. I shall see how I feel, when they ask if the venture is worthy. Or not.'

Carradine swallowed the insult. Golding was swaying, looking blankly at him for guidance.

'Very well,' Carradine said. He would have to conceal part of the profits. Honest Percy Carmady would not accommodate this wish. The man Hopestone was a possibility, though. And others in the *Sealands* might be glad to earn extra coin in secret.

'Done, Carradine?' Prothero asked airily.

'Done,' he said, vowing one day he would kill the man, but settling the contract in the nick of time, for just then a rocket fizzed into the darkness. Guests cried out in excitement. The schooner *Sealands* had come into harbour, and all rushed upstairs to the balconies to witness the fireworks Carradine had arranged.

Hunterfield was warned by Simple Tom's low whistle. He reined the mare Betsy to a stop, and waited for the first explosion. The South Toll road had wide verges with lush overhanging hawthorns. Flashes of light, and noise, caused mounts to bolt, so he kneed Betsy under the leaf shelter.

The squeals and applause from Bures House were audible. Strange that, seaward of the South Toll road, the land held grand estates, rolling lawns, herbaceous borders of almost unchallenged beauty. The inland side ought to be more prosperous, yet showed a curious dereliction. Milton Hall, of the De Foes, rested in elegant suspension with a skeleton staff. Beyond that grand gateway stood the enormous ruined estate of Shalamar.

'We shall be fortunate for a candle to light us in, Tom,' Hunterfield told his mute groom, receiving an answering whistle.

This was an odd way to come a-courting. And an even odder kind of courting to execute, Hunterfield thought.

The pallor of Tom's face showed in a burst of green and red lights. The horses were restive, but not too startled, for both were used to sporting guns. Hunterfield spoke lowly to Betsy; Tom whistled a low tune borrowed from a songthrush.

'Remember the times we circumnavigated this road, Tom?'

A sharp whistle, staccato to copy his master's wry amusement at the memory of his affair with Thalia De Foe. It had been easy – a system of signal lanterns, use of a trusted servant's staircase, Fellows De Foe away in London's Threadneedle Street. Until the stark realisation that Carradine was Thalia's sole aim brought him to his senses.

'We are almost at Shalamar. Let us on, eh?'

A long low trill, Tom's warning. Hunterfield moved Betsy into the road at a walk. For somebody mute since birth, Simple Tom expressed himself more eloquently, and was a deal less simple, than most in Sealandings.

40

Rosie and Clement proved invaluable at Shalamar. Both were excited at having the climbing boy as a new patient, and amazed at the new babe's arrival with its mother. Mehala's coach alone would have been an astonishment on any normal evening, but now it was almost ignored in the rush to provide a bed for Mistress Tyll and the newly born, and a place to lay Nath.

The vehicle was dispatched to Parker's stables on the Norwich road, and Mehala took charge. Ven sat with the boy, Barbara Tyll and the babe in the kitchen.

'We are rough, Nath,' Ven confessed gently. 'This kitchen is the only room worth looking at, except for half a room off the great hall through that corridor you see past those steps. I call that my study, but it serves as surgery, apothecary room and laboratory alike.'

'Am I allowed to stay?'

'Of course. You are now part of my family, for ever.'

'Honest?' Nath's eyes were blackened in the conjunctivae from soot, looking larger than life. He lay on the kitchen floor, Ven sprawled beside him. He had to lean close to hear the boy.

'Rosie and Clement kept the range fire going, thank goodness, or I should have been cross!' Ven smiled to belie his words, and turned his attention to Barbara Tyll and her babe in the inglenook. 'Are you well, Barbara? They will bring coverings soon, I hope! Time to get you dry and settled.'

'You are kind.' She was not too fatigued to notice Nath's condition. Ven's frown warned her from noticing too much.

'We must make a better appraisal tomorrow, Barbara.'

Nath asked, 'Will I have to leave?'

Ven cleared his throat. 'Nath. You are home, with us for ever. We are your family. Me, Mehala, Rosie your sister, Clement your brother.'

He wondered if he ought to explain the difficulties at Shalamar, and the threat looming over them, but decided no. Nath had had no certainties except the grimmest, and ought to be allowed one reassurance.

'Thank you.'

'No, Nath.' Ven took the boy's hand. 'No. Never say thanks. You deserve a home. I shall do my utmost for you; as Mehala will, and as those noisy rapscallions raising Cain upstairs ought!'

Mehala entered, carrying a blanket. 'Clement has some notion of making you a bed, Nath. He has found something in an attic that will do, until you are better. We must make do.'

She laid it on the floor. Together she and Ven lifted Nath onto it. Her startled glance told Ven of her horror at his emaciation. Ven grinned falsely.

'Time to call your other pair down, Mehala! I am hungry as a hunter, and I am sure everybody else must be also.'

'Very well, Ven.' She called upstairs to Rosie to hurry, refused Barbara Tyll's offer of help, and set to.

They had a chance to speak only when Barbara Tyll was lodged in Ven's surgery and all were fed. Ven went with Mehala to a window alcove off the corridor. It was a huge arched length. The rich ornamentation had long since crumbled. Fungus clamped every corner of the damp walls.

'You saved us, Mehala.'

She smiled and came close. 'You have not changed into your new clothes, Ven. I have wasted my largesse!'

'No, well, I am sorry, Mehala, but I —'

'Shhh!' She put a finger on his lips. 'Only my jest. You must wear them, full fig! Better than any gentry!'

He was embarrassed. 'Fashion looks ridiculous. Those enormous roll collars, extraordinary stocks, everything measured to fit absurdity! Your victuals especially saved us.'

'We shall never again go hungry!' she said, suddenly fierce. 'I shall fight for food like a tigress!'

Ven did not speak for a while. They watched the rain run down the window panes in the gloaming of Mehala's Norfolk lantern. 'This is no future for you, Mehala.'

'This? What is this *this*, Doctor?'

'Do not be angry.' He made the admission. 'I was afraid. Not that you might not leave. But wealth shows you life as it could be. Look at your life in Shalamar.'

'So?' Her hand gripped his. 'Has that not always been the case, Ven? Here is a truth that I did not reveal: my memory returned long before I said. At any time, I could have gone south and claimed my possessions. Instead, I stayed here. Because of you.'

'Mehala –' he began. She cut him short.

'No, Ven. Listen. Believe me. Believe *us*. Too many want us separated. But the only ones who can truly part us are ourselves – if we lose conviction. Believe, and all will come right.'

'I was never gladder to see you than in the barn at Two Cotts, Mehala. I am only half a person with you gone.'

She smiled radiantly at his admission. 'It is as we are, Ven. Have confidence in us. We will survive.'

She embraced him. They stood quietly for a moment, hearing Rosie call to Clement, and Clement's argumentative reply.

'What can we do for Nath, Ven? He took so little, hardly enough for a bird. I could make him chicken broth. It takes time to build up a meat stock. I must send Rosie to the Donkey and Buskin for a pot of Nelson's own stock in the morning.'

Ven withdrew, disturbed. 'Nath's cancer is typical of the killing ailment climbing boys suffer from. The cancer extends through the body. How, I do not know. I cannot stop it.'

'Can it be . . . removed, cut out of him?'

'Not without killing Nath himself. It has involved the scrotum, and the skin areas adjacent. It fungates over on to the penis. Already he has difficulty passing water. There are palpable nodes elsewhere in his body, denoting spread.'

Through tears, she asked if nothing could be done. 'He is only a child, Ven.'

'You cannot reproach me enough, Mehala. That task is mine. No, I know of no way. His cough suggests that soot has leathered his lungs. I do not know if scrotal cancer reaches into the lungs, as some cancers do. Or whether it lies dormant before leaping through the whole corpus. If we had money –'

'We have, Ven.'

He winced. 'Then I must ask you to buy laudanum for the boy. That will at least relieve him of pain.'

'Laudanum? Is that opium?'

'Yes. It is used in Lincolnshire and the Fen country against the ague. They have more ague than we in the Eastern Hundreds. Doctors are beginning to believe that the ague is one and the same with the Italians' malaria, the bad air disease of the Pontine marshes. I am ignorant. Makepeace, the apothecary in Maidborough, must have laudanum.' Ven spoke bitterly. 'This country imported over 17,000 pounds weight of the brown opium last twelvemonth!'

'I shall send to Makepeace. Blankets, food, clothes –'

'The dose will be difficult.' Ven was off, musing about the treatment. 'The pain seems to be from the inflammation near the tumour. I do not know how to treat it. We must try some lotions to allay it. The turgidity and rottenness together combine to form a feeble suppuration in spreading cancerous –'

'You must tell me. I shall make a list! Come.' She took up the Norfolk lantern.

'Unscrupulous apothecaries and merchants practise a fraud on the unsuspecting, Mehala.' He followed docilely enough.

'Do they, dear?' Down the corridor, the guttering candle in the porcelain cup made shadows leap and fall.

'Opium itself, as sold, is in chests of 150 pounds weight. It is brown-yellow, and soft enough to take your finger's imprint, though if too soft it should be rejected. Opium dealers adulterate it with leaves and plantain.'

'How cruel!'

'Hard-cake opium, if gritty and rough when rubbed between thumb and forefinger, has been fraudulently diluted!'

'Scandalous.' She linked her arm with his as they went. He leaned on her from weariness.

'You make the tincture from two-and-a-half ounces of powdered hard opium in two pints of proof spirit. Macerate for a fortnight, then strain through muslin . . .'

'Sleep will restore us for the morrow, Ven. Rosie will sleep by Mistress Tyll; Clement by Nath in the kitchen. Both know to come a-running for you if there is need.'

'Thank you, Mehala. I should surrender without you.'

'Yet you persuaded Wren the whoremistress to allow you use of her splendid barn at Two Cotts. How *did* you manage that?'

He paused at the staircase. 'I honestly do not know, Mehala. She seemed to discern some threat in my words. I wish I could remember what I said.'

Mehala smiled and took his hand. 'Perhaps it is right to forget, Ven.'

He was too tired to ask her what exactly she meant.

Judith Blaker grunted, her hands on the North Briton's scars. He felt animal-like as he worked between her thighs, though gentler than any she had ever used.

Used? Even as sweat started and her mind could no longer keep hold during his final rut, she tried to think about the sense of it. Used? That had been her way in the past. This was something different. She pressed a hand over his mouth as he strained to cry out and flailed into a gradual stillness, her gasping matching his, their bodies welded in a sweet sweat.

She was sore from the . . . from the use. He was not heavy in spite of his stocky build, yet in rut she had to bear his whole mass between her thighs. He always lifted her legs to feel her hips and buttocks, splaying her apart to drive entry. Bruises showed more on a woman than on a man. She had lately noticed Carradine's casual glance at the heavy bruising on her thighs, but he had passed no remark. Perhaps they had not registered? It was a risk. Tonight she had wanted to declare a respite. But no sooner had she met Alex in the servant's room, she was helping him to disrobe her in silence, then had knelt to shell him from his garments and started their frantic coupling.

Use, though? Was it truly that? She reached for a woollen to wipe her face free of his dripping sweat, and passed it gently across his mouth. It was extraordinary how different men were. Carradine used her mostly on her side, or raging behind her. His beatings were not a gentle susurration; they were actual blows on her shoulders, savage maulings of her breasts, buffets about her head. She welcomed them as love's passionate sincerity. Desire was the leaven of desire, and fury possession's truth.

But this North Briton was remote in his coupling, but gentle. He slid into her almost reflexly, as if prepared to explain his presence in her body should she ask.

She smiled and embraced him, pressing her hands on his scars.

They were from wounds. When asked, he had explained them away: 'People up there fight battles.'

Four knocks sounded, the signal from Prettiance.

'Alex?' Judith stirred, easing her legs wider to roll him aside. 'Alex. The firework artisans have arrived. Rad will be here to supervise the men at the harbour.'

'I am awake.'

He moved off her in silence, another curiosity. Other men gave a grunt at having to withdraw. Not this one. He was up and wiping his body all in a movement.

'Carradine has asked us to be present when he explains how he wants the celebrations to proceed.'

'The party will be at Bures House?'

'Yes. Sir Charles Golding has insisted. Everybody will be there to welcome the *Sealands*. It will be a late tide.'

'I shall be there.' He dressed with a singlular economy of movement. 'Then soon after I shall be gone.'

'Leave? Leave Sealandings?' But he was already sitting to help her lace her shaped whalebone corset.

'Yes. Two days, or as soon as the *Sealands* sails, whichever comes first.'

'So soon?' She felt sickened, but deliberately avoided showing distress. 'I thought you might want accommodation here.'

'I must go to London, at least two weeks.'

'Then you will return?'

'Perhaps. It depends on my father. He will come from Lothian, to assign revenue to my brothers.'

'Why not invite them to stay here with us? You would be back to celebrate the return of the *Sealands*.' She raised her serpents so he could fasten the latchings at her nape.

'I have an undertaking that cannot be delayed.' His taciturnity was praiseworthy. Carradine had the same reticence, if more overt passion.

'Does it include me, sir?' she asked as if offended.

He gazed at her. 'Yes,' he said flatly. 'It includes you, but is not yet ready for your ears.'

She searched his face for clues. 'Yes, but no?'

He pushed past her to the door, listened for a moment and looked back. She felt vulnerable, being only half dressed. Her smile faded at his stare. 'When I ask you, then you shall tell me yea or nay. It will then become your business according to how you reply.'

'That is singularly high-handed of you, sir,' she was saying when the door closed on her.

She sat on the edge of the bed, staring unseeing. If any soothsayer, or Petulengro from the northlands, had predicted that she would dance attendance on a North Briton, a quiet, uncouth man with hardly an elegant word, she would have screamed in derision. Now here she was, her heart thumping at the prospect of that man possibly making some unspecified proposal. It was ridiculous. She did not know what was happening to her. She had never felt like this. Oh, she was still sure that Carradine was the one for her, Carradine would enter Parliament as a Knight of the Shire, and become the most influential man in the Hundreds. Virtually all-powerful, and she his wife.

But this Alex Waite was working some sort of magic on her, perhaps inside her even. She found it impossible to judge. He did nothing unusual. He made love in a manner she would once have found irritatingly docile to the point of somnolence. Yet she wanted him now, only minutes after he had slid out of her. He had gone almost as if leaving some lady's tea-tasting.

Was this how Mehala felt for her quack? Or as Thalia De Foe felt for Carradine? Or as Mercy Carmady felt for Hunterfield? There were not too many tempestuous lovelusts in Sealandings to choose from. She would have to reason it out.

Prettiance entered, and proceeded to help her dress.

'Your lover is with the pyrotechnic men at the harbour,' she said, tying the bows with clumsy tugs.

'I shall follow.' Judith pointed to the horse-glass. Prettiance tilted the mirror for her mistress to see the hem. 'And take a letter to Miss Baring at the rectory.'

Prettiance made to speak. Judith watched her reflection.

'Yes, Prettiance? What is it?'

'Nothing, mistress,' Prettiance said. 'Will you not wear the same black shoes downstairs as you came up in?'

Judith then gave a nod. 'Yes. That would be wise. Thank you, Prettiance.'

'Yes, mistress,' the maid said without a flicker of expression.

Judith let Prettiance shoe her. She did not often make such elementary mistakes. She would have to be more careful, but as long as she had Prettiance to depend on . . . She called the maid's attention.

'How do I look, Prettiance?' She was really asking for Alex's opinion, not for Carradine or herself, she realised with that same strange feeling.

Prettiance did not speak for a moment, but stood appraising her in silence. 'Just so, mistress.'

She opened the door, handing Judith her chatelaine. It was only on her way downstairs that Judith realised that for the first time the insolent baggage had avoided speaking to her in Romany.

41

'**H**OW IS HE?'
'The babe?' Ven beamed at the mention of the scrap in the rocker.

Clement had shown an astonishing aptitude for joinery, and had adapted four old floorboards from an attic, with a fallen panel, into a makeshift cradle.

Rosie was Barbara Tyll's constant companion, rushing to serve any request. She anticipated the babe's needs almost as quickly as the mother herself. Mehala made a game out of it, trying in mock desperation to reach the door before Rosie when Barbara called. Clement abetted Mehala, laughing and holding the girl back. That their follies had to be enacted in almost total silence, not to wake the two sleepers, made it all the more laughable.

Except not so laughable.

Nath lay in a cut-down truckle bed that Clement had found in his explorations of the ruinous upper floors. His tools were the simplest: being a fragment of a rusty rip saw; an improvised hammer he himself had fashioned from an ash stick and a napped flint; and a bow drill made from waxed strips of leather and a yew stave acting on a sharpened oak arrow. The truckle's castors were removed. Nath now lay near the kitchen range. Much of Mehala's clowning was for Nath's benefit. In his clear moments he loved the kitchen activities.

Ven attributed Nath's pain to the ferments gathering about the terrible cancerous growth, not actually from within the tumour itself.

This evening, catching the excitement about the *Sealands*, they carried the truckle bed onto the verandah walk outside the huge double doors.

'There!' Ven exclaimed, collapsing theatrically. 'Your lordship will have the most marvellous display of fireworks ever seen in Sealandings!'

'We arranged them personally!' Clement shouted, pointing to where the rockets would appear over the sea.

Nath lay on his truckle. Ven held his hand, avoiding Mehala's eyes. 'We could bring out one of the new candles, Nath,' he told him, 'but that would lessen the spectacle. Have you seen fireworks before?'

Nath shuddered. 'I mislike fire, Doctor.'

Ven cursed himself for a fool. The boy could probably remember nothing except being forced to climb in the narrow chimneys, for ever in a world of fire and darkness. And he had thought this a treat, to remind the child of his brief past.

'Shall we take you in, then?'

'Inside the hall, safe behind the glass windows.'

They moved the truckle into the hall and closed the doors. The thud reverberated through the whole mansion. Rosie sat with Clement in a window, making sure there was a space for Nath to see. Mehala propped Nath up on a folded blanket.

'I shall go to sea one day,' Clement prophesied.

'It is a terrible life, Clement.'

'How do you know, Mehala?'

'Mehala knows everything about the sea,' Ven said before he could think. He sometimes said too much.

Mehala rose. 'Shall I go for Mistress Tyll and the babe? He should be fed by now.'

'In the *Sealands*?' Nath asked Clement. 'I s'll go with you!'

'But not yet!' Ven said. 'Clement must learn at his studies, and Nath must get better first *and* learn his books.'

'I want to see the great ship,' Nath said. 'Will we be able to see it from here?'

'No.' Ven clasped Nath's hand in apology, sitting on the floor beside the bed. 'Mehala offered a coach to take you down, but I thought that unwise this late. Perhaps tomorrow.'

'I will get better, Doctor?'

Ven smiled. 'Fitter than any in the land, Nath,' he lied. 'And soon.'

'It hurts now. Can I have some medicine?'

'Yes. I have it here, Nath.'

Mehala's new-found wealth had enabled him to buy the laudanum from the travelling apothecary Makepeace, who left a relative in charge of his shop while he visited the great houses in the Sealandings Hundred with his physics.

The laudanum was mixed with an extract of bitter wild lettuce tops for greater effect. Nath was unable to eat much, and was occasionally sick when in fever. Mehala maintained him so far on gruels and broths with as much sweet drink as he could take. An extract of salix, the willowtree bark, partly allayed his fevers.

'One spoonful, master!' Rosie came to administer the draught. 'We do not want you drunk on the stuff!'

Mehala sweetened the tincture with the juice of an orange. That exotic fruit was a wonder. She had taught Rosie and Clement how to extract the last drop. 'Each kikling', she showed them, 'need not be separated. Press the whole soft part out. Cut always on a plate to save the juice. And save the rind, stripped free of the white pap, to make a sweet-oil seasoning.'

They were in awe, and came to sniff the orange juice, laudanum and lettuce juice. Ven made no secret of the composition, hoping to awaken their interest.

A thump suddenly sounded in the night sky. Rosie concentrated on administering the draught to Nath before flying to the window.

'Will it come again?' Nath asked, lying back against Ven's arm.

'In a moment there will be many more,' Ven promised him.

Mehala left to bring Nath an extra cushion as two more faint bangs sounded. The whole night was lit with reds and greens. They exclaimed at such brilliance. Clement moved closer to Rosie, staring at her features in amazement, then scampering to Ven to peer, then Nath.

'It is like a drawing! All our faces go pale, then green, blue, red, and golden!'

He scurried back to the window, Ven reminding them to let Nath see. The boy seemed more frail than ever. The contours of his face were restored, drawing the eye to his illness rather than concealing it.

Nath exclaimed faintly with the other two as the trees etched in brilliance before the light faded slowly after each burst. 'It is glorious, Ven!'

'I used to see them being made, in London. It is highly

dangerous, but the workmen are fiercely proud of their art. They usually make gunpowder, but their employ is now in peaceful uses.'

'The colours!' Nath whispered. A rocket burst, and the world shone anew. 'The pain is already easing.'

Ven said. 'It seems magic, Nath. The rockets produce fiery effects by means of different ingredients added to the gunpowder in the "swarmer", as they call a firework rocket. The ingredients are only usual things: powdered glass, iron filings, common sawdust.'

Nath stared, astonished. 'So ordinary! Yet so beautiful.'

'That is the beauty of mankind, Nath. We take the ordinary, and make it glorious. Firework men call it the peacock's tail. The rockets rain a hundred colours. White from camphor; rosin for bloody rose; sulphur blue; ivory shavings for pure silver – see there!' He pointed as a cascading waterfall of glittering silver crackled above. 'The orange is from agate, a powdered stone.'

'It is a pity,' Nath said, so low Ven hardly heard.

'Pity, Nath?'

'That they are untrue, only workmen's scraps.'

'No, Nath.' Ven held the boy more closely, trying to keep the smile in his voice. 'That is called art. Don't you see? To make such loveliness is a magic thing. Put stones and shavings together, send it into the night. Create light, speed, and illuminate the heavens! That is all a star is, Nath!'

'All a star is,' the boy echoed. He lay back against Ven to watch the night made into stars.

Hunterfield knocked at the kitchen door and entered, seeing a form moving within. Mehala was startled to see the Lord of Sealandings, and made apology for the disarray as she greeted him.

'We have taken the climbing boy to see the pyrotechnics, Squire. He stays here, where we can nurse him.'

'The climbing boy?'

'You might as well know, Squire. We have Mistress Tyll, and her babe. And a climbing boy called Nath who was cast by Mr Pleasence when the sweep cut him off.' She faced him defiantly. 'I do not know why, Squire.'

'No, of course not.' He flicked back his riding cloak and doffed his beaver, sitting unasked. Mehala glanced towards the corridor. Rosie and Clement could be heard, their voices echoing faintly. 'Mehala. Your sojourn in Red Hall, and Salcot?'

She took a moment to answer. He had never seen her look so alluring. The glint of russet in her dark hair, the magnificent depth to her eyes promised such worth . . . It gave him resolve.

She was disconcerted by his look. 'It was as you predicted.'

'And your position here?'

'Will be easier. I have obtained the return of some possessions, and funds.' She avoided mentioning the dead.

'You will stay with Carmichael?'

'Certainly.'

An especially loud rocket made him pause and listen. He nodded as the crackles followed in order. 'And Carmichael?'

Mehala started folding some new linen bought for the babe. She stopped, perceiving a new gravity in Hunterfield. She felt it was a time for kindness, not defiance. He had been steadfast when she had needed support.

'He is constant in his affection, Squire, as I for him.'

'There might be a different way. For Carmichael; for you.'

'That is not possible. I speak for him.'

Hunterfield drew a breath, wanting to point out that she would be fighting his battles until her dying day.

'I could ease his road, Mehala. You know what I mean. I could place him above the intrigues that bring him down. He is a man who provokes contumely wherever he turns –'

She flashed, 'That is his goodness, Squire. They abhor his kindness. Because they lack it, while preaching about it every hour of every day!'

'There is more than a grain of truth in that,' he conceded. 'But the fact remains. If you were in a position of influence there would be no question about Carmichael's security. His work here could continue – after he leaves. His fame, as a great London surgeon or physician, in a medical institution . . .'

She paled. 'You mean that I –'

'Would stay in Sealandings, Mehala. He would leave.'

'We are married, sir. How could separation –'

'There are ways. You lacked a church wedding.'

361

'What ways?'

'Think how a wife can change.' He saw realisation dawn. 'I am not suggesting anything out of the ordinary, Mehala. You know that. Your selfmade wedding, beside the grave of the drowned girl last year, is the oddity. Abandon Carmichael, and accept a high position with me. People's memories fade, from respectability.'

'Abandon?' Her lips were blue, her face changing to red, then orange, as the sky changed with each swarmer.

'Abandon to a splendid life, Mehala. For him, fame and fortune, with knighthood a distinct possibility.'

'And I would be . . .'

'Whatever you wish,' he said evenly.

'Whatever I wish.' Her voice was dull.

'I need an answer fairly soon.'

She collected herself. 'I can answer you now, Squire, but thank you for your generosity. Would you please come, quietly?'

Silently she led him up the few steps and into the corridor. She held his gloved hand for lack of light, since the bend of the corridor cut them from the kitchen's glow. She shushed him gently, only halting as they reached the faint coloured wash of light visible through the hall windows.

She stepped aside, pulling him gently by the door.

Hunterfield saw the girl Rosie, clapping and screaming with excitement as each firework lit the sky. Beside her, the boy Wellins was pointing and exclaiming. On the hall floor lay a truckle bed, Ven Carmichael sprawled by it, his arm cradling the head of a small boy. Hunterfield could hear Carmichael's voice speaking slowly to the sick youth.

'. . . Create light, speed, and illuminate the heavens. That is all a star is, Nath!'

'All a star is!' the boy said quietly in a lull, resting back against Carmichael's arm.

'Is it pity, Mehala?'

The question was mere ritual. There was no sense in asking, but it was what susceptible mortals did. She was close to him in the gloom, conscious more than ever of his appeal, his willingness and what he was offering. Was that the reason for her resistance, that he was offering instead of asking, stating his capability and never his need? Hunterfield had been a sanctuary in the past. But she wanted Ven.

'You know it is not.' She almost called him Henry.

'Would *his* answer be different?'

That stung. 'I answer for us both.' No temptation now. He meant that Ven would not know how to reply. He would stutter, as his desire for Mehala drove him to utter his craving for her. Then he might retreat in fear that such frankness might push her into some disavowal.

'Some day, Mehala, you will wonder in quiet hours what your life would have been, as the Lady of Sealandings and Mistress of Lorne.' He was not too dignified to add, 'And wonder about the children we might have had, how you could have helped the people of the seamarshes.'

'Instead I have ordered Red Hall sold, and will buy Shalamar for Ven and his work.'

'Exchange a mansion and fine estate, for a derelict home here? Is that wise? You will be penniless.'

'If that is the consequence, so be it.'

'I advise against it.' He had difficulty going on. 'You burn your bridges. If the judgment goes against you . . .'

She smiled as the little group cried out in awe at a treble burst. 'The *Sealands* is opening a new vista for the sea folk, Squire. What notice will they take of a young doctor and his doxy?' She spoke in deliberate self-mockery.

He sighed. 'So be it, Mehala. God favour you.'

'And you, Squire.'

It was the end. Hunterfield watched them all a moment, waited for the next burst, then quietly turned on his heel and withdrew along the corridor. He ought to have said something final to Mehala, made a last declaration of his admiration, but it would have been hopeless. Using his authority to subvert her was out of the question. Mehala was lost to him.

The difficulty now would be to stay above personal grudges, impervious to his deepest feelings. The charge against Mehala and Carmichael would have to be judged without bias.

He left the kitchen vestibule calling out to Tom. The groom was holding the horses, and handed him Betsy's reins as he swung into the saddle.

'Home, Tom. To Lorne.'

Tom whistled in surprise. His mouth popped in interrogation.

'No, Tom, I will not join the firework party.' He let Betsy proceed at her own pace, though he wanted to race from this accursed Shalamar. 'I have had enough company for one night.'

Tom was a mute, thank God, and could make no reply.

42

THE SAILING MORNING was clear, blustery, with scudding clouds. The horizon was sharp, beyond the white rollers rushing into Sealandings Bay; and the crowds who had come to see the great ship were cheerful.

'She be a fast flyer.' Jervin's judgement was listened to with respect, for his was the *The Jaunty*, a Yorkshire lugger that excelled in the North Seas, always heaviest laden with the sea's bounty.

'How long will she voyage, Master Jervin?' Hal Baines asked.

'All depends on the turn-rounds, Hal. But they say they Baltic wharfers work mortal speedy.' Jervin gauged the rigging on the *Sealands*. 'It do not seem natural, with no third mast.'

'Here comes Mehala.' Hal Baines was proud of Mehala, for it was he who had saved her from sea.

Ven and Clement came down the incline, pushing a handcart on which a boy rested on a straw pallet. He was swathed in blankets, his head topped by a new beaver hat covering a soft cotton cap beneath. Mehala walked beside the cart, holding the sick boy's hand.

'Ar, a grand lady now by all accounts.'

'That be the climbing boy, sick of a growth. The sweep-master took another boy from the workhouse.'

'Then poor soul he,' Jervin said piously. 'God preserve.'

Mehala waved to Jervin and Hal, calling across the wharf, 'Where is Lack? Not here to see this grand sight?'

'Toping, Mistress Mehala!' Hal tipped his thumb towards his mouth to show that the old foul-mouthed idler was already celebrating the Sealandings Hundred's prosperity. Jervin cuffed him in disapproval, though his stern attitude had no improving influence on Lack, his deckhand.

'Why the Mistress?' Mehala chided. 'Such gallantries went at our first meeting, Hal Baines!'

'Forgive me, Mehala.' Hal was red-faced with pleasure.

'Not easily!' All smiles, she tucked in the climbing boy.

Ven was anxious that Nath should enjoy the outing. The pain had been allayed by more laudanum. This morning he had managed to eat well, to Ven's relief. His excitement at the prospect of seeing the *Sealands* depart gave them all pleasure.

The scene was one of festival, with garlands adorning the wharf and the mooring posts. Two bands of musicians were playing competing melodies on the flint cobbles by the fisher cottages. Jugglers and singers plied along the hard, trailed by clusters of children and maids. Vendors were selling ribbons and trinkets. A chapman cried that the true story of the stupendous voyage of the *Sealands*, her excellent captain and brave crew, were to be had for a penny pamphlet only available from him and no other wandering word purveyor.

Ven deliberately made a detour. He wanted to avoid the presentation. A waggon draped in blue and white silks stood ready for the ceremony, and already Carradine and a coterie of his admirers were assembled nearby. Crowds had come from White-hanger to join the melee. The seaward track from that rival harbour had been thronged since before dawn. Several still carried lanterns that had seen them safely along the foreshore mudflats before sunrise.

Carts and carriages filled Market Square. Fortunately the rain was holding off. Ladies paraded along the wharf to see the vessel and stare up in awe at her. In the harbour basin, a fleet of small boats and coastal craft was arriving, pennants flying, several carrying greenery at the masthead. Many had crossed the wide bay from Whitehanger and even further down the coast. All was relief at the promise of better times. Sealandings was at the height of its pride.

'It is a pity Rosie will miss seeing the ship sail,' Nath said to Ven as the handcart came to a halt.

'She was eager to help Mistress Tyll with the babe, Nath.'

'Because Bartholomew will call,' Clement said, unconcerned at being overheard. 'Rosie likes him.'

'See the sails, Nath?' Mehala broke in quickly. 'Square sails on the foremast, three jibs, to sail like the wind! Her holds are huge, goods of the whole country within! She will call at Hamburg, Copenhagen, Königsberg of the Prussias, and the Russian Empire!'

'Will I ever sail, Mehala?'

'You certainly shall, Master Nath!' She smiled with determination at Ven, who was nodding assent.

'I shall take you aboard one of these, Nath, when you are well. Together we will explore a ship from stem to stern. I know everything about sailing ships.'

Several bystanders smiled in disbelief. Mehala gave a tut of scorn.

'Ven knows absolutely nothing about the sea, Nath! He cannot admit his ignorance, like all men!'

Ven pretended anger, pointing to a crowd surrounding the jugglers and singers performing by the hard.

'See those, Nath? The women sing flat but contribute nothing! The men do the juggling and playing instruments!'

'Do not listen, Nath. Ven is vain.'

A cry arose at the far end of the south mole. Percy Carmady climbed from a hoy onto the paving, to scattered applause. He was in his naval uniform, but had removed the insignia of his former rank. He walked to where the *Sealands* was moored and joined Captain Hopestone. They marched in step, accompanied by a mob of people who shook their hands and cheered them to the decorated waggon. Carradine was waiting with Sir Charles Golding, the churchwardens, the petty constable and other functionaries. On signal, the bands together struck up 'Hearts of Oak' to applause, as the crowds flocked around for the address.

Ven and Clement took advantage of the space created to push the handcart nearer to the ship. Nath exclaimed in awe.

'It is huge!' he cried, in amazement. 'It is a world!'

Seamen lining the gunwales were smoking. One called down, offering Mehala his plug tobacco if she would come aboard.

'In that coracle?' she scoffed. 'Can it carry two?'

'I would make sure it did, mistress!'

'Make sure you dullards avoid that great mountain called Denmark!' She ignored the return banter, and explained to Nath, 'Denmark's highest hill is supposed to be but a hundred and eighty feet. Foolish seamen think the whole country but a wave on the horizon.'

Nath smiled. 'They like Mehala, Ven.'

'Well, be that as it may.' Ven was out of his depth. Mehala was in her natural element anywhere, nowhere more so than the sea. 'We can watch her sail from the slope above the hard. Shall we go?'

The Sealandings crier in his red robe clanged his handbell, summoning the people to hark. Clement swivelled the handcart round so that Nath could see the pomp.

In the silence, Carradine spoke briefly and, Mehala thought, well, detailing the hopes of prosperity to the Hundred. Sir Charles Golding then whined on, desperate to preach his own importance in the scheme. Carradine presented Captain Hopestone with the customary decorated sword that symbolised his achievement. It was engraved with quotations, read out by the crier, and expressed the thanks of a grateful township. Percy Carmady spoke briefly of his pleasure at being able to return to the sea.

The bands combined in a martial air. Captain Hopestone, wearing his new sword, marched with Carmady to join the ship. As the pair approached, Carmady touched his tricorn hat to Mehala. She took a pace forward.

'Mr Carmady. May we wish you safety and success?'

'Thank you, Mehala,' he replied, eyes shining with eagerness. 'This is a most felicitous dawn for me.'

'You deserve it, sir.' She indicated Nath. 'Here is one who is sick for the whilst, but who wants to go on board a great ship like your *Sealands* some day.'

Hopestone was impatiently checking his watch, gauging the tide and the growing fleet of small craft in the harbour. Percy gave him a smile of apology and came to reach out a hand to Nath, who took it shyly.

'Percy Carmady, Master Nath, late of His Majesty's navy, at your service.'

'Sir,' Nath said. They shook hands.

'I promise you will come with me.' Percy saw the caution in Mehala's eyes. 'When you are older.'

'Thank you, sir.'

'Safe voyage, Mr Carmady,' Ven said.

'I had hoped you would sail as our surgeon, Doctor.'

'My duties lie here, Mr Carmady, but thank you.'

'Could you have sailed, Doctor Ven?' Nath cried as the two went to board.

'Me? Never!' Ven shivered. 'I would be terrified crossing the harbour in a wherry, Nath!'

Mehala bent to Nath. 'Do not listen to him. He once rescued a seaman in a dreadful storm, Nath, when all the seafarers were too afeared!'

'Did you?' Nath's eyes were round in awe. Clement listened, wondering where truth lay.

'Women talk too much, Nath,' Ven said, red with embarrassment. Another reason for discomfiture was that Reverend Baring approached, prayer book in hand. With him was Euterpe.

The crowd jostled and crowded about the wharf, loud with excitement. Ven gestured to Clement to help him with the handcart, and they began to make their way towards the higher ground to gain a vantage point. There was no means of avoiding the cleric on the narrow harbour wall. To ignore him would have given offence. Ven raised his castor and bade a good morning, echoed by Nath, Clement and Mehala. Reverend Baring ignored them but Euterpe, pink from anxiety, replied with civility. Mehala noticed with annoyance that Euterpe's look was reserved for Ven alone, but mercifully they were soon past.

Clement scotched the handcart as the seamen began to make ready. There was much abuse of the harbour craft by bystanders and the officers of the *Sealands*.

It was then that Mehala heard her name called from a landau by the end of the mole.

'Is it not Mehala, Mistress Rebow as was?'

Mehala did not answer, nor did she look in that direction. Ven saw a lady and gentleman in elegant attire seated in an ornate carriage. Melissa and Bram Yale waved, angrily determined to provoke Mehala. Mehala pointedly ignored them.

'The seamen chant', she was explaining evenly to Nath, 'to keep in time, not from merriment. So they ensure maximum effort, when all hoist or pull together as one.'

Ven was interested. He would have asked for more details, but the grand lady beckoned him imperiously.

'You there! Yes, you, man! Come here!'

He doffed his hat, glancing doubtfully from Mehala to the landau. Several gentry were gathered about the vehicle, drinking as their servants offered sweetmeats and savouries among the carriages. Their conversation died away at the lady's shrill insistence. Mehala ignored her.

'Good morning, m'lady!' Ven replaced his hat, and made a pretence of tucking Nath's blankets round him against the breeze.

The silence grew. People's attention moved from the activities on board the *Sealands*. Clement and Nath were unaware, content with the spectacle. Reverend Baring began his prayer, and all hats were doffed. It was a merciful excuse. Ven removed his hat and stood quietly.

'You there!' The lady's bleat became shriller. 'Damn me if the servant does not share the harlot's deafness!'

Mehala exhaled as she came to a decision. She touched Ven's arm in apology and walked to the landau. Ven muttered to Clement that he would be back in a moment, and stepped out with her. The gentry fell silent as she halted, smiling, within a yard of the landau.

'No, Ven,' she said calmly, 'I see I am mistaken. This carriage is not one of *my* six vehicles purloined by Bram and Melissa Yale from *my* coach houses on *my* estates.'

'Of all the –'

Mehala spoke on in a mild conversational tone in spite of the shocked gasps from the company. 'It must be stolen from elsewhere, if I identify this skirt-lifting pair aright!'

The two occupants went pale, the gentleman rising in fury at the mortal insult. Mehala gave a casual inclination of her head to the frozen gentry.

'Good morning. You have my sympathy. These celebrations have foisted two reprobates on you.' She was sure of herself, inspecting the woman's dress and the horses.

'Have her taken in charge!' Yale shouted in apoplectic rage over his wife's screech. 'By God, Mehala, I shall horsewhip that oaf of yours, then I shall –'

'Let me see.' Mehala inspected them with theatrical thoughtfulness, finger on her chin. 'No, her dress is not mine, though it *does* resemble an old clementine rag I threw out a year ago! I expect this nightgowner trimmed the chantilly lace to sell on her rounds.'

Even Ven saw the depth of that insult, for the silk gauze called clementine was only ever used nowadays for bonnet linings. Distressed, he tried to lead her away. 'Mehala, please . . .'

'While I am here, dearest Ven,' Mehala continued as Bram Yale made to descend in blind anger, 'I think I recognise these horses. I swear they were among the other nineteen stolen from my Red Hall herds by these liars Bram and Melissa Yale!'

'I shall kill the brute!' Yale was spluttering.

'But no, I see I have made a mistake.' Mehala purred, stepping past Ven towards the horses. 'La Yale never wears any lace other than large-figure guipure gimp or poor-wife's filet! In any event, honourable Sealandings gentry would *never* associate with such thieves as the Yales.' She smiled impishly at Ven. He was staring at the ground. 'Bram Yale begged me to associate with him, Ven dearest. Can you imagine? His account of his own doxy's inadequacies – well known in the Tendring Hundred, for she peddles them there on the rare occasions she is not trolling them on other pavements – was explicit.'

Melissa Yale glared in speechless pallor at her husband, who made an appalled gesture of bafflement and innocence.

'Mehala, come away now.' Ven took her hand firmly in his.

'Gentlemen!' Mehala was alongside the coachman now. 'Count your sovereigns when such cutpurses come close! You ladies know only too well what *you* must watch!'

'Call the constable!' the Yales were yelling.

Mehala looked up at the coachman, and flicked a pebble at the offside horse's haunch, crying, 'Guard your reins, Hartnell!'

The coachman took hold in the nick of time. The horse shot a pace forward, but was instantly dragged to a stand by the weight of the nearside horse which then was frightened into action. Both reared, neighing, as Hartnell fought to haul both in. Ladies cried in alarm as other horses were disturbed. The agitation spread swiftly among the carriages, the coachmen calling their own calming words and struggling to calm the tumult.

Yale had fallen on to his wife as the carriage shot forward. He struggled erect. The distraught Melissa was screeching.

'Come, Ven,' Mehala said quietly as order was restored. The local gentry were withdrawing from the Yales, exchanging glances. 'We have our charges to see to.'

They returned to the handcart. Down below, the *Sealands* was already moving. Open water already reflected the early sun between the ship's side and land, a longboat pulling the ship from her mooring. Both boys were enthralled.

'Mehala?' Ven did not know what to say.

'Do not be cross, dearest.' She kept her face towards the harbour. 'I did not call you "husband" to prevent his challenging you to a duel. He would have had that right. I let them believe Melissa, that you were my servant.'

'Were they true?'

She was serene. He was astonished. A person could be hanged for slander. 'Most of them, yes. Those horses were not mine, actually. Theft is inevitable, once authority departs without heirs to take possession.'

'And the . . . ?'

'Yes. He asked me for certain favours.' She smiled. 'You alone know how far his advances carried him, or any other man.'

He hushed her, pursing his lips to warn her of the nearness of the two children. She grimaced in coquettish reply, making him look away. She took his arm. The bands struck up a bewildering variety of melodies. Ven was amazed by Mehala's quicksilver vivacity. She was laughing with a child's immediacy at the antics on the wharfside, so soon after such a terrible scene among the gentry. One band had struck up the famed *Shropshire Rounds* hornpipe in honour of the crew, but the other band, hired from Maidborough, had already started on *Kemp's Jig*. Delighted bystanders joined in the old dance. It was through Sealandings that Kemp the performer had danced the jig, all the way from London to Norwich, years and years ago.

'See the elbow pipers!' Nath cried, clapping as jugglers swelled the surging crowd. 'Everyone is laughing, Ven!'

'A brave sight, Nath!'

'Look! They are a-fight!' Clement shouted, laughing so hard at the musical squabble that he almost collapsed.

Wandering players were moving among the crowds. Ven could distinguish at least four other melodies. Several groups had started up morris dances. Mehala laughed all the more as two musicians led their morris dancers round Euterpe and Reverend Baring to the old tune, *The Parson's Farewell*, making eyes mischievously at

Euterpe and kicking their feet at the glowering rector. Ven slowly unbent and let his amusement grow, but only when he saw that Euterpe was having to hold back her own shy laughter at the prancing mummers.

'Hear what they play, Ven?' Nath was laughing excitedly, clapping in time. 'My favourite!'

'*The Dressed Ship*,' Mehala said, encouraging Ven to clap in time. 'A lovely air, to praise *Sealands*!'

Nath's eyes were shining. He caught hold of Ven's hand. 'Could there ever be a finer morning, Ven? Could there?'

'Never!' Ven clapped with Nath as the bands competed more fiercely. The crowds formed separate groups of supporting dancers. The whole concourse was one joyous mass of noise and celebration. Already one rowdy team of farm labourers was bellowing out the *We Wonnot Goo Home Till Morning* chant, and the casked beer was starting to flow.

They watched as the ship glided from the harbour between the light pillars at the ends of the moles. Thunderous shouts and cheers sounded as her first sail cracked and filled. *Sealands* drew slowly away from land out to sea. As if in omen, the sun spilled across Sealandings Bay, evoking further cries as the gold light gilded the spreading sails.

'Beautiful!'

Ven looked, and found Mehala's eyes filled with tears. 'She truly is, Mehala.'

She grasped his hands, swung to him with a face brimming with eagerness and hope. 'Dearest Ven. For once, let us expect the brightest and best! Let us praise the superb things in life! Let this day become a brilliant memory, a promise for magic and wonder for all our lives!'

'Very well,' he said, not quite knowing how to respond.

'Yes, Ven!' Clement cried out. He, like Nath, abandoned all reticence, infected by Mehala's gaiety.

'Yes, Ven!' Nath exclaimed. 'Let us see the . . .' he stumbled on the word, 'the *dazzlement* of it all!'

'For once, Ven!' Mehala danced round, leaning back, her hair shining loose in the sun as she swung. Her bonnet flew off, but she did not stop. Ven found himself laughing, pulled round and round, having to lean back, his feet moving in time. 'Today, darling, we will not think of hardships or sorrows! Today is the day of delights!'

He was swept along in the happiness. Together he and Mehala danced, the boys clapping, the crowds dancing and singing.

'Scandalous!' Sylvia Newborough said, watching.

'Was ever a lady so disgraced?' Brillianta Astell concurred. She had no illusions about Melissa Yale, or her wealthy husband Bram. But with such important backers of the Baltic scheme it was well to seem as offended as they. Meanwhile, she would store Mehala's insults away for coffee-tastings.

Mercy Carmady was in the same carriage, beside Ralph Chauncey, but said nothing. Her pride and sadness at her brother's departure amid such celebrations were tempered by the distress she felt at Mehala's battle with Mistress Yale. There was no doubt in her mind; the lady deserved to be trounced. Such a wanton, abuseful attitude to Mehala was uncalled for, but ladies need not be so outrageous before assembled gentlemen.

Mercy watched Ven dance. He moved awkwardly, and with a certain shyness. Clearly he had been mortified by the exchange between Mehala and Melissa Yale, endearingly so. But now the girl lifted his spirits by her own exuberance, moderating her own pretty dancing to match his faulty paces. She found herself fascinated by Mehala. Was it so resolute, this famed conviction of hers, that bore her up in spite of all opponents? She fought spiritedly against the Church, ignored Carmichael's ban from St Edmund's, and stayed faithful when she was desired by so many powerful men.

Envy should teach me something, Mercy told herself as gunfire rumbled out on the bay. Shouts arose and hats went aloft. The Customs frigate *Hunter* on the horizon had fired a salute to the departing *Sealands*. All dancing and music stopped momentarily in the hullabuloo. In that instant, Mercy saw Ven's expression. He was perhaps some thirty yards away from Chauncey's carriage. He seemed overcome with sadness, an ineradicable sorrow that he was trying to conceal from the sick boy waving at the sailing ship. Was Mehala truly aware of the depths in her man?

Her glance at Mehala just caught her turning away. Mercy blushed, trapped in her inspection of the little group. Mehala was as astute as she appeared, in perceiving the motives of others.

'If you please, Miss Mercy,' Ralph Chauncey intoned. The spindly cleric gave a cadaverous smile, pious beyond tolerance. 'Shall we pray for the deliverance of *Sealands* from the perils of the sea, and her safe return with prosperity for the Sealandings Hundred.'

'Yes, of course, Reverend Chauncey.'

He lowered his head obsequiously. 'Let us pray . . .' Several of the gentry and their ladies reluctantly bowed their heads. The solemn prayer he intoned was at odds with the resumption of the dancing and jollity on the wharf.

Mercy glanced under her calash at Mehala's group. It too had resumed dancing. The sick boy was pretending to play imaginary elbow pipes. Ven was laughing, determined in his clumsy capering at the morris, setting them laughing all the more. *The boy is dying*, she suddenly realised with a shock, *and Ven Carmichael knows it*. What courage Mehala must have, she thought in wonderment, to ally herself with a penniless doctor with no prospects! And how weak the woman who, loving a man, failed to claim him when every passing minute lessened her opportunity to put a final seal on the acquaintanceship.

Ralph Chauncey droned his prayer to an end. Thankfully she raised her head. Brillianta Astell was trying to send her mute signals to occupy Ralph, today as ever Brillianta's guardian, while she changed company. Carradine was approaching on foot with Charles Golding, and with Sylvia Newborough and her constant companion George Godrell. A strange gentleman was with them, tall and effete. He wore an elaborate frock coat with a fashion waist, and sported double-strap cossacks of slender design.

She ignored Brillianta's eyebrow play and decided herself to alight, as if to welcome Sylvia Newborough but with the purpose of compelling an introduction to the newcomer. Golding did the courtesies, dealing with the ladies as they were encountered.

'Miss Carmady, might I have the honour to introduce Doctor Septon Peveril?'

Mercy accepted the man's salute, with relief. She would at last be able to give Henry Hunterfield some news.

'May I inquire', she asked, 'if you, sir, are the Doctor Peveril who is held in such high esteem by the Royal Family? The whole of London has heard your medical reputation!'

'Too kind, Miss Carmady.' Peveril's eyes were on the carnival. He was not too preoccupied to notice the sombre figure of Ralph Chauncey, and added, 'I must moderate your kind observation. As the redoubtable Ambrose Pare said, I treat them but God alone heals!'

'Amen, sir,' Ralph said, coming forward. 'Ralph Chauncey, at your service. How reassuring to hear an eminent doctor express sacred conviction!' He glared down the hard to where Carmichael pranced by the handcart. 'I hope, sir, that you will influence others in your profession!'

Peveril could not take his eyes from Carmichael and Mehala. He leaned towards George Godrell. 'Is that . . .?'

Godrell said heavily, 'One and the same.'

'And as ever was!' Peveril's smile chilled Mercy.

'Do I understand you to have the acquaintanceship of Doctor Carmichael?' she asked with surprise.

'No longer,' Peveril said coldly. 'I may soon have the opportunity of correcting any familiarity that man may have claimed.'

In spite of the growing warmth of the sun and the lessening breeze, Mercy felt cold. She knew that Hunterfield had lately summoned an exalted physician from London to seek advice about news that troubled him, and had a strong premonition that Septon Peveril was that doctor.

On the wharfside, Nath was fast tiring. Ven decided to take them all off home.

'Oh, one minute more, Doctor Ven!'

Clement too begged a reprieve. Ven relented, flopping down breathlessly on the stones.

'Very well, the pair of you. One minute only!'

'Ven.' Mehala came to sit near him, sinking to the ground with an easy movement. She was so in command that it was a wonder to him that . . . Something she said caught his attention.

'What did you say, Mehala?' He surely must have misheard.

She checked that the boys' fullest attention was engaged by the departing ship before repeating her question in the same careful voice. 'Will you marry me?'

'Marry?' He almost gaped. 'But . . .'

Her colour was high. 'In church, by a rector. Before, we married ourselves. This time it will be sanctified by sacrament, valid in a way no one can gainsay.'

'I am excommunicated by Reverend Baring!'

'Not married by him, Ven. By a rector from elsewhere.'

'Will one come?'

'He will, Ven. He is known to me. A marriage licence can be taken out quickly. There need be no delay.'

Ven stared about in bewilderment. 'Where?' He realised his questions must seem prevarication, and made a hasty compliance. 'Yes, Mehala. I will. Providing that it does not lead you into more trouble than our last wedding!'

'Thank you, Ven.' She hesitated before going on. 'We already have our own chapel, the ruined one in Shalamar. It can be scrubbed, decorated. I have known Reverend Dakins in the south since my girlhood.'

'Must we not *own* Shalamar, for a consecrated private chapel to be used for a wedding?'

'Yes.' She smiled. 'I have a confession, Ven. The parson is already on his way to the Donkey and Buskin.'

'And what of Reverend Baring?'

'He is powerless against a bishop's licence.'

'When, Mehala?' He frowned at the children, and mouthed rather than spoke. 'It must be soon, if at all. You understand?'

'Yes, Ven. I plan for tomorrow. Forgive my immodesty.'

'Then so be it.' He reached out a hand and touched her cheek, then sprang to his feet. 'Come, boys. Home it is!'

'Oh, Ven!' Clement cried. 'Just one more minute!'

'No,' he said firmly. 'Tomorrow will be a long day.'

43

THE WEST WITHDRAWING-ROOM at Lorne House was the most agreeable, Aunt Faith always thought. The morning coffee-tasting was to be held there. Several varieties of the substance were to be brewed after fresh roasting. The gentlemen were excluded.

Tabitha Hunterfield was screaming inside as she descended the wide staircase, preparing herself for the utterly useless morning. She paused on the lowest step, almost weeping in impotent rage. Who wanted a bevy of hateful women, for God's sake? She wanted manhandling, the feral bestiality of someone like Carradine. She wanted her body ravished, and to ravish in her turn. She craved depravity. She glared about the hall, its marble flooring, the elegant marble patterns, the rich Normandy tapestries, the furniture from fabulous London makers, and felt stifled by the genteel world it represented. It was meant to reassure, impose, awe. Instead, it was a vast, endless tomb encircling her body, soul, mind, desires.

Light chatter of the guests wafted into the hall as somebody passed through a doorway. An attending-maid's footfalls receded down the servant corridor towards the kitchens. Another door tapped softly on the eardrums. The quiet of Lorne House was restored. This endless peace deceived. It was nothing less than a nunnery.

The women in the fisher cottages were better off. When their husbands returned from the North Sea, stinking and sex-laden, the women could strip them, wash their bodies, draw them 'naked-bed', as she had heard servants express conjugality . . . After that, Tabitha thought in impotent rage, my knowledge gives out. She was more ignorant of sex than any servant girl. She, who held the chatelaine at Lorne, was kept forcibly innocent. It was enough to drive her into the arms of any man who asked her favours. There again, she stormed inwardly. *Favours!* What a feeble word! Surely it must be something more violent, with savagery in the act? She had seen farm beasts couple, once by accident witnessed a stallion penetrating a compliant mare with great shuddering thrusts while its teeth gnawed the female's mane. Dear God, she thought, moaning audibly. *Favours* described coloured ribbons at a political husting . . .

'Keep calm, Tabitha, and join the guests.' The old lady's black dress rustled as she descended the stairs.

Tabitha had not heard her approach. 'Yes, Aunt Faith.'

'Try for graciousness, miss. It conveys a bad impression when the hostess *smoulders!*'

'Yes, Aunt Faith.'

'And creates in others a sense of superfluity. They might be essential to your wellbeing.'

Tabitha's reflex irritation lessened. She glanced at the old lady as she took her arm for support. 'You mean there is . . .' she glanced at the doors leading off the hall, '. . . expectation?'

Her aunt's lavender scent was overwhelming. She moved in clouds of fragrance. Her Honiton lace bertha must have been soaked in the Norfolk oil, Tabitha thought. How much longer before that stigma of old age heralds my own senility? And never to have lived at all!

'What expectation, child?'

Child! 'A matchmake, of some lady and a gentleman?'

The old lady paused to adjust her matching muffetees. 'Do not obfuscate, Tabitha. The servants are outwith earshot. If you mean am I about to recommend some lady to Henry's attention, you are right. That is the purpose of the day.' Her old eyes disconcerted Tabitha. 'To know precisely whether she is being overheard is a lady's first duty. Cultivate concealment, Tabitha. The brawling fish-sellers on the wharf learn that at their mothers' knees.'

Tabitha could have struck the grim old bat. 'I am Mistress of Lorne, Aunt Faith! Why was I not told the purpose of this gathering?'

'Because you *needed* to be told, Miss Hunterfield!' When Tabitha would have walked on, Lady Faith remained motionless. 'It will soon come. There are more eligible gentlemen about Sealandings than ever now.'

'When?' Tabitha exclaimed bitterly. 'Everything is Henry!'

'Tabitha! Join the tasting party immediately, and pretend you are not in a silly sulk!'

'Wait! Aunt Faith!'

Tabitha recoiled at the old lady's sudden glare. 'Silence, you ignorant chit! Keep your place! If you do not radiate charm to the company, Miss Hunterfield, you shall suffer!'

Tabitha felt her cheeks pale. This was insufferable. Nominally the principal lady, and rebuked by a crone.

'What do I hear, Tabitha Hunterfield?' Lady Faith demanded, refusing to budge.

'Yes, Aunt Faith.'

Only then would she move, her stick tapping on the marble flooring, leaning with unneccessary heaviness on her niece's arm. Tabitha felt a murderous urge come over her, hating every rasping breath taken by her determined aunt. Surely she had outlived her stay? In Sealandings, if not on earth. Had she no duties in Gloucester?

Crane emerged as they approached, and opened the withdrawing-room doors. A chorus of greetings arose. Tabitha forced a mechanical smile. Two ladies hurried forward with cries of welcome, Brillianta Astell and her friend Fenella Jepherson from Pakefield. Tabitha thankfully relinquished the dowager. Aunt Faith had assembled a colourful company. Aunt Faith herself had written invitations to the whole world, in quite the most humiliating fashion.

As the ladies settled, Tabitha registered the principals. Some were hangers-on, with the occasional married lady here. They were mere leaven in the bread, not the substance. And Sir Henry Hunterfield was at once the dinner and the eventual diner. Tabitha reassessed her own position after her scalding reprimand. Henry was *her* brother, not Aunt Faith's. Henry was *her* responsibility. Henry was within *her* gift. She herself would assess the ladies here, she decided in concealed fury. Aunt Faith could dodder back to the West Country.

Fenella Jepherson was a surprise. Her Pakefield family bred boys for military life, and she was the lone daughter of the established east coast family. No great beauty, with a candid nature that Tabitha disliked, Tabitha counted her disordered, with no sense of fashion. Today's disaster was an old-fashioned levite gown with a wholly wrong neckline with inadequate lace and leg-of-mutton sleeves that pointed up the rest of the error. Tabitha was mildly surprised that Mercy Carmady and Fenella were on friendly terms, but guessed Mercy's brother was possibly the cause. Mercy could be dismissed. She saw Aunt Faith looking for Crane, and took charge.

'I apologise for my lateness,' she said brightly. 'Duties held me. I just *know* Miss Carmady deputised perfectly! Now I can devote the whole morning to the new coffees. I insist that we *all* decide!'

She signalled to Crane, who supervised the distribution of the range tables. A senior maid had seven ground-floor maids, and a further four to see to the preserves, breads, the assortments of biscuits, cakes, creams, arranged under cover on the line side-boards and tables. Tabitha had not actually inspected the offerings, for mundanities bored her. She knew that Crane would continue Lydia's tradition. Two tables for a variety of trifles, with a centre piece of King Charles the Second's orange jellies, syllabubs and custards separate. Tables were set apart with casual anthemion chairs by the wall carrying the whim-whams, creams, flummeries and other assorted puddings and sweets.

The ladies chattered about the coffees. Tabitha put on her best manner under Aunt Faith's eagle eye. She smiled at the hateful Miss Newborough, who for once did not look too much of a mess, though her bright blue redingote was over-fussy with splayed front buttons down to the hem, screaming for attention in creamy white that drained all hues from the others. She had brought a lute which she expected to be begged to play. Well, she could dawdle in silence today. Tabitha addressed herself to Fenella Jepherson, asking about the journey from Pakefield.

'Perfectly splendid, Miss Hunterfield!' Fenella's candour made her add, 'But I dread those phaetons this far along the coast. The roads hereabouts are worse than ours!'

'Indeed,' Tabitha said, Fenella falling swiftly in her esteem. '*So* advanced, the rural pastures near Southwold and Lowestoft, are they?'

The other refused to notice the sarcasm. 'Yes, more commerce, I think. You mention Southwold. Father's brother lives on the isle. His churchwardens administered a Sealandings matter lately.'

'How can that be? We are many miles from there.'

'You have one Mehala here, do you not?' Silence spread through the room, talk dying. 'One Rebow was buried in Southwold. His widow Mehala lives in Sealandings, I believe. All sorts of tales abound about her. Documents went to your wonderful brother here at Lorne,'

'Indeed?' Tabitha, conscious of the ladies' silence, lost control. 'It is said that she lives as a doctor's servant, though she inherits –'

'How *is* Mr Jepherson?' Aunt Faith asked. 'I disapprove of his return to Pakefield. Those windmills, such draughts! And those tiresome little boys up to mischief!'

Fenella laughed openly, Mercy Carmady being amused with her. 'No little boys, Lady Faith. Seven grown men, four in regiments. And the youngest aiming for a bishopric!'

'Men's mischief disguised, Fenella! The discerning lady merely recognises it!'

'Though she might well hide the fact!' Brillianta remarked, to general laughter. 'Look at the events at Carradine Manor!'

'What events?' Georgina Bosworth's air of girlish breathlessness made her seem more agitated than she was. For all that, an impossibly heavy ruby ring announced her recent betrothal to a Midlander who owned extensive coal lands.

'You must have heard, Georgina! Our great ship *Sealands*! Carradine has established massive commerce!'

'To everybody's benefit,' Aunt Faith added drily.

'He is to be admired,' Fenella observed. 'Not long ago he was destitute from gambling. Now, his star is a comet.'

'They say he will enter Parliament.'

Tabitha angrily listened to the tittle-tattle, almost beside herself with jealousy. Fenella Jepherson was at ease. She would soon return to a household where her brothers would receive visiting officers from regiments all over the kingdom. Even Mercy Carmady was not isolated, for her brother had friends and naval officers along the entire seaboard. Brillianta's father Sir Edward was famous for his racing stables, frequently visited by London nobility.

It was then that the notion came to her crystal clear. It was like a vision. These others, even the breathy Georgina Bosworth giggling behind her ruby, had somehow taken command of their own lives. They had struck out! The tardy one was Tabitha Hunterfield, none other.

'Now, ladies,' she called, ignoring Aunt Faith's sudden mute interrogation. 'We all know that the recent reduction of import duty on the Coffea fruit from British plantations in 1825 – from a shilling to sixpence per pound weight – encourages use of this wondrous beverage! And that the lowering of duty on East Indies Coffea to ninepence, with foreign coffee only dutiable at a shilling and threepence, adds to the pleasure! The falling price – four pounds a hundredweight of Jamaica Coffea fruits this year – will make us all imbibers!'

'Not to mention a ready market for export,' the blunt Fenella added. 'Twenty-nine million pounds weight re-exported last year, my brother tells me. The Netherlands and the Baltic ports absorb the majority! Your Carradine is a visionary!'

'Therefore,' Tabitha decreed to silence the pest Fenella, 'I have arranged several different types of the Coffea today!'

Aunt Faith was waiting with a sardonic look. It was customary at this point for the hostess to announce the list of ground coffees in order. She knew that Tabitha had no idea which were to be offered.

'Ladies, you also know well that the Kingstons, the Mocas, the Hadie, the Bulgosa, and others, have distinctive flavours. This morning, the tasting is a quest! We must each guess which coffee originates where!'

The ladies clapped at this novelty. Fenella raised an objection.

'But you already know, Tabitha, so are better informed!'

'Not so, Fenella,' Tabitha replied sweetly. 'I have resisted the temptation to discover the varieties beforehand. My dear Aunt Faith can testify to that! Now, ladies, all the bean fruits are a correct twelvemonth in age, no longer! And none has been roasted in that terrible steam-fountain machine they are experimenting with in London. All have been made by my coffee maid's own slow pounding, not ground fine in mortars. And no decoction has been clarified by the addition of egg-white or fish-skin.'

She ignored Aunt Faith's wry smile at her neat evasion. From now on she would be her own mistress. She would reach for her first lover, and take him. There could be nobody but Carradine.

The coming success of the *Sealands* venture made speed imperative. Already she had tarried far too long. Henry would now find his sister decisive and purposeful in advancing her own cause, instead of everyone else's. She would enter adulthood in a leap.

Smiling, she surveyed her rivals as the coffees were poured. She had a certain difficulty in avoiding Aunt Faith's quizzical gaze, but a greater in concealing her excitement at thoughts of Carradine.

44

NATH SUFFERED THAT night. Restless and feverish, he needed sponging to cool him. The willow bark extracts lessened the pain for a time, but set his ears ringing. Ven recognised the warning signs, and resorted to laudanum at two in the morning. Nath's shouting at some imagined or remembered sweep-master were so grievous that they wakened Barbara's baby and frightened Clement, but mercifully he soon responded to the laudanum and slept fitfully.

A cool rain began about three. Ven dozed beside the truckle bed by the hearth's inglenook. Mehala retired on Ven's instruction, to be ready for the morning. She would assume responsibility for him while Ven would sleep for two hours, until the day's sick began to arrive. Clement and Rosie slept on their own pallets elsewhere.

By dawn, Shalamar was quiet. Mehala lay awake listening to the hiss of the falling rain. It trickled in the guttering, splashing where the earthenware pipings had failed. She heard the two vigorous cascades at the end of the gabled roofs where nests, lichens, and the neglect of years had collapsed the rotting roof.

She waited for Ven's summons for poor Nath. The swiftness of Clement's recovery was at shaming odds with Nath's steep decline. He would die soon, as his tumour spread through his exhausted body. The lucid glimpses of the child he might have been were a joy. She could sense Ven's grief at the tragedy of Nath's state. She felt responsible in a way she never had, being Ven's apprentice. His teaching, his limited knowledge, the ritualistic therapies, the inadequacy of drugs, brought a new understanding of the shame Ven felt.

She was committed to him, and to her course. After the coming day, she was his woman for ever. Recognised by all human laws, and divine laws churches invented. She was to be his, declared openly. And he hers. Such possession was not slavery, except to love. It was not subjection, except to the most beautiful ideal. She had wanted this day. So had Ven, with his customary puzzlement and self-deprecation, the curious mistrust that was his hallmark.

The rain increased to torrential downpour. By the fourth hour before dawn, the waterfall in the end rooms of the upper west wing had become a constant rumble. She smiled. Her wedding day, and poor Shalamar was falling into decay to welcome it! Hold on, poor home, she told it silently, listening to the rain driving on the windows. Soon will come whole teams of artisans, to build you anew. Dear house, the permanent residence of Doctor Carmichael and his bride, you will shine as you did in olden days! Your trees and lawns will be an emblem of the ordered beauty within your doors. Skilled men will bring the grey slates from Derbyshire, the lovely, warm purple, blue and yellow slates from the Isle of Eusdale in the Hebrides of North Britain . . .

Dozing, she came to with a start, and saw by the constant grey edging her makeshift curtaining that she can only have slept a few minutes. Sleepily, she struck the steel and flint from her tinderbox onto the cotton wadding, and blew gently as the spark caught like a glow worm in web skein. It flamed at the third attempt – an excellent omen on so damp a night – and ignited her night candle. She wanted to go down and see Ven.

Shalamar would have new wooden flooring, so Nath would not be troubled by noise. On the principles enunciated recently by the admirable Mr Finlayson, she would have an outer terrace in the open air; wooden paving in hexagonal patterns, each flag six to eight inches in diameter, grooved against slipperiness and retention of damp, and laid down on granite underbeds. Would the fir surfaces need to be kyanised against rot? Mr Finlayson's experiment proved that the wooden pavings he advocated for London wore less than granite when subjected to pedestrians. Of course, the tests done on the capital's speedy tramways along Commercial Road proved that the horse trams . . .

She woke suddenly, saw her hourglass set beside the candle was barely an inch above its turkshead collar, and tutted at her alarm. Lying back, her mind drifted. A housewife in these modern times needed constant self-education to manage her household. She would make Shalamar a palace for Ven to work in. Nath and

Clement – Rosie too, until her own wedding – would have a home where their young lives could flower.

And Ven's own children, that she would bear.

She would order Staffordshire stone slabs to rebuild ground floors fallen into cellars. Simple to deliver, from the fine network of canals about the Midland quarries. Rowley ragstone flags were much admired by ladies for cellar floors, being very pure basalt that outcropped south-east of Dudley. It paved growing towns like Birmingham . . .

A knock sounded. Barbara Tyll looked in, softly calling.

'Mehala? It is six of the morning! And your day.'

'Six?' Mehala swung her feet out of bed so quickly she felt dizzy and had to freeze until her head cleared. 'It cannot be, Barbara!'

'Rosie and I have unbanked the kitchen fire. The porridge is already cooked. Ven is outside at his ablutions. He and Rosie have washed Nath and seen to him.' She entered carrying the sleeping babe on her arm. 'Two gentlemen sent messages, Mehala.' She was beaming excitedly. 'One is Reverend Dakins, at the Donkey and Buskin overnight. The other gentleman is Mr Willoughby from Maidborough. Reverend Dakins will be here shortly. Nath breakfasted on bacon, quenelles and fruit. He will be resplendent in his new shirt and cravat!'

'Reverend is on his way? Heaven preserve me!'

'Be still, Mehala! All is ready. I, with young Radcliffe here, decorated the chapel. Clement has proved a tower of strength. He is waiting on Mr Willoughby at the tavern.'

'Oh, my stars, Barbara! You should have wakened me!'

'I did, Mehala.' The older woman was businesslike. 'Rosie is heating your smoothing iron and whisking starch. The ruffles must be beeswaxed. Somebody forgot, in yesterday's excitement, the pot and wax for the ruffles to be fingered!'

Mehala felt helpless for the first time in her life. 'Barbara. I do not know where to start.'

The baby mewled, snuffled, clawed the air, then quietened. 'First, rise. Then have a bite to eat. Avoid seeing Ven until the wedding hour. And *no* glancing at him through glass beforehand. You know the superstition! Clement has already wedged back the two leaded glass doors as a precaution. Today you give vows. And vows given through glass lead to mortal undoing.'

'Yes, I remember.'

'I shall send Rosie up with tea, cake breads, and porridge.'

'I could not eat, Barbara.'

'You shall breakfast as usual, madam!' Barbara reprimanded sharply. 'You shall not have vapours from the green sickness at *this* stage! You will have what Rosie brings, or there is no going downstairs! You will be little use to your husband fainting about Shalamar! Ten minutes, be up and doing.'

'Yes, Barbara.'

'Meanwhile, I shall get his lordship here to sleep and be with you.' She touched Mehala's hair. 'You have earned your friends, Mehala. Accept them now.'

'Mr Willoughby?' Mehala asked.

'Clement will bring him. He has documents that must be handed to you in person. He begs leave to wait on you before eight o'clock, and says your instructions have been met to the letter.'

'Thank you, Barbara.' Mehala watched the door close.

That door was Shalamar's. Part of the place; as was the wall, the bed, the floorboards, the window with its shredding canvas cover, the panes, the rags stuffed in the gaping hole, the ceiling with its damp. Shalamar had changed possession, if the elderly agent's report was to be believed, even as the night rain had fallen. It was as if the night's deluge had attempted to wash out the celebrations of the previous day, of her proposal, of the glorious ship leaving for the eastern sea under heavens filled with exploding colour.

Shalamar even felt different. It was hers now, hers and Ven's. She looked about, marvelling, hoping that the message was true. The house seemed to understand. It welcomed the change, but that feeling would have to be judged when there was less excitement. One day in the near future, perhaps, when Ven was out and the day tranquil, she would move alone in the great old manor house and silently express her gratitude to the place. Certainly it was a house – no, *home* – to be loved as any dwelling had to be, which was to be loved *back*, in return. There was no doubt; a house had feelings.

A knock startled her. 'Mehala? I do not hear you stirring! Must I come in with a bird-scarer's rattle?'

'Yes, Barbara!' Mehala called, leaping into the day.

She met the old agent on the first floor landing by the east wing corridor.

'Mr Willoughby! It is good of you to come at such a time!'

'Mistress.' He made a grave bow. 'It is a better visit than one I well recall from a previous occasion!'

Mehala did not smile. She did not need to be reminded that Thalia De Foe had evicted Ven from Shalamar, and had destroyed her Floral Dial. The woman had wanted Shalamar for her lover Carradine, but had been baulked by her husband's anger at her infidelities.

'You sent messages, Mr Willoughby.'

'Indeed. Am I to transact the business here, Mistress?'

The courteous old gentleman needed some explanation. He was not to blame for past events. She relented.

'I am to be married today, hence the early hour.'

His crinkled visage warmed in a slow smile. 'I wish I had words to express my delight, mistress. This ancient dwelling needs such a lady. Too long it has remained neglected – through no fault of yours.' He undid the latchings on his leather carrying case and extracted a parchment. 'Here are the deeds, mistress, giving full titlement and possession of Shalamar to you in your maiden name. Witnessed by Tayspill, who was kind enough to ride to Maidborough a week ago.'

'Witnesses, Mr Willoughby?'

'The witnesses were selected by Mr Tayspill, and are known to Sir Henry Hunterfield. My master, Fellows De Foe, wishes me to express his felicitations to the Mistress of Shalamar.'

'I acknowledge his message.' Mehala was in no mood to accept. Had that gentleman been less concerned by London's Exchange, and more alive to the events within his own doors at Milton Hall, her life with Ven would have been a deal more peaceable. 'Mr Willoughby. Have all legalities been observed? Am I now in full possession for ever of Shalamar and its Sealandings estates?'

'Yes, Mistress. I have notified all proper authorities. Sir Henry himself has given his approval.'

'You hesitate, Mr Willoughby. Why?'

Downstairs somebody was knocking. She heard Clement's voice raised in excitement calling for Ven.

'Your sale of Red Hall, mistress.' The old agent sounded

envious. 'I had the pleasure of visiting Red Hall months ago, under less auspicious circumstances, of course.'

'And?'

He coughed discreetly behind his hand. 'Forgive me. Your sale of Red Hall and expenditure of the entire proceeds on Shalamar is of course your own wish. But you have changed, from the owner in full title of a profitable estate in the south, to the owner of a, dare I say, less than perfect estate in Sealandings.'

'You wish to caution me?' She smiled at his discomfiture.

'I would never presume! But to refurbish Shalamar will take a deal of expense, Mistress.'

'It will take much more than that.'

He looked blank. 'More, mistress?'

'Yes. It will take a lifetime.' She took the deeds from him. 'And that, please Heaven, I and my husband will have.'

He bowed in wry recognition. 'I offer my joyous felicitations, Mistress Carmichael, and my prayers.'

'Thank you, Mr Willoughby. Safe journey to Maidborough.'

Drawing away from the banisters, she remained until he had descended the staircase. She heard him greet a newcomer in the great hall, and smiled to hear the familiar voice of Reverend John Dakins, rector of Saint James the Great. Flustered as ever, his voice had mellowed since she last heard his sermons in the old church on Colchester's East Hill. His rather staccato speech made her realise why he had come. She coloured. From today her life would alter completely. She would be committed to being a different woman, and would enter a new existence: Ven's medical apprentice, eventually his partner as a doctor, for her life.

She heard Reverend Dakins greet Rosie. 'Well, Miss Rosie, perhaps you will conduct me to the chapel? There are fifty minutes, I believe . . . Yes.' His familiar chuckle sounded up the stairwell. 'No marrying before eight of the clock in the morning, by the 1604 marriage law, what? We must not be tardy, not be tardy, what?'

'No, Reverend,' from a breathless Rosie. Barbara Tyll welcomed him in more measured words.

'I have Mistress Mehala's names and her soon-to-be husband's on the bishop's certificate,' Reverend Dakins announced. 'All augurs well!'

Mehala thought, listening, I have bought Shalamar *before* my church marriage. Had I accepted the transferred deeds after, even by a single minute, I should have nullified Ven's influence over me. That was the trick of cunning Welsh brides, who slyly bought a pin from a bridesmaid on the way down the aisle after the ceremony, so rendering themselves secret masters of the marriage for ever.

The footsteps receded.

Mehala looked at the unopened parchment in her hand. She went to her room and sank slowly on the edge of her bed. She felt tears try her eyes, but resolutely held them. Another superstition. A bride weeping on her wedding day would cry for life.

She smoothed the surface of the parchment.

Ven was bringing love and learning. Her dowry would be love and Shalamar.

It was eight o'clock.

Mehala waited by the kitchen vestibule door with John Weaver, taverner of the Donkey and Buskin. He was a meticulous man. Several times he had told off the time on his large fob watch. Clement waited solemnly by in a new velvet frock coat. The taverner gave Mehala an oblique smile.

'A fair distance, Mehala,' he said gently. 'A minute to go!'

'Truly, John,' she said quietly. They stood awkwardly as if about to enter a ballroom rather than leave through a kitchen garden. 'Would you have believed we should be here as we are?'

He chuckled. 'Not when you were brought in half drownded! I thought you would not last a minute!'

'I am grateful, John, for your willingness to –'

'Shush, Mehala,' he said gruffly. 'I am pleased to give you away. Besides, Sarah would have made my life a misery!'

Mehala tried to smile. 'Must we go now?'

'A moment more, I think. Nellie sends her good wishes, before I forget.' Weaver grinned, sheepish. 'You remember the day you and she fought so savagely? I had never seen Sarah so put out in my life!'

Mehala almost laughed, feeling easier as she recalled the horrid battle in the kitchen. 'That made us good friends! How is she?'

'As ever.' He grimaced, unwilling to express disapproval on such a day. 'She still provides certain services for travellers. I do not know how to correct her deplorable willingness. It goes on in every tavern in the country, I suppose.'

'She saved me several times, not least with Mr Waite the North Briton.'

'He who was present at your duel with Aggie?'

'Indeed. His pistols, too, unless I misremember.'

The taverner called to Clement, who was playing with the cat and a string. 'You know what you must do, Clement?' he asked for the fourth time.

'Yes, Mr Weaver! I walk behind Mehala, and see the doors do not bang and trap the dress.'

'But first, after we step through the door?'

'I take the boiling kettle from the hob, and pour hot water all over the threshold over which Mehala has stepped, so that Rosie will be marrying Bartholomew soon after.'

'Clement!' Rosie exclaimed, her face scarlet.

John Weaver coughed lightly. 'No details, Master Wellins! Then?'

Clement, unabashed, counted points on his fingers. 'Replace the kettle. Follow as soon as may be, round the side of the house to the main door, through which we enter, me going last.'

'Have you not forgotten something?' Weaver asked.

'No, sir. The flat cake and cloth are already by the chapel door. Mistress Tyll put them there early.'

'Good.' The taverner slowly replaced his watch in his waistcoat fob, adjusted the chain, and gave a nod. 'We leave now.' He eyed Mehala gravely. 'I wish you every happiness and heavenly benevolence for ever, Mehala.'

She tried to thank him but her throat was dry. She mouthed an expression, and let him take her left arm through his right. She glimpsed Rosie waiting outside. The girl was pretty in a white redingote with her ribbons of sky blue to match the blue and white satin ribbons on Mehala's bouquet. She caught Rosie whispering the recitation, 'No red with white, no bridegroom in sight, no fallen bride flowers, come shine, no showers.' Silly customs, Mehala thought, fighting back tears. Clement rushed for the kettle, leaping the kitchen bench. Rosie took her position of bridesmaid seriously, and had invented the rhyme the previous evening. She had examined the flowers chosen in the bridal bouquet for the slightest sign of redness, red with white being notoriously bad omens, as would be any fallen flower, however beautiful.

Mehala stepped from the door onto the path. As she did, the sun shone fitfully, bringing a smile even from Weaver.

'Sunshine, Mehala!' Rosie cried, overjoyed. 'Quickly, your face! Turn your face to it!'

Mehala had already done so, mindful of the old adage. She wanted to obey the ancient precepts, for no other reason than their observance over the ages. She went with John Weaver, adjusting her pace to his. She had accepted Barbara's deference to the same old rhymes, hence the blue ribbon on her bouquet. 'Not just Lancashire,' Barbara had warned, 'not nowadays. Even great ladies like you now conform.'

Borrowed, the silver shawl pin from Barbara. Old, an ancient fragment of a golden link Clement found in the garden when clearing brambles, on a silk cord threaded by Nath and tied about her neck as a concealed pendant. New, a pair of white satin buckle shoes. And of course her wedding dress, a superb white Venetian needle lace of dense pattern over satin, with point d'Angleterre lace to hold the veil. Let others make what they will of her superstition. She had fed the cat with a morsel of fish this very morning, the bride's traditional duty before her wedding.

They entered the main door. Mehala felt suddenly stifled. Barbara was there in a fine velvet dress of midnight blue and a paler blue bonnet. The babe was in her arms. As they approached, their footsteps echoing strangely, Barbara bobbed a curtsey then followed with Rosie. The door slammed like a thunderclap, Clement calling his apologies as he scampered to catch up. John Weaver gave a grunt of irritation, but said nothing.

To Mehala the procession along the corridor from the hall seemed interminable. Her heart was pounding. The scent of freesias was overpowering. There was no organ music. The service would be unadorned by congregation, with no floral tributes from the parish, but that was only to be expected. The doors were ajar, as Clement promised, so she and John Weaver were able to look down the small chapel.

Chairs had been placed before the altar. She saw Reverend

Dakins. He had become slightly stouter with the passage of years, but smiled a broad greeting. The little gathering rose.

Ven was in his usual old jacket. Only lately had jackets proper come into general use. It was said that in fashionable London it was even being worn now as part of a gentleman's suit-of-clothes. Previously it was the stigma of the country labourer, postillion riders, and young apprentices who could not know any better. But among gentry the new jackets were expensively fashioned. She felt a sudden smoulder of anger, that she should be dressed in such costly finery while Ven wore his only set. The breeches were mended – she herself had repaired them almost to extinction – and his shoes were failed at the welts. She had heard Clement and Ven cleaning them the night before, with Nath advising and the pair of them bickering good-naturedly. She felt her eyes prick, but caught at herself. Ven was as he was.

Sarah Weaver was there, smiling and weeping, nodding good wishes. And to Mehala's pleasure Little Jane, tiny but in her best, and lost under an enormous blue bonnet, with a blue cardinal cloak showing that she must have walked from Bures House when the early rain was abating. Nath, with his bright eyes, was near Ven in his truckle. With Ven stood Bartholomew Hast, his attire muted in thoughtful deference to Ven's garments. Against the side wall, rising with the rest, was Matilda Gould, and with her Euterpe Baring. That both had come testified to their courage, the schoolteacher risking her livelihood by attending, and Euterpe her brother's righteous anger. With a shock she realised that here stood the only friends she had in Sealandings, with the exception of Hunterfield. The presence of Reverend Dakins was the result of her position as lately Mistress of Red Hall, and the influence of her status on the bishop.

Ven moved slightly as everyone rose, wanting to watch her approach down the aisle with John Weaver. But he desisted, wondering if it was the wrong thing to do. *Look, husband*, she wanted to call out, but could only smile at him as she came to stand alongside.

Reverend Dakins nodded, his old habit to inform himself that all was as should be, and began immediately, 'Dearly beloved, we are gathered together here in the sight of God and in the face of this congregation, to join together this man and this woman. . .'

It went in a dream. The giving away, John Weaver fumbling as he passed Mehala's hand to Ven and withdrew. He almost fell over Nath, but Clement was standing beside the truckle and warned him in time. The ring was new, from Veriker's the clockmaker, who had been able to contract a gold ring near Mehala's size to fit her third finger almost exactly. It was just at this moment that the baby Radcliff gave a piercing yell and began to cry, drawing murmurs of approbation from everybody. Even Reverend Dakins smiled at this, the most propitious of all omens during a marriage service.

'. . . and are not afraid with any amazement.'

Mehala lifted her veil and Ven placed his mouth on hers for a moment. It was different from their first married bussing, when in fury she had dragged Ven towards her before the appalled gaze of Reverend Baring and kissed him fiercely. They went slowly down the aisle amid congratulations, Little Jane and Euterpe Baring slipping ahead when they reached the door. John Weaver carried Nath in his arms.

At the chapel door Mehala paused for the white cloth to be placed upon her head and the flat cake brought by Rosie to be broken over her into small pieces. They avoided struggling for a piece, but managed to obtain some and eat it there and then. The baby's piece was eaten by his mother. And Mehala received the kiss of peace from them all in turn.

'I must here give my apologies,' Mehala announced during the retreat from the chapel. 'Only the kitchen is inhabitable, so there we shall have the wedding breakfast.'

'And I trust that Barbara has managed to keep the wedding cake intact!' Sarah Weaver's mock scolding was only partly in jest, for the bride would be betrayed if the slightest flaw or crack showed when she cut the cake.

'As soon as word of my cake gets about Sealandings, Mistress Weaver, you shall lose all custom! Everyone will beg to visit here.'

Reverend Dakins laughed at this. 'Ah, Mistress Tyll, here stands one who has enjoyed the hospitality of the Donkey and Buskin. I can testify to Mistress Weaver's excellent provisions!' Always a cleric who liked his food, he hurried ahead in almost unseemly haste.

Clement and Bartholomew went for the truckle bed. The taverner carried Nath in, conscious of Ven's glances at the boy.

Ven entered the kitchen awkward at the applause. Mehala was close to him and responded to every smile for him.

'Tell me, Barbara,' she asked, distracting attention from Ven's returned stutter, 'did you or did you not somehow prompt little Radcliff to cry during the service?'

'It was Radcliff's spontaneous wish, Mistress Carmichael, I promise.'

'Mehala,' Rosie asked in a secret whisper, when all were seated and the food was being uncovered, 'will you cast your shoe?'

'Yes, Rosie.'

'Thank you!' There was only Little Jane to compete for it, since Miss Euterpe Baring was unlikely to struggle for the prized emblem, and only Bartholomew and Clement at whom the fortunate girl could make a well-aimed shy, so implying betrothal. Little Jane caught the whisper, raised a fist in mock challenge, at which they all dissolved in laughter.

Mehala was worried when she saw Ven draw Reverend Dakins aside, but merely puzzled when the cleric glanced in Nath's direction as if making a judgement. Ven listened a moment, then returned to Mehala. He asked for attention.

'I thank you, our dear friends, for coming to our wedding,' he said haltingly. 'That is my first duty, and I appreciate the welcome you gave to our married state. My second is to say that our estimable Common Law lacks the Roman Caesars' custom called adoption. In that practice, any child may be taken by a married couple to be their own, for ever and ever.'

The company fell silent. John Weaver, strangely, was the first to realise Ven's intentions. He gave a great grin of approval, starting applause before being stayed by his wife to let Ven continue.

'However, a minor child may himself elect a guardian.' Ven looked at Reverend Dakins for guidance, who nodded pompous assent. 'Thus, the law is. I therefore invite Nath, Clement, and Rosie, if they wish, to join my . . . my wife and me, and become in effect our children. If they want, I shall ask you to be witnesses a second time today.'

John Weaver led the applause. Mehala did not cry a third time, especially not now, and held on to Ven's hand even during the customary presentation of the gift of knives to the bride from those who had stood for her, quickly returning a silver sixpence in symbolic payment for the gift to stave off misfortune. All superstitions mercifully had been observed, all omens successfully made propitious by custom.

45

To Alex Waite, London was incomprehensible and unbeliev-able. The mass — mess — of threat, disorder and ruffianry presented such a turmoil that he rested in a Ludgate tavern to collect his wits before moving on. He was used to pickpockets, so was easily able to slit the wrist of a 'foist', those pickpockets who used only their nimble fingers and disdained 'nips', rival thieves who used a knife, sharpened for good luck on the stones of a London church, and a rough segged thumb. There was a hierarchy among robbers. He left the ale house, feeling his pockets and wielding his swordstick to prove he was familiar with theft.

He walked the lopsided pavements, occasionally stumbling over the up-ended paving stones, watching out for beggars and the prostitutes in league with them. Bowling alleys and gaming houses were plentiful, the dark recesses clustered about with scrofulous children and vagabonds. Villainy was trade rather than tragedy. The drunkards were reckless and boastful of their achievements. Sedan chairs, the last of their kind, fared ill in the noisy concourse of carriages and people. Pedlars seemed unaffected by the laws on wandering traders, and tinkers and hawkers abounded.

Foul waters splashed from windows on to people struggling along thoroughfares. Touts tried to drag him forcibly into the alehouse doorways, only running when he slashed with his swordstick. Hardly a single figure seemed shaped aright. People and children were warped with rickets, deformed by injury, as if mangled by some great unseen engine of God before being cast into the street to fend for themselves in rags.

The 'ordinaries', common low eating houses, worsened as he pushed his way east by Saint Paul's. He struck away from the river to avoid the crowded nightmare by the docks. Several times, near the Guildhall, he had to use his stick to force importuning women and their attendant ruffians off the pavement. The carriages and waggons were as much a risk, the enormous haulage beasts and the wheels of vehicles threatening to crush him against walls and pavement bollards. The stench was fearsome, the smoke and dirt pestilential. He gagged and retched at the stink.

In many places he stopped, led down some detour by its seeming open appearance, only to realise the sordid reason for its apparent neglect. Pools of sewage lay stinking across the narrow alleys. Trickles of filth flowed steadily into cellars. Everywhere there were flies and the sulphurous stench of the thick ochreous air.

He trudged on, wary as any man crossing a moor. Gradually as he pressed eastwards he felt the first waft of air from Moorgate which, with the burial grounds near Bunhill Fields, promised eventual release from the mad drunken throngs. He thought wryly how London was imagined, as a great city, with elegant ladies, gallant gentlemen, wonderful carriages. Instead, it was one huge press of stews, alleyways, cramped dwellings in swamps of sewage and offal, its air unbreathable and even its rain a malodorous yellow. Its fitful sun, glimpsed through palls of dense smoke, was a mere umber ball that loomed like a promised disease. Its crabbed population clawed their days away, choking and spitting, gasping and vomiting. It was a horrendous city of cess.

As he headed for the River Thames, he met Aldgate and the tramways. Here, north of the Tower, the main road followed the line of the ancient Roman exit from London. Here, commerce became channelled into a torrent flowing to the docks.

There was finally room to move, without having to batter away the fingers fumbling at his garments. He went ankle deep in a slush of horse manure and steaming piss from the great beasts hauling the tram waggons on their rumbling, flanged wheels. He followed close to one as it started down the Commercial road. He kept a safe distance, for the waggoner's mate was too liberal with his whip. It was understandable, for after each waggon came a cloud of children and scavengers picking, filching, plucking at the fastenings on each load. God, but London was a world of questing fingers alive only for theft.

A fire bell sounded. A fire machine thundered past on its way to some conflagration, horses straining under the lash. Since the Law of 1774, churchwardens had to provide fire engines in every

London parish. That same Building Act made every parish establish fire-plugs near the few inadequate water mains in water-starved London. Alex stepped into a doorway in astonishment as an enormous crowd roared out of the alleys and raced after the fire engine. A second fire engine clattered from a northerly direction.

'A race! A race!' People yelled, wagers were laid. A cripple who fell under the wheels of the second engine was ignored except to be cursed by the people rushing after. This was the result of the Law. The first three parish engines to arrive and set about extinguishing a fire would be rewarded on a sliding scale of value. Not only that, but fire insurance companies each had their own engines, with uniformed men and their own 'marks' affixed to the walls of insured dwellings. This resulted in abuse, for one company's men would stand watching idly while a warehouse insured by a different company burned.

Alex waited until the onrush abated and the street returned to its usual pandemonium. The firemen were drawn from Thames watermen and lightermen, who thereby gained protection from impressment into the King's Navy. It was a mad system. Alex's ingrained desire for urban order was outraged. Why did the system of a common insurance superintendent, established only in 1825, not work? Instead, here was a system, each for his own furrow. But, he thought as he strode towards Whitechapel, was not his interest in the *Sealands* venture and his addiction to Judith Blaker not an example of the same greed?

London gave no respite. Wherever the newcomer went, he was met with coal dust, grime, secondhand clothes shops, more dirt. He was splashed by carriage wheels, buffeted by milk sellers slopping pails of dirty milk, dripped on by carts dragging night soil and offal. And always the clatter and thunder of waggons was a constant background to the caterwauling, screams, fights, and the wailing of infants. Even Burlington Arcade, where he had taken lodgings, was built only because in 1819 Lord George Cavendish had finally lost patience with the London rabble who threw street refuse over his garden wall. It had instantly become the resort of prostitutes plying their trade above the Arcade's shops. London was the worst nightmare made real.

He made the Black Bull in Whitechapel. Sir Fellows De Foe was already waiting, and greeted him warmly.

'Your journey was not through St Giles, Mr Waite,' Fellows observed as they found the booth which his two men were keeping free of verminous topers.

'No. I came through the city.'

'You were wise. You would have been robbed of every stitch if you had. The school for child thieves there has lately excelled itself! The 15,000 trained thieves in London centre mainly in St Giles. To hire a highly trained child thief, eight years old, now costs three shillings a day. Four shillings, if the child is crippled!' Fellows De Foe was a man of sardonic humour, dry but experienced in London ways. 'An impressive advance on simple beggary! How great a nation we are!'

Alex examined the ale brought to him, but drank when De Foe gave a reassuring nod. 'I visited London only briefly before, Sir Fellows. It amazes me anew.'

'I love this great place, Mr Waite. I know the effect it has upon the visitor. The distress, the fetid streets, deformed populace, the crime.'

'I had heard that the Mendicity Society –'

'– has accomplished miracles?' De Foe did not smile. 'I am no philanthropist. In fact, I deplore it as encouraging drunkenness in the determined idle. But the sheer disorganisation of holy charities like the Mendicity distresses me, like hypocrisy among us gentry. The average price of wheat per quarter last year was fifty-six shillings and elevenpence, with over six million pounds expended on the poor of England and Wales. This year, the wheat price is rising. It will average at over three whole pounds! and the money allocated to the poor? It is *falling*! I shall be astonished if it reaches six million.'

Such candid talk made Alex wary. He redressed the balance. 'Yet London has been gaslit since 1812, Sir Fellows. The capital's energies can only be admired. I came by Horseferry Road in Westminster, where one of the first three gas stations was established. London by night is a wonder of light –'

'All operated by joint-stock companies with immense capital, Mr Waite! Like the 990,000 tons of shipping into London last year, the product of venture moneys.' De Foe signalled to his men that they could drink elsewhere but to stay within call. He waited until they had lit their light pipes at the taproom candle and gone. 'The kind of venture you and Sealandings engage in.'

'Yes.' Alex paused, but the other offered no more. 'My father wrote to you about the Baltic because he is developing the port of Leith's interests.'

'Was it coincidence, Mr Waite?' Fellows gave his visitor an opportunity to think the question through, then did it for him. 'Coincidence that Sealandings enters international commerce, a provincial harbour in rural isolation?'

Alex Waite accepted a clay pipe from a tavern servant and chose tobacco from the proffered jars. This was a more serious meeting than he had expected. He lit the pipe from a taper, tamping the rising to gain time. This Fellows was a different breed of south Britain gentry than he had become used to. The gentry seemed to be of three types: those ensconced in privilege, living from day to unremarkable day; those like Hunterfield, trying to improve a changing world; and the hellraisers like Carradine, satisfying appetites at any cost. This Fellows De Foe was possibly a Londonified Hunterfield.

'Coincident, sir?' Alex knew of the scandalous liaison between this man's wife and Carradine.

De Foe leaned closer. 'Carradine is a man hobbled and tethered, Mr Waite. He will not stay a dancing bear for ever. I knew he would burst his bonds. The nature of those bonds I do not exactly know, but they are padlocked by his housekeeper Mistress Blaker. I believe that this venture is created by Carradine to rid himself of that woman.'

Alex's instinct had been proved right. 'I too think so. My father identified the London source of the venture. Our factor in Cheapside tells me the *Sealands* was your property, sir. Hence my letter about a meeting.'

'Not my ship, Mr Waite, but, left in trust to my wife.'

'Then there is no coincidence?'

'The vessel is sold to Carradine's syndicate. Imagine the odds, Mr Waite! Five-and-a-half thousand ships entered London in 1827 alone. This year the figure will be exceeded. Too long odds – unless the dice were loaded.' Alex looked about uneasily. Carradine could duel De Foe for saying this. 'My own concern is why did my wife order the *Sealands* sold to Carradine's syndicate?'

'It would be ungallant to reply, sir.'

Fellows De Foe acknowledged the guarded response. 'I would be just as cautious, Mr Waite. I am no hotspur, no licentious degenerate who rides his prick wheresoever it wills. And duel indicates juvenile mind when the whole world is adult. Which leaves two questions, Mr Waite.'

'And those?'

'One: how to bring down Carradine. And two . . .' He shrugged.

'Two, Sir Fellows?'

De Foe smiled and tapped the bench for new pipes. 'Ah, that question is yours, Mr Waite. Can I say?'

'Yes.' Alex watched the clay pipe draw flame, the red ash swelling from the bowl, the plume of smoke.

'I heard of your first meeting with Mehala, the sea-fetched girl with Carmichael. In the Donkey and Buskin?'

Alex nodded, wondering how the man was so well informed.

'You had asked for her . . . shall I say, night services when she was serving. She declined and procured a substitute. Your next encounter was at the near-duel between two women in the Sealandings livestock field. You supervised what gunfire there was – after trying to dissuade Mehala from fighting.'

'You speak of Mehala. I have nothing to do with her.'

De Foe shrugged. 'It is, like those other odds, impossible to remain unaffected by Mehala. I would have succumbed, but am too experienced in lost causes.'

'You imply that I desire Mehala?'

'Not since this syndicate formed.'

'What is the relationship between the two, Mehala and my being here as a member of a shipping syndicate?'

'Judith Blaker, Mr Waite.' De Foe did not inhale the smoke. A group of seamen was becoming boisterous. A fight had broken out between two and a pickpocket. Someone brought out a cudgel, and the tavern servants were laying about, manhandling the cutpurse but hitting out anywhere. De Foe was unconcerned. His two men stood nearby. 'You would not investigate the syndicate unless you were involved with Mistress Blaker.'

'Is that the second question you mentioned?'

'*My* question I have told you: how to ruin Carradine and keep him shackled to Judith Blaker. *Your* question is the opposite: how to persuade Mistress Judith to relinquish Carradine, is it not?'

Alex pretended interest in the conflict across the taproom. Everyone was taking sides, yelling imprecations and offering to join in. A tankard flew across the tavern, and smashed a seeing glass by the counter.

'Yes,' he admitted finally. 'I want Judith to part from Carradine. That is why I have come. You want her to stay.'

'Mr Waite. Whether or not she remains housekeeper at Carradine Manor is irrelevant. I want her to keep her hold over Carradine.'

'Our aims are utterly opposed.'

'Not diametrically. We can find common ground.'

'Is there common ground?'

'Yes. Fetters have one quality that is often ignored. They tie the gaoler as well as the gaoled. He – or she – is as much a prisoner as the felons chained to the walls. Judith Blaker is Carradine's prisoner, as he is hers.'

'You only say it is insuperable in different words.'

'Not quite.' A prostitute tried to slide onto the bench beside Alex. One of De Foe's men hauled her away, backhanding her when she spat abuse. Idly he resumed his jocular chat with his partner. De Foe ignored the incident. Waite watched her crawl away, mouth bleeding, among the legs of the fighters. 'Carradine's ruin is called for. These are our two dilemmas.'

'I wish the man no harm,' Alex said uneasily.

'Of course not!' De Foe tutted in reproof. 'Nothing is further from our thoughts! Incidentally, Carradine once tried to proposition Mehala. Her scorn has mesmerised the man ever since.'

Alex was astounded. 'I had no idea.'

'I do not disparage Mistress Judith, but Carradine would exchange a lifetime of her for an hour of Mehala.'

'How do you know?'

De Foe inverted his pipe and rattled it on the ashbowl with a sigh. 'I am married to a rich and determined woman, Mr Waite. Her fortune is held in trust, from her kind and meticulous father, lately deceased. A wife's possessions should immediately become her husband's. I suffer – my wife's wealth outstrips mine.' He shrugged. 'I am aware of the implications. I accept them. Now, I go my own way, not entirely without success. The tie that binds is Carradine.'

'I do not see how these confidences relate –'

'I sold Shalamar to Mehala, Mr Waite. That is the reason I agreed to see you. It provides our answer, could you but see it. Today Mehala will marry Doctor Carmichael. He trained at the London Hospital across the road there.'

'How do you know all this?'

'My agent Willoughby executed the sale. Mehala, the lady of Red Hall.' De Foe relaxed, in open humour. 'The farmers in southern East Anglia are famed for having as many as fourteen, fifteen wives in a lifetime! I met one man with twenty-four! Mehala is no woman to share a tithe of any man, married or single, so Carradine's is a hopeless cause. But your Judith Blaker hates Mehala, because Carradine wants the woman more than he does Judith. Hence those chains.'

'It is even more impossible than I thought.'

'No. For the Baltic ship is already flying before the wind. One of my inward vessels signalled her. *Sealands* will come home, Carradine in the first flush of success. He will not be able to resist striking out.'

'For Mehala?'

'As God is my judge, Mr Waite. What he wants is his by rights. Anyone who gets in his way is to be exterminated.'

'You are warning me?'

'Forewarning you, Mr Waite.' De Foe rose, urbane as ever. 'North Britain might be a land of large extravagances of passion. South Britain is a land where those passions also exist, but are held tight until detonated. Then they emerge with an even greater force.' He signalled to his men. 'As in any explosion, Mr Waite, the longer the delay, the greater the destruction.'

'I fail to see what we have accomplished, sir,' Alex said.

'Do you?' De Foe smiled. 'You want Judith Blaker. We both want Carradine ruined. Then bet on the *Sealands* venture being a calamitous failure. Sell your shares in it, instantly.'

'But why?'

'If Carradine's venture succeeds, you lose Judith anyhow. If it fails, she like Carradine will be destitute.' De Foe rose. 'To whom does a woman like Judith Blaker go beggar or baron?'

'You mean I should take the risk of –'

'May I offer you the services of my landau, Mr Waite?'

The sea was in midtide when Hunterfield rode on to the hard followed by Simple Tom. He had decided to let the three ladies be driven, escorted by Ralph Chauncey. He rode apart, to inspect the harbour walls and the sea dykes. This was fortuitous, for he learned news that otherwise would have passed him. Tom as ever had slowed to hear the gate servant's gossip. He caught up with his master only when the carriage was approaching the dryland. Tom gave a robin's sharp warning whistle. Hunterfield resigned himself to yet more harrowing tidings and brought Betsy to a walk.

Tom drew both hands down his face to cup an oval.

'A beauty? A woman?'

The groom flung imagined tresses and peeped a low trill. A beauty with a little robin in her hair? Tom saw that Hunterfield understood and confirmed it by gesturing with finger and thumb into an imaginary cup. 'Leech? Mehala and the leech Carmichael?' The others could not hear over the carriage noise.

Tom nodded, drew out his groom's short knife, made an 'X' in the air, then offered the knife, his fingers in a ring.

Hunterfield stared in disbelief. The St Andrew's cross was the traditional 'X' of veracity. It was the age-old sign made on the altar steps with a knife by illiterate brides and grooms. Hence its growing use to symbolise the promissory kiss, among swains and their girls. Knives were symbolic gifts to the bride. But, Mehala *married* to Carmichael?

'A wedding, Tom? When? Where?'

The mute groom's finger pointed downwards: now, today. His hands dusted each other: the wedding was already done. He put both hands to his face: where Mehala slept, home.

'At Shalamar? How?'

Now both hands arched above Tom's head followed by a fist holding an imaginary stave, the other turning as if keying a lock. 'A bishop's licence, is that it?' Tom nodded and reined back to allow Hunterfield to catch the carriage alone.

Carradine was up ahead, waiting by the south mole and watching the single dredger at work.

'Well met, Squire,' he called to the thoughtful Hunterfield.

'Good afternoon, Carradine.'

The ladies in the landau were aware of the coolness of the meeting, but Brillianta was determined to use the day to the utmost. Ralph Chauncey was ever the drogue to her ambitions, though a simpleton in the ways of a lady's subterfuge. He had his own brand of danger. Family pressure held the maximum risk. But the day was happily free of her dear sister Lorela, whose arrival was ever impending but mercifully not often realised.

Sylvia Newborough had donned her bravest finery for the ride, with a half-riding coat dress of woaded gentian blue, a saffron bonnet and long curled hair dragons from beneath. Quite the wrongest style for one unimaginably plain. Indeed, Brillianta decided, it was sheer impudence of the harlot to be showing off her skimpy wares quite so blatantly. The dowdiness of Mercy Carmady was more preferable, with her russets and corduroy cloak, even though she could not resist showing a glimpse of richly embroidered orange silk corinna as she took her place.

'Shall we inspect the south side of the harbour, Squire?'

'I have already done so, sir,' Hunterfield replied evenly. 'Every Monday. And I ride the town every Tuesday.'

'Of course, Squire. But I should be able to state my wishes for the harbour, now that Sealandings is to develop!'

Hunterfield did not answer for a moment. His gaze took in the unloading of a fishing lugger, Yorkshire pattern, against the north mole. He smiled to himself as the fisherwomen hurried with their ready ribaldry to collect the sea harvest and fight the prices. He fervently wished he were with them instead of with this grand echelon.

'State your wishes, Carradine.' Hunterfield sighed. People of Carradine's stamp were grasping by habit. They might seem exalted rakes, to be admired for their gun prowess and horsemanship, and envied for their whoring and profligacy, he only found them tiresome. Such gentry wanted Government to substitute threat for reason, forcible repression for compassion. They understood nothing because they were determined to understand nothing.

'Yes, Squire. The advance of Sealandings is vital!'

Also, they were so damned sure of everything. They upheld morality like a gonfalon, as long as it suited. When it impeded any whim, they condemned morality as a treasonable obstacle to progress. They also forgot logick, or they would not try to impress nearby ladies with stupid questions based on ignorance. It was time to put Carradine down a peg. The ladies, sensing dispute, had fallen silent.

'Your wishes, Carradine, are *what* exactly?'

'See the small vessels there?' Carradine pointed.

'Which, Carradine?' Hunterfield said wearily. 'The hoy? The smack? The small lugger? The fly? The modified snow? The skaffie? The fifer? Pram? Sloop? Etaples lugger? Morbihan? Lug-rigged dandy? Baltic? The Bornholm? Which, sir? Or don't you know?'

'All and any,' Carradine snapped in anger, unsure. 'They are shallow vessels, laden or light. Soon the *Sealands* will come to unload cargoes. She will draught heavily.'

'Your conclusion, Carradine?'

'You must dredge the harbour out, sir! *That* is my conclusion!'

'Is it indeed.' Hunterfield turned his mild gaze on Ralph Chauncey, sitting in the landau with the ladies. 'Reverend Chauncey. Might I ask your . . . *wishes* for Sealandings harbour?'

Carradine snorted. 'Ask divine help in all our undertakings!'

'I am ignorant of docking requirements for vessels, Sir Henry.' Ralph Chauncey made it sound a blessing from above.

'But I am not, Reverend.' Hunterfield leant on his saddle. He turned on Carradine, his voice suddenly hard. 'Depth of this harbour in fathoms, Carradine?'

'Depth, sir?' Carradine said in impotent fury.

'Draught of the *Sealands* full laden, Carradine?' Hunterfield was conscious of the ladies' apprehension but did not disguise his contempt. The news he had just received from Tom did not incline him to tolerate this idiocy. 'You do understand what the term draught means, I take it? And the difference between harbour depth and the *Sealands* keel?'

'You should be about your tasks, sir! Instead of daydreaming of your coast and its history.' Carradine was made aware that he had gone too far by the gasps from the carriage. All knew of Hunterfield's liking for sealands lore.

'*My* tasks, Carradine?' Hunterfield lolled on his pommel, seemingly unconscious of insult. 'Why *my* tasks, Carradine?'

'You minister to the dryflands, the sealands, the sea marshes, the sea walls and dykes.'

'Why?' Hunterfield kept his mild manner. 'I do not have to. Why not you, Carradine? Your father did. Your grandfather assisted my grandfather. Are you too high now for such mundanities?'

'I am aware of my responsibilities!' Carradine shouted.

'Your grandfather, Carradine.' Hunterfield smiled reminiscently, looking at the harbour. 'On those sailing craft which you cannot even name, he taught me to splice a rope. Do you know *why* the ropes on land are a standard four yards long, Carradine? Your grandfather did.' He laughed gently in fond recollection. 'Your grandfather and mine sang and played on the English pipes, *A Lovely Lass to a Friar Came*, sang all the words in full! On this very hard!'

'So, sir?' Carradine was white with rage.

'So that was long ago, Carradine, when they were masters of their own souls. And houses.' His mild manner took the slur from the words as Carradine drew breath. 'I mean, Carradine, that we are no longer masters of our souls!'

'Do you mean to insult me, Hunterfield?'

Hunterfield smiled, shading his eyes against the sun's reflection. 'If I did, you would be the first to know! But my advice: To ask a sensible question, one needs learning.' He looked round at Tom's whistle. 'Not another disturbance, surely?'

'Castor Deeping, I think!' Brillianta exclaimed, turning her bonnet to see better. 'What a pleasant addition!'

'Thank heavens.' Hunterfield was relieved, guessing what news Deeping brought. It was high time the news got out. He was eager to see the effect on Carradine.

Sylvia exclaimed. 'I do hope he will stay a while.'

'Good day, ladies, Reverend Chauncey, Sir Henry, Carradine.'

Castor Deeping looked smart in his white neckstock and red riding coat. His knack of appearing untroubled had deserted him. He seemed agitated.

'Castor! Welcome. Will you join our excursion?'

'Thank you, Sir Henry. I only bring a message from Lady Faith at Lorne House. I left there an hour agone.'

'No serious cause, I trust?'

'A large deputation awaits, Sir Henry. Preacher Endercotte appears the leader. He seeks an urgent audience. Reverend Baring also, with other religious leaders, and the churchwardens.'

'Today was to be one of recovery after the celebrations,' Hunterfield sighed, scrutinising the skies and the sea. Nothing would have pleased him more than a ride along the sea dykes to Whitehanger. He could have called on his sister Letitia at Watermillock, though that would mean adding Tabitha to the party since she awaited them at the tide mill. However, with Reverend Ralph as chaperone to all, it would be proper to let them ride there together.

'Lady Faith begged me to convey the urgency, Sir Henry.'

'Very well. I obey my women as always.' He touched his riding crop to his beaver. 'Please continue the outing. I shall return to Lorne.' He waved away their protests. 'I shall expect you all for supper this evening.'

'They protest because two irreligious persons behave contrary to law. They are Mehala and Doctor Carmichael, married at Shalamar House this morning.'

'I heard.' Hunterfield was deliberately casual.

'Mehala?' Brillianta exclaimed. '*Married?* In a ruin?'

'Wed?' Carradine said the word levelly, his face expressionless, as if registering an enemy before battle.

'With witnesses.' Castor Deeping noted Brillianta's delight, from which malice was not wholly excluded.

Mercy did not look at Hunterfield, sensing the depths in the man. He was disappointed, but not bitterly. Did that mean passion was less in such a man than in, say, Carradine? She suspected that it was not so. She heard Deeping accept the invitation to ride out with them to Whitehanger by the sea dykes.

'I would be obliged if you would call at Watermillock on your return to bring my sister Tabitha to Lorne,' Hunterfield said.

The company agreed willingly. Hunterfield hesitated a moment, as if about to invite Mercy to return with him, but instead rode off at a slow canter, followed by the silent groom.

46

SHALAMAR WAS QUIETER than Mehala could remember.
By mid-afternoon the guests were gone. Barbara was crooning gently to the babe Radcliff. Clement was out in the grounds,
doubtless fishing in the old trout pools, Rosie was gone to
Bartholomew Hast's on some pretended errand.

She worked in the kitchen for a while, for some reason feeling
listless. After seeing to Nath's dressing and giving him his draught
she settled him comfortably and sat with him a while. There was so
much to do, what with the laundry, cleaning, preparation of food
for the morrow and the late supper. Of course, there were
differences. Now she was wealthy, and a wife. The cost of buying
Shalamar had been met. Maids-of-all were not out of reach. She –
that is *we*, she thought, determined to be consistent about the
plural – could afford servants. It had seemed important to remain
impoverished, and come to her husband as poor on her wedding
day as when they met.

They were man and wife, in the eyes of the law, society, all
people. Whatever the local gentry wished, whoever lusted after
whom, she and Ven were now outside their games and demands.

Soon she would improve Shalamar. Buy Ven more instruments,
take up the challenge of the books he would bring from
Maidborough. Then she would start systematic instruction.
Perhaps he might need an assistant, a young doctor. To spare him
for her? She would become his medical apprentice in fact as well as
by secret intent. Perhaps he would take her to London to sit in
lectures! No menial work simply to earn the entrance fees to
anatomy and surgery lectures from great doctors. Oh, no! She and
Ven would go together. Any lecture they wanted, to learn in any
way he wished. And she would be beside him, day by day, for ever
and ever.

Nath moaned in his sleep. He seemed more restless. Ven was on a call, to a ditch-and-dyke worker with a severe cut in his leg, a common enough occurrence. She had attended several with Ven. One, still helplessly lame, had unfortunately cut through the tendon of the right leg, giving him a flail-foot ever since. It would have rendered him a charge on the parish, but he made wooden toys for passing tinkers and, more fortunate than most, was maintained by his fishmongering wife and labouring sons.

She went to comfort Nath, who was muttering and shifting. She hoped Ven would return soon, for the boy might wake into one of his terrified deliriums. She could not cope alone. He coughed and puked a little. She fed him a little warm milk. He managed to take a few swallows, but then fell back into his fitful doze, having difficulty breathing. He seemed more at ease when she sat by his truckle and held his hand.

Shalamar's restoration would take every penny of the Red Hall moneys, but it was vitally important to live *here*, nowhere else. In time, she and Ven might migrate to London for a while, then possibly some great hospital would demand his services or . . . Who knew? But they would keep Shalamar. It was home. It was here that she had come and planted the Floral Dial of flowers, opening in sequence on the hour round the clock night and day, betokening her love.

First, she would have the roofs mended, the gables, guttering, rendering the whole place dry. Then the top floor. There would be servants here by then. Doubtless some revenue would accrue from the estate. It would be working by the end of the first year. Tayspill, she hoped, would become her chief bailiff. The fields would be planted. Moneys would increase during the second year. The third year might bring in a little from farm rentals, which could be let to tenant farmers if restored and the land was in good heart . . .

The fish ponds were a plus. She had always envisioned a windmill on the upland side of the South Toll road. Once that was built, she could rival the Quaker family Bettany. With Shalamar's estate behind her, she would give cheaper milling to Sealandings. Possibly, she might even match the lower prices of Watermillock, though that operated constantly, whereas windmills depended on the weather.

Tonight, though, she and Ven would sleep together as man and wife, safe from intrusion. She had her bride's gloves ready, new and freshly flatironed, as custom decreed for a church-wedded bride's first night. As she drew Ven into her arms, criticisms could fly like spent arrows, turned away by the sanction of Law and Church. From now on, there would be no need to be on guard against a phrase carelessly uttered, a greeting incautiously chosen. And tomorrow she would order materials, workmen, set the world to work to restore Shalamar as the pride of Sealandings.

'Mehala?'

She started. Ven was close by, looking at her with a curious expression. 'Ven!' She stammered at his sudden appearance. 'I . . . I was dreaming.'

He put his arm about her. 'I came quietly. How is he?'

'Fitful, restless, muttering.'

Ven shed his surtout. 'I will watch. You rest.'

'What is the matter, Ven?' She came to sit beside him. 'You look strange. Was the injured man –?'

'No. A simple injury. It will granulate up without loss in use, please God.' He hesitated. 'On the way home I saw a crowd of the religious making for Lorne House. None would look my way. I greeted two, but they said nothing. Euterpe Baring did not see me. She was with her brother.'

'Is it come, then, the complaint against us? Is it today?'

'I am not certain.'

She kissed him, removing his beaver to ruffle his hair. 'There is a hot kettle. Barbara will make tea. I shall walk in the garden and find Clement. Let us have as quiet a wedding day as possible.'

She left, quietly gathering up her shawl and chip bonnet, and once clear of Shalamar almost ran. If holy folk in Sealandings were making accusations against her husband, she would be there.

The assembled men and women were in a belligerent mood. They stood motionless, always an ominous sign in Hunterfield's experience. Reverend Josiah Baring carried the Book of Common Prayer under his arm. His sister Euterpe stood by him.

Perhaps about sixteen. Quaker Bettany and his wife Helen were there, grave as ever and never a smile between the pair of them; Robert Parker, running with the pack but ever needful to stay

413

where he could make a slick escape and pretend he had never run at all; his wife Bessie; the churchwardens too, he saw with a frown. Leonard Sadler stood bareheaded to show he need not doff his hat to the Lord of Sealandings. He pursed his florid lips in determination. What the principal churchwarden lacked in aggression his fat wife Jane would doubtless provide. The stout pair always argued for the quiet worriers Finch Digges and his wife Gertrude. The gamekeeper's constant production of children must provide a modicum of finance for the indigent Doctor Carmichael, Hunterfield drily supposed. And the rabid preacher Kemp Endercotte, and his wife.

'I shall see Reverend Baring, Dryden, in the second chamber.'

'Yes, Sir Henry,' the clerk said.

'Sir Henry!' Endercotte stood forward angrily, his hand raised as if appealing to the heavens.

There was an audible gasp from the others at such impropriety. Sir Henry's name was reserved for utmost formality, or familiar guests in the Lorne household.

The Lord of Sealandings ignored the man and walked on without a word.

Endercotte screamed, 'I abjure you Sir Henry Hunterfield, in the name of God, harken to the Word and punish those offenders against holy —'

Hunterfield halted and spun on his heel. 'Dryden! Exclude that ignoramus from my grounds this instant! Evict the man!'

'Yes, m'lord!'

Footmen came at a brisk pace. Hunterfield addressed the woman standing beside the aghast preacher. 'Mistress Endercotte. You may consider your good self a party to the group here, and not feel yourself excluded. If my reproof causes a conflict of choices, that is made necessary not by my conduct but by that of another.'

Endercotte was dragged out, struggling and shouting admonitions. The footmen hauled him from the main hall and down the servants' stairs. A door slammed distantly.

'Thank you, sir. I shall remain, if I may.'

Hunterfield strode on, followed by his clerk and Reverend Baring and Euterpe.

The second chamber was used for interviews and matters relating to the Lorne House estates. Hunterfield offered Euterpe and her brother chairs, then seated himself in his favourite bended-back elbow chair. Its thick upholstery should have been in the brightly coloured changeable silk, for which Tabitha thoughtlessly had insisted, only for the upholsterer to complain that changeable was too weak for such usage. He sat casually, telling Dryden to leave the door ajar for the gathering in the main hall to hear what was said.

'I agree to this meeting to conserve duty, Reverend Baring. This is neither the place nor time for an official complaint, which I understand is the reason for your visit?'

'Indeed, Squire!' Reverend Baring was uneasy after Hunterfield's angry expulsion of Preacher Endercotte. Euterpe remained quite calm, sitting with her gloved hands folded. 'I speak for Sealandings of the scandalous behaviour at Shalamar.'

Hunterfield raised his eyebrows. He, as Lord of Sealandings, was the natural spokesman, but he said nothing.

'They live in sin at –'

'Reverend. They are married.'

'Married without the benefit of sibberidge?' Baring offered the Book. 'In a churchyard, by the girl's mad shouting, without witnesses? The superstitious marriage of sinners, Squire!'

'By special licence, and a parson of your own denomination.'

'By . . . ?' The rector rose, then sank slowly, baffled.

'It took place this very day. They are now married by any measure, country custom, or Church Law. Your accusation is unfounded.'

'I see.' Baring glared at his sister, whose gaze remained fixed on the distance. He gathered himself, conscious of the listeners outside. 'I present in any case a criticism wider than status. It has come to my notice, Squire, that several people now reside at Shalamar.'

'I have seen them.'

'Then you will doubtless be aware that Carmichael has in effect been operating a lying-in hospital at Shalamar. A babe was born dead there, and buried with witchcraft ceremonies. And Mistress Tyll was delivered of a babe there. And he and Mehala abducted a sick climbing boy from the workhouse, as well as the blind boy Clement Wellins.' Reverend Baring raised his voice. 'The iniquitous couple conduct a hospital without a licence!'

'Is this true, rector?'

'Signed by two justices, Squire! And his offence makes the parish officers liable to a monstrous fine. Ten whole pounds!'

'Mehala owns Shalamar, Reverend,' Hunterfield said reasonably. 'She may invite whomsoever she wishes to her home, sick or well, injured or no, newborn or of age, may she not?'

'Illegal, Squire! He delivered Mistress Tyll's babe after removing her from her family —'

'From the whorehouse, Squire!' Mehala stepped into the room, curtseying to Hunterfield. 'Forgive this intrusion.'

'I insist that this woman —'

'Josiah!' Euterpe spoke with quiet insistence. 'Lorne House is no place to *insist*! Our apologies, Squire. We forget ourselves.'

'Mehala should hear the accusations, rector. So far you seem to lack the facts on which to base charges.' Hunterfield let Dryden bring a chair for Mehala. 'Two Cotts, Mehala? What has that to do with the case?'

'Doctor Carmichael delivered Barbara Tyll's child at the bawdy house. Mistress Wren allowed him the use of a barn.'

'Why not in her own home?'

'She was thrown out by her husband.'

Hunterfield nodded at the news, pretending a sagacity he did not possess. He could not see Mehala as married, any more than he could after she had made her own wedding in the churchyard. 'But there are many respectable dwellings nearby.'

Mehala raised her voice for the waiting group. 'Squire, where else could Ven go but to the whorehouse? To the estimable miller Emanuel Bettany, who is against him? To the schoolhouse, where Miss Gould is barred by this pious parish from helping Doctor Carmichael, since he is banned from St Edmund's? To the rectory, where the one kind soul residing there who would help is forbidden to speak with Doctor Carmichael or myself? To the stables of Robert and Bessie Parker, who side with those who want Doctor Carmichael banished from Sealandings altogether? The Saviour was given a stable!'

'That will do, Mehala.' Hunterfield reprimanded with sternness. 'I will have no brawl here.'

'My apologies, Squire.' Mehala held her anger in, conscious of her high colour. 'Doctor Carmichael had no choice. As it was, he had to force Mistress Wren.'

Hunterfield found a glimmer of humour in the image. 'I cannot imagine your husband forcing Mistress Wren to concede!'

'His determination is underestimated, Squire.'

'I am sure,' Hunterfield said courteously. 'Reverend?'

'I deplore this couple's example, Squire. I see that perhaps the charges can be taken two ways . . .'

'There is no basis, Reverend.' Hunterfield's voice was cold. 'If there had been, I would have acted with force and immediacy. As it is, to gather a group and wait on Lorne House without notice betokens a poor assessment of the niceties of society. I strongly disapprove of your high tone. I strongly disapprove of the gathering. I strongly disapprove of your having accompanied them, and the purpose for which you came. That is all, sir.'

Reverend Baring retreated, sweating and florid, trying to stutter apology, but Hunterfield bowed to Miss Euterpe and Mehala before nodding to Dryden to conduct them out. He remained standing until their footsteps receded. He sighed, wishing the feeling of impending trouble would go.

How long now until the *Sealands* returned? It had in fact only been gone a little while, and would need at least a fortnight. Then all would be eased in profitable commerce.

He would hold a supper party this evening, Tabitha to be hostess. He did not feel inclined to face Aunt Faith after the news of Mehala's marriage. In fact, he did not wish to face himself now that Mehala for him was no more.

The thought of Euterpe Baring came into his mind, so reserved, so withdrawn. But that holy brother! Sylvia Newborough, Brillianta Astell. Mercy Carmady's quiet demeanour and her brother about to be the saving grace of Sealandings, courtesy of Carradine's ingenuity, of course. His head ached. He would sit in the orangery for a while, perhaps walk in the grounds. Then the ice house, and a glass of gingered beer in ale, chilled.

47

THEY SAW THE sun's last light leach from the skies. Mehala shivered unaccountably. She tried to seem light of heart when Ven told Clement that he need not retire early tonight.

'Not early, Ven?' she asked. Rosie was tucking Nath in, and the candle already lit.

'Not tonight, Mehala.' He was forcing humour; she could tell by the strained constancy of his smile. Clement was overjoyed by the reprieve. 'We have something to say to the boys.'

'Why, yes, I suppose we have.' She was still uncertain.

Rosie was quickly done. It was nine o'clock when she retired, not looking at either. They bade her goodnight. Ven declined her offer to stay with Nath, saying instead she should wait on Barbara Tyll and the babe if needed.

For the rest of the evening Clement told them about the fish he had found in the ponds, and how marvellous it would be when they thrived again. There was a fish so big, he tried to persuade them, that both his arms could not have encompassed it about. Ven said this was clear impossibility, but Mehala argued that carp grew enormously and old as the hills.

Nath listened between fitful sleeps. His cough racked him a few times and set him sweating, though not as heavily as usual. Distantly, he followed the conversation. Clement played Ven a game of Nine Men's Morris, beating him handsomely. Mehala jokingly accused him of cheating and moving the alabasters by sleight-of-hand when Ven's attention slipped.

She brewed tea, giving Nath the first pouring with milk and a little loaf sugar newly pounded for greater sweetness. They sprawled sleepily in the semidarkness after Mehala extinguished the guttering candle, Ven on rush matting by the truckle and Clement opposite, with Mehala on the inglenook stool.

'No, Mehala,' Ven said as she made to bring another candle, 'let us stay in the firelight for a while. It is so beautiful.'

'Very well. But no cheating in the gloaming!'

'I promise.' Ven wiped Nath's forehead and put the tea to his lips. 'And I promise more honesty still. Nath?'

The boy's eyelids were closed. He raised them with effort, the eyes curiously bright and alert. 'Yes, Doctor?'

'No more Doctor this, or Mistress Mehala that for you, Nath Carmichael. You are now our son.'

'Son?' Nath's eyes went from one to the other.

'Our child, Nath. I am your father, Mehala your mother.'

'Is it true?'

'For ever and ever, Nath. So let us hear it from you. Show you understand. Who am I, son?'

Nath took several shallow breaths, Ven smiling in the ember glow. 'Father?'

'That is it, Nath. Papa or Dad if you have a mind. All are one and the same in law. And who are you?'

'Your boy?'

'Our little boy, Nath. For ever.' Ven beckoned Mehala. 'And who is this, Nath?'

'Mother?'

'True, Nath. Mama, Mum, but also one and the same.'

'And Clem?' Nath's head turned on the pillow. 'Clement also?'

'Yes, if he wishes, Nath.'

Clement and Nath stared at one another. 'Are we brothers now?'

'Of course. It may take some getting used to. But families cope.'

Nath reached for Mehala's hand. His fingers looked almost fluorescent with pallor. 'I remember my father. He shouted. They took him away. He fought them. I was left alone, until the sweep took me.'

'That is all over now, Nath.' Mehala kissed him. 'No more taking away. When you are stronger and more grown you may wish to wander, but there will always be home to return to.'

'I have a present,' Clement said shyly. 'It is a shining stick, Nath.'

He went to the vestibule and brought in a piece of rotten wood wrapped in leaves. 'See?' He unwrapped it, shielding it with his shadow. 'It glows, yet stays cold.' He gave it to Nath. 'For my brother.'

'It is a fungus,' Ven said, 'that generates light by ferments within.'

'It is magic,' Clement insisted proudly. 'Cold, yet brilliant in the darkness.'

'Father?' Nath whispered drowsily.

'Yes, Nath?'

'That is all a star is!'

'So it is, Nath!' Ven grinned, and explained about the rockets and the stars to Mehala. 'It was Nath's observation, the night the *Sealands* sailed.'

He settled Nath, whose hand held the shining wood.

'Now, I shall tell you of the things we shall all do here.'

'Together,' Nath said. 'At home. A family.'

'Of course together, Nath. One family. Mehala can explain more than I about Shalamar, so she may begin.'

'Well, there are so many things! I am not sure in which order. First, gardeners will clear the paths and make the grounds free of fallen wood. The ponds, of course, the drives, large ornamental gates –'

'Need we have gates, Mother?'

Mehala hesitated, puzzled. Ven was quick to answer. 'Actually, I rather disliked gates, Mehala. Nath has a sensible idea. Could we do without gates altogether?'

'Why, yes, no gates at all would be sensible!'

'No gates,' Nath whispered.

Clement's head drooped. He jerked upright, startled, then sank into a doze.

'And the gardens, Mehala,' Ven prompted. Realisation took hold of Mehala's mind, and she gazed, stricken, across at Ven who deliberately avoided her look. 'There is that strange circle of flowers. Did you ever complete it?'

'Yes, Ven,' Mehala whispered. 'It *was* done once, but . . . did not flourish.'

'Then we shall do it better!' Ven promised. 'And in the very centre of the gardens, near your Flora Dial, we shall have the most beautiful pond. The silver and blue of the skies will reflect in it night and day. Moon, sun, stars, the lanterns of passing coaches, all in our brilliant clear pool.'

Nath whispered. Ven bent to hear. 'That is all a star is, Nath, yes. And that is all *we* are, son! And always will be for ever and ever.'

Tears were streaming down Ven's face. He embraced the boy gently as he died. For a moment he fancied that Nath's hand tightened on his arm, that his face nestled once into his cheek, but it might have been imagined.

Mercifully Clement continued to sleep, snoring gently on the rush matting by the hearth. Mehala, Nath's hand still in hers, stared appalled at Ven and mouthed a question. Ven was unable to give the answer she already knew, and wept in silence as the kitchen fire's red embers died. Only the glow of the magic fire shone on, cold and gleaming in Nath's hand, as the darkness extended over them.

48

THE FUNERAL WAS a meagre affair. Strangely, it caused their first argument.

It was the day following their macabre first night. They had stayed with Nath, wearily keeping the night vigil until dawn promised to break the eastern sky, then silently carrying Nath's still form into Ven's surgery and laying him on the table. It was before the house woke. They spoke softly, mindful of Clement sleeping in the kitchen where he had fallen asleep the previous night. Rosie and Barbara Tyll and her babe were not yet awake.

'I will send to the Parker stables, Ven,' Mehala said. The grooms there served Sealandings as undertakers. 'Rosie will help me to wash and clean him. I want the very best for him. We must have a solemn carriage, with plumed horses and a trio of fine mourners.'

'Why?'

Mehala was startled, and looked at Ven almost anew. He seemed somehow to have suddenly grown sparse, more intent yet curiously more of a presence. The nocturnal bliss of the wedding night had been gainsaid by circumstances. Now, Ven's enduring hesitancy, his stuttered asides, and his half-nod of acquiescence, were gone. In their place was a quiet, assertive manner she found disturbing and utterly strange.

'Why, dearest?' She was at a loss. 'Why, because we loved him! Our son. We ought to let people see.'

'See what?' No pause, no doubt. It was chilling.

'See how much we loved him, even if Sealandings paid him no heed.'

'Extol him in death, when he was slaughtered by the hour in life? No.' He stroked Nath's hair from his face.

'But we can afford all the necessary —'

'*No*. He needs only his family and friends. Waken the house,

Mehala. Tell them about Nath's passing. I must prepare him, Mehala. Then you may wash and dress him.'

'Prepare him?'

'I need my instruments. Make ready as for an operation. I will do it alone, unless you have a mind to watch, which I advise against.'

'And the funeral?'

'Send Clement with a note to Reverend Baring, asking him to conduct Nath's funeral. If he agrees, we take Nath to the church. I shall be at the burial.'

Mehala did not know what to do. 'But the rector –'

'The rector can do as he pleases. If he refuses, I shall take Nath to the next parish, and the next, and the next, until I find one holy man susceptible to bribery.'

'Yes, dear.'

Mehala was shaken by Ven's adamant resolve, and his different opinion. She had never seen him like this, not even in the worst days of the cattle plague, not even when the *Dander* foundered and he risked his life in the sinking ship.

She unpacked the instruments from the cases in which they had been delivered from the London makers. He had used only four so far, relying on familiar ones, and leaving the rest until there was time to practise.

'I had better do this alone, Mehala.'

'What . . . ?'

Ven looked away. To her relief she saw his familiar embarrassment return, and glimpsed the man she loved beneath this new taciturnity. He touched her hand to his lips. 'I could do nothing for Nath in life. I shall never forget his misery, or my shame.'

'You are not omnipotent, Ven.'

'No.' His eyes shone hotly, darker than she could remember. 'But honesty is different, Mehala. From now on, that is all I must be, for Nath's sake, and the sake of the sick.'

'I have never seen you like this, Ven.'

He smiled with his usual gentleness. 'I am awake now. I intend to excise the tumour. I cannot let him be buried bearing it. So I will learn how to remove it, now he is dead. I may then help others like him.'

She acquiesced, helped him to strip Nath's body, but turned

away as Ven examined the tumour and reached for the scalpel. She quickly left to waken the others.

He worked as if in a dream, the scalpel held firmly in his right hand at an oblique angle, moving it round the tumour's corrugated edge. The growth was shaped like a flattened cauliflower, warty, encrusted with epithelial debris.

The margins of the lesion overspread the normal skin surrounding the cancer. He dissected sideways and down, intending to remove it slowly, making slanting movements with the scalpel to separate it in one piece, noting as he advanced into the tissues the induration and thickening of the deeper attached areas.

Was there a way to inspect a tumour's structure more closely, and get to the thing's sinister truth? Perhaps there soon might be, in these marvellous modern times. Perhaps, he thought, letting his hopeful imagination roam, the secrets would be found by means of these new optical micro-scopical devices. They promised to reveal the cells' activities in unbelievably minute detail. But how *did* one examine cancerous material to see within? As ever, it seemed to him as he dissected on, there would be the bafflement of seeing some phenomenon and not knowing anything more. To match the cells' structure with the changes in the patient's body was surely the mystery . . . Or was it something in the blood, the lymph, the arteries, that needed analytical examination in ways not yet discovered?

To him, it was enough that he worked instinctively, desperate to cut away the monstrous growth that had murdered Nath. The grotesque disease was an affront, a hideous insult, somehow more evil because Nath had been able to talk and even smile to the very hour of his death. All the kind wishes in the world and willingness to help had been useless.

The tumour was free at last. He placed it on a cloth and stared at the malignancy. The pressure it had exerted on the child's urinary tract, perhaps some undetected spread into the bladder or other pelvic structures, would of course have done some of the damage. But how could this cancer, seeming so circumscribed, kill? He knew from cases he had seen as a student that some patients with the spreading illness seemed to develop nodules all over their skin. He supposed that the cancer somehow reached internal organs.

Was there a way of stopping the spread? Could the growths even be prevented *before* they had begun to destroy? No doctor could answer. All disease, the senior doctors said, was an affliction from some Deity, to be faced stoically, as mankind's fate. And most diseases were the fault of the patient anyway . . .

Ven's anger almost blinded him. He almost cried out in rage at the philosophy. It was an insult. What sort of folk *are* we, he wondered, tears stinging his eyes, to teach bovine acceptance of the tragedy we call disease? We must drive ourselves to see, and in the end defeat, the murderous sicknesses. To bow before them may be pious, but there must be a different way. He had never heard of a scrotal canker in anyone except climbing chimney boys. *So why in God's name set children to that occupation?* It was an affront to humanity, condoned by all people, rich and poor alike, masters and servants. Because it had always been so, therefore it must stay so. Finally, the suffering was condoned by doctors, who concealed ignorance behind a ritual subservience to orthodoxies. Do not protest, doctors told everyone, for that way lies rebellion. Do not question the medical profession's methods, the grand London physicians preached, or you will see our ignorance, and know us for the deceivers we are. Medical fortunes were founded on that.

He wanted the cancer burned, wholly destroyed. The raised and thickened nodes in Nath's groin he left untouched. To excise every last trace of the cancerous growth would be to destroy Nath's form, and therewith his last remembrance. It would be an unnecessary offence. Ven's and Mehala's and Clement's and Rosie's memories of the little dead climbing boy were all the life Nath would ever have now.

Ven smouldered, suturing the cavity from where he had excised the tumour. It would be different for the others, the children in the workhouse and the inmates there, he vowed silently. A cold stone of certainty formed within. He stood a moment in silence, certain now.

He called out to Mehala to have Clement light a garden bonfire, and went to wash his hands and instruments in the garden pump. It was a precaution, lest cancer prove contagious, another enormous ignorance.

An hour later he had finished a preliminary wash of Nath's

body. He asked Mehala to perform the last washing for the boy, then went out to burn the wrapped cancer, and have a second, more thorough, wash in the same pump, this time using the soft soap that Mehala left there in its muslin-covered dish.

Clean at last, he went to write to Reverend Baring, and make himself presentable for Nath's farewell.

Mehala listened to Reverend Baring perform the burial service. She tried not to weep, but tears came in spite of herself. During the service she stood with Ven in the church. They took up the position of parents unbidden. There was no protest from the verger or the rector.

The service was read in a dull monotone, far removed from the minister's usual pontifical thunder. The thought came to Mehala that he was subdued by the setback to his plans to have Ven banished from Sealandings. Perhaps the resistance, if not the animosity, was over? Certainly, there had been no reluctance from Parker's stable people when their services were called upon. The oaken coffin had been immediately constructed to order. Flowers from Shalamar had been made into wreaths by Mehala, Rosie and Barbara Tyll, and the stablemen had helped Clement to load them on the handcart in spite of their ill-concealed annoyance that their hearse cart was not hired for the journey to St Edmund's.

No protest was made when Ven, unaided, carried the coffin into the church on his shoulder and lowered it with a grunt of effort on to the altar steps. Reverend Baring watched with a blank expression, and started the service without any preamble. He spoke no eulogy.

Mehala heard Euterpe Baring join in the prayers, but did not see her until she followed Ven out to the small grave, when she helped to carry the flowers. The grave had been prepared in consecrated ground, next in line to two new graves from that week; a crewman of a fishing yawl killed in some accident, and an elderly farmer from nearby Fellersham whose horse had bolted on the turnpike.

'. . . and the fellowship of the Holy Ghost, be with us all evermore,' Reverend Baring concluded.

He did not even wait for the collective 'amen' from them all before slapping his book closed and leaving without a further word.

Euterpe stepped up to Mehala and Ven. He was still and bareheaded in the wind.

'I am so sorry, Mehala,' she said. Her eyes were red. She was dressed in black, with a veil and mourning gloves.

Mehala thanked her. 'And for attending our son's service,' she added.

'I heard the stonemason from Whitehanger will bring the headstone this evening. The churchwarden . . .' Euterpe hesitated. 'I will be present, and see it set up properly.'

Mehala was not deceived. Though the rector's sister was one of her few friends in Sealandings, she had no illusions. Euterpe had always felt something more than fondness for Ven. The marriage that made Mehala his wife would no more cure Euterpe's love than the earlier improvised ceremony had.

'That is kind, Euterpe,' Mehala said evenly. 'But do not risk even more difficulties with your brother. His disinclination to remove my husband's excommunication proves his enmity.'

'I understand, Mehala. I shall use my best endeavours to improve matters.'

'I long for the day, Euterpe,' Ven said sadly, 'when there will be a Bunhill Fields, as near London's Finsbury, and other uncommitted grounds for interment like Mister Brongniart's Père Lachaise cemetery of Paris.' He ignored their alarm at his heretical view. 'Then we will be free of prejudice made malice.'

'I shall pray for Nath, Ven,' Euterpe promised, to smooth over the bitter moment. She left with a glance at Ven. Ven spoke after a brief awkwardness, brought to by the sound of Barbara's babe crying.

'I will stay a while, Mehala. Please, everybody. Thank you so much. You were a loving family to Nath. He could not have had better. It is cold for little Rad. Clement, escort our ladies home to Shalamar. Go about your duties now.'

It was a difficult moment. Clement was pale, as was Rosie. Barbara did not quite know what to say but was relieved to be dismissed for her babe's sake. They left together, Clement taking the handcart. Mehala lingered.

'What are you going to do, Ven?'

'I will stay until the sexton's work is done. Then pay him, and send the four shillings burial tax to the churchwardens.'

'Then you will come home?'

'Not for a while, Mehala.' That new assertiveness had returned, she saw with misgiving. 'I have a task to do.'

'The workhouse?' she guessed.

'That first.' He accepted her kiss, but did not look away from the open grave as the sexton emerged. 'I will be home about nightfall. Hurry to catch the others, Mehala. It is coming on to a severe blow. Ask Barbara if she will allow me to bring little Radcliff's existence to Carradine's attention, or not.'

'Very well, dearest.' She gathered her shawl about her. 'If you do not return by dusk, I will come with Clement looking for you between Market Square and the workhouse.'

He said nothing. She left him there standing bareheaded, the rising wind blowing his hair over his face.

49

VEN WALKED DOWN to the workhouse unaware of the surreptitious greetings of the inmates working in the fields.

The wind was savage now, rushing in wild frets then stilling, a typical onshore gale. It did not promise a severe storm, nothing like some he had witnessed on this coast. The more clement the better, for those too poor to make better shift for themselves.

'Pleasence!'

He banged at the door of the house and stood a yard away to scan the windows when there was no reply. He marched round to the rear and hammered on the back door. Pleasence himself opened, bleary of eye and the worse for gin. He stood, scratching his belly.

'My favourite quack, is it not?'

'Come out, Pleasence.'

Ven stepped a few paces and stood waiting. Pleasence grinned and stroked his chin stubble. 'You bring a bribe, leech?'

'No.' Ven did not need to plan his answer. He knew exactly what he was about to do, the risk he was going to take by threatening a legally-appointed officer. 'I hereby evict you.'

'You *what*?' No grin now, as Pleasence stepped out. A maid peered timidly round the door as it swung to. 'Did you say evict?'

'Yes.' Ven had his hands in his surtout pockets. He eyed the man. 'Leave tonight, Pleasence. Is that maid an inmate?'

'Maid?' The man was bewildered. He stalked to the side of the house and looked about for bailiffs. 'Yes, an inmate. She gets the best of everything, in return for a few simple chores —'

'Bring her out.'

'Who are you to give me orders?' Pleasence did not know how to respond, still stunned. 'I s'll call on the churchwardens and the proper officers —'

'Pleasence.' Ven faced him. 'I hate you, for your cruelties, your thieving and the murders you have done here.'

'I s'll not have this, leech! I s'll take you afore the magistrates for attacking a parish officer —'

'Come now, and charge me before Hunterfield.'

The workhouse master's mind winkled out possibilities. An eviction of a parish officer without bailiffs was unheard of. It needed sworn deputies of the shire reeve or churchwardens. And without criminal charges? This crime could not be perpetrated on an honest, God-fearing man like himself.

Ven watched the man's expression signal one possibility after another.

'Where are your officers? The petty constable?'

'They are yet to be summoned, Pleasence. Come, let us walk.'

'Where to?' The man was half-amused.

'The fields, the workhouse.'

'What for?'

'To survey your empire, Pleasence.' Ven was expressionless. 'Your subjects.'

'Subjects, hey?' The man was pleased. 'Like a king!'

'Exactly, Pleasence.' Ven pulled at Pleasence's elbow. They went as far as the workhouse gate. Ven could hear the coughing and the splashing from within as the rag pickers and the washers strove to keep pace with the work. The inmates in the fields ignored the worsening weather. 'Bid them farewell, Pleasence.' Ven embraced the view with a sweep of his arm. 'Today is the last you will see of them. Even a king must go sooner or later, Pleasence. Today is your demise.'

'Who says so?'

Ven appraised him for so long that the man became disturbed. 'Me, Pleasence. You have heard my wife Mehala is a rich lady?'

'All Sealandings knows.'

'This workhouse is charged to the Poors' Rate, is it not?'

'It is,' Pleasence growled. 'And cheaply enough, too.'

'From today it is free. Goodbye, Pleasence.'

'Free?' Pleasence almost laughed in derision. 'You bloody fool! *Nothing* is free! Even the poor do not come cheap! Armies, ships, profits, churches — they all come 'nation costly! I was right! You'm off your head, booy!'

'No longer, Pleasence.' Ven's deliberate stare began to alarm the workhouse master. 'This workhouse will be paid for by Mehala.'

'She . . . *pay for the whole workhouse?*'

'And lift the burden of rates from Sealandings. You will be bagged the hour I send the offer in writing to the churchwardens and the Squire. It is being drafted by lawyers now.'

Pleasence paled. 'They will never agree.'

'They will.' Ven did not need to raise his voice. 'Especially when they hear of the new hospital.'

'The . . . ?' Pleasence was visibly trembling now. 'We have no hospital in Sealandings.'

'We have now. I have applied for a licence. It will be granted by eventide. I shall merge the hospital at Shalamar with this workhouse. These inmates will become employees of the hospital, so relieving the parish. The hospital will be managed by my wife. The inmates will be paid from income. My wife will fund the venture, so saving Sealandings the enormous Poors' Rate expenses.'

'It is unheard of.' Pleasence nervously dropped his bottle, made to retrieve it but let it lie, its contents glugging on the ground. 'They will not surrender authority.'

'I shall insist that they *retain* their authority, Pleasence. On a board of management.'

'The parish cannot afford –'

'Afford, Pleasence?' Ven wanted to gloat at the man's abject terror, but could not. There had been too many disasters. 'Afford? My wife will do the affording, Pleasence. Now go.'

'Look, Doctor sir, can we not – ?'

'Pleasence.' Ven would not yield. 'I want you off the premises by dusk, or I will have you gaoled. You hear?'

'I shall protest! I shall invoke the law!'

'Against whom, Pleasence? Me? For setting up a free hospital, in my own home?'

'For the workhouse! These poor people need –'

'The workhouse?' Ven wanted to hit the man, see him suffer physically, see him cringe and beg, but this could not be done by fisticuffs. 'There will *be* no workhouse. Do you not understand? The churchwardens will concede *anything* for a farthing off the rates! They will give me everything for abolishing the Poors' Rate altogether!'

'Doctor! A week? A day? For Christ's sweet sake!' The workhouse master actually stooped to fawn, palms open in supplication.

Ven walked away a yard. 'I am glad, Pleasence. I want you to know that I rejoice. When the churchwardens come to inspect this workhouse tonight, they will see it as the charnel house you have made it.' Ven forced a vindictive smile. 'Squire Hunterfield will come this evening, as shall I, with licences and expulsion orders. An inspection will be made. You will suffer eviction. And I shall applaud.'

'Inspection? For why?'

Ven gloated even more theatrically. 'No power on earth could improve the appearance of those poor inmates, Pleasence.'

'No power . . .'

Ven saw the man clutch at hope. 'No, Pleasence. It cannot be done in time. Clean the place, give them the warm clothes which you have stolen from the parish? To feed them well, for once? No. I have promised the authorities that they will see your deprivation and filth. Then I shall paint a roseate picture of love, kindness, and affluence; the gift to Sealandings of a clean and flourishing hospital. The parish loses a costly workhouse, riddled with disease and your corruption. And gains in its stead a hospital where folk can be ill in peace.'

Ven left then, still not acknowledging the glances of the inmates working close to the path. He had not made the road before he heard Pleasence start roaring out names and orders.

He walked home, marvelling how easily confidence helped lies.

How many days since Alex Waite had gone? It seemed an age to Judith.

She had immersed herself in planning new ventures. The west wing could be extended, to balance the terraces that drew a gracious line towards the haha and the falling gardens. It would take time, of course, and expense, but with the *Sealands* having been sighted on course adequate finance would be available.

During the evenings she had organised two large supper parties, at which Sir Kennet Dropper and his wife Imogen attended, with Ralph Chauncey to provide the right degree of sobriety and Charles Golding one counterweight for Brillianta Astell and Sylvia

Newborough. The unfortunate presence of Jason Prothero was not countered enough by his meek spouse Mary, though the poor woman had slaved to mask his social blunders. The man was an oaf, bragging about his property and wealth, quite as if he had been born to them by title. The second supper had served a wider cast still, with Bram Yale and his Melissa – she of the eternal smile that increasingly irritated as the endless smiling hours of her determined wide mouth went on and on. And Rodney and Harriet Treggan, each couple outdoing the rest in fashionable dresses and new materials.

Some bother had occurred at Shalamar. Her man Bellin, doggedly pursuing news about the bitch Mehala, legal by church and law at last, had twice called to tell of Doctor Carmichael's arguments with the workhouse master. She had learned of the death of the climbing boy Nath. The immorality charge had been dropped. The odious Mehala grew in influence with every passing minute.

Worse, Carradine Manor was less tranquil than it had been. Twice Judith had had to reprimand servants. Finally she had two thrashed for laziness and insolence. Naturally, Prettiance had been the first, and naturally too her offence was outrageous sulking. The other was some kitchen skivvy beneath notice, for she was not of the tribes. The beatings had given her little satisfaction. Perhaps the repellent Thalia De Foe was right, that servants actually needed chastisement, and never by the hand of intermediaries. A whipping should be carried out by the mistress herself. Then, Judith had once heard Thalia sweetly observe in company, the abigails understood, for the offended lady was the avenger. Holy Scripture justified all.

But these were inconsequential domestic items. The syndicate was served by the supper parties, so all was well. And Carradine was pleased, though his dismissed appeal to Hunterfield rankled. He still smarted from having been made to look a fool when discussing the dredging. Judith for her part was still more than satisfied when, after sex, he finally shoved her aside and slumbered in his sweat. He was as greedy for her as ever, though she did not deceive herself. His movements could not be monitored every single moment. And he might still slip away to the whores at Two Cotts. She had had the place watched several nights, to no avail.

That Carradine used other women, when she was eager to provide him with sexual play, was enough to anger a woman. It pointed to some inadequacy within her, and she could not accept that.

The night he learned of Mehala's wedding he had been like a madman, clouting Judith when she had merely inquired why he was so irritable, and eventually taking her so bestially that she still winced. That was a man's nature, and acceptable. But his anger testified to his craving for Mehala. At the second supper, Carradine had questioned the Yales about Mehala. She had tried to deflect the conversation from the sleek-haired bitch, but Carradine had persistently questioned Melissa about Red Hall, Mehala's relatives, antecedents, her hovel of a dwelling on the marsh, and ultimately the man who had married her.

Judith seethed. The North Sea should have done its duty, and drowned the troublesome cow instead of letting her live.

The truth was, Judith realised, she was torn between Alex Waite and Carradine. The thought of losing Carradine was unbearable. His star was in the ascendent. He would be one of the Knights of the Shires in Parliament when the *Sealands* returned. Almost as bad was the fear that Alex Waite might leave. To have both was an impossibility, for sooner or later Carradine would discover her double life. Judith's mind chilled to think of her Alex going to a dawn meeting and the loaded pistols being ... No. She must protect Alex. She remembered his scarred back, his steady thrustings, his solid hands as he turned her to a more acceptable position and resumed until that final flailing and his straining into the pillow ... She went weak at the thought.

Lose Carradine, though? Lose Alex Waite? She would have to think of something soon, for *Sealands* was flying across the Baltic, fast as time. The news, of ships passing at sea, was already days old.

At her lonely tea on the terrace, she saw Carradine dismount from a ride through the orchards. He was angry from a message sent to him by Hunterfield as he joined her.

'That bastard Carmichael has renewed his warnings about the Baltic,' he told her curtly when she inquired. 'He *wants* my venture to fail! The swine once before warned the Squire by letter, and now does it again. I am damned sure he writes to every port in the kingdom for evidence, to bar *Sealands* entry!'

'Can he do that?'

'He cannot, madam!' Carradine was in an ugly mood. She recoiled, as he found the drinks table cleared and shouted for a waiting-maid to bring a glass of metheglin. 'I shall have the bastard himself barred, mark my words!'

'Will it harm the syndicate if he persists?'

'Of course it will, you stupid cow.' He sank into a chair, glowering at the maid-of-all who came at a run with a drinks tray. 'A shipping scheme dies if the ship dawdles at the whim of some dog-crocus.'

Judith moved quickly to pour for him, tutting in annoyance at the maid. 'Prettiance! I told you to have the master's drinks ready for his return! Make sure, in future!'

'Yes, Mistress,' Prettiance said, eyes lowered.

'You have forgotten the Geneva. Bring a Rodney immediately.'

'Yes, Mistress.'

Carradine drank, surveying the lawns in silent fury. 'I want him to suffer. Yet everything I do is baulked by the idiot.'

'Is there no way to force him from Sealandings?' If the Baltic venture was impeded Carradine's hope of advancement would vanish, and Alex's heavy investments with it. Success would mean she might be able to keep Carradine – away in Parliament, perhaps – and somehow have Alex here in Sealandings. She could delay the terrible decision.

He laughed harshly. 'His bitch rich as Creosus. And now wedlock strengthens her and her moneys? You stupid mare. Where is the Portugal?' He flung the glass across the terrace to smash against the house wall.

'Prettiance!' Judith slapped the maid across the face. 'I told you *always* to have the master's Portugal –'

'You did not, Mistress!'

'You insolent whore!' Judith hand-lashed at the whimpering girl until she was almost breathless. When she ceased, she realised that Carradine had gone during her temper, and resumed beating the stupid girl with still greater fury. She saw Mehala as every blow struck, and felt a glorious satisfaction. Conviction grew, as she hit and kicked the maid, that Carradine complained not at Carmichael's anxieties about diseases in the Baltic seas, but about losing Mehala.

The way, of course, was to rid the world of both. She felt a spreading bliss, and knew she had at last found the answer to Mehala. Savagely she struck harder with renewed strength.

Late that afternoon, Ven and Mehala arrived at the workhouse, announcing that they would wait for the overseers' arrival.

The inmates were sitting down at a solid meal of braised steak, dumplings, and fresh vegetables. Two puddings were ready, with fruit and nuts. As Mehala went to see the kitchens, a waggon arrived with sacks of new smock-frocks and breeches. A delivery of cloth and fustians had already come. A list of the inmates was available, with only a modicum of untruths about employment beside the names of the able-bodied.

Ven allowed himself to be persuaded by the ingratiating Pleasence, and after proper expression of doubt sighed that he could see Pleasence's heart 'was in the right place', as he put it. He promised to delay the threatened changes, and said he would postpone the overseers' visit. They left, Mehala looking quizzically at him as soon as they were out of earshot.

'Ven, darling. We could not possibly pay the whole Poors' Rate for Sealandings. Nobody could.'

'I know.'

'Nor could we build a new hospital.'

'I know.'

'And you promised Pleasence, our enemy, that he can stay on as workhouse governor. I never thought you would.'

'I lied, Mehala,' Ven said evenly.

'Ven!' She was shocked.

'Mehala, my love, lives are at stake. We can delay no longer. Today, Pleasence is repaying the inmates a little of his stolen moneys, because of fear. I shall drive him out.' He did not smile. 'When he has repaid them enough, he will be thrown out with the rubbish.'

Mehala did not smile, either.

50

THREE NIGHTS LATER, Tabitha decided to take him.

Her horseglass was superbly made, its mirror plate showing hardly any undulations. Tabitha was so pleased with her superb reflection. It showed a young woman utterly in her prime; the hair lustrous, complexion smooth and pale. The cheeks would be heightened by a pinch at exactly the right time. The dress was a blush pink redingote of chiné silk, close-fitting, buttoned down to the instep hem, the buttons hand-stitched deep pink over a rich madder coral. Her abigail's diffident suggestion that she choose a midnight blue redingote in the coming fashion – the skirt en tablier, with the risky variant of a double-breasted bodice – was utterly hopeless. Tabitha had virtually broadsided the ignorant girl out of existence. Of course, Tabitha thought with a thrill, the dolt could hardly guess the occasion. She would have been aghast had she realized that tonight Tabitha Hunterfield would become a woman, with the full carnal knowledge of the world of men.

Carradine.

After thought, she deliberately left off her half-corse, having no idea what complications those might cause when the moment came. A few years before, in 1820, she has seen Lydia's confusion when dressing. Her corset's new metal-fixed eyelets needed extensive lacing to tighten the clumsy garment and give the whalebones adequate springiness. The rule then was to reduce the female waist to a third of its natural girth, but that, she thought smugly, was the desperation of the fat. For the shapely girl—*woman*! – such artificial engines were superfluous.

The rest was gorgeous: pink silk shoes, raised heels, a bonnet of cream dressed with faintly roseate flowers of satin blonde, held with Urling's Gassed Lace; so much wiser a choice since the wretched Spaniards' merino wool used for Yorkshire cassimire, which might otherwise have served, had seriously declined and was now displaced by the Silesia wools which she hated.

Yes, she thought, moistening her lips with a flick of her tongue and rotating her exquisite form, she was simply lovely. A dark cloak, for the seemingly innocent stroll. If she encountered anyone – the risk of meeting Aunt Faith or, my God, Henry on his solitary night walk – she would explain her maid's absence by claiming a kindly reluctance to disturb the girl so late. Headache, worry about something quite inconsequential, the way women had ever escaped examination.

The figure in the Argand light pivoted slowly. Irresistible! Oh, yes, she told herself, tonight destiny called. She calculated the hour from the noisy old Harrison longcase in her dressing room. Less than one hour to go. She could wait, savouring her final moments of girlhood.

Carradine would come. There could be no doubt. She lowered herself carefully on the chaise – she could see her image from there; it deserved total worship – and went in detail over the arrangements for the tryst.

It had been well planned. She had delayed her departure from her sister's home at Watermillock. Letitia had been delighted that her sister had showed kindness in visiting, for her heavily pregnant state confined her.

The carriage had come. Carradine by some unspoken agreement had managed to escort Tabitha without the rest of the party. She had *known* it would be so. The scheme worked perfectly.

Her coachman was one of Lorne's. Carradine mounted to ride beside the vehicle. Her third attending-maid accompanied her, so propriety was satisfied. Conversation was laboured, and held single meanings only for the first part of the journey. Gradually they filled with private significances, for herself and Carradine. He rode easily, his riding castor only partly covering his long black hair. He affected a neck stock of white cambric without stiffening, which would have looked too casual on anyone else. She weakened at the thought of reaching for the garment, and returned to remember the actual words.

It was at the junction of the Watermillock road with the

Whitehanger coast track she made her ploy, and the vague whim finally became reality. The maid was surreptitiously eyeing the coachman, so her attention was elsewhere.

'It was close by here, was it not, sir,' Tabitha commented, having decided how to encourage him, 'that some lady met the, ah, stranger? They had a lengthy conversation.'

'About matters of religion?' Carradine invented casually. 'Yes, I heard the tale. But the meeting was closer to your gateway of Lorne House. The tenth hour, I understand.'

'Tenth? But was it not inclement, sir?' Tabitha shivered. 'Night gales surely gave the lady her death of cold!'

'The third night, it was, Miss Tabitha, by agreement. Should that have proved impossible, then the next third night on, and thus and thus. September always gives a Saint Thomas summer.'

'Did they not risk encountering a Saint Faith's Fair?'

Carradine hid a smile. He kneed his mount away from a deep rut in the road. The Scotch cattle drovers assembled their beasts at the village of Saint Faith in Norwich. There was widespread dissatisfaction at that event's immorality, the magistracies being incensed at the lewd scenes, when every hedgerow teemed with coupling figures. 'I wonder if the lady signalled her intention, perhaps with a favour dropped earlier in the day? Unfortunately, the folk tale to which I think you refer does not tell us!'

'Oh, but I think it does, sir!' Tabitha invented with equal casualness. 'My nurse's version is that the lady lost her pagoda fan parasol in the water. That was the place appointed.'

'Miss Tabitha. How could her gentleman-to-be know where that occurred?'

Tabitha concurred smoothly, 'Here the mystery does end. Ladies of my acquaintance always ride their favourite paths. On warm days, for example, I prefer the shallow pool above the Affon bridge. It is lovely, but too far for an evening perambulation. On a hot day, however, I pause by the woodcutter's shed in the copse.'

'Hardly an elegant summer house, Miss Tabitha!' Carradine's eyes lanced into her quickly before he pointed beyond the wall of Lorne estate. 'Perhaps Sir Henry might build you a rest in that copse, were you to ask?'

'Perhaps,' she said idly, her heart racing as she registered the place for the tryst. She now had decided the time, the place, the arrangement. No more signals were needed. The third night from now, he would be at the woodcutter's shed in the copse in Lorne House's gardens. It was unguarded, and there was no need for gamekeepers to enter. They patrolled further afield, by river, decoy ponds, pastures.

Tabitha came to and looked at the Harrison. She saw with a shock that it was almost time. Ten minutes to reach the copse? She must go now. He would surely wait. Should she be early, or deliberately hold away until he was almost demented with disappointment?

No. Caution lost opportunity. She rose, smiled approval at her exquisite reflection, gathered her dark cloak, and extinguished the Argand lamp.

For one moment she hesitated, then entered the copse gingerly. A scudding, gibbous moon gave some light. The evening had been warm, the sea breeze dying early in the evening.

She was in the moon shadow, under two large fig trees that stood incongruously on the house side. A few mansion lanterns still showed. The duty ostler's twin lamps glowed, giving direction beyond the long terrace. She felt stifled for a second, and angrily rebuked herself at the thought of retreat.

Was it like this for every woman? Some were filled with a strange certitude that moved her to envy: like Mehala, so utter in her convictions, so completely for her man. That he was a penniless leech living in a ruin never fazed Mehala in the slightest. It was admirable, in a strangely mad sort of way. Yet Mehala's madness earned the admiration of all women. Was this night vagrancy nothing but the same impulse?

Impulse, no. She had planned this meticulously. Her delay at Letitia's, the knowledge that Carradine would be compelled to offer to escort her return, the improvised story of the lady's tryst, the thrill that she was making an appointment . . .

Should she call out? She felt her heart beat with prodigious force. Surely it could be heard as far as the kitchens, still glowing and active there with the scullery maids faintly clashing coppers and irons and skillets . . .

She stepped further into the copse, suddenly impatient, and moved towards the woodcutter's shed. She had not been here for years. The night plucked at her cloak unseen. Something brushed against her bonnet, and she hesitated wondering should she raise her hood. Had Carradine found a way to ride in? Or had he tethered his mount somewhere at a distance, and walked?

There was no sound. She halted and tried to see. A denser shape blocked her path. The moon slid out briefly, slipped into darkness, slid out again for a longer moment then plunged into utter blackness. She had seen a faint sheen, as of a roof thatched with faded rushes. She and Letitia had played here. The door was on the far side –

'You came.'

She almost screamed, but his hand covered her mouth. He held her firmly until she stilled. He shushed her as grooms quietened a startled animal, shhh, shhh, shhh. She nodded once, and he released her.

'You frightened me,' she said. It came out like a testy complaint, and she amended quickly with a smile he could not see, 'I imagined you more gallant than to leap out on a lady.'

'Gamekeepers passed this way an hour since,' he said softly. 'I had to make sure you did not cry out.'

She almost exclaimed in alarm. 'Are they about?'

'No. They were heading for the decoy lake above the River Affon bridge. They will not be back for hours.'

Her heart was still almost shaking her with its throbbing, but she was almost composed. 'Are you sure?'

He took her hand and led her with confidence round the side of the building. 'The gardeners have gone. The dogs are tied at the rear.'

Suddenly she felt a desire to slow this down, settle for discussion, while knowing that she would weep tears of furious disappointment if she did. Would he agree? Men were determined, but women were also, in a different way.

'I have not long,' she said, disgusted at the timorous words.

'Nor I,' he whispered curtly. 'This way. The door is ajar.'

Its scent she remembered from when she and Letitia used it as a play house, running squealing when the woodcutters returned with their long saws and pretended to be outraged at the old Squire's children trespassing among their tools.

She stepped in behind Carradine, and was abruptly astonished when his mouth crushed down on hers seemingly from nowhere. It was an assault, as if he wanted to suck her tongue from her. His hands clamped on her waist, then mauled her breasts. An instant later he moved away so swiftly that she almost fell against the door jamb. She was bewildered in the darkness, wondering if it had really happened. Then he drew her a few steps further in. She heard him sprawl down on straw. She was still gasping from the suddenness of it all.

'I think . . .' she began to say, to her dismay showing her doubt.

'No words,' he said. 'No more words.'

He did not reach for her, though she could feel him so near, lying on the straw. His deep voice spoke the only truth of the moment. Words would only delay, obscure, deny, somehow in a mad way betray her. Either she must go and remain in ignorance, still craving the unknown. Or she must stay for the oldest learning of all.

She was astonished to hear her voice say, 'Yes, Rad. Too many delays.' Her own body forced her to her knees. Her hands reached for him. They peeled aside the leaves of his riding dress-coat, impatiently ripped aside his cut-ins, and thrust inside his shirt.

The skin of his chest made her giddy for a moment, then she was stroking her hands inside the linen, marvelling at the astonishing heat of the flesh, so much hotter than her own which his hands were already pressing. She felt her first under-petticoat tear, then her second, then she was falling on him and scrabbling his clothes away as he was tearing at hers. His teeth gnawed on her bare shoulders and his mouth sucked savagely at her breasts. For one moment she tried to withhold while she struggled to move her position, breathless as if she had run a race, but he buffeted her into compliance and she stayed even though his weight pounded down on her raised thighs. But it was wholly right and impossibly serene, even though she keened into his shoulder as he fell on her like an angel from some sinner's heaven. Suddenly capable of tremendous physical power, her body bucked as she flung herself up, to meet and clasp him in his irresistible descent.

51

THE SEPTEMBER WAS unusually warm, too clammy by everyone's agreement. Expected breezes had died days ago, and for a week the sultry air hung thick and moist. Trees seemed to loll, rather than flourish with their usual autumnal pride. Leaves drooped and clung instead of falling to make crisp carpets. No rain came, apart from occasional early seeping drizzle. The River Affon drifted indolently, even below the wooden bridge. Its noise stilled. Fish rarely broke the surface though flies hung like stealthy clouds over its oily gleam. Ven, one day walking back that way along the shore, told Mehala that even the river seemed to sweat.

The sea-coast fishing was fairly brisk, according to the season, but that too was somehow conducted with undue wariness. Barbara Tyll mentioned to Mehala that the fisher women, who hawked fish about the villages, were starting to sulk at the weather, and see portents where none existed.

Mehala was disturbed, but refused to countenance such twaddle, and openly said so. She had a kind of rejoicing to cope with, deep within, and fishwife nonsense must not detract from it. She felt proud, newly made.

They had been married a fortnight, taking the law's landmark for their conjugal state. She still felt the exhilaration of the moment when Reverend Dakins had pronounced them man and wife. Curiously, she told Barbara when the babe Radcliff had had his breastfeed, it was not possession, no. It was the converse. She immediately felt a powerful sense of belonging. She was his, far more than he was hers, somehow reversing the expected roles. She delighted in the knowledge that all social distinctions placed her in a special position. It was evident in the people. In the market she was now deferred to slightly. It was more marked among females than males. The latter still silently lusted or

443

admired. But other women gauged her, as if there were new reasons about.

Workmen were in and around Shalamar all day long now. They were brought in by Willoughby, and had been interviewed together with their masters by Tayspill and Mehala before they had been paid their earnest shillings as contract of hire.

Mehala lodged her moneys as surety. Extensive labouring work had begun on the grounds and roof, the main wings and hall. The kitchens had been excavated almost to a shell. The place was in pandemonium as days passed, trundling waggons bringing materials, timber, stone and piping.

Ven expressed misgivings about the scale of it all soon after the work was under way. Mehala was unconcerned.

'Dearest. Your worry is medicine. Mine is Shalamar.' She loved to lie propped on one elbow and watch his face, seeing him rouse into the morning. They were in bed, with the sky still wearing its pre-dawn grey and Barbara's babe not yet demanding that the day begin.

'I am worried, Mehala.' He turned to look up at her. 'Your whole fortune is draining into Shalamar.'

'My fortune is your fortune. What difference is there? We are one.'

'You have been so generous, Mehala. The surgical instruments, the optical micro-scope device, the thermometrical instrument, the medicine cabinets. It is a fortune, not to mention the obstetrical forceps.'

'Generosity? To my husband?' She smiled, drawing his hand onto her breast and encouraging it to fondle. 'That is my duty, darling, not kindness. As is this loving.'

He stirred, his palm smoothing her loin gently with an engaging diffidence that pleased her. 'What if something happens, Mehala? You recall Hunterfield's warning.'

'You are anxious about the *Sealands*,' she guessed, understanding.

'Soon I shall have Pleasence expunged from Sealandings,' he said. 'I decided during the night. I now know who will take charge of the workhouse. Lady Hunterfield has gone home to Gloucester, so I will have less clout. He will have learned of my bluff by now, but all the same —'

'All the same, the workmen will be arriving in another hour.' She lowered her head and placed her mouth on his, raising herself. 'And little Radcliff will shake the world awake even before that. We have time, darling, to bless the new day. . .'

'Thank you,' he said.

'Thanks, apologies, begging pardon,' she teased gently, laughing at his embarrassment. 'Forever the hesitant. Take me, love, is what I mean.'

He smiled, and pulled her head down. 'It is what I mean also, wife. We just differ in our mode of expression.'

The breakfast at Lorne House over, Mercy Carmady walked the terrace with Tabitha, saying how peaceful Sealandings was in spite of the heavy unbreathable air.

'Yes. We do not have this climate often.' Tabitha fidgeted then paused as a door went in the house, almost as if she were expecting an arrival. Mercy had noticed Tabitha's irritable behaviour over a number of mornings, but had been too diffident to make remark.

'I hope it does not retard the *Sealands*.'

'Would it, d'you think?' Tabitha asked anxiously.

'As all vessels depend on the weather, this still air might not bring her home faster, though how would I know?' Mercy sighed. 'It seems we women must wait for our menfolk, such is life's pattern.'

'Indeed, Mercy!' Tabitha responded with such feeling that Mercy looked at Tabitha in astonishment. 'We do, we must!'

'I had no idea you were so wrapped up in the ship's fortunes, Tabitha! Especially as Sir Henry expresses doubts about the venture.'

'No doubts at all, Mercy!' Tabitha said, too sharply for politeness. 'My brother is reserved. He carries the responsibilities of Sealandings harbour! Others want the moon, but it is Henry they ask for it!'

'Of course, Tabitha!' Mercy stammered. 'My admiration for Sir Henry's steadfastness and wisdom is unmatched, though I beg you to retain that confidence.'

Tabitha glanced at Mercy with understanding. In any other woman, the look would have implied compassion. From Tabitha it was merely knowing, and hard at that.

'Of course.' Tabitha began to find Mercy Carmady a burden. She did not seem to realise that every lady in the entire Hundred fully understood her love for the Lord of Sealandings.

Tabitha, on edge, insisted they walk the full length of the lawns, beyond the central garden copse as far as the river bank. They came in sight of the wooden bridge.

'The *Sealands* should be through the gap by today and into the North Sea, Tabitha. Percy will be so proud to have made this voyage for Sealandings!' Mercy gave a self-conscious laugh. 'Every ship I see is his, even that small vessel arriving down there!'

A single-sailed vessel was approaching the north mole.

'Do I see people running?' Mercy clapped her hands. 'Oh, for a telescopic glass! It must be news of the *Sealands*!'

Tabitha drew breath. 'If so, we shall see Rad galloping to hear!'

Mercy's excitement did not blind her to Tabitha's response. Even Carradine's name had coloured the girl's face for an instant. She suddenly knew the reason for her hostess's irritability. She craved Carradine, to glimpse the man, see him, talk to him, anything. Or perhaps she wanted more of Carradine, more again? Mercy was shocked, but two maids were running as fast as propriety would allow towards them across the grass, hands on their lace-edged mobs.

For a brief moment Mercy caught the glance Tabitha darted towards the copse as they returned to Lorne House, and knew then that Tabitha Hunterfield and Carradine had enjoyed at least one tryst, and nearby. Hunterfield surely could not know.

The maids, chattering in their excitement, managed to convey the message that a packet boat had just arrived in the harbour with news. The great schooner was in the North Sea, and closing in to home.

It was only a few moments later when Hunterfield rode out on Betsy, passing them at a swift canter with Simple Tom hurrying to keep up, that they realised the news must be serious rather than a cause for rejoicing. Hunterfield's face was grim. He failed to acknowledge either lady, which was beyond their experience.

'What news?' Tabitha called, stupidly addressing her question to Tom, but he only spurred on after his master. 'Sally, send for Dugdale. The light landau.'

Mercy felt stricken in fear for her brother. She saw in Tabitha's appalled features a mirror likeness of her own alarm. They hurried on to the front balustrade and waited on the steps in silence as their abigails rushed for driving cloaks.

52

THE CORN MART was the most ancient of the buildings in Market Square. It was filled with a noisy concourse of people of all types and origins, from pedlars with their heavy peds to tenant farmers desperately seeking news. Merchants stood apart brooding. Women pressed together, bonnets nodding. Children, released from school of a sudden, darted in and out of the crowd; the whole mass talking, calling questions, shouting, begging for word. Preacher Endercotte was one epicentre at the corner, but in the uproar he was inaudible.

'The Squire! Squire!'

Hats were raised as Hunterfield drove through in his landau, his mare Betsy trailing on a tying rein. He did not even glance towards the throng pressing about the Corn Mart. The traditional gathering centre, it was the place where Sealandings got quickest news.

'What word?' people called to the grooms, but received no answer. The coachman gave a look over his shoulder for some signal but Hunterfield made none. His groom followed the carriage out of Market Square and down towards the harbour. A straggle of people followed the merchants as they hurried to the hard.

'It is the *Sealands*,' somebody called. 'God save us!'

'Is she down?'

'The Squire is driven; he does not ride . . .'

Visiting merchants were asking local folk for the significance of these signs. They learned with horror that it would be a long and sombre day, for otherwise Hunterfield would have ridden without a carriage or merely sent Simple Tom to glean the first message. The crowd that hurried in Hunterfield's wake grew disconsolate. Sealandings emptied towards the wharfs and the harbour.

When Ven arrived the harbour was all but silent. The mass of people stood in tableau on the wharf in sultry air with hardly a breath of wind. The sky was leaden. A few faint marks showed where a breeze stirred then failed on the dull sheen of the harbour. Sealandings Bay heaved rather than ran, its currents dragging tired waves on to the long, curved beach in the distance. A few boats moved with lugsails and oars towards the harbour from the direction of Whitehanger. Several harbour vessels stayed under the shoulder of the mole, where the Lord of Sealandings had ordered the captain of the packet and other gentry to assemble.

Ven and Mehala pushed through. A gamekeeper who had carried the summons to Shalamar held his badge aloft on his long flintlock and called in a monotone, 'Lorne! Lorne!' to clear a path for them. Ven came on the group standing near the harbour light.

'Good day, Squire.' He looked about for any injured.

'Doctor. Thank you for responding so speedily. I think you know everyone?'

'Yes. I have the honour.'

'Doctors Septon Peveril and George Godrell are your former colleagues from a hospital, I believe?'

Ven bowed stiffly. 'Yes.' Neither of the two august figures deigned to notice him.

'This is Captain Nevard of the packet *Deliverance*.'

Ven reached forward to shake the man's hand. He was a stocky, motionless man, in an oiled wrap-rascal with a hood tied away over his shoulders. Ven saw that Nevard was instantly aware of the animosity between the newcomer and the fashionable pair.

'Churchwardens Sadler and Digges you know,' Hunterfield added drily.

Ven gave them both a good morning. Leonard Sadler, the stout corn merchant, gave a grunt and said nothing. The hesitant gamekeeper Finch Digges was usually an affable soul, but now seemed downcast. He merely grimaced.

'Carradine is being sought,' Hunterfield informed them. 'And Sir Charles Golding. I have summoned them to Lorne, but need your advice here in the harbour. Nevard?'

The crowd pressed about to hear the captain of the *Deliverance*. Hunterfield's own men formed a cordon about the Squire and his group, their heels rattling on the stone as they resisted the crowd's pressure.

'My vessel was beating more nor'ards than usual, for want of wind, gentlemen. Early this dawn I sighted a Baltimore schooner. In good order, Baltic Sea to Sealandings boun'. We exchanged news. She has sickness aboard, asked me to convey news.'

'What sickness?' Hunterfield asked, his steady look at Ven showing he remembered the warnings.

Nevard pursed his lips. He was not given to speculation, a deliberate man, the sort Ven admired. 'Some fever.'

Peveril heaved a sigh. 'Sir Henry, this is hardly reason to disturb our breakfasts. A chat between sailors?'

Vén ignored Peveril. 'What fever, Captain Nevard?'

'I signalled, but they were unsure.'

'You spoke to the officer?'

Nevard shook his head in seaman's style, shoulder point to shoulder point, once. 'A naval officer presently sails the ship.'

'What is the alarm, Sir Henry?' George Godrell demanded. 'A superb ship returns with all evidences of success. A vague message, some man sick of a minor ailment. The bleatings of your medical dogsbody here who hopes to aggrandise himself by screaming unnecessary alarms.' He shrugged in boredom. 'It does not amount to much.'

'How many are sick?' Ven asked Nevard.

'One when they left Pillau.' The man was candid. 'Four now.'

'All the same fever?'

'That I do not know.'

'Any deaths?'

'None that they told of.'

'Mister Nevard,' Sir Henry cut in. 'I thank you for making this call to our harbour. You will be rewarded. Visit Lorne House's counting chamber within two hours, if you please. My men will conduct you.'

'Sir.' Nevard stood aside as Hunterfield addressed them.

'Gentlemen, your advice?'

'Ignore the alarmists,' Godrell said bluntly after seeing Peveril's attitude was his own. 'These tales convey little. Every seaman ails at sea. They tend to malinger, is my experience.'

'Not only that,' Peveril drawled, supporting his friend. 'How many similar tales are there? In London, a thousand a day. Every ship carries swamp fever, the Black Death, diseases of all shades. Yet how often do we see them? Rarely, if at all.'

'Your conclusion?'

Septon Peveril shot an angry look at Hunterfield. He was not used to being quizzed. 'Ignore the tattlers, sir. Get on with life. Let your splendid little harbour do likewise.'

'Doctor Godrell?'

George Godrell gave an embarrassed laugh at the use of the title, for as landed gentry he was wealthy beyond even fashionable London surgeons. 'I agree with Peveril.'

'I mean the ship, on its arrival?' Sir Henry persisted.

'Let her come,' Peveril said. 'And now, if you will allow me to resume my day . . . Coming, Godrell?'

Ven's opinion was not asked, which was wise considering the concourse. Sir Henry thanked the churchwardens and told his men to let the visitors through.

'Doctor Carmichael,' he said. 'Will you accompany Nevard to Lorne House?'

Ven hung back. The crowd crushed along the mole after the two august doctors. There were cheers as their opinion was repeated through the mob, and hats went into the air. Somebody started a chant to pull their carriage. This was the utmost in crowd approval, where the horses were unharnessed and the people themselves drew a vehicle through the streets to receive plaudits.

The mob moved away, leaving Ven and Mehala with Nevard. One of his men shouted to him from the moored packet. Nevard signed him to silence as Ven spoke.

'Captain Nevard. What is your voyage, and what have you heard?'

'Hook of Holland, Doctor. News? There is disease in the Baltics. It comes west along Europe.'

'When will *Sealands* make port?'

'Twelve hours, God willing.'

'What is Pillau?'

'The egress from the long sea enclosure in the East Prussias.' Nevard waited, then offered the grimmest news yet. 'I heard that a Russian port was closed, but do not know which.'

'Quarantine?'

'Aye. Marseilles has it this year.'

Ven did not need to ask which disease Nevard meant. He heard renewed applause as the two distinguished visitors made the hard. The townsfolk were cheering Hunterfield also, but the names called out were those of Godrell and Peveril.

'The Mediterranean Sea alone, though?'

'I do not sail it, Doctor. But I would not sail the Baltic ports until I see ships returning hale and well. It is not long since the Tsar fought his Russia against the southern Mohammeds, who draw janissaries from the whole Levant and east. I hear of many new outbreaks, all kinds of sicknesses along the rivers north to the Baltic.'

'Thank you, Mister Nevard. Let us go to Lorne.'

Ven and Mehala went along the mole while Nevard called instructions to his vessel and caught them up to follow the Hunterfield landau.

'Twelve hours will bring us to darkness, Mehala,' Ven said. 'The wrong time.'

The counting house at Lorne had been fitted with a Herculaneum chair for Mehala's benefit. The men remained standing. Hunterfield cast off any reticence as soon as they entered.

'Captain Nevard. Might the *Sealands* carry a mortal sickness?'

'Odds I cannot give, sir. But not many would enter a Baltic port without knowing it lay clear.'

'Clear of what?' Hunterfield demanded harshly.

'Of the plague, sir.'

The seaman's candour was like a blow. Hunterfield spoke as if to himself, pacing the floor. 'Too many hopes are pinned to the *Sealands*. That is my difficulty. These hopes are not merely of the populace, but of all the Hundred.' He paused. 'Doctor Carmichael. Your warnings. On what were they based? Remind me.'

'On letters from a colleague, who died investigating a fever brought into the northern ports. He thought of a plague, but my efforts to discover more failed.'

'And recently?' Hunterfield perused Ven's latest note.

'I wrote to doctors in ports having trade with the Russias and Prussias. Two reported occurrences.'

'This Doctor Peveril. He assuages doubt.'

'I cannot answer for him, Squire.' Ven spoke with equal candour. 'London does as it likes, for power resides there.'

'I asked the advice of Godrell and Peveril on the mole. Now in my own wages house I ask you for yours. What do I order when the ship arrives?'

'Quarantine.'

Hunterfield leaned on a window. It was impossible to see out. By custom a counting house's windows were of obscured glass. 'Until . . .?'

'Until the full period is elapsed. I would not trust a clean bill of health, even if *Sealands* brings one in. My belief is that bedding and cloth goods convey the Black Death.'

'Are you sure?'

'Squire, my life rests on my belief.' Ven was almost as pale as Mehala, who rose to stand with him. 'The plague morbidity, whatever it is, seems unable to persist in the human body more than fifteen days, according to the French. They have been most assiduous in its study. But wherever it is introduced, the Black Death comes in clothes, on bales, cloth, bedding.'

'Your belief, Doctor,' Hunterfield echoed with a bleak smile, 'against the fortunes of a whole coast!'

'No, Squire. Against deaths from the plague.'

'Go on.' Hunterfield appraised Ven with detachment. He did not once glance at Mehala. Nevard listened closely.

'The Death intrudes on garments and their like. The best known lazarettos – those at Malta and Marseilles – manage to exclude it by a rigorous process. It is described by many travellers, as in the skela markets of Wallachia and Servia. Austrian soldiers rule a minimum of five days' quarantine for Wallachians, forty in times of plague.'

'Successfully?'

'Yes. Markets continue, with Austrian soldiers with fixed bayonets between partitions. Officers take the money from one set of merchants into ladles of vinegar. Goods from the other side are immersed in fumigation waters, and swapped for the money on long ladles. They never fail to exclude the Death, it is said.'

'It is said? No more?'

Ven reddened. 'No, Squire. All is hearsay with the Death. There is half quarantine sometimes, where clothes are exposed to the air and guarded apart for twenty days.'

'Twenty days.' Hunterfield realised his bitterness must have shown. 'Do you realise that payment for goods is at the moment of landfall? There would be riots at *any* delay, Doctor.'

'I know.'

Hunterfield asked Nevard, 'The *Sealands*. Was she flying any signal?' He quoted, ' "Masters of vessels to hoist certain signals when plague or infectious disease on board." '

'The yellow-and-black was not flying, sir. Come nightfall, she would have two lanterns one above the other at her masthead.'

Ven interrupted, 'The penalty for failing to observe the rule is a hundred pounds. Nothing, against the voyage profits.'

Hunterfield glanced wryly at Mehala. 'Your good Doctor learns that greed causes deception, Mistress Carmichael.'

Mehala added quietly, 'And the same paltry penalty for failing to provide a true list of ports of call, since the ruling of the first of June, 1825.' She smiled at Nevard, whose astuteness had made him sense the undercurrents. 'My husband correctly advises that the ship's goods be opened and aired. The rules say so, Squire – "with or without clean bills of health", by the King's Orders in Council of the nineteenth day of July, 1825.'

'Captain Nevard.' Hunterfield came to. 'Quarantine. Where?'

'For this coast, m'lord? Whitebooth roads, sea law says, between Hull and Grimsby. So the orders do say, for Maldon, Colchester, Harwich, Ipswich, Southwold Isle, Sunderland . . . It is Milford Haven or Standgate Creek for London-bound ships.'

'Squire.' Ven raised a hand in apology to the packet captain as he cut in. 'Summon four customs officers here, as is required. Sail out to meet the *Sealands*. Let them put the questions laid down, then decide.'

'Twenty-five,' Mehala and Nevard said together. The seaman explained. 'Twenty-five questions are required, with answers to each. Then a further thirty questions if there is doubt.'

Hunterfield seemed weary. 'They always decide for quarantine, then I am back where I started, with the populace furious and riots threatened. Every item, from apparel through the alphabet down to whisks, wool and yarn. *And all other goods.* All to be unpacked at a floating lazaretto for forty days in Standgate Creek?'

Ven spoke with sympathy. 'I know, Squire. But I urge quarantine, because of the risks to the people.'

'Very well.' The decision weighed heavily. Hunterfield shook Nevard's hand. 'One thing. Did you *see* the sick men? Was anyone identified?'

'No. I presume Captain Hopestone was in some sick bay.'

Hunterfield thanked them, and asked Nevard to wait in the counting house for a steward to pay him his reward.

Ven and Mehala bade him farewell, and left Lorne House estate near the Donkey and Buskin where celebrations seemed to be noisy and prolonged. Mehala's arm was through Ven's as they walked home. His ominous serenity had returned. Her fear also came back, with greater intensity than ever.

Mehala was first to hear the beat of hooves on the road behind, and was drawing Ven to the verge when she realised the beast had slowed. She looked round to see Carradine as he savagely reined his mount to a slithering stop.

'You bastard, Carmichael!' he shouted, almost too enraged to get the words out. He spurred his animal at Ven, raising his whip. Mehala let out a sharp scream, pushing Ven between two hawthorns and skipping to one side.

'Sir?' Ven tried to stand beside Mehala but she thrust him away and suddenly raised both arms together with a piercing scream.

Carradine's startled mount reared, wrestling for its head. The rider was in difficulties as the neighing horse wrenched at the bit. Mehala picked up a handful of flint pebbles from the track and flung them at the animal's eyes.

'Mehala!' Ven tried to restrain her but she advanced, throwing handfuls of stones at the beast, screeching and wailing furiously.

'Stay clear, Ven!' Nimbly she darted to the left, avoiding the flailing hooves as the mount reared. She flung a flint cobble, hitting the horse's nose and eliciting from it a squeal of fright.

Carradine found himself across the road before he could fight the beast to a stand. There he whipped it into subjection until blood spattered the animal's skin.

He hauled it round. It stood asplay, shivering and snorting, eyes wide in alarm. Mehala kept her eyes fixed on the enraged rider. She held one arm across Ven's chest to keep him back.

'Sir?' she said conversationally. 'If you have anything to say, speak now or go your way. And keep the King's peace!'

'Carmichael.' Carradine was breathless, his lips blue and his face white. 'I shall do for you now, as God judges all! You hear me? And as for you, bitch. You hate me because I would not, when you begged me to shag you in Shalamar's garden, before that ignorant quack had whimpered his way into your country matters.'

'You invent as you lie, sir,' Mehala said evenly, tapping together two large flint stones snatched up from the track. 'You are not a thousandth of the man Ven is. Go to your whores. Count your pennies like the born pedlar you are!'

When Carradine finally spoke it was in a sibilant whisper. 'From today, you are a dead cow. And your pox-picker. That is my promise.'

'Bested by a woman, gambler?' Mehala jeered. Ven tried to pull her away, but she knew they were safe as long as they stayed by the thick-woven hedge, into which even Carradine's mount could not go. 'As ever! My husband, unlike you, is not tied to apron latches. Go and count your usurer's coins, penny puller!'

Mehala railed on, heaping insult upon insult, jeering and shouting as Carradine ripped his mount's mouth to blood before he spurred away. She flung her last stone after the man. He did not look back. She watched him out of sight, trembling.

'Dearest, let us go home.' She shook her head gently at his attempt to speak. 'There is no truth in his inventions, dearest. You know that. His threats are balloon air.'

They started off, looking towards the Donkey and Buskin, where two ostlers were staring in awe. They must have seen the whole battle. Fisherwomen were gazing from their cottages in speechless wonder.

'Ven, dear,' Mehala said conversationally. 'Do you think Bartholomew will propose soon to Rosie?'

'I wonder sometimes what woman I married,' Ven said after they had gone some distance.

'The answer is simple, love,' she said. 'One who loves you more than life. Me!'

53

THERE SEEMED NO better day for Sealandings. The misgivings, the dread that serious news had come with the packet from the Hook of Holland, were quite forgotten in the roaring and drinking about the harbour.

The day wore through the forenoon, into a celebratory noon and afternoon. It was almost as if Sealandings had declared an additional holy-day for riotous celebration. Farmers laid labourers off. Wives brought blankets onto the slopes above Sealandings Bay and laid out their hoards. Dancers arrived, sensing a carnival with the swift instinct of their kind. Fifers and English bagpipes played to a growing swell of inhabitants and tradesfolk on the hills above Watermillock. Crowds began to cluster in vantage points to the south and Carradine's rising heathland to the north.

Several false alarms were made. In the end, joke sightings of the *Sealands* became a common trickery. A prancing bear was masked and dressed as Doctor Carmichael, who had so basely tried to quell the delight Sealandings was enjoying in anticipation of coming prosperity. The beast was dressed with a duck's beak made of crushed parchment, with black twists of paper to represent leeches draped about its neck. It was prodded to shamble to the air *Cease Your Funning* from John Gay's opera while people frolicked, mockingly greeting the animal by Carmichael's name.

There was a general call for fireworks, and an impromptu public subscription announced. Sir Charles Golding drove through Market Square to visit Carradine to roars of approval. He made a slightly tipsy speech promising musical entertainment, with liberal distribution of ale later. He was driven in his grand landau to bursts of applause. The relieved crowds streamed down to the harbour to wait for the great *Sealands* from the seas of rich and affluent Europe.

'Sir. Forgive my intrusion.'

Hunterfield looked up from *The Magistrate's Manual*, the newly published fourth edition just arrived from Butterworth's in London's Fleet Street. He saw Tabitha's expression and Mercy Carmady's concerned face, and closed the thick octavo with a thud.

'Come, Tabby.'

The diminutive was a kindness. For a frightened moment she wondered if her brother actually guessed, but that was impossible. An elder brother never did know the miniature rivalries of squabbling sisters – and some arguments were far from miniature. She gave a wan smile to Mercy, who withdrew into the corridor, entered the panelled library and perched on the stool-steps.

'I am sorry, Henry. I must tell you. About me and . . . me and . . . another.'

He nodded, unsurprised. 'Best out, Tabby. How far?'

She was shaken by his commonplace manner. Once, when quite a little girl, she had overheard Mama asking exactly that same query of a maid-of-all who had become pregnant by a groom. Her words rushed out. 'Rad Carradine and I . . . We are enamoured, Henry. I . . . we have assumed a greater privilege, sir.'

To assume marital privilege was the ominous phrase households dreaded. Henry simply nodded. 'How long since? The journey to Watermillock to see Letitia? Before?'

'Three evenings afterwards.' She felt offended. Was she so transparent, then? If so, why had he not prevented her?

'Not long,' he mused. 'What, a fortnight? I lose time's beat.'

Another kindness, allowing her some means of escape should she be lying about the duration of their affair. 'We have met three times, sir, with the same assumption.'

Hunterfield raised a finger, wanting silence. She had seen this gesture a thousand times: in games, in conversations when some supplicant was too pressing, to supplicants in court.

'His expressed intent, Tabby?'

'I do not know. He says nothing. I have every certainty –'

'Your condition?'

She coloured, partly at his directness, partly in anger at his wafting aside her supposition about Carradine. 'I believe myself to be, sir.' Too brief for firm evidence, but her conviction was total.

'Very well, Tabby.' He seemed not to need to pause and think. 'Your place is here, should you wish it. You did not correspond with your sisters or Aunt Faith?'

'I did not, sir.'

'Then I shall see Carradine as soon as the ship arrives. Have you told Mercy?'

Mercy is it now? Tabitha thought with a flash of anger. 'No, sir. I have told her I had something personal to discuss.'

'We shall wait two days, Tabby, then you and I shall arrange matters. I will be as forgiving as any brother may be.'

She went to kiss him. 'Thank you, Henry. I love you for this.'

He smiled. 'Light a candle for me, Tabby. I myself need assistance, I know not exactly what.'

For a moment she was taken aback. Brothers, indeed all gentlemen, were capable, unquestioned and unquestionably powerful and sure of themselves. They did not need help. They simply needed the right drinks at the right time, the right horse, clothes, and guns. She hesitated, saw his firm smile, and smiled with relief. He must be humorous in spite of her dire news, she concluded, so she bobbed a quick curtsey and glided from the room on air. She had braved him! Her manipulating skills had not deserted her. Her innate art always grew in the performance. How stupid her doubts! Henry had always been her darling, as she his. His concerns – the ship, the Hundred, the Law, the dullards he saw as his people – were uppermost, of course. But not when his little sister Tabby came wheedling. It was the way it should be.

Now, Henry would see that she got Carradine. Just as Henry always saw that little Tabby got the first apple, the prettiest gewgaw, the foremost seat before the travelling puppeteers. She hungered for Carradine. All else must be sacrificed – Henry's dislike of Carradine, all Sealandings, if need be the whole Hundred.

Carradine was her man. He would instantly see how Tabitha had manipulated Henry. The great and magnanimous Hunterfield might demur about the *Sealands*, but he would never go against family. Henry would favour Carradine in any way Carradine wanted.

So *Sealands* would enter harbour. Tabitha had made sure of

that. Carradine would propose marriage to his guardian angel, Tabitha. Whether or not she might actually *be* pregnant was irrelevant. She assumed not. Carradine would see that his fortune was inextricably linked to the Hunterfields. What greater prize? With a seat in Parliament virtually in the gift of his soon-to-be-brother-in-law, Carradine would wed her without hesitation.

And Henry? She smiled, paused to admire herself in a chimney glass. His problems were like the weather, there but mostly to be ignored. At a stroke she had claimed Carradine, and made it impossible for Henry not to force an immediate marriage. Carradine *wanted* her. She was the only woman in the kingdom capable of taming him. Just as some mounts were uncontrollable until they met their one destined rider, so Carradine. She was his one perfect rider. The thought made her weak. She smiled at the reflection of the triumphant Lady Carradine to be.

The girl was heavily bruised. Carradine had entered like an avenger, beating her into silence, taking her crudely with an even greater savagery. He seemed never to breathe, became as stone as he beat her open and foraged in her inner spaces. Her whimpers, when finally she pleaded for respite, he silenced by thumping a fist into her ribs so she retched even as he used her.

The storm passed. She lay in silence, too afraid to weep. She heard him reclothe, heard the belt click, its leather squeak, felt the floorboards shake as he stamped into his boots. The bed tilted as he sat. She rolled to one side. His voice when finally he spoke was astonishingly quiet, almost that of a stranger.

'Latch my boot garters, Corrie.'

'Sir!' Trying to conceal her pain, determined not to whimper, she rose instantly and knelt by the bed.

This was one task she always fumbled, always throwing him into a blind rage. She might get locked into the starvation room by Mistress Wren if the gentleman complained. She trembled, reaching for the boot garter on his right. The straps were sewn to the riding boot heel, passed round the front of the leg above the kneecap and fastened to hold the breeches down, keeping the boot in position during fast riding.

'That is right.' A silence, then, 'What is your fate, Corrie?'

'Fate, sir?' She was afraid. She had seen him bestial before, had gloried in satisfying his need. She had seen him doubting, and even quiet. His savagery was acceptable, perhaps even desirable, being uncomplicated. Troubles uttered were meat and drink to a skilled prostitute, for a clever whore could cure a milliard ills with her one physick. But these deep questions held terror. They contained a core of male silence, however loudly yelled, and that to any woman was unknowable. She began to weep. His hand came on to her head gently.

'I am not angry. How long will you stay at Two Cotts?'

'As long as Mistress Wren allows, sir.'

'And then?'

That terrible horizon beyond youth was the ultimate threat. She never looked that far. 'I know not, sir.'

'No.' His fingers guided hers so the strap garter was positioned right. 'I am dissatisfied with Two Cotts, Corrie.'

'With me, sir? Sir, I shall —'

'No. I want a new brothel. Here, about Sealandings. Could you manage such a place?'

'Me, sir?'

'Whoremistress, like Wren.' She stared at him. The offer was beyond credulity. 'I would provide you with assistance, have you taught accounts. I would buy the place, establish it. But . . .

'Sir?' She could not follow the magnanimous offer, or imagine reasons that such an exalted gentleman would do this.

'I do not want a libken, some frigging shop.'

She listened astonished, not knowing that gentlemen knew such words for a common brothel.

'Your pay would be no whore's curse. Well?'

'Well, sir!' She almost broke down. The whore's curse was a small gold coin worth five shillings and threepence. When brought into circulation a century before, it became hated in London's stews, replacing the more valuable half-guinea and so reducing whores' incomes.

'Say nothing. I shall accomplish it within the month. One word will end the promise. And I shall have you cast, and find another nightgowner.'

'On my life, sir.'

He gave a minimal smile. 'Indeed, Corrie, on your very life! Now, tell about your visitors.'

'Yes, sir.' She stammered out her news, eager to prove her worth, her mind still bemused by the change in her fortunes. She babbled of farmers, visiting drovers, merchants, the rise in the harlot's trade since the great ship venture began, a lady who came in search of sexual solace from two girls on the first floor, a gentleman who journeyed all the way from Wheatfen, the damage Preacher Endercotte did to –

'What damage?'

'Last night, sir. Preacher Endercotte beat the Saxmundham girl they call Ta, her being Roberta. She seemed nigh death, but came to this morning, praise God.' Corrie shivered, still having difficulty with Carradine's other boot gaiter. 'He is wicked as the Witch of Wickfen. The girls think him mad.'

'Was he worse than usual?'

'Oh, indeed, sir! His rage comes fast, then is gone, with him praying and weeping rivers. The girls are mortal afeared of his cruelty. Far worse than yours, sir,' she added innocently, 'for your thrashing is but passion eased in the shagging. His be worse 'n afore. It bain't natural. Girls are used to ordinary, lusty swacken men.'

'And after?'

'He had to be evicted, sir. Mistress Wren had two stalwarts come to lead him off in his ranting.'

'Ought else, Corrie?'

She thought. 'Nothing but commonplaces, sir. The North Briton's manservant rejected the tawnish girl from Lincolnshire.'

'The North Briton?' Carradine had impatiently fastened his boot gaiter for her, but now stilled.

'Yester e'en, sir.' She recoiled from his look and babbled on, anxious not to cause affront at this stage. 'He was offered the tawnish girl, that being sandy colour. The manservant, a North Briton too, supposedly fond of whores that shade –'

He quietened her with a hand. 'You must tell me a forthright tale, Corrie, not talk fourey-leet.'

'It be true, sir! The manservant wanted a black-haired whore in a white bedgown. Mistress Wren sent a replacement. The tawnish girl was mortal angry, being rejected . . .'

Carradine listened intently, made her repeat the story, questioning her to detect embellishments, then sat thinking. It was

462

unbelievable that Alex Waite had returned to Sealandings, for the North Briton had been his guest at Carradine Manor. Not only that, he was in the syndicate. For a guest to return without informing his former host was a deliberate insult. Or a deception.

'This North Briton. Whom do you mean, Corrie?'

'Why, your friend Waite, that stays at Carradine!' Corrie wanted to run from the room at the look in his eyes. She could hardly whisper. 'Sir. I intended no disrespect, sir. Please, I beg of you. I only desire . . .'

He looked at her as if for the first time, his gaze almost curiously scanning her features. The killer's look had gone. He smiled. 'Corrie, you have earned your new harlot house. I am very, very pleased.'

'You are, sir?' She knelt there, staring up uncomprehending.

'Indeed. Seal our bargain, Corrie. Holy communion.'

She smiled in relief, and reached up to unlatch him, her fingers nimble now. 'You will never be disappointed in your Corrie, sir, not as long as I have breath.'

Amiably he cuffed her and lay back, staring at the ceiling as she began lip service. So Alex Waite had returned in stealth. He had paid his manservant to vanish into the brothel at Two Cotts, and come stealthily, risking giving wounding offence to his former host. Only one reason: a woman. The woman could only be one person.

She lived at Carradine Manor, and was his own Judith Blaker. Blaker the possessive, Blaker the talented bedswoman, Blaker who chained him. As his breathing quickened under Corrie's steady work, he reached down to hold her hand. It met his. This whore had provided him with the means to rid himself of his gaoler. He could now release himself from the prison that was Judith Blaker. He closed his eyes, grunting in pleasure and the ecstasy that came.

He arrived at Carradine less than two hours later. He wanted to give them time. Deception was not clever, he realised as he dismounted and let a groom take the stallion. He entered from the terrace, ignoring the maidservants, hearing his footfalls echo. No, deception called for luck. Lose that, and you were lost. He smiled at the youngest and ugliest of the maids. He had noticed her before, even made some joke about her to Judith. Needing a quick source of irritation on hand when he met his housekeeper, he beckoned.

'Prettiance, is it not?'

'Sir.' The maid waited with a hangdog expression for the inevitable cruel jest.

'I hope to learn every servant's name, Prettiance,' he said. 'You are the youngest, what, fifteen? I shall start with you. Usher me to Blaker, if you will.'

'Yes, sir.' The ugly maid flushed with pleasure and hurried ahead, so flustered she forgot to take his riding beaver. 'Mistress is welcoming your guest, sir, just arrived.'

Prettiance knocked and opened the door, in the necessary whisper informing the elderly Hobbes of the master's arrival. Carradine smiled at the girl, who was so stricken at Hobbes's accusatory glare that she almost clawed Carradine's beaver from his hand.

'It is well, Hobbes,' Carradine said with uncustomary forgiveness. 'Prettiance here has been most welcoming. I wish all greetings would be as unspoilt!'

That would do to begin with. He even managed a casual smile to the girl as the doors closed on her delighted ugliness. He advanced, hand outstretched, to Alex Waite, still in his travelling coach-coat. The North Briton shook his hand warmly.

'Pleasant journey, Alex? Which way did you come?'

'Noisy, a little trouble near Petistree.' Alex smiled, easily. 'Did you hear that Rendlesham House, two miles from there, was bought from Lord Rendlesham for 51,400 by that man Thellusson, and the whole place changed to a Gothic style? He is to be proclaimed the new Lord Rendlesham.'

'Mmmm? Oh, he already has.' Carradine sat and accepted the Geneva spirit. 'You may leave, Hobbes.'

'Yes, sir.'

Which, Carradine noted with pleasure, lessened the dazzling smile on Judith's face. He inspected them both. They were lovers. How on earth could he have missed that? It was crystal. The betraying bitch was practically purring from love-use. No woman could ever conceal that. In truth, no woman ever wanted to hide her satisfaction. He must have been stupid. Now, the exchanged glances, the frequent double-absences, her new compliance at his own increased liberty. It fell together.

And Waite? Cool, the sense of acquiescence as the conversation drifted over the butler's withdrawal. 'The public reading room is opened in Lowestoft. Has a delightful view of the German Ocean. I admired the new bathing machines –'

'That hard, firm sand mixed with shingle is so pleasant!' Judith said brightly, sensing that all was not well.

'Sealandings should have a similar place to Lowestoft's. That chapel on the west side of their high street is exactly contiguous with the corn-cross, with a special town chamber above for transacting serious business.'

Carradine judged his moment, then rose to stand at the fireplace, rounding on them with a thunderous expression.

'The venture.' He held their attention. 'It is a disaster.'

'The *Sealands*?' Judith rose, hand at her throat.

Carradine did not need to act his bitterness. 'That dog-leech Carmichael prevails on Hunterfield to quarantine her.'

'Quarantine?' Waite glanced at Judith. Carradine wondered if she had kept Waite concealed in some cottage, where she would fly as soon as the coast was clear.

He eyed them coldly. 'The ship is due tonight, all for nothing. No shipping venture can withstand quarantine.'

'Nothing?' Judith said dully.

'Nothing. She might as well be lost with all hands.'

'It can not be.' She put both hands to her cheeks, staring in spite of herself at Waite, her lover. Carradine was gratified by Waite's abrupt edginess. He perhaps wanted to flit to London, to meet his father's treasurers and somehow opt out. A failed climber, a jack-a'horse. He felt a withering contempt for the oaf.

'It is. That bitch Mehala puts him up to it. Hunterfield is mesmerised, mark me.'

'Surely Sir Henry can see that –'

'As long as Carmichael lives,' Carradine said harshly, 'the ship will not enter harbour. A famous London doctor called Peveril – we met him – said there was no cause for alarm.' Carradine waited a moment, designing phrases that could be taken as ambiguous if remembered later. 'Hunterfield will prove adamant. No, the *Sealands* will be sent north to quarantine, and the goods and contracts ruined.'

He faced them. 'We must accept the consequences. Keep our

manner calm before the servants, and accept Carmichael's decisions.' He looked at the withdrawing room, and gestured at its luxury. When he spoke, he added just the right amount of venom. 'It is our duty to fail with grace. It is the only honour left.'

54

REVEREND BARING WAS unwilling to receive Ven and Mehala, but finally gave way when he had had time to reread Ven's note-of-hand. He came to pose in the rectory's vestibule, but did not invite them in. Euterpe accompanied him, but under duress.

The greetings were guarded. Ven said he wanted the church-wardens replaced.

'You want *what*, sir?' Baring asked.

It was almost dark. The workmen at Shalamar had almost finished for the day, except for a few still plastering a room on the first floor. Ven had said little to Mehala about his plan, but she had learned the gist when he had called to see Bartholomew at the armoury in Market Square. Rosie, radiant now she was tacitly in charge of the convalescent gunsmith, was shy but happy. She behaved almost as if the gunmaker's house was her own.

'I have two nominations for churchwardens, Reverend,' Ven told the cleric. 'I will give them now to Squire Hunterfield and call immediately on your churchwardens, unless you will perform that duty, and tell them they must resign as workhouse overseers.'

'You are mad, sir. You have no –'

Ven did not tell him that Pleasence had said the same words. 'Bartholomew Hast is one nominee; the other Mistress Tyll, currently resident at Shalamar. They will become the Poor House overseers. Pleasence will be evicted before nightfall.'

Euterpe pushed forward, ignoring her brother's restraining hand. 'Could you explain, Doctor?'

'I carry a list of offences: purloinings, deficits, frauds, exploitations, and three child deaths that were wholly preventable. The charges will be laid by myself in a sworn deposition, as soon as I have ended this conversation. Lawyers from Maidborough and

Barfenham will arraign Reverend Baring, his churchwardens, overseers, and the workhouse guardians, before the Quarter Sessions, unless that replacement occurs immediately. What is his answer?'

'You would not dare!' Baring shouted. 'To assault God's church! To take arms against the Lord! Foe of Heaven, enemy of Man! I abjure you in the name of the Most High –'

'Very well, Reverend Baring, on your own head. Mehala.'

They left, hearing Baring shouting imprecations all the way down the rectory path. Mehala was smiling. 'Does Bartholomew Hast know this, Ven?'

'He may not. And who better than Barbara Tyll to take charge of the workhouse? She knows, she is kind, she –'

'Would be near to her own husband, Mr Tyll, at the Norwich road tollgate!' Mehala smiled at Ven's casual shrug. 'They could easily be reconciled. He is a kindly man.'

'I know nothing of that sort of thing,' Ven said loftily. 'Now let us seek audience with Hunterfield. I shall give that hard-pressed gentleman one fewer problem.'

'You are learning, husband.' Mehala hugged him as they crossed Market Square, her doubts about Euterpe Baring's designs on Ven now gone.

The harbour lights glowed ahead in the early evening. The noisy dancing was continuous. The wassailing promised to go on throughout the night. Two large bonfires threw sparks from the slopes of Whitehanger, from where the lights of the *Sealands* would be seen first. A band played. Distant roars of laughter were audible. As they went from the square, a one-horse whisky clattered through at a dash, skittering and sending sparks of its own from the flint cobbles, with Sir Charles Golding laughing dementedly at the reins.

'He carries no riding lantern,' Ven said disapprovingly. 'That is highly dangerous.'

'He intends to be, to himself and all others.'

Ven looked at her face in the gloaming. 'Is your clarity of vision immediate with each person, or does it take time to come?'

'With love, instantly!' They were alone among the fisher cottages. She pulled his head down to kiss him. 'With fools, instantly also!'

'Not in public places, Mehala.' He disengaged himself, to her amusement. 'And the rest?'

'The rest I do not know.'

Only by the late afternoon, the sky already darkening, did Judith manage a few words alone with Alex Waite. Carradine had gone to bathe and change his clothes. They walked the terrace to watch the distant bonfires, and see the occasional anticipatory firework burst in the night-blue clouds.

'You will have to go with Rad, darling,' Judith said. She felt desperate. 'I do not know what to do.'

'My plans are laid waste, Judith.' Waite was out of his depth, feeling there was some elementary solution if only he could recognise it. 'I wanted the profit to buy a manor. I should have sold out of the venture when . . .' *when advised by De Foe in Whitechapel.* 'I had my father's agreement. I would be your neighbour.'

She almost groaned in distress. She would have had her lover *and* Carradine. The ship was coming tonight, and she would lose both. Carradine would lose all, and Alex would return to the northlands. . . She saw maids were carrying water upstairs from the huge coppers in the laundries to Carradine's dressing room. She had at least an hour.

'You go, darling. Behave as normal. Be sad when Carradine is sad, match his smiles and frowns.'

'And you, hen?'

Judith drew her tulle arachne shawl about her arms, hands clasped demurely before her, her face reflecting the material's gold, and smiled. She had determined to kill tonight, and must look especially demure. 'Me, darling? I shall do my duty, in the name of my loved one.'

He hesitated, cautiously looked about, kissed her with unrestrained passion, and left for the evening's wait on the headland above Sealandings Bay.

Judith watched him move quickly up the staircase. Then she rang for Prettiance, and gave her a few sharp instructions.

Hunterfield looked drawn. He received them in the main hall, listened to the account of Ven's complaints about the workhouse master, and the need to replace the churchwardens as overseers.

'I would fail in my duty were I to avoid this, Squire.'

'Your motive, though?' Hunterfield had difficulty addressing Ven, and avoiding looking at Mehala.

'I had responsibilities. . .'

'Towards a dying child,' Mehala interposed. 'The climbing boy. We declared ourselves his parents.'

Hunterfield nodded. 'I heard. Yes, I can see why you would not want him reclaimed by the workhouse.'

'As if that would actually happen!' Ven burst out angrily, but Mehala recognised the dryness in Hunterfield's words and signalled a mute apology.

'And Reverend Baring? You called on him?'

'He will not comply, Squire.'

'The churchwardens?'

'I shall lay this deposition before your clerk, Squire. The scandal will be noised all over the Hundred.'

'I am aware of that, Doctor.'

Crane entered with a note on a tray, standing patiently.

'Message from Miss Baring, Sir Henry.'

Hunterfield read and dismissed the old servant. He relaxed. 'Your luck is in, Doctor. And perhaps mine also. Miss Baring writes that Reverend Baring concedes. He will not oppose the churchwardens' immediate resignation. I confess that it is most unusual, if not unprecedented, to have a lady as a governess of a workhouse, and an overseer.'

'Mr Hast can assume that title, with Mistress Tyll his functionary.' Ven raised his eyebrows at Mehala, who nodded.

'Doctor. Will you promise to supervise also?'

'Thank you, Squire.'

Hunterfield called Crane to bring tea. 'May I have the pleasure, Doctor, Mistress Carmichael? We must rejoice in the smallest stroke of fortune.'

They followed him to the evening withdrawing-room, Ven making awkward apologies for his attire.

Mehala smiled at this sign of favour to her husband. 'Will Miss Hunterfield allow us the pleasure of her company, Squire?'

'Ah, no. She is momentarily indisposed.' He was quite at ease. 'Miss Carmady will join us, I hope.'

Indeed, Mehala thought with interest. Hunterfield left for a moment to dictate letters to his clerk about the churchwardens and the banishment of the workhouse master.

Mercy Carmady entered with three serving maids almost immediately, flustered by having to assume authority for guests at short notice. Mehala thought she looked radiant and in place, knowing the names of all serving maids and the disposition of Sir Henry's chair.

'I am supervising a meal for Henry's four customs officers,' Mercy prattled brightly. 'Happily, I have the acquaintance of the seniormost, through my brother. They will join us.'

'Customs officers?' Ven asked quickly. 'Four?'

'Indeed. They await the *Sealands* from the Baltic.'

Henry, Mehala registered. And in behaviour superseding Tabitha, who would have been only too glad to have the company of four marine officers. She made small talk, guessing that she would be seeing a great deal more of Mercy Carmady. As would Lorne House and Sealandings.

They had barely settled when Mehala raised her head suddenly.

'What is it, Mehala?' Mercy asked.

'A gun. I heard a gun, fired from seaward.'

Ven shook his head, having heard nothing. But it came again, a sharp tap on the ear followed by a distant rumble.

'Gunfire,' Mehala said. 'I am certain.'

Mercy rose and rushed to the window, calling the three waiting maids to open the curtains and casements. A distant roaring came into the room, and the sound of explosions as rockets whizzed and burst in the sky. She turned to the others, overcome with joy. 'The *Sealands*!' she cried, beside herself. 'She must be in sight!'

Hunterfield entered, smilingly heard their news but showed no sign of rejoicing. He sat with them, and told Ven that the letters had been sent off for immediate compliance.

'Pleasence is dismissed forthwith, Doctor. You will supervise the replacement.'

'Very well, Squire.'

'Unless our four duly authorised officers require your presence elsewhere.'

Mercy's delight could not be dampened, for her brother was sailing home. To cover Ven's anxiety, Mehala talked about ships. Mercy was excited, but Hunterfield ominously taciturn though he made a gallant attempt to converse amiably enough.

The four quarantine officers joined them after a few minutes. The conversation became determinedly general, Mehala managing to keep Ven from mentioning fevers, or quarantine.

Like a ghost, Bellin came from the darkness. Judith hissed his name once, but he showed little concern for stealth and smoked his pipe nonchalantly.

'*Sar shin, meeri rawnie?*' he greeted her.

She contained her impatience. 'I am well, Bellin.'

She could see him clearly as the sky shone colours over the harbour. They were in the gardens, Prettiance accompanying her mistress to legitimise her evening walk.

'You want news, *Rawnie*? There is *naflipen* on the ship, a bad sickness. *Drab-engro* Carmichael will be needed.'

'His woman, Mehala?'

'She is with the *Drab-engro* at Lorne House *kettaney*, together. They sup with the squire, who has written three *china-mengri*. One letter to Reverend Baring, and two others. The master of the *choveno-ker* is bagged, by Hunterfield's order.'

'The workhouse master? Pleasence?' The news made Judith smoulder, adding to her resolve. 'That bitch Mehala. She rules Lorne House, Hunterfield, that lunatic Doctor Carmichael, and appoints churchwardens to this or that position at whim. And her whole life is *hokkano*, a lie!'

'Four sea officers are at the house of the *Borobeshemeskeguero*, the great judge. The *Drab-engro* wants quarantine –'

'I know that! You think I am *dinneleskoe*, too foolish to see? Wait.' She stood staring unseeing at the fireworks, the bonfires spurting reds and golds. There was no other way. 'You mind Preacher Endercotte?'

She heard Bellin snort in derision. '*Avali, rawnie!* The whole world minds that *kek chusti* one.'

'It is precisely because he is "no good", as you say, that you must use him now, Bellin. You know where he is?'

'*Ava* indeed! He lies with any *lubbeny* at Two Cotts who will take a beating.'

'With a harlot?' Judith echoed. 'Find him. Use him. He is a drunkard, yes?'

'A *piya-mengro* as willing as any that ever spewed outside a tavern, *Rawnie*.'

'Tell me who lies at Shalamar, the house of the *Drab-engro*.'

'The wife of the *stiggur-engro*, the tollgate keeper, whose babe is now delivered, with the boy Clement. It will soon be grand again. A fortune has been spent on it. The workmen are all at the harbour to see the great ship.'

'Bellin. I want that *chovahani* Mehala ruined. I want Shalamar burnt to the ground. The mob will believe they do God's work. Understand?'

'It will ruin Mehala, and her *Drab-engro*. Her fortune lies in Shalamar. There are nigh on forty waggons there. The timber brought in last week cost –'

Judith smiled, feeling a sense of repletion steal through her, as gratifying as the haze after passion. Hate truly was beautiful, in a way that even love could never be. She wished her kinsman good luck. '*Kosko bokht*, Bellin. And *Ja Develehi!* Go with God.'

'*Az Develehi*, stay with God,' he rejoined politely. He knocked out his briar on his heel and scanned the sky. 'The ship will heave to in an hour. *Shom te jav*; I must go.'

Judith looked, but somehow he had already vanished. Prettiance reminded her of the time.

'You must be down at the harbour, Mistress,' she said. 'Should I run ahead, send for your carriage?'

'No. Walk with me.' Judith was pleased at Prettiance's eagerness. The beatings she had given the ugly cow had obviously taken effect. She was pleased too with the alacrity with which Prettiance hurried about her duties immediately they reached the house.

55

THE REJOICING HAD almost reached pandemonium. Many were drunk and singing, the bonfires burned and music played. Hunterfield's carriage was halted before the hard by the press of people. Many importuned the Squire, calling out advice and grinning, lifting hats and pointing into the darkness.

Hunterfield had six Lorne men with him, ominously carrying flintlocks or newer percussion muzzle-loaders, and Simple Tom. Leaving Lorne House, Mehala had joked with Tom about his livery, never having seen him wearing it before.

The customs officers and the land-waiter, who would adjudge the cargo on landfall, were driven separately in the great landau, and shared two of Hunterfield's men as escort.

'The ship is offshore, Squire,' Hunterfield's harbour man called. Scowrer was a dour but well-liked man, with his wife and tribe of little girls cottaged along the harbourside off the Blakeney coast road.

'She signs with lanterns, Scowrer?'

'Two man-o'war lanterns, Squire, supered at the mast head.'

'Give me a long-seeing glass, if you please.'

Scowrer's grim news made Mehala draw a sharp breath. She whispered to Ven, 'She signals a grave sickness aboard. Two great navy lanterns, one over the other.'

They alighted, people still cheering and waving. Faces appeared beside the coaches and vanished again into the darkness. Rockets still fizzed skywards, bursting into coloured glows and causing cries of wonder. The din was almost too much to bear. A cry went up that the *Sealands* was to dock at the north mole, whereupon a concerted rush began, only to change to groans and more mock-calls as the trick was discovered amid laughter.

'A boat! A boat!' somebody called.

'We will go out, Scowrer,' Hunterfield said, telescope to his eye. 'I see her. She carries the lights, true enough.'

'I have my tilt boat ready, Squire.'

'Very well. Carmichael?' Hunterfield nodded for Mehala to accompany them down. He paused to speak with his personal groom apart from the rest. They boarded the tilt boat with the four customs officers. Tom stood and watched the six rowers fend off as Hunterfield, the last to board with Scowrer, plumped down in the stern. The crowd cheered the harbour master's boat away. Many carried pitch torches now, and processed to rejoin the concourse, assembling in increasing numbers about the bonfires.

The tilt boat was the east coast's customary coastal passenger vessel. This one Scowrer had inherited from his father, the former harbour master, having been bought from a ferryman plying between Sealandings and Whitehanger. Mehala thought the men's features wonderfully expressive, but the picturesque image was grim, the officers and Hunterfield unwilling to voice their fears.

The land-waiter Tweedale was known to her. He had helped Ven with two injured fishermen a few months before. His purpose was to determine the values placed on each of the imports and account for re-exported cargo for the 'drawback' of the Customs duties levied. He was reputedly fair-minded and meticulous. Hunterfield caught his eye as the tilt boat moved among the anchored vessels.

'You might be saved work tonight, Tweedale.'

The man grimaced. 'I would rather have the work, Squire. Save trouble elsewhere.'

Hunterfield glanced over his shoulder at the lights, torches, and bonfires. 'Indeed. I have never seen so many strangers. Merchants, traders, fairgrounders, pedlars, the world and his wife.'

'The men are yours, Squire,' Scowrer said gruffly. 'And mine.'

Mehala scanned the rowers. They stood at their rowing because of the craft's steep sides. The tilt, a canvas awning to protect passengers in the old days, had been re-rigged, she saw with foreboding, and wetted thoroughly. It was no accident. Torches cast from a crowd could not quickly set fire to such a boat. The damping would give a chance to throw hurled torches overboard. She recognised four of the rowers as Hunterfield's watermen from Lorne. The other two she supposed were Scowrer's relatives or close friends.

The boat glided slowly through the forest of small craft. No life on board any of those anchored. Mehala gradually discerned two superimposed lanterns, pinpricks against the sea darkness, and her heart fell. Surreptitiously she closed her hand over Ven's. He smiled at her, confident he had done right, consistently drawing Hunterfield's attention to the danger. In his innocence, he thought she was congratulating him instead of showing compassion to the one whom Sealandings would blame.

The *Sealands* slowly became a single black mass on the paler gleam of the bay as the tilt boat pulled free of the harbour and started to rise with the sea. The rowers were sweating now, all six steady and unspeaking. Scowrer was at the tiller, speaking quietly with Hunterfield. The officers had assigned two other rowers to bring small pram boats from Watermillock, but they were not yet discernible. They would carry signal lanterns, like the tilt boat.

'Within hail, Scowrer,' Hunterfield said loudly.

Mehala whispered to Ven, 'Squire means to stand away, until he examines her bill of health.'

Ven nodded, eagerly trying to see across the dark sea. A distant roar sounded across the bay as some event caused the crowd to erupt in mirth. The great ship lay some two miles offshore. Scowrer's boat was clear of the land now.

'What happens if the ship is diseased?' Ven asked Mehala softly.

She whispered, 'These officers will appoint quarantine guardians. The ship is put under guard, and sailed to the quarantine port . . .' She saw Hunterfield looking in the boat's lantern light, and quietened. The Lord of Sealandings had her sympathy, but all her fears were for Ven.

'Her be in hail a few minutes, Squire,' Scowrer said, shoving the tiller slowly over. The rowers grunted at the extra exertion needed as the tilt boat headed into the cross-current. 'I s'll take her to wind'ards.'

'Very well. Hail as soon as you can.'

The *Sealands* seemed ominously quiet, no sounds of men working, though a lantern was visible moving along the starboard side as if somebody was going to meet the tilt boat.

'I s'll stay some six cables off, Squire.'

As one the officers grunted approval of Scowrer's words. They would be called upon to guard the ship constantly until she was sailed into a quarantine port, so any decrease in the risk to themselves would be welcome. Mehala held Ven as a larger wave slewed the tilt boat. Scowrer called the rowers to cease, and held his boat away from *Sealands*.

'Ahoy, ship!'

'Ahoy. Scowrer, is it?'

'Aye. You be who and bound where?'

'*Sealands*, Baltic for Sealandings home. Mister Quarles, mate o'this ship.'

Mehala gave a mute groan. Ven was shocked at the expression of grief. He wondered if he was mistaken in the poor light. The ship's lanterns reflected intermittent streaks in the water.

Scowrer bawled, 'Officers with the sea-law's questions, Mister Quarles!'

The senior officer rose, the tilt boat rocking lazily in the swell. 'Mister Quarles! Did the plague or any other distemper prevail in any degree at the place from whence you sailed?'

'Some sickness nigh the Russias, sir!'

'Are any persons on your ship suffering a disease?'

'Aye, nine are down!'

Two of the officers were already lighting a signal lantern as a light appeared out on the bay, closing in on the *Sealands* from shoreward. Mehala guessed it was the first of the prams from Watermillock.

'Have any persons died or been ill of a disease on the homeward voyage, Mister Quarles?'

'Aye. We lost Captain Hopestone, and the naval officer - Lieutenant Carmady, buried at sea the both. I assumed command . . .'

'No more, gentlemen.' Hunterfield spoke with resignation. 'I rule her quarantined. Her disposal?'

'I must go on board instantly,' Ven said quietly. 'The sick aboard need help. I intend to destroy the bedding, all materials of cloth, leathers, cottons, wools –'

'A moment, Doctor. You have no medicines, nothing with you.'

'I can send Mehala to Shalamar for them.' Ven squeezed Mehala's hand.

Hunterfield thought a moment, looking at him. The small approaching boat dipped into the swell, and nosed closer. There were two on board: one rowing, the other with a lantern. Between them and the shore, another lantern was distantly visible, the second of the two.

'I want you aboard, Doctor, and recognise the courage which moves you. But it will be more practical for you first to go ashore, then return prepared with one of the proper officers. I ask you then to sail with *Sealands* to Whitebooth roads quarantine station.'

'Very well, Squire.'

'Sir?' Hunterfield asked the senior officer. 'Nominate your superintendent of quarantine.'

'I nominate myself, Sir Henry. Scowrer, I shall need you to provide me with two boats.'

'You will have them, sir.'

'Name the landfall.'

'Point of the harbour's north mole, sir.'

'Thank you.' The officer shook Hunterfield's hand. 'You have my sympathy, Sir Henry, and my good wishes. Go with God.'

'And you mine, sir, for your courage this night.'

'Not all bravery will be afloat, sir. Much will be needed ashore, when yon crowd discovers this.'

'Scowrer.' Hunterfield indicated Ven and Mehala. 'Take me, Doctor Carmichael and Mehala ashore. Put us on the mole's point.'

'Very well, Squire. Transfer to the nearest pram, if you will, and take two rowers. That many she will hold.'

Hunterfield stood watching the boats converge as the hailed questions began coming across the intervening water. 'Let us about the land's business, then.'

Mehala wanted to question the orders but was reluctant. Hunterfield seemed sure of his decision, and the law had to be followed at all costs. Ven was unused to boats. She helped him into the first Watermillock craft, taking the oars herself to steady it as two Hunterfield men clambered in to row.

The tilt boat and the second Watermillock pram took up station windward of the *Sealands*. Hunterfield did not speak. Ven was deep in thought, listing the essential instruments and physicks needed for his sojourn on board. Mehala thought of poor Percy Carmady, dead at sea on a voyage that was to bring success to all, and now meant prosperity for none.

Endercotte was drunk. Bellin's money had kept his tankard replenished. The preacher was morosely summing the crimes for which Sealandings would be called upon to atone at the Last Judgement. They were on the heath looking down on the harbour.

'You see those crowds, sir?' Endercotte cried, pointing. 'Fireworks! Noise! Dancing! Sin, sir!'

' 'Tis sad, Preacher,' Bellin said dolefully, 'but what is to be done? Evil conquers.' He drew another bottle of pure Geneva from his wrap-rascal and offered it. The man seized it and drank as if thirsting. 'I fear for God, Preacher.'

'Fear, sir?' Endercotte closed his eyes in rapture as the spirit scraped his throat. 'Fear is for Satan, sir! Not the righteous!'

Bellin did not reply for a moment, elbows on his knees, looking at the roaring celebrations. His features were almost indistinguishable in the glim. If this night went wrong, a drunken preacher's recollections would never identify a common drover who spoke with him on a dark heathland.

'But where are the pure in heart, sir?' Bellin took the bottle, pretended to drink, then passed it back. 'In Sealandings?' He laughed harshly. 'No, Preacher! God has neglected us.'

'No, sir!' Endercotte swallowed, coughed, drank again and rose to kneel. 'No! Despair is the most grievous sin! Do not succumb! Satan is all about us! He wants you to believe that goodness has failed! Cannot you see? The opposite is the truth!'

Bellin wondered where his messengers had got to, wanting to walk to the headland and see if the harbourman's tilt boat had returned and what the outcome was to be.

'Can God ever protect a man's soul in the struggle with evil? Is it not easier to cross over, and join the revels?'

'No, friend!' Endercotte grasped drunkenly at Bellin's sleeve, his foul breath causing the drover to avert his face. 'Stand firm in the Lord's cause! You know what is over there? Lewdness! Licentiousness! Fornication!'

'Is that you, booy?' A man emerged from the gloaming. Bellin thankfully recognised the voice and called a greeting. 'All is lost! No more rejoicing tonight. The ship is held by quarantine officers. The quack Carmichael and his doxy have 'suaded the squire.'

Bellin gave mute thanks as his cousin plodded on his way. He

479

would soon be among the crowd, spreading the bad news and inciting to riot on Bellin's signal. It was perfect.

'You hear that, Preacher?' he said dully, offering a second bottle. 'The Lord deserts us! That evil Mehala has conquered!'

'She must be fought, beaten down!'

'Impossible.' Bellin called after his man, 'Here, friend! Where do they go now, this witch and her familiar?'

The reply floated from the darkness. 'To Shalamar.'

'You see?' Bellin demanded as Endercotte drank yet more. 'She has retired to her eyrie, to gloat over God's downfall!'

'She shall not triumph!' Endercotte rose, staggering.

'Can we trust God?' Bellin demanded morosely. 'To cleanse this world of sin?'

'Aye! God has spoken!'

'But who will lead us in the battle?'

Preacher Endercotte stood, breathing deeply, sweat glistening on his face. 'I shall lead the throngs of the Lord against God's enemies! I shall smite them —'

Bellin listened to the man's ravings a few more moments, then signalled to the dark. A few figures emerged. Together they followed the reeling preacher towards the harbour where the grim news was spreading among the crowds.

Prettiance was hurrying through Market Square as they passed the Corn Mart building, wearing one of Judith Blaker's long evening cloaks, the hood over her head. She had run from Carradine Manor and only paused for breath at the corner of the schoolhouse where Miss Gould's lone lantern gave direction. She heard the angry shouts begin and the chants rise. Bellin would not delay, once there was a chance to use the mob as he had been commanded. Gasping from her undue exertion, she hurried on to Shalamar.

56

'You feel the tranquillity, Ven?' Mehala asked. They alighted from the Norfolk cart somewhat shaken. She smiled at him, pleased that Clement had hung the vestibule lantern out at dusk as she asked.

'It is peaceful.' He held her in a light embrace and looked at the dark sky. 'No rockets now, Mehala.'

'The news has reached the crowd.'

They waited. No fireworks, no sound of the crowd's distant jubilation, the up-and-down surf noise now gone.

'I suppose recriminations will begin,' Mehala said. 'Will you have something to eat before we leave for the schooner?'

'Yes, love. But you will not be coming.'

'Yes, I will, dearest. Where you go, there I. Remember?'

'Love, I am afraid for you. And someone must be doctor and surgeon for Sealandings. I shall be home soon.'

'Doctor Carmichael?' Hunterfield's man called from the Norfolk. 'How long must I wait, sir?'

'Ready soon.' Ven led Mehala indoors as Barbara emerged.

'Oh, Ven! Mehala! I thought you had joined the celebrations . . .' She saw their faces and looked past them. 'Home, on a Norfolk?'

'Yes.' Mehala did not smile. The vehicle was a country cart similar to the dog cart, back-and-back seats for four passengers, with shafts running underneath and the body hung on two side springs. Ven had not noticed its significance, but to Mehala it was clear that Hunterfield wanted them to travel almost in disguise in the oak-and-mahogany two-wheeler. 'There is so much activity by the harbour, Barbara!'

Barbara saw the warning in Mehala's eyes, and smiled quickly. 'Good to see you home! The workmen are gone for the day, I suppose drinking! The *Sealands* is home?'

'No. She is quarantined. Ven will go to her, and sail north. I will doctor Sealandings.'

'God save us all!'

'Barbara. Is Clement here?' Mehala's foreboding returned.

'No, Mehala. He went down to the shore with the rest.'

'You are here alone?'

'Not now, Mehala!' Barbara's smile faded as Ven took her proffered candle and went to gather his instruments. She closed the kitchen door gently. 'Is it serious, Mehala?'

'I fear for him, Barbara.' Mehala cast about, seeing the kitchen, its utensils and crockery almost cleared and washed after the hordes of workmen had been provided for during the day's work. 'I shall go to the ship and see him sail safely. Then I will come with you. You have a new home, as Ven said. The Squire's men evict Pleasence from the workhouse. He will be gone by now. You take post as mistress of the Poor House in his place. You can go this night, if you wish. Bartholomew will be an overseer, with Ven.'

'Is it really so?' Barbara beamed with hope, her eyes shining. 'Oh, Mehala! I shall thank Bartholomew myself! And you, and Ven.' Her eyes filled.

Mehala put an arm about her. 'Use my services, and Ven's. And you can call on Little Jane for guidance about –'

A loud knocking interrupted them. Prettiance opened the door, almost falling into the room. The two ran to her with cries of alarm. It was some moments before she had breath.

'Prettiance, Mehala, maid-of-all from Carradine Manor. I come to warn.' She must have seen immediate mistrust in Mehala's eyes, for she caught her hand, and gasped, 'Please. Do not be on your guard. I am not sent by anyone, I swear. Judith Blaker sends people against Doctor Carmichael, to inflame the mob.'

'Mob?' Mehala asked. 'What mob?'

'The crowds on the harbour! They have that *rashengro*, the . . . preacher, holy man.'

'Endercotte?' Mehala guessed.

'That is he, the mad one! Judith works up the mob's anger against your *rommado*, your husband!'

'When?' Mehala almost shook the girl, who was still struggling for breath. '*When*, Prettiance?'

'I saw the *rashengro* passing the school lantern but minutes since.'

482

'Are you honest, Prettiance?' Mehala knelt and looked into her eyes, unblinking. 'Tell me true. I have the sight. Look into my eyes, and you will know. My man is life to me.'

'It is true, Mistress.'

'Why do you come, risking yourself to warn so?'

Prettiance did not answer, but glared defiantly back at Mehala, who nodded curtly after a moment, and rose satisfied. She kissed the girl's forehead. 'I see. You have done a great service, Prettiance, to him and to me. We shall never forget it.'

She hurried to the kitchen door, opened it and stepped out into the night, listening. A faint but steady roaring came faintly to her. The glow over the harbour skies was still there, but as she stared it seemed to wax, then wane and wax again, as if moving across the land, coming closer. Inland? She turned her head steadily, right to left, left to right. The night was colder now, but the heaviness in the air had gone before a light onshore breeze. It carried the distant shushing roar.

'What is it, Mehala?'

'Shhhh!' Mehala sank to the ground, pressing her ear to the stone-flagged terrace. She jumped up quickly, now sure.

'Driver?'

'Yes, Mehala?' the man replied.

'Drive to Lorne. Report what you see on the journey to Squire Hunterfield! Go now!'

'But, Mehala! I am to –'

'Go! For God's sake, do as I say!'

'Yes, Mistress !' The man uncovered his driving lantern and pulled away.

'Barbara? Get little Radcliff this instant. Stop for nothing. Bring him down immediately. I shall call Ven. We must leave Shalamar.'

'How soon? I must get his –'

'*Now*, Barbara, for his life! *Go!* Prettiance?'

'Yes, Mistress?'

'Leave us. Run to the road. Turn right, away from the town. Fast as you can, along the South Toll to the tollgate. Stay with the tollkeeper until morning.'

'But –' The girl was terrified, but glanced towards the corridor leading to the interior of the house.

'I shall call *Drab-engro* Ven, Prettiance. I shall save him now, as you have helped to save us. Do as I say. *Ja Develehi!* Go with God!'

Prettiance stared at Mehala, then slowly smiled in recognition of her own language, and answered, '*Az Develehi!* Stay with God!' She gathered her cloak about her and ran.

Mehala rushed along the corridor, snatching up a candle. She fell over a sawing horse left by one of the workmen but hurried on to the hall. Barbara was already upstairs. 'Ven? Ven!'

'Yes?' He came smiling from the darkness, the shadows of his pottery lantern stretching on the walls. 'I can hardly find a single thing! The workmen seem to have moved my bundle of artery forceps –'

'Ven. The people are coming against us –'

'The people?' He stared.

'The mobs, from the harbour. They march to the South Toll this instant.' For a moment she thought the rockets had begun again, but it was a closer light than that. A vague flickering now underlay the sky glow. 'They have reached the road. Prettiance came to warn us, darling. Barbara is bringing Radcliff.'

'The people?' He laughed at her alarm. She tried to pull him, but he resisted. Her candle fell. She left it lying there, stamping it out with a foot. 'Mehala, have you taken leave of your . . . ? *Our* people? They would never raise a hand. Me, perhaps. But you? Never!'

She let go of his arm and ran to the bottom of the great staircase. 'Barbara! Barbara! Come now!'

Barbara's distant voice answered, but a roaring outside was closing on Shalamar. Mehala ran to the window and saw torches flickering as a great crowd approached. It was all too fast. There was suddenly no time. 'They are here!'

'Mehala.' Ven spoke calmly. 'Please listen to me. All it needs is for me to explain. Take my instruments through the kitchen, if you please. I shall join you in the Norfolk cart presently.'

'You cannot explain to a mob, darling.' Tears were flowing down her cheeks. She reached to touch his face. He tried to smile as the roaring became distinct. A window broke somewhere close, the Trenchards' cottage, she supposed.

Ven looked puzzled for a moment as another pane shattered. 'They are innocent, Mehala. Uneducated, yes. But we must always suppose them to be educable. Once they understand, they will be enlightened –'

Windows crashed along the west corridor. He made an involuntary start, and pulled her to one side as stones clattered on woodwork and two hall windows smashed. Torches moved in the macabre light-and-dark images. More windows went.

'This cannot be,' Ven said with wonderment. 'They do not understand.'

Mehala shouted for Barbara again, and heard a faint scream as several windows fell in and a great whoosh of flame rose from the far end of the west wing. Ven stared, uncomprehending.

'What are they doing?' He looked at Mehala. 'They cannot mean this. I will go out on to the porch –'

Mehala was in tears, pleading with him, pulling, trying to get him away. 'Ven, darling. People are not as you think! They want blood. To burn us, for being different! Do you not see?'

'Then we must tell them, love! It is our duty! We are like their parents. We must teach, cure, protect –'

Flames crackled somewhere. Smoke crept into the light beams from the cellar doors.

'Ven –'

He stared in disbelief. 'They are firing Shalamar! Mehala? They are firing –'

'Barbara!' Mehala shrieked up the staircase.

Ven seemed dazed for a moment, then quickly came to. 'Mehala. As you love me, run from the house. You know the drugs store we are having built at the rear? Go through there, into the gardens. The walls are agape from the workmen's activities. Only canvas covers them. I will see you in the herb garden in a moment. I will bring Barbara.'

'No! I must –'

'Mehala.' He grasped her with surprising strength. 'Go, or we shall both stay to our deaths here –'

Windows everywhere were shattering. Part of the west wing erupted into flame. Ven now seemed quite calm, of a sudden accepting the calamity. He kissed her and thrust her away. 'I will stand here unmoving until you escape, Mehala.'

'Yes, darling.' She covered her head with her mob cap and ran.

Along the west wing, a thunderous crack sounded as part of the scaffolding was battered and gave way. The crowd entered with a great howl, feet hammering on the floors and the light of torches flickering ahead along the walls.

Ven ran upstairs.

'More than three, I think, Sadler!' Hunterfield called, grimly judging the turmoil.

The crowd had roared past. Windows had been smashed in Market Square but little structural damage was evidently done. They roared on their way up the South Toll.

'Yes, Squire.' The stout corn merchant was armed with a coachman's flintlock blunderbuss. His fellow churchwarden Finch Digges carried a twelve-bore Hast percussion piece.

Hunterfield sat astride his mare Betsy. Seven other gentlemen were mounted. He had them assembled by the Corn Mart. Temple the blacksmith, the brothers Parker, Prothero of Calling Farm, and Emanuel Bettany mustered about Hunterfield. Two dozen men, half wearing Lorne House livery, were armed and afoot, and stood in one group under the command of the Hunterfield gamekeepers. Another dozen stood about, the petty constable Triphook in authority.

Every second man carried a lantern staff. Hunterfield spoke.

'Gentlemen, friends. I have called you out to preserve the King's peace in Sealandings. We must manage as best we can. The high constable of the Hundred has been sent for. I expect Mills soon from inland.'

'We should shoot the bastards down, Squire!' Prothero swore, whipping his mount to order as it became skittish.

'Thank you, Prothero, but there will be no gunplay in Sealandings unless I so order! I intend to confront the crowd with your assistance, and make them desist.'

'They are too roused, Squire!' Sadler exclaimed. 'Hear it?'

Cheering was audible, and what sounded like a gunshot.

'Some reach Shalamar, Squire.' Temple cocked his head, listening.

'Not only more than three, so constituting a riot. But more also than twelve, I think.' Hunterfield's duty was to remain outwardly calm throughout any riot. 'So I am obliged to read One-George-Stat-Two. Let us about the business! Triphook?'

'Yes, Squire?'

'Lanterns shall be lit forthwith. Prepare!'

'Yes, Squire!'

Hunterfield nudged Betsy and started across Market Square. To gallop would only add to passion once he came up with the rioters. A steady fast walk with lanterns ranked behind and mounted men in pairs would seem a show of force even to an infuriated mob. He was astonished to see, as he turned in the saddle to give a marching command to Constable Triphook, Reverend Baring hurry from the rectory to join the men. He wore his cleric's hat and frock coat, and carried his book.

A few other men arrived, trotting on foot to fall in column, most armed only with staves. As the column left the Square, the clockmaker Veriker and Bartholomew Hast rode up together, the latter with one leg projecting incongruously at an angle, both men calling apologies for their lateness.

'I shall remember where not to purchase my next clocks, Veriker!' Hunterfield called, to a chuckle of amusement.

Ahead, the South Toll's slope had not slowed the mob. A forest of lanterns and torches became visible as Hunterfield moved steadily on. A hedgerow blazed a crescent of new fire. The roaring had become constant now. Flames shot skywards as the column took up the incline.

'Shalamar is ablaze, Squire, in part!' Sadler exclaimed.

'We must still proceed as we are.'

'The mounteds should ride on ahead, Squire!' Prothero was almost beside himself with fury. 'Two volleys, dispel the swine in an instant! Your damned Riot Act can come any time after, sir!'

'Thank you, sir!' Hunterfield said calmly. 'To separate our meagre force at this juncture would give the night to all and any marauders. Hold your position, Prothero, if you will.'

'That is property, Squire! The foundation of society!'

'I am aware what Shalamar is, Prothero!'

The column moved fast. The walking men were having a hard time keeping up. Triphook had the marchers trotting for a dozen paces then slowing to a walk before running again. They straggled, but stayed as one group.

'Have we a horn of any sort, Constable Triphook?'

'No, Squire,' the petty constable shouted.

Up ahead they could see flames lashing upwards among the dark trees. Figures capered in the glow between the foliage.

'All weapons primed, if you will, gentlemen. Made ready.'

They reached the ruined gateway of Shalamar. Hunterfield reined into the driveway and paused at the sight.

The house was illuminated in the blaze from a score of burning waggons in the gardens. Timber stocks intended for the mansion's reconstruction were roaring in several huge fires. Even trees were aflame. Sheds and material stores were already crumbling into ash. The west wing of the great house was ablaze, tongues leaping from the windows and glass exploding to cheers of the scores of figures running across the gardens. Many were frankly too drunk to stand. Others careered from one blaze to another. Some capered near a burning cottage. As Hunterfield looked, the central hall was engulfed in a wide sheet of flame as if from a source, the dome surmounting it rearing back before leaning down to crumble into the inferno.

A thin man rose on a mounting stone a few yards away, hand held aloft. He was babbling of hell, God, Satan, and evil.

Several stones were hurled at them, and a few figures started through the bushes. A torch was thrown at the mounted men. One of Triphook's men cursed as he was struck by a heavy flint.

'Far enough, gentlemen!' Hunterfield called. 'I shall read the Riot Act! Stand to.'

He extracted the parchment and stood in his stirrups. He shouted quickly, not needing to follow the script.

'Our Sovereign Lord the King chargeth and commandeth all persons, being assembled, to disperse themselves, and peaccably to depart to their habitations, or to their lawful business, upon the pains contained in the act made in the first year of King George, for preventing tumults and riotous assemblies. God save the King.' He put the parchment away.

Preacher Endercotte fell from the mounting stone, then clawed himself upright as with a howl a score of the rioters charged into the west wing through a part of the wall where the scaffolding had been torn down.

He raised an arm, screeching a prayer. 'I abjure thee Satan to depart! We do the work of God Almighty here —'

'Constable Triphook, arrest him, preacher or no. Gentlemen, I intend to fire one volley. Is my gamekeeper Lilley there?'

'Squire!' Lilley came forward, an elderly deliberate man carrying a heavy six-barrelled Manton volley flintlock.

'Select six men. Have them fire one shot, high as you please. Do it now, Lilley. Gentlemen, hold your horses!'

Most dismounted and led their mounts back to the roadway for when the volley came. All kept close however, for many of the rioting figures were becoming more daring. Triphook went forward, dragged the babbling preacher aside and manacled him to a sapling.

'Right, booys,' Lilley commanded. 'Fire!'

The volley was like a thunderclap. The men were prepared and looked away, partly to avoid being blinded by the flash of gunpowder and partly to avoid the shreds of copper caps from the percussion weapons, a notorious cause of eye damage.

The crackling continued at the mansion but the capering ceased. Several of the figures cast about for missiles to throw, but others began to drift away. Hunterfield waited a moment to judge the effects.

'We will proceed round the side of the house. Mounted men first, and the column of marchers extending face outwards as we near the building. Fore.'

They advanced slowly, the horses becoming nervous at the scent and sight of the vast blaze. Lilley's six scrambled to reload as they pressed forward. The penalties were death for rioters who, once the Riot Act had been read, failed to disperse, especially on destruction of any dwelling. That knowledge might convert the mob's fury into panic. Then, anything could happen.

They moved on, Reverend Baring walking soberly alongside Hunterfield's mare. A horseman cantered up to join them, the rider calling out Sir Henry's name.

'Carradine!' Hunterfield touched his riding beaver. 'You here!'

'What in God's name, sir?' Carradine reined beside Betsy, whipping his skittish horse into submission and guiding it towards the tumult ahead.

'Riot Act read, Carradine. Timed at . . . Triphook?'

'Twenty minutes to eleven o'the clock, Squire.'

'They have one hour,' Hunterfield said drily. 'Or we have.'

'We should herd the bastards into the nearest pasture, and shoot any swine that resist!'

'Thank you, no. We will go as I plan.'

'Hunterfield, let us ride round the damned building, and –'

'No, Carradine,' Hunterfield said sharply. 'The east wing remains least damaged. I remember a lawn. We will proceed there, and start apprehending them. On the move and outnumbered, we are vulnerable. I will not risk any man.'

'Damned fool, Hunterfield.' Carradine grumbled under his breath, but stayed with the column.

Two figures tried to harangue the rioters into rushing the men, but they were quickly taken by Triphook and two Lorne gamekeepers after a struggle, and shackled about a small tree. A shot sounded and a bullet hissed close. Lilley himself went after the man into the undergrowth.

It was like day near the house. The central part of the mansion and the entrance were burning now, the west wing crumbled and the windows imploded. Beams could be heard crashing down, pillars of fire and sparks shooting skywards as sections of the roof plunged down through the building.

The heat became almost unendurable. Hunterfield led the column away from the building to reach the comparative cool of the overgrown lawns by the east wing. The smoke rolled densely from the main building, but at least the risk was reduced.

He called a halt and suggested the men dismount. 'Lilley, Triphook. Take half-a-dozen men and start bringing in the rioters. This is your base. Sadler, Digges, start preparing for prisoners. Stakes, a waggon or two if they be saved, ropes, leather straps, any means of restraint.'

'Squire! Sir!' Mehala came from the darkness at the edge of the lawn, her dress torn and mob cap lost. She was in disarray. The men stared. 'Please. Ven and Mistress Tyll are in the house!'

'Where, for God's sake?'

'I do not know.' She was broken. 'Ven went upstairs to recover Barbara and her babe –'

'There! Squire! You see?'

A man was pointing upwards. Mehala rushed closer. 'Ven!'

'Lornes!' Hunterfield called. 'Make a step-mast, with hanks of rope the length of your storeys! Sharply now, if you please.'

Smoke was fuming upwards in pale streams from each storey of the wing. Flames were leaping at the rearmost windows, though the panes had not yet given. Mehala was frantic. She could see Ven against the ominous background of shifting red-gold light. He was struggling to open a window. He finally smashed it through with a chair. Another figure, hunched as if carrying something tightly to her, was behind him. Mehala saw Ven push her forward so she got the air through the broken glass.

The men used scaffolding poles, all wood, lashed together as if making an extension to a broken mast at sea. They worked swiftly, even joking in a steady mutter, and raced it as a battering ram to the base of the wall, lifting it in one concerted heave at the last moment so it was thrust at the window. Ven pulled Barbara and her bundle aside as he realised their purpose. It held a sack, tied to the tip.

'Carmichael! Use the sack to contain the infant!' Hunterfield's voice failed, and the petty constable took up the command, bellowing the instruction over and over.

'Bag the babe, sir!' Triphook bawled. The men took up the cry.

A window near the front façade blew out with a shudder and the men on the lawn scattered, calling warnings. Pieces of glass falling twenty feet could pierce solid mortar.

'Tie the rope to the tip,' Lilley yelled up. 'Let it out as it takes the weight!'

Ven waved. He had trouble persuading Barbara to let the babe go, but finally stuffed the child into the sack tethered at the mast-head.

'It comes, men!' Triphook's instructions were superfluous now, for the fishermen were now under the command of the elderly Jervin, master of *The Jaunty* from the harbour. Three were sent to hold the base of the step-mast firm as a fulcrum while the rest craned upwards to see the sack lowered on the step-mast. Two gamekeepers had cut a long ash branch, and reached up to take the pole's weight in the fork.

Mehala took the sack, seizing a knife from a Lorne woodcutter and slicing through the rope that bound it fast, hurrying away from the fire immediately with the babe. A second window blew, shooting flames and shards of glass and masonry into the night, followed instantly by a third. The floor below was now burning. The wall started to crack.

'Ven!' She shouted up desperately to the figures at the fourth storey window. 'Make a double rope if you can! Lower Barbara along the mast! Then on to the ledge!'

He had already begun to edge Barbara out of the window, lashing the rope about her. There was no time to use the mast now. Barbara swung aimlessly, feet flailing the air. She swung against the house's side as she came down. A pulley, Mehala thought desperately, a pulley would have got them both down instead of her man waiting among the flames for the woman to be rescued first. She examined the child, unbelievably sleeping. She put her face to it and felt its breath.

'Now, sir! Come now!'

The men were all shouting, yelling, bawling frantically.

'Now! Come now! The house is going!'

Ven came slithering down the rope, his flexed elbow shielding his face from the flames licking from the third and second floor windows. He landed with a thump on the grass and was dragged clear, coughing and retching, his hair and coat burning.

Men beat at him, clawing his smouldering clothes away. He was almost unrecognisable, hair singed and face black with grime. His half-jacks he himself wrenched and cast away with bloodied hands. They smoked on the grass.

Mehala rushed to him, but Hunterfield was among them, gesturing and calling orders to get away from the house.

'She goes, Squire!' Triphook called. The men scrambled away, shouting warnings as the east wall of Shalamar crumpled and fell. The top storey separated to fall outward, and the floors below seeming simply to dissolve in the flames. Smoke billowed now, golds, and greys among the red, a bright yellow glare engulfing the whole of Shalamar.

They withdrew to a furlong's distance from the burning building. Barbara held her babe, weeping with relief. Mehala in tears embraced Ven, examining his ripped palms.

'We are all saved, Mehala!' He was excited, elated, amazed at the events. 'The threat of death, then your rescue of us!'

'Doctor,' Hunterfield called. 'No more in there, I suppose? The boy Clement?'

'At mine, Squire.' Bartholomew limped across to smile at Ven. 'With my percussions, my apprentice, and old Gomme, to defend the gunsmithy and the kingdom.'

'Thank God.' Hunterfield examined the sky. The men murmured, pleased. 'Now we have no need of it, here comes the rain. Too little too late, or too much too early, rain on these damned sealands.'

'Never trust a nor'easterly, Squire,' Mehala said. 'And thank you for rescuing my husband.'

He looked away, understanding her meaning. Ven rose, looking at his hands. 'I fear I shall be little use on the ship, Squire, with these palms, and now no instruments or physick. But I had better be off, or she will sail without me!'

'Ven.' Mehala silently begged Hunterfield to be the one to explain. 'The *Sealands* has already sailed.'

'Already?' Ven could not take it in. 'But I was asked . . .'

'I thought it best, Doctor,' Hunterfield said evenly. 'The quicker to the Whitebooth quarantine, the safer for the men on board.'

Ven remained silent a minute, looking askance at the inferno that had been Shalamar. 'You mean the safer for me, sir?'

'Both. But it was for me to decide.' He gestured to Triphook. 'Constable. That derelict cottage is dowsed. Give these people one man as guard, and get the babe and its mother under shelter somehow.'

'No, Squire.' Mehala reached to the stack of long arms and selected a flintlock. 'I can stand guard at the Trenchards' cott.'

'Very well.'

On the lawn a sorry mass of rioters was being assembled. Many were already in custody, roped or shackled together, the ring-leaders manacled back to back. Mehala led the way, telling Ven that she must find a way to bandage his injuries somehow. Some of Hunterfield's men were mounted again. The discovery of rioters was proceeding apace.

As they passed the prisoners, Mehala stopped with an exclamation.

'Hal? Hal Baines? Be that you, booy?'

Baines was seated disconsolately on the grass, begrimed and worn. He was tied with a rope to three others. 'Yes, Mehala.'

'Among *them*? Who wanted to burn *me*? Why, Hal?'

'Everybody said.' He shrugged. 'So I.'

Mehala felt tears start. She tried to speak but could hardly manage a word for a moment. 'Hal. You were the one who rescued me, fetched me drowned from the waters safe to the sealands . . .'

'I am sorry, Mehala.'

'You could have burned Doctor Carmichael. Mistress Tyll. Her baby Radcliff, that is a newborn innocent!'

He said nothing more. Mehala led on to the broken cottage. One wall only remained standing. In the firelight she examined the space. Thatch had been stripped from the place, so no roof shelter was possible. The rioters had used the thatch for torches, the timbers to help the conflagration, but the wattle-and-daub wall held at one corner.

'Please stay here, Ven, Barbara. I shall get a cloak, or brush for cover.' She went outside, and came face to face with Carradine.

He dismounted and stood against the flames, tall and with his drawn sword in his hand. He spoke just enough to be heard.

'You spoke of a babe, Mehala.'

'Yes.' She was drained, too exhausted to fight more. Her duties lay with her man.

'Its name. You said a name.'

Mehala did not hesitate. The rain streamed down her face, streaking her hair across her eyes. She scraped it aside. 'Radcliff.'

'Radcliff. As mine. Tyll's babe?'

'And yours.'

Carradine obstructed her path. She made to step round him and go in search of some canvas. He removed his cloak at a single gesture and handed it to her. She took it, and returned to the ruined cottage leaving him there silhouetted against the dying Shalamar.

57

T HE UNIFORMED SOLDIERS were distantly visible against the sunlit fields. The grass was still wet from the night's steady rain, but the mound of ruins that had once been Shalamar still burned desultorily. Every so often a smouldering timber fell with a crash, or an interior wall toppled with nothing more than a steady grumbling noise into the embers, causing a cloud of ash and dust to rise, speckling the sunlight.

'Your arrival was timely, Lieutenant Pordage.' Hunterfield offered the compliment graciously.

Pordage was appreciative. 'I could not have come faster, Sir Henry. Your mute servant was excellent. I had no idea these coast lands had so many trackways! Perhaps when the Ordnance get round to completing their land survey, we may all share his knowledge!'

'Report the damage, then.' Hunterfield stood where the rioters had been assembled. 'Mehala, I have the honour to present Lieutenant Pordage.'

Mehala greeted the military man. He seemed so youthful, trying to assume an air of gravity to emphasise what years he had. Ven was by the ruined cottage, splinting a rioter's broken tibia.

'My report is hardly worthy, Sir Henry,' Pordage said in apology. 'The house Shalamar you see totally destroyed. The burned remains of some fifty waggons lie in the orchards, which are salted and beyond recovery these several years.'

'The new trees, sir?' Mehala asked.

'Burnt, m'lady, if by that you mean the sacks beyond the first orchard, all that can be found. Gardeners have identified the place they lodged the new apples, pears, soft fruits. Sadly, not a twig left.'

'The trout pools?'

Pordage glanced at Hunterfield. 'The dams broken, the ground salted. The pools are emptied. The paddles, I think they call them, burned.' They were costly wooden retaining gates, built on the pattern of canal lock gates.

'The farming implements?'

'Stolen or broken, m'lady. The dray horses were driven out, several of them shot, including a hand of mares in foal.'

Mehala felt turned to stone. 'The two cottages a-building?'

'Gutted and burnt, m'lady. It is as complete an act of wanton destruction as I have ever seen or heard, and we are just returned from the northern manufactories. They are a veritable vision of hell.'

'Is anything left, Lieutenant?'

'The land, m'lady, but that ruined, salted, despoiled.'

'I thank you, on behalf of my husband and myself. Please thank your soldiery. I wish I had largesse to give them.'

The officer touched his hat and left with his sergeant to transport the remaining rioters.

Mehala paused. Hunterfield swung into the saddle before he spoke. 'You received warning last night, Mehala?'

'Prettiance, the maid from Carradine Manor, came moments before the mob.'

'Then good girl she.'

'Squire. Please convey condolences to Miss Mercy on the death of her brother. He was a brave and pleasing gentleman.'

'He was my friend.' Hunterfield looked across to where Ven was straightening up from his work. 'You, Mehala?'

'My friends will survive and do well, Squire. Mistress Tyll will occupy the workhouse master's post this morning.' A final wall fell in Shalamar with a growl, flinging more dust to dapple the smoke and sun. 'Miss Matilda Gould, Miss Euterpe Baring, Bartholomew Hast –'

'You will not stay to see Miss Rosie and Hast wed, Mehala? That *will* be their fate?'

'It seems happily ordained.'

'Where will you go?'

Mehala thought a moment. The officer's words came into her head. 'A veritable vision of hell,' the north where manufactories abounded.

496

'We shall walk north, Sir Henry, and see what God brings.'

'North? Who can survive there? And away from the sealands, Mehala? They are your life.'

'Shall we survive here, Sir Henry?' Her voice was bitter. She saw Ven talking to the recumbent man. She started to walk slowly across the grass to join him. Hunterfield kneed Betsy to pace alongside.

'You will die of a broken heart, longing for Sealandings, Mehala.'

She looked up at him against the sunlight. 'I shall mind my man better and safer than I have here.'

'*He* should mind *you*, Mehala!'

'No, Squire. That is a man's foolish thinking. We women know better. We are protectresses to our loved ones.'

'And this one?'

Prettiance was approaching from the drive, staring about her in amazement, pausing to let a rider pass before coming on.

'She can come with us, if she has a mind.'

'That hornet's nest at Carradine will require investigation, and the part the woman Judith has played, by all accounts. Carradine is enraged, and has already gone in search of her. She has flown.'

'His child was almost murdered from her intrigues.'

'*His* child?' Hunterfield's tone made her quiz him a moment. She thought of Tabitha's transparent hunger for Carradine, but said nothing. Perhaps matters had moved on faster there than she or Sealandings supposed. 'I see.'

Well, Mehala thought, some problems would remain. She thought of poor Euterpe Baring trapped in her brother's rectory, of Mary Prothero's spirit crushed under her husband's vehement ambition, Reverend Baring himself and his lonely obsessions, Sir Charles Golding's drunken blunderings towards ... what? And the great ship *Sealands* sailing into quarantine with the fortunes of the whole Hundred lost as surely as if she had sunk off the Goodwins.

'Clement will possibly want to come with us. I shall give him the choice of remaining with Bartholomew as his apprentice.'

'Let him stay, Mehala. I shall discover his parents, God willing.'

And the Yorkshire school Ven wanted to improve. The hatred of the Goat and Compass taverner Ben Fowler for her friends;

John and Sarah Weaver of the Donkey and Buskin who took her in when she was brought ashore . . . But the child she now carried for Ven would come with them, be born where she and Ven lay, and share their wanderings.

'Very well.' She stood waiting as Ven joined them. She looked up at the Lord of Sealandings. 'Goodbye, Sir Henry.'

'Goodbye, Mehala. Doctor.' He pulled Betsy round and set her at a slow walk to rejoin his men and the officer of foot.

'Mehala?'

'Yes, darling?'

Ven nodded to Prettiance who was standing a few paces away. 'We are destitute, I think.'

'Indeed. The land is despoiled. The fertile areas will no longer grow under the salt broad cast last night by the rioters. Our home is gone. The estate is devastated, for years to come. Our clothes, your instruments, notes, everything.'

Ven shivered. 'As if the poor house had no hope, Mehala. I should have been stronger, wiser.'

'No, Doctor!' Prettiance burst out. 'You are kind!'

Mehala smiled. 'Prettiance has a woman's view of matters. It is time to leave Sealandings, Ven.'

'Leave?'

He stared at the smouldering ruins, the grounds, the land. Mehala's Floral Dial was trampled and obliterated. The herb garden, the terracing, even the valuable new flagstones from the Midlands and north were broken.

'Everything, darling.' Mehala took his hand as the soldiery marched off towards the road and harbour. 'There *is* no longer any "everything", except ourselves.'

'I see.' She said nothing, giving him time. 'You are right, as ever, Mehala. Gather what we can carry. Barbara?'

She had come from the ruined cottage carrying Carradine's cloak and the babe. 'I understand, Ven. Constable Triphook will bring a cart to take me to the workhouse residence. I shall have a maid! To help with little Rad!'

'Remember Little Jane, should you falter, Barbara.'

'I shall, Mehala.'

'And the Weavers are our friends. And Miss Gould.'

'I know.' Barbara was in tears.

'Prettiance. Will you stay, perhaps to work for our friends, should we find you a place?' Mehala let the choice sink in. 'Or you can take your fortune in your feet, with Doctor Ven and myself. I might need help, sooner than we think.'

'Let me come, mistress. There is nothing here for me.'

'We shall rest part of the day, during this fine weather, then leave later and put a good foot under us. Decide.'

It was four o'clock in the afternoon, the sun lowering and the smouldering ruins still sending blue-grey smoke up in a drifting column, when they picked up their peds and started down the drive.

The remains of the burned waggons were strewn everywhere. It resembled a battlefield. Two Lorne gamekeepers seated on a mound of stones raised hands in farewell. Ven and Mehala waved. Prettiance gave a shy flap of her hand.

Mehala had managed to get them all dry and re-clothed somehow, with the help of the Weavers. They had washed in the brook, and she had fed them eggs and bread obtained from Little Jane. She had obtained a muslin bag of supplies, three scallop shells for scooping drinking water from crevice pools and from leaves in pilgrim fashion, and a spare oiled cloth for cover. They had said their goodbyes to Clement, Bartholomew, Rosie.

Ven had foraged for his instruments. He found one scalpel, and nothing else.

'Exactly what I arrived with, Mehala!' He was almost laughing at their penury. 'Sealandings has allowed me to keep one thing! A stroke of good fortune!'

'Sir?' She pretended affront.

Ven now really did laugh. She meant he had gained her. 'I quite forgot you, Mehala!'

They reached the road and started north, striking across Market Square by the lich-gate, passing the schoolhouse where Matilda Gould waved, handkerchief to her eyes. Mehala ran to kiss her farewell, and Ven doffed his beaver to her.

They started up the slope, aware of the quiet figure of Mary Prothero at the gate of Calling Farm, alone in her whisky carriage. She gave no sign, looking after them. They saw Euterpe Baring raise a flower from the churchyard near Nath's grave. Ven felt tears start to his eyes, remembering his silence there an hour before when he had bade goodbye to the climbing boy, to Bella the drowned whore from Two Cotts, and to Rosie's stillborn baby. He waved, not looking at the still black-clad figure of Reverend Baring standing before the porch of St Edmund the Martyr's.

They walked up the Norwich road, past the brothel at Two Cotts, Quaker Bettany's mill, the livestock ground, Parker's public stables, the gates of Carradine Manor, and the tollgate where Barbara's husband farmed the toll but did not emerge to bid them goodbye.

Then they were at the bend of the road as it curved north and inland. Ven paused to look back, but Mehala kept on with Prettiance. A whistle sounded from the direction of Market Square. He scanned the area, and finally glimpsed Simple Tom on his mount, waving his hat to and fro in slow farewell.

Ven raised his hat, slowly waving it side to side. Then Mehala did look back with him, and together they waved for a moment.

'Come, Ven,' she said, taking his arm, 'you who gained nothing but your rusty old scalpel from Sealandings!'

'We could use the journey, Mehala!' he said seriously. 'I could conduct another lecture. What would you like? Perhaps this time, the incisions to be made for gangrene of the extremity?'

She kissed him, causing Prettiance to blush and look askance. 'Should we not speak of our hopes for the future in the north, Ven, at least a little while?'

'We know those, Mehala: to do our best for the sick.'

'And to find a good home, make a place for ourselves, find friends for Prettiance and any children of our own that come.'

'Meanwhile, we must keep on learning, Mehala!' he said seriously. 'Now, suppose a woman of fifty years had a gangrenous limb, with the line of demarcation extending from the medial malleolus circumferentially to the mid-point of the . . .'

Mehala smiled at him with love, matching her pace to his.

She saw in her mind's eye the sealands' desolate beauty, the shot satin of the thrift over the low marshes in colours lily white to madder rose. She saw the purple sea lavenders, the royal sea aster's hues. The transparent emerald green of the glasswort, melting with the spring into carmine. She had heard for the last time the sea mews, the royston crows, the cry of the grey geese, the trumpets of the whooper swans, the quiet splash of the stately heron, the barking of the brent geese over the still blue waters of the fleets and sedges. But the sealands had turned against her love. She walked away from them, with him.

Prettiance walked alongside, naming the roadside flowers to herself in Romany and the common English tongue. Ven frowned, speaking on his lecture.

They walked north.